THE WITCH'S TAROT

THE TOWER

KRISTIN BURCHETT

MILTON & HUGO L.L.C.
4407 Park Ave., Suite 5
Union City, NJ 07087, USA

Website: *www. miltonandhugo.com*
Hotline: *1- 888-778-0033*
Email: *info@miltonandhugo.com*

Ordering Information:
Quantity sales. Special discounts are granted to corporations, associations, and other organizations. For more information on these discounts, please reach out to the publisher using the contact information provided above.

Library of Congress Control Number:	2024915930	
ISBN-13:	979-8-89285-218-0	[Paperback Edition]
	979-8-89285-217-3	[Digital Edition]

Rev. date: 07/30/2024

Dark and foreboding, the Tower is the embodiment of disruption and conflict. Not just change, but the abrupt and jarring movement caused by the unforeseen and traumatic events which are part of life.
- Trusted Tarot

Note to Reader

If this were a movie, it would definitely be rated R! There is a lot of death, blood, and gore associated with all ages, that some may find disturbing. There are several sexual situations ranging in intensities that some may find offensive and/or disturbing. There are a few religious phrases such as 'his God', 'the Gods', and 'higher and lower powers', that are used several times throughout, which some may find offensive. While part of my goal for this completely fictional novel *is* to disturb you, my dear reader, it is in no way my intention to offend you. With that being said, I advise those of you that are faint of heart, squeamish, deeply religious, or easily offended to simply find another novel.

Contents

Prologue

"Please, let me!" She pleaded with him, but he would only roll his eyes for the umpteenth time.

"Ain't all that for your customers?" he asked, slightly exasperated.

"Well, yeah, it is…" She replied, "…but it's such fun, and would be good practice, too." She finished with a small, sly smile.

"Practice." He repeated in an amused tone. "You? Need practice? Unlikely." He continued soberly.

"Such a flatterer, you are." She told him playfully. "Now, appease me."

With another exaggerated roll of the eyes, he relented. "I suppose I can endure one of your readings, though I cannot say that I understand why you wish to do one. My future lies with you, my love, and only you." He told her sweetly.

The radiant smile he received in return was worth more than all the words his vocabulary contained. "I'll be right back." She told him excitedly, then leaned over and kissed the tip of his nose before hopping off the bed and taking off.

She returned only moments later with an ancient deck of cards in hand. Once settled back on the bed and comfortable, she carefully began to shuffle the deck of cards by separating the deck into three smaller ones and then restacking them. She did it repeatedly until she was satisfied that they were thoroughly shuffled. With that done, she had him place his hand over the deck and say his name, loudly and plainly three times, before having him cut the deck into three sections and then restack them as she had just done.

She drew the first card of three and laid it on the quilt between them. The picture before them instantly mesmerized him, enchanting him with its exotic, ancient beauty. The card depicted a stunning glass tower, that dwarfed the forest of gnarled, bent trees in the background. Trees that still showed brilliant green, thick foliage that he was sure buzzed with life. There was no sun in *the picture but the brightness enveloping the background and the multicolored reflections on the glass tower, gave the impression that a high, burning bright sun sat just beyond the edge of the hand-painted picture. At the base of the pastel-rainbow hued tower, laid a carpet of assorted wildflowers. Some only had three or four petals, while others contained intricate layers of them, each breathtakingly beautiful if only for the delicate patience placed into each one. Every color one could imagine could be seen among the meadow leading to the magnificent tower, allowing for the beautifully reflected colors against the transparent dwelling among them. A breeze seemed to blow through the meadow, for the flowers appeared to almost bow toward the ethereal tower, as if in a worshipping, or maybe mournful, gesture. He could not fathom, however, that such an exquisitely painted picture would, or could, contain the latter.*

As he intently studied the beauty of the card, he did not notice that she sat across from him staring at the six little letters plastered across the top of the card. She forced herself to swallow the gasp that had lodged in her throat when she realized what card it was because she knew what that card meant. She tried to shake off the sudden unease that washed over her and steeled herself for the drawing of the second card.

She stole one final glance at the card, before forcing her eyes toward her beloved, reading the Latin name atop the tarot card.

Turrim.

The Tower.

Chapter One

The Valley's End

1

The budding trees and sickly, coming-back-to-life pines pass by in a rush of browns and greens and grays and all the other natural colors of the Earth, as the train operated by Jimmy and Toby heads northeast on the Appalachia Railroad. They are, literally, going through the mountains where a small old mining community awaits the first train shipment of the year. They expect a large crowd, possibly the entire able population, by the tracks when they pull up to the Miner's Nook train station. What they find upon arrival, however, is not at all what they expect and leaves a lasting impression upon them both.

Tobias Medlin became Conductor Jim's assistant a few years back. Jim has never regretted walking into that office and telling the higher-ups that he would *take on the boy*, as they had so eloquently put it. The boy in question, Tobias Medlin, is what some would consider mentally challenged. He does have an immense interest in trains and seems to be able to retain information about them much easier than most other things. Even in Jim's vilest of thoughts, he doesn't regret becoming a mentor to Tobias Medlin. Tobias loves Jim, unconditionally, the evidence displayed proudly upon his slightly deformed face from time to time. Jim is his first and only friend. None of the guys they work with are mean to him, they don't tease him, and they always invite him when they go out for drinks after work. They are all real nice folks, but Jim is his partner, and even more, his friend.

The mountains they are travelling through are riddled with various mines: salt, gold, silver, and coal, and the valley, known to the 'outside'

1

world as Miner's Nook, allowed miners to access them easily enough. A touch over a century ago, a small mining community was built and as news spread, the community grew to cover the whole valley. What was once a bustling little mining town of approximately 850, filled with American dreams and satisfied dust-smudged faces, is now a much smaller, barely-hanging-on community of less than 200. When the mines stopped producing the enormous shipments so many of the miners had gotten used to, most of them packed up their families and headed out with the train the next chance they got, some holding out longer than others. The population dropped to its current state within a few decades and somehow, miraculously, has managed to maintain it all these years since. Those that remained there learned how to care for their families with what the valley and surrounding mountains provided them. They passed this information down through the generations, who improved on most of it, creating their own little more-or-less self-sustaining community. The train just ensured that they could maintain it.

But all that changed over the winter.

It was as if a curse of the blackest black had been cast upon Miner's Nook and if some of the rumors Jimmy had heard were true, maybe that's just what happened.

Miner's Nook sits in a small valley nestled deep between three monstrously, looming forest covered mountains, one on each side of the valley and one on the northern end. A branch of the Collis River runs through the western half of the valley out of the mountains and joins the branch that cuts through the eastern side. The river continues to run south toward the open mountain-less end of the valley, ending in a magnificent waterfall. A bird's eye view, so to speak, shows that the valley is shaped kind of like a human torso. The north end is slightly wider and the way the mountainside curves in toward the valley gives the illusion of a ribcage. The two Collis River branches running through each side of the valley, joining to form a Y, have a sullen, depressing likeness to that of an autopsy incision and it only increases the grimness of the aerial view.

The old but well-built railroad tracks emerge from a tunnel carved through the mountain and run east on a slight downward curve at the southern end of the valley. It runs over the Collis River, even stopping on the bridge because the train is almost as long as the valley is wide, and into another tunnel carved into the mountain on the opposite side. The similarities are eerie, almost like looking at a mirror image of itself. The tracks also give the illusion of sutures running along the base of the torso shaped valley, almost as if it has been reattached to its lower half with large dark threads in a perfectly stitched pattern.

There's a wide strip of forest on both sides of the river that separates the railroad tracks from the waterfall. The waterfall can't be seen from anywhere in the valley or even the tracks, but it can be heard easily. It is a constant sound in the background of the valley and the only time the residents really pay any mind to it is to miss it when they leave and despise it when they return, for a little while, anyway. The river and waterfall, in the opinion of those who live among them, are infinite and immortal. They have never dried up or even so much as seemed to slow. The water moves quickly and seamlessly, churning in tight little swirls at the junction point before resuming its smooth ride off the mountainside. It is a narrow, yet powerful waterfall, falling several hundred yards before cascading into a small pool at the bottom. Or maybe it is a large pool, it's hard to tell for sure from this height.

2

Toby doesn't notice the smoke billowing and puffing toward the west until he sees that Jim is looking at it as they emerge from the dark already beginning to slow down. Before entering the tunnel, they pull the brake levers that stop them in the right place on the tracks. Toby's eyes are still adjusting from the gloomy darkness of the tunnel to the bright afternoon sunlight, but the smoke couldn't be missed. "Dat uh foo'rul fi'ya, 'im?" Toby looks up at Jim with honest curiosity in his eyes, torn between wanting to be right and wanting to be wrong. Right because he is wrong about so many things, so much of the time, that he enjoys being right when he can be. Wrong because that means that death has occurred. Tobias doesn't like death. Tobias doesn't like to think about death. Tobias gets very upset around death.

"I suppose so." Jim says after a brief hesitation. It's in the right area for a funeral fire but something is nagging Jim about it. He just can't quite say what, though. Tobias picks up on his unsurety and lets out a long slow, kind of raspy sigh, saying no more.

The cab of the train stops several hundred yards ahead of the ramshackle train station and very close to entering the east tunnel, the rear car just barely clearing the tunnel entrance they had arrived from. Within seconds both men are leaning out of the small rectangular window, observing the station. Jim stands a solid four inches over Toby, and while standing beside him, hip to hip, crammed in front of the narrow window, he leans his tall body over Toby's head, his midsection twisted at an uncomfortable angle. Jim pays no attention to this, however. The smoke, at least, made the lack of attendance at the train station make sense. *Something isn't right, though. McGrath isn't even here.* Jim can feel it and he thinks Toby can too, even if he doesn't know what it is he is feeling.

The poor lad is looking around outside, his head snapping from side to side. His eyes are alert but overwhelmingly confused, sweeping over the, somehow, strange panoramic view of the southern end of the valley, trying to take in everything at once. A narrow but dense patch of evergreens line the river on both sides, obscuring the fire blazing through the Slums and into the Lot. The problem was that there was nothing to take in, which was, in itself, the problem. Miner's Nook felt *unattended. Abandoned. Breathless.*

Jim notices the small beads of sweat popping out on Toby's slightly misshapen forehead, glistening like the morning light shining through a dew drop caught in a delicately spun spider web. The sweat would be understandable if not for the cool breeze swirling around their heads. "Alright, Toby." Jim straightens up from the window, grabs Toby by the shoulders, pulls him away from the window and upright in front of him in one swift motion.

The surprise of it startles Toby badly and for a few moments, he is in danger of crying. Crying in front of his friend, Jim. Toby's parents tell him he's too old for tears now, that he needs to be a man and men don't cry. But Tobias does cry. But only in the comfort of his room at home. So, with considerable concentration he wills the tears away and stands in Jim's fearful grasp trying to understand what is happening. Jim sees the tear forming on his lower right eyelid, trying to bead on his fine dark eyelashes but he blinks it away almost as quick as it forms.

Shame overcomes him. *What the hell is wrong with me?* Jim relaxes his grip on Toby and speaks in a softer tone with the intention of soothing the young man. "It's all right. Nothin to be ascared of, boy." Toby's strained face relaxes a little, but Jim thinks it is more the tone than the words. "I'm goin to walk on over to the station and try to find Frank. I want ya to stay here like ya always do." Toby's face tenses again, panic stricken. He opens his mouth to protest, Jim is sure of it, and continues in that same comforting voice before he can so much as utter a sound. "I know it seems spooky cause ain't nobody here, but with the funeral fire goin, I'm sure that's where everyone is. So, I'm goin to hop offa here and go find someone to unload them two cars down yonder, and right quick too, so we can get the hell outta here. Sound like a plan, boy?" Jim pauses, waiting to see if Toby's expression changes, but it doesn't falter. So, he adds, "Everything's going to be fine, Toby, I promise."

Toby stands there for several long moments, Jim letting his hands slide off Toby's shoulders to hang at his own sides, seeming too heavy to lift for the time being. Slowly, Toby's expression changes to one of understanding and then quickly over to worry as he recognizes the doubt laced in that last statement. One of the things Toby is good at is reading other's emotions. No one knows this, though his parents have suspected on more than one occasion that their son can pick up on their emotions, more so than most children, at any given time. That isn't quite right, though. If Toby had a mind that could articulate comprehendible sentences and he had an actual education that extended beyond the mere basics, he would best be able to describe this *emotional empathy* as something like echolocation. Bats use it to travel by emitting a sound that bounces off its surroundings, returning the sound waves to the bat giving it the ability to detect what's around it. Tobias Medlin's emotional empathy works in the way the sound waves bounce back to the bat. Except in his case, colorless scented waves of emotion emerge from those around him and bounce in his direction. The stronger the emotion the more powerful the wave and therefore, the stronger the scent is. It turns off and on, almost as if an invisible force is flipping a switch inside his head, sometimes staying on for as long as several hours but mostly just a matter of minutes. Toby cannot control this ability, nor does he have any desire to, but he has dealt with it enough to know the scent of just about every emotion a person can feel. The aging gent standing in front of him reeks of a wretched combination of odors. Doubt smelling like a moist, mildewy rag. Shame smelling like burning rubber, a horrid acrid smell, and currently the stronger among the mingle of scented waves. Confusion smelling like vinegar and sour fermented apples, appalling and nauseating. And fear smelling like sex; hot, rough, sensational, sweaty sex.

Tobias takes a step back, meaning to take another but backs up into the window instead, trying to get away from the overwhelming scents that Jim is unintentionally expelling. "I 'ay," he says, looking down at the dirty floor of the cab not wanting to meet Jim's eyes. He doesn't want Jim to leave, he is scared, and something is wrong, but he can't stand that aromatic bouquet much longer and he doesn't know how to *turn it off*. Besides, he trusts Jim and knows that he wouldn't let anything hurt Toby. So, he agrees, reluctantly, but he still agrees.

Jimmy Moran lets out a long, exaggerated sigh of relief. He is certain that Toby wouldn't want to stay on the train this time given the current atmosphere. Whatever is going on around here can be felt in the air; thick enough to cut with a butcher's knife. "Okay, Toby. Good! Thank you!" He really is relieved. Jim knows that certain things can set Toby off on one of his fits. Luckily, Jim has only had to deal with two of them in the few years he's known Toby, but he still doesn't know them all. And it's better to be safe than sorry, his mama had always told him.

Jim takes a step forward, with the intention of giving Toby a reassuring hug, but stops before taking another. Toby is trying to take another step back even though he is already against the wall but ends up cowering in the corner instead. Jim, unaware of the horrendous scent oozing out of him, mistakes the disgust on Tobias Medlin's face for that of terror. Jim's heart breaks and for the first time since *taking on the boy*, he imagines it is his son standing before him instead of the feeble-minded Toby. "I'm sorry I scared ya, son." Jim says softly as a tear slips from his eye, slowly running down the graying stubble on his cheek, before dripping off his strong jaw and on to his dark blue overalls with the large front pocket. Toby doesn't see the tears though; the last word is still hanging in the air when Jim steps off the bottom step to the cab of the train.

Lost in thought and trying not to spook himself along the way, Jim makes it to the large two-room shack with the attached lean-to that serves as the Miner's Nook train station, much quicker than he has expected to. It's eerily quiet, with no birds or bugs. The air is ripe with the smell of the burning fire, circulating in the steady light breeze swirling around the valley. He doesn't see or hear anyone around, no dogs barking, cows mooing, or chickens clucking. *It just keeps getting creepier and creepier.* He thinks to himself as he makes his way, slowly, across the hard-packed dirt platform, immediately noticing the lack of noise coming from inside the station. Eerie. He has run this exact track for well over a decade and stops here on every single weekly run. Not once has he ever showed up, funeral or otherwise going on, and there not be at least one person awaiting the shipment. *What in God's good name?!?!*

He veers slightly to the left to get a full view of the bench placed under the lean-to, notes there's no one there, and corrects his path toward the door leading into the front room of the train station. That's when he sees the flames in the distance spreading across the Lot and edging toward the train station. *Gonna have to make this quick.* He tells himself, trying not to think the worst. He sighs heavily, hoping to find someone, anyone alive.

The front room of the train station runs the width of the building but is quite narrow. The door opens in the center of the long front wall. On the left side of the room is a square table with four chairs scattered around it. All unoccupied. He takes a step inside, noting the plain door on the far-right end of the room on the back wall. This door leads to the big warehouse-like room where the shipments are taken and distributed. A sturdy oak desk sits to the right of that door and a small square window, the only one in this room, sits smartly behind it. A single chair sits behind the desk while two more sit in front of it; all, also, unoccupied. Floor to ceiling shelves beginning at the door on the back wall, wraps around the room, breaking for the outside door, only to resume on the other side and stopping in the corner opposite the door by the oak desk. The wall with the single window is the only wall unoccupied by the cluttered shelves. Almost every shelf is being utilized to hold something. Lots of books. Lots of paper. Lots of wooden crates. And a lot of dust. Thick dust.

But no people. No indication anyone's here or has been here.

No noise. Silence.

Silence.

Silence....

SILENCE!

No. Noise. None.

THE WATERFALL! I don't hear the waterfall! All at once it comes crashing down on him why it is so quiet here, aside from the lack of people, of course. There is no waterfall roaring in the background, no birds chirping hither and tither about, no bugs singing lazily in the lengthening grass, no sounds of men at work or children at play, no talking or crying over the funeral. *Something is definitely wrong here.*

He turns and rushes back out into the dooryard, but his rough worn boots slide easily through the thin layer of dirt that puffs up around them as he comes to a skidding stop. He stands there, astounded, watching a man run through the rows of dilapidated homes that serve as the 'Residential Area', known as the Lot to the valley folks, toward the front of the train. It is from quite a distant, the man quick as can be, and looks like he is carrying something in his arms. The sight of the man is lost to the train and Jim thinks, *was he bleeding? Did I see that? Could I...* His thoughts are broken off by a shrill, piercing screech that reverberates off the mountains intensifying its already undeniable rage. Jim's nerves immediately electrify at that terrible sound, sending panicky jolts throughout his, seemingly paralyzed, limbs. Several seconds later, a woman in a long dark hooded cape jets by obviously following the man that had appeared moments before her. She disappears behind the front of the train before he can notice anything more about the mystery woman, and when the last of her flowing cape disappears with her, Jim is able to regain his senses.

He finally breaks free of his temporary shock and fear-induced coma and bolts for the front of the train. Praying that the man and/or woman doesn't board the train and begging that they don't find Toby if they do.

Please God! Please! Jim prays to his God as the dust puffs up in clouds from under his worn-down work boots with every lengthy stride.

3

Toby stands at the only window in the cab of the train watching Jim Moran walk quickly toward the train station. Part of him is okay with the fact that he is gone because of that wretched smell but Toby is very, very, afraid of this place and desperately wants Jim to come back to the train. Stench be damned. He is already aware of what Jim will be a minute or so from now. The waterfall has been silenced or stopped or something. Toby isn't sure because he can't see the river from here, but he knows he doesn't hear it, even though he should. He is sure that it is a bad sign. His yearning for his friend's return grows stronger and stronger with each moment Jim isn't on the train.

Toby watches as Jim becomes partially obscured by the shadowy doorway of the train station as he steps into it and panic tries to set in. Jim just stands there, however, not disappearing entirely into the room, and this helps Toby settle himself. Then Jim does begin to move deeper into the shadows. One step, Toby's already obvious frown deepening even further. Another step, Toby's heart quickening evermore, the panic trying to return. "'im" Toby mutters, breathlessly. And just like that, Jim's out the door in a flash now standing in the dooryard with a mixed expression of confusion and exhilaration plastered across his face. Toby leans out the window a little further wanting to give Jim a wave, so Jim knows that Toby is staying on the train like he's supposed to. Before he can get his hand up, though, movement catches his eye, and he turns his head to see a man running straight toward him.

The sight of the man startles Toby badly and he jerks hard enough to crack his elbow on the window ledge straightening up from his leaning position. He doesn't notice because now he can see the man running across the front of the train through the large solid pane of glass that serves as a windshield. It is covered with splatters of dead bugs and small mud clods, sprinkled with dust and pollen, yet still clear enough for Toby to see that the man is carrying something bundled up in a cloth. He is streaked with ash and soot carrying the pungent aroma of the fire burning in the valley with him. Toby, unsure of what to do or how to react in such a situation, takes a couple of steps toward the top of the stairs exiting the cab then stops dead on his feet.

The man is standing at the base of the steps, panting heavily, sweat dripping off his face in strange gray droplets. The bundled pale-yellow cloth held tightly to his midsection is dotted with black fingerprints and smears. Toby does not sense any danger or malice from the man, the empathy thing isn't working on him, or it turned off again, either way he doesn't need it because the feeling is strong. The man's eyes dart toward the front of the train and back to Toby. The man takes a small step forward and quietly asks Toby if he has a mother. Toby still unsure of how to react to this situation answers this question impulsively, promptly, and truthfully. "'es, I 'ommuh' 'ack 'ohm' 'it I 'ahhee. 'Ommuh 'ake ook…" The unknown man seems to have no trouble understanding Tobias with his terrible speech impediment. *Translation: yes, my momma back home with my daddy. Momma make cook…*

A heartfelt and murderous shriek cuts throat the air. Toby, entranced by this strange man, barely notices but ceases speaking because the man's face is changing. The man standing below him sighs heavily, nods, then tells Toby that he is to give this to his mother as a gift. He steps up on the bottom step leading into the cab and reaches the bundled cloth up toward Toby. Toby instinctively takes a few steps forward and wraps his arms around it. The filthy man still holding a piece of the cloth flicks his wrist violently, gracefully jerking the cloth off the thing now laying in Toby's arms. He turns, bends, grabs a chunk of wood from the rack by the door and a moment later is running at full force through the trees in the direction of the waterfall. The entire ordeal is over in a matter of seconds. Toby looks down into his arms, smiling with absolute glee at the gift he is to give his mother. All his fears, first overridden, and then vanquished completely by this unexpected, absolutely delightful gift. She will be so pleased. He steps through a door at the back of the cab, leading to the cabin where they sleep, turning sideways as he walks through the doorway so not to bump his arms possibly causing him to drop this magnificent present. He very gently and carefully lays it down on his cot.

Toby does not see the woman in the long-hooded cape run past the front of the train, he has already turned toward the cabin to tend to his Momma's gift. He does, however, hear Jim screaming his name franticly, moments later, so he leaves it where it lies, careful to close the door behind him. Toby is standing in the same place he was just moments ago, looking halfway panicked, when Jim comes bursting across the view through the windshield, turning and coming to another skidding stop, this time at the base of the train steps. Jim is panting much heavier than the man was, looking gassed and ready to kill over but relieved, nonetheless. The boy is safe. "Oh, Toby! Thank Heavens!" Panting, a little slower now. "Ya'll right? Ya certainly look'it." Jim finally managing to catch half his breath. "Stay here, I need to try to talk to them." Then he turns and runs off into the trees toward the waterfall, not giving Toby a chance to respond, just as the two did before him.

Jim runs through the thick tangle of tall trees: pines, spruces, oaks, elms; in the back of his mind, he's thankful that the underbrush has just recently begun to reappear for the spring season. He unnerves himself with irrational fearful thoughts, but with a considerable expenditure of energy, Jimmy Moran pushes these horrid thoughts away. He is tiring quickly and feeling well older than his actual age. *Can't stop! Gotta keep goin!* A sudden sense of urgency, growing stronger and stronger as he approaches the waterfall, bears down on him with every step. He can't quite grasp why but he feels as though he will miss his chance to find out what is going on if he doesn't get to them soon. Some or any information is better than none. Or so he thinks.

Jim can hear voices, or maybe just a voice, as he emerges from the trees, still several yards from the edge of the cliff where the waterfall once drained its constant flow of water into a pool at the bottom. Jim can see that there is no water for the usually rapidly flowing waterfall. Just a mere trickle that falls in heavy droplets to the drying pool below. The man and woman, apparently too caught up in their own mess, to hear or see Jim step out of the woods line, is standing off to the right of him. The river creating the waterfall divides the forestland they have just emerged from in two the same way it divides the rest of the valley. All three of them are standing on the left side of the waterfall. The *silent* waterfall. Jim stands, unflinching, watching their exchange from

11

a distance. Too far to see the details of their clothes and faces, except for the hooded robe which is a deep royal purple instead of the dark brown or black he had originally mistaken it for, but close enough to hear some of what is being said. The man, his back to the waterfall, facing the trees and just mere steps from the edge of the cliff, is shaking his head violently, the bundled cloth trapped between his soot smeared chest and scraped, crossed arms. The woman, standing before the man with her back to Jim, lets out a long, agony-filled scream of fury, her hands upraised with her fingers spread, palms out, fingers bent in a clawing gesture. The force of the scream, blows the man's sweat drenched hair across his forehead, causing him to first rock back on his heels and then take a staggering step backward.

Jimmy Moran's heart skips a beat, his breath catching in his throat. *He's going over.* He thinks in a panic then quickly realizes that he doesn't. The man simply readjusts his footing never taking his eyes off the female or loosening his grip on the bundled cloth. Jim exhales, the pocket of air caught in his throat comes bursting out in a loud gasp as the man settles on his feet. Jim's heart pumping harder, as if to catch up with the missing beat. The robed woman snaps her head in Jim's direction, most of her face hidden by the enormous hood, and eyes him with a quick look of distaste and hatred. He has time to register a dark colored eye with a narrow strip of eyebrow above, set upon naturally tanned skin. It disappears with a snap of the head as quick as the first and she lets her hands fall to her sides, disappearing in the flowing folds of her robe. A puzzled look comes across the man's face as the woman's voice rises with every line.

"Dust into disintegrate patois thy beware thus…"

"Must thee if name thy speak…"

"Pimpernel the of virtue the…"

"Tell can tongue no, heard hath ear no."

Her left hand appears from her robe and then disappears in front of her face in an instant. She blows on the palm of her hand, as if blowing a kiss to her sweetheart, and a whirlwind of dust puffs up and out into the man's face like a tiny sandstorm. The man, immediately cries out in surprise, drops the bundled cloth at his feet, and begins scratching at his face in a failing attempt to get the dust off.

The woman snatches the bundled cloth just before it hits the ground with a squeal of delight and triumph. Her moment of joy is quickly staunched, though, by the unraveling of the blanket to reveal a chunk of firewood rather than what she is truly after. "You hid it from me! I need it! I will have what is mine!" She squalls at the man with an undeniable hatred. The man grabs her by her upper arms and lifts her up until only the tips of her heeled boots are touching the weather-worn rock under their feet.

Jim does see a broad grin appear on the man's black smeared face, giving him a much more bizarre appearance. The man leans even closer to the woman, his hands lost in the fabric of her billowing robe, and Jim believes he means to kiss her. He may have for all Jim knows. He hears the man whisper something but the only word he catches off the breeze is *never. Never what?* Shockingly, with a simple pivot of the hip, the woman goes flying out over the emptiness of the void beyond the waterfall, the bundled log still held tight against her chest. She screams as she begins her descent, the murderous squall echoing off the cliff walls.

Jim bolts to the edge of the cliff. The woman is still falling, and he makes it in time to see her hit the ground. It's a massive cliff and everything, even the monstrously tall trees look tiny from up here, but Jim just about knows that the woman lands on her feet by the way she immediately takes off running. And at an incredible speed. *What the hell did I just see? There ain't no way! She should be nothing but blood and bone splinters down there on a rock! There ain't no way! There just ain't no way!*

"Yeah, ya just seen dat same as I did." The dirty man standing beside him says raspily, as if he has read Jim's mind. The man looks familiar to Jim, but he can't quite place him by name. The man is covered in ash and dirt, his shirt lays in tatters across his thin chest and shoulders. In years to come, looking back, Jim Moran will wish he would have asked the man his name before anything else, but that's not how it happens. Jimmy Moran has a lot of sleepless nights in the following years because of this odd day in Miner's Nook.

4

It just so happens that the first question Jimmy asks the man is the wrong one. "Who da hell was that? And why did ya just throw her off the damn cliff!" Shocked and still trying to process the events of the hundred years, it seems, that he has been here.

The man looking down toward the trees the woman has disappeared into, turns toward Jim, and asks if they can head back to the train. Jim agrees immediately and the two of them start back into the tree line, walking slowly and clearly exhausted. Jim gives the man a few moments to give him an answer but when he doesn't, Jim asks him again.

"Ya really wanna know?" the man asks with an undeniable exasperation.

"I need to know!" Jim shouts back. "I need to know what in the goddamn hell happened around here! I know it's been a tough winter but where is everyone? What the hell happened to the river and waterfall? I can only assume that since you threw that woman back there off a fuckin cliff, that she must have *somethin* to do with it, so start there, would ya?" Jim stops walking, causing the man to stop a few steps ahead of him. He is glaring at this man with an intensity that, ultimately, seals the poor man's fate.

A heavy sigh. "Alright. Her name is Uhblubbuha and she….," the man begins.

"Wait, what'd ya say? It was all jumbled up and I…." Jim cuts off mid-sentence. His eyes grow wide as he watches the man's face contort into one of horror and pain. The terrified man parts his lips, exposing a radiantly bright light unlike anything Jim has ever or will ever see. This light, or whatever it is, can only be described as *black*. So excruciating bright, yet, being of the darkest of black. It seems to be emerging from his throat, too bright to look at. Jim raises his arm to shield his eyes from this oddest of lights, but it blinks out a moment later. A narrow tendril of silver smoke escapes from his parted lips and when the man tries to inhale his next breath, he immediately begins coughing, ash flying out of his mouth in small mushroom cloud shaped bursts.

The coughing continues for several long moments before starting to abate but not before the man loses consciousness. Jim watches as the man's eyes turn up into his head exposing only the veiny white and then slumps to the pine needle coated forest floor in an uncomfortable heap. With a determination he isn't even sure he has, Jim drags the man's body through the timbers and back to the train. By the time they get out of the trees Jim is sweating profusely but the ash-covered man is no better, remaining unconscious.

Jim gets the man to the bottom step of the stairs leading up into the cab of the train, panting hard. Toby grabs one of the man's arms and drags him to the back of the cab toward the cabin, where his Momma's gift is nestled in an empty drawer in the built-in bureau on the cabin wall. Toby lays the man on his own cot, not wanting to leave him on the floor, and then leaves to retrieve a small canteen of water.

Toby comes back to the cabin a few moments later to find Jim sitting on the same cot as the dirty man wearing rags and looking into the man's slack mouth. It is quite a strange sight, indeed. Toby walks over, the canteen in hand, and stands behind Jim to see what he is looking at. What they should be seeing is a set of teeth set in gums, a tongue, and that weird hanging ball thing in the back of the throat (the uvula). This mouth is missing the tongue, though. Just gone. No trace of one whatsoever, as if he was born without one. Toby is confused but doesn't ask any questions, his thoughts constantly returning to the gift he is to take to his mother. The gift he tells Jim nothing about.

Jim is fascinated, in shock, unable to believe what he is looking at. He knows what has happened to this man's tongue - it flash-fried in his mouth - he seen it happen even if he didn't know that's what was happening at the time. The only thing Jim can think to do is get the man back to Albany and as quick as they can. He could stop in Portland and find someone better equipped to help this man, but he doesn't know anything about Portland beyond its train station and the diner across the road from it. He would end up wasting a lot of valuable time just trying not to get lost. He knows Albany and knows he can get the man help a lot faster there. This man needs help, he doesn't know what kind or who can give it, but the man needs help. So, Jim tells Toby to feed the fire and keep it fed to the max the rest of the ride because they are going straight back to Albany. No more stops on this trip. Those stops left on the route will have to survive another week because Jim doubts that they are any worse off than the unconscious man in the cabin behind him. And if the company wants to fire him for it, well then, to hell with them.

5

Approximately twelve hours later, Jimmy Moran, Tobias Medlin who still has his Momma's gift, and the tongueless man, arrives at the Albany, New York train yard. This middle-of-the-night, much-earlier-than-normal arrival is startling and unheard of, drawing quite a bit of attention quickly.

The tongueless man is handed over to the New York State Police who take him to the local hospital. No matter what they try, they are unable to wake him. A few days later he is transferred to the N.D.A.M.A. due to lack of beds at the hospital. Jimmy Moran is questioned multiple times, over the next few weeks, about this strange man and the even stranger circumstances surrounding him. He is finally left alone when they realize that his story does not change in the slightest. Tobias Medlin, being the feeble-minded young man that he is, wasn't even considered for questioning. If he had been, they would have learned of the gift Toby was to give his mother. Then maybe, just maybe, things may have turned out differently in the end.

Toby gets in the car, slings his pack over his shoulder and tosses it on the floorboard, but keeps a tightly wrapped blanket pressed against his chest with one hand. Mr. Medlin is cautiously surprised to find his son in such a pleasant mood given such unpleasant circumstances. "Watcha got there, Toby?" his dad asks, but Toby simply shakes his head and informs him that it's for his Momma. No amount of pressing will get Toby to spill the secret in the blanket, so Mr. Medlin lets it go, knowing he'll find out soon enough. Toby keeps asking his father where his Momma is, every few miles on their way home to the Medlin residence. Once they pull up to the house, Toby is out of the car and running toward the house before Mr. Medlin turns the ignition off. "Ohmma! Ohmma!" Toby yells more excited than ever. Mrs. Medlin, standing in the kitchen finishing up the dishes, turns toward her usually loving and currently ecstatic son's voice. He crashes into her, wrapping one arm around her neck and squeezing her tight, almost knocking her over backwards spilling them both to the spotless kitchen floor. She notes that his other hand is holding something wrapped up in a moth-eaten blanket.

He releases her before she can return his startling but warm hug. A huge smile spreads across his face and his mother can see the little boy he once was, the one she still gets a momentary glimpse of from time to time. The face that is now trying to grow a stubbily little mustache and few chin hairs. Her heart swells with love and adoration for him all over again. "'Ere Ohmma!" Toby says excitedly and grabs her hand leading her over to the small table she keeps in the kitchen corner. Toby lays the blanket carefully down on the table as his father walks in and approaches his son and wife.

Mrs. Medlin asks Toby if it's for her and Toby nods his head eagerly. Excitement dances across his eyes as his mother grabs a fold of the blanket and lays it back, then doing the same thing to the fold on the opposite side, revealing the treasure underneath. Mrs. Medlin gasps loudly and her husband, shocked into silence but not paralysis, places his hand on the small of her back in both comfort and support. Toby, gleaming with joy, looks from the table to his mother and back over and over.

Laying on the kitchen table in the Medlin's home, is a beautiful healthy baby boy, barely six weeks old, a few remaining splinters of umbilical cord stub still lingering around his tiny navel, swaddled in a light blue baby blanket. A tuft of dark brown hair sticks out from under the blanket tightly hooded around his tiny head. He has flushed rosy cheeks as if with a full tummy and fierce green eyes. Eyes so bright, so intense, they were unforgettable. His eyes will remain with him for the entirety of his life, sometimes as a blessing and sometimes, ultimately, a curse. He has all the right parts in all the right places; he is perfect in every way... almost.

"Oh, my...." Mrs. Medlin gasps, placing her hand over her mouth.

Chapter Two

N.D.A.M.A.

1

"His execution is set to take place at 11:00 a.m. tomorrow morning. This will mark the fourth execution in the state this year." The pretty blonde woman on the screen announces from her seat behind the long wooden table, her fingers entwined in front of her laying on a stack of papers. The television displaying this vocal beauty is mounted high up on the wall, close to the ceiling, in the far corner of the common room. The middle-aged man standing behind one of the sofas placed strategically around the television set, is more interested in the newswoman's appearance than the news itself. At the call of his name, though, he reluctantly tears his attention away from the screen.

"Here's your medication, Mr. Patrickson." Another blonde. This one much younger and right in front of him, not on a screen. She is standing beside a pushcart on wheels with rows of small paper cups, half containing a diverse selection of pills, while the other half contains a swallow's worth of water. She is smiling cheerily at him, holding a cup with several pills, of varying sizes and colors, in one hand and a cup of water in the other. He returns the smile and takes the cups, first tipping the small cup of pills into his mouth and immediately chasing it with the water so he can swallow them down before they have a chance to dissolve on his tongue.

The young blonde in the white nurse's uniform, complete with matching knee-high white stockings, white pumps and a small white cap that must be pinned in place atop her up-done hair, broadens her smile and retrieves the empty paper cups, placing them on a stack of other empty ones. "You have a wonderful day now, Mr. Patrickson!" she says as she begins pushing the cart past him.

"Ya seed Joe dis mownin'?" Gregory Patrickson asks in his thick, husky voice. Joe isn't really his name, no one knows the man's real name because he's never spoken to anyone, and he mostly refuses to communicate through writing or any other means. He has been known to write down simple requests, that are almost always fulfilled, even though no one really understands why. Joe asks for his own room and a week later he is moving into one. Joe asks for stationary supplies, and he receives them within days. Joe asks for a writing table, and one gets bolted down in his room the following day. There have been rumors circulating the asylum about Joe since he showed up some three decades ago. That the head doctor, Dr. Gerard to his youthful employees and the 'warden' to some his more unruly patients, took a liking to him and the way his tongueless mouth feels on his junk, is probably the most common rumor circulating. All that stupidity aside, and that's exactly how he sees it all, Greg considers Joe a friend, anyway. They play cards together, eat meals together, and try to volunteer together when able to. They have a simple life and Greg likes it just fine, as long as Joe is around.

Her cheery smile fades quickly and a frown line forms across her forehead as she furrows her brow in sudden confusion. "No... now that I think about it.... no, I don't believe that I have." She's looking around the large room, scanning the couple dozen or so faces scattered around, her mind automatically registering their familiarity and dismissing them. After concluding that Joe is not in the common room with the rest of the patients, and not being able to recall giving him his medication this morning, she snatches the clipboard hanging off the side of the cart and runs her finger delicately down the side of the paper. She quickly scans the first page, flips it up from the bottom to scan the names on the following page, and repeats the process to check the last page. She finally locates Joe's name on the last page of the list and, just as she suspects, it's missing the check mark indicating he has received his morning dose of medication. She looks up from the clipboard into the troubled, worried eyes of Greg Patrickson, back down at the list of names and then back up to Greg, "Let me go find out where he is. I'm

19

sure he's still in the cafeteria, probably just late to rise this morning." She lays her petite hand on Patrickson's arm in a comforting gesture and gives him, what she hopes, is a reassuring smile, one that says everything is fine and you're worrying for nothing. The young blonde nurse doesn't really think it's nothing though, she wishes she could think that way, but something is nagging at her that it's something, and that something probably isn't good.

Greg lays his hand over top of the nurse's hand for the brief moment it rests on his arm. The smile is convincing enough for Gregory Patrickson because relief cascades over him. "Thank ya, miss! Thank ya!" he praises as she slips by, awkwardly turning the wheeled cart and heading in the direction of the nurse's station, her tight hips swaying rhythmically, like a pendulum in motion. Greg watches as she stops the cart, leans over one of the desks, speaking to a frizzy red head with bright pink horn-rimmed glasses, who then leans to her left and speaks to the woman sitting at the desk next to her. It seems every nurse has the same response, the same lackadaisical shake of the head. He watches as she raises from her leaning position against the desk, a troubled look upon her face, she speaks something else to the frizzy-haired woman and turns to walk down the long hallway, slipping beyond Greg's line of sight. He ambles over to an unoccupied, small, round table for two with a deck of playing cards on it. He pulls up a chair and begins shuffling the deck of cards, looking back over his shoulder every few minutes waiting for Joe, the pretty blonde nurse, or both.

2

The young blonde in white, who should have been wearing her name plate pinned to the left breast pocket on her nurse's uniform, pops her head into the cafeteria, hoping to catch sight of Joe eating a late breakfast with sleep gunk still hanging from his eyelashes. No such luck though, just the janitor; an old bald man with a few thin gray hairs sticking out of his ears, pushing a broom across the floor. She continues down the long, white-washed hallway toward the locked corridor that contains all the patient's rooms, her pumps producing the only sound in the quiet, echoey space. *Clack! Click! Clack!*

She runs her hands down the front of her uniform brushing out any wrinkles and straightening her short dress by the bottom hem, once again, noticing her missing name plate. If she had been wearing her nameplate it would read **Sabrina Lowell** in white against a plain black background. She isn't, though, she has left it in her room at home and didn't realize it was missing until she was more than halfway to the asylum this morning. It is Sunday, however, and Dr. Gerard has the day off. On any other day, she would have been late for work just to go back and get it; knowing that according to Dr. Gerard, tardiness is a forgivable error while uniform mismanagement is an unforgivable sin. Dr. Gerard is funny about certain rules and regulations and the nurse's uniforms are one of them. They must be complete and unblemished at the start of every shift. Sabrina, an employee of the asylum for just under two years now, watched one lady get fired on her first day for wearing ivory-colored stockings instead of white. That's how funny the "warden' is about certain things.

Dr. Gerard is, also, funny about the whereabouts and welfare of his patients at any and all times. This is the real reason, unbeknownst to the greater population of The Navea Dwighton Asylum for the Mentally Afflicted, that most of the patient's requests are accommodated to, not just Joe's, within reason of course. Most of the patients here lack the mental compacity to understand simpler matters than this, though, and all the patients are consistently heavily medicated for their own protection as well as everyone else's. Gerard believes that they should be allowed what few dignities and pleasures they can muster.

Sabrina Lowell turns right, takes several more steps forward before stopping at a set of locked double doors. She enters a four-digit personal identification code, hers is 1833, into the small square numbered panel on the wall to the right of the doors, then pushes through them after hearing the muffled click as it unlocks. She stops and takes a deep breath trying to get her racing heart and whirling thoughts under control. She needs this job and therefore needs to find this unaccounted for patient. She exhales slowly, closes her eyes, and draws another deep breath. This exhale is just as slow as the last but more helpful. Her heart is beginning to slow, so she opens her eyes, taking in her surroundings.

This corridor consists of two lengthy hallways, crossing in the middle like a large plus sign. There are ten relatively large rooms in each of the four hallway sections, five rooms (all even numbered) on one side and five rooms (all odd numbered) on the other. All of them numbered with gold-plated metal cutouts, for a total of 40 constant resident suites. At the ends of each hallway, the same set of locked double doors at each one, there's a list of names with room numbers beside them. She finds the name JOSEPH DOE, notes room number 32 beside it, then takes off walking again. Unlike the plain white walls making up majority of the asylum, these hallways are painted in bright warm colors: reds, oranges, and yellows. Smarty-pants scientists say that colors affect moods, so Dr. Gerard decided to have the residents' rooms and hallways painted in bright colors to help promote positive behavior and attitudes. Sabrina wasn't here before they added the colored paint, but she doesn't believe it helps with their moods much. Most of the patients are stoned, nonresponsive, or just hateful as hell. She guesses she can understand why, though.

The room numbers increase toward the intersection. Sabrina has just passed room number 10 and stops momentarily in the intersection to check the closet room numbers. On her right the closest room number is 40 and to her left is 30. She turns right and the room numbers begin descending, 40 now on her left … 39 now on her right… 38 on her left…, until she finally approaches room number 32, the next to last room from the end of the hall and the last room on her left. She can see the double doors exiting this end of the corridor, a half dozen or so steps away, from the man's welcome mat in front of his plain white door with the gold-plated numbers 32 bolted to it.

She takes another deep breath, counts *one-two-three*, and exhales slowly. She raises her hand and knocks loudly on the door. "Joe… Joe!" she waits, listening. Nothing. *Rap! Rap! Rap! Rap!.... Rap! Rap!* "Joe!" A pause. "You need to wake up!" Pause. "Joe!" Nervous pause. "Please answer me!" She waits, listening, her ear pressing against the door hard enough to turn it snow white, panic building and threatening to boil over. She fumbles a shaky hand into her dress pocket, a few strands of her golden blonde hair falling out of place hanging around her paling face, and after several long moments, comes out with a master key to all the patient's rooms. All the nurses have them and are under strict instructions only to use them if the situation demands it. Well, she thinks this situation demands it! Sabrina feels certain Joe is in there, she doesn't know nor care how she knows it, but she does. She also feels that something dreadful is behind the door and these feelings only exacerbate her terror.

3

After what seems like a century of jerkily missing the keyhole, Sabrina finally manages to slide it in. She turns the key, unlocks it, and lightly pushes the door, letting it slowly swing open. Her heart hammering, she can feel beads of sweat forming on her nose. Her stomach feels as if it has knotted itself and her tongue and throat have dried out to equate to the Sahara Desert. She is sick with anticipation and dread by the time the door comes to a slow silent stop a few inches from the wall. She can feel the scream rising in her throat before her eyes have completely registered what she is seeing.

Blood. Blood on the floor. Blood on the walls. Blood soaking through the thin mattress under and around him. Blood in the sink and splattering the toilet. Blood beaded in his thin hair. Blood running out of his eyes. His ears. His mouth and nose. Blood drenching his knit pajama pants to his feet and pooling under him. Blood beading on his shirtless thin chest like drops of sweat.

Within a few seconds, Sabrina sees all of this, screams hysterically, or thinks she does, anyway, and abruptly faints. As she falls the heel of one of her white pumps clips the lower corner of the door just hard enough to bounce it off the wall, engaging a spring-based set up that swings the door closed, locking it bolt tight... literally. It can be opened from the inside, but the outside cannot be unlocked without a key. A key that only Dr. Warren Gerard and his half dozen or so nurses have.

Sabrina lands on her side, her hip taking the blunt of the fall but not saving her lolling head from quite a hard hit on the tiled floor. A small knot quickly starts to form but Sabrina is unaware of it or the pain.

Chapter Three

Doc's Day Off

1

At twenty after nine on a beautiful Sunday morning, Dr. Gerard is just sitting down at his eight-person dining room table to a hearty breakfast of two glazed doughnuts and a cup of coffee, black with sugar. He settles into his chair at the head of the table, his robe sliding open to expose a chest full of dark thick curly hair, closely resembling a shag carpet, a pair of plain gray boxer briefs complete with a couple small piss dots, and mid-shin high, white socks over legs as hairy as his chest. Scientists could possibly discover the missing link between humans and monkeys if this man appeared before them nude. He is a short, stout man with a few strands of gray spotting his prided thick black hair. Warren Gerard has already showered and combed his hair for the day. He always combs his hair the same way, almost a cross between a combover and slick-back, a bit odd but it seems to suit Warren just fine. He unfolds his Sunday paper, scanning the headlines for anything interesting, one hand holding the newspaper and the other reaching for one of his donuts.

Bbbbrrrrrriiiinnnggg!!!!!

The sound deafening in the morning silence. Gerard's hand stops shy of the donut, the other one jerking, rattling, and thus wrinkling the paper. His heart leaps at the sound, skips a beat and resumes at a quickening pace. "Gosh darn phone!"

Bbbbbrrrrrriiiiiinnnnnnggggg!!!

"Oh, shut up already, would ya?" He rises from his chair, setting the paper down beside his coffee cup and walks, lazily across the dining room and into the kitchen.

Bbbbbbrrrrrriiiiiinnnnnnggggg!!!

The ring much louder in the spacious kitchen, echoing off its undecorated walls. He quickens his pace, hoping to catch the phone before it bellows another mind-numbing squall, but he isn't quite fast enough. He picks it up mid-ring, still hearing it for several seconds after putting the phone to his ear. "Yes! Hello! This is Dr. Warren Gerard speaking. How may I help you?" He spurts, automatically, before giving the person on the other end of the line a chance to speak.

"Dr. Gerard!!!!" a feminine voice, so loud Warren pulls the phone away from his ear, slightly, stretching the tight spiral cord. He returns the phone to his ear after a momentary hesitation. The voice is calmer, but the seriousness is evident. His heart beating ever faster at the urgency in the woman's voice. He listens carefully for several seconds, his eyes growing larger in their sockets as each one ticks by.

"What do you mean *unaccounted* for!? And when did *that* happen!?" Dr. Gerard shouts into the telephone. A cyclone of emotions threatening to take over this normally calm man, his mind racing in the confusion of the current situation. He listens some more. "Has anyone…." He begins, stops, listens again. "Okay, good. What about…" and stops again, listening. "Well, it's good to know I haven't hired a bunch of *completely* incompetent fools! Keep Ms. Lowell there, I'll be in soon." He finishes not attempting to mask the irritation in his voice and slams the receiver back into its cradle hanging on the kitchen wall.

Warren Gerard dresses quickly, his Sunday paper and glazed doughnuts long forgotten. He grabs a final sip of barely lukewarm coffee as he passes the dining room table, then goes through the kitchen and into the mud room. He grabs his jacket off the hat rack in the corner, slips his shoes on that sit neatly beside the door, and grabs the keys off the hooked plaque hanging about a foot above the back porch light switch.

Approximately 20 minutes later, Dr. Warren Gerard, the founder, the head, and the only doctor at The Navea Dwighton Asylum for the Mentally Afflicted, struts into his office. His gait combining with the stern expression that is plastered on his face, gives him the aura of a man who means business. A man who means to get everything figured out and back in order as quickly and quietly as possible. And that is just what Dr. Warren Gerard *intends* to do.

2

Sabrina Lowell, the pretty young nurse with the golden blonde hair, wakes from her fainting spell in complete confusion. She looks around the room unsure of where she is and what has happened. Then everything comes crashing down on her in a cold rush, goosebumps popping out across her body, a slight shiver runs up her spine. She's laying in a hospital bed, in what appears to be one of the examination rooms they use for new arrivals, monthly physicals, and the occasional wound or ailment. She remembers everything. Mr. Patrickson, the poor soul who's mind broke when he lost his wife and four children in a car accident a few years ago. He was looking for Joe. She found him in his room. The blood. Oh my God, the blood. Just. Everywhere. She doesn't remember screaming but her sore, hoarse throat is enough proof on that subject. She doesn't remember fainting either, but who ever does?

She raises up on her elbows, from her semi-sitting position, when a brilliant piercing pain bolts through the right side of her head followed by a wave of dizziness so intense, Sabrina immediately lays back down, panting harshly. The air tears at her dry throat, seeming to rub it raw as it makes its rough way into her lungs. Slowly, the panting stops, and the dizziness subsides but the pain in her head is now a constant dull throb, and her throat feels as dry as sandpaper, each breathe drying it evermore. She carefully turns her head to the right and sees her best friend since the third grade, Patty Bollier, the woman with the naturally red, teased hair and pink horn-rimmed glasses, sitting in a chair beside the bed. A magazine lay open upon her crossed legs, a considerable amount of her legs noticeable below the white dress uniform hiked high up around her thighs and chewing her signature bright pink bubble gum. Patty reaches beside her out of Sabrina's view and reappears with a cup of water, carefully handing it to her. Sabrina wants to drink it all down in huge gulps and demand more, but she sips on it slowly instead, letting the water lubricate her sore, tattered throat a little at a time. Patty gives Sabrina a small tight-lipped smile. "Took a helluva fall, didn'tcha?"

"Yeah, I reckon, I did." Sabrina replies trying to raise herself up into a sitting position, much slower and much more carefully this time. Patty closes the magazine, sets it on the floor beside the chair she's occupying and gets up to help Sabrina. She places a couple pillows behind Sabrina's back and head for support, then plops down on the bed beside her. She grabs Sabrina's hand, once she's as comfortable as she can be, and notes that her hand is cold to the touch and trembling enough to feel but not quite see.

"What happened?" Patty inquires concernedly but continues before giving Sabrina a chance to answer the question. "All dey tole me is dat a couple of maintenance men found ya lying in da 'rainbow corridor' in a faint." This is the name most nurses use for the restricted hallways of the patient's rooms, for the obvious reason of the bright colors. "I rushed on down here just as quick as I could. Didn't e'en ast da other girls to cover my desk, just came right on down to see my Bri." Bri is Patty's nickname for Sabrina and Pats is Sabrina's nickname for Patty. Just silly little names they came up with in grade school, shortly after becoming the best of friends, but they stuck like glue.

"Well, Pats, it's still a lil fuzzy but I do remember Mr. Patrickson askin me...." Sabrina begins.

"Mista Patrickson, da one who lost his wife and kids in dat horrible car crash?" Patty asks, slightly shame-faced for interrupting.

"Yeah, dat's the one." Sabrina answers patiently, she has been dealing with Patty's interruptions since they were nine years old, and she has grown used to them. Sabrina takes a sip of water as Patty nods to show she knows who Sabrina is referring to and then continues. "Well, he asts me if I'd seen Joe this morning. I tole him no and came and asted ya'll. You remember don't ya, Pats?" Patty nods, her voluminous red hair bouncing as she does. "I tole you I was gonna go find him and that's what I did. I checked the cafeteria first, but he wasn't there, so I thought he might still be in his room. I got to his room and knocked but..."

The door to the exam room Sabrina Lowell and Patty Bollier are occupying opens and Dr. Gerard's head appears from behind the ajar door, stopping Sabrina midsentence. "Ahh, Sabrina, you're awake. How is your head?" Dr. Gerard asks, relief and concern mingling in his tone.

"Throbbing and sore." She reaches up and touches the nickel sized pump knot protruding from the right side of her head, winces and drops her hand back into her lap. "Really sore."

"I'm sorry to hear that. We'll see what we can do about that, though." He responds sincerely, and looks over at Patty, and then asks her to fetch Sabrina some aspirin and a soda with a thanks and a light pat on the bottom. One of the many physical gestures of his that his employees must endure. He enters the room as Patty exits it and lingers a few steps away from the bed Sabrina is laying in, stuffing his hands deep into his pockets. "Think you're up to a conversation? We really do need to discuss this situation before I am able to make an educated decision on how to handle this." Dr. Gerard asks sympathetically, yet pleadingly. He doesn't want to make Sabrina talk about it, but he will if he needs to, if she pushes him to pull the power card, he will. He's hoping she will agree willingly and cooperate to the fullest. And that's exactly what Sabrina does.

3

An hour later, Dr. Gerard is sitting behind his desk in his office. His eyeglasses laying on a couple papers of current unimportance, both hands planted firmly on his head, the heels of his hands pressing achingly into his eye sockets. He is trying to process everything Ms. Sabrina Lowell has just finished telling him. She discloses everything that happened between her encounter with Mr. Gregory Patrickson in the common room to waking up in an empty, sans her and Patty, exam room. Twice. He has her go through it the second time, searching strenuously for any inconsistencies, but there aren't any. *Not. A. Single. One.*

Warren sighs loudly, roughly rubs his eyes and drops his hands with a *plunk* on the well-made sturdy desk. He looks across at Sabrina, several strands of blonde hair hang around a beautiful face with green almond-shaped eyes. She is pale from the shock of it all, apart from two bright red patches on her cheeks, as if she is blushing. When in fact her blood pressure is elevated and she's feeling quite woozy from the knot on her head. She's rather lovely, though, most of the nurses Dr. Warren Gerard employs are of a certain age group and build. But they are all generally good, caring, and trustworthy.

"Let me get this straight," he begins, "you couldn't find Joseph Doe in the common room or the cafeteria this morning, so you went to check his room where you found him dead? Covered in blood? Looking as if he has been murdered?" Dr. Warren Gerard finishes. His tone of voice insisting that he is torn between disbelief and pique. His hard eyes, unblinking, seeming to stare right through her, as if she has suddenly become transparent, are searching for the reason behind this despicable lie.

"Yes!" she shouts at him, her own disbelief apparent at his insinuation that she would spin such a horrible tale. "Patty said two maintenance guys found me in the patient's corridor fainted dead away on the floor, didn't ya talk to them? They saw him in there, didn't they?" Sabrina asks trying to get her emotions under control again. The man sitting across the wooden desk from her who not only founded but heads the institution, also, signs her paychecks. If she oversteps because she lets her emotions get the best of her, he won't be signing anymore paychecks with SABRINA LOWELL printed on them.

"Of course, I spoke with them." He remarks with an irritated wave of the hand. "They said they had just finished up repairing the sprinklers in B wing when they heard a woman scream from the patient's corridor. They rushed in and found you lying in the floor. No one was around, there was no sign that you were injured other than the bump you took to the head, and we all assumed it was from the fall. And we were right to assume that, apparently. All the doors were closed and locked tight, like they should be. One of them carried you out while the other found a couple nurses to tend to you. That's all any of us know, and now you're telling me all this craziness."

"Ya think I'm crazy? That I'm just making this all up?" She shouts at him once more, angry all over again because, honestly, part of her thinks she just might have gone crazy. This time, however, she doesn't care if her emotions take over or not. "Why? Why would I do such a terrible thing?"

He sits there looking at her patiently, as if she were a fibbing child. Despising that this is how he must spend his day off.

Sabrina ascending beyond anger shoots right to furious with this man. *Fuck him and fuck this job! I don't need this stupidity!* Tears prick her eyes and roll slowly down her cheeks; she refuses to wipe them away, afraid that wiping the tears away will wipe the fury away with it and right now it is easier for Sabrina to be furious than it is for her to feel anything else. She takes a few deep breaths, exhaling slowly, settling back into her more composed tone but the fury still quite evident, "Go look for yourself if you don't believe me." She stares at him from her chair in front of his desk, deliberately not blinking or looking away.

"Ms. Lowell," Dr. Gerard begins. The formality of using her last name means that he is getting irritated and in a hurry, too. "I am very aware of our missing patient, and I have a few nurses and the security team searching the grounds for him, as we speak. We have attempted escapees all the time, you know this. You haven't even been here two years yet and you, yourself, have witnessed several." Dr. Gerard reminds her, almost pleadingly now.

"And has anyone bothered to check his room since ya'll discovered that he was missing?" Sabrina inquires, ire morphing with a grave coldness that radiates from her in waves.

"Now, Sabrina!" Back on a first name basis, that's a good sign. "You know darn good and well that we never find escapees in their rooms. Hence the term *escapee!* They are always out around the grounds and rarely very far from here." He rubs his temples with the index and middle fingers of both hands, simultaneously, as if coming down with a killer headache. "Look, we almost always find the ones who try to escape, you know this too, and when they haul Mr. Joseph Doe back in here from wherever it is they find him, you'll see for yourself that your claims can't possibly be true." His gaze has softened and he's looking at her with an exasperated, I'm-running-out-of-patience look combined with the stern look saved for children who act on impulse and ignorance rather than common sense. "Besides, the video feed for his room shows that it is empty. That was my first check. He's not it there, Sabrina, that's why he's been labeled an escapee." He maintains that same despairing look meant to conjure shame in the looked upon, but for Sabrina Lowell, it only intensifies her fury.

She stands up, leans over, and slams her hands down on the center of his desk, raging over the look that disappears into confusion at her standing. Warren shrinks back in his chair, away from Sabrina, sure that she means to knock him a good one. The outcome is starling yet relieving. "Then fucking humor, me!" She screams at him. The red splotches on her cheeks darkening to a purplish tint, her bright green eyes huge and glaring at him with pure rage, no more tears pricking her eyelashes. She can smell his aftershave and is close enough to see the blackheads on his sharp nose. Her intensity and anger bring out a hidden glowing beauty, one with a pulsing crimson light streaked with jagged bolts of onyx black. Glowing with the red scorned rage only a woman can conjure and spiking it with the sudden, relentless, extremely short-lived black hatred women can feel for the male race from time to time.

Warren Gerard doesn't see her equally gorgeous glow, but he undoubtedly sees her beauty. In any other situation and during any other conversation, his eyes would be firmly set on her breasts and the considerable amount of cleavage her ample bosom provides. But right now, his eyes are locked on hers. He feels a familiar yearning way down low and feels a twitch in the crotch of his pants. He casts these thoughts aside quickly, telling himself he will add this to his *fantasy files*, later. By the time it's all said and done, though, *or rather all said and read*, this memory (to turn fantasy) will receive no more than a passing affectionate glance.

He swallows with an audible click in his throat and sighs heavily. "Alright." Dr. Gerard reaches between her hands and retrieves his glasses that her right one missed by fractions of an inch. He stands up while cleaning the lenses of his glasses with the handkerchief he pulls from his back pocket. "Let's go." He puts on his glasses and gives her a very hard and convincing don't-even-try-to-protest-coming-with-me look. Warren isn't the most observant person, except when it comes to his patients, he's quite thorough in his examinations, but he does notice the way her face instantly changes from fury to panic and knows she will have something to say about it. The look he gives her tells her not to and she listens, reluctantly.

By the time they arrive at the double doors at the end of the hallway Joseph Doe's room occupies, Sabrina is snow white without so much as a trace of red on her cheeks. Her stomach is rolling over in tumbling loops and she is desperately trying to gain the upper hand on her gorge. She is trembling on her feet by the time they make the half dozen or so steps to the door with the gold-plated numbers 32 on it.

Chapter Four

Where Did Joe Doe Go?

1

Dr. Warren Gerard stands in the doorway of Joseph Doe's room for an undeterminable amount of time. Moveless. Thoughtless. Timeless. The earth seeming to stand still while his mind spins endlessly. The cogs of his, normally faultless, trains of thought have ceased to rotate due to what his eyes are showing him, but his mind keeps insisting that he can't possibly be seeing. A mental conundrum is what Warren is currently experiencing. *A joke. Just a sick joke. Someone's idea of a joke. A very sick person's idea of a joke. It must be because this isn't real. It just can't be.* And yet, his eyes, consistently registering the excessive amount of blood sprayed and splattered across the part of the room he could see from the door, was insisting that this is indeed reality; insisting that this is indeed NOT some sicko's idea of a fucked-up joke.

"Wha,,," Dr. Warren Gerard begins, breathlessly. Quite literally at a loss for words.

"I tole you!" Sabrina Lowell suddenly screams from beside him, in a panicky ragged breath. Quickly turning her half-enraged, half-terrorized face toward him, bringing him out of his own thoughts. Jerking his head in her direction, a startled look of surprise appears and disappears from his face in a flash. He had forgotten all about little, lovely Sabrina Lowell, momentarily, in his state of unbelief.

"I tole you! Do ya believe me now!?!" She asks him rhetorically, screeching. Her voice rising higher and higher into hysterics. Employees throughout the asylum catch wordless, meaningless snatches of the echoes from her screams. Though screaming is quite common in the asylum hers had a fearful, anxiety-inducing quality that most others lacked. Had any of the employees had the desire to talk about those terrible bursts of echoes, later, they would have mostly all agreed on two things. One, that it slightly resembled a banshee from one of those creepy Friday night movies they liked to play at the drive-ins. And two, that they hoped to never hear such a fear-inducing sound again.

Tears stream helplessly down her young, pale face. Her entire body seeming to vibrate compulsively, as is she has just stepped out of an ice bath or a frozen pond. "I tole you! I tole you! I tole you! Why'd ya make me come back here??" Sabrina continues, slowly winding down, the rising pitch in her voice now decreasing with each word. The last word lingers around them, like an unpleasant scent. Shock, already having a firm grip on her, squeezes, puncturing her tough exterior layer with its numbingly painful talons. Sabrina covers her face with both of her hands and begins to sob quietly.

2

Dr. Gerard stands there, silent, unblinking, and seemingly unaffected by her rant. He watches her turn away from him, hands still hiding her face, and take off at a steady jog before disappearing down the left hallway at the intersection. Warren turns back toward room 32, the deceased body of Joseph Doe, and the unbelievably incredible mess accompanying them.

He takes a long deep breath, exhales slowly and repeats this action until his mind is somewhat clear again. He is unaware of how long he stands here and does not have the energy to care if anyone has seen him. Had Sabrina not taken off down the hall, she may have been able to see and recognize Dr. Gerard's breathing-induced pause, for what it really is. The fear of the unknown trying to rip its way through his mind while he tries desperately not to let it. And it looks like he's winning this round.

Dr. Warren Gerard steps through the door. His senses seem to heighten and take in every part of this despairing room. It smells strongly of coppery blood, much like corroded, wet pennies. And there's the underlying, unpleasant smell of urine and excrement. The air seems heavy with the scents, but Warren is grateful because he knows it could be much worse. It is chilly in here, almost cold. The temperature for each patient's room is set separately, manually, and by the patient for their preference from an inside thermostat mounted on the wall by the door. This thermostat controls both the heating and air conditioning for maximum patient comfortability. A glance at the thermostat in room 32 shows that it is set to 58 degrees and the vents are serving a constant flow of cool air, dampening the smell.

The door opens on the left of the largish room, divided into wall-less sections by its furnishings. The left side, a simple undecorated wall covered in pastel orange and yellow stripped wallpaper. The wallpaper now speckled with dark red spots, some small and some as large as misshapen baseballs, some in clusters and some in random lonely places, some on the bottom by the tiled floor and some way up high mixing with the spots across the plain white ceiling. The splotches of dried blood stand out like a waterfall in the desert. Immediately to the right of the door is a large box bookcase, that looks as if several wooden crates have been stacked floor to ceiling. A thick wire mesh covers the back of the shelves, the side Warren can see. It takes him a half dozen steps to clear the bookshelf and be able to see the other side of it. The shelves are crammed with books and papers and curios and magazines and only Joe knows what else. Every shelf has contents with blood spatter dried upon them. *It almost looks like one of those paintings where the artist slings a paint brush at a canvas, letting the paint fly, splatter, and dry where it lays. Then have the audacity to call it art. Well, this artwork has been done primarily in red, and it is quite distasteful if I should say so myself.* Dr. Gerard thinks to himself, horrified and dismayed.

A decent sized, metal table sits bolted to the floor to the left of the makeshift bookcase, its tabletop neat and uncluttered. In fact, the only thing on the table is an unmarked yellow manila envelope bulging with its contents, sitting primly in the center of the desk. A couple of blood droplets, now a dark maroon color, have dried on the shiny metal tabletop. If it wasn't for all the blood splattered around the room, it would be difficult to place exactly what those dried spots could be. But Dr. Gerard doesn't need to guess, he knows. Knows it is blood. Of course, it is, it's everywhere. *Everywhere.* Yet, oddly, the metal table sitting bolted to the left of the bookcase is the only clean*ish* area in the entire room.

Warren slowly, very slowly, makes his way around the room, trying desperately but failing, nonetheless, not to disturb the *crime scene*. A crime scene he shouldn't even be witnessing, and yet, here he is. He moves away from the metal table, toward another, smaller, shelf running parallel to the giant floor-to-ceiling bookcase on the opposite side of the desk. This one sitting on the floor, attached to the right-side wall it sets against. The top two shelves have a variety of approved snacks: chips, bottles of soda and juice, cookies, crackers; nothing that requires heating, a utensil, or anything in a can. On the bottom shelves, there's stacks of unused paper, a small cup of dull pencils, a shoebox left ajar but not enough for Warren to see inside, two pair of slip-on shoes and a pair of slippers. There's a massive amount of blood that has oozed down the front of the shelves and a bloody handprint smeared down the wall above it. It looks as though Joe may have stood in front of these shelves bleeding out, but for what reason, Warren can't say. Blood lays in a large pool that has seeped under the shelf; that end of the pool cut off from Dr. Gerard's field of vision. He notices something settled into the coagulated blood coating some of the items along the top shelf. Leaning over to get a better look, he avoids stepping in the large puddle of blood but almost stumbles into it, anyway, when he realizes what he's seeing. It's a tooth. A molar, to be exact. Laying on its side, one of its three roots lost in the mess it lay in, the others pointing indifferently toward the body with the mouth they inhabited not long ago.

3

Continuing his counterclockwise tour through room 32, Warren next comes across Joe's padded rocking chair with the matching footstool. A small end table sits beside the chair with a stack of newspapers on it. There is an open book laying with the cover facing upward, the spine silently creaking as it splits under the strain, atop the stack. He sees it's the recently released biography of a man named Owen Ray Houston. The book looks relatively new but well read. And that name seems to ring familiar in Dr. Gerard's mind. He isn't sure why, though, and it surely isn't important right now, anyhow. The padding of the chair is completely soaked in blood, as if Joe had sat here for quite some time before making his way over to the bed. It is pooled under the chair and table and soaked through a few of the top layers of newspapers on the table. The book cover is relatively clean, however, in comparison. There are only two spots, one on each end of the cover, about the size of smeared fingerprints.

Intrigued and curious, he reaches out to touch the book, possibly to turn it over, but retracts his hand at the last moment remembering he has a protocol to follow. At least to some degree. Technically he shouldn't be in here right now, he should be back in his office on the phone calling every Tom, Dick, and Harry across the board. But this… this… this is just astounding; this dumbfoundingly, mind-numbingly, bloodcurdlingly (no pun intended) grim situation. He is still trying to comprehend what his eyes are showing him, so there's no way he could explain this to anyone else yet.

The rich smell of blood in the air, combines with the grisly images his eyes are constantly feeding his brain, and Warren's stomach begins to make large, galloping flops. He casts his eyes to the floor, fighting to hold down whatever is trying to force its way up. His eyes immediately fall upon several white specks and a few larger pinkish globs in the discolored blood that is still tacky wet in the center of the puddle. More teeth. And possibly… some flesh? The very thought is enough to send whatever is forcing its way up his esophagus flooding into his mouth. He makes an awkward long stride/leap that lands him on the opposite side of the large blood pool surrounding Joe's wall-less sitting area and in front of the stainless-steel toilet bowl. If anyone had been around to witness his acrobatic-like, swift footing he might have reminded them of a child playing hopscotch. He retches loudly into the toilet, turning the clear water to a very pale sickly yellow with the stomach acid he has just vomited. Even in the roughest grips of his retching he takes pains not to touch the toilet seat or lid, both of which are splattered with beads of dried blood.

Dr. Warren Gerard straightens up from his bent position in front of the toilet bowl and turns to his left with the intention of rinsing out the soured taste lingering in his mouth in the matching stainless-steel sink. He quickly reconsiders, however, upon seeing all the drying blood in the sink basin. Another tooth and a few more of those pinkish fleshy globs get his stomach flip-flopping all over again. He quickly turns away from the wall-less bathroom, fighting his gorge, and ultimately winning this round. After a few deep breaths to ensure his stomach is settling, he faces the only part of the room that he hasn't carefully observed yet: the bedroom area.

Straight ahead of the door is a single-person cot pushed against the wall with a small end table placed beside it. Next to the end table is a large portable wardrobe where all of Joe's clothes are hanging off clothes hangers. These are no ordinary clothes hangers, though. They are specially made for people with highly unpredictable behavior or extreme impulsiveness, such as those housed at the N.D.A.M.A. They are made of a synthetic rubber that is extremely flexible so that it cannot be broken, yet durable enough to hold up the weight of the outfits given to the patients. Several other items found throughout the asylum are made or covered with this same rubbery material. At the foot of the bed sits a long narrow ottoman, the length of the single bed, covered in padding closely resembling that of his rocking chair and footstool. The lid of the ottoman is closed tightly but Warren doesn't need to see inside to know what's there. All the patient's rooms are set up more-or-less the same way and he's had to search his fair share of rooms. He knows that this is where their undershorts, undershirts, socks, etc. are kept and usually along with a nudie magazine or two, or the occasional cucumber. The latter can be quite uncomfortable considering this is the men's section of the asylum. The women are housed on the opposite side and headed by an elderly female doctor that resembles a ferret more than a woman. The two sides rarely interact for the safety of the patients.

Dr. Gerard takes a few steps closer to the cot where the body of one Mr. Joseph Doe lays with his left foot propped nonchalantly on the pillow, the right stretched out and lax on the floor, an inch or less from the end table. His head hanging off the end of the bed, caught by the ottoman, his blank and unblinking eyes staring vacantly into nothingness. Joe is wearing a pair of knit pajama bottoms and nothing else. There's something different about this section of the room, aside from the dead body, that Warren can't quite put his finger on. He closes his eyes, counts to ten and opens them. The moment before his eyes open, he is almost overwhelmed by a feeling of utter fear and certainty that he will see this bloody grotesque man standing before him ready to make him bleed the same way he is. But, of course, no such thing occurs. When he opens his eyes, everything is exactly as it was when he closed them - right down to the nagging but unidentified difference.

4

His head is beginning to throb, seemingly coming from the center of his brain, the pain increasing with each throbbing wave. He rubs his eyes with the thumb and index finger of his right hand, sighs deeply and turns to leave. His eyes cast about the front half of the room, partially divided by the large bookshelf and all the blood splattered and pooled about. The mostly dried, various reddish-purple hues plastered everywhere about the room. All the dried blood. *Dried. Blood.*

He snaps back toward the body on the cot realizing, suddenly, the difference he missed moments ago. It is so obvious. The blood on and around the body is all a vibrant vital shade of red, the exact shade of fresh blood. The contrasting shades are so subtle yet so spectacularly different that Warren is usure how he missed it the first time he looked around the room. *But how could this be? How could the blood everywhere else in the room be dried or drying to the point of discoloration, yet the body and its immediate surroundings bathed in the bright red of fresh spilt blood? It doesn't seem possible. It can't be.*

Another step closer, edging into the pool of blood circling the cot, disrupting the edge of it with the toe of his shoe, leaving a light pink crescent shaped indent. He leaned forward, careful not to overbalance and fall face first into the corpse. He watches a bead of blood slide down the slanting curve of Joe's torso and disappear into the cot joining the millions of other drops of blood already soaked into the cot mattress. Another bead begins to form almost immediately after the first departs, and a few moments later the cycle repeats itself. He expands his concentration beyond this singular drop of blood and notices that several drops were sliding and rolling down the sides of his chest, abdomen, arms, and neck. His eyes are still rolling with bloody tears and for a single moment, Warren is convinced Joseph Doe is still alive.

Dr. Gerard in his stress-induced lapse of judgement reaches out and grasps the cold, ashy gray wrist of the body laying before him, meaning to feel for a pulse. Of course, he doesn't find one just as the logical portion of his thoughts, that has been momentarily shoved to the back of his mind, knows he won't. He changes his mind about touching the body the moment before he does but is unable to stop himself and knows a moment too late that he has made a terrible mistake. As if the clammy skin of Dr. Gerard causes a chemical reaction with that of the cold, tight, pale gray skin of the corpse's wrist, a tingling sensation occurs between the two. This sensation is followed by a couple thin tendrils of smoke that float up around the curved sides of his clawed hand. He jerks his hand away in fearful surprise rather than pain, looking at his palm with strange curiosity dancing in his frightened eyes.

More small tendrils of smoke begin to rise from random places across the body of Joseph Doe, spreading out toward the cot and the blood pool below. Warren is in a temporary shock-induced paralysis, never blinking or averting his eyes from the phenomenon occurring in front of him. The same thing is happening all around the room and less than a minute later every drop of blood, tooth, bit of flesh and the body itself has thin streams of dark shiny gray smoke emerging from them. Tens or even hundreds of thousands of thread-thin strips, merging in their density, form an eerie low-lying fog over everything. Seemingly, the same type of fog they show floating along the ground in cemeteries, thick enough so that the audience is only able to catch glimpses of the headstones, before the decayed and grotesque hand of the living dead reaches up to snatch at the ankles of the love-sick teenagers walking by. The room seems to be swimming in the odorless, burnt charcoal colored smoky fog.

Some of the smoke threads, the ones coming from the small specks of blood splattered across just about every surface in the room, including all four walls and the ceiling, are already dissipating. The blood spot disappearing into the smoky grayness, all evidence of its existence evaporating with the smoke into nothingness. Several moments later, there is noticeably less blood splattered about but still enough to fill the bodies of at least four healthy young men, and probably with some left over. The amount of blood in this room, really is astounding.

Warren's eyes are still glued to the fog covered body, only a shadowy humanish figure laying in the murkiness of it. His heart is thumping in his chest hard enough to echo inside his skull and his glassy staring eyes thud with each beat. His stomach rolls in large jerky tumbles, and he has a slight tremble in his sweaty yet cold hands. He stares at the body, oblivious to the rest of the room that is, also, enveloped in this strange wispy vapor. Oblivious to the person that has appeared in the doorway of room 32, as well.

'Lost in thought' is the wrong phrase to use for Dr. Warren Gerard's current mental state only because it implies there are logical and coherent thoughts running through his mind. A much more accurate phrase is 'at a loss for thought' because that is exactly what he is. His usually calm, logical, and almost flawless train of thought has not only been knocked off course, but completely derailed, bombed and the ashes salted just for good measure. He is brought out of this stupefaction with a suddenness so forceful it, literally knocks him off his feet. His eyes register a flash of light so excruciatingly bright, shooting razor sharp rays of light directly into his corneas, that the extremity of his pain makes him wish that he were dead. A moment later and only lasting a moment, he feels completely weightless as he goes flying backward toward the wall-less bathroom. Even in his intense and unbearable pain a partial thought rises from the back of his mind, trying to push its way, unsuccessfully, forward. *Blood.... land in... all that blood!* And then the darkness swallows him in one quick gulp as he hits the floor. Taking the blunt of the fall with his right upper arm and shoulder, his head bounces off the tiled floor with an ugly thwack. His limp body finally comes to a sliding stop a few inches from the wall next to the stainless-steel toilet. Laying on his side in a somewhat natural position, eyes closed, and breathing deeply and consistently one could easily mistake him for a sick, passed out, drunk.

He regained consciousness a few minutes later, just to have it threatened by yet another astonishing sight.

Chapter Five

Trickery of the Eyes

1

Sabrina Lowell had disappeared down the other hallway but hadn't gone far. She cried hard, sobbing, and weeping into her hands. After several long minutes she was able to calm down and get control of her emotions, again, not entirely but enough.

Now, she can hear the echoes of Dr. Gerard retching and thinks about how much he deserves it for making her look in that room again. She can feel the anger trying to boil back up and pushes it away before it can begin to fester. She feels bad for thinking that way and decides to go check on him, as a way of atonement, she supposes. She assumes he is still in the hallway, anyway. She quickly notes that he isn't there, however, once she rounds the corner heading down the hall she ran from earlier. Her stomach begins to tumble lazily, her heart quickens, and sweat pops out on her forehead. Her eyes, puffy from the waterworks, are wide and alert, yet fearful. She considers turning back, leaving him to deal with this on his own since he is so eager to do so, but ultimately decides to return to room 32.

She reaches the doorway but stops just a step shy of being able to see inside. Sabrina calls his name once... twice... thrice. No answer. She takes a deep breath, exhales, and bravely takes a step forward. Her eyes immediately find Dr. Gerard standing by the cot with a lost, dazed, deer-in-the-headlights look in his eyes. Following his gaze toward the cot, she gasps loudly when she sees that the body is shrouded in a strange sparkly gray mist. Almost immediately after, she notices that it's all over the room, as well, leaving very little visible among the dense fog.

Unlike Dr. Gerard's intense concentration on the strangeness of the room, Sabrina is utterly overwhelmed by it. She takes two staggering steps forward, now closer to the locked double doors, bends at the waist, placing one hand on her knee while the other supports her using the wall to her left. She is panting deliberately, a desperate and somehow successful act to abate the hysterics that are trying to force their way upon her. This small ritualistic action saves her from the initial ferocity of the flash of black light that spontaneously encompasses the body and every other bit and spot that is seeping that mystic gray vapor. Sabrina sees the lighting around her change, forming new shadows that weren't there a second ago and dissipating pre-existing shadows just as quick. They dance and jerk in their places, flickering in the odd, unnatural light.

She straightens from her bent position, waves of curiosity and fear crisscrossing their way through her senses. She turns, takes a step forward, then leans toward the door to peek inside. She instantly squints and jerks her head back away from the dazzlingly bright light, partially due to the unexpectedness of it. After taking a couple deep breaths to try to prepare herself, she closes her eyes tightly and leans forward again. This time she deliberately turns her head toward the floor and opens them a little bit at a time, her eyes adjusting quickly. She squints them again and slowly turns her head toward the cot, trying and failing to see Dr. Gerard. She has just enough time to see the silhouette of the body still laying on the cot. A bright black light radiating out of his entire body, rays of this unnatural light stabbing its way in every direction. Then the light winks out. Just like that, literally in the blink of an eye, and it's all gone. The blood, the gore, the body. It's all gone, not so much as a trace of the nightmare left behind.

If she was standing on the opposite side of the door, around the place she stood upon first arriving back at the room, she would be able to see the lower half of Dr. Warren Gerard's unconscious body lying on the floor by the toilet. But he has been temporarily forgotten as Sabrina struggles with her conflicting thoughts on what she has just witnessed. *It all just vanished!* Impossible. *It was never there to begin with!* I'm going mad. *You're hallucinating from your head injury!* Matter-of-factly. Logically. *Ya done lost it!* Probably the most accurate. While lost in these thoughts, her body running on a kind of autopilot, Sabrina slowly walks into the now neat and tidy room of the former Mr. Joseph Doe, recently deceased and more recently displaced.

2

There's a light moan, barely more than a whisper but eerily loud in the deafening silence.

Sabrina is startled out of her thoughts, and gives a small jump and a tiny, frightened squeak that escapes her slightly parted lips. She looks toward the bathroom area, sees Dr. Gerard laying there and two thoughts come to her mind almost simultaneously. *When did I come in here?* and *Why didn't I see him when I walked in?* Both unanswered. She rushes over to him and gently rolls him over on his back. His eyes are closed, and he is breathing normally. She doesn't see any open wounds or blood and takes that as a good sign. He looks as if he is sleeping or has, maybe, passed out.

Another low groan.

Sabrina gives him a startlingly rough shake of the shoulders bringing Dr. Gerard back to a groggy semi-consciousness. His head rolls lazily on his neck, partially opening his eyes only for them to roll in their sockets from the too bright after the darkness, overhead fluorescent lighting of the room and he closes them tightly. His mind is more alert now and everything is rushing back to him. His eyes still squeezed shut he tries to raise himself up on his elbows but only slides on the tiled floor. Sabrina grabs one of his arms; using her support and his other arm he's able to sit up, leaning his back against the colorful wall. His chin resting on his chest, he slowly opens his eyes and blinks a couple of times, the crotch of his pants coming into focus.

After a long moment he raises his head to look at Sabrina. He watches as her eyes grow large in her head, the color rises in her cheeks, her mouth opening to expel a scream. One escapes but it's underwhelming, more of a small gasp/squeak, compared to what he was expecting. She falls backward onto her hands from her squatted position, kicking her feet but sliding on the tile, trying to use them to propel herself backward and away from him. Startled by her strong and strange reaction, he sits up straight, his back no longer against the wall. 'Sabrina," he croaks from his dry sandpapery throat.

"No! Please! Don't touch me! Please!" she pleads in a frightened harsh whisper, still kicking her feet to get away from him.

Sabrina increasing the distance between them, a little at a time, with each push of her feet, causes Dr. Gerard to notice his surroundings and the pool of blood that she is kicking her way through to get away from him. He looks down at the tiled floor he is sitting on to find that half of his body is sitting on the edge of the pool of blood surrounding the rocking chair and matching footstool. The palm of his left hand is coated in a thick coat of tacky coagulated blood. *Not as dry as it looks, I see.* He thinks to himself disgusted, wiping it on his already ruined slacks that are now splotched with patches of dry*ish* blood from the ankles to just below his crotch, up both legs now.

He looks up at Sabrina again, who is now several feet in front of him but just a few feet from the cot and the dead body. She has stopped moving backward but as soon as she sees that he is looking at her, she starts again. "Sabrina." He croaks almost inaudibly. He clears his throat and tries again, this time with more success. "Sabrina! Stop! Look, you're all covered in blood! Please calm down? You're about to touch the…" But it's too late, her back is firmly against the side of the cot. Dead Joe's arm, hanging off the side from the elbow down at a downward angle, rests comfortably on her shoulder; his limp hand almost close enough to cup her breast.

There is blood all over her, her lower body completely coated in the fresh blood surrounding the body and its death bed. It is soaked through the lower half of her white uniform giving it a grotesque red-on-white retro dancing dress vibe. Her hands and lower arms up to her elbows match her lower half and there's blood splattered across the upper half of her dress, her neck, face, and hair, which is now more down than up. She reminds Warren of a horror movie victim. He looks away from her, scanning the room trying to remember how it was before and wondering if there is any change.

She is completely unaware of it all, though. Sabrina can't see the blood and the body, and all the other gore spread about the room. She can't smell the rich coppery blood in the air or feel the dead weight of Joseph Doe's arm resting on her shoulder. She can't see the blood drenching her clothes, slowly soaking its way up her white uniform. She can't feel the warmth of the fresh blood that is coating her hands and forearms. And in her, seemingly irrational, fright she doesn't hear him trying to soothe her or the part about her being covered in blood. She probably wouldn't believe him if she had; she can see with her own two eyes that she is as clean as a whistle.

3

What she does feel is the utter terror Dr. Gerard's eyes are inducing in her. Sabrina doesn't know what happened in this room only that everything disappeared before her eyes... literally. She doesn't know why it all disappeared with the strange light when it blinked out, and she doesn't know that he seen that light.

His eyes, normally the light brown of black coffee with a splash of cream, are now an almost supernatural, pale silverish opalescence that is only distinguishable from the whites of his eyes when the light hits them a certain way. He looks almost completely devoid of pupils and irises, as if the colors had been burned out of them.

Even in her borderline hysteria she notes that he is looking around the room as if he is taking in all his surroundings. *He's blind! He has to be! How is he being so calm right now!? Why isn't he panicking!? Screaming at anything and everything for answers nothing or no one can provide!?* These thoughts and questions and more swirl and spin around her brain like a carnival carousel, while he continues to glance around the room with his colorless eyes.

"D-D-Doctor...." Sabrina whispers, drawing his attention and his eyes back to her, causing her to turn her head and look away from him quickly.

"Sabrina? What is it, Sabrina? Why are you acting that way?" Dr. Gerard inquires, curiosity and worry mingling together in his tone. "I don't know what happened. I was standing there looking down at his body," he points a bloody finger that she can't see at the body laying just behind her head, partly resting on her petite shoulder, which she cannot feel, "and the next thing I know you're shaking me awake. What

46

happened?" Warren finishes this last sentence with a raspy half-sigh, half-sob that is utterly unlike his normally composed behavior, the worry in his tone quickly turning into fear.

The fear Sabrina hears in his voice is what breaks her fright induced inability to look at him. Her fear is slowly being replaced by pity. She turns her head, eyes cast toward the floor, in his direction, not quite ready to investigate those creepy, depressing eyes with her own. "Your eyes... there's... there's something wrong with your eyes." She responds barely above a whisper but audible enough for him to make out her words in the silence of the room.

"My eyes?" This is not the answer he was expecting. Dumbfounded, he reaches up with both hands, the right one splattered with blood and the left slathered in it and touches his eyes as if he can't feel that they are in his sockets where they belong. He leaves a large fingerprint smudge on one of his eyelids, looking like a splotchy birthmark or a healing bruise. Unspeaking, he slowly gets his feet under him and using the top of the toilet tank to brace himself, stands up. A couple of seconds later, allowing the wooziness of the unconsciousness to fade from his body, his mind had shaken it when Sabrina began her freak out, Warren walks over to the sink with the reflective surface set in the wall behind it. A glassless mirror; for safety reasons, of course.

He steps carefully around the larger spots of blood, unable to dodge every drop because there are so many. To Sabrina he looks quite odd, taking half-a-step here and a small leap there, concentrating hard on each move he makes. She is flabbergasted, unsure of what to think about such an odd set of movements. It reminds her of a childhood game her and her friends and siblings played where they pretended the floor of the house was on fire and they had to make it from one side to the other without touching or falling into it. Dr. Gerard looks like he's playing that game, right now, walking the few steps to the sink basin and glassless mirror. Even though he is covered in the dead man's blood, he is still taking every precaution now that he was before and therefore doesn't rest his hands on the edge of the sink basin for support. He needs to; there are small gray spots threatening his vision, the wooziness in his mind apparently still lurking. Instead, he takes a small step backward, bends and places his hands on his upper legs taking deep breaths through his nose. His forehead less than a half-an-inch from the edge of the sink basin.

Sabrina straightens up. Unbeknownst to her, Joe's lifeless arm slides limply off her shoulder to dangle freely over the side of the cot once more. She draws her feet up under her readying herself to stand when Dr. Gerard stops at the sink his head down and unmoving. He bends over and she's on her feet ready to move if he goes to faint, still very leery of him because of those eyes and not wanting to get too close. She knows, however, that if he faints again then he will undoubtedly hit his head on the sink on the way down. She inches closer to him with each passing moment, hoping against hope that he won't look up at her again with those acid-washed eyes of his.

He doesn't and she silently whispers a prayer of thanks a few minutes later when the wooziness passes. He slowly straightens himself in front of the mirror, his head still hanging before him as if defeated, his eyes never looking in Sabrina's direction. Slower still, Dr. Gerard raises his head until he's looking into his own eyes in the reflective surface hanging on the colorful orange and yellow wall of room 32.

Sabrina can see his face clearly in the mirror from where she stands just a few steps away and slightly behind him. She watches as his face slacks into a, under other circumstances, comical expression of shock and awe. His *colorless* eyes open as wide as one can possibly open them, almost bulging out of their sockets and his mouth agape in a large O of surprise. He reminds Sabrina of the cute little pumpkin faces they put of the plastic Halloween buckets for small kids. She doesn't see anything comical in his expression though and there is nothing humorous about any of this situation. She pities him, sympathizes with him. She can hardly imagine how she would feel if she had woken up from her fainting spell looking like someone poured whitewash under her eyelids as she slept. But what troubles her the most is that he can still *see*. Despite the obvious lack of pigmentation, he still has his gift of *sight*. It just doesn't seem possible. Then again, it doesn't seem possible for a dead body to wink out of existence, but she watched *that* happen.

Warren, seemingly unaware, places both hands on the edge of the sink basin gripping it hard enough to turn his knuckles white, the tendons standing out prominently under the skin. He leans toward the glassless mirror close enough for his nose to touch it and stares into it for several long moments. Sabrina grows more and more nervous, the longer he stands there, becoming more unsure and anxious of what his reaction may be.

He stares. Expression unchanging and it's unsettling.

Sabrina contemplates saying something, if for no other reason than to break this relentless feeling of anxiety she is experiencing, when she hears him sigh loudly. "I don't know what happened," he whispers shaking his head, finally pushing himself away from the sink and standing up straight again. "I just don't know," he repeats sadly, looking down at the blood spotted tiled floor. "I understand why you reacted the way you did now. I apologize for frightening you." He says barely above a whisper in a raspy, quavering voice. Slowly, he shuffles his way toward her, causing her to flinch away from him out of nervous reaction, but she just as quickly relaxes when she sees that he means to walk right by her.

"Doctor…" she says suddenly, momentarily regretting opening her mouth when he raises his terrifying eyes to meet hers. He notices her sudden terror and casts his eyes toward the floor again, ashamed.

"It's okay, Sabrina. I understand. I'd be scared too." And he means it, even if she thinks he's just saying it to make her feel a little better about the situation. "I'm leaving now anyway."

"No, wait! Don't leave." She says as she reaches out, impulsively, grabbing his arm just above the elbow. He looks down at her hand and she removes it quickly as if she has offended or insulted him with her touch. A look of exasperated disgust forms on his face from the bloody smeared handprint now quite evident on his shirt sleeve. Sabrina mistakes this look for something else and now it's her turn to look at the tiled floor, ashamed. "I'm sorry. I just want to make sure that you are okay. Maybe you should have your eyes checked out, make sure your eyesight isn't impaired or anything." She suggests, hoping he will answer the question nagging at her mind without her having to ask it so directly. It seems rude, under the circumstances, to be so direct about a question that has such an obvious answer.

Dr. Warren Gerard sighs heavily, the end of it dragging out into a half-sob. After a long pause he answers her. "Yes, I think you're right. I should have my eyes checked. I don't think I can see the same way you do or maybe we're not seeing the same thing. Heck, I don't know." Throwing his arms up in a gesture of cluelessness and then lets them drop back down to his sides limply.

"What do you mean by us not seeing the same things?" she asks, clearly curious and clearly beyond her fear of his eyes…for now, anyway.

"Well, I can only assume," he begins, sounding like himself again for the first time since opening the door to room 32, "that you can no longer see the blood all over the walls and floor and splattered across the ceiling. Or the dead body still laying over there," He pauses pointing his finger toward the cot, "that had its arm on your shoulder. Or that you are almost completely covered in his blood." He pauses again. Seeing the confusion on her face simply ascertains his assumptions. "You see, I can see all those things and more. I, myself, am covered in the same blood you are, mine's just in the process of drying and not nearly as fresh or brightly colored as what you are wearing." He finishes looking down at his blood-soaked pants.

Sabrina is taken aback, to say the least, at his absurd claim that he can still see everything that she watched wink out of existence before her very eyes. "That can't possibly be right…" she says in a hushed under-her-breath voice that he barely hears. Fear creeps into her, spreading, darkening her mind with all the things he has just told her. *Everything still here? His dead arm on my shoulder? Covered in his blood? Fresh blood?* Unsure of why, but grateful for it nonetheless, she can feel the fear turn to anger, and she instantly, irrationally, convinces herself that he's lying. "That can't be true!" she yells at him, suddenly. He takes a step back at the unexpectedness of her response. "You're as crazy as your eyes make you look! There's nothing here! I watched it all disappear! Just poof and gone! Just like that! You lie! Why would you lie?!" the last word hanging in the silence surrounding them.

Sabrina realizes that much of her fear hadn't changed to anger; it was in fact, just fear. Plain outright, fear and now she is nearly hysterical again. She turns from him, once again, covering her face with her hands, and runs out the door, leaving him alone in the room with the dead body of Mr. Joseph Doe. Only this time, instead of disappearing down a different hallway at the intersection, she runs to the locked double doors about a half dozen steps from the room Dr. Gerard is standing in with his whited-out eyes. It takes her three fumbling, shaky tries to get her pin number entered in the door pad so she can get out of this nightmare corridor.

That is the last time Dr. Warren Gerard ever sees Ms. Sabrina Lowell.

Chapter Six

Bri and The Escapee

1

It's been a week since the strange contingency in room 32. The details of which are only currently known by one living being, Dr. Warren Gerard. The only other soul that knows of the events in that room, took them with her to her grave. Literally and quite recently, in fact. They buried Sabrina Lowell in her family cemetery just yesterday. Warren didn't attend but allowed all his nurses the opportunity to attend the services. Most took the offer, but a few chose to work instead, unwilling to attend on principal due to her manner of death, quite reasonably ruled a suicide or as a coping mechanism, staying busy to help soften the heartache. He was short staffed by almost half of his normal schedule but the patients, most of which were too drugged out to be able to care, were quite calm yesterday allowing the small staff to work efficiently and smoothly. The only issue the staff has had in the past week, aside from the issue with the *escapee*, is that of his friend, Mr. Patrickson.

Dr. Gerard knew moments after Sabrina left the room that day a week ago, that this was going to be a very difficult situation to navigate. Panic tried to overtake him, but he fought it off, struggling to find an answer to this predicament when one presented itself to him. He had turned back to face the body that only he could see, fresh drops of blood trickling from every orifice of the dead man's skull and still beading like sweat on his naked chest and arms. The blood on and pooled around the cot still fresh as ever, just the faintest touch of discolor along the outer edges. A deep male voice from behind him, startled him out of his thoughts, "Sir? Ya find anything?"

What an ignorant question. Dr. Gerard thought to himself, clearly irritated with this interruption but aware of the problem-solving possibility before him. "What do you think? Please, tell me what you see?" He insisted, throwing some heavy annoyance into his tone. Without turning to face the man, the doctor extended his arm moving it swiftly in a sweeping motion, offering the man to step inside and have a look for himself.

The young man standing in the doorway didn't notice the way the doctor wouldn't look at him or even turn in his direction. He simply obeyed, a soldier at heart, and walked just far enough into the room to pop his head around the floor to ceiling shelves. After a quick glance around he turned back to the doctor, only able to see his back, one ear and part of his cheek, with his answer. "There's nothin here, sir. It looks like a cluttered but well-kept patient's room… cept without the patient."

"Well, young man, you have your answer." Dr. Gerard responded, unmoving. He was kind of relieved that he was the only one that could see it. This was just too bizarre to try to explain. So that just left Sabrina, but something told him that he wouldn't see much of her after this. She would almost certainly terminate her employment and he was almost as certain she wouldn't speak of this. Probably not even to her best friend, the frizzy red head with the sensuous legs, Patty Bollier.

It turned out that he was right.

The rest of that day and the following day was a blur of phone calls, interviews and questions, questions, questions. So many questions and so few answers. Dr. Warren Gerard informed the rest of the staff, via intercom, of the *missing* patient, the man named Mr. Joseph Doe that had attempted and apparently succeeded in escaping from his fine institution. Everyone was to be on high alert, keeping an eye out for the escapee. Then came the flurry of phone calls to everyone from the local police to the governor. Locked in his office, everyone he had to call asked some variation of the same three questions: *How did it happen? When did it happen? Why did it happen?* He gave everyone the same three answers to all three questions. How was still under investigation, when was sometime between lights out and wake-up call – yes, there's someone at the monitors but no, they don't have someone to cover the camera's during their breaks – and why could only be answered with the obvious, the man was mentally ill, or he wouldn't be in this institution in the first place.

By the end of the day, his head was in misery, and he had almost forgotten about the drastic change to the appearance of his eyes. He had seriously considered making an appointment with the local optometrist but decided against it because he didn't have a clue in the world as to what he would tell the doctor. This wasn't some common eye strain or a minor infection. This was something unnatural... maybe even supernatural. Who knows? Warren surely doesn't. He had taken pains all day not to talk with anyone in person. He certainly didn't need any more questions, things were crazy enough without everyone questioning him about his eyes. The couple of people he couldn't avoid talking to in person, had only stepped into his office for a moment or two. He kept his chair turned away from them, hiding his face from view, on both occasions, rushing them out quickly with the excuse that he was incredibly busy dealing with the recent escapee. No one at the Navea Dwighton Institute for the Mentally Afflicted envied Dr. Warren Gerard's position of power during times like these and no one really questioned him when he finally left three hours later than normal at almost sundown with dark sunglasses on. His *almost unbearable* headache being his very reasonable excuse for them.

Before returning home that first evening with his newly colored, or colorless, eyes he stopped at the local drug store, still donning his dark shades. Luckily for him, there were only two shoppers in the store at the time and both seemed to assume that he was blind. He bought a pair of colored contacts almost the same shade of light brown as his original eye color. The cashier gave him an odd look but let him leave without any questions. So, that solved *that* problem.

2

The news of the missing patient made the front page of the local newspaper the following day, as it always did during situations like this. Dr. Gerard spent that day, shades free but with itchy eyes that were struggling to adapt to the new contacts, doing interviews and answering even more questions over the phone. About halfway through the day between a phone call with the city's mayor and waiting for the third reporter of the day to show up, Patty Bollier knocked on his office door. A momentary instance of panic and guilt flooded his mind, but he abruptly pushed it away as he motioned her in to take a seat in the same place Sabrina had sat just the day before.

"Well, hello, Ms. Bollier! You look wonderful as usual!" He said in the pleasant tone all his nurses have come to associate with his 'good moods'. "As I'm sure you know I am quite busy today with everything going on, but I always try to make time for my faithful staff. So, how may I help you today, Ms. Bollier?" he asked with a mouth as dry as sandpaper. Every fiber of his being told him that this discussion was going to be about Sabrina, and it made him very nervous.

Sitting in the chair across from Dr. Gerard in her white well-kept nurses' uniform, much of her long legs evident for his viewing, Patty fidgeted with her prettily painted, manicured fingernails, reluctant to speak at first. Finally, she asked very low, "What happened to Sabrina?"

"What do you mean?" Growing more nervous by the second, he decided the best way to go about this current conversation was to answer a question with a question. See what she knows before giving her an answer.

"Well..." she begins, still reluctant to speak forwardly with him.

Seeing her reluctance and wanting to be done with this conversation as quickly and effectively as possible, Dr. Gerard says in his most soothingly, charming voice. "Ms. Bollier, please, your nervousness is unnecessary. Honestly, it is." He stood up from his desk chair, walked around the side of the large wooden desk and sat in the empty chair next to her. He reached out and grabbed her hand, embracing it in both of his. A flicker of alarm flashed in her eyes, there-and-then-gone-again; then she realized it was a comforting gesture. A big difference from his usual leg rubs, ass pinches, and boob grabs. One of the other women they work with who's been here for almost five years told her and Sabrina once that the only reason he treated them that way is because his checkbook still wasn't big enough to cover his ugly ass and tiny prick. Not today though, he was being sincere, truly trying to comfort her.

She cleared her throat, straightened up in her chair a little, adjusting the bottom hem of her uniform, noting his eyes never left her face as she did so. This made her a little bit more comfortable with the situation, so she opened up. "Well, I haven't seen or spoken with Sabrina since ya brought her in here yesterday for yer discussion. She was tellin me about what happened fore ya came in, but she didn't get very far. We talk every night after work but not last night, even though I tried four times. She didn't show up for work this mornin either. It's just not like her. I thought that since you were the last person, *I* know of that she spoke with, I'd ask ya about it."

Listening attentively the entire time and organizing his thoughts into intelligent sentences, he seems to consider the information she has given him before answering. Rubbing his thumbs along her knuckles, he gives her an explanation. "Well, we had our discussion and then went to Mr. Doe's room in the patient's corridor. While there she started acting sort of strange so I told her to leave for the day so she could go see her doctor about that bump on her head. I even offered to take her myself or call an ambulance over from the hospital, but she refused. She said that she was going to go home, take some more aspirin and try to rest. I advised her against that in case she was suffering from a concussion. Whether or not she took my advice I cannot say, Ms. Bollier, but I walked her out myself and haven't seen her since. I know that she didn't call this morning to let us know she wouldn't be coming in today but given yesterday's circumstances, I hardly think such trivialities are important." His tone, comforting and soothing at the start became mingled with professionalism as he finished up.

Patty nodded. A glum look upon her face, worry in her eyes. "Okay. I was plannin on stoppin by her place afta work, anyway." She told him then let out a small chuckle, surprising Dr. Gerard.

"Something funny?" he asked, astounded.

"Yeah, kinda. She forgot her name tag yesterday mornin. I thought maybe ya mighta fired her for it." She confessed, another small laugh escaping from between her slightly parted smirking lips.

Dr. Gerard is even more surprised. He hadn't even noticed she was missing her nametag yesterday. Given everything the two of them had witnessed, it was quite a funny thought that he would have fired her because of it. "Oh, yeah... I still might." He says in that same professional tone but gives her a quick wink, indicating that he is joking. Then he's the one giggling. A few seconds later, realizing he really was just joking, she joins him. As they sat there giggling together like young girls ogling at a shirtless bodybuilder, the first of many flies had targeted the body of Sabrina Lowell.

3

Patty is the one to find Sabrina, stopping at her place on her way home from work later that day. She knocks several times without an answer before retrieving the spare key from the inside of the bell, disguised as the clapper, hanging by the screen door. She lets herself in, calling Sabrina's name repeatedly to no avail. Patty finally finds Sabrina in her bathroom lying in the tub with thick white and green foam dried on her neck, chin and the inside of her gaping mouth. Her eyes are mostly closed but already slightly sunken into her skull, her skin a pale, yellow jaundice-like color. There are several small jewelry bags laying around the bathtub on the floor. All just large enough to hold a small handful of pills. All the insides coated with the white powdery residue of any number of medications. And, aside from the few loose pills scattered about, all of them are empty.

Patty screams and screams and screams some more, until her throat is raw and sore. She goes into hysterics that prevent her from calling the authorities, but a couple of officers arrive several minutes after Patty finds Sabrina, anyway. Apparently, 'a concerned neighbor' heard her screams and called it in. She is grateful, nonetheless.

Patty can't tell them why she is there upon their arrival due to her current mental state. After seeing the body of Sabrina Lowell, the two officers call in the coroner for the deceased and an ambulance for the hysterical. Patty is taken to the local hospital where she is sedated and evaluated for a possible psychiatric hold. Once she has her wits about her again, Patty tells the psychiatrist what happened and how she had found her best friend in the bathtub. She isn't required to stay for the hold, but she does leave the hospital the following morning with the name of a trauma counselor and the intention of keeping the appointment.

Patty Bollier attends Sabrina's funeral three days later with over half of her former co-workers. She never works for Dr. Warren Gerard again or steps foot in the Navea Dwighton Asylum for the Mentally Afflicted. She sticks around town just long enough after the funeral to find out the results of the autopsy Sabrina's family had insisted upon. The initial ruling is suicide given all the evidence and the way she died, but her family insisted, nonetheless.

The autopsy reveals everything one would expect from a healthy young woman in her early twenties, apart from the 15+ almost fully intact oxycodone tablets found in her stomach. This number did not include how many her body had already dissolved and absorbed or the amount that she had thrown up before consequently passing.

An investigation of the circumstances surrounding Sabrina's death was completed but it ultimately rules in favor of the coroner's results that it is, indeed, a suicide. The only fingerprints, aside from Sabrina's, were on the baggies. They belong to a man in his mid to late twenties that goes by the name of Reef on the streets. He smells strongly of marijuana and spiced cider but when he is searched, he comes up clean. He speaks and acts sober, not giving either officer so much of a hint that he might be intoxicated. The reality of it is that he is on Cloud Nine and rising, they just don't need to know that. The officers question the man for several hours before being satisfied that he is telling them the truth. By the end of the interrogation, the man is obviously irritable, his buzz long gone. They release him and marijuana man heads home to his Mary Jane.

Turns out that Reef is just a small-time seller/pothead. They had asked him about the baggies which he admitted to handling during the drug deal, but he swore that he didn't know they were for her OR for that reason. Reef seemed to be very sympathetic to the situation and even teared up when they informed him of Sabrina's demise.

A few days ago, he had met up with Sabrina and handed her more than 30 of those tablets. She gave him the right amount for them and then they went their separate ways, even though she did not strike him as the Oxy type. She certainly didn't look or act the part. He never even considered that she was going to take them, just assumed she was the deliverer or was going to resell them for a bit of extra cash. So, it really did hit him hard to find out she used them to commit suicide. Neither officer could detect any signs of untruth or deception in Reef pertaining to Sabrina Lowell. They pick Reef up, again, a couple of days later, charge him with distribution in connection with her death, knowing that he would just post bond quickly and return home to lay low for a bit.

4

Sabrina Lowell's death makes the local newspaper due to the surrounding circumstances and the unexpectedness of it, but she is not connected in any way to the *escapee*. They only briefly mention that she was employed but don't mention where, as if it is irrelevant. It's a small town and gossip abounds, but no one ever suspects what really happened to Sabrina Lowell. The only person that knows only had to tell his lie once to Patty Bollier, but never again.

A week to the day, giving up another one of his only days off a week, Dr. Warren Gerard still has security scanning the grounds in shifts looking for any sign of the *escapee*, everyone knowing he is *long gone already*. Dr. Gerard just wants to make sure they have checked twice, thoroughly, and then once more for good measure. Just in case. The local papers have simply kept up with an updated version of the original article about the *escapee*, Mr. Joseph Doe, throughout the week. All updates have said a variation of the same thing, that the escapee still hasn't been apprehended and that an investigation into the matter is underway. Dr. Gerard has every intention of keeping the *investigation underway* until the local papers finally find something else to talk about. *He* knows that Joe Doe will never be found but he can't tell anyone such a thing, especially not a reporter for the local paper. They wouldn't understand. He *witnessed* all that strangeness and doesn't understand it. Just thinking about it makes him feel like a lunatic, so he can't imagine trying to explain any of it, to anyone.

Chapter Seven

No Mo' Joe

1

Dr. Gerard sits at his large wooden desk, going through a mental checklist of everything he has and still needs to address pertaining to Mr. Doe and the oddity of his parting. A scenario to cover Mr. Doe's disappearance: check. *A little white lie never hurt anyone.* Sabrina's knowledge of the situation: check. *Unfortunate but it resolved a major issue.* His.... His eyes: check. *If only these darn contacts weren't so dang uncomfortable.* His sixth sense: check? *Well, I only see things in room 32, so it hasn't gotten worse, I suppose?* Room 32, itself: X. *Need to get all his personals out so they can lock it up.*

The most recent and pressing issue, however, is Mr. Gregory Patrickson, the man that originally sent Sabrina looking for Joe. The usually mild tempered, acquiescent man attacked one of the maintenance men earlier today sending him to the hospital with multiple lacerations where he is currently being evaluated and treated. Mr. Patrickson was sedated during the attack and moved to his room in the patient's corridor. Now, this is hardly a unique situation; Warren deals with similar situations on a bi-monthly average. What troubles him the most about it is how the man kept screaming "Where's Joe?!" and "What'd you do with Joe?!" at the maintenance guy as he lashed him with his clawed fingers. At the end of each finger were fingernails, much longer than they should be, and each fingernail had been bitten into very sharp tipped points.

Greg Patrickson, for no known reason, knocked the maintenance man off the ladder he was standing on while washing one of the common room windows. He immediately leaped on and began swinging and slicing at the man, screaming the whole time, tearing skin and hair from the man's face with every successful blow. The maintenance man, scared and confused during this unprovoked attack, raised his arms to protect his face but only got his forearms sliced and shredded for the defensive act. The tatters of clothing and flesh being ripped from the man's arms were soon mixed with a considerable amount of blood.

Mr. Patrickson's last successful blow, accompanied by an earsplitting "Where the fuck is Joe!!", landed over the maintenance man's left eye and cheek; his eerily sharp middle fingernail punctured the man's eyelid right below the eyebrow. When a nurse in the onlooking crowd was finally able to inject Mr. Patrickson with a fast-acting sedative, he jerked back reflexively, lifting the man's eyelid up and off his eyeball, momentarily. Simultaneously, he jerked his arm away from the man's face bringing his attached fingernail with it, ripping the man's eyelid straight down the center. Miraculously, the fingernail missed his eyeball by fractions of a centimeter, only slicing the eyelid that had parted just enough to be visible. When Greg was torn away from him, the maintenance man blinked reflexively. His eyelid, partly closed from the attack, finished closing but instead of ascending to open his eye again, the two halves of his eyelid folded up to just under his eyebr0w. His right eye, seemingly unscathed but splattered with blood from a cut around his temple was bright and alert, jittering with adrenaline. His left eye now resembled a window with curtains hung but pulled back to the sides. It was an incredible, undeniable sight witnessed by about half a dozen staff members and more than a dozen patients.

2

While Greg Patrickson is sleeping off the effects of his sedative and Dr. Gerard is contemplating disciplinary options for him, two of his nurses are going through everything in the former room of Mr. Joseph Doe, room number 32. This is a common assignment for the nurses at the Navea Dwighton Asylum for the Mentally Afflicted. On the rare occasion that a patient can return home, the patient usually packs their own belongings and everything else is disposed of after they have been discharged. On the occasion that a patient has died, another common event but not occurring nearly as often as the situation like Mr. Patrickson has found himself in, the personal effects are sent to the next of kin and everything else is disposed of. A lot of the patients that end up hospitalized here, die here; usually due to the natural aging process, a suddenness physical sickness (most patients haven't been and/or can't be vaccinated due to the complicated web of medications they are on), or they succumb to their mental illnesses, resulting in the death of the mind that eventually leads to the death of the body.

The Navea Dwighton Asylum for the Mentally Afflicted has a long running, prided reputation for never having a patient commit suicide on the grounds. Plus, in it's more than triple decades of existence, it's only had two attempts both of which unsuccessful in themselves, but successful in reevaluating protocols and guidelines to better care for the patients. The last attempt was more than fifteen years ago.

However, when a patient manages to successfully escape the grounds, allowing seven days from the time of the disappearance, the patient's personal effects are gathered, labeled, and placed in a storage area in the basement. This allows them to be accessible if the patient is eventually apprehended and returned to the asylum. The room is then cleaned thoroughly, everything sans personal belongings, replaced back in their original positions. Once a month a janitor is permitted inside to do a quick clean but otherwise the room is left locked and untouched. If after five years the patient has yet to be apprehended or returned to the asylum, the remaining contents of the room are disposed of, and the patient's personal belongings are sent to the next of kin.

Room 32 will be no different in that regard. It'll be locked up for the next five years, untouched, until the allotted time passes so that they can actually clean it out. That is if they can get it sorted through and cleaned up the first time. The two nurses, Ms. Beckett and Ms. Roberts, are working diligently, one clearing off shelves and wiping everything down with a cleaner dampened rag while the other sorts through every item, scanning it all for personal belongings. They have been in here for more than two hours and have only gotten through five of the twelve wooden box crates making up the floor-to-ceiling bookcase. To make it more exasperating, there were only four items sitting in the dated box marked:

Personal Effects
Joseph Doe (40s–50s), Birthdate: unknown
Room #32, East Hall

Three of the four items are pictures that had been taken from a book or magazine. One is of a random, beautiful, dark-haired woman with piercing green eyes, like emeralds glistening in the sunlight. The second one is of another slightly older woman, this one a ginger with hazel eyes and a pale freckled complexion, beautiful in a simpler, more motherly way. The last one being of a small sleeping baby swaddled in a blue blanket and wearing a blue hat, a small tuft of dark hair laying across its smooth forehead. These pictures, ripped carefully around the images, don't really seem like personal items to either nurse but she tosses them in the box anyway because they are so out of place from everything they have found so far. A lot of books, a lot of notepads filled with odd drawings and little notes that are written in such atrocious handwriting that they can't be read, and a lot of newspapers and magazines. Since everything must be wiped off and scanned through before being replaced on the shelf, it is proving to be quite a daunting task.

The fourth item is the sealed manila envelope they found lying on the desk. Even though there's no name or address anywhere on the envelope it feels like the most personal item in the room. So, it was the first to get tossed in the small, labeled cardboard box.

Time passes for the two nurses. After the first hour, they accept that this is going to be an all-day job instead of the usual few hours. They stop once to go on their lunch breaks and are right back at it as soon as they are done. About an hour after their lunch break, they realize that they might have to finish this room tomorrow. Not going to happen, they decide. Kicking it into high gear they rush through the rest of the room, making sure to check everything but being a little laxer about the cleaning.

They finish up about 20 minutes before the end of their shift with Ms. Roberts putting fresh sheets on the cot while Ms. Beckett completes the mopping. They grab the box of personals, flip the light off and close the door. The lock engages leaving the contents of room 32 in limbo for the next 1,825 days. The two nurses head toward the double doors exiting the 'rainbow corridor', bound for Dr. Warren Gerard's office.

3

There's a knock on his office door and before he has a chance to respond, a petite black-haired young woman opens the door, stepping in with a stack of papers in one hand, pulling the door closed behind her. "Ms. Beckett and Ms. Roberts are here to see you before they leave for the day." She tells him in her pleasant business-like tone.

Warren, up until she knocked on the door, was scanning through the company handbooks for advice on his Mr. Patrickson debate. He leans back in his chair with a small sigh of relief. A headache is forming behind his eyes from the concentration and focus he's applying to the situation. A temporary pause, with a solution instead of another problem, is guiltily welcome. "Send them in, please." He tells her kindly.

"Yes, Dr. Gerard." She turns to open the door, but he stops her before she can.

"Oh, Ms. Lancing?" she stops and turns to look at him with her hand remaining on the door handle. "Have you heard anything on the condition of Mr. Gordon?" He asks her, knowing she would have told him already if she had.

"No, Doctor. I will call the hospital and see what I can find out, though." She answers quickly and politely, careful not to sling all the insults forming in her mind at him.

"Thanks, doll." He says as she steps back out. Dr. Gerard does not notice her roll her eyes at his sexist pet-name.

A moment later the nurses that cleaned room 32 come walking in with a labeled cardboard box indicating the room has been finished. "Hello, Ms. Beckett! Ms. Roberts! Please come in and sit. You two look exhausted and I have no doubt that you are." Both ladies move to take a seat in each of the two chairs sitting in front of Dr. Gerard's desk. The one holding the box hands it over to him before sitting down with a sincere look of relief. "I have been in that room, and it is quite full. I can sympathize with your anguish." He pauses knowing there's a lot more in that room than they know, and a silent awkwardness tries to settle in on them. "So, have you initialed the box yet?" He adds quickly, looking across the desk at them as they both shake their heads.

"We did the inventory list and stickered everything as we went, though. We just haven't double checked that everything is in there and correct yet." The one that handed him the box, Ms. Beckett, replies.

"Okay. Usually, I would insist we get it done this afternoon but since you two have had such an exhausting day you can wait and go through it tomorrow morning if you prefer." He informs them, feeling an odd guilty generosity since it is technically against protocol.

The nurse that didn't carry the box in, Ms. Roberts, yawns and covers her mouth with the back of her hand. She lets her hand fall back into her lap and says, "Oh, there's only a few things in there. It won't take but a moment." To elaborate her point, she reaches out and grabs the box, setting it in her lap as she leans back in her seat. She takes the lid off the top of the box and turns it so that the inventory list, held in a plastic sleeve attached to the outward facing side of the lid, faces her. She glances from the list to the box five or six times and rummages through it once. When she finishes, she leans forward steadying the box in her lap with one hand and grabs a pen out of the cup sitting on his desk. She slides the inventory sheet out enough so that the top quarter of the paper is out of the plastic sleeve and scribbles her initials R.R. on it before sliding it back in place. Without replacing the lid, she hands the box over to Ms. Beckett who repeats the process just as swiftly. After signing her initials P.B. she replaces the pen they used back in the cup it was retrieved from, puts the lid securely on the box, and places it back on his desk in front of him. The cardboard box had only left his desk for approximately 40 seconds.

With a look of unbelief, he eyes both ladies suspiciously, his contact-covered eyes darting from Ms. Beckett over to Ms. Roberts and back. They shrug in unison, their eyes or expressions never faltering indicating truthfulness. "I guess you two were being serious." He finally says.

They nod, the exhaustion of the day evident on their emotionless faces and slumped postures.

"Well, I see no reason to keep you two fine ladies from the rest of your evenings." He tells them as he stands from his chair behind the desk. In response, the nurses also stand. "Thank you kindly Ms.

Beckett. Ms. Roberts. As always, I appreciate each and every one of my staff members and all the hard work they put forth for this great institution. You two have done a phenomenal job with all your hard work today. Again, I thank you!" Dr. Gerard tells them as he walks them to the door.

They both turn to look at him before exiting the door he is holding open for them. Ms. Roberts catches his attention, and they lock eyes momentarily. Then her face contorts into one of confusion that she quickly masks with another tired yawn. "You're welcome, Dr. Gerard. I mean, this is what you sign our paychecks for." Ms. Beckett replies with a girlish giggle.

Dr. Gerard gives her a small chuckle even though he didn't quite catch what she had said, just felt it an appropriate response to laugh with her. He missed it wondering about the change of expression on Ms. Roberts face just a moment ago. For a second there it felt like she had seen through him and everything he had been hiding the last week. *But that would be impossible, it's probably just my guilty conscience messing with me.*

The nurses leave his office and Dr. Warren Gerard returns to his desk. He sets the box on the floor beside his desk and goes back to scanning through the handbooks trying to find a solution to yet another problem.

4

As the nurses walk down the hallway leading back to the main nurses' station where they will clock out and head home for the day, Ms. Roberts asks Ms. Beckett, "Did you notice that the Docs eyes seemed different, somehow? Like they were a different color or something?" She asks this with a solid mix of genuine curiosity and sheepish regret, waiting for Ms. Beckett to laugh at her idiotic question. She doesn't though, just eyes her curiously before answering with another question.

"And just how do you know the exact color of the boss' eyes, huh?" Ms. Beckett asks Ms. Roberts with a slight crack of a smile.

"Oh, don't you start." Ms. Roberts says, giving her co-worker a small shove. All the nurses like to tease Ms. Roberts like this because they all know that she is still a virgin. "I'm being serious! There was something odd about them, I just can't quite seem to put my finga on it." She whispers to Ms. Beckett, loudly. They are now standing in line with all the other day shift nurses that are clocking out and heading home too.

"I'm just teasin ya, girl, don't go gettin your panties in a twist, now. It was probably just the lighting or something. I wouldn't worry about it." Ms. Beckett advises her, stepping up to punch her personal code into the computer. Once that's done, she steps aside so Ms. Roberts can do the same.

"Yeah, I reckon you're right." Ms. Roberts says with a loud sigh. "I really am exhausted. I'm sure that was part of it, too. Like my mind playin tricks on me or something." She finishes as she enters her personal code into the computer.

"Coulda been." She pauses, looking at the uncertainty pasted all over Ms. Roberts face. "Hey, how about we stop at that little coffee shop on the corner on our way home and grab us one of those lattes you like so much?" Ms. Beckett asks, hoping the offer alone will help take her mind off it.

Ms. Roberts stands there a moment, seeming to weigh her options. Finally, she gives Ms. Beckett a mischievous grin. "Screw coffee, lets' go to the bar."

"Even better." Ms. Beckett replies without hesitation, and they both start laughing. Walking into the locker room, she says, "Seriously though, I'm gonna jump in the shower fore we go. I don't know why but stripping and remaking that bed made me feel really disgusting. I won't be long." Then Ms. Beckett turns toward the showers, grabbing a towel on the way, leaving Ms. Roberts to sit and wait for her much needed drink.

5

A few hours later, it's just about time for Dr. Gerard to head home for the day when he finally puts away the handbooks and other law references, he has acquired. There's not much he can do right now. He can and is keeping Mr. Patrickson from harming himself or anyone else to the best of his staff's ability. Aside from that, all he can do is wait. Wait until Mr. Patrickson is coherent and stable enough to speak with him about his actions. Wait to find out about the extent of Mr. Gordon's injuries. Wait to speak with Mr. Gordon about the attack. Wait. Wait. Wait.

He will check on Mr. Patrickson in the morning, he is done for today. His headache is in hurricane mode and thudding raptly in his temples. There's another quick rap on the door before Ms. Lancing steps into his office for the last time today. He has been expecting her because she always informs him when she's leaving for the day. "I called the hospital earlier like you asked me to, but they didn't have any information to give at that time. However, I just got off the phone with one of the nurses that tended to him. She informed me that he had to have more than 20 stitches in his forearms, over 45 in his face and is currently in recovery from a repair surgery on his eyelid by an oculoplastic surgeon." She sighs sadly, seemingly wishing she could give him better news.

Warren sighs loudly, wishing that she had given him better news. This is worse than he expected. "And she said that they have him on IV antibiotics to prevent infection. They are treating him like he was attacked by an animal instead of a sick, disturbed individual!" She adds, her voice rising into a yell at the end of the last sentence.

"I understand your frustration with others perception of our patients, Ms. Lancing, but I must insist that you calm down, my dear." Warren rises from his chair behind his desk and walks toward her. He continues, "The antibiotics are a good thing regardless of whatever reason they have, for giving them to him." He reaches her, putting his hands on her upper arms, gently caressing the smooth skin with his callused thumbs.

Ms. Lancing has an overwhelming feeling that the doctor is going to try to seduce her… again. She is in no mood for this creep and his insistent groping. "Well, I must be going." She tells him, icily, while grabbing the door handle. In a small series of quick movements, she opens the door and wriggles out of his grasp as she steps out of the office, closing the door behind her. She walks as quickly as she can out of the office and to her car because she knows he won't follow her out of the building.

Warren watches as Ms. Lancing closes the door behind her, he sighs heavily and returns to his desk with a disappointed look on his face. The doctor was, in fact, hoping to seduce the young and appealing Ms. Lancing this evening. Lord knows he's been trying for quite some time. All the stress of the past week has gotten Dr. Gerard... pent up, one could say. He was so hoping that Ms. Lancing would have provided him with some release. From behind, preferably, so she wouldn't notice his eyes.

Maybe another time.

Dr. Warren Gerard, head of the Navea Dwighton Asylum for the Mentally Afflicted, decides to head home for the night. The box of belongings with Mr. Joseph Doe's name on it, tucked under his arm as he turns off the light in his office and closes the door behind him.

Chapter Eight

Nightmares and Other
Personal Belongings

1

Gregory Patrickson sleeps the night away in his room. He is watched closely on the monitors by the night shift nurse that was informed of the situation upon arriving for her shift. Two guards are stationed in the rainbow corridor in case Mr. Patrickson decides to attack someone else. But the night proves uneventful, for the night nurse and guards anyway. The most eventful part of the guards' night is escorting another patient to the smoking area for a late-night cigarette. The night nurse observing the monitors watches Mr. Patrickson stir restlessly in his sleep several times throughout the night. If the cameras were equipped with audio too, she would have been able to hear him mumbling incoherently in his sleep.

Mr. Patrickson is plagued by the eerily vivid nightmares of his friend, Joe, screaming in agony and pure terror. Brief flashes of Joe being tortured in the most heinous of ways flip through his mind like a patch-work home movie. A screaming Joe is strapped to a table as a blood-soaked 'doctor' in stained sterile whites, with dark red eyes and long clawed fingers, reaches into Joe's split open chest cavity, removing another organ. The 'doctor' tosses it into a pit to the right of him where a three-headed dog-like beast snatches up the bloody organ. The head on the right has the organ in its fanged teeth when the center head snatches it violently away, leaving only small scraps behind. The right head angrily snaps at the center head's ear, catching it with a fanged tooth, ripping it in two. The center head yelps in pain as its black blood patters to the stone floor, allowing the left head to snatch up and devour the organ while the center and right heads snarl and snap and bicker with each other. The scene changes and now Joe's blood curdling screams die down to a choking gasp as he is being ripped apart, limb by limb, by some man-like creatures that are not at all men. They have large hands and feet with long claw-like fingers and toes, grotesquely disfigured bodies bent in incomprehensible ways yet agile and fluid in their actions. All the creatures are clearly male with very large appendages, some hanging half-way down to their feet, swinging between their unclothed legs. Their faces resemble humans in most ways but look melted, which grossly dislocates, and distorts their features. They are vile and repulsive to look at, yet he cannot avert his eyes from them. Greg has never seen the Devil or a demon to know what one would look like, but he's certain those man-like... things... are demons of some sort.

He stirs in his sleep, mumbling the Lord's Pray.

The next scene shows Joe strapped to a metal chair, blood trickling down his face. The top portion of his skull has been cut and removed, exposing the grayish-pink noodle-like structure of his brain. The 'doctor' with the dark red eyes stands behind him, tools in hands, slicing, dicing, and cutting chunks out of his brain. The 'doctor' turns and places the chunks of brain on a tray being held by one of the man-like creatures... the demons. The demon takes the tray across the dark room and out of sight. Soon after, the sound of sizzling meat and the smell of searing flesh carries toward him, turning his stomach. He looks sadly at his friend as tears stream from Joe's bloodshot eyes. The scene changes again with Joe on his hands and knees, unbound, but seemingly held in place by some invisible force. One of the grotesque demons appears behind him and that's when the screaming starts. Joe screams with all the pain and humiliation one can muster as the demon savagely sodomizes him with a baseball bat... wrapped in razor wire. Blood seeps from the tatters of his nether region, pooling under him, and Greg is more than relieved when the scene finally changes again.

The final scene before the nightmare, mercifully, ends is of an incredibly beautiful woman, by far the most beautiful woman Greg has ever seen, with deep purplish-blue eyes. They are magnificent but there is a darkness in them that makes him nervous. She laughs, seeming to mock his nervousness. "He can show you, but you can't help him. He will finally be mine... when *He* decides his punishment has been suffice, of course." She laughs, again, and enjoys the knowledge that this man is suffering having had to endure those scenes. The image of the tantalizingly beautiful woman fades along with her evil, malicious laughter.

Mr. Patrickson stirs again but falls into a deeper, dreamless sleep for a while. When he wakes up come morning, he can only dimly remember the nightmares from the night before. Not that he really wants to remember them but because he feels like it is somehow important. If only he could remember.

2

After eating his breakfast and taking his medication, all from his room in the patient's corridor, Greg is escorted into Dr. Gerard's office. "Please have a seat, Mr. Patrickson." Dr. Gerard insists from his chair behind his desk, beckoning him to sit with an outstretched hand. "You two may leave us. I'll call for you if any issues arise." He tells the guards that escorted Greg to his office, giving Greg a quick look before glancing at the guards and waving them out. They nod and walk out, without comment, closing the door softly behind them. "Now then, Mr. Patrickson, you have placed me in a very delicate situation with that little... stunt... you pulled yesterday." Warren puts a disgusting amount of emphasis on the word *stunt*. "What do you suppose I do about that?" The doctor asks his patient.

Knowing a rhetorical question when he hears one, Mr. Patrickson declines to answer. He sits with downcast eyes, stealing quick glimpses of the doctor's stern face.

"At least tell me why you attacked one of our maintenance men. What in the heavens did that man ever do to deserve such a malicious beating?" Dr. Warren Gerard asks the man, sincerely curious as to how he will respond.

Warren waits for quite some time before Greg finally gives him an answer. He sits quietly, contemplating and fidgeting with his neatly trimmed, short, fingernails. Finally, he softly tells the doctor, "I thought he did somethin to Joe. I really thought *he* was da reason Joe is gone."

"What do you mean? Joe escaped Mr. Patrickson." Warren pauses. "Do you think Mr. Gordon helped him?" He asks.

Abruptly, almost not allowing Dr. Gerard to finish asking his question, Greg sits straight up in his chair and yells, "Dat's bullshit and ya knows it! Joe didn't 'scape! He disappeared! I don't know how or why or all dat, but I knows he didn't 'scape!" He sits back, trying to get his anger in check, doing so quickly.

Dr. Gerard arches an eyebrow in question. "And you are no longer convinced Mr. Gordon had anything to do with Joe's... disappearance?" He almost chokes on the last word of his question, a simultaneous lie and truth.

"No, sir. Not anysmore." Greg replies sheepishly.

Warren waits for further elaboration, but none comes. Exasperation evident in his tone, he asks the man sitting across the desk from him what changed his mind.

Another long silence preludes Greg's reply. "Ya wouldn't believes me if I's told ya, sir." Fragments of the vile nightmares streaming through his confused mind. The fragments themselves, pointless; the importance of the message, astounding. He just doesn't know what the message is to decipher its importance.

"Now, what makes you think I wouldn't believe you?" Warren asks, the words escaping his lips mere moments before realizing the ridiculousness of what he has said.

Gregory Patrickson looks at the doctor dumbfoundedly for a moment before shaking his head, his anger threatening to return, refusing to dignify his idiotic question with an answer. Dr. Gerard, clearly embarrassed and slightly irritated from the lack of information this conversation has produced, stands and yells for the guards to come escort the patient back to his room where he will remain until further notice.

With a guard on each side of Mr. Patrickson leading him out of Dr. Gerard's office, he stops and turns back to look at the middle-aged man sitting behind his desk. "I's sorry bout dat man I hurt. I hope he's gonna be alright." Then he walks out, one of the guards pulling the door closed behind them.

3

Warren sighs heavily, rubbing his face with the palms of his hands. After taking a few deep breathes and trying to clear his mind, he calls his secretary, Ms. Lancing, into his office to inquire about the maintenance man, Mr. Gordon. "I haven't spoken with anyone this morning, but I'll call the hospital and see what I can find out for you, Dr. Gerard." She tells him from her place right beside the door. Any farther inside the room and he would probably think she's coming on to him.

"Thank you, Ms. Lancing. If you speak with someone, find out when I will be able to talk with Mr. Gordon, would you please?"

"Yes, sir." She answers quickly, abruptly leaving the room before he could molest her with his eyes, again. God, how she hates going into his office. How she is beginning to hate him.

About an hour later, Ms. Lancing taps on his office door and enters after his admittance. "Sorry it took so long to get back to you, but I had to wait for Mr. Gordon's doctor to return my call. Anyway, our maintenance man only has a 60/40 chance of coming out of this with any sight in his injured eye and he won't know until the eyepatch comes off in two to four weeks. Even if he does retain his sight, he will need to wear glasses for the rest of his life." She pauses.

"I wish him a full recovery and intend to tell him so when I can go speak with him. When is that?" the doctor inquires.

"About that, Dr. Gerard, and this is why I had to wait for the doctor to return my call. The nurse I spoke with at first told me about his eye but when I asked her when you would be able to talk to Mr. Gordon, she refused to answer me. She told me that she would have the doctor call me, wished me a good day and hung up. The doctor calls awhile later and informs me that a few of the gashes in his face are rather deep. One of which is deep enough to have cut through one of the tendons in his jaw. They sutured it before closing the gash, but they had to wire his jaw closed so that the tendon can heal."

Dr. Gerard grimaces at the mental images flashing through his mind of the sliced tendon. His disgust turning into alarm at the news that his jaw had been wired shut. "For how long?" he asks, a little more harshly than he intended.

"The next six to eight weeks, minimum." She tells him, trying to hide an amused smile at his reaction. He is quite comical when he's upset, but she can't tell him that and she can't damage his precious ego by laughing at him. Not if she wants to keep this job. He might be a creep sometimes, but he pays well, it's a reliable job, and it's close to home.

"Alright, Ms. Lancing. Thanks." Warren huffs and waves her out. She takes her cue to leave and steps out of his office with the trace of a smile on her smooth, pouty lips. Dr. Gerard is pulling the handbook and law books back out as she does.

A few hours after his normal workday usually ends, Dr. Warren Gerard finally sets the books aside, mentally exhausted, and no closer to an answer to this Mr. Patrickson/Mr. Gordon situation. He sits at his desk, rubbing his temples, fighting a lingering headache. Quickly becoming lost in thought. *I'm looking at this the wrong way. I have to be. I need to step back and look at this from another angle.* He replays the attack on Mr. Gordon, thoroughly. Then does the same with his conversation with Mr. Patrickson this morning. *Maybe it's a cry for help? Maybe the attack was just a way of getting my attention so we would find Joe?* Dr. Gerard can't answer any of these questions but it's a theory he can work with… for now, anyway. *But I know where Joe is. I just don't know why he's there or what happened to him before he came here all those years ago. His past must have something to do with… well, whatever the heck is going on around here. But how to find out?*

He is still trying to figure out how to find out who Mr. Joseph Doe really is, or was, as he leaves his office and makes his way home for the night. The answer to all his questions sitting unnoticed in a lidded box in the back seat of his car.

4

Greg is once again plagued by the horrendous nightmare scenes of Joe being tortured in the worst of ways. Each scene is different from the ones he had seen the night before, but the final scene is the same, the same beautiful woman with the same dialogue. Come morning he will, once again, only remember fragments of the nightmare he had. The feeling that the nightmare holds some importance, a little stronger.

Dr. Warren Gerard falls asleep in his bed, after masturbating vigorously in the shower to erotic fantasies with the beautiful dark-haired Ms. Lancing. He dreams of a beautiful woman, whom he has never laid eyes upon, but very much wishes he could. She whispers in his ear, sending a tingling sensation through his body. The immense beauty takes him by the hand guiding him toward a large, padded platform that is covered in fluffy pillows, lit candles, and vined flowers of exotic beauty. The perfect set up for some serious love making.

Suddenly, though, the dream fades to black and Warren rolls over on his side, kicking the blankets from him.

He hears a hiss, quite feminine, come out of the darkness that is followed by a hearty satisfactory laugh, quite masculine.

"Stop your meddling!" The feminine voice screams.

Another masculine laugh, this time taunting.

"You can't stop this! It is written!" She screams.

The laughing that follows this comment is of utmost amusement, dragging out and finally slowly fading. The female voice suddenly screams loud enough to shatter glass, fading and dying out in the darkness.

Dr. Warren Gerard suddenly wakes from his strange dream, his heart pounding in his chest. The dream is already fading from his memory, and he will have no remembrance of it come morning. He walks to the bathroom, urinates, and returns to his bed, sleeping soundly until his alarm wakes him.

5

He gathers his belongings resting in the passenger seat beside him and prepares to walk into the asylum to begin his day's work. He lays his wallet on the arm rest, a few seconds later knocking it into the back seat floor with his elbow. Warren finishes gathering his things, steps out of his car and opens the back driver side door. There sits Mr. Joseph Doe's box of personal belongings. Another potential solution presents itself. *This could be helpful.* He grabs his wallet and slides it into his pocket, then grabs the box and swings the car doors closed.

About an hour later, Dr. Gerard has the contents of Joe's box laid out across his desk. He carefully examines each one. A picture of a lovely woman with long blonde hair, carefully ripped out of magazine. *Why would he have this? Maybe she reminds him of someone from hist past? A sister, mother, or lover?* A picture of another ginger-haired woman with freckles, a little older than the first. This one has, also, been carefully ripped out of a magazine. *Another woman but of a completely different type.* Another carefully ripped out picture of a beautiful baby wrapped in a blue blanket. *A baby? Now this is certainly interesting. A sibling, a child, or just wishful thinking? So many questions.* A small white cross that had been hand woven together with tiny threads. *I didn't know Joe was religious. I didn't really know anything about Joe, come to think of it. Not even his real name.* A pocket-sized bible bound in black leather with a gold crucifix embedded into the front cover. Dr. Gerard flips through the book and finds that every page had been written upon, some lines overlapping others making them harder to decipher. *Looks like a manic writing episode. I'll look at this much more closely a little later.* A manila envelope stuffed full of papers. No writing on the front, just packed full, the envelope still sealed, unopened. *This too requires further examination.* The last item being a hardback book titled *The Life of Owen Ray Houston: Born Evil or Raised That Way?* Warren flips through the well-read book, noticing that certain words and phrases had been circled and there were the occasional notes scribbled here and there. *Another item that will need extensive examination.*

Warren sits back in his chair, letting his eyes skirt and dance across the miscellaneous items strewn across his desk. After a few moments of contemplation, he picks up the pocket-size bible and opens the front cover. FUCK YOUR GOD! is written in large red letters across the first page, almost deep enough to rip through the thin paper. Dr. Gerard quickly slams the small book closed, his heart pounding in his chest. *Okay. Maybe Joe wasn't religious. But even those who aren't religious wouldn't do…. this!* He takes a few deep breathes to still his racing heart and then slowly opens the bible cover again, quickly turning the first page. A small irrational part of his mind, imbedded from years of growing up in the church, is convinced that if he reads those words again, the Lord above will strike him dead with lightning. No such thing would or did happen, of course.

The book of Genesis is filled with blood red scrawling's proclaiming God a liar, a fraud, a cheat, and a sinner. There are vile comments about defiling the first woman, Eve and sodomizing the first man, Adam. There are crude drawings among the comments and scribblings. Some of hideous beasts and strange symbols, some of sexual depravity and tortures unimagined by even the most creative out there. Warren Gerard hadn't even made it out of the book of Genesis before the handmade contents became more than he could handle. In one swift motion he slammed the small book closed, made the sign of the cross, tossed the black leather Bible into the box he had retrieved it from and immediately doused his hands in alcohol-based hand sanitizer.

Even after several applications of hand sanitizer and a few trips to the men's room to scrub his hands, he can still feel the nastiness of those words and pictures upon him. That book has made him feel… unclean. He hates this feeling and leans over his desk to apply a couple more squirts of hand sanitizer. A tiny droplet splashes from the palm of his hand into his eye, searing his eyeball as if it were a lit ember. He hisses through the pain, knowing he can't rub his eye with his hands, so he begins blinking rapidly, almost fluttering his eyelashes. The burning tames with the blinking, but his colored contact catches his eyelid, folding it over, and causing it to pop out onto his desk. He can see the contact lens laying there; he sighs heavily and carefully picks the lens up, setting it in the palm of his opposite hand. He stands from his chair with the intention of heading into the men's room, unconsciously scanning the items on his desk.

Dr. Gerard stands at his desk for several moments before collapsing back into his chair, not taking his eyes off the manila envelope stuffed full of papers. A few minutes go by before Warren finally blinks several times and rubs his eyes. It changes nothing. He can still see the distorted words on the front of the envelope. He closes the eye that doesn't have the contact in it, looking through the colored contact in the opposite eye. The words disappear, confusing the doctor. He opens his eye, blinks a couple of times and then closes the eye with the contact, now looking through the strange silvery-blue hue that is his new eye color. The words on the envelope not only reappear but come into focus. The handwriting is unlike anything Warren has ever seen, seemingly written with a multicolored velvet marker that glistens and glows in the light. It reads:

To: Dr. Warren N. Gerard
Immediately!
Imperative!
J.O.C.

Dr. Gerard reads the instructions multiple times before opening his other eye, forcing himself to look away from the words. An odd feeling has swept over him, an anxious unnerving feeling, something he can't ever recall feeling to this extent. He sits in his chair for several long moments before finally deciding on what to do.

He returns from reapplying his colored contact, reaching success after two failed attempts. Warren places the hand woven cross and the three, magazine tear-outs back into the box with the defaced bible, replaces the lid and leaves it sitting on the floor behind his desk, just out of sight of visitors. The manilla envelope and the biography are slipped into his briefcase, tucked away until he can take them home and read them. Read them without the restrictions of contacts and judgement.

The remainder of his workday drags by slowly but is uneventful, nevertheless.

Several hours later, Dr. Gerard sits down on the suede sofa in his den clad in his boxer shorts and gray silk robe. His eyes, devoid of any itchy contact lenses, faintly glow with an eerie softness in the dim light given off by the den lamps. He has the manilla envelope in one hand

and a scotch on the rocks in the other. He sets his drink on the table beside him, only a single relished sip taken from it, and then Warren rips the seal from the envelope, releasing the truth but sealing his fate in doing so.

Chapter Nine

The Beginning of The Beginning

1

The seal of the envelope flutters wistfully to the carpeted floor of the den as Warren carefully pulls a large stack of papers from the manila envelope. He lays them neatly on the coffee table, picks up the envelope and inspects the emptiness of the inside, ensuring he has left nothing unaccounted for. Satisfied that the envelope is empty, and all the contents are before him, Dr. Gerard looks carefully at the top page on the stack of papers. His eyes scan over the page, it seems to be loose-leaf notebook paper, the whole stack, college-rule, so there's more lines per page. The handwriting is neat but small, almost illegibly small, two handwritten lines to every line on the paper, small. There is no title or heading of any kind, not even a date written in the upper corner. There is no spacing between lines or paragraphs and only enough between words to distinguish one from another, the paragraph indents are shallow and barely distinguishable. Warren leans over the stack of papers, not touching them, squints his uncolored eyes, straining to make out the first couple of sentences. He cannot so he sits back on the couch slightly annoyed, staring at the mysterious stack of papers sitting on the coffee table before him.

Irritably, Warren picks up his drink and sips it as he loses himself in thought. *Now what the heck is all this junk? Why would Joe leave me.... whatever the heck this is... but make it so hard to read? It just doesn't make sense.* He abruptly sets his drink back on the table, half gone now, and sits up as straight as his middle-age posture will allow. His colorless eyes grow wide in their sockets as realization overwhelms him momentarily.

How did Joe know to address the envelope to me in a way that only I can see? He was dead when my eyes changed so how did he know I would be the one to end up with... with... heck I don't even know what to call it? Did he know what was going to happen? Did he know that I would be the one to... to... to...

He sits silently for several long minutes, finishing his scotch on the rocks, leaving the ice to melt in the, now, scotch-less glass. Finally, Dr. Warren Gerard decides that even if he doesn't know what to do in his current situation, he might be able to find the answer to that and many other questions by simply following instructions. The instructions given to him by someone or something beyond his current understanding. The instructions, only he can see, that are written in the multicolored velvety ink on the front of the manila envelope. He will read this, whatever it is... somehow. *It doesn't matter how difficult it is or even if I go blind trying.*

Unconsciously, Dr. Warren Gerard is slowly becoming obsessed.

He positions himself on the edge of the sofa in front of the stack of papers and sighs heavily. That odd feeling has swept over him again, the one he can't quite pinpoint. He tries, unsuccessfully, to shake the feeling. He ignores it instead and picks up the top page. What he worries would be a very difficult reading session, turns out to be the most tantalizing, horrific, insightfully addicting experiences of his life. With the page in hand, Warren again focuses on the first sentence. Almost immediately, the tiny handwritten letters on the page begin floating off the paper, changing from the flat gray graphite they are written in, to the mesmerizing ink of the unknown. The letters merge into words, the words into sentences, and the sentences into paragraphs. Initially, he is frightened but curiosity overcomes the fear, and he adapts to this new form of reading very quickly. He soon becomes enrapt in the reading, his obsession growing with each paragraph. He delves into the tale, into the answers, into the unknown. He delves into a past that he never knew existed and will ultimately wish he never had.

2

It begins:

> Dr. Warren Gerard, you know me as Joseph Doe only because I have refused to inform anyone of my name. Or anything else about me, for that matter. I am still reluctant to do so but please know that you will learn that as well as many other important things as you read this. I believe it will be lengthy, but I assure you it will be worth the abundance of information you will procure. I need to tell you a story, a true story. Everything I am about to tell you; I believe is 100% true but before I begin that, I need you to know a few other things beforehand.
>
> The first is that like your newly acquired 'sight', I have been blessed and cursed with nightmares and dreams of the events I intend to tell you about. I have had them every night since soon after I lost my tongue. I feared them at first, cursed them and even tried on numerous occasions to go for extended periods of time without sleep to avoid them.

Dr. Gerard pauses in thought, recalling Joe's arrival shortly after the facility had been opened. *I think he had trouble sleeping shortly after he got here. I need to pull his file to be sure.*

> They were relentless though and eventually, I realized they had a purpose. They were replaying that long winter, scene by scene, so that I could better understand the circumstances I had found myself and my infant son just barely surviving.

Another pause. *A son? The magazine photo of the baby. Of course!*

I understand a great deal more about the tragedies and losses that occurred during those fearful months in the mountains. So, the things that I couldn't have known from simply living through the experience, I know now. Some of them I wish I did not know but one cannot unknow such things. You are a logical man, Dr. Gerard, so please trust that I am wholly telling you the truth because I have no reason to lie. I know death, as you know it anyway, is waiting for me the moment I scribble the last word of this letter. I cannot change it, and even though I am uncertain of what awaits me after 'death', I have accepted that my end, here, is near.

Warren shudders and his heart quickens in pace for several moments before returning to normal.

The next is the purpose behind this letter. My son. I cannot tell you who he is at the present time, but I hope you will come to know him quite well before this... situation, is concluded. As a show of my credibility and truthfulness, I am informing you now, days beforehand, that there will be three new patients taking up residence in your facility. One of the three is innocent. One is a cold-blooded murderer, and the third is mentally afflicted and desperately needs your help. It is your job to determine who's who, so to speak. You will understand more as you continue to read why I insist upon you believing what you're reading. I will speak of this again later.

And the final thing you need to know about is the Witch.

Warren's eyes grow wide as he backtracks to read the last word again and again, trying to comprehend it. He finally continues.

Yes, Dr. Gerard, you read that correctly. Again, I must reiterate that everything I have, am, and will tell you is 100% true. The Witch is the reason for the decimation of an entire village, the loss of almost every life there, the loss of my son, the loss of my tongue, the loss of my love, and soon, the loss of my life. She is a powerful sorceress that deals in black magic, fucked up enough to be Satan's right hand...

He gasps, swallows with an audible click, and realizes how parched his throat and mouth are. He sets the paper down on the top of the stack, momentarily regretting it. *Dang! What if won't work when I pick it back up?* A few seconds of quick deliberation. *Heck with it! I need a drink, it'll work, or it won't.* He shrugs it off and walks over to the glass-top table where multiple decanters are placed, filled with a variety of top-shelf liquors. As he refreshes his glass with fresh cubes from the lidded ice bucket, he looks up, trying to mentally digest everything he has read so far.

Suddenly, his heart leaps into his throat, perspiration springs out on the bridge of his nose and forehead, and he draws back his fist out of reaction. It takes Warren a moment to realize he is looking at his reflection in the large mirror hanging on the wall behind his minibar. His eyes have an eerie glow about them that initially startles him. He assumes, correctly, that it is a 'side effect' of his newly acquired eyes and the things he is able to see with them. *This is hardly the most distressing thing you have dealt with lately, so quit being so dang jumpy.* He scolds himself as he sips his drink. He returns to the sofa, takes the top page off the stack careful not to look at it just yet and settles back against the couch. As soon as his eyes concentrate on the small, neat handwriting the letters begin flowing from the page again.

...and she wanted my son. I was able to keep him away from her for some time, but I know now that she found him. Now, her creation concerns her, for he is out of control. That's all I can say for now about that but know that as you read this you will learn much more about the

Witch. It is crucial that you learn what you can about her, as well. Your life will depend on it.

I know you have an abundance of questions and I hope that by the time this is over, they have all been answered. I also hope that you will still be here because of the information I was able to give you. I know you were chosen for this because it was shown to me in my dreams, but again that's all I can say about that for now. I only vaguely know by who, but I know for what, and you will too, soon enough.

3

As Dr. Warren Gerard begins to read the story, Joe insists he needs to know, the words start to mingle and tangle before his eyes, making it impossible to read any further. Quickly the jumbled words start forming an image, indistinguishable at first but becoming clearer with every passing second. Then one image becomes two and soon a sequence of them has formed. The scenes slowly take over his mind, enveloping him. Now, instead of reading the letter, it is showing it to him, like a movie and the nightmares/dreams that plagued Joe and are plaguing Greg Patrickson. He is shown an ariel view of the small mountain community known as Miner's Nook to those few on the outside world that know they even exist at all.

The most logical place to begin is the village. It sat in a small clearing tucked into the side of the Appalachia Mountains. The only village in the area, sitting several dozen miles from any other community in any direction, was almost completely isolated. The clearing being only half a dozen miles, give or take about a mile, east to west, and about fifteen miles north to south. was only accessible by train or extremely rough, usually impassable hiking trails. The eastern, western, and northern sides of the valley ended at the timber-crowded mountainsides. A beautiful river ran diagonally through both the east and west sides of the clearing, coming to a point toward the southern end and widening out into a larger, swifter river. The river ran under the railroad tracks that entered and exited the valley through tunnels dug into the mountainside. On the southern side of the railroad tracks was a grove of large trees that prevented a lot of undergrowth. The lack of sunlight gave it an eerie, ominous feeling. The river ran through the middle of the small forest that ended at a drop off, the river feeding a magnificent waterfall that fell several hundred meters before cascading out into a seemingly small, beautiful lagoon at the base of the cliff.

The village itself was divided into three sections, naturally due to the course of the river. But each section had sturdy, wide bridges running across the river to connect them. The western side of the clearing, sectioned out by the mountainside, the river, and the railroad tracks, was a massive farm. In the center of the farm was a barn that butted up against the mountain, with a giant fenced in area for various livestock. Cows, goats, pigs, ducks, and sheep. No horses, though, the terrain was too rough to ride them so the villagers couldn't see the point in keeping them around. The few they did try to bring to the valley were all put down shortly after for broken limbs. A full grain silo sat behind the barn, also butted up against the mountain. A large henhouse sat on the eastern side of the farm, close to where the two rivers join, the hens and roosters were scattered about the property. Multiple homes sat at the north end of the farm indicating generations of family that lived on and tended to the property. Along the river were a handful of small one-person shacks, shelters for the seasonal farmhands. The entire southern end of the farm was an enormous garden filled with almost full-grown fruits and vegetables of all kinds. Corn, cabbage, beans, sugar snaps, wheat, watermelon, cantaloupe, peppers, tomatoes, potatoes, and a few others. It had to be enormous, this farm had to supply the entire village.

The eastern side of the clearing, also sectioned off by the mountainside, river, and railroad tracks, consisted of rows and rows of houses. Like a modern-day residential area but much more poorly constructed. Some of the homes hadn't been occupied in years, if ever, based on their decaying state. Literally rotting on the stone foundations, most of this magnitude were uninhabitable. Other homes were habitable given some much-needed attention, and few were actually occupied. The residents tried desperately to make their homes look a little brighter against the dullness of their surroundings with little success. Toward the northern end of the section sat a large fence enclosing an area for the dozens of hunting dogs the villagers kept. A building, essentially a giant doghouse, sat within the confines of the fence. The giant dog lot separated the rows of houses from one much larger and much nicer home than any other in the village. This home was built to honor the founder of the village, a man named Eustice McGrath, who convinced a handful of miners to bring their families and settle down in this valley in the mountains. They could be self-sufficient, he told them. And they were, for the most part. Behind the large home sat two small, sturdy shacks. One was a single, two-person jail cell, very rarely used. The other, sitting right bedside it was what you would call a guard shack; also, very rarely used.

The entire northern end of the valley, more than double the size of the eastern and western sections, was naturally sectioned off by the timbered mountainside and the river. The southern-most point of the section was where the two rivers merged into a singular flowing unit. Several shops were scattered around the western and southern sides of a large square area, outlined with stacked flat stones. There was the butcher shop in the bend of the conjoining rivers, the mercantile, the fabric shop, the hostel, the grainery, the woodworkers mill, and the orphanage. The rock-outlined section was known as the common area to the village folks. In the center of the common area was a big circular area on the grass-free earth that was scorched black, with a tall wooden tower-like structure placed in the center of the scorched area. This was the Funeral Alter where they burned their dead so their souls could fly into the heavens. Two lines of small stands were set up for the farmer to use for his garden produce and the gatherers to use for their findings, along two of the stacked rock walls on the outside of the common area. On the northern side of the common area sat the schoolhouse. A long narrow one room building that accommodated the school aged children long enough for them to learn how to read, write, and do arithmetic. Once they had mastered that, regardless of the age, the child would then be taken on as an apprentice for any trade of their choosing. Every able-bodied villager, and even some that weren't, had a job. Everyone contributed to their society in some form. That's how it had always been and that's how it would always be, so they all hoped. The eastern side of the common area consisted of the church across from the schoolhouse, the apothecary and infirmary tucked between the common area and the river, and the one and only bar in the valley setting a little further off to the east.

The western side of the northern section of the valley ended at a rounded natural corner where the river met the mountainside. This large area contained the sawmill and lumberyard, the coal flat with a fenced in section for the mules they used to pull the carts in and out of the surrounding mines. There was a salt flat in the northwestern most corner, a fisherman's shack with a dock next to the river, a large strawberry patch, and a fruitful apple orchard. There were fishing nets set up strategically up and down both rivers running through the valley. The nets stopped shortly before the rivers met because the current was too quick for them. There were a handful of hunting lodges spread out across the valley along the wooded mountainsides to accommodate the hunters after a kill or to rest up between hunts. There were also various types of mines, scattered around the valley. Each mine was accessible only by following the carefully cleared paths leading to them. There was silver, salt, and coal mines. The miners carefully led the mules with the freshly mined cargo loaded into the cart behind them, out of the mines and back into the valley. The gatherers would not only tend to the apple orchard and strawberry patch but would search certain parts of the wooded mountains for mushrooms, berries, flowers, herbs, etc. The villagers knew how to utilize the surrounding land and everything it offered them. They respected it and tried hard not to misuse or abuse it in any way.

The eastern side of the northern section was composed mostly of makeshift shacks, tents and teepee-like dwellings densely packed together, leaving little room for much else. Many of the dwellings were uninhabited and uninhabitable after being picked over by the villagers for recycled housing materials. In the village, almost everything was used and what was used was used to threads. This section was where the less moral resided. Not to say that all who dwelled in this section of the village were all the same. Some were there by circumstance, some due to work, some to devotion. There was a row of five, somewhat sturdy shacks lined up not far from the bar that was known as 'Hussey Row'. Eight women and two young men would 'service' anyone who made a deal with the boss man. Against the mountainside, nestled between two hunting lodges, set one of the few well-built homes in this little area. The resident made his living making and selling moonshine out of the still behind his house. Over by the river, in another well-built home resided a man who made his living by growing and selling marijuana. He had a small two-acre plot that produced more than enough each harvest to supply the entire village and then some. The northeastern most point formed a natural corner where the mountainside met the river, and there set a plain well-built shack. A knee-high wall, built of flat stacked river rocks, started on each side of the entrance to the home, came out from the shack about a dozen feet and then arched out in both directions. One ending at the moss-covered mountainside, the other ending at the river. The entire area nestled between the knee-high rock wall and the mountainside behind the shack was covered in thick foliage. Every inch of the ground behind the rock wall was occupied by a tree, bush, flower, herb, etc. of various, exotic kinds. This mini jungle defied all logic with its diverse vegetation, having bushes and flowers from separate continents growing side by side. Plants from all climates with varying care details all grew and thrived within the walls around the shack.

A few dozen feet from the rock wall are a handful of teepees lined up facing the shack. These few were the most devoted to the Witch.

4

Dr. Gerard sets the page on the couch beside him, 'pausing his movie', as he lets the heaviness of everything, he has taken in this evening settle down on him. He feels as though he has been lost in that strange place for hours. Slightly alarmed at the ideation he swings his head around the den looking for a clock he doesn't have. He goes to glance at his watch instead and sees that his scotch-on-the-rocks, only half drunk, still has ice cubes clinking lazily around in the glass. No more than a few minutes have passed since his 'movie' began. *That's odd. But then again, what isn't odd about all this?* His head swirls with unanswered questions, names, and bits of information. It is overwhelming and only adding to his mental exhaustion.

He downs the remainder of his scotch in two big swallows, sets the paper on the stack with the rest of them and carefully slides the stack back into the manilla envelope. He takes the envelope to his briefcase meaning to return it to the office the next morning, thinks better of it, and decides to leave it sitting on the coffee table in the den. Trying hard to ease his racing mind, but failing miserably anyway, Warren makes his way upstairs to his comfortable queen-sized bed. He worries, while tending to his nightly needs, that he will struggle to fall asleep and be restless when he finally does. However, minutes after his head hits the pillow he falls into a deep restful dreamless sleep.

The following morning finds Dr. Gerard well rested, energetic, and feeling better than he has in two decades. He strolls into the office with a confidence that rivals the egotistical. *Gosh dang do I feel good! This is my lucky day; I can feel it.* And so, it is. The best day he's had in years, in fact, one of those days where everything is just right, almost as if the world itself is trying to appease you for a time. But it's a scam, an illusion, a way to lure him deeper. He just doesn't know it yet. He will though, but in the meantime, he still gets to relish the last 'best day of his life' he will ever have.

Come later tonight, however, when he 'un-pauses his movie', it's going to be downhill on a slippery slope from there.

After doing some simple, almost mindless morning paperwork Dr. Gerard pops his head out of his office and asks Ms. Lancing to have

Greg Patrickson brought into his office. She complies, immediately placing her hand on the telephone receiver. He thanks her kindly and returns to his desk to wait for his patient. He doesn't have to wait long, approximately five minutes later there is a small tap on the door with Ms. Lancing appearing to inform him that Mr. Patrickson is here to see him. He again thanks her kindly, and as she walks out of his office, she reciprocates with a beautiful smile and... was that a wink he just saw? No. Not her. Not Ms. Lancing. Warren watches her, curiosity beating at him, even as she is blocked from sight by the two security officers escorting Mr. Patrickson into the office. He, reluctantly, pushes his fine young receptionist out of his mind for the time being.

"Good morning, Mr. Patrickson!" Dr. Gerard greets the patient good-naturedly. Greg's only reply is an irritable grunt as he plops down in one of the chairs. The two guards that had just escorted him into the office, stepped back against the wall. A lean built, handsome young man on the left of the door and a broad, mean-looking short-haired woman on the right.

"How have you been holding up, given the circumstances, Greg?" Warren asks trying to coax some conversation out of the man. No grunt this time, just an unreadable stare from blood-shot eyes. That stare causes him to realize just how poorly this man really looks. His hair and clothes are disheveled, his eyes are blood shot, heavy and watery, and his complexion is more ashen than normal.

Greg Patrickson doesn't reply because he doesn't know how to explain to the doctor how badly the nightmares are affecting him. *He can't stop the nightmares and he can't keep me awake all the time. So, what's the point in telling him?* Greg thinks to himself as he recalls last night's vivid, awful scenes of Joe's relentless torture. One of a shirtless Joe tied to a chair while the evil doctor in white used a blow torch to slowly, agonizingly deliquesce each of his eyes. Joe's screams reverberated around the filthy room, but Greg could still hear the sound of it, like bacon sizzling in a hot skillet. Thankfully, there was no detectable odor. Another of Joe strapped in a standing position by his hands and feet, arms and legs spread into a human X. The doctor stood off to the side by a large switchboard, laughing hideously as he flipped various switches causing Joe to jerk and spasm and groan, exhausted from the intense pain. The cords running from the switch board were connected to different things located on Joe's naked body. Large metal clamps with wires hanging from the ends of them are firmly attached to his tongue, pecks, and testicles. Long thick probes with protruding wires were snugly inserted into his anus and urethra. And small quarter-inch spikes with attached wires were located, in pairs, at his temples, neck, wrists and ankles. A tiny trickle of blood escaped from beneath the insertion of the spikes. One of Joe sitting in a large glass tank with two smaller tanks attached to it. In the two smaller tanks were hundreds of rats, not mice, rats as large as some small-breed dogs. It was obvious that the rats hadn't been fed much or at all in some time by the number of dead, eaten upon bodies of their own kind laying around the bottom of the tanks. A couple of demons appeared and pulled levers by the smaller tanks that allowed the rats to enter the large tank with Joe inside. The rats rushed him, cutting off his screams before they could begin. He was unidentifiable in less than three seconds and there was very little of him left when the rats had finished feasting. The scene switched with a rat crawling out of what was left of Joe's mouth, a chunk of his esophagus hanging from the rat's jaws. The last scene Greg can recall is a naked Joe hanging with his hands tied over a large tub of liquid. The evil doctor stands by laughing as the demons slowly lower him into the tub. First his toes, his feet, then up to his ankles. Joe began to scream and jerk, trying to raise his legs out of the tub. He succeeded for about five seconds before he was zapped with a cattle prod in the right ass cheek, temporarily immobilizing his legs down past his knees and halfway up his back, The doctor signaled them to raise him out of the tub and the only thing left of Joe's feet was some slowly dissolving metatarsals. The doctor clapped giddily and ordered them to lower him further. Each morning Greg remembers a little more about the previous night's nightmares and is more and more convinced that Joe is having to endure such things

Dr. Gerard clears his throat, slightly uncomfortable under Greg Patrickson's eerie stare. "Have you been taking your medications? Eating? Sleeping? You don't look to good, Greg." He pauses, waiting for an answer he doesn't receive, so he continues. "I ask because you are my patient, Mr. Patrickson, and because I care deeply for all my patients and staff members. I can't help you if you don't tell me what's going on, though. Please, allow me to help you?" Just another irritable grunt in reply.

Warren stands behind his desk, nodding at the two guards standing by the door. "Well, I can see this conversation isn't very productive. Maybe you will be more inclined to talk at a later time, Mr. Patrickson." Directing his gaze at the guards, "Please escort this gentleman back to his room." Greg Patrickson leaves the office without speaking a single word to the doctor, but Warren isn't going to let this minor inconvenience ruin his day. He is feeling too fine for all that.

Chapter Ten

Temptation Day

1

As the guards are escorting Greg out of the office with the female guard in the lead, the male guard hesitates before stepping out. Warren has already reseated himself at his desk and the young man's reluctance to leave goes unnoticed. After a few brief moments of last-minute contemplation, the guard, by the name of Ryan McCane, faces Dr. Gerard and nervously asks if he could speak with him for a moment about a personal matter. Momentarily startled by the unexpected presence, Warren shakes it off and stands behind his desk, once more, offering for the young man to have a seat. By this time, the female guard and patient have noticed his absence and are standing in the receptionist's office waiting for him to join them.

"I'll be brief sir." Ryan begins, stammering at first. "Ya see… my momma… she's real sick… got the diabetes… done lost one foot and a couple toes on da other. She needs her insulin real bad and my checks usually cover it… but, uh… last week… well last week, my car broked down and I had to spend da money for her meds and then some to get it fixed. I feel real bad dat I did dat but I can't get to work without my car, ya know?" Dr. Gerard nods in agreement, knowing that Ryan is telling him the truth and what his next question will be. Ryan goes for it. "I was wondering if ya would give me… uhh…" he fidgets restlessly in his chair before continuing, "… like an advance or even a small personal loan… sir? I just really need the money to get her meds, sir." Ryan finished almost breathlessly.

Warren was right in his assumption of what Ryan's next question would be. He leans back in his chair, seemingly lost in thought. A few moments later, he leans forward, placing his forearms on his desk, and looks thoughtfully at the young man before him. "I'm sorry to hear that about your mother, Ryan, being sick like that. Of course, I will help you. Come back during your lunch hour and we will discuss this more thoroughly. This will allow me some time to work out the details, so to speak." A sigh of relief escapes Ryan as renewed hope cascades over him. He rises from his chair, leans over, and shakes the doctor's hand enthusiastically.

"Thank ya, sir, Thank ya. I'll see ya again later, sir. Thank ya! Thank ya, sir!" Ryan gushes, overwhelmed with gratitude. He's smiling ear to ear as he walks out of the office, back to the patient and his coworker. Dr. Warren Gerard follows the guard to the door and as they walk out of the receptionist's office, he asks Ms. Lancing if she has heard any recent updates on Mr. Gordon. She sadly says no but she would find out if she could. He thanks her and she reciprocates with another beaming smile and a wink. A small, but unmistakable wink. *Yes! Definitely my lucky day!* He walks back into his office to return to his paperwork and the next item on his agenda, wondering what the rest of this day has in store for him.

A couple hours later, he's silencing the jangling phone midway through its second ring. "Dr. Warren Gerard speaking." He listens. "Yes, of course. How is Mr. Gordon?" Listens. "Wonderful. So, is this call about the insurance because if I recall correctly everything should be..." He cuts off. Listens. "Oh, he wants to see me? Fantastic. I can come by this afternoon." The rest of the details were made, the meeting set. *This is going to either be a really good meeting or a really bad one. Maybe my luck will hold out for it.*

2

The lunch hour arrives, as does Ryan McCane. The greetings aside, both gentlemen seated across from each other, Dr. Gerard begins. "Well, Ryan, I have given this some thought and I am curious as to whether or not you are going to be able procure enough money to pay me back a short time from now?"

The young man shifts in his seat uncomfortably and casts his eyes toward the floor, not wanting to meet his superior's eyes. "Well, sir..." It comes out as an inaudible croak. He clears his throat and tries again. "Well, sir, honestly, I can try to come up with da money to pay ya back, but I really don't see how I could. Short of winnin the lottery or somethin as equally miraculous." He finally meets the doctor's eyes, a sad disappointed look upon his face.

"I suspected as much." Warren sighs. "I suppose I could withhold so much out of each of your paychecks." At this suggestion, Ryan opens his mouth to protest but he is waved silent before he can get out a single word. He continues, "But that would ultimately put you in a never-ending cycle of owing me more and more money and that would make me no better than a loan shark." Ryan is obviously relieved but keeps his mouth shut, the realization of diminishing hope hitting him hard. "So, where do we go from here Ryan? I didn't get where I am today by charity or taking handouts. I have repaid every cent I have ever owed and earned every cent I have now. I don't believe anyone can get anywhere in life on handouts. So, with that being said, how do you plan on repaying me?"

Ryan McCane sits silently for several long moments, his mind and heart racing, trying to fight off the panic boiling up in his chest. A sudden, desperate, unnerving idea comes to him. He swallows with an audible click in his throat and leans forward, his forearms resting on his thighs. With a strange look in his eyes, he tells Dr. Gerard, "I'm sure we can work *somethin* out..." and lets the words drift among them, their eye contact unbroken. A few moments of silent communication pass between them before Gerard nods his head ever so slightly and young Ryan McCane stands from his chair.

Apprehensive yet determined, Ryan walks around the side of the desk toward Dr. Gerard, trying to rationalize his coming actions. *This is for Momma, she's gotta have her meds. Besides, I've done this before. It's not my favorite thing to do, but, oh well. The old pervert is probably gonna bust the moment I touch him, anyway.* But that is just wishful thinking.

Dr. Warren Gerard slowly turns his chair to the side of his desk, as if to stand, but doesn't, matching Ryan's pace as he slowly makes his way toward him. *This really is my lucky day! Never been sucked by a man before. I haven't been with anyone for so long I just don't care. How often does an opportunity like this present itself, anyway?* He continues to rationalize his behavior as Ryan kneels in front of him. The young man hesitates for only a moment before reaching out and fumbling to unzip Warren's slacks.

More than twenty minutes later, Dr. Gerard hands Ryan a personal check for three months' worth of his mother's much-needed insulin. "Oh, goodness, Dr. Gerard, I cain't accept dis." Ryan says, his words slightly slurred from his partially numb mouth, staring wide-eyed at the numbers on the slip of paper he holds in his hand.

The doctor laughs, heartily, for the first time in ages. "After today, I think you should call me Warren." He tells Ryan, with another small laugh. Ryan smiles at him but says nothing, uncomfortable with the way the doctor speaks of it so casually. "Honestly, Ryan, that was the best dang blow job I have ever had. You earned that, sincerely earned it, young man." Warren claps him on the back as they both recall Ryan briefly struggling to take him fully in his mouth. Chocking and gagging on the large appendage several times before Warren finally erupted with enormity. Ryan had managed through it all though, and both were happier for it in the end.

Warren had no way of knowing and Ryan, preoccupied at the time, didn't see that Warren's eyes glowed brightly behind his contacts during his... release and faded out upon completion. Just another one of those 'side effects.'

Ryan McCane thanks Warren again, many times, shaking his hand. He walks out of the office, the check safe in his wallet, rubbing his sore jaw and swallowing repeatedly trying to soothe his aching throat. He heads for the vending machine to get something to wash the taste of Dr. Warren Gerard's unborn children out of his mouth. He then returns to his duties, feeling not in the least bit ashamed or guilty for what he did. Why should he feel guilty or ashamed for doing whatever he can to make sure his Momma is taken care of?

Warren sees Ryan out and returns to his desk, exhausted. He could really use a nap but knows that's unrealistic. So, he straightens and organizes the papers on his desk, then ventures out of his office for some coffee before heading out for his next appointment. Mr. Gordon.

3

He sits at a well-cared for, naturally beautiful dining room table; the matching China cabinet, buffet table, and tall grandfather clock scattered around the well-lit parlor in Mr. Gordon's home. "How are you doing since you've been home?" Warren asks the man sitting across from him.

After a few moments of watching him scribble on a small notebook, Mr. Gordon shows the paper to him. NOT BAD. THIS JUST ALL SUCKS. THE WIFE AND KIDS ARE A BIG HELP.

Yes, his two kids, probably at school right now, are going to have to grow up with a father that does and probably always will look like a patchwork quilt. Warren thinks before answering. "I'm glad you've got help. If you need anything, and I mean anything at all, you just let me know, Mr. Gordon."

The silent man stares at him thoughtfully for a moment before scribbling something else on another sheet of paper. CALL ME SAM. HOW'S GREG?

Surprising. The man is permanently disfigured but still asking about the well-being of his attacker. He's either genuinely concerned or vengeful and hoping he's suffering. "Well, I don't think he's handling this very well, to tell you the truth, Mr.... uh, Sam." He pauses, trying to gauge Sam's reaction but there isn't one, not one that he can read anyway, so he continues. "I can't say exactly what is going on with Greg, but he doesn't look very good, and he refuses to speak to me. Not just about what's going on with him, he won't say anything at all. Probably just a case of delayed shock, he has been through a lot lately." Warren stirs, then sips at his iced tea, compliments of the lady of the house, looking away from the man uncomfortably, realizing the irony of what he had just said. No response or reaction comes from Sam, so Dr. Gerard finishes his run-down. "I think Joe... escaping is affecting him much harder than even he realizes. He is remorseful, though. Sincerely remorseful." He lets his last words drift between them, waiting for Sam to respond.

After several long moments, Sam Gordon begins to write. DO YOU KNOW WHY HE ATTACKED ME? THAT'S WHAT I CAN'T SEEM TO GET PAST. IT DOESN'T MAKE SENSE.

"Yes, I do. For whatever reason, he was convinced that you had done something to Joe. Helped him escape, is what I believe was going through his mind at the time. But sometime between him attacking you and me speaking with him the following morning, something convinced him that you had nothing to do with Joe's escape. And before you ask, Sam, no I don't know what it is that convinced him either way."

Sam sits thoughtfully for some time, allowing his wife to come in and refill their glasses, a sturdy straw sticking out of the top of Sam's tea. Shortly after the lady of the house left the two men to their selves, once again, Sam shows Warren the notepad. I UNDERSTAND. I HOPE YOU WILL BE ABLE TO HELP HIM.

Warren is dumbfounded. Sincerely caring about the welfare of another person, even one that has done you wrong, is understandable, noble even. But understanding the motive when the victim is truly innocent, doesn't seem to make sense. "So, you're not going to press charges?" he blurts before he can stop himself.

Sam's brow furrows and his jaw tenses even more, the first major change in his facial expression since Warren had arrived. He scribbles furiously on his notepad then shoves it aggressively under Warren's nose. I'M OFFENDED YOU WOULD EVEN SUGGEST SUCH A THING! THAT MAN IS SICK! Warrens sighs with relief but is still slightly stunned at Sam's outrage.

"Mr. Gordon... Sam... I apologize for offending you, that was in no way my intention. With the viciousness and severity of your attack, I just assumed that would be the course you would take. Please try to understand that it wasn't an assumption based on anything personal, it was merely based on statistical averages and my experiences with such circumstances. I do apologize, sincerely, Mr. Gordon."

The man with an unmoving jaw, an eyepatch, and numerous cuts and scratches all over his face, some of them stitched, visibly relaxes. He takes back the notepad, flips it to a clean page and writes something else. I JUST WANT TO SEE THE MAN CARED FOR SO THIS DOESN'T HAPPEN TO SOMEONE ELSE. He shows it to Warren, flips to another clean page and writes. DOC SAYS I SHOULD BE ABLE TO GO BACK TO WORK IN A COUPLE WEEKS, ONLY GOING TO HAVE ONE EYE THO.

"Your job will be waiting for you, with some restrictions of course, whenever you feel you are ready to return to work, Sam. And if there is anything I can do for you, please just let me know." The two men talk for another half hour or so, say their goodbyes and Warren leaves, making it back to his office with only three hours left of his 8 a.m. to 6p.m. workday.

4

Ms. Vivian Lancing squirms in her office chair, needing a release. Her usual lunch date couldn't show up today and relieving herself just won't do. She must be extremely careful about her... disorder. She is a closet nymphomaniac and is careful about who she hooks up with and when, fulfilling her cravings to a degree on average three times a day. Occasionally, she will organize an all-night orgy with three of her well-endowed male friends. Then she will be okay for two or three days before setting up another round of multi-day trysts. But it's all done in secret. None of her coworkers know of her disorder and she intends on keeping it that way. That leaves only one option, and he wants her so bad, he won't question it. *Desperate times call for desperate measures.* She convinces herself as she stands, straightening her modest, knee-length dress and approaches Dr. Gerard's office.

She raises her hand to tap lightly on the door but before she gets the chance, Dr. Gerard opens the door, startling them both. "Oh, my goodness!" they say together, then giggle shyly. "Forgive me, Ms. Lancing. Are you alright?" Warren asks as he places a large, meaty hand on her side. A touch she normally shies away from, and it doesn't go unnoticed that she isn't this time. *Is she finally starting to come around to my advances? A beautiful young woman like, Ms. Lancing? No, she's not. She's probably just in an exceptionally good mood today or something. But what if I really could...* and Warren allows his mind to drift, only momentarily, to that sweet place between her thighs. His arousal is immediate and obvious.

"That's quite alright, Dr. Gerard. I am fine. You just gave my heart a small jump start, is all." She giggles, girlishly, covering her mouth with a petite, well-manicured hand, and slightly bowing her head. She almost immediately notices his canopied groin and her eyes widen from the shock of it. She was not expecting him to be so well-endowed. Until this moment she had believed all the rumors going around among the nurses about Warren being so ill-equipped. Boy, were they wrong.

Dr. Gerard realizes that he has a very apparent erection at the same moment his secretary notices it. He is overwhelmed with embarrassment and shame, never having had this issue before despite his many advances toward her. Before he can begin to stammer out an apology or attempt to conceal himself, Vivian says "Oh, goodness, Dr. Gerard, let me take care of that for you." He has no chance to respond before she places one hand on his chest and uses the other to grab a handful of his crotch and gently pushes him back into his office. He swings the door shut and it closes with a quiet thud as she stops him at one of the two chairs for guests. She undoes his slacks and jerks them to the floor before shoving him into the chair. He no longer has any desire to respond, and his embarrassment and shame dissipate. *Oh, my God! I must be dreaming. There's no way this is happening right now. Not with her.* She raises her dress up high around her thighs and slips out of her panties. *No dang way this is real. I'm dreaming. Well, at least I think I am.* Carefully maneuvering around his protruding gut, his sexy young secretary guides him into her silkiness. *Oh yeah, this is real. It must be. This feels too flipping good not to be.* This fulfills just one of his numerous fantasies involving Vivian Lancing. Another one is fulfilled several minutes later when he bends her over his desk, as she begs him to put it in her ass.

Almost an hour later, both satisfied, redressed and refreshed, Vivian tells Warren that she is pleasantly surprised with his size and 'skill', as she puts it. He chuckles and tells her she can come see him anytime. He is still very much in awe that this encounter even happened and doesn't want to risk ruining a chance at a second affair by questioning her motives. Honestly, does why even matter? Dr. Gerard doesn't seem to think so, or care.

Vivian, pleased and satisfied, returns to her desk to inform the guards watching over Patrickson that Dr. Gerard will be there to speak with him soon. Warren gathers Greg Patrickson's file, as well as a few other forms, and then suddenly remembers Joe's file. He places the file for Joseph Doe in his briefcase, grabs up Greg's papers, and makes his way through the asylum.

5

In the rainbow corridor where Greg Patrickson is being detained in his room, Warren pauses outside the door to ask the two guards if there have been any issues with Greg. They inform him that there hasn't been and as far as they can tell he is still eating, drinking, sleeping, and taking his medication. They think he's just depressed, and in a way, they are right.

Dr. Gerard stands several feet away from Greg, who is sitting in a small recliner with a blank look in his eyes. *There is something wrong with this man, aside from the obvious. Maybe this whole Joe thing 'rebroke' him and he's slowly having another breakdown? I need to find out. Or at least try.* "Alright, Greg, I understand if you aren't ready to talk but I need you to listen to me. I went and spoke with Sam… uh, Mr. Gordon, today." That broke Greg's blank stare and he shot his eyes at Warren. *Okay, good. I have his attention now.* "He's doing as well as he can be given the extent of his injuries. He was understandably confused about why you attacked him and once I informed him of the reason that you had given me… he forgave you." Greg Patrickson's eyes widened, then softened, glassing over while tears touched his eyes. "He has absolutely no intentions of pressing charges, was even offended by the idea." He let that sink in for a few moments before finishing. "What he does want is for you to get the help you need so that you don't hurt yourself or anyone else. That's what he is concerned about, your well-being. I want to help you, Greg, I really do. But I can't do that if I don't know what's going on."

Greg sat still facing Dr. Gerard but looking down toward his feet, silent and unmoving, for so long that Dr. Gerard was about to just walk out. Finally, Greg says, "I want a rosary."

"I'll see what I can do. Anything else I can do, Greg?" Dr. Gerard asks.

The disturbed man turns back around to stare at the floor ahead of him, the doctor forgotten.

Joe returns to his office, refusing to allow Greg Patrickson and his stubbornness to ruin his amazing day. He pushes all that to the back of his mind, willing it to stay there. Instead, he reflects on the better parts of his day while he signs all his staff's paychecks. By the time he finishes signing the last one, he is feeling so good he decides to open the wall safe and place a crisp hundred-dollar bill into each of their envelopes. *My wonderful staff deserves a bonus.* He reflects.

He stops at the locked mailboxes for each staff member and personally places each paycheck into the appropriate box using his master key. Feeling quite good about himself he saunters out into a beautiful evening, heading toward his car with the intention of trying his luck.

Warren goes to his favorite restaurant for supper, a reservation-only place, on a whim and lucks into a table due to a cancelled reservation. His favorite meal was cooked to absolute perfection. The waiter accidently spilled a couple drops of wine on his tie, and he was given an aged expensive bottle of wine as repentance. It was rather enjoyable and paired well with his meal. His bill paid, he heads home to shower, settle in, and decide what he's going to do about this whole Joseph Doe situation.

Chapter Eleven

Blood Splattered Walls

1

A nightcap in hand, Dr. Warren Gerard settles on to the sofa in his den, the manila envelope still sitting on the coffee table where he had left it the previous night. *Now, what to do? What to do? This whole situation is so confusing I don't know where to begin. I know the letter, story, whatever the heck it is, keeps saying that I need to pay attention and gather as much information as I can, on different ones, but I don't understand why. None of this makes any sense. Do I keep reading, watching, whatever, and play this out or do I burn it all and go about my life?* Warren stares at the unlit fireplace on the far wall of the den, sipping his drink, seriously considering throwing the manila envelope, Joe's file, and everything else he can find on Joseph Doe into it. Then he, once again, recalls the almost perfect day that he had had. *One thing is for sure, I don't believe my wonderful day was such an accident or coincidence. I think someone or something beyond my understanding had something to do with it. I haven't had a day this good since... I can't even remember when. So, it stands to reason that my newly found luck could be a repayment of sorts for taking on this challenge. Okay, I'll accept that. It's one of the few things about this whole situation that makes any sense right now.* And with that it is decided. "Okay, I'll play your game." He says aloud to the emptiness of the room.

Sitting his drink aside for a moment, he carefully removes the stack of papers from the manila envelope, setting the couple of pages he had already 'read' to the side. Before he begins, he refreshes his drink and makes himself more comfortable on the sofa, stretching out with the intention of putting a dent into this stack of papers. He grabs the page he had left off on, concentrates on the first word and soon the mental scenes are rolling. He is instantly enveloped by the vividness and clarity of it, by its *realness*, almost as if he's really there. Without his knowing, his obsession grows a little more as his 'movie' begins to play, again.

Now that you know the layout of the valley it will make telling this just a little easier. This story began almost half a century ago today with a young boy just a few days past his seventh birthday. Not that his father had allowed it to be a happy birthday, and that was just one of the many reasons that the boy hated him. That one dreary, stormy evening changed the boy's life forever, he just wouldn't know to what extent for several more years.

The young boy cowered in the corner of the filthy, trashed kitchen of the only home he had known since birth. With his eyes closed tightly, his knobby, skinned knees pressed tightly to his chest, his thin hands with scabbed knuckles pressed tightly to his ears, a trickle of blood leaked from one nostril, and he could feel the tender bruises all over his body begin to throb. He was scared, confused, and sore, knowing that if he moved it would only draw his father's attention back to him.

His eyes popped open, and all his emotions amplified as he watched his mother run through the rickety old house into the kitchen, tears streamed from her swollen eyes, her face puffy and bloody, the bruises already making an appearance. She screamed at her husband to stop as he came stomping through the kitchen after her, his large hands curled tightly into brutal fists. The battered woman turned to face her brutish husband, having nowhere else to go in the enclosed room. Even if she could have made it to the only door into or out of the house, going outside during one of her husband's 'fits', was unthinkable. She had tried that only once, before the boy was born, and she almost didn't survive the beating he had given her for it. She wasn't sure she was going to survive this one, either.

She begged and pleaded with her husband as he backhanded her multiple times, rocking her head on her shoulders, blood from her mouth and nose splattered the walls and floor of the kitchen. They would eventually dry and blend in with the rest of the blood splatter throughout the house. One particularly hard hit knocked her to the floor where she instinctually curled up into the fetal position. The large angry, violent man began trying to kick her in the chest and stomach, but because of her protective position he was unable to inflict the damage he wanted, which angered him all the more. He screamed his rage at her, brought his heavy booted foot back and kicked her as hard as he could in the face. Her nose exploded in a shower of blood, a couple of broken teeth fell from her mashed lips, and an impression of the sole of his boot was immediately present around her mouth and nose. The force of the kick contacted mainly with her nose, ramming splintered bone, and cartilage into the front of her brain, killing her before she knew what happened. Her husband believed her only unconscious and began kicking her in the abdomen several times.

2

Their young son, temporarily forgotten among the brutal chaos, watched in horror as his mother fell unconscious from the brutal kick she had just received. All the fear, pain and confusion quickly turned into a roiling rage that overwhelmed him to an extent that he could not comprehend. Later he would describe his actions as having been done by someone else. He was temporarily not in control of himself, but instead seemed to have watched it all happen. The small, thin boy stood from his crouched position, his sore and aching body temporarily forgotten. There was a strange, cold look in the child's eyes that would cause even the largest of predators to hesitate. He took a couple steps forward, his father oblivious and preoccupied with putting a few more marks on his wife, paused to pick up a lengthy piece of wood from the chair that had been hurled at his mother, but smashed against the wall, instead, earlier in the evening. The wood was narrow but solid and fit well in the boy's small hands, blunt on both ends it would make one hell of a club.

The brave, irate child approached his father, taking no pains to be quiet, with the wooden club held firmly in his hands, swung back over his shoulder, ready to swing. Only one thought filled the boy's mind, and he would not be stopped until he accomplished it. As the monster that was his father was knelt beside his wife delivering a few final punches to her face, the young boy raised the club a little higher and swung as hard as he could. The club landed with a loud thud across the man's shoulder blades, causing him to flinch away reflexively, with a grunt. He stood, turned, towering over the small boy, his wife forgotten. The child, having no fear, swung again, not allowing his father a chance to react, and connected with the side of his face. The force of the hit caused the, now confused man, to stagger backward. Trying to regain his footing, he stepped on a shattered jar, the jagged pieces slick with its contents, bringing his foot out from under him. He crashed to the floor of the kitchen, landing on an assortment of broken jars and dishes, and broken furniture.

The large man groaned as he raised himself up but was met with the hardest hit yet. That one smashed into his temple, his eyebrow split into a deep gash that gushed blood over his eye. Not quite unconscious, the dying man watched through glassy eyes as his son moved to his side, raised the club high over his head and administered his final blow to the face. The young boy in his outrage continued to hit his father in the face, releasing all the years of pain and torture that man had made him, and his mother endure. He released all the hatred, all the anger, all the fear. When he had finished, more exhausted than he had ever been, his father's face was completely unrecognizable. What was once the center of his face with all the normal anatomy, was now a bludgeoned, bloody shallow crater. The young boy, panting from exhaustion, dropped the blood-soaked wooden club, spat on his father's corpse, and rushed to his mother.

He knelt in the same place his father had been just minutes before and gently rolled his mother from her side onto her back. A single look of the battered, bloody woman was enough to tell her son that she was no longer among the living. As the steady rain beat ceaselessly on the rusted tin roof of the house, silent hot tears streamed from his eyes. He was a whirlwind of emotions. Fear of what he had done to his father and what would become of him without his mother. Fear of the violent outrage that was still slowly abating. Grief and sadness over the loss of his mother, who always tried to protect the young boy from his devilish father. Hatred for his father and everything he had done and put them through. Hatred for the violence he had to inflict upon his father. Hatred of the knowledge that he had the potential to be just like that monster.

It took the boy a long time to sort out his emotions so that he was able to think straight enough to decide what he should do next. He didn't want to leave his mother; it made his heart ache even more at the thought. However, he knew that as a child he would not and could not survive alone. After several long minutes of deliberation, he finally decided that he would go find Rebecka, the only friend of his mother's that his father had allowed her to have.

He trudged up the short ladder to the two-room loft where the three of them had slept and entered his small bedroom to pack what very few belongings he still owned. A pair of patched trousers, two shirts, a pair of socks and undergarments, and two old, well-read children's books. He tossed all the items into a knapsack then slowly walked into his parent's bedroom, scanning the scantly furnished room with red-rimmed, puffy eyes. He spotted his mother's small nightstand in the dark shadows of the unlit room and approached it, hoping and praying that it was still there. That the monster hadn't found it and destroyed it with the sole intention of hurting his wife.

A couple of minutes of increasingly panicky searching finally produced what he was looking for, a small hand-carved wooden figure of a woman cradling a bundled child. Once a treasured gift, given to his mother by his father, was now his precious keepsake. When his mother informed his father that she was with child with him, he had been so elated that he spent three days pay to have one of the woodworkers carve it for him. He presented it to her proudly with all the promises that he would quit drinking, work regularly, and stop knocking her around. His mother was so elated about the one and only gift (aside from her precious son) and his promises of a better future that she wept tears of joy. A couple days later she wept tears of fear and pain, again, after he had drunk away all his pay then come home and smacked her around. He stuffed the wooden figure deep into the sack and made his way back down the stairs and into the kitchen.

He, once more, knelt beside his blood-soaked, beaten mother. A few tears fell from his cheeks, splashing against her battered, once-beautiful face as he bent over and kissed his mother lovingly on the cheek. He leaned over a little more, whispering in her ear, his sincerest apologies for not being able to save her from the monster she had married, and then telling her how much he loves her and always will. Moments later, he stood in the doorway of the rickety old house, refusing to look back over his shoulder at the life he once had, and trying to accept the changes ahead of him. A bright flash of lightning followed a rumble of thunder, as he stepped out of the house and into the pelting rain.

3

A lovely brunette with a slim figure and small, round face sat at the table in her kitchen, hemming one of the few dresses she owned. She paused to sip her tea but was interrupted by a knock at the door when it was only part of the way to her lips. Irritation coursed through her, and she set her cup down hard enough that a swallow's worth of tea splashed out and onto the table. She arose from her chair, aggressively, stalked to the front door and began yelling and cursing before she even touched the door handle. "Now, God damn it, Donnie, ya son-of-a-bitch! I told ya to leave me the fu..." her words stopped dead on her tongue when she opened the door and saw a small, thin child with dark hair and piercing blue eyes staring up at her. The child was soaked from the heavy rainfall, their hair and clothing plastered to their frail body. In the dim light of the late evening, the dark gray clouds overhead added to the darkness, making it impossible to tell if the child was male or female. She stared at the silent young child in disbelief, then shook her head and said, "Oh my." It was the only thing she could think of saying at the moment.

"Ms. Rebecka?" the child asked her. A flash of lightning revealed that the child was a boy and combined with the orangish glow of the firelight behind her, for a moment the little lad looked as though he were soaked in blood rather than rain. The heavy rain had washed all the actual blood, sweat, and tears off the boy's hands and face but it only increased the coverage of the blood stains on his shirt and trousers, adding to the colored illusion.

"Yeah. Come on in young man, outta that rain. Come on in and sit. I'll go find ya a blanket then gathers up something for ya to eat." She told him as she ushered him into the house and into the chair opposite hers at the table, the only other chair at the table. She walked out before the boy could so much as utter a word of protest or thanks. She returned moments later with a wool blanket with only a few moth-eaten holes, wrapped it around his shoulders snugly then walked across the room to search her meager pantry.

It was full dark by the time the boy had finished eating and drinking his fill. Wrapped snugly in the wool blanket, he was only half dry but no longer cold from the lengthy walk from his home by 'the Lot' to Rebecka's place in 'the Slums'. While she watched him eat, she realized who he was. He was George and Marianne's boy, and that realization made her very uneasy.

113

Since he had eaten, she decided to try to find out why he was sitting in her house instead of his own and where his parents were, particularly his mother. The boy sat silent for several long moments before finally beginning with a heavy sigh. He began with how his father had spent the morning working only to blow all his pay at the bar. Then came home to beat his wife for not having supper ready for him three hours earlier than normal and his son for not being at school even though it was a Saturday. Finishing with the death of his mother and the summation of his own anger against his father.

Rebecka sat quietly, listening intently the entire time. She shed tears at the news of her friend, inwardly rejoiced at the news of his father, and reassured the boy that he was not at fault in his actions. That he had in fact, done the valley and his mother, even in her death, a favor by killing that monster. "I know he deserved what I did..." cried the boy helplessly, "...but my momma didn't deserve that! I want my momma! I miss her." He put his face into his hands and wept like the young boy he was. Rebecka walked over to the crying child, wrapped her arms around him and silently held him tight for a few moments. As she stood, she kissed his forehead and told him to stay put, that she would return soon.

She left her shack and returned in less than five minutes, finding the boy asleep with his head cradled in his arms, resting on the table. She gave him a faint smile and resumed her position across from him. Rebecka finished hemming her dress as she waited.

The knock was expected and answered immediately. Roy McGrath walked in, the irritation evident on his face. He glanced at the sleeping child, still resting on the table, then quickly turned his attention to Rebecka. "You better have a good god damn reason why I had to trek my ass through this damned old storm, Rebekka. I mean someone best be fuckin dead, cause there's gonna be a god damn funeral pyre tomorra one ways or another." The overweight man ranted.

Rebecka expected Roy to be this way, he always was until he was able to assess and handle the situation, but he seemed to be in an exceptionally poor mood that night. She didn't care how pissed off he was or who he was, she wasn't going to allow him to speak to her like that. "Now you listen here Roy, before you come up in here makin a damn fool outta yourself, threatenin people and whatnot, you'd do best to remember where you at." She gave him a measured look that dared him to contradict her. He wisely kept his mouth shut, so she continued. "Now, this little boy here showed up at my door a while ago now and told me a very sad, disturbing story. You want me to wake him so he can tell ya what he told me?" she asked.

Roy McGrath looked at the boy for a few moments before answering, with much more control in his voice. "No. He looks exhausted, let him sleep for now. Tell me what he told you and I'll reconsider then. Who is this kid, anyway?"

"That's George and Marianne's boy. So, he tells me that his father had went to the bar and..." Rebecka began and finally finished after some time.

Roy stood in the middle of the shack, silent, taking in everything Rebecka had told him. After taking the time to collect his thoughts he asked, "You are tellin me that there's two dead bodies down in the Lot? The boy's parents and they're both dead? The mother killed by the father and the father killed by the... the child?" he asked with genuine disbelief.

"Yes on all accounts," was his answer.

"Damn it!" He hissed. He looked at the boy for a few long moments. "Just let him sleep and I'll be back in the mornin to talk with him." He cast his eyes to the floor, then looked up at Rebecka, his sad eyes locked on hers. "I must apologize for my ravings, Rebecka. Know that I meant you no harm, now or ever. You were correct in having your friend come to get me. I will tend to the matter at once, and bodies or no bodies, I'll be back in the mornin to see the boy. I, also, need the child to remain with you until I have a chance to speak with Charlotte at the orphanage."

"Yeah, that's fine and all. I'll see ya in the mornin, careful out there." She told him as she walked him to the door. Once Roy McGrath was gone, she went into the only other room in the shack, the bedroom, and laid extra blankets on the floor beside her bed. Once they were laid out, making it a cozy-ish place to sleep, she carried the small boy into the bedroom and laid him gently on her bed. She removed his muddy boots, covered him with the wool blanket, then settled into the place she made on the floor. They both slept soundly that night.

Fifteen years went by in the valley...

Dr. Gerard 'pauses his movie' and sits dumbfounded for a moment. *Fifteen years? What the heck? You can't just skip fifteen years in a story like this, what the heck is up with this crap, Joe? You better fill in some blanks along the way, old boy or you and I will be having a serious sit-down when we meet again.* Feeling confident that he would, indeed, meet the man he knew as Joseph Doe again. Sometime. Somehow. He will, he has no doubt.

Chapter Twelve

Aunt Frieda's Letter

1

Taking advantage of this little intermission, Warren makes his way to the bathroom to relieve himself, then returns to make himself another one of his signature scotch-on-the-rocks. He settles back down on the sofa in the den, knowing he must get up for work in the m0rning but not ready to call it a night, yet. He is too enthralled and eager to find out what is going to happen next. His unknown obsession, growing a little more. He picks up the page he had stopped on and resumes.

> ...but unlike the rest of the world, time seemed to stand still in the valley. Very little had changed but much had remained the same. Some died and some were born. Few left and even fewer arrived. The folks of the valley continued to live off and respect the land as they always had. The train still came once a week from April through October. The same family still tended the farmlands on the western side of the valley and most situations were still dealt with by those involved, usually leaving McGrath out of it.
>
> Roy McGrath retired five years ago, so naturally his son Franklin took his place. He was fair but known to use more severe punishments than his father. When the elder McGrath died, just a little over two years ago, Franklin became cruel. Not to just anyone or everyone, to those that had to be

brought to his attention. The last incident and, definitely the most atrocious one yet, was when he was brought to a very badly beaten young woman who was begging the doctors to save her young daughter. The three-year-old girl was quickly bleeding to death after being savagely raped by her father. When the mother tried to stop him, he beat her unconscious. Her husband was gone when she regained consciousness, but her daughter laid trembling in a semi-conscious bloody heap on the floor. She scooped her daughter up in her arms and ran straight to the infirmary by the common area.

Dansford Keeton, Franklin McGrath's right-hand man, was making his way toward the bar when he seen the bloody woman and child go running by him. He immediately took off at a run toward the bridge connecting the Lot to the Slums, to get Franklin. Whatever happened to that woman and child, Frank needed to know about it. Frank had the woman tell him, as best she could what had happened to her. She did, quickly and bluntly, not mentioning her daughter who she was extremely anxious to get back to. With a ferocity in her eyes she glared at Frank, "Ya betta fine dat man an make sho I's never have to see him again. Not afta what he did to my baby."

Frank knew the child was injured but he also knew that children get hurt plenty on their own. She wouldn't be the first wife to get beat up on for not watching the children close enough, lack of completed housework, burnt supper, etc. He asked what exactly happened to the child, hoping against hope that it hadn't been inflicted by the father. Frank personally knew the man, even considered him a friend, but decided, almost immediately, that wouldn't save him. Not after what he did to that little girl. "I'll take care of him; you take care of that baby girl in there." Franklin told the weeping woman, trying to conceal the rage that was boiling up inside him. Then he nodded at Dansford Keeton and walked out of the infirmary, Dan at his heels.

"I'm gonna go collect the boys then we'll go find that sick son-of-a-bitch." Dan, who was equally as outraged as Frank, told him once they were outside.

"Yeah, unless he's passed out somewhere, he's hidin. Maybe he will do us all a favor and go die in the mountains. Anyway, while you get em, I'm gonna walk on over to the bar and see what I can find out." Frank replied.

Half an hour later Dan Keeton, Frank McGrath and four other men they knew well stood outside the bar, dividing up in pairs to spread out and search the valley. It took several hours to find him and several more for the man to die. The group of six men drug him out of hiding and into the common area, stripped him naked, and tied him to the tall wooden tower that would be used for the next funeral pyre. Frank asked the man how he could have done such a horrid thing to such a beautiful young girl. The scum of a man, his intense fear masked by outrage at his treatment, replied, "She's my fuckin daughter. I made her, I raised her, and I'll do as I damn well please with her." Emphasizing his point by spitting on the ground at Frank's feet. Frank, in a single fluid movement, snatched the man's penis and testicles in one large rough hand, unsheathed the knife on his belt with the other and with one brisk swipe, loped his manhood right off. It happened so fast the man was only aware that his junk had been grabbed rather forcefully for a moment or two. The realization brought all the terror he was experiencing to the surface, and he opened his mouth to scream in pain. It was cut off mere moments after it began when Frank shoved the man's appendage into his mouth, gagging and choking him.

Frank stepped back as Dan and the rest of the men took turns cutting and slicing at his exposed skin, head to toe. Then they all took turns first rubbing handfuls of salt into his open wounds to slow the bleeding, then they smothered the man with thick syrupy sorghum to attract all sorts of hungry insects. It was a slow and miserable death for the man who raped his young daughter and beat his wife. He deserved nothing better before being sent to spend eternity under Satan's cruel hand.

Frank ordered that the man be left to hang in the common area for three days after he finally succumbed to death. He was and the valley folks looked at the insect infested body with outright disgust every time they passed by the common area. Disgust at what the man had done to deserve such a fate. Very, very few people in the valley disagreed when something like that needed to be done. It certainly left an impression on those who had a similar way of thinking. The man was finally cut loose, then drug and dumped way out in the timbers of the mountains. He did not deserve to be sent heavenward via pyre, and most of the valley folks agreed.

2

Frank McGrath was an easy man to befriend, he knew everyone in the valley and made a point to get to know those few who arrived. In the five years that Frank had been 'the Law of the Valley', he had only met three newcomers. The last and only one of the three, Alvin Danson, stuck around. The young man showed up a couple years before, an orphan, never adopted, that aged out of his facility. He had paid off one of the train conductors, a man by the name of Jimmy Moran, and this little valley was as far as his meager amount of money would take him. He wanted to work and was eager to try anything, proving to be quite a valuable asset to the farm. The O'Reigan's farm. What he found in the valley was so much more than he had anticipated; a job, a home, and the love of a kind beauty, so he decided to stay.

One scorcher of a day in the middle of August brought the valley and its residents a fourth and final visitor. This one was a lovely young lady, in her early twenties like himself, with long light auburn hair that flowed to the small of her back. She had bright green eyes and smooth tanned skin the color of coffee with a splash of milk. She had small, fine features and an excellent full, curvy body. She was a beauty. Head to toe and front to back. She was a total knockout.

She stepped off the train and onto the bare dirt in front of the make-shift train station. Oblivious to all the eyes on her, she arched her back, twisted slightly and raised her arms high over her head, trying to stretch out her aching back and legs. That movement caused her knee-length dress to rise high on her thighs and press the fabric of her dress tighter against her bosom. She straightened herself and her clothing, now aware of everyone staring at her. Slightly uncomfortable, she began to make her way toward the station.

The mysterious newcomer turned every head of every person, young and old, male and female, as she walked over to the shade of the lean-to that was attached to the train station. Some stared in curiosity, some in awe, some in envy. The young woman stopped in the meager shade of the lean-to, unsure of where to go or what to do. As the sun beat down on everyone in the valley, sweat began to pop out on the bridge of her nose and her forehead. She scanned her surroundings with a brisk swivel of her head, she was unimpressed with what little she was able to see of the valley. The train station stood not far from the tracks and all that the young lady was able to see were the tracks themselves with a river running pleasantly underneath them that disappeared into a wooded area that stretched as far as she could see.

3

Franklin McGrath made a point to be at the train station every Wednesday when it ran, for a few reasons. Greeting the rare newcomer was just one of them. Overseeing that everything was distributed to its proper place and/or owner was another and the final was to deescalate any issues that might arise. Like everyone else standing on the dirt platform that day, Frank had also noticed the beautiful young woman. He decided on her looks alone, that he was going to give her a very in-depth tour of the valley.

As he walked up to approach her, he noticed that she looked confused, or flustered, or maybe a combination of the two. Regardless, he knew from watching his father interact with his mother and his own personal relationships, that if he didn't tread carefully, he would eliminate any chance he could have with just a single wrong word. He steeled himself, trying to calm his thudding heart with deep breaths, as he made the final strides to stand beside her. "Hello, young lady. You must be lost." He told her with his most charming smile.

She eyed him curiously for a few moments, seeming to come to some inner conclusion, before returning the smile. "I might just be." She replied, a hint of worry in her voice.

"Well, now. Where is it that you are trying to go? If you ain't in the right place, then you can just hop back on the train and head on down yonder." He told her with another winning smile.

"I'm looking for... Oh, what was that name again... Miner's... Miner's Crook, yeah that's it." She told him with a victorious smile.

Frank laughed. He couldn't help himself. "It's Miner's Nook, not Crook." He laughs a little more before finally sobering. "But we don't call it that. Folks round here just call it the valley. And if that really is the place you're lookin for, then you are not lost at all. You have arrived. Being that we are such a small community with very little to offer the outside world, I must ask why it is that you have come here? I don't mean to pry, Miss, but it is a question that is asked of all the new arrivals."

"It is a fair question, too. I'm sure you don't have many visitors in these parts. Hell, I'm prolly the first one in some time." Frank nods his head in agreement at her statement, and she continues. "As for the reason I am here, I received a letter from my great aunt Frieda informing me of her death. I was asked to make the trip and pick up what precious few keepsakes she had. My life back home was shit being disowned from my parents and all, so I figured I'd just move on out here. Start a new path, so it's said."

"Yes, the letter is customary for the valley. Most have letters written to any family they have livin out there..." Frank gestured toward the mountainside with his thumb as he continued. "...and give them to someone else in the valley, usually a younger someone, that is instructed to send it out upon their deaths. In Frieda's case, she had asked her neighbor Ruth to hold her letters." He was silent for a few moments. "We sure are glad to have another fine young lady

123

joinin our valley, though. I'll show ya around the valley endin at your great aunt Frieda's former home."

She looked around uncertainly, most of the people had gone about their business, probably gossiping about her all the while. A few others stood staring at her making her quite uncomfortable. She concluded that it was because the valley hadn't had a new arrival in such a long time. She was the type of woman that knew she was attractive but humbly didn't realize the extent of her beauty. Everyone noticed her, she just didn't know that. "What about my bags? I have a couple that Conductor Jim said Toby was going to bring out to the platform for me. I am not about to pack them all over this valley." She told him.

"Of course not. There ain't no sense in all that." She noticed how thick the attractive young man's drawl was, and how it kept popping out even though he was trying so hard to hide it. Trying to sound proper for the new girl, she mused. "I'll have a friend of mine take them to Frieda's place where they will be waiting for you at the end of the tour. You have my word that your belongings will be safe and unbothered." He assured her.

She sat down on the wooden bench under the lean-to, quietly pondering his request. She finally decided that she would try hard to make it work here in this small valley. A new life, starting from scratch. "Alright, I need to get a feel for the lay of the land, anyway. My name is Sarah, by the way, Sarah Maisse. And you are?"

Frank hesitated before answering, thinking to himself how odd a comment that was, but he quickly pushed the thought away. "I'm Frank McGrath. I'm the closest thing to law there is around here, and that scrawny fella walkin this way is Dansford Keeton. He will be takin your bags." He pointed out Dan in the thinning crowd, walking up to meet Toby with her things.

Sarah stood from the bench and watched as the tall stalky young man took her bags from the obviously, mentally challenged young Toby. Dansford looked over at Frank and Sarah standing under the lean-to, gave Frank a single hard nod and then took off toward the Slums where Frieda's now empty shack sat. Sarah didn't notice the interaction between Frank and Dan Keeton, not that it had any importance, because she was more focused on Toby.

Sarah observed how Tobias Medlin, kind of like Conductor Jim's assistant, jerked his hands quickly away from Dansford when handing him the bags. As if simply touching the man would cause Toby harm. Toby watched the man walk away, staring after him with such a strange look upon his face. Sarah found this very odd, her curiosity taking precedence over everything else momentarily. Unbeknownst to Sarah, Toby's echolocation-like emotional empathy had clicked on and the scent he picked up from the man was confusing him. Toby knew almost every scent to every emotion one could put off, but this scent was new to him. It was a disgusting combination of dead fish and overly ripe, sickeningly sweet fruit. He could not understand this new scent and because he didn't know anything about the man, he didn't know what it could mean. So, Sarah watched Toby watch the man walk away, his empathy clicking back off, and he turned to walk back toward the train.

Sarah suddenly realized that she was staring, probably rather rudely, at the mentally challenged young man and felt a flood of shame pass over her. She quickly pushed that and the oddness of the young men's interaction out of her mind.

4

Frank stood watching the beautiful young Sarah Maisse as she, seemingly, stared out into the breathtaking timbered mountainside. Several thoughts raced through his mind about the lovely lady, mostly erotic, but he was gentleman enough with his women not to share such personal ideations. His pleasant thoughts quickly took on a more serious tone, though. This girl was going to be a challenge, he thought to himself. He didn't know how he knew, but he knew she would be. He also knew that she would be worth that challenge... if she stayed. That would be the first part of the challenge. The valley wasn't for just anyone and not just anyone was for the valley. It took a special breed to live in the valley the way they did, and Frank sincerely hoped she was of that breed. He was quick to come out of his thoughts when Sarah turned toward him and with a small smile asked him if they were going on that tour.

A little while later, Jimmy Moran and Tobias Medlin left the valley via the eastern tunnel in the mountainside, headed for their next stop down the tracks. Not long after they had pulled out of the valley, Sarah looked at Frank and said, "I think I was on the train too long. I can still hear it's rumbling or whatever you call it." Frank informed her of the waterfall, which she found fascinating. He assured her that she would grow used to the constant background noise. He also promised he would take her to it one day if she decided to stick around in the valley.

Dansford Keeton took Sarah's bags to Frieda's old place, leaving them just inside the door and headed toward the common area. He didn't know where Frank was but he knew he wasn't at the house so he would eventually find him there.

Unless he was out doing something for Frank, he was always close by him, even when Frank didn't know he was.

Dansford and Frank had literally grown up together. Neighbors since birth and only days apart, they had spent almost everyday of their lives together. The entire valley knew the boys were as close as brothers, but only Mr. and Mrs. Keeton and Mr. and Mrs. McGrath knew that there was a very likely chance that the boys were, in fact, brothers. It wasn't a love affair, scandal, or anything so dramatic. It was just two happily married couples that enjoyed weekly group sex with their neighbors. It was a secret that went to the grave with all four participants and no one in the valley ever knew or expected a thing. Not even Frank and Dansford. Knowing the possibility was there may have prevented Dan's unhealthy, borderline obsession with Frank. Knowing could have prevented certain events that had taken place as they grew up.

Dan glimpsed Frank walking alongside the new pretty girl, heading away from the schoolhouse, and he felt an irrational pang of jealousy in the pit of his stomach. He waited until the pair got several yards ahead and then followed behind, blending into the surroundings.

It took almost four hours to make it to Sarah's new 'home'. If one could call a shack a step above in shambles a home. Frank had taken her down the track toward the western tunnel and cut down into the O'Reigan's farm. After some introductions they cut across the bridge into Town, and he walked her around, showing her where all the different shops and facilities were. He explained that their currency was a solid mix of money and trade, whether that be trade of property or services. He walked her through the Lot, showing her the rows of homes and those that resided there, the dogs, and reluctantly informing her the largest home in the valley was his. In the valley that made the women feel inferior which just pissed them off. Sarah didn't make much of the information, didn't seem to care one way or the other, which relieved Frank. He brought her across the bridge into the Slums, walking her around the area, introducing her around to different folks. Sarah lingered as they walked by the little shack with the lovely, exotic garden. It intrigued her but since she was new, she decided not to ask too many questions right now.

Sarah and Frank had arrived at the small three-room shack that was once the home of Sarah's great-aunt Frieda. The first and largest room in the house was a kitchen/living room combo. On one side of the room sat a wood and coal burning stove with two cook burners on top, a large wash basin, a wall with rows and rows of shelves (mostly empty sans a few chipped and cracked dishes) and a small wooden table. The opposite side of the room contained another small table with two wooden chairs, a rocker, and a wooden bench covered in animal hides. The next room was the bedroom, complete with a single bed draped in more animal hides and a rickety old chest of drawers. The last, the smallest room of the house, was the 'bathroom'. Which was essentially an outhouse attached to the home. The toilet was a board with a hole cut out in it that allowed access to a small barrel underneath that someone came around once a week and dumped in the river.

Sarah found that the valley was very primitive compared to the rest of the world. They didn't have running water. Almost every shack/tepee/house/etc. had a wash basin that had to be hand filled via buckets of water drawn from the river. They didn't have electricity.

They used torches and 'coal lights' to see by at night and everything was done manually. They didn't have automobiles of any kind. Their only form of transportation, aside from their own two feet, are the mules; and they are strictly used to transport the mining loads back to the valley. They didn't have guns or firearms of any kind. Most people had a knife of some sort for a multitude of reasons but the only actual weapons in the valley were bows. Made from timber cut from the mountainside and hand crafted by the woodworkers for the hunters of the valley. The bows and arrows were a step above primitive but well-built and did the job they were intended to do. Crime was extremely low. There was no such thing as poverty as everyone was the same 'financially' speaking. Everyone in the valley that was able was employed; and those few that couldn't work were cared for by family and friends in the valley. There was no racism, no bias, and no extreme judgement. What Sarah didn't know yet was that there were almost no secrets. The very few secrets that were, were all connected to the woman who lived in the little shack with the magnificent garden.

Frank helped Sarah with the stove, showing her some tips and tricks to get a good hot fire going for heating and cooking. She found a tea kettle on one of the kitchen shelves and after Frank went and drew her some water, she made them a cup of tea. Sassafras tea, gathered from the woods and dried to perfection. Sarah had never had sassafras tea before and fell in love with it instantly. Which was good because it was the valley's version of coffee. After some small talk between the two, Frank told her that he would be back in the morning so they could find her a job and that she should think about what she would be best at it, until then. She seen him out, wishing him a good night with a lovely smile, then proceeded to unpack what little she possessed and placed it throughout her quaint little home.

5

The following morning, Sarah woke up refreshed with the breaking sun. She was only partly surprised that there were already quite a few people out and about starting their day. She washed her face with water she had gathered the evening before and dressed for the day. Opting for a pair of shorts, mid-thigh length, and a tee shirt instead of a summer dress like what she adorned the day before. In the kitchen she boiled water for tea and attempted to fry a couple of eggs for breakfast. The result was a half raw, half charred slimy disaster that she couldn't stand to eat. She had just finished scraping the abomination out of the pan when Frank McGrath knocked on the door. She met him outside and they took off in the direction of the common area.

As they walked Frank asked Sarah, "You give any thought to what you'd like to do round here?"

"Sure have. I'd like to hunt." She told him bluntly.

Frank started laughing, convinced she was joking. He quickly sobered up when he realized that she not only wasn't sharing in his humor, but she was being serious. "Oh. Well, I... uh... don't you think you would rather help the seamstresses? Or the gatherers? Or the cooks?" he asked, stammering, unsure of how to go about the conversation.

Sarah smiled at him patiently. She anticipated such a reaction, had been through them too many times. It's as if men can't handle the idea of a woman being good at something 'made for men'. "I do not know how to sew, Frank. Never wanted to learn so I never did. Hunting is the same as gathering in the sense that we're all helping to feed the valley. I can spot an animal that can be eaten. I would poison someone trying to decipher plants. As for cooking, you wouldn't have even asked me that if you had seen how bad I managed to screw up a couple eggs this morning."

Frank smiled at her but still couldn't fathom a woman out in the timber hunting a huge animal and then managing to haul it back to the valley... alone. "Come with me. We will go talk to some of the other hunters about this. It's their territory so informing them of your desire to hunt with them is only respectable. We should be able to catch them before they head out if we hurry." He takes off toward the hunting lodges at the base of the mountainside on the northern side of the valley before Sarah has a chance to accept or reject. Knowing she wouldn't opt for the latter.

The pair arrived at the lodges just as the men were tossing sheaths full of well-made arrows over their shoulders. Frank quickly introduced Sarah to the hunters and informed them that she wanted to hunt too. They all stared at her. Some in awe, some in curiosity, some in disbelief. But no one would say anything in response. Finally, Sarah suggested, "Let me show you that I can use one of those bows." She looked over at Frank. "You go set up a few targets about 60 yards out." He eyed her curiously. "I'll hit my target." She told them all confidently.

The group of men looked around at each other, seeming to silently communicate before one of them nodded their head at Frank. He walked over to the lodge looking for something to use as a target. By the time the targets had been set in place, word had gotten around, and a generous crowd had gathered around to watch Sarah shoot. She placed her feet, accordingly, taking her shooting stance. Her sharp eyes scanned the area around the targets, locking in on one. She raised her bow, drew back, released the arrow, and dropped her arm back to her side in less than two seconds. Her speed alone was impressive. The arrow flung over the targets and landed with a thud twenty yards behind them. "You missed." Frank told her flatly.

"Did I, though?" She smiled at him slyly. "Let's go take a look."

The pair of them walked to where the arrow landed, the hunters tagging along behind. All of them, except for Sarah, were completely stunned by what they were seeing. Sarah had shot a squirrel from almost a hundred yards, the arrow entering one eye and exiting the other. The only blood evident was a mere few drops on the very tip of the sharpened stone arrowhead. It was the cleanest kill any of them had ever seen. Sarah stood holding the squirrel up by the tail, proudly before the men. "Does this prove my point, gentlemen?" she asked rhetorically.

Sarah took her prized shot and headed back to her scant little home to have a proper breakfast. Frank remained with the awed hunters and gossiping crowd trying to decide if she could hunt or not. After enjoying some fried squirrel, she took the hide with her to the common area. She took her squirrel pelt to the woodworkers first, knowing they liked using them to polish their finishing products. She sold the hide, sans the tail, to a Mr. Ron Hellman for enough money to get some food into her small home. She took the squirrel tail to the seamstress, Mrs. Rebecka Marlow, who not only took the squirrel tail enthusiastically but bargained with Sarah to get some more. The agreement was that Rebecka would make her a camo hunting outfit in exchange for eleven more squirrel tails and five rabbit tails. She was going to be adding fur cuffs to the coats for the coming winter. They also agreed to do further business should they both hold up to their end of the bargain. It was the beginning of a good business relationship. Later that evening, Frank showed up and told Sarah that the hunters agreed that she should hunt and believed she would be a very valuable asset to the valley.

The beautiful, young Sarah Maisse was the talk of the valley for some time after she had arrived. If not for being the first newcomer to the valley in years, then for her impressive knack for hunting. Whether it be small game or large, there wasn't a single day that Sarah ventured out into the timbers and returned to the valley empty-handed. After the initial shock of seeing such a beauty handle a weapon as well as she did, the hunters had gained a healthy respect for the lady. That respect, however, was laced with threads of jealousy. Not vengeful jealousy where they wished her gone, but more of a competitive jealousy that resulted in the male hunters stepping up their game, so to speak. They were still men, and they wouldn't be outdone by no damn woman... if they could help it, that is.

Now that you have gotten to know one of the two leading ladies, Dr. Gerard, it is time for you to meet the main leading lady...

Chapter Thirteen

Young and Ambitious

1

Dr. Warren Gerard sits up straight on the sofa in his den. *Another 'leading lady'? What the heck does that mean? What happened to the little boy from fifteen years ago? Is it Frank McGrath? The age seems to fit but it doesn't feel right.* He sighs heavily and rubs his eyes in weariness. *Well, I reckon the only way I'm going to find out is if I keep reading. But not tonight! I've had enough for one day.* He recalls his amazing day with a sense of pride and ownership, feeling as if it had occurred days or even weeks ago now.

He places the stack of papers back into the manila envelope, leaving it on the coffee table as he makes his way to bed.

The following day passes by uneventfully. The previous days standards had been set to an all-time high in Warren's mind, so he had no expectations that today would be anywhere near that good. He doesn't see the young man that he has helped finance his mother's medication and Ms. Lancing treats him as she always has, as if nothing at all had occurred between them. He admires her professionalism and tells her so on one of her visits to his office door. Her only response is a slight smile and quick wink.

On a subconscious level, Warren spends most of his workday anxious to get back home. To get back to that letter… story… whatever. Question after question after question swirls their way around the back of his mind. All unanswered. He has been promised answers that he wants more than he is willing to admit. He is much more emotionally involved in this situation than he cares to say as a medical professional. As a well-respected doctor, part of the job is being able to detach yourself from cases and patients. It is more a means of survival than anything else. Doctors, like everyone else, can only handle so much heartache and loss. This time is different, though, in every aspect. He just hasn't been able to admit it, yet; especially to himself.

Later in the evening, at home and comfortable, Dr. Gerard decides to start in on the letter early. He orders a pizza, something he hasn't had in three years, since he started his diet. He has a nip of whiskey as he waits for the delivery man to show up with his pizza. The delivery man ends up being a tall, lanky, pimply lad that is several minutes early, so Warren is generous with the kid's tip. Apparently making the kids day, if not his whole week.

He sets his place at the dining room table, always eating there regardless of the meal. With his greasy pizza (eaten straight out of the box) and his signature scotch-on-the-rocks, he pulls the stack of papers out of the manila envelope he retrieved from the den while he waited for the pizza. He has read/watched about eight pages of the manuscript, so far, so he slides those back into the large envelope. With a slice of pizza consisting of pepperoni and sausage with peppers and onions in one hand, Warren picks up the page he had left off on the night before and begins to read. The words immediately form into pictures, the 'movie unpausing'.

2

...the main leading lady. I cannot, as of yet, reveal her name to you. She is the witch that resides in the small shack with the magnificent garden. At this point in the tale, she is a good witch, commanding her strength and powers from the light, helping those of the valley. So, I shall address her as you now know her, the Good Witch, for now anyway.

She has a lengthy past stretching back centuries. A second-generation sorceress born to one of the original sorceresses of time and an unknown father, witchcraft is all she has ever known. Of course, she was schooled in all the basics, but sorcery of every kind was taught above all else. Even the dark side of sorcery, only as a tool to learn how to disable curses and hexes and be able to identify what they can undo and what they cannot. Her schooling was extensive, finally completing it after 80 years. Her schooling led to an apprenticeship of sorts, under a supreme coven member for another 50-year stretch.

It took another 20 years after she completed her apprenticeship for the Good Witch to be initiated into the coven that she had mentored under, and she was belated when she was. As one of her first acts as a new coven member, with the strength of her powers coursing through her, she ventured out into the night for a place of silence and peace. Being young and ambitious, her attempt at conjuring a spell that she was not nearly powerful enough to handle, was both commendable yet irresponsible. The result was a completely exhausted and drained young witch that didn't even have the strength to stand. There was no way she could make her way back to the coven house, so, she had decided to lay under the tree where she attempted the conjuring, and rest for a while.

A short time later, three men came walking by and noticed the sleeping woman, weak and alone on that humid night. The three men assaulted her in the most vile and depraved ways one can imagine. She tried to fight them off but weakened very quickly, giving them the chance to restrain her before she could get away. They left her bleeding, bruised, and battered under the tree they had found her and then went about their way as if no more than a casual greeting had taken place.

The young witch had suffered some severe injuries from that assault, taking several weeks to recover even with the aid of healing teas and potions. When she was finally healed, the handful of head coven members met with the young witch to find out precisely how she came about her injuries. An elder sorceress hypnotized the young witch, mentally drawing the events out of her traumatized mind, and projected it to the other head coven members. They all watched the events unfold much like you are now. The Good Witch was excused for deliberations and after a very lengthy and at times heated conversation, the elders finally came to an agreement. The young witch would have the use of her powers suspended for five years and remain under close supervision of the coven.

The young witch stormed out at the news of her punishment. Before that though, "Punishment for what?" she demanded an answer. She already knew why but she wanted to hear them say it.

"You are not being punished, young one." One of the five elders told her.

"We are only trying to ensure your safety." Another one added.

"Then why the loss of my powers?" she asked angrily.

The elders hesitated before finally giving her an answer, stammering over their words. "Your growing powers is what... uh... had you out there alone to begin with." A third elder told her.

"Yes. We are simply removing your temptation until you are able to gain some self-control." The first one said as the other four nodded their heads in agreement.

The Good Witch didn't respond, just got up and walked out. She was furious! The rage seeped and boiled deep within her, slowly spilling over, sending waves of fury to radiate from her. She went straight to her room, slammed, and locked the door, then sulked in her newest misery until the first thoughts of venomous revenge seeped into her mind.

And with them came a brilliantly malicious idea.

The rage, an unknown driving force, had her calling out to any and all forces for the power to punish those that had wronged her. Eventually, she received an answer... but the force that answered her, drawing from her rage and desire for revenge, was one of Satan's own. The young witch refused to come out, eat, sleep, or drink. The coven members were becoming very concerned for the girl when she finally came out of her room well into the fourth day. She looked completely refreshed and pristine. Somehow.

She wouldn't speak about what had occurred during those four days she spent alone in her room, and after a few days everyone decided to stop questioning her about it, realizing all attempts were pointless. Something in her eyes told them to back off, as if sending out a warning signal.

The truth was that she had spent the first 52 hours out of the 109 she had spent in her room, conjuring, and enduring the process of the ritual. On the 48th hour, the witch's request was finally granted. It was short-lived, however, the immense power that she could feel coursing through her was overwhelming and frightening to her young and still fragile mind. She began rejecting the power before she even used it, not trusting herself to handle it properly.

She had been able to fully expel the power by the 52nd hour, the light in her, the goodness, overcame the darkness, the evil, that threatened to consume her. From there, she spent another six hours in a heated discussion with the evil force that granted her the powers she eagerly got rid of. This lengthy argument wore on them both and eventually progressed to more physical altercations, the evil being confident that it could take her by force.

They fought for 26 hours.

The Good Witch weakened multiple times, but still managed to fight it off. The evilness reluctantly accepted that it had been beaten... this time... but it vowed to return. "You belong to me, now, and I WILL have what is mine!!" The disembodied voice of the demon roared at her. Its thick, gravelly voice reverberated around her room, knocked pictures from the wall and trinkets off the shelves. The Witch, in her extreme exhaustion, refused to rest until she was sure the evil had departed.

After four hours of waiting and receiving no signal that the being was still watching her, she reluctantly laid down for some much-needed rest. 18 hours of it, to be exact. She spent her remaining three hours making herself presentable enough to face the coven. It worked because everyone was amazed at how good she looked. Underneath, however, she was screaming from the pain and soreness that coursed through her body at every movement.

3

Even though the Good Witch had rejected the powers that would have granted her revenge, those that had wronged her were punished. 'Something' served each of them their individual consequences. The three men that had raped and beaten her and the three of the five head coven members that wished to punish her for it. One of the three men was caught trying to rape another woman, was then castrated, and ultimately exiled. Another one accidentally stumbled upon a small dragon's nest. Several hours later, the elephant-sized dragon shit out what remained of him. The last of the three men was attacked and mauled by a pack of dogs when he attempted to break into a wealthier person's home. The scummy bastard survived, but the maimed man would bear the scars and disfigurements for the rest of his long life.

Two of the five head coven members had stood at the Good Witch's defense against the other three. Those three wanted the Good Witch to be completely turned out from the coven. To strip her of her powers and exile her for her blatant disobedience. They considered her to be defiant, arrogant, selfish and an outright fool. They didn't want to initiate her into the coven when they did but had run out of excuses as to why she shouldn't be. The three of them just did not like her and that was going to be their reason to get rid of her.

The truth of it was that they were not only jealous of the young witch but were also fearful of her. The head coven members were all old enough to remember the power that the Good Witch's mother had held and knew that according to the prophecy she was to inherit and amplify her mother's powers. She was young still and if the three coven members could help it, she would never realize her full potential. The other two coven members still held the Good Witch's mother at a very high regard, having the utmost respect for her. They very much wanted to see the young witch blossom to her full potential, use it for good to make the world a better place. They knew that one day she would be able to do some utterly incredible things or some devastatingly terrible things.

The two defending coven members refused to back down or yield to the other three. They would not accept her dismissal and encouraged them not to punish the girl but to help her continue to heal emotionally and mentally. The three would not hear of any such thing. It took a long time before a compromise was reached and it was reluctant on both sides, neither side trusting the other.

The consequences of the three head coven members wasn't as extreme as it was for the three men. One of them slipped on a stone staircase, tumbling down a couple dozen steps before landing in a heap at the bottom. She had a nasty gash on her head from the fall and could no longer move anything from her breasts down. This left the bitter old sorceress bedridden and riddled with pain from excruciating reoccurring headaches for the remainder of her life. Another member suddenly had the Drops (what you call a stroke) which resulted in her having fits (seizures) for the rest of her lengthy life. The remaining member, a man, soon began suffering from what you know as erectile dysfunction that quickly turned into outright impotence. His formerly promiscuous life was no more, causing him to spiral into a deep depression. He tried to dull his depression with drugs and alcohol, but it only intensified it. He became what you would call a bipolar alcoholic. None of the three would ever be the head of any coven ever again.

The Good Witch didn't know that any such consequences had occurred because she had already left the coven and was off to find the next one. They had shamed her, so she crossed her name out of the book, left her former mentor a short and sweet thank you note, then packed what few belongings she owned and headed out into the world.

4

The decades turned into centuries as she bounced from coven to coven. Spending no less than fifteen years but no longer than sixty with each one. Each coven offered its own relationships, experiences, mistakes, and teachings. Some were much worse than others, but she regretted none of them. Some were even exciting; like the time she narrowly escaped being hung during the Salem Witch Trials. Damn was that a close one! While some were sad and full of heartache, like her beloved Jacobi from Guyacinth. Anyway, after having been a part of dozens of different covens and mentoring under multiple solo sorceresses, with ties to everything from angelic conjuring to voodoo, throughout the centuries, none of which she truly felt she belonged to, the Good Witch decided to go solo for a while. So, for 137 years she has been a solitary sorceress, roaming the country helping those in dire need or those willing to pay.

She would not dabble in the dark magic, harming or cursing, but if someone came in who was hell bent on revenge, the Good Witch's dark side would surface momentarily to advise them on the best way to handle said need for revenge. Which was to follow through with it. You want to poison them? How about some belladonna, hemlock, or some henbane? You want it to be physical? Choose a weapon and maintain the element of surprise.

Every time that dark side of hers surfaced, the demon that 'owned' her would muster a spark of hope only to watch it die out as the light pushed the evil way back down deep. The Good Witch had all but completely forgotten about the evilness that lurked after her for most of her life and she was unaware the demon was watching her or that it vowed relentlessly to have her. She had become its obsession as well as its currently untouchable possession. And it would have her.

The Good Witch had travelled all through the mountains, coming across small migrant communities or families trying to establish their own land. She would help them if she was able, and they were able to pay. Very few did she consider charitable. Sometimes she granted wealth, luck, health, or happiness. Sometimes she would aid in fertility, behavior, or love issues. Every encounter was different (even if it wasn't) and each one had to be handled in a different way according to the issue and the person enduring it. What worked for some wouldn't work for others. She would stay for a short time, ensuring that she had held to her end of the bargain. Every successful spell, potion, chant, etc. that she completed strengthened her powers just a little bit more. Most of them fueled and strengthened the light that shone so bright within her; but the actions that border-lined dark sorcery and the advice she would give to those seeking revenge strengthened the evil within her. Once satisfied she would pack up and leave when she felt she had accomplished all she could for those she encountered.

5

One day while roaming, she came upon the valley in its very beginning stages of development. They barely had the foundations up for their homes. The waterfall and its lulling roar were soothing yet empowering. She knew she would be able to draw and maintain a lot of natural strength from this area, that would in turn strengthen her overall powers. She scanned from the thick timbers on the western side of the valley's mountainside and seen several small groups of people. She decided to wait and watch them before presenting herself. In the meantime, she would find her a place to call her own.

She did. She discovered a decent-sized cave at the northeastern corner of the valley. It had a natural wall, complete with a tall doorway into another larger cave. It was like a two-room home built into the mountainside. The second larger cave had a jagged opening in the ceiling of the cave, vine covered, allowing little sunlight to filter through. She made a mental note to find and clear that hole so that she would be able to read the moon. On one wall, running almost the entire length of the wall, was a natural rock shelf that she could use as her altar. There were notches and handholds scattered across all four slightly curved walls to hold a multitude of candles. Plus, there was an ample amount of space on the floor so she could sketch out and put down a permanent magic circle. The mental pictures were snapped, and she was planning everything already. When night came and she knew no one would see her, she ventured down into the valley and instead of going into the cave, stood back from the mouth of it determining where she would put her home, whatever structures they were building would suffice. More mental pictures were snapped, and she visualized putting up a rock wall to house her magnificent garden.

For the first time in literal ages, she wanted to settle down and just enjoy life without moving constantly. She decided she would make herself known the next day and the next day she did. They accepted her with open arms and very few questions, just excited to have another member added to their tiny community. Her small two room shack was built, mostly on her own but needing help with the roof. Quite a few young men were happy to help her, and she blessed them with excellent health. All seven of the young eager men lived long healthy lives, finally passing well into their ninety years and all of them passing peacefully and painlessly. She collected and built the stacked-stone hip-high wall that came out from the entrance to her shack and then out in opposite directions, ending at the incline of the mountainside and upper eastern branch of the river. Once that was completed, she started creating her magnificent garden.

After decades in the valley, the garden constantly thrived from its enchantment and the enchantment always thrived from the garden. It was a continuous, beautiful cycle that birthed a place of near perfection that could rival the Garden of Eden. It was lush with exotic plants of every species and was home to some mythical, long-believed extinct creatures. Only the Good Witch knew for sure what all creatures resided in the enchanted garden, but there were rumors around the valley of strange sightings and sounds from the garden. Almost everyone in the valley had visited the Good Witch for one thing or another over the years, even the newcomers came to her even if at first only out of curiosity. Very few of those people had ever been in her garden, for their own safety, she had told them, then added that she had some highly deadly plants in there. The few that she had allowed into her garden were brought there as a warning or worse yet, a punishment. Those few also now resided in the tents set up in a long arch dozens of yards from the garden wall.

More about that later though...

Chapter Fourteen

Terrible Tea

1

The movie pauses. Warren has finished all but two slices of his pizza and is now suffering from some highly uncomfortable heartburn. He takes a half hour break to tame his heartburn and clean up his dinner mess. When he finishes, he walks into the den to settle in but reconsiders and decides to take it to his bedroom instead. Warren steps into his upstairs study and grabs the scotch bottle from the cabinet under his decanter set, this one much less valuable than the one in the den. He heads to his bedroom and decides to grab a quick shower before settling in.

Drinking his scotch straight out of the bottle and nestled comfortably in his bed, he 'un-pauses the movie'.

More about that later though. The Good Witch, being of immense beauty with her short blonde pixie cut hair, dark blue eyes and a body modeled by Aphrodite herself, was irresistible to most men. She could and pretty much did have any man, and occasionally a woman, whenever she wanted. It was always just sex though, no emotions other than basic physical sexual attraction. Nothing more.

Until she really noticed Johnathan Colmes for the first time, the spring before the young Ms. Sarah Maisse arrived.

Something or several somethings about him reminded her of her lost love Jacobi and she

146

quickly fell head over heels in love with him. She wanted to spend the rest of her life with him, no matter how short or long that may be. He was a young man, early twenties, the valley butcher since the death of old Mr. Henry Jolen, and handsome in the rugged, backwoods kind of way.

It took much longer than one would expect for the two of them to interact, being that the valley was such a small place. He had heard numerous things about the Witch all his life, of course, mostly good, and she had heard of the new butcher but was unsure of the name. The Good Witch had been vegan for a couple hundred years now but would weaken from the lack of protein and had to occasionally resort to eating a couple seared fish and a very bloody steak. They always perked her back up and maintained her for quite some time. She had not had to enter the butcher's shop for well over two years after the death of Mr. Jolen, and it had been months or more since she had been in there then.

She knew the moment she laid eyes on Johnathan Colmes, though, that she wanted him. It was an immediate and strong attraction that she couldn't deny. He was a hormonal young man that was utterly intoxicated by her scent. It was like an aphrodisiac to him, so he embraced it. They spoke for some time, he gave her the fish and steak she wanted, and then she invited him over later that evening so she could pay him for the food. This last was said with a seductive wink.

So, of course, the young Mr. Johnathan Colmes went to the Good Witch's shack that evening. He didn't know exactly what her payment would be, but he had heard rumors his whole life about the incredible feats the woman had accomplished for others in the valley. He wasn't expecting anything spectacular. Just hoping to get a little love on that fine night.

And he did.
And again.
And then once more.

She finally let him leave just mere hours before dawn. He crawled into his own bed a little while later completely exhausted and completely satisfied. He fell asleep almost instantly thinking about the sexy woman and hoping she was equally as satisfied.

The Good Witch was, indeed, satisfied, but she didn't drift off to sleep like John did. Instead, she waited until she could no longer hear his footsteps before she got out of bed, slipped into her off white ritual robe with nothing underneath, and exited her small shack out the back door. She took the half dozen steps to the covered cave entrance and entered it without a thought that anyone would or could see her. Her sixth sense would have alerted her to any spying, and it was always spot on.

She stepped into the smaller of the two caves, glanced around the cluttered room then stepped to the side to acknowledge her squawking friend. The Good Witch had found and adopted an abandoned fledgling. It was not sick or injured, but it had been born with partial albinism, so the mother raven rejected the fledgling and left it to die on the forest floor. The Good Witch had raised it since it was only a couple days old, the now beautiful raven very near death when it was found. Knowing that the Good Witch had rescued it, the raven remained very loyal to its master, its albinism making it slightly more intelligent than others of its species which allowed it the ability to be loyal to the Good Witch.

THE WITCH'S TAROT

She reached into a small, lidded box and brought out a couple wiggling maggots in her fingers. The raven pecked at them gently, taking care not to harm its master, as the witch stroked its neck and back with a single finger. She admired how beautiful the bird was with its deep black feathers highlighted by the contrasting bright white with the light pink undertone. The raven had a splotch of white around one eye reaching around the back of her head. That eye was bright pink and very clearly affected by the albinism. There were a few white feathers strewn into its narrow tail, the tip of its tail and wings were all tipped with bright white feathers, as well. The good witch was still amazed that she had been able to save the young bird and have it not only survive but thrive so well. She cared deeply for the unique animal and hoped it lived a full and happy life.

She left the comforted bird and entered the second and larger of the two caves. A snap of her fingers illuminated the cavernous space as almost every candle in the room lit simultaneously. She walked over to the alter where she displayed her copy of the 'Opera Magicae' and flipped through the yellowed, brittle pages until she found the spell she was looking for. The Good Witch scanned the page quickly, taking in all the ingredients and tools she would need. She only had a few hours until sunrise, so she needed to hurry if she was going to complete it while she still had the power of the moon.

The Good Witch walked back into the first cave room and with a mental list at the front of her mind she began searching for everything she needed. She grabbed two different colored candles, two small bottles of liquid and several more with a variety of dried and ground herbs. She grabbed the mortar and pestle, grinder,

149

a knife, and a long narrow spoon. As she took things off shelves and out of cabinets, she placed everything in a wooden bowl, using it to carry everything she needed into the alter room of the cave.

She read over the instructions for the ritual much more carefully. She placed the candles on the floor, one pink and one red set on either side of the center of the magic circle set into the floor of the cave. She placed the wooden bowl in between the candles and arranged all her tools and ingredients in front of her. The Clove had to be run through the grinder, leaving a dense course gravelly substance. She dumped the newly ground Clove into the bowl and set the grinder aside. Then fresh Rose petals and Chamomile flowers had to be processed using the mortar and pestle, the resulting mush scraped into the wooden bowl with the ground clove. She added ground Mugwort, John's Wort and Lemonbalm to the bowl and gave it a quick swirl with the long wooden spoon.

Once the concoction of herbs was readily mixed in the bowl, the Good Witch stood up, stepped forward, hiked her robe up around her thighs, and squatted over the wooden bowl. She stayed that way for several long moments before she finally felt Johnathan's seed drip out of her and into the herbs below. Five drops were plenty enough for the ritual, so she returned to her place in front of the bowl and added the remaining ingredients. A few drops of Jasmine oil and a few more drops of Rose oil. Using the knife blade, she pricked her finger to add a few drops of her blood, which completed the potion. She mixed it well, defying logic by turning it into a syrupy-like solution. The bowl was placed back into the center of the magic circle and the Good Witch readjusted her position so that she was kneeling before the potion. She recited the chant.... in Latin.

"I Naturae et spirituum vires circumfer,"
I ask the forces of Nature and Spirits around.
"Deos rogo ut abundet amor adiuvet"
I ask the Gods to help love abound.
"Hac amoenitate herbarum,"
With this charm of loving herbs,
"Adiuva hanc caritatem ab interiori parte canvalescit et canvalescit."
Help this love grow stronger and stronger from within.

With the ritual complete, she took the bowl filled with the herby potion over to the altar and left it there to steep. The longer it steeped, the more powerful it would become.

The Good Witch returned to her bed a few moments later, shed her ritual robe and slipped into her bed, nude. Pulling the blanket up over her, she fell asleep only minutes later.

2

She awoke well after everyone else in the valley and immediately set about getting ready for her day. She dressed and boiled water to steep some tea to mask the potion she intended to give her new love. The Good Witch approached the butcher's shop come early afternoon, two cups of the unique tea in her hand. She had been careful not to drink any of her part because the potion would only work properly if the first drink was taken simultaneously.

She quietly stepped into the shop, glancing around the front room, and quickly registered John's absence. She carefully placed the two cups of tea down on the wooden counter and waited for John to return. She studied the room as she waited, very aware of the prominent smell of blood and the tangy salt in the air. The wooden counter sat out from the walls several feet, allowing for a wide walkway behind it. It spanned three of the four walls, angling sharply at its corners. It was expertly polished and clean as can be. An array of hooks hung from the sturdy ceiling over the counter with an assortment of cured meats hanging from them. Some of the hooks held large fish of various kinds, some headless bodies that could have been a squirrel or rabbit, and some just had large slabs of unidentifiable meat. She could hear the buzzing of the flies that floated on the weightless air around the room. Then she heard the squeak of the door located on the back wall of the front room. The door that she correctly assumed led to the back part of the shop where he done all his actual work.

Johnathan Colmes stepped through the door, wiping his bloody hands on his stained apron, and stopped halfway to the counter when he realized he had a visitor. His eyes lit up at the sight of the Good Witch and a surprised smile stretched across his face. She admired his rugged handsomeness from across the counter. His thick dark hair, slightly damp form perspiration, had a slight wave to it. His piercing blue eyes had an almost aural quality about them that fascinated her. His squared jaw was still prominent under his stubble of a beard. He had a very large but well built, muscled body that was currently hidden behind his khaki shorts, tee shirt and stained apron. She was undressing him with her eyes when he interrupted her thought process.

"What are you doin here?" he blurted before realizing how rude it sounded. Before he could apologize for his tone, he heard her giggle, and then visibly relaxed.

"I was hoping to surprise you." She told him with a pleasant smile. "Here I brought you some tea." She slid the cup across the polished surface of the counter toward him and continued. "It's not sassafras, though. It's my own recipe. This is the first time I've ever made it and I wanted you to be the one to try it with me. If you would, that is?" The Witch gave him a mischievous little smile and lifted her cup.

John picked up his cup, investigated the dark liquid, and then gave it a good sniff. "Well, it smells good. I'll give it a try." He tells her and lifts it to his lips. She quickly raised hers too and they both drank at the same time. Then they both proceeded to grimace as the awful taste of the potion hit their taste buds, souring them. "It's... uhh... well... it's..." Johnathan stammered not wanting to hurt her feelings.

"It's fuckin terrible!" The Good Witch exclaimed.

John stared at her for a long moment, laughed, and then agreed with her. "Yeah. It is." He laughed again and she joined him.

The spell had been cast and the potion consumed by them both. If the ritual worked, then the effects would be noticeable before dawn of the following day. So now all she had to do was wait.

They talked for a little while before the witch left, her inviting him over again that night. He accepted. His eagerness evident. She informed him that she had "a job" that night as well and that he had to wait until she settled that before he could come over though. He was slightly disappointed, but he understood and agreed to wait until she was finished.

Chapter Fifteen

Ametrine

1

After closing the shop for the night, Johnathan went back to his little tepee shaped home and napped for a few hours. When he woke up with the sun falling behind the horizon, he decided to go see the seamstress, Ms. Rebecka. Like a lot of others in the valley, John had known her his entire life.

As he was walking into Rebecka's home, the Good Witch had her own visitor. Mr. Joseph Brenner. Old Joe to most everyone in the valley because even though the man wasn't a day over 40, he looked a couple decades older. He claimed that his dear old daddy had aged earlier than most too and that it was just a family trait. Most everyone in the valley knew better though; they knew it was from his 25 years of daily Shine and Smoke intake. Not that anyone really judged him for it, hell everyone in the valley would or had partaken in some of Mr. Robert Daniels' Shine and some of Mr. Jiminey McAvay's Smoke. There just weren't very many others in the valley that enjoyed them as much as Old Joe.

Joe Brenner was a stout, strong man regardless of his aged appearance. He could outwork most men twenty years his younger and he was damn proud of it. His bodily physique did not match well with his leathery, wrinkled skin and full head of silver hair. As he settled in at the round wooden table the Good Witch had placed over the magic circle on the cave floor, he informed her as to why he was there. He recently began having intense pain in his side and lower back and decided to go to the infirmary. Th valley's doctor, the entirety of his medical training being a six-month volunteer job at a hospital over in Georgia, told him that it was probably his liver from all those years of 'being addicted to the Shine'. Joe, having a rather successful business, and no one to pass it along to, took this news very seriously. He finished with, "I don't tink dat I'm strong nuff to handle the withdraws without any... uh... outside hep." Joe was one of the few people in the valley that hadn't come to her for help before. They knew each other very well but had never had any business interactions until then.

The Witch nodded thoughtfully at him. "Is this something you are serious about overcoming?" she asked him.

"Oh, yessum." He answered and she noticed the fearful glint in his eyes.

"Alright then. A quick reading will tell me with more certainty if you are being truthful. If I find that I cannot help you, there will be no deal made. Understood?"

Joe nodded his head in understanding and waited patiently as she entered the first and smaller of the two cave rooms. The Good Witch returned with a short stack of cards in her hand, but Joe immediately noticed that they were not the same type of cards they played with at the bar. They were larger in size, very old, and oddly decorated. Among other feelings, he was intrigued by them. "These are Tarot cards. They will tell me if you really are willing to end your addiction."

155

Joseph Brenner swallowed hard and nodded his head. Her intense stare made him question and doubt himself. He was visibly relieved when she cut her eyes to the cards in her hand. He watched her carefully shuffle the deck of cards repeatedly by cutting it into three smaller sections, stacking and restacking. Then she had Joe place his hand over the deck of cards and say his name three times in a row. She placed the deck gently on the table before her and had him cut the deck of cards into three smaller sections and restack them. With that done, the Good Witch flips the top card over. It shows a brightly colored picture of a man carrying a knapsack walking down a dirt path that leads off into the horizon. The top of the card read 'STULTUS', The Fool.

She looked down at the card and then instructed him to cut the deck once again into three and restack it. The next card had been divided diagonally into halves with a large heart traced in the center. The upper part of the card was brightly colored with flowers and butterflies while the lower half of the card was dismally shaded, the only color being the bright red of the blood dripping from the pierced heart. A silhouette of a desolate land filled with death and decay set eerily in the background. The top of that card read 'AMANTIUM', The Lovers. She observed the card and again had the cards cut and restacked. The final card had a very detailed drawing of the head of a lion with wide-stretched jaws, exposing razor sharp teeth. The eyes had an undeniable fierceness in them that radiated confidence. The top of the card read 'VIRTUS', Strength. The witch sighed and fear threatened Joe.

Joe had no idea if the cards on the table meant good or bad or anything at all. He hoped it would tell her that he wanted, no, needed this. He needed to quit drinking. He was afraid to die even if he refused to admit it. He grew more nervous the longer he watched her study the cards; anxiously waited for her to tell him something, anything. Finally, she looked up at him and pointed at the first card. "This is The Fool." She began and a look of instant disappointment creased Joe's face. "The name is misleading; it means the end of one thing and the beginning of another. In your case it is a good card. Now this one..." she told him pointing to the next card. "...is The Lovers card. I'm sure you're thinking it's because of your line of work but I assure you the two are unrelated. This card signifies the hard choices and painful hardships that must be endured. Not necessarily an indication as to how the withdraws will go but it does indicate your willingness to endure them." Joe nodded, not understanding most of the large words she was using but he understood enough to know what she was talking about. The Witch pointed to the final card with the ferocious lion and said, "This one says Strength. Strength of all kinds. Physically, mentally, emotionally, spiritually. In every form. In your case it will come in confidence and resisting the inevitable urges." She looked at him thoughtfully for a long moment, contemplating before finally telling him that she would be able to help. His offer for payment was a free night with anyone of his eight employees but she politely declined. She simply told him that he would owe her a favor in the future, and he happily agreed.

It took several minutes for the Good Witch to gather and prepare everything she needed. She had gone into the first room once again and came back out with a burner plate, a pair of ornate silver scissors, a small gem wrapped in thick twine, and three jars of herbs. Mugwort. Sage. Sandalwood. The fire under the burner plate was bright in the dimness of the candlelit cave. She had added the herbs to the plate then stood and approached Joe, the scissors in hand. Weariness intensified in him as she raised the scissors and then was washed away with relief when he realized she had just snipped a lock of his silver hair. She returned to her seat across the table from him, carefully laying the scissors back on the table, she added the lock of hair to the herbs on the burner plate. Within moments the contents were smoking, emitting a pungent odor that she instructed him to breathe in. Reluctantly he obeyed. The Good Witch laid the twine wrapped gem in front of her and chanted in Latin as Joe inhaled the acrid smoke.

"Ad copias,"
To the forces that be,
"Eos in conatibus adiuva."
Aide them in their endeavors.
"Da illis fiduciam et fortitudinem,"
Give them confidence and strength,
"Libero et expedita ut."
And the clarity to be free.

She stood once more, that time with the gem in her hand and again approached him. He wasn't fearful this time, though; he was almost overwhelmed by a sense of confidence he never knew he could possess. He was ready to face the world and whatever came with it. The good witch unwound the twine revealing the full beauty of the gem beneath and placed it around Old Joe's neck. He lifted the lavender colored crystal, tracing the dark purple veins running through it with his eyes. He was fascinated by how powerful it made him feel. "This is called an Ametrine, and you must not take it off. It will give you the strength and confidence you are convinced that you need to get through this. Anytime you feel weak, just hold the gem, and ask it for help... it will. You get through the next

48 hours, and you'll be free of your drinking habit." She told him as she walked him to and through her shack to the front door. He thanked her sincerely and repeatedly before heading back to his own shack located behind Hussey Row in The Slums.

Old Joseph Brenner made it through his withdraws and the 48 hours the Witch told him it would take to get over his addiction. She was right. The evening of the second night brought sweet relief in the form of no more hallucinations, tremors, or sweats. The following morning, after a dreamless, restful night's sleep, Old Joe woke up feeling better than he had in a decade or more. It was, he knew, all thanks to the Good Witch of the valley, and he would be forever grateful to her for it.

2

The Good Witch stood at her front door watching Old Joe walk away and got the sense that someone was close. A moment later John stepped out from the shadows cast by her magnificent garden, startling her with his suddenness. He approached her, held her tight against him, and apologized. She melted into his warm embrace, becoming intoxicated by the scent of him, unaware that her sixth sense had failed her. He told her how he just simply could not wait to see her any longer. The ritual worked. He was hers and she was his. She jerked him into the shack with her and slammed the door behind them.

After almost four hours of stop and go sensual, intense love-making John finally, reluctantly left for the night. Comfortably in their own beds, they both spent the wee hours of the morning in a deep exhaustion fueled slumber.

Within days the valley knew about their not-so-discreet relationship.

Unbeknownst to himself, John was spellbound to her. He loved her immensely, or so he thought. Love induced by the potion and lust induced by his loins. The latter feeding the former like fuel on fire. He was intoxicated by her, addicted to her, and that's just the way she wanted it. She occupied his thoughts throughout the day, his arms throughout the evening, and his dreams throughout the night. She needed no potion to intensify her feelings toward Johnathan and she was finally convinced that she loved John much more than she ever had Jacobi, pushing him from her mind for good. She was the happiest she had ever been in her long, long life and vowed to cherish and hold on to her love... no matter what.

The months passed and John's relationship with the Good Witch stood firm, both seemingly madly in love with the other. It had become common knowledge that the two of them were a couple and it harbored very little gossip amongst the valley folks by the time Sarah Maisse made her debut in mid-August.

3

Johnathan Colmes, being first the butcher's apprentice and eventually the valley's butcher, knew all the hunters better than most in the valley. He had an outstanding agreement with them all that stated that they could come in every day and have their pick of anything in the shop if they provided him with large game a couple times a week or small game every other day. Most were able to keep their end of the bargain, but he didn't hold it against them if the hunt didn't go well. That did happen from time to time.

Because of his profession, it was no surprise that John had heard of Sarah and her impressive hunting abilities soon after her display of skills. He had heard all the hunters mention her and talk about how skillful she was with the bow. So, John thought it odd that he had yet to meet this mysterious young lady after knowing that she had been in the valley for well over a month now. If she was as skilled as he kept hearing, then why hadn't she come to him with her kills? That's how it worked in the valley; the hunters and fishermen brought in the meat and the butcher cleaned and cured it all, allowing the valley a variety of protein-filled options. He had plenty to do with the hunters and fishermen he already dealt with, anyway, so one hunter dealing with their own kills wasn't much hurt on him.

Chapter Sixteen

Storm's Abrewin'

1

Less than a week into October brought the first few signs of autumn to the valley and the beautiful mountains that surrounded it. Unbeknownst to those in the valley, that was the day that everything changed. A markedly cursed day. One that contained a few incidents that started the domino effect resulting in the decimation of the village and all those in it. The events of that day caused a ripple effect that is still being felt today. For the longest time I believed that it was all just coincidence the way it all fell together. Now, after the vivid dream-visions I was shown, I am certain that a higher (or lower) power had a hand in those events that played out so delicately.

The sun was warm and welcoming that day but the wind blowing out of the north had an icy pang to it that chilled the elder folks down to their bones. Hundreds of miles south, beyond the magnificent flowing waterfall, dark clouds began to gather, slowly building into a monstrous storm. It slowly... very slowly, inched its way north across the sky heading in the direction of the mountains. At the same time, way up north, a cold front was making its way, slowly down south toward the same mountainous area.

The outside world was watching the pressure system and the storm closely, but all were almost certain the two would not meet. They believed that the cold front would hover just north of the massive storm and that the storm would begin to dissipate soon, weakening as it did. Storms almost always started to dissipate once they peaked and surely, as large as that one was, it was at its peak or very near it. Only when the cold front and the storm merged and mingled did they realize that they were wrong. It would go down as one of the worst storms in history.

While the storm, still a few days off, brewed in the south, a large portion of the valley's population stood on the dirt platform in front of the train station. All but a handful in the crowd had their bags packed and in hand or at feet awaiting the conductor's okay to board the train. There was a large fall festival held in New York every year and most of the families, especially those with children, would pack up and go off to enjoy the week-long festival. They would return via the train the following Wednesday. The valley prepared for the week by doing extra hunting and gathering to make up for the lack of work while most were gone. Then work would resume as before when they all returned to the valley. During that week of the year, right before Harvest season began, the valley seemed almost deserted with only a third of its normal population present.

The train brought its usual cargo of flour, sugar, soap, etc. and once unloaded, the valley folks were able to board the train. Those few left standing on the platform, Frank McGrath among them, watched the train disappear into the eastern tunnel, not knowing that it was the last time any of them would ever see it again. The valley's population went from 189 to 65, both a blessing and a curse.

2

As several of those that remained in the valley dispersed the train's cargo to its various locations, Sarah Maisse had just gotten the largest kill of her hunting career, a moose. She stood over the massive carcass, admiring her miraculous kill shot. And miraculous it was. The arrow she fired at the animal was a sure miss, she thought, the moment it left her bow, but the moose raised its head at the very last moment, literally, and the arrow pierced its skull right below the start of its enormous antlers. She watched the large animal flick one of its ears, sway gently on its long legs, and then drop where it stood. Sarah was still trying to comprehend what she had just managed to do when she let out a series of high-pitched whistles that carried throughout the timbers, reverberating off the mountains. The whistle was a signal to the other hunters that one needed help of some sort. Each hunter had a specific whistle and hunting area of the mountainous area surrounding the valley. Those that heard her whistle would come to her side as soon as they were able to get to her.

Almost half an hour went by before the hunters showed up to help her. It was Roy Hoarding and Ben Fariday. "Where's the rest of em?" Sarah asked the men without looking up at them. She was elbows-deep in the moose's chest cavity trying to get a good grip on its other lung.

"Dey left wit da rest of em dis mornin." Roy told her as he glanced over at Ben to see if he looked just as shocked as he felt. With wide eyes and a gaping mouth, Ben fit the shocked description to the letter. "You... uh... ya killed this with a single shot?" Roy asked her with a note of disbelief in his voice.

"I watched it happen and still can't hardly believe it. Don't take it personally, boys, I couldn't do this again if I wanted too." She told them with a sweet little laugh. She stood from the carcass, blood soaking into the sleeves of the camo she wore, perspiration evident on her nose and brow. "Think ya'll could help me carry this big ass beast outta the timbers?" she asked them as she wiped her blood-stained hands on an old rag she kept in her back pocket. "There's all the meat you wanna keep in it for ya'll."

"Sure, we will." Ben answered for both men, speaking for the first time.

"Dere's so much meat on dis thang, da tree of us could eat well for half da winter or more." Roy said. "But I knows I'd get tired of it right quick."

"Yeah, I think I would too." Ben replied. Sarah, alongside the two men, pulled her weight of the large, heavy carcass and listened to the men's verbal exchange.

"If it were my kill, I'd take it over to John afta getting my share." Roy told them.

"Yeah, could get all kinds a stuff for this much meat." Ben added.

Sarah engaged in the conversation for the first time by asking, "Ya'll talkin about the butcher, John?"

"Yessum, John the butcher." Roy answered her.

The subject changed many times before they finally lugged the giant carcass out of the timbers and to the hunting lodge. Typically, the kill is brought to the lodge before it is gutted, the entrails fed to the dogs over in the Lot. The dogs are taken when the hunters are looking for smaller game. Birds, rabbits, squirrels, etc. Sarah had taken a couple dogs out a few of the times she hunted small game. They were primarily for seeking out the smaller creatures, but they were very good at retrieving the fresh kills too.

Sarah, with the help of Roy Hoarding and Ben Fariday, got the carcass hung and the antlers removed. The men went about their own way when Sarah began skinning the moose, having to stretch from a chair to reach the legs it was hung from. She quickly ran over to Jiminey McAvay's place, knowing he used one for his harvests, and asked to borrow his hand cart so she could get the moose over to the butcher's shop. He allowed it in return for three days' worth of meat. When she later returned the cart, she handed him four days' worth as a goodwill gesture.

The cart was carefully stacked with giant slabs and chunks of moose. The brain had been removed with the skull, placed in a bowl, and carefully wedged between the chunks of meat so it would not spill from the bowl. Finally, she tossed the hide over the cart and set out toward the common area, pulling the wagon-like cart behind her. The first stop was to see the seamstress, Ms. Rebecka. Rebecka, already having dealt with Sarah on a multitude of occasions, welcomed her excitedly. She was quite pleased with the lovely moose hide Sarah had brought her and in exchange Sarah was given the promise of a scarf and glove set for hunting this winter and five gold pieces.

For the sake of understanding its worth, a gold coin in the valley was equivalent to the outside world's hundred-dollar bills. Most of the currency in the valley was bronze, some silver, and very little gold.

The next stop was the apothecary where she delivered the moose's brain. She hadn't the faintest idea how, but she was told that they extract hormones or something from the animals' brains to use in serums and elixirs. Whatever or however they made their products, they usually worked. The brain was exchanged for a future favor if she were to be injured or fall ill. The Aides at the apothecary eagerly accepted this arrangement.

Sarah's final stop before returning Jiminey's
cart was the butcher's shop where the final event
took plac....

The scotch bottle well over half gone, slowly slid off the side of Warren's protruding stomach, resting between his legs, his left hand still snugly wrapped around the short bottle neck. His right hand slowly falls across his stomach, papers still in hand.

The doctor is snoring.

Chapter Seventeen

Convulsions and Catatonia

1

The following morning, sporting itchy, watery eyes and a headache the size of a horse, Dr. Gerard enters his office hoping the day will go by quickly and uneventfully.

He slides his chair up to his desk, immediately noticing a small stack of memo notes sitting neatly in the center of the scatter of papers. He allows his eyes to glance over the top memo but puts no effort into reading the words on the small paper. He sighs heavily, opens one of his desk drawers, and rummages around inside it for a few seconds before emerging with an aspirin bottle in his hand. He takes two, adding to the three he had taken before leaving his house this morning, and swallows them down with the lukewarm coffee he had brought in with him.

A few minutes later, he reluctantly picks up the memos and reads them carefully. The first one reads:

IN RELATION TO GREGORY PATRICKSON
EVIDENCE OF NIGHT TERRORS @ 01:27 A.M.
r.m.

Okay. This is typical, nothing to get alarmed about. The second memo reads:

IN RELATION TO GREGORY PATRICKSON
MILD CONVULSION @ 02:41 A.M.
r.m.

A convulsion? He doesn't have a history or even a family history of convulsions. Did the night terrors cause his seizures? Surely not, there's never been such a case or anything like it to my knowledge. A tumor then maybe? The third memo reads:

IN RELATION TO GREGORY PATRICKSON
MULTIPLE MILD CONVULSIONS (4 WITHIN 17 MINUTES)
SEVERE CONVULSION @ 03:04 A.M.
MULTIPLE FAILED ATTEMPTS MADE TO PHONE YOU AT HOME
r.m.

Worried now, the doctor thought, *Severe convulsion? How severe? I would have heard the dang phone if I hadn't taken that gosh darned bottle to bed with me. I won't make that mistake again.* Still silently scolding himself, he read the fourth and final memo:

IN RELATION TO GREGORY PATRICKSON
RELATIVELY UNHARMED FROM FIRST SEVERE CONVULSION
SECOND SEVERE CONVULSION @ 03:13 A.M.
CURRENTLY IN A STATE OF CATATONIA
MULTIPLE FAILED ATTEMPTS MADE TO PHONE YOU AT HOME
r.m.

All four memos were written and initialed by the same guard. R.M. Ryan McCane. The handsome young guard that persuaded Dr. Gerard to help him pay for his mother's much-needed medication. He makes a mental note to find and speak with Ryan before the end of the day. He needs more information than what he read in the memos and what he could find in Mr. Patrickson's chart.

Warren leaves the memos lying on his desk and walks out of his office. He stops and asks Ms. Lancing if Ryan is still on duty, and she tells him that she isn't sure but can find out in a matter of moments.

He waits as she picks up the phone, occasionally pressing buttons and speaking politely to whoever is on the other end. Less than a minute later, she replaces the receiver and informs him that Ryan has already left for the day and isn't due back for three days. "Call him at home and tell him I need him to come in and speak with me before I leave this evening. It is important that I speak with him." He tells her as he walks out the door and heads down the hall to find Mr. Patrickson.

Checking his room in the rainbow corridor but finding it empty, he heads toward the infirmary section of the asylum. There he finds Greg in one of the exam rooms, lying seemingly fast asleep on a cot. There is an IV tube running out his left arm to a bag of clear fluids hanging from a metal pole beside the bed. There are cords running out from under the blanket pulled up to Greg's shoulders; Dr. Gerard doesn't need to move the blanket to know that the cords are attached to the machine monitoring his pulse and respiration rate. A nurse comes in to check his blood pressure every 15 minutes. All his vitals indicate that he is healthy and only sleeping. The issue lies in the fact that Greg Patrickson cannot be aroused. They tried everything short of giving him epinephrine with no success. His eyes don't dilate with the light, but all tests show he hasn't had any type of brain injury from the convulsions, no stroke, aneurysm, etc. They know the convulsions are what caused his catatonia, but they are baffled by what caused the sudden convulsions in a physically healthy man like Greg Patrickson.

Out of everyone that knows about the case with Gregory Patrickson, Dr. Gerard is the only person that considers, even if only briefly, that the night terrors are the cause of the convulsions. He quickly disregards the thought as foolish, though, and therefore, never mentions it to anyone.

Dr. Gerard performs his own exam on Greg and comes to the same conclusion as his nurses; it just doesn't make any sense. He sits at Greg's bedside for quite a while, thinking over... well, everything. He finally walks out of the exam room more flustered and no closer to any answers than he was to start with. It is disheartening and irritating in his currently intolerant mood. He returns to his office, hoping the day doesn't bring any more issues than he already has.

2

Ms. Lancing stops him at his office door and informs him that Ryan McCane will be in later this afternoon to speak with him. He thanks her and she gives him a little smile and a wink. *Well, at least that part is taken care of. I will find out from Ryan what happened to Greg last night. I need to find my rosary this evening and bring it to Greg tomorrow. I kept putting it off and I shouldn't have.* He plops down in his chair and sighs, wishing his headache would go away. It isn't quite as strong as it had been earlier but still bad enough. He is rubbing his temples with the tips of his fingers when the phone jangles beside him. The harsh ringing ripples through his skull and a moment of intense rage urges him to rip the phone from the desk and hurl it into the wall. It would smash into dozens of pieces that would scatter about the room and he would never again have to endure that wretched racket.

Instead, he picks the phone up before it can jangle once more and places it to his ear. In the politest voice he can manage through the pain, he makes his introduction. "This is Dr. Warren Gerard at the Navea Dwighton Asylum for the Mentally Afflicted."

"Good morning, Dr. Gerard. This is Calvin Powers at Georgia Insanus Domus Institute down in southern Georgia. Our building has recently been deemed a historical landmark because of its age. The courts have allowed us the next six months to relocate. We are desperately searching for another building, but the search is bleak. We have been able to find other asylums, like ours, to take in a few of our patients, temporarily of course, while we find a new place and relocate. Would you be able to help by taking in a few of our patients, Dr. Gerard?" Calvin from Georgia finishes.

Warren is silent for a few seconds before answering him. "I think we have a few rooms available. How many men should I expect and when?" He asks the man on the other end of the line. Between the suddenness of the phone call and the dull throbbing pain in his skull, he did not recall the letter and it's warning of the three new patients he would have coming to his asylum.

"We thank you kindly, Dr. Gerard." Calvin begins sincerely. "There will be a total of three men sent to stay with you over the course of the next four to five weeks. I know that seems like a lengthy amount of time, but we have found that moving too many of the patients at once creates much more stress than necessary. We send one patient, allow a week to ten days for the adaption phase, and then send the next one."

"I completely understand. The patients we deal with can be rather sensitive to such situations as these." Warren comments.

"Indeed, they are, Dr. Gerard. You can expect the first patient, by the name of Walter Paulus, in three days, on Monday."

"Alright." Warren responds jotting down the man's name on a clean memo sheet. "What's his story?"

"Poisoned his entire family, including himself. Wife and three young children. Been here about four years now. Cooperative with only a few minor disciplinary issues. The file will be sent along with the patient, of course, complete with the detailed accounts of all involved before, during, and after the incident. The same will be done with the other two patients. Ray Melbin and James Kitchen." Calvin informs Warren.

Dr. Gerard sits silently for a moment; his pen halted in the middle of writing the letter b in Melbin. His voice is low and quizzical when he asks, "Did you say Ray Melbin? As in the alleged serial rapist and murderer, Ray Melbin?"

"The very one." Calvin replies seriously.

There is something nagging at the back of Warren's mind about that name other than the countless headlines he had seen recently about the man. *SERIAL RAPIST STILL AT LARGE. RAPIST FINALLY APPREHENDED; RAY MELBIN NAMED AS SUSPECT. PUBLIC WANTS DEATH PENTALY FOR MELBIN. RAY MELBIN TRIAL A DISAPPOINTMENT TO THE PEOPLE. INSANITY CLAIM PREVENTS DEATH PENATLY. RAY MELBIN TRANSPORTED TO LOCAL ASYLUM FOR TREATMENT.* He tries to bring forth whatever it is that is nagging him but to no avail. "Well, I have certainly never had a patient as infamous as him." He finally responds.

Sensing his nervousness, Calvin reassures him by saying, "We haven't had him long, but he's been a very cooperative patient though... almost ideal. The press surrounding his trial and transport was an absolute nuisance, however. Damn vultures."

Dr. Gerard laughs at the seriousness of his tone, not so much a hint of humor in it. "So, what's the story on Mr. Kitchen?" he asks Calvin once he sobers.

"Another case of insanity plea. This guy was on the fast track to being a serial killer, though. He killed four of his coworkers while working at a construction area a couple years ago. Details are in the files. He's been here almost a year now. Not our most cooperative patient but certainly not our worst either. He's very sly, Dr. Gerard, so keep a watchful eye on that one." Calvin warned him.

"Thanks for the heads up, Mr. Powers. I'll be seeing you Monday afternoon with Mr. Walter Paulus." Warren tells him before ending the conversation and disconnecting the line.

He sits at his desk, headache forgotten, trying to conjure that nagging thought lingering just out of reach. After several long minutes he stops trying and begins hoping it will conjure itself. He tries to pull his focus toward his paperwork and succeeds long enough to accomplish some of it.

3

His focus breaks with lunch approaching. Almost everyone in the asylum is in the cafeteria enjoying salads and sandwiches but Warren opts to sit at his desk in his small office. He's still kind of queasy from all the scotch and pizza from the night before. He had decided that morning he wouldn't eat anything until he returned home that evening just in case he took to vomiting.

Warren is filling out insurance papers when Ms. Lancing knocks softly on his office door. He beckons her inside and when she closes the door behind her, she locks it. Before he can say anything else, she slowly crosses the room to join him at the desk. Her hips swaying exaggeratively, the top buttons of her knee length dress undone bringing more attention to her ample bosom, her seductive eyes locked on his. He turns in his chair as she rounds the desk and stands to face her. She immediately grabs his crotch, enlarging at her touch, pulling herself tight against him. Gently massaging the engorging appendage between his legs, she runs her tongue lightly up the side of his neck to tickle his earlobe. "Fuck me" she whispers softly in his ear. His hands immediately find the button of his pants, getting them around his knees in less than three seconds, impressive. He lifts her effortlessly, surprising her, setting her gently on the edge of the desk for a better angle. Vivian Lancing is just as eager as Warren Gerard in the moment, both overwhelmed with lust. She moans with pleasure as he pushes his way into her with a grunt. It is an intense, borderline rough, satisfying affair.

Both are looking as if nothing ever happened less than half an hour later and after some light small talk, with a slight lingering awkwardness, she is ready to resume her place as the secretary. Warren stops her before she does. "Call a staff meeting at shift change today. Make sure you take plenty of notes at the meeting because I'll need a letter posted on the wall for those that are off today."

"Yes, Doctor." She replies. She had called meetings many times for him, and very rarely did she know what they were about until the meeting was held. Asking is futile.

"Thank you, Ms. Lanc..."

"Call me Viv... when it's just us, of course." She interrupts.

"Alright. Thank you, Viv. What time should I be expecting Mr. McCane?"

"At two o'clock and the meetings at five, so there is no conflict."

"Yes, of course, my wonderful secretary wouldn't allow such a mishap." He tells her teasingly. She simply smiles sweetly and walks out. Warren admiring the natural sway of her lovely curves with each step. *What a woman.*

4

Try as he might, he can't refocus his attention on his paperwork after his tryst with the lovely Vivian Lancing and before he knows it, she's knocking on his office door informing him that Ryan McCane is here. Dr. Gerard welcomes him, standing as he enters. Once the formalities are over and both men are seated, Dr. Gerard asks. "Do you know why you're here Officer McCane?"

"Yeah, I dink so sir." Ryan answers, the uncertainty evident in his tone.

"Wonderful. Can you please begin with your recollection of last night's incident with Mr. Patrickson, Officer McCane?"

Ryan shuffles his feet and clasps his hands together in silence for a moment. When he finally speaks, it's almost too low for Warren to hear him. "He had me awful scared for a bit, sir. I really thought we was gonna lose him for a minute."

"Well, thank goodness we didn't. Take your time, now, we've got all the time you need." He tells Ryan reassuringly, noticing his apparent anxious tone and fidgety manner.

The young man sits fidgeting with his fingers for a few minutes, trying to get his thoughts in order. Warren's impatience growing with every passing moment. Finally, starting with the monitors and ending with the infirmary, Ryan tells Dr. Gerard what Gregory Patrickson went through the night before. "I was gettin ready to start my rounds agin when Stacy radioed tellin me to go check on da patient in room 17. It was Greg, acourse and I fount him thrashin round on his bed, damn near fallin outta it. He wasn't hollerin and screamin like he shoulda been, he was makin some kinda whinin sound but real low, like a whispa. It was turrible, sir, just turrible. His face was all screwed up and turnin purple. I was scared for him, so I radioed the nurses. I was tryin to wake him up when da nurses came runnin in. Dey all gathered round him ready to start checkin him when he just went limp all a sudden. He quit thrashin round and makin that awful sound, but he didn't wake up. Just kept sleepin as if he hadn't just been attacked by someone or something in his nightmares. Dat's what I dink happened. Anyway, he had a couple more of dem fits fore we could finally wake him up. He was kinda outta it at first but no more dan normal. He didn't member nothin bout da nightmares and seemed kinda angry dat we woke him up. Da nurses checked him up and down and dey couldn't find nothin wrong with him. Hell, we was talkin bout lettin him go back to sleep if he wanted but den he had his first seizure. Lord, was I scared den. I ain't never seen nothin like dat fore. I just stood dere starin at da poor guy as all da nurses started movin him round and diggin round in his mouth and talkin all at once. It only lasted a few seconds, but he woke up and was just fine. I don't know how but he was. Never seen nothin like it, sir, not never. I radioed Stacy and told her to call ya at home, she tried a buncha times but could never reach ya. Dat's how it went for a while, he'd have a seizure den wake up fine, over and over. Den he had da first bad one, it was just bad cause he shook so much and it lasted so much longer dan da first ones. Da secont bad one almost kilt him, though. I didn't dink it was eva gonna be over. Dere was white foam comin outta his mouth like he was rabid or somethin and dere was a tiny trickle of blood comin outta his left ear. I had Stacy on da phone for anotha rounda calls tryin to reach ya, He finally stopped shakin and foamin and bleedin but he wouldn't wake up. We waited bout an hour fore we tried movin him from his room to da infirmary, thinkin he might have anotha seizure. But he ain't had nomore dat I knows of since da last one he didn't wake from." Ryan lets it all out, without a break or a pause. He doesn't think he missed anything; he hopes he didn't anyway.

Dr. Gerard sits silently for a few moments, mentally digesting everything Ryan has just told him. He is scanning over the notes he jotted down during Ryan's verbal account. *Foaming at the mouth is a common enough symptom of severe seizures, but the bleeding from the ear doesn't fit. All his scans show that everything is normal, so what caused the bleed? It doesn't make any sense. Maybe some follow-up questions might help shed some light on it.* "During his night terror, you said he was whispering. Was he trying to speak? Was there anything comprehensible to the sounds?" Dr. Gerard asks.

"No, sir. Not dat I could hear. It just sounded like a small animal whimperin from aways, but I knows it was him makin it." Ryan responds.

"Alright." He jots down another note while nodding his head. "You said you think he was being attacked by someone or something in his nightmares. Can you elaborate on that please Officer McCane?" Ryan stares at him, not understanding the question. "Can you explain what you mean by that statement?" Rephrasing the question, unable to keep all the exasperation out of his voice.

"Well, dat's what it certainly looked like to me. I don't know what he was dreamin bout, sir, but it sure looked like he was bein attacked or choked or somethin. Ask Stacy bout it, she prolly watched it all on the monitor." Ryan answers.

"I'll make a point to do that." Warren tells him while writing her name on his note page. "How many seizures did he have in all?"

"Five." Ryan says after counting on his fingers for a moment. "Wait... no, six." He says confidently.

"Okay. One last question, Officer McCane. Were there any other symptoms, like the foaming at the mouth or the bleeding ear, during his last seizure?"

Th young officer sits silently in thought for several moments before answering him. "I don't know if it's a synonym or whateva ya call it, but his eyes were strange. I'd never seen nothin like dat fore so I really don't know but they didn't act da same durin da last one as all da others."

"What do you mean they didn't *act* the same?" Warren presses.

"Well, da first ones his eyes were open but dey would roll upwards like he was tryin to look toward da Heavens. But on da last one dey didn't move upwards but moved back and forth really fast, like he was tryin to see everythin at da same time. I don't know if any of da nurses noticed his eyes or not." Ryan explains.

"Interesting." Dr. Warren remarks. He scribbles 'eye darting' on his notes, his head spinning with unanswered questions. He thanks Ryan McCane and wishes him a safe and enjoyable weekend, walking him to the office door.

Once Ryan leaves the receptionist's area, Dr. Gerard asks Ms. Lancing if Stacy Farris is on duty tonight. It takes less than a minute for her to find out and she informs him that Ms. Farris is scheduled to start at five today. He thanks her and walks back into his office, making a mental note to talk with Ms. Farris after the meeting.

He spends the next couple hours preparing.

Chapter Eighteen

Disregarded Connections

1

"Alright, everyone, listen up, please." Dr. Gerard says not quite loud enough to be considered a shout. He waits until the last of the whispering and murmuring ceases before continuing. "Now that I have everyone's attention, I would first like to say how grateful I am to have such a wonderful team of employees. Each and every one of you are excellent at your jobs and I thank you, sincerely, for everything you do." A few claps their hands, several others roll their eyes, and a couple yawns can be heard in the minimal crowd. "The reason I called this meeting is to inform everyone that we will have three new arrivals within the next few weeks. I know we don't get new arrivals often, so three new residents seem like a lot. They are only temporary residents, however, waiting for the relocation of an asylum in Georgia. Luckily, they will be arriving separately to allow for an adaptation phase to the new surroundings. Unluckily, the first one will be arriving on Monday." The small crowd breaks out in whispers, knowing all too well that it would be extremely difficult to get everything prepped for a new patient by Monday. Dr. Gerard waits out the soft commotion before going on. "I know what you all are getting at. It's going to be almost impossible to prepare everything for his arrival in the short amount of time allotted to us. However, I believe that it can be done. I believe in my wonderful employees and their dedication to their workplace and the broken-minded men we care for. Be that as it may, if my wonderful, dedicated employees can pull off this task of 'impossibility'..." this last said with extreme sarcasm. "...than they will find a pleasant little bonus alongside next week's paycheck... as a token of my appreciation, of course." He watches almost every set of eyes in the crowd widen at this incentive and believes that is just the push they need to ensure it all gets done. "Any questions?" He waits but no one speaks, most still with looks of shock upon their faces. "Well, you know where to find me if you do. I'll be here all weekend, and if a problem arises let me know so it can be handled quickly. We can do this." He finishes. The small crowd erupts in different conversations as they split off into small groups.

Warren searches the crowd of nurses, maintenance men, pharmacists, janitors, cooks, etc. for several seconds before finally spotting Stacy Farris in the slowly departing crowd. He quickly makes his way to her, unintentionally interrupting the conversation she is having with two other nurses. "Ms. Farris, I need to speak with you in my office, please." He tells her.

She looks at him, at the two other women standing with her, and back at him. "Okay." She says softly, an almost guilty look upon her face. The one of a small, confused child being yelled at by the teacher. She follows him out of the conference room and back to his office.

Stacy Farris is a petite, short woman just over five-foot tall. Her small frame proportions well with her narrow hips and small breasts, giving her subtle womanly curves. She wears small rectangular-shaped glasses that draw attention to her bright sky-blue eyes. Eyes one could get lost forever in. She is the most competent and confident woman he has ever known and that to him is the epitome of sexiness. She is stunning but unreachable, it would be blasphemous to even try. So, she is one of the very few nurses that are spared of his misogynistic tendencies.

Stacy doesn't know this, however, and is understandably weary of Dr. Gerard. She has heard many of the other nurses talking about the comments he makes to them and the way he puts his hands on them. He has never said or done anything like that to her, but she sure as hell isn't going to give him the chance to either. She sees Ms. Lancing sitting at her desk outside of Dr. Gerard's office and feels much better about the situation. Ms. Lancing would hear her screaming if the doctor tried anything.

Once in the office and seated, Dr. Gerard and Ms. Stacy Farris have a conversation much like his earlier one with Ryan McCane.

"Ms. Farris, can you please recount what you observed on the monitors during last night's incidents with Mr. Gregory Patrickson?" He asks her from across the desk.

"Oh..." she shifts in her seat and crosses her legs. "Well, at first, he just looked restless, tossin and turnin a bit, nothin out the ordinary. Then he flopped over on his back and started thrashin around. I radioed Ryan to check on him. Then, Greg's arms go out to the side and start jerkin, like he couldn't hardly move them or somethin. Then he starts thrashin around again. I see Ryan come in the room and a few seconds later he's radioin in for the nurses. Honestly, I couldn't see much of the actual convulsions... not that I wanted to... Ryan said it was just awful. I saw Greg sittin up awake on the bed after several attempts at trying to wake him. Then he would fall back, the nurses would swarm him, and I couldn't see anything til he was sittin back up. Those camera's ain't too good anyway, sir, so I wouldn't be able to tell you anything in detail. Ryan was there for the whole thing, you should talk to him, but I think he's out til Monday." She tells him.

"He is, but he graciously came in today to speak with me about last night's incident, at my urging, of course. He's the one that pointed me in your direction. He mentioned a few symptoms of Mr. Patrickson's convulsions that I was hoping you would be able to elaborate on." Dr. Gerard tells her.

"Honestly, sir, have you seen the feedback on those monitors? I wouldn't even know who's who in which room if it wasn't for the room numbers bein assigned and charted." She reiterates, truthfully.

Dr. Gerard sighs heavily, knowing she's right about the monitors. "Yes, I suppose you are right. I will have to look for a better monitoring system, one with recording and audio functions." He says more to himself than her. "Is there anything else you can remember about the incident last night, Ms. Farris?"

She sits thoughtfully for a few moments before answering. "No, sir, I sure can't. I'm sorry that I can't be of any more help, though. I like Mr. Patrickson, he reminds me of my crazy uncle." She tells him, reminiscently, with a high-pitched girlish giggle.

"I think we all have an uncle like that," Warrens says lightly. He walks her to the office door, thanks her kindly and tells her to call him if she thinks of anything else about last night, no matter how small or unrelated it may seem.

He returns to his desk to finish up his paperwork before heading home for the evening. He hasn't had a day off since the week before the disappearance of Joseph Doe and he isn't going to get one this weekend either. *Oh, well. Maybe next weekend?*

2

The first thing he does after kicking off his shoes, when he returns home from work, is take a couple more aspirins for the looming headache creeping around in the back of his head. Then he goes searching through the attic, the basement, and most of the closets before finally finding what he was looking for. The rosary his grandfather had given him for his seventh birthday, tucked securely into the small velvet pouch it had been gifted to him in. A wave of shame washes over him at having to have spent so much time looking for it. Before he moved into his current home, which he has been residing in for almost nine years now, he always knew where his rosary was. He credited it and his deceased grandfather to his diehard willingness to finish med-school. Every time he became overwhelmed with his studies, wanted to quit, or just thought he couldn't handle it all, he would hold his rosary in both hands and talk to his grandfather (the emptiness around him). It always helped get him through his dark thought processes and he walked away with a new-found confidence.

The shame is very quickly replaced by a flood of memories that sweeps him through a whirlwind of emotions surrounding his grandfather. *Anxiously awaiting his arrival as a young boy. Fishing off the creek banks. Catch in the backyard. Long walks in autumn evenings. The rosary. The wicked illness that threatened to rob him of all their memories. His untimely death at his own hands. The overwhelming sadness and rage that entwined itself in him afterwards.* The memories are too much for Warren, so he puts the velvet pouch in his briefcase and pushes the memories away.

After all the scotch last night, he has no plans of consuming any alcohol today, not even his usual nightcap. The memories have him undeniably shaken, though, so he relents and pours himself a shot of whiskey. As the burn hits his stomach, the warmth showers him, calming his nerves. He considers returning to the asylum so he can give the rosary to Greg tonight. After a few moments of contemplation, he slips his shoes on and grabs his car keys.

Dr. Gerard was in and out of the asylum in less than ten minutes. He simply slipped quietly into Greg's room and slid the rosary between his folded hands resting comfortably on his chest. He did not speak to Greg or to anyone else that he passed in the hallways or parking lot.

Back at the house Warren sits restlessly trying to get his jumbled thoughts into some sense of order. After several long unsuccessful minutes, he decides to do something that will numb his mind for a bit, allow him to relax before getting back into the letter. He turns on the television and begins flipping through the channels.

Well, that's enough of that. Warren thinks as he flips the television off less than an hour later. He was starting to worry that the mind numbing had hit the next level of dropping his IQ. He makes his way to his bedroom where he had left the manilla envelope lying on the dresser this morning. He had awoken to a scatter of papers and one slightly crumpled page. He reorganized them and slid them back into the envelope before leaving for work this morning.

He settles into bed, without the bottle of scotch this time, and flips through the papers before finding the last place he could remember reading.

The movie un-pauses.

3

Sarah's final stop before returning Jiminey's cart was the butcher's shop where the final event took place that allowed the inevitable domino effect. The meeting of Sarah Maisse and Johnathan Colmes. Even a skeptic could not have denied the instantaneous connection that developed between the two of them. It was literally love at first sight but neither one of them dared admit such a thing. Johnathan was with the good witch and Sarah had been seeing Frank McGrath. The whole valley knew of both relationships.

The moment their eyes met, the spell bound young man standing behind the counter in the butcher's shop, was no longer spellbound to the Witch. He felt something break within him, but it was a relieving, freeing sensation that he became temporarily high on. He gazed into the gorgeous green eyes of the woman standing in the door pulling in a hand cart filled with the large chunks of meat. He rushed over to help her with the cart.

The Good Witch, tending to some of the herbs in her garden, felt the spell break at the very moment Johnathan did. While his was euphoric, hers was dismal and pain filled. She had no idea what happened or why. All she could feel was heartache and betrayal, her sixth sense in overdrive. She rushed into the cave, hurriedly checked several glass bottles with corks for lids before finding the one she wanted. She reached inside and gently pulled out a few dried petal leaves, almost crumbling with aridity. She placed them carefully on her tongue, snapped her jaws shut and sucked at them greedily, the calming effects of the Chamomile evident in her loosening muscles. When she could think clearly again without the overwhelming wave of unprovoked emotions, she decided to wait and see how Johnathan acted when he arrived later that evening.

Sarah left all the moose meat, sans what she owed the men and was keeping for herself, with Johnathan at the butcher's shop. In return, she got the same deal as everyone else, except she could come in daily. They were both overly polite, almost awkward with each other, during their ten-minute business exchange. Both departed feeling somewhat relieved that the encounter was over and both secretly hoping for another, less awkward, one.

Sarah made her way around the valley, looking for and eventually finding, the homes of Roy and Ben, to deliver their cut of the moose she had promised them. She took what she kept for herself to the valley cooks, the only two that hadn't left for New York, Samantha and Brenda. The cooks could and would cure, salt, smoke, stew, cut, slice, dice, etc. whatever you wanted, however you wanted. Next to the butcher and the hunters, they were the most skilled in the valley when it came to using a knife. Sarah had a few days' worth of the meat stewed and left the rest with the cooks to be cured and salted. She paid the cooks with two of the gold pieces she had attained, took her stewed moose, and left to return the hand cart to Jiminey McAvay. She returned to her little shack in the Slums long enough to freshen up before meeting Frank at the bridge over the eastern branch of the river. She spent the evening at the side and in the arms of Frank McGrath, but John the Butcher kept creeping into the back of her mind.

4

Johnathan Colmes slowly ambled his way toward the Witch's shack, lost in thought. Thoughts that for some reason kept circling back to Sarah Maisse. He had never met her before today and was relieved when she finally left the shop, so why did she keep popping up in his head? He chalked it up to innocent curiosity because she was still the 'new girl in town', and left it at that... well, he tried anyway.

When he knocked on the door to the Good Witch's shack, she didn't greet him there like she usually did, and he found this a bit odd. He heard her beckon him in from the other side of the door, so he just walked in. The first room of the two-room shack was unlit but the dim, dusk light seeping in through the windows was enough for him to navigate safely through a combination main room and kitchen. The second room was the bedroom, where he found his beautiful lover sprawled upon a mess of animal hides, wrapped only in a robe made of the sheerest cloth he had ever seen. He could see everything she had to offer, and he briefly wondered what the use for such clothing was. For a single there-and-then-gone-again moment, Johanthan visualized Sarah laying on the bed instead of the Witch. It was such a quick glimpse that he questioned really seeing it the second it ended. Pushing thoughts of Sarah away, again, he quickly became mesmerized by the Witch's beauty. Everything about her was flawless and perfect.

Neither spoke as he approached her. He slowly discarded his clothing, piece by piece taking in every inch of her. Her slender, perfectly pedicured toes were curled tightly, the muscles in her legs taut from her thighs down into her feet, stretching her flawless, perfectly complexioned skin, tight against the curves of her long, smooth legs. She had the perfect hourglass-shaped body, that was perfectly proportioned to her meager five-foot-seven height. Her broad hips, flat stomach, and voluptuous breasts were as enticing as her eyes that were locked on his. He could see the waves of ecstasy ripple through her body at the intensity of her orgasm. Perfectly timed to meet his eyes as he walked in.

John yearned for her, feeling that familiar stirring and twitch in his loins. He crawled onto the bed as her explosive orgasm ended, their eye contact unbroken, and he softly kissed her lips. There were spots of perspiration on her nose, and she was lightly panting, but she returned the kiss. They laid on the bed, side by side, for a long time, kissing and fondling each other. Intent on exploring every inch of each other. They were both slow and meticulous about it, ensuring the utmost pleasure.

By the time the real foreplay started, John was visualizing Sarah more than he was seeing the beauty before him. He fought it until he realized how ineffectual it was and stopped trying to stop it. When they finally finished, both climaxing together in a momentary euphoric bliss, he was almost completely convinced that he was with Sarah and not the Good Witch. Shame and a sense of betrayal crept into him and for the first time since he started seeing the lovely Witch, he wanted to leave her bed and return to his own.

Chapter Nineteen

Rain's Acomin'

1

Two days passed in the quiet, mostly deserted valley uneventfully. Everyone that remained in the valley got up each morning and went about their work as if much of the valley wasn't currently in New York for the week. The hunter's hunted, the seamstress's sewed, the cook's cooked, and the fishermen fished. The butcher butchered, the woodworker's built, the miner's mined, and the gatherer's gathered. The O'Reigan's and their farmhand's prepared for the coming harvest, Jiminey McAvay tended his fruitful marijuana crop, and Robert Daniel's distilled his Shine. The Good Witch worked her magic, the merchant sold, the priest and his trio of nuns prayed, and the bartender served. Life was pleasant and beautiful in the valley during those two days as autumn approached gracefully, without malice.

Johnathan still spent the evenings with the lovely Witch and Sarah seen Frank on both nights, the weather perfect for evening strolls. He had made several moves at her to no avail. They kissed, held hands, and occasionally made out like young teenagers; but the moment he tried to cop a feel she stopped the whole bit. She refused to give him a reason, stating that she didn't need one and if he couldn't respect that then they shouldn't be seeing each other. He respected her decision to wait but he couldn't help himself around her sometimes. He returned home almost every night with an uncomfortable bout of what you would call 'blue balls'. She was proving to be more of a challenge than he anticipated her to be.

The third day after the train exited the valley through the eastern tunnel with most of the valley folks, the massive southern storm blew in. It mingled sweetly, almost lovingly, with the northern cold front, creating a historically devasting storm that unleashed the extent of its wrath on the valley.

Those remaining in the valley woke that morning to the warmth of the sun trickling in through the quaint windows of the shacks and teepee-like structures. All except for the small handful of elderly, folks went about their day dressed for the late summer/early fall weather they had grown accustomed to. The elderly in the valley, equaling less than half a dozen, could feel the needle-sharp claws of winter scratching at the innermost sanctions of their joints and bones; but not one of the five expected winter to hit so suddenly or violently.

That morning began as the previous two had, with most in the valley heading out to start their day's work. Johnathan Colmes opened his butcher shop while the Good Witch prepared to address and utilize her five devout followers. They thought her almost God-like and were undoubtedly as loyal to her as her faithful, rescued half-albino bird. Sarah Maisse met up with Roy Hoarding and Ben Fariday at one of the hunting lodges, gathered their weapons, then headed in their own directions out into the timbered mountainside. Mr. O'Reigan, his eldest son, his eldest daughter's husband and his three farmhands: Alvin Danson, Danny Bailey, and Betty Jones, were gathered around the pecking chickens discussing what work needed to be accomplished that day.

The six remaining miners met up at the coal and salt flats, paired up and parted ways. One pair headed out to the salt mines located on Mining Road 1, starting at the northwesternmost corner of the valley, winding its way a little less than two miles into the timberlands. Another pair headed for one of the several coal mines surrounding the valley, on Mining Road 3, starting almost directly north of the schoolhouse. This one about a quarter mile farther up the mountain than the road to the salt mines but not as hard on the mules hauling the loads. The third and last pair also went out to a coal mine on Mining Road 7, this one starting on the eastern side of the valley, directly to the east of Frank McGrath's home. It was less than a mile to this mine, but it was rough enough to become impassable much faster and for much longer than any of the other roads. They all assumed that the previous days of good weather would hold out for another one, allowing them a fairly good load from the not-quite-used-up mine before the day's end.

Ms. Rebekka Lane opened her shop and waited for her fellow seamstress Ms. Carol Jewell, and her two hide-makers David Bailey and Earl Redley. Harvest season marked the beginning of the seamstresses work on winter wear. They put a lot of time and attention into the shirts, trousers, jackets, coats, socks, undergarments, mittens, scarves, camo-wear, and everything else they pieced together for apparel. Hardly anyone in the valley could complain about the quality of the clothes Ms. Rebekka made and when there was, she addressed and rectified it quickly. The two remaining woodworkers, Ron Hellman and Porter Siddle, were preparing their tools to begin their work. The four remaining fishermen met up at the western pier, spoke of the day's work, then promptly set out to it. The gatherers: Abigail Fariday, Sue Ann Bailey, and Catherine Weston, met at the train station, spoke of their mornings briefly, then headed south, destination: the forest beyond the tracks.

Gary Brown, the owner, and merchant of the only mercantile in the valley, kissed his wife on the cheek before heading out into the morning sun, going over his mental to-do list for the day. The priest, Father Robin, who as it turned out wasn't very priestly, held a small mass among his trio of nuns: Sister Grace, Sister Virtue, and Sister Harmony. The cooks, Brenda Daniels and Samantha Lane, were preparing their large kitchen-like room to start cooking whatever meats they were brought or had waiting in the damp, borderline-icy coolness of the kitchen cellar. Frank McGrath and Dansford Keeton were beginning their rounds to check up on the elderly, tending to any chores or errands they might need.

Jiminey and Patty McAvay sat at their small wooden table in their little shack of a home, passing a well-crafted, polished, wooden pipe packed with the smoldering odorous herb he was known for, between them as was part of their normal morning routine. Robert Daniels was waiting for Sledge, the broad and strong young man that helped him run the Shine distillery. The bartenders, twins Nonna and Nonni Brookes, were resting peacefully in their rooms at the back of the bar. Being that most of their customers can't make their way to the bar until well after noon, the bar is only open from 5 p.m. to 3 a.m., plus an additional hour or more for clean-up. Old Joe Brenner and his escorts followed the same schedule as the bar plus an hour more, so they too were all deep in sleep resting for the coming night's work.

The morning went as it should for all, apart from the increasingly more painful bouts of arthritic flare-ups in the elderly. The clouds began to gather overhead minutes after noon. The valley folks and those working in the timbers around it, were blissfully unaware that their countdown to fatality was already ticking.

2

Very few of the folks in the valley noticed the gathering clouds grow darker and darker with each passing minute. Those out in the timbers, the sky shielded by the thick canopy of trees overhead, weren't aware of the gathering clouds at all until the first rumbles of thunder were heard echoing around the valley. Of all the miners, already deep in the mines by noon, only one of the six knew of the storm moving in. He just happened to be close enough to the mine's opening to hear the thunder. Thinking little of a passing autumn storm, he casually mentioned it to his partner who brushed it off as casually as the first. The hunters, knowing the storm would drive their prey into their dens and holes, began heading back toward the valley after hearing the first bit of thunder. They could always return to the hunt when the storm had passed. The fishermen had similar feelings to those of the hunters, but with a shared fear of being hit by lightning while out on the water. So, the four of them gathered their things and headed for the piers. The three gatherers, collectively, decided to keep at their work. It wouldn't be the first time they had been caught out in a storm.

Mr. O'Reigan kept one eye on his bunch of workers and the other on the eerily darkening clouds that had begun appearing several minutes earlier. He could feel the icy chill in the wind that was beginning to stir around the valley and hear the low, deep, gravelly rumble of thunder. He decided to just keep an eye on the ominous clouds, trying to get as much work in as possible before harvest started next week.

John had stepped out the back door of the butcher's shop to toss an armful of meatless bones into the wooden barrel out back that he collected for the dogs. He noticed the lack of warmth on his skin the moment he stepped outside, and his attention was immediately drawn to the layered, dark upon darker clouds that plastered the valley's horizon in every direction. The sun, not even a glimpse of it, was nowhere to be seen and John picked up on the same icy chill in the wind that Mr. O'Reigan had.

Dansford Keeton was several houses down from Frank helping Old Man McAvay walk back to his little teepee-shaped home in the Slums. He watched the sky thicken and darken above them, awaiting the first few drops of rain, and hoping that he would be able to get Old Man McAvay back inside before the downpour began. He did, but just barely.

The Witch and her followers were too heavily involved in their ritual to notice the ominous clouds or the thunder.

The first pitter-patters of falling rain could be heard as the first of the three hunters, Roy Hoarding, emerged from the western mountainside. He had just stepped into the closest hunting lodge when the downpour came, noting how cold the rain felt. Sarah was out on the eastern side minutes later, soaked to the skin and shivering, utterly relieved when she entered the dry warmth of the hunting lodge. Ben Fariday was last to return to the valley and, much like Sarah, was soaking wet and half froze. The fishermen had all made it back to the piers before the rain even began, a pair in each, waiting out the storm. Another collective decision of the gatherers was to head back to the valley when the downpour started and showed no signs of relenting. By the time they made it back to the train station, they all three were cold, wet, and miserable; regretting their decision not to leave at the first sign of thunder.

The pair of miners in the salt mine on Mining Road 1 and the miners in the coal mine on Mining Road 3 had no idea what the weather was like outside. They just kept swinging their pickaxes and working their shovels, determined to fill the carts. The pair of miners on Mining Road 7, however, weren't afforded the same luxury. That road was short but rough and escalated steeply uphill for most of the way. The incline finally topped off at the ridge, then immediately began slanting downward where the mine set several hundred feet away at a downward diagonal direction. The downpour lasted for more than 40 minutes, saturating the ground quickly and causing the excess ground water to accumulate and rush downhill toward the river. In their case, it rushed right into the mine, trying to fill it with water slowly but steadily. The two of them headed for the entrance to the mine but couldn't even make it close enough to hear the thunder that now roared in the sky or the heavy pattering of the rain. The rushing water was like trying to wade through a river rapid; they both knew it would be a futile attempt that would more than likely get them hurt, or worse. They prayed that the storm would cease before the mine filled up.

3

The torrential downpour relaxed to a steady drumming rain, finally abating, but the roaring thunder, dazzling lightning, and gusty winds did not. A partially rusted thermometer smacked against the wooden post it was nailed to in the almost constant breeze, the mercury level resting on the 78-degree mark. It was almost half past one in the afternoon. Everyone remained sheltered in place, waiting for the storm to pass so they could go about the rest of their day.

An hour later the mercury was resting at 63-degrees and the rain was still steady and relentless. Those in the valley were slowly becoming impatient with the rain, knowing it was useless but feeling it, nonetheless. None of them had noticed the temperature drop or thought anything of the six miners still up in the timbers. The four men on Mining Roads 1 and 3 were now aware of the storm but continued with their work in the dry, coolness of the Earth. The pair on Mining Road 7 weren't fairing as well as their workmates, though. The rushing rainwater flowing into the mine eroded away at the walls causing a cave in several dozen yards deeper into the mine than the men were. The densely packed debris allowed very little water to trickle through causing the water level in the cave to rise from ankle deep to chest high in less than ten minutes. Panic was quickly closing in on the two men and as they floated in the chilly water, they prayed to every God, Angel, and Saint that they could think of for the rain to stop. It did...eventually.

Another hour passed and the mercury then read 48-degrees. The valley folks were very much aware of the drop in temperature now, noting that the rain was slowly turning to ice. No one in the valley was dressed or prepared for winter, they usually had several more weeks before anything more than a snow squall came through, and even those had never come that early in the year. Some watched the transformation with dismay, feeling the icy claws of winter wrapping around their soul. They were filled with a sense of dread, like impending doom, but most just ignored it. Others watched with curiosity, wondering what happened to cause such an enormous shift in the temperature; while some looked on confidently knowing that it would be over in time for them to be home by sundown.

Around four o'clock the temperature had dropped enough so all the fallen rainwater and everything drenched in it was beginning to freeze. The constant rain was now a steady drum of ice falling across the mountains, aiding the falling temperatures in freezing the lands below.

The mercury was just dipping below the 33-degree mark on the battered thermometer about 30 minutes later. The temperature had been dropping 15-degrees an hour for the last four hours and the now freezing folks in the valley were hoping it wouldn't get any colder. Then the snow started, blending with the falling ice, eventually taking it all over. It continued to fall steadily with no waver in intensity.

The temperature finally stabilized about half past six in the evening at three degrees Fahrenheit, the wind chill making it feel like seven-below, though. The snow, dropping an average of about half a foot an hour, fell for sixteen hours straight before finally tapering off and ending. Almost eight feet of snow that thickly covered a couple inches of ice was dumped on the valley during that 20-hour timespan. The folks in the valley... those that survived the storm... wouldn't be able to emerge from their shelters for many more days.

Chapter Twenty

Snow Drifts

1

When the snow enveloped the sleet, most folks not sheltered in their homes ventured out of their shops and shelters to make their way there. Abigail, Catherine, and Sue Ann decided to make their own way home when the snow started. Abigail and Sue Ann lived by the Lot but on separate ends of it and Catherine had her own little teepee in the Slums. Abigail's shack, that she shared with her husband Ben, sat an empty shack away from being right up against the mountain. Its stone base was weatherworn, and moss covered in places, the walls, floors, and roof a single earthy brownish gray color courtesy of the timber cut and used to build all the homes and buildings in the valley. The three of them walked together to Abigail's, Catherine and Sue Ann intending to move on once she was in the warmth of her home. By the time they made it to Abigail's, all three of the women were shivering uncontrollably, teeth chittering, and ice crystals forming on their damp clothes and hair. Rushing into Abigail's they dropped their baskets, snatched up animal hide blankets to wrap themselves up in, and began working on building a fire praying their shaking hands would allow it.

All the elderly were safe in their homes. Dansford, still with Old Man McAvay, had built him a toasty little fire when the old man kept going on about his bad joints. When the snow started Dan told the old man that he needed to go check on the others and that he would be back to check on him again soon. Dan headed out into the icy wind in search of Frank McGrath. He found him with the elderly couple, Mr. and Mrs. Jones. Frank had also built them a toasty little fire and made them some sassafras tea before leaving them to check on Old Man Daniels and Old Miss Jewell. After their fires had been built and they too were temporarily settled, Dansford and Frank headed toward the Lot to check on the hunting dogs.

The massive lot was surrounded by a five-foot-tall wooden fence meant to keep the couple dozen hunting dogs in. There were two entrances into the lot and the feeding stations were set up by the gates. The dogs' kennels were cleaned regularly but they hadn't been winterized for the year yet, so the animals had no solace from the rapidly declining temperature. Frank entered the lot first, Dan right behind him, bracing for the stampede of barking, yapping excited hounds, they expected to come barreling at them at the sound of the gate latch. None came, though, worry instantly washing over both men.

After a few minutes of searching the massive lot, Dan called Frank over to where he was standing, showing him the place in the ground at the fence edge where the dogs had dug their way out. There were already a couple inches of snow coating the ground, so any signs of the hounds would be gone within minutes if not already. The two men, shivering in the thin coats they wore, headed back to Frank's house for warmth, clothes, and food before going back to check on the elderly again.

The Good Witch and her followers had completed their ritual and were no longer oblivious to the strange weather occurring before them. The five followers: Rachel Smith, Beth Redley, Leena McAvay, May Frederickson, and Anna Weston headed back to their teepees just outside the garden walls when the snow began. They all made it to their respective places and immediately wrapped themselves in layers. The Witch stood in the doorway of her shack debating whether she should try to find Johnathan. She knew he would either be at the shop or in his home and she would have to pass his house to get to the shop anyway. Ultimately, she decided to stay where she was, though, knowing she could make him come to her instead. So, she drew her mind inward, closed her alluring eyes and mumbled a power amplifying chant that made a signal of sorts emit from her that only Johnathan would be drawn by. Then she waited.

Since the spell broke three days ago, Johnathan Colmes had thought about the lovely Witch less and less. His thoughts of her and her alone were slowly being replaced with thoughts of Sarah Maisse, whom he had not seen since their first and only awkward meeting at the shop. When the snow began though, his thoughts were not of Sarah but of his lover. He was almost overwhelmed by the need to go to her, to find her, to protect her. He had only a light jacket with him and decided to leave his apron on as an added layer of clothing, even if it only covered his chest to his knees. He left the shop, doubting he would see anyone in there today, but still battling guilt and regret for it, nonetheless. It was a worrying relief when he seen Ms. Rebekka Lane and Ms. Carol Jewell walking out of the seamstress's shop, the hide-makers: David Bailey and Earl Redley right behind them.

John trudged through the slush and snow, trying to will himself to stop shivering through the icy wind, knowing it was going to take him much longer than normal to get to the Witch's shack. He would have to stop at his place first to warm-up and layer-up before getting back out in the snow. He had already made it past the Infirmary and the Apothecary but still couldn't see the bar through the thick falling snow. The constant breeze kept the snow falling at an angle, the gusts swirling the snow in small tornado-like funnels. There were already snow drifts beginning to form around the buildings and residences. John was exhausted and freezing but he refused to stop and rest before getting to his own place. The need to get to his lover kept the determination from eroding. He could see the bar, a promising sign he was still going in the right direction. He knew once he passed Hussey Row, on the other side of the bar, that he only had to count the shacks before he arrived at his own.

2

Sarah had not gotten any kills that day, so she left all the hunting gear at the lodge and trudged out into the freezing cold snow to make her way home. She quickly realized that would be no easy task with the lack of visibility and slippery underfoot. She had to get home, though. She couldn't stay in the lodge; she would freeze to death in her still damp clothing. Sarah slowly made her way past the empty Orphanage and then the empty Schoolhouse. She shook constantly from the cold and decided to stop at the bar long enough to warm up enough to get home.

She had only been in the bar for about ten minutes when she decided to try for home again, so she thanked Nonna and Nonni Brookes, the twin bartenders, and walked out of the bar. Dark had fallen on the valley quickly, Sarah noticed when she walked out, lessening the visibility that much more. It was still bright enough for her to see the man walking past the bar, though, shivering in the chill of the wind and the swirling snow. She took off toward the man but couldn't see who it was until she was within talking distance of him. He knew she was there, and he had watched her approach him. A part of her regretted that approach the moment she realized who it was, but the other part of her tingled with anxious excitement. Her feelings toward this man she barely knew were an enigma. "It's plenty warm in the bar, John, you should go in and warm up. You look awfully cold." She shouted so she could be heard over the constant wind. He wouldn't speak, just shook his head. "Your choice." she told him with a shrug. They walked side by side through the thickening snow in silence.

John had seen someone step out of the bar as he walked by it but didn't pay much mind to them until he noticed that they were approaching him. He watched them out of curiosity, first realizing it was a woman and then quickly realizing it was Sarah. Sarah Maisse. The moment he knew it was her, the pull of his lover lost most of its potency and he no longer felt that overwhelming need to go to her. Those feelings were replaced with the flitty butterflies-in-the-stomach feeling that mingled with an irrational reluctance to be around her. His feelings toward this woman he barely knew were puzzling him. She told him about the bar, but he only shook his head in reply because he didn't trust his voice at her sudden appearance. His thoughts kept trying to drift back to that night with the Witch the day he met Sarah and shame began to threaten him. When they got to Hussey Row John turned and walked toward the other one room shacks, eight of them lined up in a row facing the east and only a short walk from the bar. He made it to the fifth house in the row, turned again, and walked straight into the Slums from there.

Sarah followed along beside him, violently shaking again, even though she should have turned at the second one-room shack. She didn't know how long John had been out there before she had run into him, but she was worried about him and wanted to see for herself that he got home. She hoped that he, or anyone else in the valley, would do the same for her. They would have, she was confident of that. She kept pace beside him, noting he had slowed down some and his strides were becoming shorter and heavier. The weariness of the cold and trek was apparent in the blistered red patches on his nose and cheeks, the inevitable numbness in his fingers and toes, the restricted movements of his exhausted body. She watched as he stumbled, landed on one knee, but kept himself from falling face first in the snow. Sarah helped him to his feet and then had him lean against her so she could guide him home. He was too weak to make it on his own and he knew it. "What number you on and what number you goin to?" she asked him, panting from the added weight, as they walked. She knew he was counting the shacks to make his way home because she was going to do the same thing to get back to her place.

Clearly exhausted, he leaned his head toward her ear and with considerable effort gave her the information she needed in short, choppy sentence fragments. "The one... comin up... is number three... and I'm... goin to... number seven." He breathed in her ear just loud enough for her to make out his words over the gusting wind. He was completely exhausted; it threatened to steal him away into its foggy darkness. He knew he couldn't submit to it, he had to stay awake, to stay conscious, so he could get home, out of this weather. He would put on layers and layers of warm winter clothes, then head back out to get to his lover.

It took Sarah almost half an hour to get John past the remaining four shacks and into his own. She knew that he was just on the brink of unconsciousness, so she took him straight into the bedroom and carefully lowered him down on to the bed. He fell back against the animal hides, no longer shivering from the cold. Contradictory, he was coming down with the 'wet shivers' (hypothermia). Sarah knew that was a bad sign so she quickly built a fire, willing her hands to stop trembling so she could. Once it was blazing, she stripped John of his half-damp, half-frozen clothing, noting how well-endowed he was, even in the cold, with surprise, and swaddled him in the animal hides that lay across his bed. She watched him sleep for several long moments, watching his ragged breathing start to regulate as the warmth and strength slowly encompassed his body. He was deathly pale, ice crystals clinging to his thick eyebrows, the tips of his short-kept dark hair, and lacing through the stubble of his beard. There were large dark patches under his eyes and his lips were dry and cracked. Aside from that he looked like he was sleeping peacefully. Sarah shed her clothes, hung them by the stove to dry and wrapped herself in one of the extra blankets she found in a large wooden chest in the living room/kitchen. She put water on to boil, sat by the fire and waited.

Ms. Rebekka Lane decided they should all try to head home since the rain and ice finally started to taper off. They wrapped up in what few winter items they had left over from last year, which was considerably more clothing than everyone else in the valley was wearing trying to get home. Rebekka walked out with Carol Jewell at her side and the two hide-makers behind her. Rebekka lived alone in the Slums, her younger sister Samantha Lane, in the shack right beside her. Carol Jewell lived with her mother, Old Miss Jewell to the valley folks, over by the Lot. The women parted ways, and both made it to their respective homes.

Rebekka sat by her small fire, facing the window, waiting for her sister's return.

Carol, grateful for the warmth inside her home, added more wood to the now dying flames, and tended to her forgetful mother (dementia).

The hide-makers David Bailey and Earl Redley, headed in the same direction as Carol because they too lived by the Lot. A mere five shacks away from each other and they usually met up to walk to work together every morning. They both made it home safely, but David was worried the moment he realized that his wife Sue Ann, hadn't made it home yet. He sat amid the warmth of the fire and waited for her. Earl Redley lived alone in one of the places over by the river. His concern was being able to stay warm with no wood or coal to burn. He made his plans to go and retrieve some as he warmed himself beneath his thick black bear hide blanket.

Mr. O'Reigan rushed his family and farmhands into the barn when the rain started. He knew none of them would get much work done if they took ill from being caught out in the rain. When the temperature began to drop and the rain turned to ice, and then to snow, Mr. O'Reigan became that much more nervous about the weather. He sent Alvin Danson, Danny Bailey and Betty Jones, his farmhands, back to their one-room shacks by the river, informing them the pre-harvest work would have to be postponed until the weather cleared. He just hoped that the cold wouldn't kill out all his crops before he had a chance to harvest them. The whole valley could very nearly starve if that were to happen. Mrs. O'Reigan felt much better when she seen her husband walk through the door and immediately inquired about their boy, their son-in-law, and their hired workers. He assured her that he sent them to their own places when he left to join her, as he sat down by the fire to warm his aching, aging joints.

The farmhands returned to their shacks across the farm at the river's edge. Alvin Danson, who had found love in Anna Weston, worried for her safety, knowing she lived in one of the tent-like teepees outside of the Witch's place. For the life of him, he couldn't understand his love's borderline obsession with the magical woman. Danny Bailey, the younger brother of David Bailey, waited about ten minutes inside his little shack to ensure that Mr. O'Reigan was back in his own place. Once he was certain, he cracked open the front door, peered out into the falling snow and soon realized that he couldn't even see the barn through the thick, large snowflakes drifting steadily from the clouded sky above. He stepped out into the icy wind, securely closing the door behind him and quickly made his way over to the next little shack where Betty Jones resided. She welcomed him eagerly with a long, sensuous kiss.

The eldest O'Reigan boy wandered into his childless home, reluctantly kissed his wife on the cheek, and went to sit by the fire. She returned his display of love with a nasty scowl and a breathless insult.

The O'Reigan's son-in-law, married to the eldest O'Reigan daughter, was named Joshua Jones. He was Betty Jones older brother and the only one in the valley, besides the two of them, that knew of Danny and Betty's relationship. Joshua stepped into his home and into the welcoming, loving arms of his beautiful wife. He hugged her tightly, released her, then knelt, and kissed the navel of her swollen belly. Their first child, carrying like a son would at almost seven months along, was already his pride and joy.

The miners in the salt mine and those in the coal mines on Mining Road 3, were throwing their last few shovelfuls into the carts around the time everyone else was trying to get home in the snow. The closer the two pairs got to the opening of the mines, the quicker they realized what they had missed during their long hours of work. Both pairs, not knowing what the other pair was doing, mimicked each other's actions without ever being aware of it. Both decided to abandon the carts and walk back into the mine far enough not to shiver in the cold to discuss their next moves. Both talked it over, weighing the option of staying in the mine with essentially no food or supplies against the option of trying to make it back to the valley in the freezing wind and falling snow before they froze to death. The second option would have been a sure bet if there was any way for them to warm up between the mines and the valley, but there was none.

The pair in the coal mine took a little longer to make their final decision because they were farther from the valley than the other two pairs in the mines were. Ultimately, the two set of men came to different decisions. The pair in the salt mine decided to try to make it back to the valley. They untied the two mules from the carts, content with abandoning their hard day's work, and set the mules to fend for themselves knowing animals had better instincts than they did. With that done, they stepped out into the winter wonderland, a couple of inches of snow over quickly freezing ice, crunching under their boots.

The pair in the coal mine decided to stay in the cave and wait until the snow stopped before trying to leave. They, too, untied the mules from the carts and led them deeper into the cave where it was considerably warmer. The torches lined along the walls, allowed the men to have adequate lighting and extra warmth in the damp, dark mine. Waiting out the storm in the mine would be agonizingly boring but waiting it out in the dark would be absolutely terrifying.

The two men in the flooded coal mine on Mining Road 7, were neck-deep in cold water. Standing on the tips of their boots they sucked at the air, knowing that their heads would soon be bobbing against the ceiling of the mine. They both were trying desperately not to panic when one noticed that the water had stopped rising and the roar of the rushing water wasn't as loud. He hushed his partner and they both listened with rising hope as they heard the rushing water lessen and lessen. The water level wasn't lowering but they could no longer hear the water moving so they slowly made their way toward the mouth of the mine. The below-freezing temperature immediately sent gooseflesh rolling across their air-exposed bodies. The water, as cold as it was, was considerably warmer than the air. The men were shivering violently, almost seizure-like, by the time they stepped foot out of the mine. Slowly, step by step they headed for the valley.

Mr. Ron Hellman and his mentor, Mr. Porter Siddle, worked through the storm and rain under their sheltered shop. Porter whittled while Ron polished, both content with their tasks until the cold became too much for Porter's aging joints. They had everything cleaned and put in their proper places by the time the snow was falling. Since they both lived in the Slums, Ron in a teepee by the river and Porter in a shack by Jiminey's place, they decided to trudge through the icy shit together.

The Woodshop sat closest to the flats where mounds of coal, salt and timber were kept and all in the valley could take what they needed when they needed it. There was more than enough for everyone as long as no one became greedy, and rarely anyone did.

They first passed the Church, then the currently empty Orphanage and Schoolhouse, all on the north side of the common area. It was a quick and easy decision to step into the Bar and warm up with a nip of Shine before heading back out. Once warm and on their way again, Ron told Porter that his little teepee would make for a poor shelter in the snow, and he was worried that it may collapse. Naturally, Porter told Ron to come stay with him until it was over, which probably wouldn't be long. They found their way to Porter's place by counting their way there and immediately built a fire to warm themselves.

The four fishermen were sheltered in the pier shacks, two to each one, where they brought and gutted their fish before taking it to the butcher. They were both foul-smelling, cramped places that reeked of rotten fish and mold, but the fishermen had grown accustomed to the smell and hardly noticed it. Unknown to each other, the two pair of men decided to wait a while longer for the snow to stop before heading home. They occupied their time with trivial games and the Shine they kept stashed under the counter.

Gary Brown, the merchant, shut up his shop minutes after Johnathan did and safely made it home to his concerned wife.

In the Church, Father Robin insisted that the Sisters keep the door locked, refusing to allow anyone into the warmth of the Church. They were reluctant at first, but obeyed, nonetheless. He led them into the altar room, where the masses and sermons were held and sat the Sisters in the front row. He began an hours-long 'sermon' insisting that one or all of them had sinned and this was God's punishment; that the entire valley was being punished for the sins of one. He demanded to know who it was that angered God and what they had done to do so. The longer the snow fell, the louder and more upset he became. By the time he had tired from his rantings, the Sisters were in tears, sobbing and begging for his and God's forgiveness.

Jiminey McAvay and his wife Patty laid nestled and panting under the animal hide blankets on their bed. Afternoon sex after a chubby hemp blunt was addicting and a very pleasant part of their daily routine.

As Jiminey and Patty fondled each other in the warmth of their bed, Robert Daniels was trying to talk Sledge out of going back to stay in that teepee he lived in. Sledge was adamant though but told Robert he would come back if he didn't think his place would hold up in the snow. The homes, like the dog kennels, hadn't been winterized yet. Robert watched from the window, surrounded by the warmth of his living room, as the young man stalked his way through the thickening snow in the direction of the bar and Hussey Row.

Brenda Daniels, Robert Daniels baby sister, and Samantha Lane, Rebekka Lane's little sister, had both put in a full day's work in at the kitchen. The thunder, during the storm, had blended into the cacophony of sounds amid the running kitchen and the dropping temperatures and frigid wind were no match for the warmth of it. The women, exhausted from their hard work, stepped out into the falling snow which surprised them both. With a quick knowing glance from the other, the women stepped back into the kitchen content with staying in its lingering warmth while, what they assumed was an early snow squall, passed them.

The bartenders, Nonna and Nonni Brookes, had awoken around half past three that afternoon, as was their usual routine. Nonni stepped into the connected outhouse to relieve herself and immediately noticed that it was cooler than it had been when they had gone to bed that morning. Finding that very curious, she mentioned it to her sister who was already standing at the window, watching in disbelief as the rain started to turn to ice in the freezing cold wind. The twins quickly dressed, set a fire to warm the chilled Bar up, and reluctantly set out toward the river to fetch several buckets of water. They hoped between the water they carted back in the freezing rain and the two rain barrels that had been topped off by the recent downpour, that they would have enough to keep up with the slew of tea and stew they were going to have to keep on hand. The first few patrons had already walked through the doors several minutes before opening time to warm up; the water for the tea and stew had yet to begin to boil.

Old Joe Brenner had awoken shortly after the twins had and watched, with astonishment, as the two identical lovely ladies trudged back and forth through the cold, wet freezing mud packing buckets of water. He had already built a fire and was plenty warm in his little shack, but the Gals shacks hadn't been winterized yet, so they were probably freezing their half-naked asses off. He knew he couldn't leave them out there like that. He, personally, didn't give a tick's shit about those disease-riddled ugly broads out there, but it would be a real bad financial choice to let them get sick. They couldn't work if they were hacking and coughing all over their customers. He was a businessman. and the women were his selling product. Reluctantly and mumbling curses all the while, Joe dressed in layers, shoved his cold feet into thick wool socks and then his boots, and headed toward the shacks. He stopped at the second of the eight shacks, knocked until he heard a voice on the other side of the door, Lacy, and informed her to be dressed as well as possible and ready to leave when he came back. He repeated the same information to Sugar at the third shack then continued down to the fifth shack where Kat resided. He knocked, told her to get ready and that she only had a matter of minutes, and waited outside in the sleet and wind gusts that cut like ice. She came out, wrapped in an animal hide blanket that served well against the wind, and they set off to get the other two. Once Lacy and Sugar had joined them, Joe told the girls, loudly to be heard over the wind, that they were going to the Bar to wait this out. He had all the provisions at his place, but it wasn't nearly big enough for four of them, so the Bar was their only option. They walked into the Bar, the warmth of the place wrapped them in a tender embrace, minutes before opening, and waited as the water boiled for some nice warm tea. Joe had already spoken with Nonna and Nonni about the four of them staying in the Bar to wait out the weather. They agreed on the condition that Joe opened a tab for the duration of their stay that would be settled whenever they returned home.

4

Few tried to leave once they were sheltered again. Sarah Maisse tried a couple hours after she had gotten John into bed, finally content with his returning color and evened breathing. She went to open the door, but it wouldn't budge. Shoving a little harder, she heard a muffled cracking sound, like glass being broken under a blanket, and the door cracked open; enough for her to get her arm out but no more. Regardless of how hard she shoved on the door she couldn't get it to open any more than that little bit. The cold air rushing in from outside dropped the temperature in the shack drastically and John began to shiver in his bed. She closed the door and stepped over to the window trying to see through the blanket of snow still falling steadily. She could faintly see the outline of the nearest shack; she squinted her eyes and forced them to see through the haze and blur to see a few more of its scant details. She could then make out the door and one of the windows of the place. The lower half of the door was hidden behind a thickening snowdrift, continuing to grow in the gusty winds. She rightfully assumed the same had happened to John's door as well. With a loud, nervous sigh she checked on John, built up the fire and started scanning the shelves in his kitchen for something to eat.

Frank McGrath and Dansford Keeton didn't make it to check on the elderly the second time.

They attempted to but couldn't make it across the east bridge because of how icy it was. It took them 20 minutes and they had only made it a quarter of the way across. They had no choice but to return to Frank's house, defeated, exhausted, and freezing.

Earl 'Red' Redley, Beth Redley's older brother, took off toward the same bridge that Frank and Dan couldn't pass. The only connection between the Lot and the Slums. He knew he needed to get wood and coal so he could stay warm through this cold spell, so he was on his way to the Flats on the western side of the common area. It was quite a walk from there to his place on a regular day, but as young men tend to believe, he thought he could handle the cold and the intense trek there and back. He made it to the bridge and started across completely unaware of the sheet of ice covering the entire structure, from the waist-high handrails to the squeaky floorboards.

One gloved hand slid easily along the rail as he took step after step with growing confidence. His confidence faded as the tread of his boots packed with ice and slush and became as slick as everything else out there. Red's slick bottomed boot stepped on a similarly slick patch of ice that sent his foot out from under him. He felt himself falling backwards and grasped for purchase with his gloved hand on the railing, the other arm pinwheeling, straining for balance. He managed to grab the railing long enough to get his foot back under him but in doing so he nudged his other boot, sending it skidding on the ice. He tumbled to the side and his hip connected painfully with the waist-high handrail. It sent him head-first over the side of the bridge and into the swiftly moving river below. As he fell, he sucked in a mouthful of air he intended on releasing in a throat-splitting scream for help, but his mouth filled with water before any sound passed his lips. The water thrashed him around violently and he endured an abundance of pain before he was slung into a rock that jutted from the riverbank. The jutting rock, mercifully, knocked him unconscious before the rushing water swept him through the merging point of the river branches and south toward the gushing waterfall. Earl Redley's limp body shot off the cliff like a projectile and then plummeted to the small wading pool below. His body landed at the water's rocky edge, leaving a splattered undistinguishable mess of blood and gore that flew yards in every direction.

With that, the storm claimed its first victim.

Chapter Twenty-One

Bustin' Out

1

Most folks in the valley woke up the following morning confused because only darkness was present in the windows that should have had bright, glowing sunlight illuminating from them. The bartending twins and Joe and his escorts were the only ones that weren't confused. They had sat up throughout the night, getting increasingly drunker as the time ticked away, and watched the snow steadily build until the windows were completely covered. They knew the others would figure it out soon enough.

Around eight that morning, the steadily falling snow finally began to taper off. Those sheltered in the valley were unaware of this, however, because there was almost eight feet of snow, with snow drifts as large as 20 feet. The tips of teepees and chimneys could be seen above the snowline but nothing more. The thick snow that entombed the shacks and teepees was both a blessing and a curse. A curse for the obvious reason of being stuck inside with no way of attaining food, water, fuel, companionship, etc. There wasn't a door in the valley that could be or would be opened for six more days. It was a blessing, however, because the snow acted as insulation and kept the shacks and teepees, that had fires before they all got snowed-in,

214

relatively warm. The snow insulation made the difference for several people in the valley that were able to stretch out their fuel sources for longer than they should have been able to. Some even survived what would have been a hypothermic death because of it.

The temperature rose slowly but consistently, stalling but not dropping during the darkest hours of the night, until well above freezing and comfortable in the mid-sixties. It took the first 36 hours for the temperature to get above freezing so the snow could start to melt, averaging an increase of one degree an hour. By the sixth day a lot of the snow had melted, except for the larger snowdrifts, leaving behind a half-frozen, half-muddy-slushy-mess. It will take another nine days of no rain for the valley to completely unfreeze and dry out.

2

The first to force their way out was Alvin Danson. He had run out of the precious little food he had in his one room shack two days ago. He was famished and weak but managed to plow through the door, breaking it loose from the ice-covered ground that kept it in place. He landed heavily on his hands and knees, panting from the multitude of attempts that finally paid off. He could feel the ice under his hands and the knees of his trousers soaking up the mud beneath them. He stood up, squinting into the brightness of the sun, and smiled broadly, genuinely glad to be alive. His thoughts kept returning to Anne, worrying him, but he continued to tell himself that she had stayed with the Witch through the storm, and she was just fine. Weak, hungry, and pale maybe, but all right, nonetheless. He had lost a noticeable amount of weight, himself, living on the meager rations he had, and his muscular physique now resembled that of a scrawny young man's puberty-riddled body. A slight breeze blew across the valley, and he shivered from the chill of it even in the warmth of the sun. He stood motionless for several long moments, allowing himself to become fully immersed, even if only briefly, in the beauty and elegance of mother nature. She could be sweet, kind, and loving at times and at others, she's vengeful, cruel, and merciless.

He turned toward Danny Bailey's shack, approached it carefully due to icy patches, and knocked several times. He didn't get an answer and he was too weak to get the door open all on his own, so he walked over to Betty Jones' shack instead. He was trying not to worry about Danny, trying to convince himself that he had left before it got bad and was safe elsewhere. Alvin knocked on Betty's door a couple of times and sighed with relief when she answered from the other side. From outside the door, Alvin instructed her to push, while he pulled. It took an effort he couldn't spare and what seemed to him like an eternity, but they managed to get the door open.

It swung open enough for Betty to step out into the warmth of the sunshine, and before Alvin could tell her that he couldn't get an answer over at Danny's, the man had materialized behind her. Alvin, with a look of utter surprise, stared at Betty, then at Danny and back to Betty again, dumbfounded. Betty realized what was going through Alvin's mind and began stammering for an explanation while Danny stood behind her with a slight, knowing, smirk upon his face. Before Betty could get out anything coherent enough to be understood, Alvin just shook his head at them with a broad, goofy smile. "C'mon. Let's go see if the Bossman is still kickin.'" He said light-heartedly, fully expecting the Old Man to be ready and waiting when they knocked on his door.

"I hope his Old Lady's got some grub on." Danny remarked, walking up behind Alvin. "Ain't had nuttin but her snatch to munch on for a few days now." Danny told him with a chuckle, throwing a thumb behind him in Betty's direction.

"Oh, you!" Betty shrilled; her face flushed a deep red with embarrassment.

Alvin laughed with Danny at her expected reaction. "I see the cold hasn't effected your sense of humor any."

They made it to the O'Reigan's homestead, where a small group of shacks sat huddled together, only three of them currently occupied. The three of them decided that they could cover more ground if they split up, so each picked a shack and started knocking. Alvin Danson knocked on the door to Mr. and Mrs. O'Reigan's place for so long he almost gave up when he thought he heard a faint, weak whisper from the other side of the door. He tried for several minutes to coax the whispering person to the door but only failed. Struggling to open the door on his own only weakened him further and he had to stop. He sat with his back against the shack, mud soaking the seat of his pants and waited for the others to return.

Danny Bailey knocked on the place belonging to the eldest O'Reigan daughter and her husband, Joshua Jones. His knock was answered immediately by a frantic masculine voice that was begging him to help his wife. "Please!" Joshua pleaded. "I need to get my wife to the infirmary. She's with child and has fallen ill." Danny could hear the pain and sorrow in the man's voice. "Please! Help me get her out of here." Danny pulled while Joshua pushed in a frenzied moment of adrenaline-fueled exertion and the door popped open with an audible crack of splintering wood. A small chunk of the base of the wooden door was still firmly frozen on the ground in the doorway.

Danny rushed in, Joshua recognizing him immediately and he guided the farmhand to his wife. The young woman, her pale complexion increasing the visibility of the dark circles under her eyes and the deep red feverish blush high on her sharp cheekbones, was resting fitfully in the only bed in the shack. Her eyelids fluttered, her breath was raspy and shallow, and there was a light sheen of sweat evident across her nose and brow. There was a slight, almost unnoticeable ripple under her light nightgown and Danny realized that the baby was moving around inside her. There was more than one life at stake here and Danny needed to get them some help. Joshua wrapped his wife in a blanket and Danny swept her up into his arms and headed out the door. Danny immediately took off toward the chicken coop since the west bridge was right behind it and told Joshua to let Alvin know where they were going and why. Joshua did and was back at his wife's side before Danny had made it to the nauseatingly odorous coop that was filled with dead, maggot-covered chickens.

Betty Jones knocked on the door of the eldest O'Reigan son and his wife. Betty had only ever seen the man's wife a couple of times from a distance and had never spoken to her. She had heard plenty of stories about what a hateful bitch she was, though, to everyone, all the time. In fact, Betty had never heard anything remotely positive ever said about that woman. She knocked and knocked but no one answered. She didn't think she would be able to get the door opened by herself and didn't want to burn what precious little energy she had, trying. She walked back to Mr. O'Reigan's, where she found Alvin waiting for her to return. "Anyone?" he asked as she approached him.

"No answer but I'd like to get in there and make sure. I can't get the door open on my own though. I came to get you and Danny to help. You find anyone?"

"Danny found Joshua and his pregnant wife. She's real sick, I reckon, so their takin her straight to the infirmary." Alvin informed her.

"Why? No one's there. The doctor took off with that nurse he's been seeing and that kid of hers. His other four nurses all have kids too. Hell, I think there's only one Aide in the Apothecary, and she will be probably next to useless." Betty responded querulously.

"Damn" Alvin cursed. "I reckon they'll figure that out once they get there. I need your help here too. I thought I heard whispering earlier, but I couldn't be sure."

3

Alvin and Betty decided to open Mr. O'Reigan's place first, then go check the one Betty knocked on. They knew something was wrong the moment they got the door open. The shack was too cold, even with the sun beating down on it, and the stench was atrocious. There was definitely something... or someone... dead or dying in there. Neither one of them wanted to go in there and find out, though. Their stomachs tumbled and rolled, nausea rushing them in intense waves, but nothing would or could make it up and out. Together, slowly, they stepped into the shack. The rooms were lit up by the brilliant sunlight, plainly revealing Mr. O'Reigan's corpse lying face down on the floor, across the threshold of the bedroom and main room/kitchen. His lower half was closest to them, and they could see his upper half leading into the bedroom, but their sight was abruptly cut off by the wall. They took two steps forward and could see Mrs. O'Reigan sitting on the floor, just inside the bedroom, with her dead husband's head in her lap. She was staring at the wall, rubbing his head, her mouth moving as if speaking rapidly in a foreign language. Occasionally a hushed whisper would escape her lips but nothing comprehendible. She looked as if she had aged ten years in the past six days; pale, thin, and fragile.

Betty and Alvin looked at each other, knowing she had gone mad when her husband died but didn't want to say it out loud. Betty walked over and knelt beside her; she couldn't help but look down at the corpse's face. He had been dead for a few days, at least, because the ivory-colored skin on his face and hands were leathery, dry, and shriveled. The dull gray eyes stared lifelessly away from her as a plump, yellowish maggot fell from the parted shriveled lips. She fought back a gag but just barely and reached over to grab the mad woman's hand off the dead man's head. The woman didn't acknowledge that the pair even existed, but she allowed herself to be lifted all the floor and led away. Alvin walked over to help Betty get the woman off the floor, she had been sitting for so long that her knees and hips retained the same bent position. They tried to plead with the woman to try to unbend her legs, but she was not responding to anything they said or did to her. So, they carried her over to the bed and sat her down. Very carefully, they laid her back and began gently massaging the muscles of her calves and knees; the woman had no reaction whatsoever. This went on for some time before the two of them were able to get her legs somewhat straightened out and separated. They both knew that she wouldn't be able to walk for some time and neither one of them had the strength to carry her out, even together. So, they made her as comfortable as they could, given that she gave them no reaction, and assured her that they would be back for her, which they were given no response to.

Alvin and Betty went back to the shack where the eldest O'Reigan son and his wife lived. After what they had just witnessed with Mr. and Mrs. O'Regian, they didn't think it could get any worse... but they were wrong. It took them several tries in their weakened state to get the door open, and they immediately regretted it when they did. Fresh waves of nausea assaulted them as they took in the gory nightmarish scene before them. Large spots of brownish-red dried blood were scattered about the floor, it streaked the walls and ceiling, and splattered the meager furnishings that had been toppled and tossed about the room. In the kitchen, several maggots wiggled across the muscles and tendons of a severed wrist and hand that laid on a small wooden table, a large, discolored place beneath it. The rotting, coppery smell of the dried blood permeated and overwhelmed their senses. There was an evident blood trail leading into the bedroom and it was obvious to them both that whatever had happened here, began in this room, and ended in the bedroom.

Forcing their feet to move, they walked to the bedroom door where they found the bodies of Mr. and Mrs. O'Reigan's son and daughter-in-law. The woman was propped up against the far bedroom wall, her head laid over on her shoulder in an unnatural way, and a very large butcher knife protruded from the side of her blood-soaked neck. There was a trickle of dried blood at the corner of her mouth. Aside from the obvious knife wound, no other wounds were visible. A blood covered hatchet sat just out of reach of her limp hand. Sprawled across the blood-soaked bed was her husband. He had one hand over his stomach as if he had tried to hold his protruding organs in place. There was a very large, deep cut across his abdomen that had long ceased trying to hold in its entrails. His other hand, or lack of, laid across his chest. Flies flew and landed, flew and landed, everywhere in the shack but there weren't any signs of maggots on the bodies yet.

Betty and Alvin quickly left the shack, the entire ordeal lasting less than two minutes but feeling like hours to them. It was horrible and they prayed this wasn't how the rest of the valley would be found too. There was nothing else they could do at the farm then, so they went back and checked on Mrs. O'Reigan. They found her sleeping and then headed for the west bridge, the same one Danny crossed when he left with the eldest O'Reigan daughter.

Chapter Twenty-Two

Shack to Shack

1

Danny Bailey had to stop shortly after they passed the Butcher's shop and had Joshua carry the sick woman the rest of the way. He couldn't do it; he was too weak. Joshua, on the other hand, was warm and well-fed until his wife got sick a few days ago. Then he was still warm and fed just no longer well. He got her to the Infirmary with Danny right beside him only to be welcomed by disappointment. The Infirmary was deserted, the doctor nowhere to be found. Danny helped Joshua get his wife inside and laid down on one of the few small beds, then told him to stay with her while he ran over to the Apothecary.

About 15 minutes had passed before Danny returned from the Apothecary with a short, plump, middle-aged woman named Doreen. She was as pale as the rest of them, and even with her rotund shape, one could still see that she too had dropped some weight over the last week. Poor appearance or not, Joshua was highly relieved to see the Aide. "The doc ain't here." Danny told Joshua concernedly. "Apparently he's been seein one of his nurses and took off with her and her kid to New York." Joshua could only shake his head dejectedly as Doreen pushed her

223

way between the men to see what condition the ailed woman was in.

"You didn't tell me she was with child!" Doreen turned toward Danny accusingly, with a motherly scolding expression upon her face. It took both men by surprise and Danny looked from one to the other, hesitant before answering.

"I apologize. I thought I said that when I first approached you. I know I gave you quite a start comin up on ya like that, but I coulda swore you heard me with the way you come rushing out to help me." Danny explained apologetically.

Doreen recalled her heart thumping wildly in her chest when she turned the corner in the Apothecary and there stood a very pale, sickly looking fellow. He was rambling on about something, she could see his lips moving, but the only sound she could hear for the first several seconds was the persistence of her own pulse thrumming in her ears. When the roaring noise finally dissipated and she was able to concentrate on what the man was saying, all she caught was 'she's sick. Please! You have to help her.' Doreen's response was simply, "Where is she?" Danny asked about the doctor's whereabouts, and she explained on the short walk from the Apothecary to the Infirmary.

Snapping back from her short tryst down memory lane, she looks at Danny. "No. It is I that should apologize for my tone. I believe we have all been under a great deal of... stress... these past days. It is catching up with me, I'm afraid. I no longer doubt that you told me of her... condition. I must have misunderstood what you said." She turned back to the woman lying on the bed, sighed heavily, and turned back toward Danny and Joshua. "I am unsure of what ails this woman, but due to her condition I don't wish to even venture a guess. If I am wrong, and the chances are high that I would be, there could be dire consequences for both the mother and child. I'm sorry, Mr. Jones, but I cannot help your wife." Doreen told the men with sincere sadness in her voice. Danny could tell it bothered her deeply that she could do nothing in this situation.

Joshua, in a frantic panic at the news he had just received, grabbed Doreen's arm just above the elbow. He gave her a quick hard shake. "What do you mean you can't help her? You won't even try! What kind of person can just sit there and not try?" There were hot tears stinging his eyes and he was shouting just mere inches from her upturned face. Her expression didn't show anger or fear, it was stern and unreadable from the moment he grabbed her arm.

After a long moment of looking deep into Joshua's eyes, with a calmness that she struggled to maintain, Doreen asked him a question. "Do you want your wife and son to die?"

Joshua's grip on her arm tightened, it was almost painful, but she refused to show it. He was taken aback by the directness and coldness of the question and for the first time in his life he wanted to strike a woman. Even in his frazzled state, he resisted the impulse, ground his teeth, and answered her. "Of course not. Why would you ask such a thing?"

"I know about as much about her condition and sickness as you do, which is next to none. If I try to treat her, not knowing what I am treating her for, it could and probably would kill her and your unborn child. If that's truly a risk you want to take, toying with the lives of your loved ones, then I offer you to do it yourself. You wouldn't get it anymore wrong than I would." Doreen maintained that stern look, glaring at him the whole time.

"I understand." he said softly, tears running down into the stubble of his beard. "There's gotta

be someone that can help her, right? Anyone?"
he asked her, pleadingly, releasing her arm.

Doreen was quiet for a few moments,
collecting her thoughts and debating internally
before finally answering him. "I, personally, am
skeptical of her but if anyone in the valley
could help your wife, it's the Witch."

"Yes! The witch!" Joshua shouted with
newfound hope. "We can go get her, bring her
back to treat my beloved, and then everything
will be fine." He was already getting up to leave
when Alvin and Betty walked in. They had
followed the sound of their voices, echoing
through the empty hallways, and had heard
everything since Dorren said, 'not knowing
what I'm treating...".

"We need to find somethin to eat, for everyone's
benefit, get our strength back up. Then the three
of us..." Danny indicated himself, Alvin, and
Betty. "...will go find the Witch. Joshua, you
need to stay here and be with your wife. Doreen
can stay with you til we return. I don't think
any of us want to be alone much right now."
Everyone nodded in agreement, even Joshua. He
was antsy about getting her help, but he didn't
like the idea of leaving her. In her weakened
state, taking her along with them was out of the
question, too. He knew he had to trust that the
farmhands would find the Witch and bring her
back to help his wife.

2

Leaving Alvin with Joshua and Doreen to
rest, Danny and Betty went out and over to the
kitchen where Betty had to endure yet another
horror. The door had opened much easier than
the others they had opened already, but neither
thought much of it. They were both anxious to
get their hands on the food they knew would

be in the kitchen. Even if a dozen people had sheltered in the kitchen during the week no one could get out, there would still be plenty of food in there. Their stomachs rumbled eagerly and impatiently. They stepped into the dark room and the lack of light initially went unnoticed. They realized, Betty just mere moments before Danny, that something was wrong. "Shouldn't it be brighter in here?" Betty asked casually as Danny stepped over to one of the few windows in the building. His eyes had slowly adjusted to the dim lighting in the room, but he had to lean close enough to the window for his nose to almost touch it, before he realized that it was thickly coated in a dusty black substance. He ran his hands along a long wooden table that stood between him and the window until his fingers felt the softness of a rag. He used it to wipe clean a single wide strip on the dusty window and the sunlight that flooded into the room momentarily blinded him. When his eyes readjusted to the new-found light, he finished wiping the window clean. Betty had already found another rag and cleaned another window by the time Danny had finished with the first. All they could do, standing in the sunshine drifting through the windows, was stare at the filth that surrounded them.

The kitchen was one large room with only two doors, one led outside and the other led down to the cellar; both of which stood wide open but unnoticed. There were three wood and coal stoves, equipped for cooking and baking, that sat spaciously apart against three of the four walls. Closer inspection showed that the metal piping running into the stone chimneys had come out to the wall... on all three of the stoves. Long wooden tables, scattered with bowls, pots, pans, cooking utensils, etc., were set meticulously around the room to allow for the most use in the limited space. They lined the walls on either side of the stoves and formed aisles in the center of the room. All the tables were in use, except for a small, square, wooden one, complete with two chairs, that sat empty in the corner. Everything, from the floor to the ceiling and everything in between, was covered in a thick settled layer of back dust and ash.

The couple walked slowly through the kitchen, feeling the padding of the soot under their booted feet, moving toward the cellar door that would lead them to the food they desperately needed. They had walked along the first two aisles before they found the body of a woman. She was lying on her side, her face against a table leg and out of their line of sight, on the floor between the second and third row of tables. The amount of soot that coated her body made her unidentifiable, but it was obvious that she was dead.

The sight of the dead woman made Betty Jones want to scream but it lodged in her throat before she could release it. She swallowed it down instead, along with the acidic bile creeping up her esophagus. Panic tried desperately to sink its claws into her traumatized mind, and she tried even more desperately to fight it off. She couldn't lose it, or she wouldn't be any help to anyone. She had known most of these folks her entire life, quite well, and it pained her deeply to see that all of them had died in such terrible ways. She wasn't sure who the woman was lying on the floor, but she believed, rightfully, that it was Brenda Daniels. Under her breath she prayed that she wouldn't have to endure anymore death today, tomorrow and for years to come.

Danny Bailey, who as a farmhand had had his hands in some very questionable places more times than he cared to speak about and had

had to dispose of dozens of dead farm animals in the eight years he had been working for the O'Reigan's. He was not a squeamish man by any means, but the sight of a dead body up close made his stomach flipflop and burn with a hidden fire. At that moment, he was glad that he hadn't eaten recently because it all would have ended up on his boots. He knew that Betty was just as sickened as he was, so he moved a little closer and wrapped his arm around her waist.

With Danny's arm around her and Betty still uttering her silent prayer, they turned together and took a couple more steps in the direction of the cellar door, realizing with a sinking feeling that it was open. Another step brought them into an overwhelming pungent smell of death and rot and another dead woman. This one was lying on her stomach in the cellar doorway, hand outstretched and hanging over the first step leading downstairs. It looked as if she were trying to crawl down the stairs but collapsed before she could. Her hair covered her face, making her unidentifiable as well, and neither Danny nor Betty could summon the courage to touch the dead woman to move the thick, dusty strands of hair.

Danny stepped first around Betty, who was frozen in place, and then the dead body, to peak his head into the cellar stairwell. He abruptly jerked his head back, knowing by the increase in the strength of the smell that nothing in the cellar was salvageable. He ushered Betty outside and they both stood trembling. The sunlight and fresh air brought them out of their mild shock, and they both stood taking deep breaths of the mud-scented mountain air.

It would take longer than they had planned to be out, but they decided to go to the Butcher's shop in search of food. They were both utterly exhausted by the time they made it there.

Some of that was restored when they opened the door and found a normal building with no death, blood, or gore. Large chunks of salted and cured meats hung silently from the hooks in the ceiling. A few flies buzzed around and there was a slight hint of rot in the air that was seeping from the door to the back room. Danny and Betty were absolutely elated. He found a knife behind the counter and sliced a couple large chunks off the salted leg of a large animal. It was the most amazing thing either one of them could ever remember tasting. They sat and enjoyed the first half of their chunk of meat, grabbed a leg and a couple other pieces then headed back to the Infirmary.

They had been gone for about 45 minutes, when it should have only taken them twenty at most to get back to the Infirmary. Alvin was worried when he returned from fetching water to find that they still weren't back yet. That was fifteen minutes before, and he was on the verge of going out to search for them. The three of them waiting for the couple were pleasantly relieved to find that they had found food. Everyone, sans Joshua's pregnant wife, was ravenously hungry and ate their fill for the first time in days.

3

With newly replenished strength, Alvin Danson, Danny Bailey, and Betty Jones left Joshua Jones, his ailing pregnant wife, and the Apothecary Aide, Dorren, in the Infirmary. They headed east toward the bar, Hussey Row, and the Slums beyond, on their way to the Witch's shack at the northeastern most corner of the valley. As the trio approached the Bar, they seen the haggard, pale face of a young woman in the window, and knew that those in the bar would need their help getting out.

Once the door was open, Nonni and Nonna Brookes offered them some Shine, but they opted for tea instead. They needed the nutrients in the sassafras more than they needed the nerve-numbing calmness of the Shine. Old Joe Brenner thanked the trio profusely for finally getting them out of that damned old Bar, as he had put it. "It's startin to stink something awful in there." He told them as he stood just outside the door taking deep breaths of the fresh air. "Kat died a few days. We was all sittin round, sippin Shine and swappin stories. Then, she just fell over dead. No rhyme or reason why. It was the damnedest thing, boys, I tell ya."

Betty chose to stay outside with Old Joe, Lacy, and Sugar while Alvin and Danny walked through the Bar. They went to the back room, where they found the deceased woman's body covered, head to toe, with an animal hide blanket. Neither man wanted to pull the blanket back to see the state of the body, so they sighed deeply, trying to remember to breathe through their mouth rather than their nose, and walked back out.

Before they left, the three of them informed the bartenders, the old man and his two remaining 'employees', of Mrs. O'Reigan and asked if one of them could go get her and take her back to the Infirmary. They also told them that they knew there wasn't anyone else alive on the farm, but they hadn't checked the rest of the shops. Alvin, Danny, and Betty left, and the five others decided to split up so they could cover more ground. The twins went to the farm to retrieve the now-loony Mrs. O'Reigan, while Joe Brenner and his girls started checking for any more survivors in the shops.

There were only two places they found that were used as shelters from the storm and cold. The first was the fishing shack on the western pier, or what was left of it. The small one-room shack had collapsed in on itself under the weight of the ice and snow. The only reason they knew that it was being used as a shelter was the blood-splattered hand sticking out from beneath the rubble. After several minutes, and some heavy lifting, they had moved enough of the rotted-fish-smelling debris to be satisfied that there were only two dead bodies. Both men and both known fishermen in the valley. There was nothing they could do for them, so they moved on.

The second place was the church where they found a very angry, raving preacher and three battered, terrified Sisters. All four were alive, though. Sugar and Lacy tried to calm the three shaking women that would flinch every time Father Robin raised his voice, but the effort was fruitless. It took some convincing, but Joe finally got Father Robin to agree to go to the Infirmary where there were other people and plenty of food and water for everyone. They knew the Sisters would not abandon Father Robin but they were not safe with him either. It was for the benefit of the women that they all go to the Infirmary. Joe and the two young women, escorted Father Robin and the three Sisters back to the Infirmary where they had a bite to eat and refreshed themselves with some hot tea before leaving to search the Lot.

They had decided on the Lot first because even though it was a larger area, fewer people live by the Lot than they did in the Slums. They would be able to tell quite easily which shacks were occupied and tend to any survivors. Once they finished there, they would double back across the bridge and check out the Slums.

Nonna and Nonni Brookes had made it to the infirmary with Mrs. O'Reigan who was tended to by Doreen. Doreen knew what was wrong with Mrs. O'Reigan after hearing what they had deduced from the way Alvin and Betty had found her. She set about tending to her, while Joshua Jones sat at his wife's side and held her hand. Nonna and Nonni left with Joe and the girls to help look for others. They walked along the riverbank and crossed the east bridge into the Lot without incident.

The first place they checked was Frank McGrath's and was answered by him on the first knock. It took a little more effort to get his door open because it was larger and heavier than the rickety doors that hung on the shacks throughout the valley. It was almost a full minute before Frank walked out to join his five rescuers. He looked as if he were flustered, or guilty or maybe it was shame. Dansford stepped out behind him which wasn't any surprise that they were together whenever the snow got bad, but he looked upset, almost angry. It was odd seeing this reaction from the two men since the valley knew that they were as close as brothers and had been since they were very young. But aside from being pale, they had stayed warm and ate well, leaving them well enough to help search.

The seven of them split up and covered the whole Lot in less than two hours. Nonna and Nonni went west and found Roy Hoarding and David Bailey. David asked if anyone had seen his wife, Sue Ann, and tears formed on his eyelashes when they said they had not, but they all assured him that there were still a lot of places they hadn't checked yet. They would find her; it was just a matter of when. Roy was just glad to be outside. Both men were thinner and paler but well enough.

Dansford and Sugar went down the center row of shacks noting that several of them had fallen in under the weight of the snow they had received. It was going to take a lot of work to get all the destruction cleaned up.

The pair came across Gary Brown and his wife, and Carol Jewell. Gary and his wife were pale but okay. Carol was distraught over the death of her mother. She said that her mother, Old Miss Jewell, went to sleep a few nights ago and didn't wake up the next morning. Carol assumed she died of old age, that it was just her time to die, but it didn't make it hurt any less. Her mother was all she had and now she was gone. She didn't know what she was going to do.

Joe, Frank, and Lacy went east, along the mountainside and came upon Abigail Fariday and Sue Ann Bailey at Abigail's place. That's where they found the body of Catherine Weston, too. As the five of them made their way back toward the bridge, Abigail and Sue Ann explained to the trio what happened to Catherine. They said that she kept going on about how she didn't feel right and that she thought it had something to do with her twin sister, Anne. Then a few days ago, she just started screaming No! over and over, wailing and sobbing the entire time. She went on like that, relentlessly, any attempt to soothe her was futile, and after almost an hour, the hysteria killed her. Neither woman had any idea what she was talking about or why it had occurred, only that their heart ached at the loss of a dear friend.

The five rescuers and the eight survivors, met at the empty lot not far from Earl Redley's shack. There was a heartfelt, temporarily joyous reunion between Sue Ann and David Bailey, both elated to be in the arms of the other. Abigail asked about her husband, Ben, but no one had seen him yet. Carol Jewell asked about Rebekka Lane and received the same answer as Abigail. Joe, Sugar, and Lacy told the group of the collapsed pier shack and the two deceased fishermen beneath the rubble. Nonna and Nonni informed them of Mrs. O'Reigan's whereabouts and her current mental state. The group also discussed those found in the Church, Joshua Jones' pregnant wife, the trio on their way to find the Witch, and searching the Slums for more survivors.

As the rush of information swirled among them, there was a lot of gasping and sighing. It was a lot to take in at once and some of them were struggling. The rescuers stayed quiet on the way back, so the survivors had time to digest everything they had just been told. It seemed to work, or they were in a mild state of shock and speechless.

The group went back to the Infirmary where they found a feverish mother-to-be and a peacefully resting middle-aged madwoman. Old Joe Brenner was exhausted and needed to rest, so he stayed with the survivors at the Infirmary, while Frank and Roy went back to the Butcher's shop. They needed more food to accommodate for the increase in empty stomachs. Dansford and David Bailey went to get bucket after bucket of water from the calm gently flowing river.

4

Old Joe Brenner, Roy Hoarding, Sue Ann and David Bailey, Frank McGrath, Dansford Keeton, and Abigail Fariday all went out to search in the Slums. They had precious, few hours before dark and those left undiscovered would have to endure another night alone, hungry, and thirsty. Possibly the deciding factor in life and death for some. They split up from Hussey Row, going door to door, except for the Witch's shack because Alvin, Danny, and Betty were handling that.

Sue Ann and David Bailey and Abigail covered the section by the river. The elderly move there once they are no longer able to work and take care of themselves. They are not isolated in any way and are helped by all. They have earned the right to not have to barter for their needs, so everything is given to them. They once took care of the valley, so the valley returned the favor. They started at Old Man McAvay's place, finding his deceased body in his bed. The next shack was Old Mr. and Mrs. Jones, and they were both found... alive, but very weak, pale, and exhausted. Sue Ann and Abigail helped Mr. and Mrs. Jones walk, very slowly, to the Infirmary.

On their way back they met David helping Old Man Daniels to the Infirmary, but they went back to look for others without him, knowing he would catch up soon. After searching several shacks and teepees that were still standing and finding no one, dead or alive, they came upon the east pier shack. Abigail knocked several times and was about to give up when they heard slurred mumbling from the other side of the door. David appeared around the side of the shack they had just passed and just in time to help the ladies get the flimsy wooden door open. The mumbling person inside the shack was of no help. When they got the door open and were able to see inside the small shack, they understood why. There was one deceased man, propped up in the corner, looking like he had been slung into it, and another laying drunkenly under the wooden table. The drunken man was almost delirious with alcohol-poisoning, and they couldn't understand any of the incomprehensibility coming out of the man's mouth. The trio sighed and shook their heads, then helped get the drunk fisherman up off the floor and out into the waning sunlight. He winced in misery, tried to retreat into the foul-smelling shack but David caught him before he could. They had to practically drag the man the first quarter of the way to the Infirmary before he stopped resisting them. By the time they made it back to the Infirmary with him, they were so exhausted from the search that they were grateful that the pier shack was the end of their section.

Roy Hoarding and Dansford Keeton took the center section of the Slums, going from shack to teepee to shack, checking them all before moving on. They found Sarah and John first. They both walked out of John's place like it was the most nature thing in the world that they were together. Everyone in the valley knew that Sarah was seeing Frank and John was seeing the Witch, so it was no surprise when Dansford eyed the two of them suspiciously. Sarah stared daggers at him, and John looked away as if uninterested. After a long and strung-out awkward silence, Roy urged the small group on to the next place.

A few minutes later John came across an out of place scrap of material lying stuck in the mud. He picked it up gingerly, turning it over in his hands, finding it odd. A few feet away, moving toward the mountain, he seen another piece of cloth the same color and material. A few more feet away showed a few more, smaller pieces of the same cloth. He gathered them all up, looking around for anymore in the immediate area but not finding any, and caught up with the other three. He showed the scraps of material to the trio, they too found them odd and out of place. No one had an explanation, so he slipped them into his pocket, and they went about checking more places.

They only found two more survivors, Jiminey and Patty McAvay. This couple was found, higher than the clouds, as they usually were and just as bubbly and full of life as ever. "Thanks for

237

gettin the door opened for us, boys." Jiminey told the three men standing in the main room/kitchen. "Want a toke fore ya'll head back out?" he asked them all as they stood there in mild shock, trying to figure out if they had heard him correctly. 'Why wouldn't they come with us?', they all thought to themselves. Jiminey sat with his arm extended, offering them a large, well rolled hemp blunt. Roy took it gratefully, having run out of his own supply a few days ago, and sucked deeply on it before passing it to Sarah. Half an hour later, pleasantly stoned, and ready to head back to the Infirmary, Roy inquired of Jiminey and Patty. "Ya'll sure that you don't wanna join us back at the Infirmary? We got plenty of food and water, and there will be others."

"Lord no!" Patty exclaimed as she went to stand at Jiminey's side. "We're just fine right here, ain't we honeylove?" She asked her husband.

"Sure is, babycakes." He replied with a loud smack of her ass. "We will probably venture on out tomorra. We will be fine ya'll. Still got plenty of food. A little light on the firewood but that's alright, this little hot mama here will keep me warm tonight." He told the group standing before them.

"Dat's right!" she proclaimed with a girlish little giggle. The six of them said their goodbyes and parted ways. Roy, Dansford, John, and Sarah left the still-honeymooning couple, even though they had been together for 28 years and had sent two wonderful, brilliant children out into the world, and checked the few remaining shacks for more survivors. They found no one so they headed back to the Infirmary, arriving mere minutes after Abigail, Sue Ann, and David.

Frank and Old Joe Brenner took the mountain side of the Slums and returned with the largest group of survivors almost half an hour after Roy and Dansford's group. The first was Rebekka Lane, thin and looking much older than her middle age, she immediately asked about her sister Samantha. Frank and Old Joe knew of the two dead bodies in the Kitchen, but they didn't know who they were and didn't make the connection, even though both men knew that she worked there. They told her they didn't know where she was, but there were others searching too, so she would be found.

Much like John had, Rebekka came across a scrap of cloth, a little while later. She found another large piece and two much smaller pieces that were in tatters. A brief bout of anger shot through her, seeing the clothing she had created treated in such a manner. Then she seen the small spot of dried blood on the first piece she had found, and all that anger melted into fear. She gathered the pieces and took them to the two men. None of them had any idea what might've happened or who the clothing belonged to, so she hid it away in her pocket.

Several places away they found Ron Hellman and Porter Siddle at Porter's place. They had run out of food on the second day and were extremely weak. They also had to conserve their water intake and therefore were extremely dehydrated. Had the snow not insulated the shack, the two men wouldn't have been able to stay warm and surely would have died. Frank escorted Ron and Porter back to the Infirmary. They were weak but still able to walk, it just took quite a bit longer than it should have because they had to stop and rest every few dozen yards. Frank had lost much of his patience and most of the daylight by the time they made it to the Infirmary.

Joe and Rebekka went on a little way and found Robert Daniels, the Shine maker. He looked haggard and distressed, but otherwise healthy. Much better than most. He joined the search party and Frank caught up with them before they came across the followers in the teepee. The first one had the deceased body of Rachel Smith, as well as the last two, which contained the bodies of May Frederickson and Anne Weston. The only two survivors, Beth Redley and Leena McAvay, were deathly ill, too weak, and feverish to leave the teepees they could have gotten out of two days ago.

Frank carried Leena because she was considerably taller and therefore naturally heavier than Beth, while Robert carried Beth back to the Infirmary. Doreen immediately went about asking questions that no one could answer but started mixing elixirs and herbs to treat the symptoms. The followers were the end of their section, leaving the Witch's shack the only place unchecked.

Chapter Twenty-Three

A Blast of Fury

1

Alvin Danson, Danny Bailey, and Betty Jones approached the Witch's front door at about the same time that the bartending twins, Old Joe and his two money-making ladies were crossing the east bridge into the Lot. Alvin knocked on her door and it opened before him before he had time to drop his hand back by his side. Startled he stepped back, eyed the woman standing in the doorway cautiously and curiously before asking her who she was. She smiled sweetly and told him that she was, indeed, the same person he had come to find, she had just had a 'transformation' of sorts.

The woman residing in the shack, the one that they all remembered before the snowstorm, was completely different now. The basic underlying facial features were the same but everything else, down to the color of her eyes and skin, had changed. Her complexion, once the color of silky cream was now darker, more tanned, almost as if she had spent too much time out in the sun. Her dark onyx colored hair cascaded around and past her shoulders, thick and full, stopping at the small of her back. The last six inches of her hair were a deep royal purple that perfectly matched the new color of her eyes. Before, her hair was the golden color of sunlight, kept short in a cute pixie cut, and her eyes were the soft radiant blue of the clear sky. She was considerably taller, more filled out, if such a thing were possible, and glowed with an unseen grace and confidence.

"You can't be." Betty objected. "You look nothing like her."

She smiled at them innocently. A sweet, soft smile that masked the malice. "Of course, I am, you silly girl."

Alvin and Danny remained silent as the two women continued with their tension-laced conversation. Betty stood eyeing the woman carefully, studying her. After a few long, drawn-out moments, Betty finally responds. "Alright. If you are who you say you are, then tell me, when was the last time I came to see you and why?"

The witch hesitated thoughtfully before answering her. "It was a couple months ago around the time you started developing feelings for your boytoy there. You came to see me because you weren't sure if he reciprocated those feelings or was just trying to get you in bed."

Betty turned bright red, knowing Danny was looking at her, but too embarrassed to return the gaze. She was mortified because she had not expected her to know that. "You really are the Witch." Betty replied in a soft whisper, almost inaudible.

The Good Witch only smiled at her sweetly and ushered them in.

The trio was invited into her small home, led directly through the shack and out the back door. Instead of continuing forward into the cave, she turned left and led them into her garden. They walked for about five minutes through exotic plants and flowers of every shape, size, scent, and color. The trees created a canopy that allowed the light and shadows to ebb and flow endlessly around them. It was as if they had been transported somewhere else in the world because the garden that they were walking through was nothing like the environment on the other side of the knee-high stone wall around it. The air seemed sweeter and warmer, bugs darted and zipped to and fro, the unusual sounds of the enchanted garden blended into a soft melodic tune, and the colorful foliage surrounding them was almost surreal compared to the drab colors of death and rot in the winter. It was a truly magical place and all three of them could feel the tingle of the enchantment around them, pleasant and exciting.

When they finally stopped, they were in a large clearing furnished with an extravagantly crafted iron table and four matching chairs. There was a large archway erected off to the right, indicating the start of the smooth stone path that snaked out beyond it. The same intricately designed pattern stretched across the whole of the furniture. There were rosebushes at the base of the four archway legs, all four about a third of the way up and in full bloom with their large dazzling multicolored roses. Every color of the rainbow and many more could be found, a different color for every petal. They were astonishingly beautiful, immediately catching the eyes of the visitors.

The clinking of glass brought their attention back to the Witch who was setting the table with a beautifully painted, fragile, and obviously aged, glass tea set. The tall-backed iron chairs they were instructed to sit in were cushioned and comfortable. What the Witch called Ginseng tea sat before them and they all tasted it, reluctantly, finding it quite pleasant. The quartet sipped at their tea, engaged in small talk, and admired the enchanted elegance of the garden that surrounded them. The Witch gleamed with pride as the three spoke of her garden with such awe and, maybe, a hint of envy. They could not fathom how the garden had remained untouched by the savage snowstorm they had survived. It was as if an invisible dome of sorts had been placed over her tiny corner of the valley. "It is kind of like that, yes." The witch told them, picking up on their thoughts, clearly making the three of them uneasy. She giggled girlishly and innocently before continuing. "Forgive me. I cannot read yours or anyone else's thoughts, so rest easy, please. It was merely painted upon your faces and quite evidently, I must add." Alvin and Danny relaxed visibly but Betty eyed the Witch cautiously. "As I am sure you all have figured out, my lovely garden is enchanted. It needs to be, so that all these exotic beauties can coexist. It was merely the enchantment that kept the cold from killing them. The snow still fell here, as it did throughout the valley, it just could not harm my garden."

"You must be some powerful." Danny said awestruck, staring nervously at the sensuous woman sitting across from him. He forgot all about Betty whenever he looked at the immense beauty of the Witch. She smiled sweetly at him in response, but the smile did not touch her eyes. There was a malicious provocativeness in her eyes, unmatched by any other.

"So, what brings you to my door? Anything specific or are you just out looking for survivors?" She asked anyone that would answer.

Alvin cleared his throat before answering. "We were lookin for survivors and found some, so they started lookin while we came to get you. There's a very sick lady over at the Infirmary that is also carryin a youngen. The doctor is gone with all the nurses and most everyone else in the valley and the only person we found was an Apothecary Aide that can't help cause she don't know how. You're the only one that might be able to so we are asking you to return to the

Infirmary with us so you can maybe help that poor lady and her baby."

The whole time Alvin explained the situation to the Witch, Danny found himself swatting at some kind of buzzing insect by his ear. It reminded him of a bloodsucker, so he kept waving his hands through the air by his ears trying to get it to leave him alone.

The Witch's eyes kept darting from Alvin to Danny while still listening to Alvin. When he finished, she sat thoughtfully for a few minutes watching Danny swat at the air around his head. "I wouldn't do that." She said looking directly at Danny.

"Do what?" he asked naively as he continued to wave his arms around, almost constantly now. "Anyone else dealin with these damned old bloodsuckas?"

Before Betty or Alvin could answer him, the Witch said, "They are not bloodsuckers. They are not even bugs. If you harm one of them, they will retaliate. My advice is to just endure the buzzing. They are merely curious creatures and will leave once they are satiated." Danny looked at her strangely for a long moment, his arms and hands frozen in mid-air. Finally, he nodded and slowly lowered his arms, resting his hands in his lap. He did not say another word until long after they had left the Witch's shack.

"As for your request for help, I cannot return to the Infirmary with you..." She could see the hope die in their eyes and secretly relished it. "...because I cannot treat her there. She must be brought to me here." She told them, as a torturous ploy swirled through her mind. She didn't want to help the woman; she couldn't care less if that bitch and her bastard child died. She could use them though, to inflict pain on others. Someone obviously cared about her, or they wouldn't be pleading for her help right now. The Witch

245

wanted the whole world to feel her pain and anguish, wanted to burn it to the ground, but she would settle for just the valley and those in it, saving her two favorites for last.

"She can't be moved..." Betty began. "...or we would have brought her with us. We considered every option we had, and this was her best chance." There was a little more than just a touch of coldness in her voice that made Danny and Alvin wince.

The Witch gave no reaction to Betty's tone, though, as if she was completely uninterested in anything she had to say. The Witch stood up and motioned for the three of them to follow her out of the garden. They did and ten minutes later were heading back toward the Infirmary, without the Witch but with a small vial of bile-yellow liquid and a few simple instructions.

They were simply to pour the yellow liquid on the ailed woman's lips and wait 30 minutes. The Witch told them that it would make her extremely cold and that they would have to wrap her in as many blankets as they could find before bringing her to the Witch. They had to leave as soon as the 30 minutes were up because they would only have an additional hour to get the lady to the Witch's shack where she could be given the elixir needed to bring her body temperature back up so that the Witch could treat her. It took Alvin, Betty, and Danny almost 45 minutes to get back to the Infirmary so having to carry someone was going to cut it close... real close.

2

The Witch stayed at her place to prepare for the sick expecting mother's arrival. She sauntered back and forth between the two caves. She would carry armfuls of different tools, herbs, concoctions, etc. from the smaller cave into the larger one where the rituals and such were held. She would set everything on the round wooden table, then flip through the spell book before returning for more supplies. As she gathered, organized, and prepared, her thoughts wandered off to the night of her 'transformation' and a whirlwind of emotions slammed into her. The memories were so vivid and the feelings so raw that it was almost as if she were experiencing the entire ordeal all over again.

She had been sick with fret and worry over Johnathan's absence. She could not understand why he hadn't made it to her. The signal she was emitting should have been strong enough to pull him from 50 miles away. She had convinced herself that the only explanation was that he was injured and dying out in the snow. She wouldn't even begin to allow herself to think of their broken connection and that he might have been able to disregard her lulling signal because of it. The thought was unfathomable to her so she would not allow herself to even entertain the idea. The concern deepened with each passing hour.

On the morning of the third day after the snow had ceased to fall, the Good Witch would have been almost unrecognizable to anyone in the valley. She was ghostly pale and much thinner than anyone else in the valley, even though she had more than enough food to last her. Her blue eyes were foggy, bloodshot, and sunken in, making the dark circles under them that much more apparent. Her hair was tangled, matted and unwashed. There was an earthy, sweat smell that lingered around her, strong enough that she could smell her own odorous body. It sickened and revolted her, but she could not bring herself to care beyond that thought. Almost every ounce of her energy had

247

went into worrying over her beloved and she was just about spent.

After several long minutes of foggy-brained thinking, a brilliant idea occurred to her and then she scolded herself for not thinking of it sooner. She knew she would need considerably more energy than she had, so she forced herself to go back into the shack and lay down in bed. Between her endless concern for Johnathan and her excitement at her latest idea, she expected sleep to elude her. It didn't, though, and she was sound asleep within seconds of throwing the blanket across her filthy, stinking body.

She awoke well after sundown, rested, refreshed, and ravenous. She cleaned herself up, changed clothes, ate enough for a few people, and then sat down at the round table in the ceremony cave with her book of magic and a cup of tea. It took her quite a while to find the incantation she was looking for. Her eyes scanned the page quickly the first time and then once again, more carefully. She cleared the table, walked into the supply cave, and returned with a silver candle, a small bundle of various incense tied together with twine, and a small metal cage containing her unique black and white raven.

She placed the caged raven in the center of the table, placed the candle on the right of it and the bundle of incense on the left. She carefully removed the bird from the cage, setting it aside gently. The raven squawked and flapped its wings a couple of times but remained on the table where the Witch had set it down. In the candlelight of the cave, the albino white covering its one eye, shone with a ghastly, eerie glow. With a snap of her fingers the silver candle sparked a single flame that glowed brilliantly momentarily before settling into a more natural soft flame. She picked up the incense bundle,

248

held it over the candle flame, and then slowly and methodically waved it over the raven's head. The pungent, aromatic smoke lingered heavily in the dense air of the cave as she began her Latin incantation.

"Hoc carmine unum sumus," With this spell we are one,

"Donec ac dictum est." Until the task is over and done.

"Ostende quid sit quod scies," Show me what it is you will know,

"Per oculos tuos crescet sapiential mea." Through your eyes my wisdom will grow.

The Good Witch closed her eyes, the incense fell to the wooden table, extinguished the few smoldering sticks upon impact, and she slumped into the chair behind her. The raven took off, arrow straight, up through the hole in the cave roof, leveling out high enough above the trees that the entirety of the valley could be seen. The raven circled the valley twice, giving the Witch a nice ariel view on both trips before swooping down lower, mere yards above the chimneys.

Through her closed eyes, the Good Witch could see the tops of every shack, teepee and building throughout the valley. It distressed and disheartened her to see the amount of snow piled up among all the dainty little homes. She could sense death lingering in the air, waiting... or perhaps already beginning to feast. As the raven flew above the rooftops, occasionally becoming entangled in the silvery whisps of smoke puffing from various chimneys, the Witch scanned the snow for any sign of her lover. She found nothing, making several sweeps from the Butcher's shop to the Witch's own shack. The bird rested on the bar's roof peak, while the near-panicked Witch considered her options. Door to door would be the only option, at least she would know he's alive and safe. The most obvious place to start would be his shack so that's what she decided. The raven rested for a few more minutes before taking flight again and landing on the windowsill of Johnathan's shack.

The window looked diagonally through the main room/kitchen, giving a wide view of the entire room, and directly through the doorway into the bedroom. Johnthan had his bed positioned so that one could see almost the whole bed from the window, given the door was open. It was... entirely open... revealing a heart-shattering scene of intense love making. The Witch, shocked to her core, sat unmoving as she watched as her beloved pushed himself off Sarah Maisse, turning over onto his back as she lifted herself up off the bed. She watched as John cupped both of Sarah's breasts while she positioned herself across his lap. She moaned as he entered her again and the thrusting resumed. She could see the glimmering sheen of sweat across both of their bodies, could hear their thick, heavy panting, and smell the tangy odor of sex in the air. She knew they had been at it for a while and probably would be for a while longer.

<h1 style="text-align:center">3</h1>

As her thoughts returned to her, the shock began to wear off, and the anger began to snake the start of its tendrils into her soul. It quickly coiled its way through her, the hurt and betrayal merging and strengthening the fury that was quickly settling into her heart. A heart that, once long ago, had momentarily let in the darkness. She knew that she had expelled that darkness soon after she had welcomed it, as well as she knew that the darkness had left a long, jagged, ugly scar where it had once been. The hideous scar now trembled and quivered, waiting for its moment to burst open and swallow the light within her for the first and final time.

A split-second thought told her that if she let her fury take control, then the light would be lost to her forever. In her enraged mind the thought was quickly replaced with tainted, wretched thoughts of revenge and soon forgotten. Subconsciously at first, she began begging the powers that be for the strength and power to exact the revenge she sought against those that had wronged her. The longer she enticed the dark forces, the more meaningful and powerful her request became. Mere seconds after her consciousness realized who and what she was asking for, the black scar on her heart erupted, spilling evil straight out of hell into her soul. She felt the darkness swallow the light that burned so bright within her, felt the darkness fill her mind, then her heart, and finally her soul. She felt the power swell within her, the same power that had frightened her so badly when she was young. This time she embraced it and let it fulfill her wholly and completely.

When the Witch opened her eyes, the wrath that she was enveloped in, burst from her in a shockwave that rippled across the valley. It affected everyone, some slightly and some severely, but no one knew what it was. The moment her eyes opened numerous things happened simultaneously.

The Witch's uniquely beautiful, half-albinism inflicted raven squawked fiercely, flapped its wings in a frightened flurry, and fell dead from the windowsill. Its tiny heart had exploded in its chest from the sheer intensity of the Witch's ire.

Still tangled lovingly in each other's arms, John and Sarah continued their guiltless intimacy, inching closer to their climax. The shockwave rippled over them and they both spasmed in ecstasy as fluids were released and entwined. It was the most mind-numbingly euphoric experience either one of them had ever had or ever would have. It was in that moment that Sarah and John fully accepted that their destinies were entangled, but had they known what fate held in store for them, they may have reconsidered.... Maybe.

In the bar, Nonna and Nonni, Joe, Sugar, and Lacy watched as Kat slumped slowly forward in her seat, her glass of Shine tipping and spilling to the rough lumber hardwood floor. Her laugh had faded halfway through, and it caught the attention of those around her, who at first thought she was simply passing out from too much Shine. None of them attempted to catch her or move her before she smacked the floor with an echoing thud in the empty Bar. Lacy knelt beside her, brushing Kat's shoulder-length dark hair away from her face. She tried to shake Kat awake so they could get her into a corner that way she could sleep it off. After a couple of tries, Lacy noticed that her lips were turning blue and that she wasn't breathing, panic setting in almost immediately. Joe seen the panicked look on Lacy's face and quickly knelt beside Kat. It only took him a few moments to realize that she was dead and with a heavy heart he informed the rest of them. What they didn't know was that an aneurysm in her brain had burst whenever the wrath-wave swept over them, killing her instantly. It took Joe several hours to calm Lacy down enough so that she could sleep and allow the rest of them the same privilege.

Brenda Daniels and Samantha Lane were asleep on the cold wooden floor of the kitchen, between two of the middle aisles. Brenda had not slept well the night before and was utterly exhausted by the time they had decided to lay down for the night. She was cocooned in a dreamless, rest fulfilling, sleep that drew her in and kept her there for eternity. The stovepipes leading into the chimneys all came loose from the walls at the same moment, instantly filling the room with acrid, pungent black smoke. Brenda never even stirred, but Samantha had heard the pipes clatter against the chimney bricks. The room was already full of smoke by the time she opened her eyes, pointless as they were in the blinding, thick soot. She crawled to the left of her, knowing the cellar door was close by and groped out for it frantically. She could feel the poison smoke searing its way into her throat and sizzling her lungs and she knew that her time was quickly running out. Her trembling hand grazed the door, and her heart gave a tiny jump for joy. She managed to get the door open but no longer had the strength or the air to go any further. Samantha drew her last breaths lying in the cellar doorway.

Old Man Daniels, Beth Redley, Carol Jewell, and the merchant and his wife were all asleep in their own beds, in their own homes. However, all five of them shared the exact same, extremely vivid nightmare. In it they encountered a tall, broad-shouldered man with unnervingly dark eyes, and a startlingly deep voice. His presence invoked seemingly irrational fear in them that they could not understand. They watched as he appeared before someone draped in a large concealing robe, only their back visible, and inaudible words were exchanged before the scene changed. It was nothing but ruin and decimation, entire towns and cities gone. The outside world in purgatory, with no known survivors. Her immense fury radiated like the sun from every scathed mark upon the earth.

She had unleashed her wrath and allowed it to destroy everything in its path. They would have only simple vague memories of the nightmare the following morning but the fear that it had imprinted on them was never forgotten.

On the O'Reigan farm, Mr. O'Reigan's heart attack was directly caused by the wrath-wave, and it did indeed drive his wife mad. She had held him in her arms as he struggled and gasped for his last few haggard breaths. Her mind broke the moment his heart stopped. Their eldest daughter, married to Joshua Jones, took ill suddenly, and remained bedridden after that. Joshua was in a flustered, worried state trying everything he could to get his wife out of the semi-conscious feverish sleep she almost constantly remained in. He feared for his love, and he feared for his unborn child.

The eldest O'Reigan son and his wife were a very unhappy couple. She had been with child whenever they got married, but no one else in the valley knew that. Seven months later, she gave birth to a very small, sickly baby boy that was full-term but did not look the part. The first O'Reigan grandchild died just a few hours after birth, and it utterly destroyed her. Since the valley did not recognize divorce, a married couple remained that way until the death of one or the other, so that left the unhappy couple stuck with each other. They played the part while in the company of others, used each other for their most basic needs, but behind the closed door of their little shack the tension could be severed with a knife and the words seared like fire. His wife openly blamed him for the death of their son because she wanted to wait until after they were married but he pressured her into it before she was ready. Which was true. The result of his impatience was their son, and she believed that God took their son from them as a form of punishment for his sins. When she was not berating or belittling him, she sat in her chair in the corner of the room and silently prayed. When she wasn't at home, she was at the Church listening to Father Robin preach.

His wife sat glaring at him from across the room. He was sitting at the wooden table cutting small pieces of meat off a bone and the few wilted vegetables and herbs they had left. He could feel her eyes boring into the back of his head and could sense the intensity of her hatred for him even from the distance. He heard the squeak of the floorboards and knew she was walking up behind him, probably to see and berate what he was doing. He stepped to the side of the table and sat down in one of the chairs, continuing to cut up vegetables. She approached the table, using both her hands to lean against it and watched him closely but without comment. He had left the hair splittingly sharp meat cleaver laying on the table, like he always did, and it was about equal distance between the two of them. He reached his arm across the table to grab a small bundle of basil, when the wave passed, and brought it back to him as a bloody stump. His wife's mind had broken with that wave, and in one swift, hit she had severed straight through his wrist. She had been filled with a momentary, non-human-like strength that allowed her this incredible feat. The strength passed as quick as it came; her rage and hatred toward him, radiating from her very soul, remained constant and yearned for an unfulfilled revenge.

Blood poured from his amputated lower arm, the pain had not caught up with his brain yet, but the panic had, and he knocked the wooden chair over behind him as he raced to get away from his wife. She laughed shrilly, manically, as she watched his severed hand twitch on the table. Keeping his eyes on her, he slowly backed himself into the bedroom but before he could step out of sight, she swung around toward him. The look in her eyes frightened him to his core and he knew that he was going to die that day. The only question that remained was whether he would be able to take that hateful bitch with him. She shrieked at him and then bolted in his direction, swiping the meat cleaver back and forth in a long arch in front of her. He stood his ground, waiting for her to get closer before he tried to evade her. As soon as she was within arm's reach of him, he waited until she swung the cleaver away from him, then shoved her as hard as he could with his one hand and sprinted out of the bedroom. She landed, sprawling on the bed, and let out a small giggle before chasing him back into the main room. Unbeknownst to her, he had grabbed a large butcher's knife from the kitchen and held it close against his leg as he watched her come at him from across the room. She ran toward him again, the cleaver held high above her head, and he ducked the high-arched swing just in time. The cleaver lodged in the wall in the same place his forehead had been less than a second before. He frantically ran back into the bedroom, his heart thrashed in his chest, his mind was a mess of jumbled half thoughts, and the pain in his bloody forearm swelled with every heartbeat.

It took her a few long seconds to wrestle the cleaver out of the wall and then she returned to the bedroom to finish what she had started. She walked in and found her pale husband standing at the foot of the bed, blood dripping steadily from his missing hand. He still had the knife pressed against his leg, out of her sight, but knew he had to wait for the right moment to use it. Not only was her weapon larger and sharper, but he was fighting one-handed, literally. The odds were definitely not in his favor. He tried the same evasion maneuver that had worked for him the first time, but she expected it. She faked the same move as the first time but pulled it back at the very last second when he began to move around her. She swung the cleaver, as hard as she could, in the opposite direction and sliced right through his abdomen. The skin and muscles of his lower stomach separated, spilling a small portion of his intestines out onto his blood-soaked shirt. She shrieked in a victorious triumph that was cut short by the knife that he impaled in the side of her neck. He shoved the knife into her throat up to the hilt and then immediately dropped his remaining hand to catch his seeping organs. She stared at him with a strange, surprised look on her face as the meat cleaver slid from her hand, landing with a muffled thud on the floor. She fell back against the wall, her eyes still fixed on his, and slowly slid down to a sitting position where she would be found a few days later. Her husband fell to the bed, unconscious, seconds after she took her last breath and died several minutes later from excessive blood loss.

4

The two pair of fishermen stuck in the pier shacks had different experiences. The pair in the west pier didn't have time to react before the walls crumpled and the roof collapsed on top of them. One died instantly from being impaled on a broken board that pierced his right lung. The other died hours later, slowly suffocating from the excess amount of weight on his chest and the lack of clean air.

The pair in the east pier shack were sharing yet another bottle of Shine and having a friendly conversation about some of the women in the valley. That friendly conversation instantly turned to words of anger when the wrath hit. After a few minutes of back and forth bickering, one swung a right cross at the other. It was half-hearted and easily dodged but enough to cause him to shove the guy that swung at him. It took the man by surprise, and he stumbled backwards, his legs tangling in the chair legs, and he toppled to the floor. On his way down, he spun to the right hoping to land on his shoulder rather than his head and impacted with the small coal stove. The sick crunching sound that followed was deafening in the room and the man's body lay unmoving on the floor. The one still standing knelt beside his friend's body, shaking him, and calling his name. The jostling lolled his head to the side, and he could see the trickle of blood creeping out of his ear and the large, deep indention in his scalp right above it. He knew he was dead, and he tried desperately to recall what caused the argument to begin with. He couldn't and eventually returned to the bottle where he hit the bottom and wouldn't resurface until discovered as a survivor.

Jiminey and Patty McAvay, David Bailey, and Rebekka Lane could all hear the wind pick up outside, blowing fiercely across the valley, rattling windows, and whistling chimneys. It swirled down their chimneys, like tiny tornadoes and extinguished their toasty fires, but that was the extent of the effects of the Witch's scorn for them.

Old Man McAvay, Old Miss Jewell, and Ben Fariday all died in their sleep when the wave swept over them. Old Man McAvay and Old Miss Jewell were both resting peacefully when their hearts stopped, and they both drifted slowly into the depths of forever. In the case of Ben Fariday, he too had slipped on the bridge and fallen into the river. Except he was on the west bridge and was carried by the rushing current as far as the railroad tracks. He was thrashed around quite a bit but was able to keep his head above the water enough to keep his senses. He knew that he wouldn't have any hope of getting out of the river once he passed the tracks. When he got to them, he grabbed desperately at the riverbank, pleading with his fingers for life. For one uplifting moment his fingers caught, then almost immediately slipped, but then caught again, that time for good. He dragged himself out of the water, practically by his fingertips in the silky, stinking mud of the riverbank. The bank on that part of the river had a steep three-yard-long incline that flattened out for a couple yards before inclining another five yards and flattening back out into the valley. The deep riverbed was a natural part of the mountain, and the high banks allowed the valley a natural flood defense. He tried for several hours to no avail to climb the crazily steep riverbank and screamed for help until his throat was raw and his voice was hoarse. He woke up the morning of the third day with a high fever and terribly sick. He spent the remaining hours of his life in a half-conscious delirium before finally relenting to death's enticing kiss. The loose, starving hunting dogs found his body two days later and drug it off into the dense woods between the railroad tracks and the waterfall. He was never found, but rightfully assumed dead.

Roy Hoarding, usually a laid back, good-natured, comical man, sat in front of the small fire alone in his shack. For the first time in his life, he considered trying to kill himself. He didn't think about the details of the act itself, he focused on every depressing thing in his life and every reason he had to go through with it. The thoughts both repulsed and intrigued him, but only lasted a few minutes. When he was finally able to think of something other than suicide, understandably shaken and confused, he smoked the last of his stash. He had no memory of the heinous thoughts from the night before but a small part of him regretted indulging in the last of his Smoke.

Leena McAvay, one of the Witch's follower's, rose from a sound sleep and became violently ill when the wave passed. She dry-heaved for over an hour, having nothing in her stomach, she could only produce the smallest amounts of stomach bile. She felt feverish and faint, her muscles tensed and ached. When the dry heaving finally abated and she was able to rest, she fell asleep quickly and awoke the next morning feeling as though she had dreamt the whole thing.

The miners on Mining Road 3, sat in the dim, foul smelling cave waiting for the snow to melt enough for them to get home. Both men were awake, sitting around the fire, not saying much of anything when what felt like a small earthquake caused the ground to tremble. The cave groaned from the sporadic movement, and it echoed through the mine. Tiny pebbles rolled down the rock walls and dust drifted from the ceiling. Both men tensed and waited for what seemed to them like an inevitable mine-collapse. It never came though and after a couple hours the two men slowly started to relax.

Danny Bailey and Betty Jones, still in the lust-filled stage of their new relationship was enjoying each other when the wrath hit. For several minutes after that, their playful love making was replaced by rough, animalistic, borderline-savage fucking. They bit and clawed at each other, screamed and insulted, pinched and jabbed; tried to inflict pain. They both awoke the following morning with marks from that strange session but no memory of it.

Every time Frank McGrath thought about Sarah Maisse his heart would ache for her and he thought about her almost constantly. Sometimes those thoughts would take on a more provocative nature and his body would naturally react. By the third night, this having happened multiple times since the snow began, he was in a considerable amount of pain. Dansford had offered to help him with a release but until that night Frank had refused. They had done that and every form of playing one could imagine but never went all the way. Frank still wasn't sure how he felt about it all and had therefore rejected Dan on the few occasions he had mentioned it. He knew how Dansford felt, though, and knew that he was just waiting for Frank to admit what they were and what they should be. Frank tried not to let those thoughts bother him while he sat on a cushioned bench in front of the fire.

Frank tried much harder than the action usually required, to concentrate on Dan kneeling before him and how his mouth was making him feel when the wrath wave swept by. Suddenly, Frank wanted Dan, right there and right then. He wanted to be inside Dan more than he had ever wanted anything and he was going to have it. He didn't say anything to Dan, just shoved his head off him and didn't flinch when Dan instinctively tensed his jaw. Startled, Dan moved backwards as Frank stood up and the look in his eyes made Dan very nervous. He rolled over to crawl away, but Frank grabbed him with one arm around the waist and used his other hand to jerk down Dan's pants. Dansford struggled under Franks grasp, but it was useless because Frank was a couple inches taller and quite a bit heavier than him. He didn't stand a chance given the awkward position Frank had him in. It took only seconds for Frank to force his way into Dan, him begging Frank to stop, pleading with him not to. Frank reminded Dan of how he had always wanted it as his entirety slammed into Dan over and over. "Not like this!" Dan cried, tears streaking his cheeks from both the pain and the humiliation.

It didn't take Frank long to finish, guilt and shame washing over him immediately. He apologized profusely to Dansford, who only regarded him cautiously, and swore to himself that he would never do that with Dan or any other man ever again. As it turned out, it did happen again. Once more before morning but with Dan's consent that time, and several times before Old Joe and the girls found them. The last of which came to completion less than ten minutes before the knock on the door.

Robert Daniels, the Shine maker, hadn't had a drink of alcohol in a quarter of a century but had his first one when the wave hit. It was the most overwhelming urge he had ever experienced, and he couldn't resist it. The impulse to take another drink overrode the shame of doing so and he was drunk within the hour.

Old Mr. and Mrs. Jones were cozily asleep in bed with a small fire still burning in the front room. Mr. Jones woke up, without warning, and for the first time in well over a decade, his manhood was standing at attention. He wanted to hurriedly wake up his wife but thought better of it and decided to wake her the way he would decades ago when they were much younger and more able. It worked and Mrs. Jones woke, pleasantly surprised, and more excited about his hardness than he was. It was fun and playful, making them feel young and nostalgic.

Knowing it was their last time they savored every moment, every touch, every pleasure.

At Porter Siddle's shack, him and Ron Hellman were engaged in a conversation about the best way to polish wood when Ron began jerking and spasming, falling from the chair he was occupying. Porter panicked, dropped to his knees but was unsure of what to do or how to help Ron. It lasted several long seconds before Ron slowly stopped jerking, twitching once or twice, and his entire body visibly relaxed. Porter was relieved and in mild shock from what he had just witnessed, and Ron woke up on the floor, dazed, trying to understand what had happened. He didn't believe Porter when he told Ron about his shaking because nothing like that had ever happened to him before, but Porter had no reason to lie or make that up. He was confused but eventually they both forgot about it because it never happened again.

In the church, Father Robin was losing control. He had never been known as an understandable or understood man and a lot of people were leery of him. If he had been a patient of yours, Dr. Gerard, then you would have considered him for mania or schizophrenia. As the days continued, inside the church, his rantings would become longer and more incomprehensible. The Sisters were confused and scared but had nowhere to go, so they could only endure. On the third morning he finally ended a night-long rant about sin and forgiveness and disappeared into his own quarters for the rest of the day. The Sisters had grown accustomed to this new routine of his, the hours-long rantings that abruptly ended with him ignoring the Sisters for quite some time before calling them back for chores, food, or another sermon. The three Sisters were all still young, the oldest only being 23 years old but they had all been with Father Robin, a man well into his 40s, since they were in their early teens. Since their arrival he had instilled in them that they would only be worthy of his and God's love if they maintained undying faith and loyalty. He was the vessel in which God spoke through and, therefore, his happiness was God's happiness. The Sisters believed this with every fiber of their being, and since Father Robin was so upset and angry, God must be too.

Father Robin called on the Sisters quite a while after the wrath wave rippled across the valley. He called them to the same room he held all his sermons in but instead of being instructed to sit in the front row, he told them to stand at certain places around a wide area created by moving the long wooden benches toward the walls. There was a large circle formed by lit candles in the center of the open space and each of the three Sisters stood equidistance from the other, with Father Robin at the top of it. He was clad in a long white, preacher's robe worn for funerals only, which further confused the three women. "God sent me a vision earlier today..." he began. "...and this vision told me that by sacrifice alone can you fully repent for your sins and bask in the Lord Almighty's precious love and grace once again. Much like how..." he went into a 30-minute-long mini sermon about all the followers in the Bible that had presented sacrifices in the Lords' name. Finally, feeling that he had justified his coming actions enough to the Sisters, he instructed them to remove their habits. None of them moved. "Repent or be damned! You sinful wenches!" He screamed at them, his voice reverberating off the stone walls of the Church, making them all flinch then clumsily begin to fiddle with the buttons of their robes. All three of the women were quietly sobbing by the time they dropped the last of their clothing.

He dropped his robe, as well, his maleness jutting out from him, and all three women gasped simultaneously. They had never seen a naked man before, and wished they never had. He was uncircumcised and it reminded Sister Virtue of an eel, which revolted her. "Now is the time, Sisters, to pay for your sins... and you will pay with your virginity. The virgin blood will wash away the resentment God and I feel toward you. Once the sacrifice has been accepted, your sins will be absolved, and you will be loved by God once again!" He explained to the stunned, nude ladies standing before him. They had studied the Bible since they were very young and knew about the sacrifices mentioned in the Bible. They just never expected to have to participate in one. None of them wanted to do it but they didn't believe they could get away from him or the situation, so they continued to endure. Virgin blood was spilt that night, by all three of them, but no matter how many times Father Robin told them their sins had been washed away, they felt more guilty, ashamed, and full of sin. Luckily for the Sisters, nothing like that ever happened again.

Three of the Good Witch's followers: Rachel Smith, May Frederickson, and Anne Weston froze to death in their teepees.

When Anne Weston took her last breath, her twin sister Catherine knew, and it shattered her heart and mind. Catherine went into hysterics, leaving Abigail Fariday and Sue Ann Bailey to try to calm her. It was fruitless and her heart gave out from the exertion sometime later.

Alvin Danson, who had been seeing Anne Weston for a few months, thought he was starting to fall in love with her. His heart ached for her, so he tried to keep his mind occupied with other things. When the wave hit and Anne died and Catherine went hysterical, Alvin grieved and wept for his love. He was unaware of her demise, simply missed her and wanted to hold her more than anything in that moment. The tears lasted only a few minutes and then he was back to occupying his mind and trying to avoid thinking about her.

The only ones in the valley, and surrounding it, that weren't affected by the Witch's blast of fury were those that were already dead. Earl 'Red' Redley was also never found and rightfully presumed dead after some weeks. Sledge, Robert Daniels apprentice, had been making his way home carefully with no issues. The wind picked up, rattled the shacks around him, and abated. The next gust of wind brought a large chunk of wood sailing off the roof of the shack Sledge was walking by, and it crashed into the side of his head, knocking him unconscious into the slush and falling snow where he froze to death a few hours later. He remained there until the dogs found him. The scraps of clothing Johnathan found were what little remained of Sledge.

The pieces Rebekka had found belonged to one of the miners from the salt mine on Mining Road 1. They had made it less than halfway back when one of them fell and broke his leg, making him unable to walk. The other guy could barely keep his own footing on the slick ice and in the blinding snow, so they agreed that he would go back to the valley and get help to carry the broken one off the mountain. The guy with the broken leg froze to death propped up against a tree waiting for help to arrive. The other guy made it most of the way to the valley when he finally lost his footing, sending him crashing to inch deep snow with a thick layer of ice underneath. The fall stunned him, but his exhaustion drew him into an unrestful slumber. He woke sometime later, surrounded by the vicious dog pack, snarling and obviously hungry. He forgot all about his friend on the hill, about his fall, and needing to get to the valley. He just wanted to survive, but the dogs attacked the moment he made a move to get away. He died a very painful, brutal death.

The soaking wet miners out on Mining Road 7 that made their way out of the flooded mine they had been trapped in, made it about a third of the way back to the valley before the shivering stopped and they no longer felt cold. Minutes later their bodies rested in the falling snow, and they drifted into oblivion. Days later their bodies would be found and used to nourish the pack of dogs, but no person would ever find any trace of them.

Chapter Twenty-Four

Powerless Magic

1

The Witch had never felt anything like the power that coursed through her. She could feel the electrifying tingle in every part of her body. She enjoyed it, savored it, let it devour her. She felt like the most powerful being in the world, she felt invincible and unstoppable. Right up until he appeared, and everything changed. The feeling of immense power within her slightly faded, as did her feelings of invulnerability and she stood before the man that wasn't a man, dumbfounded by his sudden and unnoticed appearance, everything else momentarily forgotten.

The being standing before her resembled a man, a very handsome man, in every way except for his eyes. His eyes were the immediate giveaway that he was not what he appeared to be. He stood well over six feet tall, with every muscle in his arms, legs, shoulders, and torso prominent and outstanding. With dark hair, a strong jawline, and masculine features he was the most handsome man she had ever laid eyes on. His eyes, however, resembled those of a snake or another cold-blooded being. They were more elongated than normal, and the pupils were much smaller than they should have been. When he blinked, his eyelids did not fall and

THE WITCH'S TAROT

retract back up like anyone else's would. They
closed sideways, meeting in the middle over his
too small pupil and retracted back into the sides
of his eyes. It was one of the most bizarre things
the Witch had ever seen.

The man smiled down at her sweetly and
when he spoke, his voice had the soothing
quality of a loving mother cooing at her fussy
infant. Just the calming tone of his voice helped
her relax the slightest bit. "Please do not fear
me. I have come to grant you what you desire
most in this world. The revenge you so wish
you could inflict on a certain Loverboy that
has scorned you and the deceitful cunt that
made him do it. Am I wrong?" the strange man
asked her.

She said nothing but shook her head
indicating that he was not wrong. That sweet,
charming smile again. "I have desired you since
the moment you let me in all those decades ago,
no matter how brief it was. It was your inner
strength and confidence that intrigues me so,
and I have been watching you ever since. I have
been hiding in wait gathering my strength,
longing for the time when you would beg for
my help once more. You finally have and I have
granted your deepest desire."

The Witch visibly tensed once again and eyed
the man carefully. Her thoughts took her back
to those long, excruciating hours of fighting off
that terrible darkness. She had almost convinced
herself that she had vanquished the demon all
those decades ago. The knowledge that she hadn't
summoned fear deep within her that she had
to willfully repress. She could not allow fear to
take over because she would surely fail. "So..."
she tried, her voice catching in her throat. She
swallowed hard and tried again. "So, you're the
one that gave me this power?"

269

His sweet smile changed the smallest bit, hiding a slyness behind that was kept just out of sight. "Well, give is a strong word, dear. I am merely allowing you to use a fraction of my own power. Of course, a payment of sorts will be required later, but you mustn't worry yourself about all that right now." With that the subject was closed and the Witch took the hint. "I say..." he said changing the subject. "... we must do something with your hair. You're too... too... angelic looking." He said the last words with such disgust that it left a bad taste in his mouth. He recreated her, changing everything about her he found distasteful, into his version of the perfect sorceress. Now he just needed her to act the part.

He held a mirror before her stunned face. She was speechless at the astounding transformation she had just endured, barely recognizing her own reflection. She stared for several long minutes and the handsome fellow stood by quietly until the shock wore off. When it finally wore off and she was able to communicate again, he told her that she was the most beautiful and powerful woman in the world and could remain so as long as she stood by his side. She looked deep into his strange reptilian eyes for a long moment but said nothing.

The man/demon, named Malum, tried to read her eyes and expression, probing with unseen fingers for any indication as to what her reaction could be. Her prolonged silence had begun to play on his nerves when she finally answered him. The following seconds were a complete shock to both the Witch and the handsome man with the strange eyes. "I will stand beside no man... or demon!" she proclaimed with the flick of her finger. That flick would have blown any other being through the cave wall and landed them somewhere in her garden to be dealt with by one of the many magical creatures that occupied it. The man-demon never flinched, moved, or blinked. He simply stood before her with a look of astonishment on his face. An expression that screamed, 'I can't believe you dared speak to me in such a manner!' She stared at her finger, speechless and awestruck, then tried again, a little more forcefully. Again, nothing happened and Malum offered no reaction. The third try was done with her entire hand flicking her wrist and concentrating all her power upon the demon. Nothing.

2

Confusion turned to anger when she figured out that her magic was more-or-less ineffectual against Malum, and that anger churned and fueled the rage that burned deep within her. Using both hands and her newly acquired power she concentrated and aimed. The powerful current of magic surged at Malum, discoloring, distorting, and rippling the surrounding background. The beam of magic, about the width of a ruler and glowing an intense black that was almost too bright to look at, would have incinerated a grown adult in less than ten seconds, but Malum only stood and smiled at her. Completely unscathed and unfathomed by it, as if it wasn't even happening.

She held the beam on him for almost a full minute, finally allowing her hands to drop and dangle exhaustedly at her sides. She was spent and she knew it. She also knew that it had been a futile attempt and that angered her all the more. She slumped heavily into a chair, trying to regain some of her strength. She caught movement in her peripherals and watched as Malum slowly approached, that same smile spread across his face. She noticed that everything about a yard out from where Malum stood had been burnt to ash or blackened. There was an evident path where the magic beam had been projected. The magic had penetrated the cave wall around Malum leaving a man-sized rock cutout attached at the top and bottom of the wall. It went out into the garden, the enchantment spared the foliage, and it tapered out on the mountainside.

He sat down in one of the other chairs, his eyes never wavering from her. "You must have missed the part about how the power you contain is only a fraction of the power that I possess?" he asked her, putting unneeded emphasis on the phrase 'only a fraction'. She said nothing and only glared at the demon with hate-filled eyes. "Of course, you couldn't have harmed me I am much too powerful for that." He sighed heavily, as if distressed. "Are you aware that I could force you to do as I please?" he asked, in a softer huskier voice. "I could take your very mind from you. I could make you my stringless puppet, to do with as I please." His tone taking on a hint of sinisterness. "But that's not what I want. I want you to want to be by my side." Malum reached over to grab one of the Witch's hands, but she jerked her arm back and quickly stood up before he could try again. She did not want him to touch her, no matter how handsome he was or how many times she had wondered what he was packing, just the thought of his hands on her skin made her feel dirty and gross.

The Witch walked to the opposite side of the table and started fiddling with the bundle of incense she had left lying there. "What if I don't want that?" the Witch asked Malum, a hint of defiance in her voice.

Malum sat silent and thoughtful for a few moments before answering her. He decided to answer her question with a question and asked, "Why would you not want that?"

The witch stared at him with a look of astonishment on her face. "You... are... a... demon." She told Malum, saying it slowly and deliberately, as if speaking to a young child or a confused great-grandparent. "You are evil, and you want me to be evil with you. I'm not like you. I'm not a bad witch or a bad person. I'm good and I always have been!" She hailed the last statement proudly, but a tiny part of her deep down knew that it was all a lie. "You can have your power back if that is the cost. I do not want it! Take it back!" she demanded, and he watched her struggle to keep her emotions under control.

Malum sat in the chair and watched the display of defiance and naivety to its completion before he could retain his laughter no more. When the long moments of laughter had subsided and there were only a few giggles remaining, he told her what he found so amusing. Knowing she was curious simply by the look on her face. "I can't take it back. You lost that chance the moment you gave into the power, and let it overtake you. You are mine whether you want to be or not!" He told her, rising from his chair. "You will obey me!" He took two steps away from the chair, eyes locked on hers and his voice was getting deeper. "You will stand by my side!" Two more steps around the table toward her. His voice deepened and took on a slight rumble that sounded like he was speaking through a throat full of pebbles and stones. "And you will thank me for this opportunity as many times and in as many ways as I see fit!" He was standing right in front of the Witch, and she could feel the fear trying to snake its way through the rage.

The Witch glared at him, the rage seething in her eyes and voice. "I am no man's... or demon's fuckin puppet! Not now and not ever!" She took

273

a step toward him, and even though he towered over her she felt herself a formidable match for the evil, vile being that stood in front of her. "You will never control me! As you said, I am the most powerful woman in the world, and I will not be brought to my knees! Especially not by the likes of you." She was panting by the time she completed her rant, the fury within her threatening to boil over again. She fought mightily to keep the upper hand on it.

Once again, Malum waited until she had finished her spiel before laughing at her ignorance. The laughter rolled out of his mouth and off his tongue, the shrill sounds drilling their way into the Witch's mind, enraging her even further. She could take his cockiness and arrogance no more. She raised her delicate-appearing hand and slapped him hard across the face. The sound echoed through the caves, the strength and suddenness of it rocked Malum's head back, and she knew she should regret what she had just done. She just couldn't quite bring herself to feel that guilt, shame, and regret though.

Less than a moment later she felt her airways being restricted as if something had just been wrapped around her throat. She clawed at her neck, only to find there wasn't anything there to claw away. Her face started to turn red and puffy, her eyes slightly bulging from the pressure, and she fought desperately for the trickle of air she was able to suck into her lungs. Her vision had started to become splotchy and shaded when she noticed the black flames in his eyes. She watched the fire pop and crackle in all its strangeness. She knew at that moment that she had made a terrible mistake, but she still could not bring herself to regret it. Malum took a step toward her, the tip of his nose mere centimeters from her cheek. "I'm going to make you regret that!" He told her in a harsh, raspy whisper. "I'm going to make you wish your mama would have swallowed you instead! Oh, yes! You will regret that!" His breath was hot on her cheek and foul in her nostrils. He smelled like death and his breath indicated he had been feasting on it. It sickened and revolted her which only added to her fury.

With a strength she wasn't aware she possessed, the Witch resisted the demon's powers enough to turn her head and take in a few meaningful breaths of air. "Never... regret... it", it came out as an almost inaudible whisper, but Malum had heard her loud and clear. Then she smiled at him through purpling lips. He wasn't sure which one was more astounding, her strength or her audacity. Regardless, he had grown tired of her insolence and disrespect. She needed to be punished; she needed to be broken; she needed to be taught.

He stared at her through his unnerving eyes for a long moment and then returned her smile, which surprised the smile off the Witch's face. She felt whatever had been restricting her airways release her and she began taking full deep breaths again. Malum suddenly snapped his fingers and the Witch collapsed into a lazy heap on the cave floor. She appeared to be sleeping but was in a coma-like trance that swallowed her consciousness and sent it into a dark oblivion. This oblivion landed the Witch in what she could only assume was Hell itself.

Chapter Twenty-Five

Internal Battlegrounds

1

She must have been one tough broad if she could survive Hell. Warren Gerard thinks to himself as he slides the papers back into the manilla envelope. He knows it's late and he knows he's going to be tired in the morning. He had tried several times tonight to stop reading, to put it away, and finally succeeded when the Witch was taken to Hell. He had even contemplated calling off work tomorrow so he could binge read the rest of the night. However, he knows he can't process that information on top of everything else he has already read. *And if I don't get some dang sleep then I won't be able to process anything tomorrow, either.*

The next day is hectic and borderline chaotic, but at the end of the day Dr. Gerard returns home with a sense of relief and a lot of confused thoughts. It starts out groggy with lots of too strong black coffee. A meeting is held first thing and assignments are doled out accordingly. The biggest issue is getting the room furnished, set-up, cleaned and sanitized before Monday. Usually, they are given a couple weeks' notice and have ample time to order and retrieve all the furniture and items required for the patient's rooms. They would use a week to furnish and set up the patient's room, a day to clean and two to sanitize. That is not the case this time, so everyone is scurrying around trying to find everything needed to meet the asylums requirements. This is a rush job, but it would be completed according to the specifications, just not done to the lengthy and extra careful extent they would usually take.

The first issue of the day is brought to Dr. Gerard's attention shortly after he returns from the morning meeting. A bed has been located but it is in poor condition, needing a few new nuts and bolts to replace the rusted ones that is making it unstable. He sends a maintenance man out to the nearest hardware store to retrieve some and get it fixed. Problem solved, just like that.

Halfway through his morning paperwork the second issue arises. Ms. Lancing knocks on his office door and informs him that he is needed in the Infirmary because Greg Patrickson had awakened and is wanting to see him. Naturally, Warren rushes down the hallway to speak to the newly conscious man. "It's good to see you awake Mr..." Dr. Gerard says as he walks in the room and approaches the chair placed beside Mr. Patrickson's bed. Before he can finish though, Greg interrupts him.

"Burn it!" Greg tells him in a hoarse, cracked voice. He takes a long sip from a lidded cup with a rubber straw sticking out of the top of it. "Burn it, Doc!" He repeats, his eyes large and almost bulging from the sockets.

Warren sighs heavily and loudly. *Manic.* He thinks to himself while mentally scolding himself for believing even for a moment that he was going to come in here and have a conversation with a sane man. "Burn what?" he asks Mr. Patrickson, trying to keep the exasperation out of his voice.

Greg stares at him for a long moment before answering. "Da letta, acourse. Da one Joe left for ya." Greg tells him with a don't-play-dumb-with-me tone.

Dr. Warren Gerard is speechless. No one else knows about that letter except for him, not even the nurses that cleaned Joe's room knew what was in that manilla envelope. So how did this mind-broken fool know about it? He swallowed hard around a growing lump in his throat. When he is finally able to find his voice again, the doctor asks, "How... how do you know about the letter?" in a small, weak voice.

"Joe tole me."

"Joe?" Confusion. "Joe came back?" *But that's not possible, he is dead! He can't come back... can he?*

"Acourse not!" Greg eyes the doctor with the same don't-play-dumb-with-me look and goes on. "He's dead, doc, or have ya convinced yaself of yer own lies?"

In this moment, Dr. Gerard realizes that Gregory Patrickson might be able to give him information he hasn't or won't be able to find elsewhere. A slight tingle of shame touches him for his actions, and he apologizes to Greg. "If he didn't come back then how did he tell you about the letter?" he asks.

"He tole me last night in muh dreams. Since he died I's had turrible nightmares bout him bein hurt an tortured in da worst ways I's eva seed an some I's couldn't even imagines. Night afta night I keeps seein doze hurrible thangs an I taut I's gonna go crazy from it." Warren had to stifle a giggle at the unnoticed irony of the man's statement. "Den las night one of da nightmares was a lot different dan da rest of em. A real purtty lady was dere insteada creepy lil demon thangs dat done all the hurtin an whatnot. She ast him ova an ova who he left da letta wit an fo a long time he wouldn't answa her. She done thangs to him without even touchin him, makin him squirm an scream. She broke him, finely, an he whispaed yer name. Da smile on her face was pure evil, doc. Den, Joe turned his head real slow like an, I's don't know how, but he looked right ats muh an den I woke up. Been awake eva since an tinkin bout how to tell ya bout all dis. I tink dat purtty lady might be lookin for ya now. Ya gotta get ridda dat letta fore she finds ya wit it!"

Dr. Gerard sits speechless once again, trying desperately to process and comprehend what Greg was telling him. *The Witch could be after me... as in' The Witch', all because an unnamed man wrote a ridiculously long letter telling me an outrageous fairytale? Thinking about it like this makes the whole situation seem completely ludicrous. Why am I reading that unbelievable tale? Why am I talking to this clearly insane patient that just woke up from an unidentifiably sourced coma? Why am I looking into this at all? I don't even know who he was, so why did he put this burden on me? I must be losing my mind! I must be. It's the only thing that makes any sense right now. I've done lost my mind and as soon as someone who isn't already a patient here figures it out, I'll be Greg's next-door neighbor. All because I opened that gosh darn envelope!*

"It's a lot to process, ain't it, doc?" Greg asks rhetorically and Warren comes out of his own half-mad thoughts. He doesn't answer his question.

"I don't believe you." He told Greg half-heartedly but with some conviction, after a few moments of silence. He needs more time to think over everything and decide what to do then. Hopefully he would be more rational then because right now his thoughts were anything but.

Gregory Patrickson simply gazes at Warren through bloodshot, sunken-in eyes that burn with vitality. He is pleading with the doctor for him to heed his warning but is unsure if the message is received because there is no reaction from the doctor. After several long moments, Dr. Gerard stands up from the bedside chair, hesitating at the foot of the bed before walking to the door. "I hope you enjoy the rosary I left you." He says to Greg but Greg only stares at him and says nothing so Warren walks out.

As soon as he is out of sight, Greg looks down at the cross-shaped burn on the palm of his left hand. The blackened edges make the bright pink of inner flesh stand out in comparison. The area around the outside of the edges is a lighter shade of pink with bright red tendrils streaking in several directions. There is no pain, and he only came across it because he rubbed his hands together and felt the unfamiliar, raised edges of the scald. It is a nasty looking wound and now he knows how he got it, but not why.

2

Warren Gerard collapses into his office chair, breathing heavily, sweat popping out on his forehead. He reaches up and loosens his tie. Then, a few moments later follows that up by unbuttoning the top of his shirt. He feels like everything is coming unraveled around him and he can't get a grip on anything. The more he thinks about it the stronger the feelings of despair, depression, failure, etc. try to overwhelm him.

He is still trying to catch his breath when Ms. Lancing gives a quick tap on his door and then abruptly opens it. "Not now, Ms. Lancing, please." He says without looking up at her.

"But sir..." she says hurriedly, not getting very far.

"I said not now, Ms. Lancing."

"Doctor, please! You're nee..."

"I said not now!" he screams at her, rising from his chair and slamming his hands on the desk with a loud smack that startles a jump out of his lovely little secretary. She quickly composes herself, standing up straighter, almost rigid, but her eyes glare with a ferocity that screams how angry she is. She turns and walks out of his office, softly closing the door behind her.

Warren sighs heavily, feeling ashamed for yelling at her, and slowly relaxes back into his chair when there is another knock on his office door. He says nothing, hoping Ms. Lancing will get the point and handle whatever she thinks is so important right now. Another knock and his irritation grow into anger, but still, he says nothing. The third knock and he is out of his chair and across the room in two swift, almost-agile movements. "I TOLD YOU…" he screams as he flings the office door open, expecting Ms. Lancing to be standing there. She isn't though, she's standing off to the side with a knowing smirk on her face, enjoying her asshole boss get served a nice little dose of instant karma.

Dr. Gerard's eyes widen, and his mouth snaps shut when he realizes that the Governor is standing in his office doorway, and he immediately knows he screwed up by not listening to his secretary a few moments before. Standing behind the Governor is a younger man carrying a briefcase and wearing a suit that is supposed to look expensive but really isn't, and two other gentleman that look more like professional fighters in business attire. Dr. Gerard's frightened eyes take in all four of them and he swallows around the knot swelling in his throat before stammering out an apology. He steps aside so the four gentlemen can step into his office.

The Governor and the man with the briefcase sit in the only two chairs in the office and the two mean looking men stand by the door much the same way the guards do when they bring a patient in to see him. With everyone situated, Dr. Gerard sits in his seat behind the desk and smiles uneasily at the Governor.

The Governor of Georgia, Matthew Bourdan, sits in the uncomfortable chair and eyes Dr. Gerard carefully, as if he is sizing him up. His first impression of the man was a poor one and he isn't sure if he should give him the opportunity to amend it or justify his demeaning actions. When he finally speaks to Warren there is an icy note in his voice. "Is that how you speak to all your employees, Mr. Gerard?" Emphasis on the *mister.*

"I'm a doctor, sir." Warren begins, his tone indicating his disapproval of the Governor's lack of respect. Bad first impression or not, he is still a very successful doctor. "To answer your question, no I do not. That was an isolated incident, sir. I deeply regret and apologize for it and assure you that Ms. Lancing will be told the same. My actions were inexcusable, but if you ask anyone that works for me, they will tell you that I am generally mild tempered and not easily roused." Warren finishes in a softer, apologetic voice.

Mr. Bourdan eyes Dr. Gerard for a few more seconds before telling him that he might just do that and then changes the subject. "I have been gettin more letters than I am comfortable with, about how some of my fine folks are gettin a bit nervous where your name and asylum have been in the papers so much lately. First an escapee, now three new patients in just a few weeks. One of them being the infamous serial rapist that's shaken my state! I understand their concern, which is why I am here. I want to know what the hell is going on around here. If it's safe to say, there isn't going to be a bunch of psychos running around all over the damn place. Why the increase in patients? I need to be able to tell the folks that voted for me what they want to know. So, help me out here."

"That's a lot of questions at once, sir." Warren says, overwhelmed by the rush of inquiries. "Slow down and ask me one at a time. I will answer anything you want to know..." he hesitates a moment, "...within reason, of course." The Governor arches an eyebrow curiously, but Warren only shrugs. "Patient confidentiality and all that kind of legal stuff. I've got to honor my oath, wouldn't be a very good doctor if I didn't." Warren tells him with a nervous little giggle.

"Right." Matt Bourdan responds with a hint of obvious sarcasm. "Well, what happened with the escapee? Let's start there." They do and they speak for almost two hours before the Governor, his assistant and his two security guards leave. Warren tells him the same story he told the police and the media about Joseph Doe and tells him about how his room had been cleaned and locked up, as is procedure, on the seventh day. He tells Matt that he still has men out looking for him, a private team that he hires for those that manage to get past all the obvious blockades around the asylum, and the Governor seems satisfied with this lie.

Warren briefly tells Matt about the incident with Greg and the maintenance man, Sam, but is quick to assure him that it has been settled. They speak of the three temporary patients which greatly relieves the Governor, and he has his assistant make a note to check on the relocation of the other asylum. Then Dr. Gerard reassures the Governor that there is absolutely no need to worry about the patients getting out because most of them don't even know where they are. So, they wouldn't know how to get out of the labyrinth of a building the asylum is to anyone unfamiliar with it.

Warren did not mention his eyes, the items found in room 32, Greg Patrickson's coma, or anything else that might have alerted any of his guests that something strange was going on. He isn't in denial about it, he just understands that it is unbelievable and trying to convince someone that has nothing to do with the situation just seems like more effort and energy than Warren can spare.

The Governor leaves satisfied with the information he received and is relieved to have answers for his voters.

3

Once again, Dr. Gerard falls into his chair, sighing heavily, a headache threatening to start pounding at his temples. *It's just one thing after another today. I need to catch my breath, dang.* He thinks to himself when there's a knock on his office door again. Another heavy sigh and he permits entrance. It's Ms. Lancing informing him of yet another problem.

"The thermostat in the room isn't working. One of the maintenance men has already started looking at it while the other finishes up with the bed." She tells him bluntly and coldly.

"The problem is being resolved, though?" He asks but she only nods. "Okay, thank you. And Ms. Lancing I would like to apolo…" but he stops because she is already walking back out of his office, closing the door behind her a little more forcefully than normal. He gets the point and doesn't pursue her.

A couple hours later, Dr. Gerard is informed that they can only find less than half of the items needed to accessorize the room, so Warren sends two of his friendliest nurses over to the women's asylum to ask if they could donate any extra supplies they have. The nurses return a short time later with a few more of the things they need but are still short of toiletries such as toothpaste, comb, deodorant, etc. and some more bedding. Reluctantly, he sends a couple nurses to the closest market to get whatever else is needed.

Still no news on the thermostat.

It's almost time for the night shift to start trudging through the doors when Dr. Gerard calls all his employees together for a quick end-of-the-day meeting. He gives them a quick rundown of their day's progress, informing them that the room is completely furnished, and all accessories have been acquired. The thermostat still isn't working but Warren has already called an electrician that would only come in for double pay since it is Sunday, and he is going to have to miss church for it. Warren had begrudgingly agreed to pay through gritted teeth. He thanks them all for their hard work and positive attitudes and reminds them of the bonus with their next check.

As the shifts change, Warren goes back to his office to finish up the rest of the day's paperwork. He finds Ms. Lancing standing at her desk, gathering her things to leave, and he can feel shame wash over him. He starts to apologize again, but she waves him away and he knows it's useless. She grabs her bag off her desk and shoves her way by him, without speaking or making eye contact. He reaches out and grabs her arm, just above the elbow to beg her to please speak to him and to please at least allow him to apologize even if she won't accept it. But before he can get a single syllable past his lips, Vivian flings her arm back and slaps him across the face. It is hard enough to rock his head back and stagger him a step, leaving a stinging, red, whelped, handprint where she made contact. Warren is flabbergasted momentarily before it all converts to fury like he has never felt before. He releases her arm but then grabs her by both shoulders and shakes her until her head bobbles, lost in vile thoughts all the while. *How dare she lay a hand on me like that?!? No woman has ever struck me like that, and I will not let this... this... this little WHORE go unpunished. Oh, no! She will not...*

His thoughts cease immediately when he feels her lips on his. She draws back, stiff in his grasp, and he releases her. She throws one arm around his neck, drawing her mouth and body closer to his and runs the fingers of her other hand across his groin. The confused look on Warren's face quickly disappears and he wraps his arms around her waist, drawing her even closer to him, trapping her arm and hand between them. She kisses him forcefully, biting his lower lip, and squeezes his crotch just hard enough to send a twinge of pain into his lower abdomen. "Show me how fuckin sorry you are!" She whispers in his ear as her tongue laps playfully at his earlobe. He lifts her off the floor, and she jerks the hem of her skirt up high on her thighs so that she can wrap her legs around his waist. He carries her into his office, barely getting the door closed and locked before she starts clawing at his clothes.

It ends much sooner than either one of them wants it to, but it has already been over an hour and they both have plenty of sore rug burns. He tells her about his house and how he lives alone and extends the offer that if she ever wants to come over, she is more than welcome. That way they would have plenty of space… and a bed… and as much time as she would allow. She thanks him as she wipes his juices from her thighs and ass, off her breasts, her chin, and the small squirt that got in her hair. They dress and depart, going their separate ways, until the next time.

On the drive home, Warren thinks about Greg Patrickson and what he said about burning the letter. *Should I burn it? Should I finish it first? Should I finish it at all? Surely there is no Witch and it's all just a made-up story out of the screwed-up mind of a mentally disturbed man. Right? None of this is real. And I never believed that it was. I have just been reading the letter out of mere curiosity and once it is finished my curiosity will be satiated. Right? Yes. That's right. It must be. Its simple curiosity brought on by the lack of information we have on a man that had been there as long as Joe. I was just trying to find out more about the mystery man. That's all. There is no Witch and Gregory Patrickson is a crazed man that talks out of his head. I will finish the letter only to satisfy my curiosity on the subject and then that will be the end of this whole strange situation.* With that, Dr. Warren Gerard makes up his mind on the subject.

Once home, showered, and settled in, Warren sits in his den with a shot of whiskey that he is swirling around in one of his decanter glasses.

Even though he is sure in his decision to finish the letter, he is reluctant to pick it up and 'un-pause' the movie. A small part of him, shoved way back in the recesses of his mind, thinks he should listen to Greg and just toss the manilla envelope into the burning fireplace. That small part of him is being very loud, vocal, and adamant about his opinion on the matter and Warren is locked in an internal battleground for it.

4

A knock at his back door brings him out of his self-conflict and back to reality. He looks around the room, his heart racing, unsure if he really heard a knock at the door or if he had only imagined it. He hears it again and is relieved to know that he isn't losing his mind... yet anyway. The relief turns into confusion when he looks at the time and sees that it is after 9:30 at night and full dark out, but that confusion turns to curiosity as he walks to the door to see who it is.

He is pleasantly surprised, but somewhat embarrassed, to find that Vivian Lancing is standing on his back porch. *Oh, my God! I can't believe she actually showed up. What am I going to do?!?!* He asks himself in a mild panic. He had only ever vividly fantasized about such encounters with the lovely Ms. Lancing and in every one of them he is the cool, flawless, stud that he has always wanted to be. Now that she is actually standing on his back porch waiting to come into his home, he feels like the exact opposite of that cool, flawless stud. He can feel his testicles shrivel, his heart quickens, his temples pound, and a few dozen butterflies take flight in the pit of his stomach. All immediate symptoms of lovesickness. He is a nervous wreck but can't quite understand why since they've already been together more than once. Just another item to add to the list of things he doesn't understand.

Standing at his back door, he feels like a fool, hesitating so long before answering the door. Since she hadn't knocked anymore, and hasn't left yet, she must know that he is in here. With a strength he isn't sure he can muster he opens the door for the beautiful woman. She looks up at him with a fire in her eyes that could rival the flames of Hell and a yearning in her loins that he could sense from the doorway. He knows, beyond a shadow of a doubt, why she is here. He extends his hand, and she places her much smaller one in his so he can lead her into his home.

There isn't any greeting or small talk. No drink or evening meal. No movie or walk or date of any kind. He simply leads her into one of the guest bedrooms, where he takes all his flings, and quickly shows her around. Normally he is very uncomfortable with this part of the night and watches for distinct signs and changes in their behavior. With Vivian though, he shows her his 'sex room' with a sense of dignity that borderlines on pride. There is a massive four-post wooden bed, king size, swathed in a plush sherpa comforter with matching pillowcases. Shag carpet underfoot is equally as soft, and a large velvet area rug lays out in front of a beautifully crafted fireplace. There is a nightstand on both sides of the huge bed, both containing a drawer full of condoms and various types of lubes. On the right side of the fireplace is a large wooden chest filled with an assortment of sex toys. Dildos and vibrators, cock rings and ball gags, whips and handcuffs, anal beads and nipple clamps. Anything one could want could probably be found in that wooden chest and if it couldn't be, then Warren would find one. On the left side of the fireplace is a door leading to a small bathroom. It is almost spotless with a slight lingering odor of cleaner. There is a small sink, toilet and stand-up shower, all matching in an off-white color.

Vivian takes in her surroundings with wide, hungry eyes that jump with excitement at the box of toys. *This could definitely satisfy a few of my kinkier cravings.* She thinks to herself as Warren says, "I'll be back in 15 minutes, unless you would like more time than that."

She looks around the room, taking her time before meeting his eyes again. "Be back in ten." She tells him flatly, and then walks into the small, not-quite-white bathroom and closes the door.

Ten minutes later and after several nerve-calming shots, Warren Gerard stands outside the closed door to the guest bedroom where he knows Vivian is waiting for him. He was able to get his racing heart under control once he left her in the guest bedroom but now it was worse than before. He knows all this excitement can't be good on his aging heart and he wonders, not for the first time, how it is that he has been able to have sex as much and as well as he has been lately. Another item on the rapidly growing Do Not Understand List. He reaches for the doorknob, but his hand pauses just before his fingers touch the cool metal. He hesitates for a moment, then opens the door and enters the room.

Their sexual rendezvous goes on for almost three hours when Vivian Lancing finally calls it a night. Warren is relieved because that had been the kinkiest, craziest sex he had ever had. He had no idea Vivian even knew about some of the things they had done and quickly realized that she may just be too much of a woman for him. He endured though, with only a trace amount of regret, because those anal beads did not feel the least bit pleasurable when she jerked them out of him like she was pulling on a lawn mower cord. That was one of the few times she made him squall like a wounded banshee. Viv had taken two sets of nipple clamps and attached one to each of her nipples and fastened the other clamps on Warren's balls while he pounded her doggy style. He squalled when she clamped them on him, and he begged her to take them off, but she told him no that the pleasure would overcome the pain soon and to go harder. The pain did not turn to pleasure, but he did go harder. The last time was when she surprised him with the horse-cock sized dildo she had found at the bottom of the chest, almost forgotten. It took her using both of her hands to hold and maneuver it properly. She had cuffed him to the bed, on his stomach with the guise of a sexy back rub and some wax play. Warren was so sexed up he didn't really care why she was tying him down on his stomach instead of his back, he was just going with the flow and enjoying the ride along the way. He did enjoy it too, right up until she penetrated him with half of the massive dildo in one quick shove. She didn't even use any lube.

Warren is asleep minutes after he returns to his bed from walking her out. He offered to give her a ride home, but she declined, so he offered to walk her home instead, since it was after one in the morning. She declined that offer too and he settled with walking her to his back door and giving her a quick kiss goodnight.

He sleeps until morning, but it is a restless sleep, tossing and turning all night, the nightmares more vivid than any he has ever had. His first thought upon awaking is not of the horrid nightmares from the night before or of the lovely Vivian Lancing, but of the letter. He can sense a nagging sensation at the back of his mind urging him to pick it up and un-pause the movie. The nightmares fade with the light of the morning sun, and he is grateful for the lack of memories because the fear they instilled in him is still very fresh. So is his exhaustion from the previous evening and night's activities with Vivian, as well as his tiredness from his restless sleep. He trudges into work on this beautiful, warm Sunday morning anyway.

5

It starts out much like the previous morning with much-needed coffee and the morning meeting. The letter lingers in the back of his mind all the while. With all that out of the way, Warren is in his office starting on his morning paperwork when Ms. Lancing taps on the door, looking fresh and well rested, informing him that the electrician has arrived. Warren, begrudgingly, writes out the man's check for double his usual pay and walks out to greet him. The electrician earns his day's pay because the problem ends up being much bigger than either of them had anticipated. It takes him almost six hours to get the job done but the thermostat is working like new when he leaves The Navea Dwighton Asylum for the Mentally Afflicted with his check in his pocket.

The fact that the electrician took most of their last prep day rewiring half the building to get one thermostat working worries Dr. Gerard. He has never missed a deadline and has no intention of starting now but the nagging sensation for the letter is fogging his thoughts. After some deliberation, he calls another meeting two hours before shift change, piquing the curiosity of the volunteer employees that are working for overtime plus the bonus promised on their next checks. He divides his employees into two groups, one group larger by three people, and gives them careful instructions on what to do next. The larger of the two groups are set with the task of cleaning the coming-patients room. Everything; floor to ceiling, wall to wall, and everything big and small in between must be wiped down with a weak antibacterial and hypoallergenic solution. The group of seven are told, with adamancy, by Dr. Gerard that the room should be clean before they leave for the night. They all know that if they work diligently, they will be done by shift change. The smaller group of four are instructed to mix and prepare the sanitation solution so that it will be ready and waiting when everyone arrives in the morning. If they are going to be ready and prepared tomorrow afternoon when the patient arrives, the sanitizer must be ready. They too are told that they should finish the task before leaving for the evening.

All tasks are complete, and all employees go home at shift change. The room is furnished and stocked. Everything is in working order. It is clean, quickly done but properly done. The sanitizing solution is ready and stowed away in one of the janitor's closets for the morning. A group of seven can sanitize the room in approximately the same amount of time it had taken them to clean it this evening. Everything is going to work out, and they will be ready when the patient arrives tomorrow. Feeling relieved and much calmer, Warren leaves the asylum trying to push the increasingly more intrusive thoughts of the letter tucked away in the manilla envelope out of his mind so he can focus on the few errands he needs to run before going home for the night.

Chapter Twenty-Six

Malum's Abode

1

A few hours later, errands ran, dinner eaten, showered, and settled in, Warren sits on the couch in his den with a scotch-on-the-rocks in hand. He is staring at the manilla envelope lying on the coffee table in front of him, once again locked in that mental battleground with the annoying voice in the back of his mind urging him to heed Greg's warning.

Just throw it in the fireplace. You know it's dangerous and will only bring you despair!

That's absurd! It's just a story, a fairytale created in the mind of a crazed man that refused to even tell us who he was... for 30 years!

If you're as certain as you say you are then why am I here? I am a figment of YOUR mind; therefore, my mere existence is proof of your doubt.

(Long hesitation) You're right. You are a figment of my mind and only exist because of my own doubt. You could be right about everything. Maybe I should burn it... but something keeps nagging at me to finish it.

Joe sent you a warning using Greg as the messenger. Why do you refuse to believe that? Why would you not heed a warning sent by the man that wrote and left the letter to you and you alone?

The man was in an asylum! The letter is just a made-up story he wrote, and for all I know he actually did believe it all happened, and everything was real! I don't! I don't believe in witches and magic and demons! It's all way too unbelievable to be real.

Explain your eyes then.

Simple. They are flash burned from the sudden bright light that occurred when Joe spontaneously combusted in his room. Yeah! That's what happened to him. That's the only thing that makes sense... sort of.

(A heavy sigh) ***You are impossible! Terrible things are coming! Mark my words! Please, I implore you to burn the letter now, be done with it, and maybe... just maybe she won't find you.***

I... I can't.

The inner voice dissipates, and Warren is left in the silence of his den still staring at the manilla envelope. He knocks back the last swallow of his scotch and goes to get him another glassful. He tells himself that he really shouldn't read tonight since he is so exhausted and decides that he can wait one more night. He grabs the envelope to take it and his nightcap to the bedroom with him. By the time he gets to the bedroom he feels somewhat rested, as if he has just awakened from a few hours nap. Taking it as a sign that he should at least read a page or two, he starts to get the feeling that time is running out, almost like a feeling of impending doom.

He brushes the feeling aside and slides the letter out of the envelope. He shifts through a few pages trying to find the one he left off on. He does. Warren settles into bed and un-pauses his movie.

...only assume is Hell itself.

The Witch spent, what felt like, several lifetimes in her own personal Hell with the demon, Malum. He had intended to break her will, to make her submissive and obedient. It took much longer than Malum initially thought it would, but the longer she refused to bend to his will, the harder he fought to control her. She was, by far, the strongest Witch he had ever encountered and for a short time, he was almost convinced that he couldn't beat her. Until he did... or so he thought.

The Witch had been beaten with everything from spiked clubs and knotted whips to razor-sharp barb wire and mangled body parts. She should have died a thousand deaths from the beatings alone, but she didn't... couldn't die.

She could only endure the pain and wish for death that never came. The Witch had been dismembered dozens of times with different objects, the strangest of which was something that resembled a shank made in prison. She was savagely raped and sodomized by creatures that could have only come from the depths of Hell. Some were cloaked, hiding their grotesqueness, with long sharp talon-like fingers that ripped at the very flesh they tried to caress. Massive humanish beings made of solid metal with appendages that were overly proportionate for their bodies. Feminine creatures with fierce red eyes and horned, disfigured snakes for hair. Large, grotesque creatures that she could only describe as ogre-like. Skeletal creatures. Some that resembled humans but were limbless, eyeless, faceless, etc. and some that were just too hideous for description.

2

Of all the hellish creatures that she encountered, Malum was the most wretched and evil of them all. Their final meeting in her own personal Hell was her worst experience yet and it broke her... just not to Malum's will like he had so hoped. He had summoned her to his quarters of Hell, and she had been bathed in fire and dressed in rags before being presented to him. Even with her scalp charred and smoking, her skin blistered, red, and swollen and clothed in filthy, stinking rags, she was still stunning. As the burns began to heal and her hair regrew at an unfathomable pace, Malum searched the darkest depths of her mind and drudged up her saddest, most unbearable moments. The death of her mother, her long-ago love, the men that raped her, on and on the memories played out in her brutalized mind. The Witch hated Malum with every fiber of her being and between the horrid memories, she vowed to herself that she would have her revenge against this demonic being too.

The rush of emotions from the memory replay had her in tears just moments later. Her weeping turned Malum on and he slowly undressed as she sat with her face in her hands. When she finally looked up, she gasped loudly at the sight before her and immediately lowered her eyes. No longer the incredibly handsome man with the odd eyes, he had reverted to his natural, revolting form, which was the only way the demon was able to copulate. Unable to stop herself, the Witch took in the being's appearance starting at the large hooved feet. Her eyes ran up the long, muscular legs, that were covered in thick black fur. She seen the head of its penis long before her eyes reached its pelvis, where the black fur began to thin out right above its groin. Her eyes paused on its limp, massive member, easily as long as her arm with a base as thick as a two-liter bottle, and testicles the size of baseballs. Her eyes widened and she gasped loudly, then quickly looked upward. The thick black fur continued up the sides of the torso, covering the armpits and moving down the underside of the arms. Its chest, back, shoulders, and the upper part of its arms were all hairless, the exposed flesh a disgusting, sickly yellowish green. The color of gangrenous pus. It was dotted with oozing sores, blisters and boils, and maggot filled craters of black, rotted flesh. She could feel the bile rising in her esophagus and she fought to keep control of it. She did not want to give this bastard the satisfaction of seeing how disgusted she was by it. It wanted her to be repulsed and scared. It wanted to break her mind. She wouldn't allow that though... she couldn't.

The Witch finally allowed her eyes to rest upon the true face of Malum, the powerful demon. It was as monstrously gruesome as she thought it would be. The skin on its face, devoid of any fur, was as ravished and despicable as the rest of its bare flesh. It had a long-pointed chin and high, sharp cheekbones that were almost visible beneath the overly stretched skin. Long pointed ears that were punctured with small bones, metal hooks and beautifully colored gems on spikes. The mouth was too large for its face, with plump bright red lips, accommodating for rows upon rows of tiny, fanged teeth. Where a nose should have been was only two small holes surrounded by cancerous sores and blisters. Its eyes had not changed, but it no longer had eye lashes or eyebrows, making its features even stranger. The high forehead led to two long antler-like horns protruding from both sides of its head. The base was in a spiral formation that continued straight out, unraveling the further it went. There was a slight upward curve at the end of the horns, and they branched off into several razor-sharp spikes. The skin on the scalp was rotted, black, and peeling off in chunks. Huge pieces of dead flesh hung by mere shreds to the scalp and maggots squirmed about, munching on it. At the base of the back of its mishappened head was seemingly a clump of hair, tied off in a ponytail. The ponytail fell down its back, finally stopping at its thighs, and ending with the head of a large, black snake.

The snake head had raised and positioned itself right above Malum's shoulder and it glared at her with red eyes, its large mouth open in a hiss, venom dripping from its long, sharp fangs. The snake is what took the witch aback. The rest of it, no matter how revolting, did not surprise her, but she was not expecting that.

Malum looked down at her with a tight smirk upon his large lips. "Remove that filth you're wearing." he demanded of her. The disgust evident in his tone.

"You put me in this fuckin filth!" she spat at him but started removing the ragged clothes anyway for fear of what the snake head might do. She knew what Malum was about to do and even though he was much larger than any of the other creatures she had already been raped by, she thought that she could handle it because of what she had already been through. She tried to mentally prepare herself as she finished removing the rags and stood nude before Malum.

Malum stood for several long moments admiring the witch's beauty. It acknowledged and congratulated itself on the fine job it had done on her transformation. She had completely healed from her fire bath and was as radiantly beautiful as before. Malum let its eyes take in every inch of her body before finally succumbing to the urges. It reached out and grabbed her arm and she instinctively tried to pull away. That was good because it wanted a fight, the fucking was better when they fought. But she immediately stilled herself, knowing that fighting would only make it hurt more. Malum surprised, grabbed her other arm, his disfigured four-fingered strong hands gripped her tightly. The Witch sucked in a breath and squinted her eyes but nothing more. Malum was becoming angry at her lack of participation and struck her across the face in frustration. She landed on the floor but was immediately jerked back up by her hair, blood dripping from her torn lower lip.

The Witch groaned as Malum twisted her hair in his hand and jerked her head cruelly to the side. Its long, narrow split tongue snaked out of its mouth and gingerly licked the side of her neck. She could feel its foul, hot breath on her skin and could hear the hiss of the snake head very near even though she couldn't see it from the unnatural angle Malum had her head in. The residue left behind from its tongue left a slimy, stinging sensation on her neck, one that was more uncomfortable than anything else. This confused Malum because he could sever a thick iron chain with just a few drops of its acidic saliva. The lack of reaction angered him even more, so he slung her, with all his strength, across the cavernous room. She smacked into the far wall with a disgusting crunching noise and slid lifelessly to the floor. Malum roared his outrage, an unhuman sound that echoed about its quarters.

The demon stalked over to the Witch and jerked her up off the floor, once again, by her long black hair. Her eyes fluttered and she moaned as she drifted in and out of consciousness. Malum shook her until she was more conscious than not and when it was sure she was able to hear and comprehend what it was saying, it began insulting and belittling her in every way it could think of. It called her nasty, vile names and told her how weak, useless, and pathetic she was. It told her how her mother's death was her fault, even though it wasn't, but in her distress, a small part of her mind believed it. It told her how degrading it was for her to fall for mere mortals and how she had deserved the brutal rape she had endured at the hands of those men all those years ago. The Witch admirably fought back the tears that welled in her eyes at all the terrible things the demon said to her, but what Malum had said about Johnathan was what caused her to break down sobbing and weeping. The demon told her that her beloved, Johnathan Colmes, had never loved her, not even a little, and had simply used her as a 'jizz disposal', as Malum had phrased it.

Hearing and seeing her tears of pain renewed Malum's sexual urges and it approached her with its erectness jutting out before it. It almost doubled in size from being soft. A small squeak escaped her surprised and frightened lips when Malum threw her to the hard rock floor of its quarters. It was only a matter of moments before he was shoving his way inside her, moving deeper and deeper with each thrust. She bit her bottom lip and endured through the first few inches but could contain her screams no longer. She wailed in misery and pain as the searing heat of his gigantic member melted her flesh from within. She could feel the flesh it touched inside her, char and burn, the pain almost unbearable. The demon paused mid-thrust knowing it had reached the limits of her womanhood but was still several inches away from being fully inside her. Malum simply adjusted the angle and applied a little more force to each thrust and within minutes was able to feel the damp warmth of her flesh on his testicles. Blood seeped from beneath them, hot and sticky, and Malum used it as lube. The snake's head in all the excitement, struck out and bit onto her breast, the fangs sinking deep into the flesh around the areola. It stayed that way, flicking its tongue, teasing playfully, and hardening the nipple. The volume and intensity of her screams increased, reverberating off the stone walls, drowning out Malum's evil, pleased laughter.

The Witch wished for death, wished for unconsciousness, wished for anything that would take away the unendurable pain. Nothing did though, and it went on and on until the demon had had her in every way one could imagine and several they couldn't.

She was splattered with foul smelling pus that oozed and squirted from the rupturing boils that plagued its gruesome skin. Maggots fell and caught in her hair, squirming to be freed, and later she would remove a few from between her legs. Malum left her in a bruised, battered, and bloody heap on the floor, laughing as it wiped himself clean and walked away. Just as it walked out of the large room, it snapped its fingers, and the Witch was back in the cave behind her shack in the valley.

3

The Witch laid in the same heap Malum had left her in, for a long time before she had built up enough strength to get up off the cold, damp cave floor. She slowly, very slowly, made her way into the shack and into her bed. Ignoring the soot, grime and dried blood that streaked her wounded, aching body, she pulled the covers over her eyes and cried herself to sleep. Feeling for the first time that she was everything Malum had told her she was and worse.

She awoke sometime the following afternoon but refused to get out of her bed. She wallowed in her filth, stink, self-pity, and depression, first cursing Malum, then Johnathan and finally, taking accountability, cursing herself. The anger turned to sadness, the tears returning for a while, and then reverted to anger once again. The anger was fueled by recurring memories of everything Malum had said and done to her. By thoughts of Johnathan and that bitch, Sarah, that stole him away. By thoughts of sweet, sweet revenge on every entitled soul in this valley that came whining to her to fix all their problems. The anger grew into the rage she felt before Malum presented himself and she called out to Satan himself, for she knew of no other being strong enough to deal with Malum. Except the Gods of course, but they were part of the Light. The Light that she no longer possessed because the darkness had extinguished it; and she was glad. She was relieved to feel no guilt or shame at her thoughts and actions, it felt good to be free of the restrictions and rules set in place by those that follow the Light. This path would be darker, much darker, but ever so much fun. The blackness in her soul deepened in hue, darkening even more.

She called upon Satan, begging, and pleading for a mere moment of his time. She called his name, praying and worshipping him, for exactly 666 minutes (11 hours, 6 minutes) before the ruler of Hell finally acknowledged her. "You arrogant, entitled whore! Who are you to call upon me?" Satan's voice bellowed from nowhere and everywhere all at once. She held back a startled scream at the suddenness and ferocity of the voice.

"Please! Your foulness, I need your help. I beg of you! Help me get the revenge I seek, and I will be forever yours. I am a very powerful sorceress, the only one left of the first generation from the originals, I can do wonderfully hideous things for you. Please! Just name your price and it's yours." She pleaded in a low but strong voice.

Satan was silent for a long moment before responding. "If you are as powerful as you say you are, and I believe what you say is true, for I can smell the magic on you, then why haven't you taken care of the matter yourself?"

"I was tricked into a deal with the demon, Malum, and it..." the Witch stopped, interrupted by Satan laughing at the mention of the name.

"That filthy cockroach turd is a blight even to Hell. Very few can make a dismal, miserable place even worse and Malum does. Normally, I enjoy the company of such souls but even I have my limits." The voice of Satan paused as if in thought and the Witch remained silent. Finally, Satan finished. "I will listen to your story, nothing more... for now."

With a glimmer of hope, the Witch told Satan the story of her overwhelming rage and the rape that brought it on and everything that had followed that, all the way up until the conversation she was presently having with Satan. She went into vivid detail and left nothing out. She told Satan that she could handle John, Sarah, and the rest of the valley, but she was no match against Malum, even if she had thought she was once upon a time ago. "You are much stronger than you think you are, and much more powerful too. You are right, however, Malum is much more powerful than you... for now, anyway. I will think this over and come to you if, and when, I am ready."

The Witch thanked Satan profusely, praising the powerful being's many names but Satan had left her in the fading sound of her own voice. She crawled into bed during the darkest hour of the night and slept until mid-morning. Her wounds, especially the internal ones, had yet to heal and this frightened the Witch very much. Had any other being inflicted those wounds, she would have been healed by the time she got herself up off the cave floor.

The Witch settled into a chair at the wooden table in the large cave with her book of magic before her. She flipped through page after page, careful not to worsen the more brittle pages, for quite a while before she finally found the healing potion she was looking for. With the potion made and drank, the Witch settled back into bed to allow it the time it needed to work.

When she woke several hours later, as the sun was setting, she felt better than she ever had, physically. Mentally, she was content in her constant state of rage, dwelling on all her pain, humiliation, and anguish. She waited for her new Master, hoping it would reveal itself to her again, even if only in voice, and soon.

Satan did. Only in voice again, just the night before. "I wish for another offspring. A son this time." Satan told her bluntly.

"I do not believe that I am able to give you or any other man or being a child." She swallowed a swelling lump in her throat and blinked away the tears. "I was born without that ability, your ugliness."

"Then find one. An unborn that I can mark for my own. The autumn and winter seasons, with all the death and rot, are my domain whereas the Light have the warmer, brighter seasons. The child shall be born before the spring comes. I will destroy Malum, in whatever manner suits you, when the unborn has been marked."

"I know of only one pregnant woman in the valley, rumored to be having a boy, but with this weather I'm not sure she is still alive." The Witch told Satan, unaware of what her wrath had done to the valley folks. Realizing that sounded like an excuse, she quickly added, "I will not fail you, Master. Allow me adequate time and I will find you a son. How will I mark the unborn?"

"Like this..." Satan began and she noted everything that was said. Every ingredient, every word, every instruction. When Satan had finished with the instructions, she was given the only ingredient she did not have. A small, corked vial filled with the black, rotted blood of Satan.

"One more thing, Defiler of Souls, if Malum decides to take me back to his quarters again, I would surely miss multiple opportunities to fulfill your wish." She told Satan, knowing the voice would soon leave.

"I will ensure that does not happen." Satan said after a few moments of thoughtfulness. "However, should you fail to mark my unborn son before the winter solstice, I will hand deliver you to Malum's quarters myself. After I am through with you, of course." She could hear the rise and fierceness in Satan's voice, and it frightened her.

"Yes, Master. Of course. Thank you!"

"Stop that damn sniveling, its unbecoming!" Satan scolded her and then returned to Hell.

Everything flashed through her mind in a matter of moments, the timeline of painful memories that she would never be able to forget. She cleared her mind, storing the boiling rage down deep and continued preparing for the pregnant woman's arrival.

Chapter Twenty-Seven

Death and Other Failures

1

She didn't have to wait long once she was finished preparing everything for the arrival of her new master's soon-to-be marked unborn. She sensed the incoming group several minutes before she heard the frantic knocking on her shack door. She ushered them all in, through the shack and out into the cave. Almost everyone present had been in the ritual room at least once, for one reason or another.

Joshua Jones carefully laid his wife on the damp cave floor, in the center of the massive pentagram carved into the stone. She was still shivering under the weight of the dozen blankets she had been wrapped in. The Witch quickly knelt at her side and began rubbing her lips with a potent herbal concoction that almost immediately took the bluish purple-tint from the ailing woman's lips, fingertips, and toes.

Those in attendance watched as the Witch slowly uncovered the eldest O'Reigan daughter and begin her evaluation. Alvin, Danny, and Betty had returned with Joshua Jones. Danny determined to see the ailing woman through her ordeal and Betty determined to be with her brother, to comfort him no matter the outcome. Alvin was hoping to find his beloved, Anne, believing that she had stayed with the Witch through the storm but not having had the chance to ask her amid the commotion. Old Joe, Sugar, and Lacy were also there, but only so that they could get away from the raving preacher and the now, hysterical O'Reigan widow. Johnathan Colmes completed the group, there out of obligation since the valley last knew of his and the Witch's relationship. In the rush of getting the

303

woman into the ritual room and treated, the Good Witch had missed his presence, though. He considered slipping out of the cave and going back to the Infirmary but decided that would be untasteful, even given the current situation.

Joshua was almost out of his mind with worry and dread by the time the Witch finally stood from her place beside his sick, pregnant wife. She approached him slowly with a, seemingly, sorrowful look upon her face and asked if she could speak to him in the other room, away from the rest of them. With a heavy heart and tears in his eyes, he agreed, and she led him into the smaller of the two caves. They walked right by Johnathan and when the Witch's eyes met his, it took much more strength than she would have thought to restrain the urge to rip his eyes out where he stood and shove his testicles into the bleeding, empty eye sockets. She smiled sweetly at him instead, but Johnathan knew that smile did not touch her eyes, and he did not care much for her new appearance either. It made no difference to him that she was much, much more attractive now than she was before the storm. Deep down, Johnathan Owen Colmes knew that the Witch knew what he had done, and the first tiny tendril of fear, not shame or guilt or regret, but fear began to wrap itself around his heart. Not for himself, but for his love, Sarah.

"I really do regret having to inform you of such things, Mr. Jones, but I am afraid that you have a very difficult choice to make, and it has to be soon." She paused, inwardly pleased at the sight of the tears streaking down his long, saddened face. "Your wife is suffering from one deadly ailment while your unborn child is suffering from another one. I only have the time and ability to save one of them. You need to choose, and soon, or they will both surely die." She turned her head from him, as if concealing a tear but it was really to conceal the smile that crept upon her face as Joshua started openly sobbing and weeping, grieving for his wife and child.

"How? How do I make a choice like that? How do I live with myself knowin I chose one over the other? Oh, Lord! Help me! I don't know what I am supposed to do." He cried out loud, speaking directly to the Heavens. No answer came. He wept for several long minutes before the Witch pressed him for an answer.

Reluctantly he told her through a cracked hoarse voice, "I know that my wife would never forgive me if I chose her over our child... so save the child. Just allow me a few moments with my wife first please."

She allowed him only a few moments using the excuse that time was of the essence. The sooner she could mark the unborn child and please her Master, the sooner she could enact her hate-fueled revenge. She was almost giddy with the anticipation, putting much effort into not looking or thinking about Johnathan, so not to ruin her present good mood.

2

The Witch put the finishing touches on the potion for marking the unborn boy-child as Joshua Jones said his final good-byes to his best friend and the love of his life. When he kissed her too warm, cracked lips for the last time a tear fell from his eye and rolled down her cheek causing her eyelids to flutter. He whispered in her ear how much he loved her, how much he would treasure their child, and how he would be with her again one day. Then he walked out of the caves to wait outside, unable to endure the gory birth that he knew would follow. Johnathan followed him out and the Witch was grateful that he wasn't there to be a rage-fueling distraction to her during her important task.

The Witch mixed an herbal concoction and carefully coaxed the dying woman into drinking it as a sedative. Which technically it was a sedative, the Witch had just given her enough to put her in an eternal sleep. However, she would slip into a temporary coma first, allowing the Witch time to remove the child from her womb. She was far enough along in her pregnancy that the Witch would be able to keep it, not only alive, but healthy. If everything went the way the Witch was expecting it to go, then she would be able to hand deliver a marked son, already born, to her Master, the Lord of Degradation. Then he would see her willingness and eagerness to serve and please him.

She told the remainder of the group that if they stayed, they would have to stand back and out of her way. They all obeyed, standing back far enough so that they could see but not what was happening between her raised, bent legs. Joshua's dying wife whimpered softly, still deep in sleep, when the Witch slit open her lower abdomen from hip bone to hip bone. It was a clean, straight cut through. She dropped the knife and sunk elbow-deep into the open wound, pulling and tugging on the placenta, carefully ripping it open rather than risking Satan's unborn by cutting it. Sweat popped out on the bridge of her nose and her eyes shone with confidence and determination. A little more tugging and a little more pulling and then out popped a foot, a knee, a second foot, and finally the entire bottom half of the child, from the umbilical cord down.

The shine in the Witch's eyes dulled significantly as she realized that the child she was birthing and about to mark was missing the most important physical male feature. She held the half-birthed daughter of Joshua Jones in her hands, and it infuriated her, resurfacing all the tampered rage. She felt the heat grow in her face, reddening it, then felt it dissipate just as quickly when an evil, wicked idea occurred to her.

The not-so-good Witch grabbed the umbilical cord, reached up into the sac where the upper half of the girl remained unrevealed. With a single swift motion, she wrapped the cord tightly around the baby girl's neck, pulled it tight and twisted. She continued to act as though she were still pulling and tugging at the placenta, trying to free the baby. After several, tiring, long minutes she finally pulled the purplish-blue swollen infant out of her very-close-to-death mother's body and wrapped it in a blanket laying nearby for just the purpose. The Witch was neither gladdened nor saddened by killing the child. She was indifferent to it and therefore decided not to do it again. If it brought her no joy, then what was the point? She sighed heavily, forcing a tear to form in her eye as she approached the others and told them to go get Joshua.

The man's agony could be heard and felt in the anguish of his screams. First pleading with God to give him back his wife and daughter, and then cursing him for not returning them. He refused to hold his daughter, a quick glimpse at her color told him he could not handle it. He tried to flee from the Witch's shack and Alvin reached out to stop him. In his misery and grief, Joshua swung his fist at him instinctively, connecting with his lower jaw and knocking Alvin backwards, into the Witch who was still holding the 'stillborn' child. She stumbled, her arms jerking outward, releasing the child, all accidental. It landed with a sickening splat on the rough cave floor and everyone in attendance knew the poor baby's face was no more.

Joshua screamed loud enough to rupture his vocal cords and then he darted out of the cave, straight through the shack, and out the door. No one tried to stop him but all of them, except for the Witch followed him out. He had already disappeared among the multitude of shacks and teepees before any of them made it outside. No one had any idea where he went or even which direction, he went in.

They searched for Joshua to no avail the whole time Alvin and Danny prepped Joshua's wife and daughter to be carried back to the common area. The Witch accommodated to all their needs and materials. Alvin asked the Witch if any of her followers had stayed with her during the storm and she informed him that she had sent them home when the snow started, obviously unaware of what the outcome would be. Alvin's heart sank and he sighed heavily, trying to fight back the tears as the realization that his love was more-than-likely dead, hit him.

The Witch was quite pleased with the lovebird's depressing reaction. She was quite pleased with the agony and pain that Joshua was enduring. She was quite pleased with the sickened reactions to the infant falling. The best reactions often come out of the most spontaneous, unplanned incidents. She wasn't quite sure how she felt about the baby falling though. It didn't bother her that it happened, she had just expected to get more pleasure out of causing death and pain. Maybe it was just because it was an infant. She would have to test the theory. She, also, had to come up with another plan to get her hands on an unborn male child, and soon.

The small group left, Johnathan included, leaving the Witch to herself once more. Johnathan causally asked if she wanted to go back with them...not him... them to the Infirmary.

When she declined, he didn't push the issue and told her he couldn't stay. He knew she didn't believe him when he said he needed to go look for Joshua before he did something he would regret. She told him that she understood and that he was needed elsewhere. She didn't offer to kiss him, and he made no effort to kiss her. Simply said good-bye and walked away.

She was fuming when she closed the door behind her, the rage swelling once more. The Witch was humiliated and ashamed by the tears she felt stinging her eyes. How could he not see the pain I am in? The pain that he caused. He knows I know; I can see it in his eyes! Why would he do this to me? The angry answerless questions swirled through her mind.

It took some time for the Witch to calm down enough to get her emotions and thoughts back under control. With that done, she freshened up and called on the Master of Madness and Mayhem to admit and atone for her failure with the unborn child. Satan laughed long and hard on the part when the baby landed on the cave floor. When he was finished, he amended her for admitting her failure but insulted her for failing, for not using her magic to know it was a girl-child beforehand. The Witch was unaware that she possessed such gifts and told him so, but he scoffed and told her that she was much more powerful than she knew and would never know unless she toyed with it. She intended to take that advice.

"I am sending you a new pet..." the voice bellowed at her, after a few moments of silence. "...one you cannot destroy as you did the raven." Satan's laughter echoed through the cave, knowing he had struck the Witch with a bit of shame. Suddenly, an average sized python, seemingly a solid, glistening black with bright red eyes came slithering out of the shadows at the far end of the cave and straight at the Witch. Her heart rate quickened, and her respiration increased as it grew nearer. "Don't be frightened," the voice laughed, "it is here as both an aid and a punishment, but it will not harm you." Satan explained, not soothing her whatsoever. The black snake with the blood red stripe down its back and glowing red eyes, slithered closer to the Witch, who had backed herself up against the cave wall and had nowhere else to go. "He will be my eyes and ears while you're tending to your end of the deal, that's the punishment. However, he will obey your commands if they do not go against my wishes." The snake, its color so black it vanished in the shadows, had made it to her feet, and began wrapping itself around her ankle. Its fanged mouth was closed but its tongue darted in and out of its mouth, tasting the air around it. The Witch was stunned, speechless. and motionless. "I will leave you two to get acquainted then, but before I leave, I must say..." the voice of Satan paused, chuckled as she began to whimper because the snake was moving its way past her knee, then the gravelly voice continued. "...I must say, Vipera WILL find the warmest place around..." the python was swirled around her thighs, "...and that would be..." she could feel it's tongue slightly nipping at the slit between her legs, startling her. "...right about there!" Satan's roaring laughter slowly faded with its voice.

As if by signal, the snake lunged, burying its upper body deep within her. She screamed in surprise and what she anticipated would be pain, but it never came. It was slightly uncomfortable at its worst and quite pleasant at its best, as it slithered and snaked around inside her until it was comfortably curled up and nestled inside her once useless, but now useful uterus.

Chapter Twenty-Eight

Forever in the Light

1

Joshua Jones had been much closer to the searching group than any of them had realized. They also, hadn't realized that the sight of him running madly out the door of the Witch's shack was the last time they would ever see him. He had made a sharp left, running in the direction of the river along the stacked-stone rock wall. When he was about to the halfway point, he hopped over the rock wall, landing in the middle of a large plant that resembled an aloe vera. Luckily for him, Joshua was able to step out of the plant without breaking any of the leaf-like stalks. If he had, and any of the jelly-like substance inside the stalks had gotten on him, it would have eaten through his clothing and skin like the most powerful acid on earth.

He hid behind a tangle of young saplings and watched as the others searched for him for a long time before finally heading back to the Infirmary, believing he had fled in that direction. That was fine by him, he wanted to be left alone anyway, left alone to grieve for the family he'd never have. He wandered off into the dense foliage behind him, aware that he was in the Witch's garden, but unaware that it was enchanted, moving deeper into a magical jungle.

Joshua stumbled around, confused, for hours among the exotic plants and flowers of every size, shape, and color one could imagine. Some were beyond beauty while others were something seen only in nightmares. He sometimes wondered if he was just walking in circles, but he never came across anything that looked familiar to him. His confusion only deepened.

Finally, he came to a small clearing where some of the grass had been trampled down in a large ovoid shape. Leery of the unknown, he stayed to the outside of the clearing, trying to look in every direction at once. He circled the area several times before resting by a small creek that trickled nearby. It was the sweetest, cleanest water Joshua had ever tasted. He was aware of the peacefulness of the area, the hushed babble of the water, and the softness of the grass beneath him. Slowly and reluctantly, he dozed off in the clearing.

The enchantment over the garden was consistently fueled by the Witch herself. When she was a Good Witch, following the rules of the Light, her enchanted garden was vibrant with life beyond the magnificent plant life. There were fairies of every color and shade, that helped tend to the flowers and plants. There were gnomes lurking about, stout and mischievous, playing harmless pranks and jokes. Tree-elves that were very welcoming to newcomers, an astonishingly beautiful white unicorn that shone with grace and power, and many, many more. When the Witch accepted Malum's power, she accepted the darkness, thus changing the enchantment's power and the mythical creatures within.

Joshua was brought out of a dreamless sleep by a strange sound he had never heard before. It most certainly wasn't a human sound, but it wasn't quite animal either. It was similar to, but not quite, the sound of a snorting horse, and he could see flames licking across the ground near his face. Flames that were coming from the nostrils of an onyx black unicorn standing mere yards away from him. He was shocked, motionless, unsure of the massive creature's intentions. The unicorn was easily the size of a moose, its shining silver horn protruding several feet from the center of its forehead. It would raise its foreleg, occasionally, to stomp at the ground and large flames leapt from each impact.

He scurried to his knees but feared standing in front of the massive animal may cause it to attack so he awkwardly made his way backward on his hands and knees. The unicorn, blacker than night, maintained its pose and breathed fire through its nostrils that scorched the lush green grass beneath it. Joshua had made it to the stream but knew getting in the water would mean his death, so he remained in his awkward position, nervously watching the creature before him and trying to figure out what to do next.

Then, suddenly, seemingly out of nowhere, Joshua heard a small, tinny voice speak but he couldn't understand what it was trying to say. He did not react or speak, and the voice didn't repeat itself, making Joshua wonder if he had even heard it all. The unicorn took a single step forward, keeping its head lowered to the ground as before. Joshua jumped at the sudden movement. He could hear his racing pulse in his ears and feel his temples throb in unison. He had to figure out what to do and soon. "This way! Follow me!" he heard, plainly, as if spoken into his ear. He instinctively turned his head in the direction of the voice, for the first time taking his eyes off the unicorn but found no one there. Just a few flying insects buzzing around. Realizing what he had done, he quickly swiveled his head around to see the unicorn trotting toward him, quickly gaining speed, with its head still lowered to the ground, as if meaning to impale him.

The element of surprise and the sheer sight of impending death locked up Joshua's muscles and he was momentarily paralyzed from fear. He watched the unicorn charge directly at him, the large spiral horn tapering off to a finite point, aimed straight at his face. He felt as though he could do nothing but watch this unimaginable tragedy unfold before his very eyes. "Move!" that small, tinny voice bellowed into his right ear and Joshua obeyed without question. He rolled to his left and kept rolling until he felt the ground angle downward and then relaxed as he rolled down a small embankment and into a tangle of trees. He jumped up to a crouching position as soon as he was stopped enough to do so, swinging his head back and forth, trying to fight off the dizziness and disorientation while trying to look in every direction at once. There was no sign of the unicorn anywhere in sight. He sighed with relief and leaned back against one of the trees to catch his breath and slow his thumping heart.

The onyx unicorn pranced around its clearing, the Light within it was failing to fight off the Darkness that was overpowering it. It fought the urge to kill the intruder, but the Darkness became too much to resist, and it charged the two-legged being. It was able to evade the unicorn, then the Light overcame the Darkness momentarily, so the unicorn did not pursue the being. In a matter of hours, the Light within the unicorn would be completely extinguished, replaced by the Darkness. The last of the mythical creatures of the enchanted garden to fall to the extinguished Light and the Darkness that promised forever. It will no longer be able to resist its homicidal impulses, and the bloodlust will be evident in the black, vibrant flame that will glow from its eyes.

2

Joshua, reluctantly, got up and cautiously made his way through the trees, constantly watching and listening for the return of the unicorn. He never did see the unicorn again, but sometime in his very near future, he will wish that the unicorn had killed him. It would have saved him a lot of pain and humiliation.

He sensed movement in his peripherals which drew his attention to his right, then there was movement on his left, then his right again. Either it was really fast or there was more than one out there. Whatever they were. Then he caught a glimpse of one. It was hard to see any details through the swarm of flies or gnats or bloodsuckers that were gathered around him. It was about knee-high and hiding behind a tree. A movement from the treetops above showed him a smaller creature with long pointed ears perched on a branch several yards off the ground. He looked from one creature to the other, unsure of what to do. He didn't fear them because of how small they were but he didn't want them to fear him. He just didn't know how to go about telling them that without scaring them. He just kept an eye on them as he slowly continued his, seemingly, never-ending trek through the never-ending garden.

After a couple hours of walking without incident, Joshua came across a small fire up ahead in another clearing. He rightfully assumed it to be the camp where the knee-high creatures resided, even though he couldn't see any of them. He cautiously approached the fire and sat down to warm himself in the sunless garden, utterly exhausted. He could see the knee-high creatures slowly and reluctantly creep closer to him as the minutes ticked by. After about half an hour a single creature approached him. It was an elderly version of whatever it was, standing only a couple feet tall, with a long narrow face, a small round bulbous nose, tiny circular eyes, and a long silver beard that dragged along the ground beside him. When he spoke, Joshua could see the small blood red lips by the light of the fire, its mouth a small hole in the center of its voluptuous facial hair.

"What are you?" the creature asked Joshua, its tone indicated that it was offended by his mere presence.

"What are you?" Joshua spat back.

"Are you as the Witch?" it asked a little less hostilely.

"The Witch? Oh, no. She has powers and all that. I can't do any such things. I'm just a farmer." He said pathetically.

A strange little smile creased the short creature's lips and a twinkle of evil sparkled in its eye. "So, you are weak." he stated rather than asked, intentionally prodding Joshua.

The irritation rose along with his voice when Joshua told it. "I am not weak. I could just about step on you, as small as you are and you're calling me weak."

"You believe that to be true?" the creature asked with that strange little smile still plastered to its lips, unnerving Joshua.

He couldn't handle that stupid little smirk and he was going to wipe it off the smug little bastard's face. Anger built up inside Joshua and it quickly turned to rage at having lost everything he loved. He jumped up and charged the knee-high creature standing on the other side of the fire, with the intention of kicking him like a ball. Just as he raised his foot to kick the creature it stuck out one hand, grabbed Joshua by the ankle and slung him into the nearest tree. There was a muffled thud and then the creature watched as Joshua slowly sat up wheezing, knowing he had fractured a couple ribs when he hit the tree. He lifted his shirt and could see the skin begin to darken into a tender bruise and desperately wanted to make the creature pay for it. Any rational thinking was overtaken by the pride-hurt rage only men can experience, and he charged the creature again, this time more slowly.

Joshua swung his fist, but the creature was faster and dodged it easily. Joshua swung several more times, but the creature dodged every one of them, laughing at Joshua the whole time.

Tired, aching, and gasping for breath due to his battered ribs, Joshua kept swinging, determined to hit the damn thing. It was a fruitless effort, and the creature grew tired of his masculine display of strength. The creature's long silver beard shot out toward Joshua, wrapped itself tightly around his throat and lifted him several inches off the ground. His feet dangled and kicked at the air for a nonexistent purchase as he clawed at the millions of hairs that were cutting off his air supply. His face had begun to turn a dark shade of red, he could feel the blood vessels in his throat burst and his eyes bulge from their sockets.

His vision was blurred through tears of fear and pain, but he could feel himself being moved, swaying gently through the air. Suddenly, the millions of strands of hair released him, and he gasped for air, taking deep, rapid breaths that were immediately knocked out of him upon impact with the stone he was dropped on. Before Joshua had time to realize what had just happened, he felt dozens of small hands grab him, pinning him down to the stone on his back. He wasn't given enough time to scream, beg, ask, or even get his breath back before a rock just large enough to fit, but too large for him to swallow, was shoved into his mouth, chipping a front tooth, and cracking two back molars. A piece of cloth was wrapped around his head, covering his mouth, so he couldn't spit it out. He thought he felt ropes being thrown across him in several places, Joshua fully aware of his situation. He was on the verge of all-out panic, making his feelings of suffocation much worse. He had to concentrate on breathing through his nose, calmly and consistently, eyes closed, finally catching his breath, and calming his shuddering heart. Usually, he would have prayed to God for help but since He took away his wife and daughter, he didn't see why God would bother with him. The way Joshua looked at it, God, apparently didn't love him, why else would He take everything that he loves away from him like that? Instead, he simply whispered, "I'll

315

see you soon my loves.", then opened his eyes, thinking he had accepted and made peace with what was to come.

3

When the Witch and the enchantment were of the Light, the gnomes were playful and silly, like happy children in an endless game. Often dirty, they lived off what they could find off the garden floor, sleeping under the stars every night or in the hollow of a tree when the cold came. They enjoyed all things fun and loved to laugh, mischievous but benevolent. The tree elves were more sophisticated, being almost overly hospitable to newcomers. Taking them in, feeding them hearty meals and giving them soft, fluffy beds. They would send them off with gifts and food and were more than happy to help or accommodate. They lived in small treehouses in the canopy of the trees, finding their food from the branches. They were clean and civilized and had the Witch over weekly for dinner and drinks. They hosted parties and holidays and generally enjoyed caring for others. The fairies were small, about the size of a dime, and were very fast with their hummingbird-like wings. They would dart from one flower to another, tending to each one's induvial needs. Each one a different color or shade and no two were the same. Their wings glowed with their unique colors and hues, indiscernible during the day. At night, however, the colorful fairies would glow vibrantly in the darkness, like multicolored fireflies. They did not eat or drink and only needed to sleep for two hours out of every twenty-four, simply perching on a quiet branch when needed.

Since their Light had been extinguished, the fairies' brilliant colors faded to black and various shades of gray, their glowing colorful auras swallowed by the black flame. Instead of tending to the needs of the plants, their purpose was to spread the darkness that overwhelmed them. They destroyed beautifully magnificent plants and flowers, turning them as ugly as they felt, and turned the ugly ones outright hideous. Believing that they were much too small, even in large numbers, to effectually harm, much less kill, they left the two-legged being alone, content with being a nuisance to him.

The only change in the gnome's appearance was in their eyes that glowed with the same bright black flame as the unicorn, but their thinking had matured greatly. They were the new sophisticated species, but much pickier about what they would eat and drink. The human had been easy once they knew what he was, all the humans were weak, especially in the presence of their awesome powers, meager as they may be in comparison to others. They were grateful for this human that they had strapped down to the stone table using long hand braided vines, and they all awaited eagerly for their share of him. That night they would feast, and the anticipation called to the gnomes and tree elves alike.

The gnomes had slowly and methodically bled the human down to a mere few pints of remaining blood and had selected only certain parts of his anatomy to be served and eaten that evening. Among the picks, aside from every organ and entrail, were the meaty part of the hand at the base of the thumb, a large strip taken from both thighs, the meat along the jaw, the left buttocks (because the right one felt too fatty), and the penis. They nibbled at the well-cooked meat and sipped at their still cooling blood as they laughed and conversed amongst themselves. All with that evil black glow in their eyes.

The tree elves had changed drastically in appearance, becoming clawed, fanged, rabid abominations that were much more animalistic than civilized. When the gnomes had harvested the two-legged being for what they wanted, the dead body was tossed to the tree elves so their feasting could begin. The body was hauled into the treetops where a savage, vicious sight could be seen. They were ripping, tearing, and shredding bloody flesh from the bones with their jagged claws and needle-sharp fanged teeth. Their only thoughts were to eat, eat, eat! When the flesh was gone, the elves snapped the bones and sucked out the sweet, spongy marrow from inside, savoring it as if it were an after-dinner mint.

4

Joshua Jones had quickly realized that he hadn't accepted his fate and wasn't okay with any of it. Panic, once again, overwhelmed him, wholly and completely, when he seen the various knives laid out for filleting him. That was when he wished that the unicorn had killed him. Mercifully, he was more unconscious than conscious during his time with the gnomes, but the periods of consciousness were excruciating, until finally, mercifully, he was able to die. He died a hard, terrible death, resembling a meaty skeleton rather than human being. It was sickening and unimaginably painful. He begged for death when it finally came for Joshua Jones.

Joshua walked up to the most beautiful woman he had ever laid eyes upon, his wife. As he grew closer to her, he seen that she was holding a sleeping baby girl in her arms, his daughter. With tears of joy in his eyes, Joshua hugged his wife and child, fiercely, holding them closely to him. Giggling, his wife pushed herself and their daughter away from his grasp. He took her hand and they walked into the Light, together.

Chapter Twenty-Nine

Preparations for Paulus

1

Warren forces himself to look away from the half-read page, putting another pause on his in-mind movie. He yawns loudly as he slides the stack of papers back into the wrinkling manilla envelope, trying not to think about the horror he has just finished reading. Hoping that his thoughts will wait until he is asleep, or maybe tomorrow, before they try to process this new information and file it away with the rest.

He turns off the bedside lamp and rolls over to go to sleep, going through a mental checklist of things he must have ready before the new patient's arrival tomorrow afternoon. He has an important day tomorrow and knows he needs to be well-rested for it, but his mind won't allow him the luxury of sleep. He lays there until the early morning hours, his mind a jumbled mess trying to connect and understand the current mystery he is a part of. Exhausted from the constant confusion, he finally falls into a dreamless, mildly restful nap that he wakes from less than two hours later because of his bleeping alarm clock.

Dr. Gerard walks into the asylum feeling much better than he had the day before, but still not quite his usual. He knows he needs more sleep, but he will manage for today. *I'm going to be busy, busy, busy today and won't have time to be tired.* He thinks, attempting to convince himself of his own words, as he sips at his strong, black coffee.

Most of the day-shift employees go about their usual Monday morning tasks without prompting or issues, but he has Ms. Lancing bring in the group of seven that cleaned the new patient's room the day before. He tells them of the sanitation job and asks if any of them refuse or have any other assignments that are more urgent. One of the nurses tells Dr. Gerard that she is supposed to be prepping the medication cart, which is a higher priority task than sanitation. Warren steps out to speak with Ms. Lancing, asking her to shift around a few employee's tasks to cover the cart preparations. The nurse is grateful, she finds that task very monotonous and boring, like most of the daily tasks. This is a change in her routine, and she welcomes it. He tells the group where to find the sanitizing solution and when the task must be completed.

The group finishes sanitizing the room with plenty of time to spare before the patient arrives. Dr. Gerard does a walkthrough of the room, ensuring all criteria are met for the room to pass inspection, and it does. He locks the door to room 6 and slips the key in his pocket, then he walks back to his office to wait.

A few minutes before the clock strikes two o'clock, Ms. Lancing, looking young and vibrant, steps into Dr. Gerard's office and informs him that the patient has arrived, and all his information is being processed. He thanks her, stands from his chair behind his desk and straightens his tie before walking out to meet his new patient, Walter Paulus. Warren meets the small group in the hallway, where they pause to make introductions and shake hands before returning to his office.

Warren takes his place behind his desk, quickly scanning and assessing the group crowded in his office. The two seats directly in front of him are occupied by Calvin Powers, the man he had spoken with on the phone a few days prior and a seemingly bored young man with a laminated card pinned to his shirt pocket that states he is an Inspector. Walter Paulus is sitting on the small sofa to Warren's right, wearing an off-white jump-suit, very much resembling prison garb, that has **TRANSPORTEE** stitched on the back. Beside him on the sofa sits a middle-aged, strongly built, homely-looking woman, a well-respected nurse, that travels with all patients being transported. Completing the group and standing on both sides of the office door are the two guards that have been escorting Mr. Powers, Walter, and the others across the state.

After a little small talk among the three gentlemen, Calvin lifts his briefcase off the floor beside the chair he is occupying and pulls out a yellow file folder, handing it to Dr. Gerard. The file has some weight to it, but it is not nearly as thick as others that Warren and Calvin have seen. "That is Mr. Paulus's psychiatric medical records." Calvin tells Dr. Gerard as he pulls out another, much thicker file, this one in a white file folder. "His medical records, including injuries sustained in the military." Calvin hands it to Dr. Gerard, who lays it on top of the first one. "His police record..." Calvin hands him a navy-blue file folder that is much, much thinner than the other two. Finally, a dark green file folder is pulled from the briefcase and handed to Warren, who adds it to the growing stack on his desk. "...and finally, his military records. All copies of course, that will need to be returned with Mr. Paulus upon his return to Insanus Domus."

"All right." Dr. Gerard says as he lifts the large, weighty stack of files and sets them on the side of his desk. "I will make sure to look at these as soon as we can get Mr. Paulus settled in." Before Warren can say anymore, he is halted by the man on the sofa.

"My name is Walt." The dark-haired man says icily. He refuses to turn his head to look at Dr. Gerard but he side-eyes him, glaring.

"Okay, then...' Warren says politely. "...it's nice to meet you, Walt." The man on the couch only grunts in reply.

Calvin Powers, slightly embarrassed by Walter's attitude toward the new doctor quickly adds, "He's shy. He will warm up in a day or so."

Dr. Gerard smiles, his eyes darting between Calvin Powers and the patient on the sofa. "No worries. Walt, there, will get along just fine." *But will he though? Something's off about the man. I can feel it, but I can't explain it. Maybe the files will help.*

An awkward silence falls upon the group, unsettling Calvin in its eeriness. "Well, uh, I think everything is in order, except the inspection, of course, and we do have a long drive back." Calvin says, letting the last trail off. The Inspector looks up at the word 'inspection', looking slightly more interested than a moment ago.

"Right. Yes. Of course." Dr. Gerard stands from his chair, everyone else doing the same, shuffling out of the office door and into the hallway. Dr. Gerard leads the group through the labyrinth-like hallways to the rainbow corridor. At room 6, they are all standing together as Dr. Gerard fishes the key out of the same pocket he had slid it into earlier today.

Warren opens the door to room six, the Inspector standing beside him ready to enter the room, but they both stop mid-stride at the sight of the room. The Inspector turns his scowling face toward Dr. Gerard's wide-eyed, open-mouthed, caught-off-guard reaction. "Is this a damn joke, Doctor? Because I have better things to do with my time…"

Dr. Gerard, slowly, as if the Inspector isn't speaking to him, steps into the trashed, disgusting room. He can barely believe what he is seeing. All the furniture, items, clothing, everything that could be ripped, torn, broken, etc. is and is scattered across the room. Except for the rubber-like items, they are unharmed just thrown about. The mattress is stripped, flipped off the frame, and slashed open in multiple places, while the bedframe is leaning against the opposite wall. Animal excrement has been thrown and slung everywhere around the room and the smell is overwhelmingly putrid. Everything that his employees worked so hard to accomplish has been ruined, completely undone in the few hours between his inspection of the room and this one. Someone has done this, and he is going to find out who.

He walks back out of the room, back to the small group of people wondering what happened. He is wondering the same thing. "Gentlemen, ma'am…" the nurse smiles and nods, "…we need to return to my office and discuss alternate arrangements for Mr. Paulus." Leaving it at that, Warren heads off in the direction of the double doors leading out of the rainbow corridor and the rest of the group follows suit.

Dr. Gerard excuses himself momentarily, leaving the small group waiting in his office so he can inform Ms. Lancing of what happened and what he needs her to do. She is to inform whoever is watching the monitors today to find the camera covering the door and hallway of room six and inside the room itself. Next, she is to go to the room herself, Warren apologizes profusely for asking her to go around that filth, but she is the only one he trusts to do this and take plenty of photographs of the inside of the room. Then, she is to find two nurses that are willing to clean the room up so the maintenance men can get in there to try to salvage and fix what furniture they can. Finally, he has her search the other unoccupied rooms in the rainbow corridor for another suitable room that hopefully won't require a lot of preparation.

Ms. Lancing takes off to check the first task off her to-do list as Warren walks back into the office, apologizing to them for his absence. Almost an hour later, after some back and forth about what to do with the patient in limbo, a plan has been made. Walt sits in silence, on the sofa, for the duration of the discussion, finding it unbecoming that they speak about him like he isn't sitting mere feet away from them. Walt finds it very offensive and disrespectful, in fact. Everyone in the room stands and Dr. Gerard shakes hands with all the men, sans Walter Paulus, and escorts the group out the door as two of his own guards' step in. They have been waiting outside the office door to escort Walt to the Infirmary where he will spend the night in one of the examination rooms. Only temporarily until another room can be prepped, cleaned, and sanitized.

2

It is only minutes after his office clears out, Walter already in his temporary room, that Ms. Lancing is knocking on the door having completed her to-do list to the best of her ability. "The videos have been found but there is something wrong with them, I'm not sure what, before you ask, and she said that she doesn't know how to fix it. She's only been here a couple months."

"Darn!" Warren shouts, his refusal to curse something to be acknowledged. He drums his fingers roughly and rapidly against the desktop, deep in thought, for several long moments. Vivian stands by the door in silence, knowing to speak would only earn her a brutal tongue lashing, and not the kind she enjoys so much. Finally, he says, "Call Stacy Farris. I know she's not supposed to come in until six but call her in anyway. Tell her if she is here by four o'clock, I'll give her time and half for the night."

"Alright. I took the pictures like you asked, three rolls of film worth that I will drop off after work and pick up in the morning." She says, relieved to have some good news for him.

"Excellent! Thank you, Viv... Ms. Lancing." He catches himself and blushes. Hoping that would not give her the wrong impression. He still found her very attractive, sexy even, but she was too much for him. His being almost twice her age wasn't helping the issue either; he couldn't keep up with her. Just another thing he would have to figure out and resolve.

"Don't thank me just yet, doctor…" Warren sighs. "…I can't find a single nurse that is willing to even walk in that nasty ass room, more less clean it."

He rolls his eyes and considers the situation, finally telling her to ask around again but give them the same offer as Ms. Farris. "They'll have to work well past their shift tonight, but I will pay them time and a half for the hours spent cleaning the room, plus they can have tomorrow off."

Last on the list she tells him about the room she found. 'Room 18 has… potential… yeah, that's the right word for it. Bathroom fixtures in place, some salvageable furniture, a mattress but no frame. So, yeah, I'd say it has potential compared to the emptiness of the rest of the rooms."

"I'll check it out, Ms. Lancing. Thank you." He says as he rises from his chair. "Let me know how the offers go."

They walk out of the office together, Vivian reaching for the phone before her ass touches the cushioned chair. Dr. Gerard walks back to the rainbow corridor for the millionth time in the past few days wondering who had done that to room six and why. Room 18 is just as Vivian said. She is right, the room does have potential. He walks around, the mental list of things to do, things to get, things to fix, forming in his mind; the planning process beginning.

Once back at his office, Warren looks for Ms. Lancing, but she isn't at her desk, so he leaves her a note instead. It says: *Need 3 nurses and maint. men (N shift) for prep of room 18. All 5 in office @ 6:30p.m. - G* He returns to his office and waits to see if Ms. Farris arrives, hoping she does. Even if she can't or won't help him at least he will be in her almost-Goddess-like presence for a little while. Something about her does something to him, but he can never bring himself to act upon it. She is above him, way out of his league, untouchable. Strange as it is because based on physical appearances, Vivian Lancing puts Stacy Farris to shame, yet there's something about Ms. Farris that gets to him.

Stacy Farris agrees to the time and half pay and shows up two minutes before four o'clock. Ms. Lancing had given her very little information about why Dr. Gerard needed her so badly and what was so important that it couldn't wait another two hours before her shift. She sits in Warren's office, listening carefully as Dr. Gerard explains what happened, what the situation is with the monitors, and why those videos are so important. She agrees to help but is adamant that she isn't sure she is going to be able to recover the videos where the system is so old. She will do her best, though, and Warren believes that.

Stacy Farris gets to work on recovering the two videos. Ms. Lancing finds two nurses that are willing to clean the room, coincidentally the same two nurses that cleaned room 32, not so long ago, Ms. Roberts and Ms. Beckett. They almost reconsider when they see and smell room six for the first time, but the thought of time-and-a-half pay for a job they can take as long as necessary on, wins out. Donning elbow-length thick rubber gloves, aprons, goggles, and masks that cover the lower half of their face, they enter the room with a cart loaded down with cleaners, buckets, mops, rags, etc. and begin cleaning up someone else's mess.

Night shift clocks in and day shift clocks out, allowing Vivian only half an hour to find the two maintenance men and choose three nurses to clean room 18. She had seen Warren's note about ten minutes after he had written it and after she made a couple phone calls, she took out the night-shift schedule and started going over the employees and their tasks. After some rotating of tasks, she had three names in mind and a fourth in case one doesn't show. Vivian doesn't need the extra name and has all five employees sitting in Dr. Gerard's office by twenty after six.

Warren is quite pleased and impressed with her ability to handle everything he has thrown at her today, and quite eloquently too. *She listens well, maybe she just needs some boundaries put in place.* He pushes all thoughts of Vivian Lancing out his mind for now, knowing he needs to focus on getting yet another room ready for Walter Paulus. He looks at the small group before him and then explains what needs to be done. They already know about room six and why it needs done so he didn't have to explain that part. When he is finished, they leave the office, heading to room 18 to begin cleaning and repairing.

3

Finishing up paperwork before heading home, Ms. Lancing knocks on the door telling him that Stacy Farris has just called from the monitoring room and is ready for him to see what she found. He's up and walking through the halls, once again, this time with Vivian striding in heels alongside him. He asked her to tag along stating that another set of eyes can only help figure out who it is.

The three of them in the small monitoring room, Warren snug between the two incredibly gorgeous women, his senses very aware of their womanly aromas. Stacy sits before a keyboard that connects to the larger of the several screens on the wall behind the keyboard. Every five seconds the scenes on the screens change to another poor-quality video recording from another security camera. Stacy has fixed the video of the doorway and hallway outside room six, well enough for it to play but there is nothing more she can do to take out the glitches or make it any clearer.

She doesn't say a word to either of them; both noting how pale she seems. Stacy plays the short clip of the black and white, grainy video, pressing the button and immediately swiveling the chair away from the screen, intent on not seeing the clip again. It only lasts a few seconds, but Warren remains standing in front of the screen for several long moments after it's over. In the video, a figure can be seen entering from the right of the screen, approaching the door, carrying a large bucket in each hand. The video is of such poor quality that no details can be seen or determined. The figure is large with hunched shoulders and wearing a long coat or robe. They could make out nothing else about the person, until they stopped directly under the camera, obscuring it from view. Suddenly, a hand pops up on the screen with a glowing cross burnt into the palm, the palm covering the entirety of the camera lens, filling the monitor screen. The cross glows brighter and brighter, making Warren and Vivian squint at first and finally shield their eyes against the glare. It is too bright to look at but neither of them can seem to take their eyes away from the harsh light radiating from the screen. The light intensifies, blinding the pair before winking out, the monitor screen fading to black.

Vivian Lancing faints, crumpling to the floor in an uncomfortable heap. Dr. Warren Gerard stands and stares into the black screen, unmoving and unblinking, as his subconscious is swept away. He finds himself floating in an abyss of nothingness, just darkness all around him, eerie, silent darkness. Out of the silent darkness, comes a startling voice that spikes fear through him. A woman's voice, a very sexy woman's voice. One that sounds oddly familiar, somehow, but that seems unimportant right now. "You will be given this opportunity only once so hear me well! Burn the letter, this need not concern you, you cannot help him." The feminine voice tells him.

"I know I cannot help him; he is beyond anything a mortal can do." Warren replies, having come to that conclusion when he locked the door to room 32 with Joe's body still laying in the bloody, disgusting mess.

"Then what is your purpose for pursuing this?" Clear irritation in the tone.

"Is that why you want the letter? Because you think it can tell me something that can upend your plans? You're not sure if I can help him or not and you're afraid that letter might tell me how I can." Warren challenges the voice, showing no fear or disrespect.

Thoughtful silence for a long moment. "You are a clever one, Dr. Gerard. I do not nor do I have the ability to know everything. I have ways of finding out certain things, but those ways are restricted. So, to answer your question, no I do not know what information the letter holds and therefore fear what I do not know. It is a natural sorceress trait. Burn the letter, be done with this all, right now, and you walk away from this just fine. One time only offer!" The voice giggles, then continues to speak, "Think on it, Doctor. I'll be back soon for an answer, and you better have one." The voice fades away before Warren has a chance to say anything back.

Warren's subconscious is suddenly thrown back into himself. He staggers, catching himself with the desk edge in front of him. A wave of light-headedness hits him, and he is forced to sit in a chair or fall over, he chooses the chair and waits for his head to clear up. The conversation is still vivid in his mind, the voice is the only part of the hallucination, or whatever you want to call it, that he can't quite recall. He knows it is a female voice and he knows he remembers that it sounds kind of familiar, but he can't remember what it sounds like to draw a name or face to the voice. The lack of recall is quickly forgotten as the words of the conversation play on repeat in his mind, making it so he can think of little else.

Vivian regains her consciousness before Warren's subconscious returns and Stacy helps her off the floor. She is a little weak from fainting but otherwise unharmed. Warren returns and recovers to the panicky voice of Stacy and Vivian moaning as she attempts to stand up in her weakened state. "What the hell was that?" Stacy asked.

"A clue." Dr. Gerard calmly answers the two women. Now that his thoughts have cleared, the logical part of his mind is currently running in overdrive, processing, sorting, and connecting even more pieces to this complex puzzle. At the same time, it is distinguishing between reality and unreality, forming and discarding several theories about what he had just seen before finally settling on one that makes sense... well, enough sense, anyway.

"A clue? What are you goin on about, Doc? The video mess with your head, or somethin?" Stacy asks, a southern drawl coming out with her exasperation.

A thoughtful pause before answering. "To see who vandalized room six of course." Both women stand staring at him dumfounded, speechless that, after what they just witnessed, he was worried about what the person did to the room instead of that same person having a glowing cross on the palm of their hand. He could see their astonishment at his statement and smiled sweetly at them, having quickly devised a cover story to account for what the video showed. "I know what you think we just saw was something to be marveled at, but it was only a lighting mishap as the figure disabled the cameras." He watches as their astonishment turns to apprehension and knows it's a step in the right direction. "The light within the camera reflected off the palm of the figure's hand giving it the illusion that it was glowing, the more the figure messed with the camera, the brighter the light got, thus increasing the illumination back into the camera." He explains, knowing they are believing enough of it to soothe their wagging tongues.

"Explain the cross, then." Stacy demands, still reluctant to fully accept the illusion bit.

"Simple." Dr. Gerard begins with a sweet but slightly condescending smile across his lips. "A tattoo. Several of the guards, maintenance men, and patients have them. I'm pretty sure even a couple of the nurses have them." He explains with ease. Vivian accepts his explanation fully, feeling much better about the situation, deducing that her fainting spell was caused by the mere intensity of the lights. She figures that Warren was in the twilight zone for a few moments, looking at all the flashing lights that come along after a sudden bright light. Stacy stands looking at Dr. Gerard for a long moment, searching for any sign of a lie or untruth in his tone or eyes, but seems to find none. Reluctantly, she accepts his theory, admitting to herself that everything he just explained makes sense. "Now, were you able to locate the video of inside of room six?" He asks a calming Stacy.

"I haven't found it yet. When I came across the hallway video, I wanted you to see it before I went searching for the next one. I just hope it isn't as... creepy as that one." She says indicating the ended video clip behind her.

"I understand your reluctance to continue with this task, given what we just watched. It was creepy, initially, but once you consider what I just told you, it doesn't seem so creepy now, does it?" He asks Stacy, further soothing her with his charm.

"No, I guess it doesn't." She agrees after a few moments of thoughtfulness.

"If you feel that you can't accomplish what I'm asking..." Warren begins, letting the last word drift between them, knowing it would strike at her ego.

It did. "Of course, I can find the video." She says more harshly than she intends. Checking her tone, she adds, "I'm just a little spooked, that's all."

"I think we all are after watching that." Vivian chimes in, finally having regained most of her strength.

"Well, we will leave you to it then, Ms. Farris. Thank you for your cooperation with this assignment." Warren tells her. Stacy says nothing to either of them as Dr. Gerard helps Ms. Lancing down the hallway and back to his office.

When she is certain that the couple has left, her bright sky-blue eyes darken into a deep purple, an evil grin forming on her blood red lips. "Clever one, you are..." She whispers to the darkness of the monitoring room. "...but let's see you explain this one." She giggles menacingly as she presses a button on the keyboard and the video of the inside of room six begins playing on the large screen.

4

Back at his office, Dr. Gerard insists that Vivian go home and get some rest from her fainting spell. She agrees with only a little argument, grabbing the three rolls of film to be dropped off for development, before turning to leave. She gives her ass a quick, sexy little shake for his entertainment. He can't help but stare, it would be rude if he didn't. Then she walks out, smiling at him over her shoulder, the scent of her enticing perfume trailing behind her as she leaves him alone.

He sits down heavily in his chair, sighing loudly and loosening his tie. *I'm done. Whatever it is can wait until tomorrow. I'm just going to sit here for a few moments, gather my things and go home. Lord, do I need a day off. A man can only handle so much, and my plate was full before all this started. Why me? Why...* His in-mind self-pitying rant goes on for almost half an hour before he realizes how long he's been sitting in his chair. Time slips right by him as he has his much needed, stress-induced mini-meltdown. His mind is clear, really clear, for the first time in days as he walks out to his car to go home.

Warren returns home, all his usual evening routine accomplished. He's standing by the fireplace in the den with a scotch-on-the-rock in one hand and the manilla envelope in the other. Now that he can think clearly, he understands why he should throw the whole thing into the fire and forget about it all right now. He's been given that chance but the same something that was nagging at the back of his mind to burn it in the first place, when Gregory Patrickson told him to do the same thing, was now telling him that he couldn't trust that sexy woman's voice. He didn't listen to that little voice the first time, and maybe he should have, but it's too late for that now. He lowers his hand with the envelope in it toward the flames.

Stop! You can't! That could be your only hope.

You told me burn it, now you're telling me not too?

It's too late for that now. The voice you encountered was the Witch, the same one from the letter. She is an evil, scheming, sorceress and that's just what you have read so far. You want to trust her? The absolute absurdity of it!

She told me that if I burn the letter and forget what I know that I can walk away from all of this. She has given me no reason to doubt her sincerity, what purpose would it serve her to lie?

She is going to kill you! As soon as you burn that letter, or she can get her hands on it, you will die because of what you already know. You were never supposed to be a part of this, and you know it!

You're right! I shouldn't be a part of this, so I should just toss this into the fireplace and be done with it.

No! That letter really could be the only thing you have to make any of this make sense. It could be the difference between this ending with you walking away or being put in the ground. You're already in it, too deep to get out, so keep the letter and see it through.

The little voice returns to the depths of his mind, and he withdraws his hand before the envelope can catch fire. He walks back toward the sofa, tosses the envelope on the coffee table and heads for the decanter for a refill.

A knock on his back door stops his hand midway to his refilled glass. He leaves the drink sitting there as he goes to answer the door. He knows who it is and why they are here, but with his mind clear he sees how their fling could never amount to anything, due to a lot of reasons. He knows he needs to draw some lines, so to speak, with Vivian and the sooner he gets it done, the sooner he will have another issue resolved.

He invites her in but pulls away from her when she immediately throws herself at him. He tells her to follow him into the den so they can talk, and she gives him a comically, girlish pouty look but obeys. Warren offers her a seat on the sofa. She eyes him carefully as he snatches up the manilla envelope and disappears into another room for a few moments before returning without it. He offers her a drink that she refuses, so he grabs his own and sits in one of the armchairs across from the sofa. He takes a sip of his scotch and sighs heavily before beginning. "Vivian, look... I... I know this is going to sound confusing considering how openly I have been about my attraction toward you, but if you will just let me explain..."

"There's nothing to explain..." she interrupts him. "...I know this isn't and never will be anything more than what it is, and I don't really want it to be. Can I be honest with you? And I mean brutally, crudely honest?" she asks. Warren looks at her strangely for a moment and then nods his consent. "Plain and simple, I like to fuck. A lot. More than most anyone else, really, and it takes a lot to satisfy me. You have an exceptionally large dick that does satisfy me, and I intend to use it until it doesn't." Vivian Lancing tells him matter-of-factly.

Warren sits, deep in thought, for several moments before asking his own question. "What if I refuse?"

"Wel... that would be a regrettable decision, but I would understand. I have found so few like you that satisfies me so. I am neither vindictive nor judgmental, however. I know who I am, like it or not, and I am not ashamed, just careful. I don't want to lead you to think anything more about this and that's why I was so forward about using you. Now you know and I understand, no ill will or hard feelings whatsoever, if you would like me to leave." Vivian answers him truthfully, casting her eyes to the floor as she finishes speaking; silently awaiting the verdict.

Warren sits in the armchair, swirling his drink around in the glass, his mind slowly beginning to fog as he contemplates everything she has said. It, initially, angers him but once he thinks about all the women he has used solely for the same reason, he knows he has no right to get upset with her. She is just being more honest with him than he ever could have been with any of the women he has done the same thing too. He knows it's just karma making sure he reaps what he sowed. Upon further speculation of the situation, he really couldn't find anything to be upset about. He has a very fine young lady that has a very overactive sex drive on steroids, ready and willing to give him literally whatever he wants, whenever he wants it. He just needs to put some rules and boundaries in place. So, what is there to be upset about?

Warren looks across the room at her, her eyes meeting his, a silent communication passing between them, and Vivian knows that she has him wrapped, even if only temporarily. She stands from the sofa and approaches him while slowly unbuttoning her blouse. Warren sits his drink on the end table beside the chair as she does. "Viv, listen, I've really got to get up in the…" he begins as she straddles him in the armchair.

"Hush!" she whispers in his ear, sending chills through his body that elevates the blood flow to other parts of his anatomy. "So do I. I have no intention of being here long, a quickie and I'm out for tonight." She pauses, then adds. "We can talk about your boundaries and rules and whatnot tomorrow, if you want… but not tonight."

"How…" Warren begins but is interrupted once again. Uneasiness is trying to overcome the sexual desire, trying to warn him. Desire prevails though as Vivian presses her bare, open-shirted chest toward his face, enticing his tongue with her breasts, while she runs her fingers through his thick hair.

"Body language, baby!" she answers in a hoarse whisper. "Now, read mine and fuck me!" So, Warren wraps his hands in her hair, drawing her face to his while her hands search to free his throbbing manhood from its cloth prison.

The fog continues to work in his mind, clouding his thoughts during his pleasurable romp with Vivian. When they are both satisfied… enough, Vivian leaves, and Warren's muddled thoughts return to the letter. He walks into the den to retrieve it from the coffee table, his initial recollection telling him that that's where he had last seen it. It isn't there and a moment before panic sets in, he remembers that he moved it after inviting Vivian in. Where, though? He couldn't remember where he had put the envelope. He remembers picking it up as Vivian sat down on the sofa and he remembers walking out of the den with it. However, everything between then and walking back into the den to offer Viv a drink, was blank. As if it had been erased from his memory.

Now, the panic sets in and Warren exhausts himself searching through the entire house. He even goes and checks the attic, knowing good and well he hasn't been up there since he found that rosary for Greg, and he certainly hadn't taken the letter up there when he did. He can't find it anywhere. Time ticks on as he searches from one end of the house to the other, up and down, side to side, just to repeat the process all over again. Tears stream from his eyes in frustration and loss. His heart aches and it feels as if his soul is being ripped from his body. He has never in his life experienced such great sadness and sense of loss, even during the death of loved ones. He doesn't understand these feelings but doesn't fight them, either; his only mission is finding the letter.

Chapter Thirty

Play Her Game

1

Hours after Vivian has left, a tired and weary Warren collapses on the sofa in the den, passing out from lack of sleep and utter exhaustion. It is a restful, mercifully dreamless, sleep that is cut short by the jangling of the telephone. He comes awake with a start, falling off the couch from initial confusion and fright before everything comes crashing back to memory. He rushes into the kitchen and jerks the phone off the wall, unaware of the bright morning sunlight flooding in through the draped windows. It's Vivian Lancing asking if he is coming to work today since he's already an hour late. He can hear the concern in her voice. He glances at the kitchen clock, first thinking that it is a trick of sorts, and is astonished to find that she is right, he is in fact late for work for the first time in almost twenty years. "Yes, of course, I will be in. Just a little mishap this morning with the... uh... water pipes. Yeah, one of the pipes was leaking and the plumber was late. I meant to call but it slipped my mind." He lies, hoping she believes him.

"Oh, is that all? We were beginning to worry, it's not like you to be late, Doctor." She replies and Warren sighs in relief. The fog that had clouded his thoughts, had cleared some as he slept. In his rush to get to work and the shame of being late, all thoughts of the letter are pushed aside.

Half an hour later, Dr. Gerard strolls into the Navea Dwighton Asylum for the Mentally Afflicted looking much better than he should considering the lack of time for his normal hygienic self-care morning routine. There wasn't enough time for him to shower, shave, or eat. He threw on the first suit he could get his hands on while brushing the morning breath out of his mouth. He hastily put on some deodorant and cologne and out the door he went. His hair is slightly mussed, not his normal carefully styled do, and there is a dark stubble across his jaws and chin. His stomach rumbles from lack of food and the dark circles under his eyes still very prominent from the lack of morning caffeine. Last night's unwashed musk still clinging to him, mingling with the smell of cologne, creating an odd, yet alluring personal aroma. He turns heads as he walks through the halls, heading to his office, either because of his appearance or the smell he is omitting.

He asks Ms. Lancing to follow him into his office but stops her before she can say anything. He politely asks her to get him some coffee and a double shot of espresso before they begin, and she obliges. While she's gone, he notices Walter Paulus's stack of files and makes a mental note to begin reviewing them. And *speaking of files, I need to get those transfer papers out of his briefcase to complete.* He opens his briefcase and there sits the manilla envelope, the transfer papers temporarily forgotten. Tears of joy and relief spring into his eyes and he picks it up carefully, as if it is an ancient fragile relic, wanting to feel it to ensure its reality. He, now, remembers putting it in his briefcase when Vivian came in, but he hasn't the foggiest idea why he couldn't remember that when she left. He sits it back in his briefcase and lays several other papers on top of it, just in case. He remembers and finds the transfer papers and the briefcase is back on the floor beside his desk where it always is, when Vivian comes walking in with his coffee and espresso.

Ms. Roberts and Ms. Beckett realize shortly after starting to clean room six that they will not need to milk the job for the hours. This job is much worse than they originally thought but since they had already agreed they just set themselves at a steady pace and work constantly and consistently. It takes them well into the night, finally getting to leave the asylum less than three hours before day shift is due to start. They are filthy, disgusted, and exhausted but go home without showering anyway. Even as filthy as they are, Ms. Beckett still doesn't feel as gross now as she did when she changed the bedding in room 32 after Joseph Doe 'escaped'.

A few minutes later, with the espresso and some of the coffee gone, Warren is feeling much more focused. Ms. Lancing informs him that Ms. Roberts and Ms. Beckett completed cleaning room six, leaving just a few hours ago. Room 18 has also been cleaned and re-furnished. It is about two-thirds of the way from being completed so it can be cleaned and sanitized. *Alright. All good news so far.* Warren thinks to himself. Then, she informs him Stacy Farris has found the second video. "She says it's weirder than the first, way weirder." Vivian says, lowering her voice to a loud whisper.

Warren sighs and sits thoughtfully for a few moments, trying to figure out the best course of action. "Okay, Ms. Lancing, is there an inventory list of everything still needed to complete room 18?" She nods and hands him a paper with a couple dozen items listed on it. He scans it quickly and nods. "Send a couple nurses over to the women's side and ask them for more donations please. If any questions are asked, just tell them to tell that weaselly-looking old bat that it was vandals."

"Very well, keep it simple without lying or volunteering too much information." Vivian adds.

"Exactly. Whatever else is needed can be sent out for." She nods and jots a note on the legal pad in her arm. "I want room six locked up and kept that way." Another acknowledging nod. Finally, he asks, "Is Ms. Farris still here?"

"No, sir, she left with the rest of the night shift crew..." She pauses, noting Dr. Gerard, looking mildly irritated with this news, begins drumming his fingers on the desktop. "...but she left me step-by-step instructions on how to find and play the video." Vivian tells him, seeing the evident relief wash over his face.

"Excellent. We will see to the video a little later once I have been able to get my morning work caught up."

"Yes, sir." A pause. "There's just one more thing I should bring to your attention." She tells him mysteriously.

I knew it! I knew there would be something else, and I know it's going be awful! Better brace yourself. "Go on." He urges her exasperated.

"Well... it seems that... uh... Mr. Patrickson..." she says, nervously stammering.

"It's alright, Ms. Lancing. Whatever it is, I will figure it out. Just take a breath and tell me what's going on with Mr. Patrickson." Warren says, soothing her.

"Yeah, you're right." She says nodding, then takes a long, slow, deep breath. "Well, sir, it appears that Mr. Patrickson slipped back into a coma... yesterday." She informs him, timidly, and then steps back toward the door, waiting for the inevitable blow up.

"Yesterday!" Warren screams, jumping out of his chair. "Yesterday! Why wasn't I informed of this YESTERDAY?!?!" His face bright red, eyes wide and wild, Warren Gerard is fuming with anger.

"Apparently, Mr. Patrickson became violent with one of the nurses yesterday, so they sedated him. He was still sleeping it off at supper last night, so they didn't think much of it until he still hadn't woken up for breakfast. They tried to wake him but couldn't, so they ran the tests, and they show that he's comatose." Ms. Lancing explains the situation as it was explained to her.

"Sedated? Why was a man, that recently came out of an unidentifiably sourced coma, being sedated? He could have died! Why wasn't I informed of his sedation yesterday?" Dr. Gerard asks.

"Well, sir, you know we only inform you of such matters in person if the situation is... substantial, such as the one with Greg and the maintenance man. The rest are filled out according to protocol and sent to you to be signed off on. You sign at least a dozen of them daily. They are currently sitting on your desk, the one for Mr. Patrickson among the stack, I'm sure." Ms. Lancing tells him, hoping she has kept her tone in check, not wanting to anger him further.

"Yes, you're right, but that man was in a COMA! This is an unprecedented situation here and any change in his behavior should have been brought to my attention, immediately. Immediately!" Warren yells, stalking back and forth across this office, clearly furious.

"Yes, sir." She whispers, flinching away from him.

Dr. Gerard sees the fear on her face and takes a deep breath, calming down enough to lower his voice. "I am not upset with you, and I apologize for shouting. I want those infirmary nurses in my office as soon as possible."

Ms. Lancing, being exceptional at her job as a secretary, had anticipated this request and had already found the schedule, locating the three nurses running the infirmary yesterday. One is at the front station, one is on janitorial duties, and one has the day off. She informs him of this and has her call the third one in, to be here at noon. "Tell her I said tardiness or absence equals unemployment!"

"Yes, sir." She says and hurries out of the room.

Warren closes his eyes and takes several long deep breaths, calming his thudding heart and lowering his increased blood pressure. Once calm, he finishes his coffee in a few gulps and starts on his morning paperwork. He plows through all his desk work in great time, enjoying the caffeine buzz along the way.

He still has over an hour before his meeting with the infirmary nurses and decides to grab Vivian and head down to the monitoring room. Dr. Gerard sends the day shift monitoring nurse out for an extra break, which the bored young woman accepts gratefully. After Vivian follows the instructions Stacy left to the letter, the video plays for the pair. Vivian thinks that Stacy is right the whole time, it is way weirder. Warren watches it, unbelieving, the logical part of his mind scrambling for a sensical reason for what he is seeing.

The video shows the same figure from the hallway outside of room six entering through the door with the two large buckets. The figure sets them on the floor, in the middle of the room and steps back. There isn't any audio to the video and the figure is standing with its back to the camera, so they don't know if the figure is speaking or not. They both feel strongly that it is, though. The figure raises its arms, holding them above its head as objects around the room begin to lift off the floor and break into pieces. Everything floating in the air then flies in every direction, smashing against the walls and ceiling, crashing to the floor in littered heaps. Next comes the excrement. They watch it rise out of the buckets, suspend in air momentarily, and then fling in every direction as well, splattering various animal's feces and urine all over the room. All that is hard enough to process, nevertheless explain, but what draws their attention the most is the way the flinging objects; whether it be wood, rubber, or shit, would just travel right through the figure as if it wasn't standing there. Seemingly satisfied with its work, the figure lowers its arms, lifts the now empty buckets, turns, and walks out of room six.

The video clicks off. The pair sit in stunned silence, staring at the now blank monitor. Vivian Lancing and Dr. Warren Gerard are both trying to process what their minds have just seen. Unbeknownst to the other, they both had the same line of thinking. Not in any exact text but the point remains the same. They can't believe that the video is anything more than a trick of sorts. Even with everything Warren has witnessed and experienced so far, magic is still an unbelievable topic for him. They won't believe it is anything more than that because that would open a door to the unexplainable and neither of them believe in any such thing. They believe in the tangible and that everything can be explained, sometimes it just takes a while to find enough information to explain it. After some brief, hushed discussion about the video they convince themselves that that is the case this time, that it can be explained... somehow... they just need more information to do so. "It's still eerie as hell, though." Vivian comments as they leave the small, dimly lit monitoring room.

2

Vivian sits at her desk, trying to refrain from giggling because he might hear her if she does. She can't help it, though. He keeps contradicting himself and she can only imagine the confused expression on the faces of those three nurses standing in there, right now. That's what she finds so amusing, it's the imagined faces more than the words. Nevertheless, though, she would do well not to get in his fury path. She's already been yelled at once today and she didn't even do anything, but that was just a textbook case of shooting the messenger.

"During your next three days of suspension, I hope you three think long and hard about what you have done! The man could die! Do you want to live with that on your consciouses!? Now, when you three come in tomorrow you better toe that dang line!" Vivan hears Dr. Gerard scream at the three admonished young women. *There he goes again.* She thinks with a small smile. *I think he's fired them twice already and are currently on their third suspension... or is it the fourth. He's been going on for 15 minutes now, it's getting hard to keep up.*

Another five minutes of shouting later and the three nurses are sent about their way. Dr. Gerard follows them out of his office, his anger still evident. He tells Ms. Lancing to schedule the three of them for two weeks of hygienic care, which involves cleaning up patients who have accidents, showers, grooming, etc. The patients aren't the problem, it's just a nasty, degrading job. The nurses aren't the least bit pleased about it, but they are grateful to still be employed.

Warren calms down and heads to the Infirmary to check on Greg himself. Nothing has changed, but all vitals and tests are coming out okay. They don't know why he has lapsed back into this coma, Warren being strongly suspicious of the sedative. Gregory Patrickson looks as if he is sleeping peacefully, hands folded much the same way they were the first time. Dr. Gerard sits with Greg for a time, not speaking, just sitting with him in silence. Believing that Greg can sense the presence of another.

Time ticks by him slowly, the quiet of the dim room enveloping him, and he dozes in the chair. The same sensation he had after watching the first video rushes through him, and he knows what is happening. His subconscious is being swept away to the dark emptiness, which meant the Witch wants her answer. The realization panics him momentarily, but he quickly pushes through it, definitively deciding his fate.

"Your decision?" The disembodied feminine voice asks from the depths of the darkness.

Warren intends to tell the Witch that he will take his chances with finishing the letter, but before he can speak, a voice that only he can hear tells him to play her game against her. To simply tell her what she wants to hear, the same way she did him the day before. If his subconscious could smile, it would have, but that smile does not transmit to his body sitting with Greg in the Infirmary. "I tossed it in my fireplace last night. I was tired of reading the danged old thing anyway. It was some kind of crazy, poorly written story that didn't make much sense. Well, at least I couldn't make much sense of it or why you'd be so worked up about it. I don't know who you are or how any of this concerns you, but I know it doesn't concern me. I don't want any part of this. I did what you asked, the letter is gone." Warren says, hoping he sounds convincing enough but not desperate.

He does because there is an obvious sound of relief in the feminine tone when she responds. "Very well. You kept your end of the bargain and I, too, shall keep mine. Enjoy the rest of your life." She says with an inflection on the last few words, an eerie inflection. Then Warren's subconscious is sent hurtling toward his body again.

The Witch reaches out to her Master, the Prince of Profanity, ensuring him that she has resolved the issue with Johnathan's letter. She informs him that the doctor is still alive and claims he knows nothing about the situation, but she intends to keep an eye on him to see how much he really knows. Her Master approves of her plan and sends her on her way.

Dr. Gerard jerks violently in his chair, jarring himself awake from his nap. He has no idea how long he has been asleep and has no recollection of even dozing off. He looks at his watch and sees that he's been in the Infirmary for about an hour. He stands, his back and knees popping as he stretches. He still has several things to take care of today, and that was before he lied to a supposed Witch. It has yet to occur to Dr. Warren Gerard how easily he has accepted many aspects of this highly unusual situation or of his contradictory belief that magic simply does not exist.

Before walking away, Warren spontaneously reaches over and grabs Greg's hand, giving it a small comforting squeeze. His fingers brush against the jagged ridges of the seared flesh on the palm of Greg's hand. Instinctually, Dr. Gerard unfolds Greg's hands revealing the burnt imprint of the cross. The cross that is the exact same size as the rosary he had given him. Warren is taken aback by the sight of the grotesque wound and quickly, folds Gerg's hands back together, hiding the hideousness. Warren rushes out of the room, his heart racing and his hands trembling, the scenes of the fiercely glowing light omitting from that cross on the palm of Greg's hand play repeatedly in his mind.

Thankfully, Vivian is away from her desk when Dr. Gerard bulls his way through his office door, closing it quickly behind him. He collapses on the sofa, loosening his tie, trying desperately to catch his breath. Along with his shaky hands and rapid heartbeat, sweat has popped out on his forehead and nose and there is a lingering nausea in his abdomen. He can feel the quivering tension in every muscle of his middle-aged body. It feels like all the oxygen is being sucked out of the room and the walls are slowly moving in on him. His mind whirls without incoherent thoughts, just mere thought fragments and random words, nothing is connecting or making any sense to him. It only adds to the crushing anxiety he is experiencing.

Warren closes his eyes, fighting to clear his mind, and begins taking long, slow, deep breaths. After a few minutes, his mind calms and he can feel his body start to relax. His breath and heart rate even out, the perspiration ceases, and the nausea subsides. It takes almost half an hour, but Dr. Gerard is mostly himself again.

3

He has only been back at his desk for a matter of minutes, looking haggard and exhausted, when Ms. Lancing taps on his door. Before she can say anything, she notices how much worse he looks compared to the last time she had seen him, less than two hours ago. "Doctor, are you alright? You look, well, awful." she asks, trying hard not to sound too bluntly cruel about it.

He disregards her question with a wave of his hand. "What is it, Ms. Lancing?" he asks irritably.

She looks at him strangely for a moment before answering. "I came to inform you that room 18 is completely furnished and being cleaned as we speak. The cleaning will probably roll over into the night shift, in which case that group will finish cleaning and then sanitize the room. It should be ready for the Inspector by mid-morning and for Walter Paulus by the afternoon."

"That's good. I'll make the call to the Inspector directly." He says shortly.

"Yes, sir, and room six has been locked, as per your request." She tells him but he only nods. She can see the dark circles under his eyes and the overly tired, glossiness in them. "You know you don't have any more meetings until tomorrow, maybe you should go home and get some rest. You are clearly exhausted or getting sick or something. You really do look… well, terrible, I'm sad to say."

Dr. Gerard can hear the worry in her voice but is reluctant to care. He looks at her sternly and asks, "Are you quite finished?"

Fury courses through her and she literally bites her tongue to refrain from insulting the hobbit-looking egotistical bastard to tears. She nods, rolls her eyes, and walks out, closing the door forcefully behind her.

Warren sighs, feeling kind of bad about speaking to her that way and knowing he should apologize, but he just doesn't have the energy to do so. He doesn't have the energy to do much of anything but that doesn't change the fact that things need to be done. So, he pulls himself together the best he can, makes his quick and to the point phone call to Mr. Powers and the Inspector, then slowly makes it through his evening paperwork. He still hasn't cracked open any of Mr. Paulus's files and that is a must-do before his meeting with Walt tomorrow. He sits back in his chair, considering his next move.

He decides to take the files home with him. Vivian is already gone for the day and the night shift will soon be clocking in. They all know what needs to be done so he heads out too. He stops at the local deli and grabs him a sandwich for dinner and takes a shower as soon as gets home, leaving his briefcase and dinner laying casually on the table. The shower made him feel refreshed and the food energized him, giving him the confidence to tackle the files of Walter Paulus.

Chapter Thirty-One

The First of Three

1

Dr. Gerard starts with Walter Paulus's medical records and finds the only major childhood injury was a broken arm resulting from a baseball incident, but the follow-up appointment wasn't kept. Not very uncommon but noteworthy, nonetheless. His military physical had checked out and he was able to join the Marines, his military records indicating that he had fulfilled his four-year contract and was discharged with Honors. No major injuries reported during his military stint, but his psychological test showed very minimal sympathetic and empathetic traits. The psychologist noted that Mr. Paulus could have merely acted out the few emotions he had shown and that there was a high probability that the man may have sociopathy. Not an uncommon trait in the military, but the extent of it is worth noting. According to Walter's medical, psychological, and military files he seems to have ended his four-year contract harder and more resolved than most. Compared to most others, he is seemingly completely unaffected by the horrors they witnessed and experienced during active duty.

Walt went on to college, with the help of the military, and became an oncologist. That is what the files tell Dr. Gerard, but what he doesn't know is that Walter met his wife, JoAnne, during his junior year and they were married three months after his graduation. JoAnne was the only person at the wedding that knew she was already pregnant. It was a shock, but time went on. In the eight years they had been married, Walter's reputation as an oncologist had elevated him to a highly comfortable status, a status that he refused to share with his wife. He was always working or out entertaining others as influential as himself. He owned a lovely home in a secure, beautiful neighborhood and his children were dressed in nice clothes, even for being small children. His wife, however, owned one decent dress, a Sunday church dress, and the rest of her clothes looked as though she were a mere step above homeless. Very few of them fit her properly and they were riddled with moth-eaten holes. She looked much more like a housekeeper than a wealthy oncologist's wife.

Dr. Geard doesn't know about Walter Paulus' secret medicinal cocktail for his patients that had a very high success rate, in the high-eightieth percentile. Many had tried to get their hands on it only to fail time and time again. The patients given the cocktail would live much, much longer than they should have been able to. Spending decades in and out of remission, hovering on the brink of death and then recovering to that place of contentment, so it can be ripped away in a torrent of agony and misery time and time again.

From what Dr. Gerard can determine from all but his police file, Mr. Paulus seems to be a hard military man that decided to help others by becoming a well renowned oncologist. He wouldn't be the first man on Earth to have his woman step out on him for not being attentive enough to her. Warren has seen it many, many times. A couple of his exes had done the very same to him. He pieces this together solely with the information that he is an oncologist, knowing the grueling hours doctors like that work and the fact that he poisoned his family. Dr. Gerard sets the three other files aside and opens the dark blue file folder containing the reports, photos, and witness statements pertaining to the Paulus family incident.

Warren scans the page noting the time, date, and address of the incident, but reads the report carefully and studiously. A mental recreation of events plays through his mind as he reads. An ambulance was requested at the Paulus home and when the medics entered the house to tend to the sick man that had requested them, they immediately notified the police. The house stank of vomit, defecation, and death, but the smell isn't what made the medics call. It was the lifeless body of the seven-year-old Paulus girl, Jenny, sprawled out on the couch, laying on her stomach with one arm hanging over the side. Her sightless eyes were half-open, and her skin had a sickly yellowish tinge to it. There was a dark reddish-brown stain on the back of her pale pink nightgown and bloody vomit was crusted to her mouth and chin. A puddle of bright pink foam, looking like bloody carbonated slime, sat drying in the floor below her slightly open mouth.

The medics, highly nauseated by the sight, rushed the sick man with the same-colored foamy vomit drying on his shirtless chest and knit pants, out of the house and into the ambulance. They were still preparing Walter for transportation when two police cars, carrying three seasoned police officers, with lights flashing but no sirens pulled into the driveway. It was late evening so the lights flashing off the police cars could be seen from quite a distance, drawing curious pedestrians to the streets. Two of the three policemen entered the Paulus house where one immediately ran back outside, vomiting on the lawn from the sight of the child and the smell of the home. The officer wiped his mouth, puffed out his chest and walked back into the house unashamed of his involuntary reaction.

The ambulance had left with Walter Paulus and the coroner had arrived by the time the officers had completed their search of the home. Besides the young girl in the living room, they had found three other bodies. One was the five-year old son of Walter and JoAnne, found in the second story bathroom bathtub, lying on his side, knees slightly bent, with his eyes closed. He had one arm pulled free of his dinosaur pajama shirt, it lay bunched up on his shoulder and neck, while the other arm lay pinned beneath his small, fragile body still clothed. His free arm was extended toward his waist, his little hands gripping the sides of his pajama bottoms, the upper side of them pulled halfway down his thigh, exposing half of his buttocks. The child appeared to have been trying to remove his soiled pajamas when he had either fell asleep from exhaustion, passed out from weakness, or died from whatever caused all of this. Both officers had children of their own and both were highly infuriated and disgusted by the sight of the children. I took much more control than normal to maintain a level, unbiased opinion of the situation as they continued through the house.

JoAnne Paulus was the next to be found, alone in her bed in the master suite of the large two-story home. She was wearing a thin nightgown that she had had for many years, the blankets pulled up to just under her breasts, with her head propped up slightly on the pillow. If it wasn't for the sickly yellowish tone to her skin, one could almost believe that she was only in a drug or alcohol induced deep sleep. JoAnne's head was bent at an uncomfortable angle and her mouth was slightly ajar. There were no traces of vomit on her mouth or the front of her nightgown, but there were a few small drying spots of the pinkish foam on the edge of her pillow. It seemed she had leaned over and vomited on the floor, judging by the large puddle of it beside the bed. The cleanliness of the connecting bathroom indicated that she had made no attempt to get out of bed to make it to the bathroom. When the coroner pulled back the blankets to move JoAnne's body, they found half the mattress soaked in the watery, vile, and bloody foulness that had leaked from her lower body. The coroner's assistant, unlike JoAnne, did run for the bathroom when the wave of violent vomiting overcame him.

The final body to be found, and perhaps the worst of them all, was the youngest of the Paulus children, a thirteen-month-old baby girl. At the age of not quite walking and talking yet but trying to. This one was different than the other three victims. The youngest didn't have the sickly yellow color the rest of them had, instead she was blue. Her eyes were wide, frightened and glossy, the tears having dried to her tiny, thin eyelashes, clumping them together in places. Her tiny lips were puffy and a couple shades darker than her oxygen deprived skin, almost purple. Lying in her crib, wrapped snugly and gently in a fuzzy pink blanket. There was no vomit anywhere in the room, but further investigation found a few stains on the baby's onesie, the same faded red as the vomit, that had been wiped away and cleaned carefully. When the coroner was gingerly lifting the lifeless child out of the crib, the lighting displayed the darkening bruise of a handprint that covered the entirety of the lower half of the baby's face.

By the time the two officers had walked out of the house, concluding their search, it was almost impossible for them to control their outrage of emotions. Both men walked directly to their vehicles, sat in the driver's seat, turned off their lights, and closed and locked all the doors. A crowd of a couple dozen had gathered outside the Paulus home and the single deputy that remained outside was struggling to handle the nosy gawkers alone. He called in back up and done the best he could until they arrived. He had known the other two officers for years and had dealt with many nasty cases with the two gentlemen, but he had never seen them react like that before. He left them to deal with whatever they were feeling on their own, despite how much he could have used their help with the growing crowd.

2

Autopsies come back that all, including the youngest child, had been given rat poison. Cause of death for JoAnne, Jenny and the only Paulus son was death by poisoning, as a matter of murder. The youngest's cause of death is suffocation and, also listed as murder. Witness statements indicate that JoAnne may have been having an affair with a neighbor a few houses down because said neighbor had been hired by Walter on several occasions to fix things around the house. The neighbor was reluctant to be found due to his shady past, but when he was, the affair was confirmed. He even confessed to the possibility of the youngest being his rather than Walter's and how JoAnne had confided in him about the immense guilt she felt over the affair and the youngest child. They pressed and pressed the man, but he would not admit to killing them. He hadn't so why would he, he had an alibi and everything. That line of questioning stopped whenever his alibi had been confirmed.

The youngest of JoAnne Paulus's children was DNA tested and it was confirmed that the child was indeed the neighbor's daughter and not her husband's. The more information the investigation uncovered; the more nervous Walter became. He knew he didn't poison his family, including himself, but everything was pointing to him anyway. It was like some unknown force was trying to lock him away any way it could. Walter isn't a big man, only five-foot-ten and maybe 170 pounds, but muscular and stronger than his appearance indicates. His hands were just the tiniest bit bigger than his wife's hands, so it was hard to determine whose hand it was that smothered the baby. Walter knew it wasn't him, he could never have done anything like that to a child, his or not, but he still struggled to believe that JoAnne could have either. That was one point against him.

Another was the fact that he had had one of his rare days off and had decided to spend it at home. He did not get very many of them but unless he was with a dying patient, he was home for dinner every night. That was when he talked and advised and reprimanded and bonded with his son and eldest daughter. It was when he would play peek-a-boo and make funny faces at the youngest just so he could hear that adorable little giggle of hers one more time. JoAnne would sit quietly at the end of the table and only speak when spoken to while the family ate the dinner that she alone prepared. Then she would set about cleaning up after everyone else while they sat around at the table. What Dr. Gerard didn't know was that she would watch them from the kitchen doorway. There was no malice or loathing of them in her thoughts because this is how it has always been for them, not for her, but for them. Instead, she felt a love for her husband because of the immense love he felt for his children. He was an amazing father, when he could be around, but he couldn't give them, us she corrected herself, he couldn't give us these beautiful things without working. She would simply sigh and return to the kitchen.

Very seldom was he able to spend an entire day at home with his children and since they adored their father, it meant the world to them. He cherished moments like that with his children because he was granted so few of them. On that day, they played ball in the backyard, went for a hike in the stands of trees around the city park, then watched movies in the den all afternoon as it stormed outside. This was typical behavior of those that commit murder-suicide, another mark.

When the time came, on a whim, Walter had decided to send the children off to their rooms and headed off into the kitchen to help his wife cook dinner. Something he hadn't done since Jenny was potty training. Walter Paulus had told the investigators this himself, it was highlighted in his official statement. Another mark against him.

He had stepped out of the kitchen on a few occasions to check on the children and get the baby set up in her highchair. He was adamant about this point once he realized that he had dug his hole a bit deeper by disclosing the 'opting to help with dinner out of nowhere' bit. In hindsight, the adamancy may have aided in that extra mark against him, but one would never really know for sure. The coincidences only continued to add up from there, and that is exactly what they were, coincidences. The defense, however, will argue, truthfully, that twice is a coincidence and any more than that is a pattern, and this pattern leads directly to the hard ass ex-Marine, Walter Paulus. His lawyer could not argue that point, the defense was right, almost all signs pointed to Walter.

During dinner, it just so happened that Walt received a call from his neighbor directly across the street and he had to leave his dinner, partially eaten, sitting on the table so he could go help his neighbor repair a busted pipe in their laundry room. Off he went and he came back a little more than an hour later, his plate still sitting on the table, a cover placed over it, awaiting his return. Another mark.

He was feeling a little queasy, assuming it was from all the excitement with the busted pipe, so he left it sitting on the table. He checked on the children, who were laying in the den floor watching an animated movie on TV, the baby lazily sprawled between the older two. He thought they looked a little pale but assumed it was only the lighting from the TV and thought nothing more of it until explaining everything to the investigators. He didn't see JoAnne or know where she was but thought little of it. He went to his home office to catch up on a little paperwork before his morning meeting. And another mark.

It was in his home office that the sickness sank its claws into him, and he vomited in his trash can the first time, most of it his mostly digested supper mixed with some clotted stringy blood that went unnoticed. The second time he vomited, not only did he miss the trash can but was even denied the time to reach for it. He had no notice of it erupting from his mouth until it was, and he vomited all over the top of his desk. Initial rage, that he felt only for a moment, consumed him before it was consumed by mortal fear. All he could see was blood, bright red fresh blood splashed across his desk, splotches of it were sudsy, paling the color to a bright pink. Immediately and utterly convinced that his death was near and imminent, he pushed the panic back knowing he could not let it take control and went for the phone to call an ambulance. Walter was unaware that his wife and children were enduring the same cruel symptoms, but worse, and didn't want to alarm them. So, he called the ambulance himself rather than calling for his wife. He went and sat by the front door, everyone was asleep upstairs, or so he thought, but he didn't have the strength to make it up there and wake his sleeping wife. Another mark.

The pain and the trips to the half bathroom/laundry room down the short hallway to the right of the living room where the front door was located, required all his strength and attention, and fogged his focus. Mercifully, he did not see his beloved daughter laying on the den sofa or her take her last few shuttering breathes before falling into the eternal abyss of death. Walter has stated on more than one occasion that he didn't even know they were dead until the following day when the officers came in asking him why he had poisoned and killed his entire family. No one believed him, though and few believed his grief and mourning. Walter was and is sincere in his grief, sadness, and regret surrounding the situation and those involved, it was and is just hard to see through the hard military exterior he wears like a plate of armor against the world. Walter realized only too late that that plate of armor couldn't stop his heart from shattering or his world from falling to ruin around him.

3

It was a quick and unanimous verdict: incompetent of standing trial, criminally insane, send him to the asylum. The speculation was that Walter knew about JoAnne and the neighbor's affair, as well as the youngest daughter not being his child, even though he insistently denied it. Everyone believed that he poisoned his family with the dinner that he helped his wife prepare, eating only enough of it to help his 'I'm innocent' plea. Some thought that maybe he really had meant to kill himself along with the rest of them and just chickened out at the last minute. For a short time, the neighbor that had called asking for Walter's assistance with the busted water pipe was harassed by several of the less upstanding members of the community, some believing that he had been in on Walter's plan to murder his family the entire time. The harassment was short lived, however once the police were notified.

So off Walter Paulus went, as a guilty man, to a place he could not thrive in. He had and has maintained his innocence ever since, denying all accusations surrounding the Paulus family tragedy. Still yet, no one believes him. There are just too many signs screaming of his guilt to be ignored. Now, he sits in Dr. Gerard's asylum.

Warren closes the last of the file folders on Walter Paulus and places the stack back in his briefcase. He kind of feels sorry for Walt, understanding the man's entire world, everything he had built, his family, career, life, etc. came crashing down on him in a single night. If the speculations are true, and Warren isn't so sure that they are, then the man deserves everything he has gotten, but something about the entire situation feels off to him. Something is nagging him about the tragedy Walter survived, the one he may or may not have caused. He leans back in his seat and rubs his face with his hands, sighing loudly.

The nagging in the back of his mind won't turn off; it seems like it hasn't shut up in years, bitching about one thing or another. Finally, Warren gets up, makes himself a stiff drink and returns to his seat, where he glances into his still open briefcase. His eye catches the corner of the manilla envelope and before he realizes what he is doing, it's already in the hand opposite the one holding his drink. *What in the...* is all he manages to think before he realizes that he has set his drink down and is sliding the letter out of the envelope, the page he had left off on resting on the top of the stack just as he had put it in there the last time. A previously unknown sensation creeps over him and he cannot understand why he has no immediate control over his own being. He feels like a prisoner trapped in his own mind, watching himself from a first-person view. It is a surreal feeling that he doesn't much care for. He watches himself settle onto the sofa, letter in hand, and then feels what little control he had managed to maintain, relinquish as his in-mind movie begins to play again.

Chapter Thirty-Two

Body Recovery

1

The group returned to the Infirmary, short the eldest O'Reigan daughter, her husband, and their newborn daughter. They informed the rest of the storms survivors about the events that transpired at the Witch's shack and that they were unaware of Joshua's whereabouts. The news was met with teary eyes and a few shocked gasps. The preacher, his trio of nuns and a few others joined hands in prayer while others whispered among themselves.

The preacher had ceased his ranting's a short time ago, mercifully ending the suffering of all that could hear him. Father Robin, the three Sisters, and a small handful of others were currently enrapt in prayer that border-lined an outright sermon.

The O'Reigan widow had been sedated and was sleeping as restfully as possible. Whenever she was awake, she had begged and pleaded with whoever would listen to her, for them to give her husband back to her. When they finally told her that was not possible, she flew off into a violent fit of rage that resulted in her sedation.

The drunk fisherman found in the pier shack was snoring loudly in a far corner, still sleeping off his massive Shine intake. The rumbling nasal sounds echoing through the dimly lit corridor both irritated and oddly soothed all those in the room. A couple hours later, while some were sleeping, he woke up, leaned over and vomited on the floor beside him. The change in the consistent droning background noise caused several of the sleeping valley folks to stir and a few to awaken. His vomit smelled of Shine and rot and it sickened the fishermen even more. He crawled away from his own disgust before the urge to vomit struck him again and when he felt he was a safe distance away, he curled up on the floor and went back to sleep. Within minutes the snoring resumed, and all slept a little more restfully.

Most everyone else was split up, of their own accord, into small groups scattered about the large room, some asleep and some not. Sarah Maisse, Carol Jewell, and the merchant's wife were walking around the room offering food, water, medical aid, blankets, or anything else anyone might need.

Danny and Betty went to find Alvin, when they did, they found him silently weeping for his lost love, Anne Weston, one of the Witch's followers that froze to death in her meager little teepee. Alvin Danson hated the thought of his beloved lying out there another night but knew he had to wait until morning to move her to the funeral pyre. They would all have to wait to be moved.

Johnathan immediately began helping Sarah and the others, trying desperately not to display any outward or extra attention to her. As far as the valley folks were concerned, they were both seeing other people. He, the Witch and her, Frank McGrath. He wondered though, if anyone would or did suspect anything since they spent six days alone together in his shack. He felt that only time could answer him.

Frank McGrath and Dansford Keeton were off to themselves in an intense whispered conversation, both looking quite angry. No one thought anything of the pair off talking alone. It was Frank and Dan, they were always together, everyone knew that. No one saw the looks of anger between the men either. Everyone was coming to terms with the fact that they survived a monumental snowstorm, so they had no interest in minor quarrels or gossip on that night.

The following morning everyone gathered to discuss what should be done, but before anyone could say anything, Father Robin declared that he "...wasn't going to take orders from any sinful heathens that were damned to rot in the fiery pits of Hell for all eternity!" No one spoke, they all simply regarded him dumbly. "Follow me, brothers and sisters, and we shall pray for our Lord God the Almighty to heal the wounds he has inflicted upon us with his wrath!" Again, no one spoke. Even his most faithful attendants could not walk out that door with him. They thought that now was a time for unity and a sense of community. Besides, praying only helps when the resolution is out of your hands, doesn't the Bible say something like God only helps those that help themselves? Praying isn't going to remove the dead so the live don't get sick or feed the dozens of mouths here. We must do that... together.

When no one answered him, the preacher simply grunted his disgust and turned his back to them, the Sisters mimicking the motion like little toy soldiers. Father Robin, Sister Virtue, Sister Grace, and Sister Harmony all left the Infirmary together, walking the short distance back to the Church where they shut the doors to the rest of the valley. Later that day a sign would be hung from the front door reading: All Sermons Cancelled Until Faithful Congregation Can Be Found The valley folks that seen and read the sign would only shake their heads and walk away, uttering to themselves what a petty son-of-a-bitch their 'Godly' preacher was.

2

With that bit of drama over, the discussion began. Roughly an hour later it had been decided that the dead should be the top priority and so it was. Most of the group was divided into two large groups. One group, led respectably by Ron Hellman and Porter Siddle, the valley's only remaining woodworkers, was set to build layers and additional sections to the wooden structure in the center of the common area, in the middle of the scorched earth, that would send the dead to the Heavens or welcome them to pits of Hell. Every time they thought that they were caught up and had enough lumber to accommodate all the dead bodies, someone would show up saying they needed to add a few more. There were fourteen bodies in all and each one had its own platform. It looked like a rectangular cube full of death when it was all said and done.

The other large group, led by Alvin Danson and Danny Bailey, were to begin on the West side of the valley at the O'Reigan farm, scanning the entire area. Alvin had woken long before the sun had risen and went to Anne's shredded teepee that would forever mark her tomb. He gently and gracefully carried the stiff, partially decaying body back to the common area. Tears streamed down his eyes the entire time and he silently cursed God for taking his love. She was the first on the funeral pyre, having undressed and prepared her body himself. As she lay among the dried grass and branches that would be the fuel to the fire, he absent-mindedly knocked one maggot out of her hair and another off her lower lip that had wiggled from the hollow of her slightly gaping mouth. Then he leaned over and kissed the dry, cracked, receding lips of his beloved, with a final tear in his eye.

All the dead bodies were transported via wagon to the common area where a group of five young men and women, Old Joe Brenner's sensual female employees Lacy and Sugar among them, were waiting to retrieve and prep the bodies. All the dead animals, all partially rotted and inedible, were tossed into the river and there turned out to be quite a few of them. It took the large group all day to search the entire valley. Making it to the Witch's shack and finally being able to turn back right as the sun was disappearing behind the mountains. They were smelly and exhausted but felt mightily accomplished. They were welcomed to the common area where the largest funeral pyre they had ever erected would be set aflame while the rest of them feasted and rejoiced in the lives that their loved ones lived, as was their custom.

Frank McGrath, who was more-or-less running the show, was walking around supervising, one could say. He never really has done much of anything, but he can sure get others to accomplish the work needed done though. Frank's father knew from the time Frank was just a small tot that his place was in management and leadership. Frank had a way of pinpointing most people's best qualities and setting them to be used to the best advantage. Sometimes that advantage was for the betterment of others and sometimes it was for more selfish reasons. This was for the betterment of the valley. Frank shoved all other thoughts, thoughts of Sarah and of Dansford and of all those that have been lost to this tragedy, to the back of his mind and singularly focused on rebuilding their quaint little community, one board and body at a time.

Dansford Keeton and the fisherman that still smelled strongly of Shine but had a much more sober look in his eyes, were sent to the train station to take inventory of what the warehouse was currently storing. Everyone knew the train hadn't come through this week but with as much snow as they got it, it wasn't much of a surprise. The surprise came a few weeks later when the reality set in that they were completely on their own until spring rolled back around. Not that they weren't used to that part of living in the valley, it was the lack of supplies that concerned the valley folks. The train would always return with those that had gone to the festival in New York and a fraction of their winter supplies. The following and last week the train ran for the season would bring the largest bunch of supplies, usually taking upwards of four hours just to unload off the train. That train day was always a busy and hectic one for almost the entire valley. The effort was worth the reward because they were usually able to comfortably sustain the valley through the winter months if their food supply was in order. Water was never an issue because the river had always run, never dried up and never frozen. It was as faithful to the valley residents as they were to the valley. They had none of those supplies this winter and it was already freezing cold by the time the realization about the never-coming train came upon them. As frightened and unnerved about the coming winter as they were, there was still an overall sense of hope, a need to fight for their survival against the odds and the elements.

Doreen, the apothecary Aide, remained at the Infirmary with the O'Reigan widow who was currently drooling from the side of her mouth, eyes half open, starry-eyed, staring at only she knew. Doreen tried to get her to eat and drink but the mad woman refused. She wasn't being violent or begging for her husband, so Doreen just left her to her thoughts and kept an eye on her as she tended to the severely ill women that had been brought in the day before. She had been able to break their fever in the night, only for it to come back with a vengeance by morning. Doreen wasn't sure if Beth Redley and Leena McAvay were going to make it, but she wasn't about to give up on them. Between the mad woman and the sick women, Doreen also had three elderly folks to look after.

Luckily, they could do mostly for themselves, but she still had to endure their impatient attitudes and hatefulness at the situation that they could only direct at her or each other.

Roy Hoarding and Sarah Maisse, Ben too if they knew where he was, were sent over to the Slums to have Jiminey and Patty McAvay and the Witch head on over to the Infirmary. Then the pair were to try to find the six missing miners that, as far as anyone knew, were still up in the mines they left for a week ago. They were tasked with this job due to their tracking skills from hunting. If they could track an animal, surely, they could track a person or two. So, Roy and Sarah set off east while the large group of body recoverees went west.

3

The ice and snow had completely melted away leaving the ground a soppy, slippery mud that would swallow your boot in some places. As Sarah and Roy headed toward the McAvay's place, they noted how much worse the destruction of a lot of the shacks and teepees had gotten with the melting snow. Roy was looking to his right, past Sarah, examining a shack with a caved-in roof, paying no attention to his next step. The toe of his boot caught the face of a rock jutting from the muddy ground, and he stumbled to his left, his arms outstretched grasping for and at anything his hand grazed. He caught the door frame of a very unsteady looking shack that held his weight just long enough for Roy to breathe a sigh of relief. Then the wall supporting the door frame collapsed under his weight and he fell inside the crumbling shack, his arm still outstretched and grasping a section of the rough wood door frame.

The wind was knocked from his lungs, and he laid there gasping and pining for breath, surprise overwhelming him. Then the panic set in as he heard the first groanings from the unstable ceiling hanging above his head. The fear and panic rendered him motionless as distant memories fragmented in his mind, knowing that his life would be over in the next moment or two. Suddenly, he felt a tightness around his ankles and a jerk that, pleasantly, popped over half of the vertebrae in his back. Just as his outstretched arm cleared the fallen doorway of the shack, there was a loud crash and a small puff of dust billowed out from around the now imploded structure.

Finally starting to get oxygen back into his lungs, Roy sat up and started taking long deep breaths of the slightly dusty air, trying to understand what had just happened. He raised his hand, the one that had caught the door frame and had been outstretched before him, to run his fingers through his hair. His hand stopped most of the way there due to a sudden, sharp, stabbing pain just above his temple. At the same moment a searing pain shot halfway up Roy's forearm. He lowered his hand and could feel the blood trickle down the side of his dirty face. His eyes widened in astonishment and horror as they registered the eight-inch long wooden mini-stake that had pierced through the palm of his hand. The center of the wood shard was about the same size as a cornstalk, which was going to leave a considerable hole in his palm. The sight alone caused him to feel woozy, as if he were going to faint.

Sarah stared at the wound fighting to keep her meager breakfast in her stomach, then tore off a part of his shirt to carefully wrap around his hand, trying hard not to nudge the wood in any way. With that done, she was able to carefully help him to his feet and they slowly walked to the McAvay's place. There, Sarah quickly explained to the couple what had happened to Roy and that he needed to get back to the Infirmary. She still had to go get the Witch to tell her to get to the Infirmary, at least they knew that building was safe. The rest of them would need to be properly checked and stabilized. As if to emphasize on her point the McAvay's shack shuttered with a gust of wind. Jiminey and Patty startled by the coincidence of it all, didn't question, just grabbed up a few things, tossing them into a knapsack, and then on both sides of Roy, they walked out and toward the Infirmary. As they walked westward, Sarah went east with a steady uneasiness, that she couldn't quite explain, growing within her.

Chapter Thirty-Three

Confusion and Despair

1

The Witch could sense that someone was drawing near her shack, as well as she could sense that someone had stupidly snuck into her garden the night before. She did not and could not, in any magical sense, know who either of them was. The intruder made no difference to her because her incredibly devious garden had taken care of them for her, but the one that was approaching intrigued her.

The Witch was infuriatingly, yet pleasantly, surprised to find who was connected to the other end of the hand that was knocking on her shack door. The moment she realized that it was her lover's mistress standing in her doorway, the Witch twitched her finger, which went unnoticed by Sarah. Suddenly, a confused look washed over Sarah's face as if she couldn't remember how she had gotten to the Witch's shack or why she had showed up in the first place.

Sarah Maisse approached the Witch's small shack, the smell of decay still heavy in the mountain air on the east side of the valley. The uneasiness she felt leaving the McAvay's place had only strengthened the closer she got to her destination. Sarah assumed the uneasiness was just a sign of her guilty feelings about falling for and sleeping with the Witch's beloved. Neither of which she had had much control over. Not that Johnathan had forced himself upon her or any such thing, it was just that the connection between John and Sarah was stronger and more powerful than anything either of them had ever experienced. They had been drawn to each other since the moment they first met, and neither of them could explain or understand the undying love and commitment they felt for one another.

Since the surviving valley folks had banded together at the Infirmary, Sarah had only been able to briefly speak with Frank McGrath, something she was quite thankful for. He seemed to have been preoccupied with something involving Dansford Keeton, but he hadn't mentioned anything about it, and she hadn't asked. Truthfully, she didn't much care what was going on as long as it kept him occupied a while longer. She harbored much more guilt toward hurting Frank than she ever could have harbored for the Witch. That was simply because Sarah had never met the Witch before, had only seen her in passing, and even though she didn't love nor had ever been intimate with Frank, Sarah very much cared for him. Frank was the type of man that she could have grown to love... one day, someone she could have been content with settling for. Settling wasn't in Sarah's nature though, which is part of the reason why she had moved to the valley on a whim when she received that letter. She had refused to settle for her shit life before she came to the valley, and she refused to settle for a man she didn't truly love. With that acceptance came the realization that she would probably never feel for anyone the way she felt for Johnathan Owen Colmes.

Sarah shoved all thoughts of Johnathan and Frank and the Witch and the whole fucked up situation out of her mind as she walked up to the shack door. She sighed heavily, sucked in a gulping breath, and knocked. Seconds later the Witch opened it and the two women immediately locked eyes. Sarah was momentarily startled by the seemingly furious, hate-filled eyes boring into her own and for a split-second Sarah knew that the Witch knew about her and John. The knowledge slipped from her mind as the Witch smiled sweetly at her, a smile that didn't quite touch the eyes that still seemed to burn with loathing and malice.

Suddenly, Sarah's mind blanked out, confusion taking over. She stood staring dumbly at the woman before her, brief recognition dawning, only for the confusion to wash over her again. The Witch's facial expression changed to one of 'put-on' concern and she reached out, placing her hand low on Sarah's back, to walk her inside. Sarah, try as she might, could not remember coming to the Witch's shack or why she was there. She could almost get the answer to come forward, only for confusion to take its place. Unsure of what was going on, she allowed herself to be led inside.

The Witch, taking advantage of the woman's temporary confusion, ushered her into the shack. As she walked her across the room, one hand on the small of her back, Sarah tripped over a chair leg. The Witch, instinctually, reached out with her free hand to catch the woman from falling. Her hand, by sheer and utter coincidence, landed on Sarah's lower abdomen. That one, happenstantial touch alone was enough to tell the Witch all she needed to know and with that knowledge she believed she had found the answer to all her problems.

2

She sat Sarah down at the small wooden table in the front room of her shack, seemingly concerned. "You look distressed, child. Let me make you some tea to help calm them nerves of yours. I'll only be a minute, dear, I keep all my herbs in the back." The Witch told her, but before Sarah could accept or refuse the tea, the Witch had disappeared into the other room.

She gathered dried leaves, stems, and flowers from various herbs out of various vials, bottles, and lidded containers. The Witch could hardly contain her giddiness at the way everything had fallen together for her. An evil, hate-filled sneer stretched across her lips as she let her rage and suffering boil uncontrollably, enjoying the vivid fantasies of revenge that played through her head.

When her hand rested upon Sarah's stomach, the Witch could feel the process of conception occurring within her. She could feel the energy ebbing and flowing from the miniscule life form trying desperately to survive and thrive. The Witch intended to not only ensure the conception was successful but to progress the pregnancy so that her Master's marked son would be born within the time frame that she was given.

For the herbal concoction and the evocation to work, the ingredients had to be prepared properly. She tossed the flowers of a Balm of Gilead into the ceramic mortar for success of the

363

ritual, followed by dry Bistort leaves to ensure the success of the conception. Carnation flowers for added energy to aid in the pregnancy and Clove leaves to protect the unborn and ensure the pregnancy's survival. The flowers of Rue to progress the pregnancy threefold, Lemon Verbena stems for added power in the progression and Vervain flower petals to increase the intelligence of the unborn child. The Witch lifts the pestle to grind the herbs only to set it back down and grab one more. She adds just a pinch of dried Camphor leaves to the mortar, an herb that should cause Johanthan to be repulsed by Sarah and bring an end to their unfaithful deceitful affair. It was an impulsive, jealous-and-wrath-fueled action that couldn't have been undone during those following second thoughts that the Witch did not have.

She ground the herbs to a fine, dusty powder and left them to rest in the mortar while she gathered the rest of the tools necessary to complete the ritual. The Witch took everything into the larger of the two caves, her ritual room and set everything on the altar. The appearance of the altar had changed drastically along with its owner. What was a clean, plain stone altar, cluttered only with a couple white candles, her Book of Majic and the elemental symbols, was now draped in a heavy black cloth, covered with candles so black they melted into the shadows, while others were the nasty yellowish green of disease. Decaying bodies of small animals, some for sacrifice and some for pleasure killing, had been thrown nonchalantly about the altar, left to rot wherever they lay. The smell was atrocious but pleasant to Witch's senses. The good that had been within her, the Light, had been quickly consumed by the darkness. Every beautiful, kind, gracious, loving, amazing trait, memory, and likeness about the Witch, had been consumed and/or altered until there would be nothing left of the Good Witch.

As the Witch scrambled between the two cave rooms, Satan's asp, the viper sent to monitor the Witch and her doings, slithered out of its warm and cozy home within her, slithering down her leg in a spiral. The midnight black snake with the glowing red eyes and the crimson streak along its back that radiated like fire, lazily made its way over to the altar. There it feasted on the rotting corpse of what was once a ferret or weasel and then dined on the slightly cool entrails of a large field rat that had been ripped in half only hours before. The python-like viper flicked its tongue several times, as if licking its lips confirming it was, indeed, a fine meal, as it slithered its way back up the Witch's leg and then between them.

The Witch had experienced this retreat and reentry multiple times already, even though it had been less than 18 hours since the snake had been given to her, but this was not always for it to eat. Sometimes it would wander around, as if searching for something while other times it would simply sit and stare at her. The latter would make her very uncomfortable; it would give her the sensation that the snake was searching her for something as well, probing her mind. After the first couple times experiencing the viper's movements, they were no longer bothersome to the Witch, but she would still pause in whatever she was doing as it entered or exited her. Mainly because the girth of the python could be almost painful or quite pleasurable depending on her stance and position at the time. She didn't necessarily opt for the pleasure but, the human part of her, as miniscule as the magical part had made it, insisted that she avoid the pain. So, she would stop, quickly position herself for the least amount of discomfort and once the asp had slithered either up or down her leg, she would resume her task.

A flick of her finger set the candles on the altar alit, and they cast just enough shadowy light so she could read the evocation chant from her book, 'Opera Magicae'. She set the mortar of herbal powder in front of her but put the silver chalice that was older than herself and three small, corked vials to the side. The Witch flipped through the yellowing pages of her spell book, found the one she was looking for and read it carefully. Then she picked up one of the vials and let several drops of Rose Geranium oil fall into the mortar. The drops beaded up instantly in the fine powder giving it an exotic water droplet on the sand look. The second vial contained Vanilla oil that was also added liberally, adding to the beads of oil on the finely ground bed of herbs. Lastly, a half-full vial of Satan's blood was added to the mixture, where the contact with the herbs sent up a tiny mushroom cloud of reeking, putrid foulness. Its vile stench engulfed the large nature-made room.

Whether using white or black magic, the Witch always called on the help of the elements during her more difficult rituals. The burning candles signified Fire and a dash of salt was dropped into the mortar signifying Earth. The Witch lit her incense bundle, waving the heavily aromatic smoke above the almost-complete potion, signifying the element, Air. Finally, water to signify Water was splashed into the mortar with the rest of it. The witch used the pestle and mixed carefully, so not to splash any of the precious potion onto the altar. With it mixed well, she poured the dark red liquid into the silver chalice and left it sitting as she read the four-line evocation chant over and over until she could recite it flawlessly with ease.

The preparation of the potion and memorizing the chant took well over an hour, but time meant little to the Witch. The risk of spending that time to get the ritual right was worth not screwing up a second time, and so soon. Besides, Sarah Maisse was still in a state of confusion where time was nonexistent.

3

She was right. Sarah had watched the Witch leave but she didn't know how long ago that could have been. As long as Sarah was in the state of confusion that the Witch had cast upon her, time was meaningless. Sarah had no idea, no concept of how long she had been sitting there. It could have been three minutes, three hours, or even a day or more. Sarah didn't know and didn't care. She didn't need any more questions; it would only make the confusion worse. So, Sarah just sat at the wooden table, trying to push through the confusion and waited for the Witch to return.

It would be too hard for the Witch to get Sarah back into the cave where she would normally have done a tarot reading before anything else. She would have to skip that part because the added confusion could drive Sarah mad, and she just couldn't have that... yet. For the sake of Satan's son, of course. Once the child was born, however, the story would change. The Witch brought the silver chalice, the chant still fresh in her mind, to the small wooden table in the front room where Sarah sat. She carefully set the chalice on the table before Sarah. "Here, child, drink your tea. You look frazzled. It'll help clear that foggy mind of yours." The Witch told her sweetly.

Sarah watched the Witch enter the room carrying something in her hands. She watched her set the thing on the table before her. Sarah knew she knew what that thing was but in her whirling mind of confusion she couldn't find the word for it. Then her mind began to clear of its fog of confusion, still not remembering how or why she was at the Witch's shack, though. The confusion was replaced with an imagined scenario that was not only blurry but glitchy. Sarah didn't know what was happening, though, didn't know that the Witch had finally removed her confusion but replaced it with a glamour spell. Sarah was looking at the thing the Witch had placed on the table before her, but it was slightly distorted, like she was looking through a very smudged lens. It was a teacup, which is what she had seen but couldn't name. For a fraction of a second, the teacup blinked and was suddenly a tall, wineglass looking goblet made of a metallic material encrusted with beautifully colored gems, some of which that were colors never known to exist. She didn't know the word for a chalice, but goblet was close enough. Then the goblet blinked back into the basic tan colored pottery made teacup it was less than a moment before.

Sarah looked down at the chalice strangely. "It's tea, dear, you really should drink some to calm them nerves." The Witch insisted, and reluctantly Sarah obeyed. The blink had only happened that once so Sarah wasn't entirely sure what she had seen or if she had seen it at all. Reluctantly, she lifted the chalice with trembling hands and as she took her first sip, the Witch's eyes started to glow with the brilliant black flame associated with Satan and his followers, as she began to chant the evocation backward, as was the way she was taught:

Own your as son their take
Blood your and herbs these with
Mark your with unborn the defile
Flies and fowlness, filth of master oh

As the dark red liquid spilled into Sarah's mouth and down her throat, her body demanded more of it, and more until she had drunk the entire goblet full without pause. In her mind, however, Sarah had just chugged the best cup of tea she had ever had. She could taste the elderberries, the cranberries, and the sassafras. There were others too, too many to name, but it was wonderful. Sarah was unaware of it, but the teacup had blinked once more, while in her hands and pressed to her lips, where the dark red liquid stained them blood red.

Sarah set the teacup to her, chalice to the Witch, almost ashamedly back on the table. The Witch immediately lifted the chalice and returned it to its place in the caves. By the time she returned, Sarah was looking much more alert but almost frightened about what had just come over her. "How do you feel, child?" The Witch asked, as if they didn't look the same age, even though the Witch was centuries older than the stunning young Sarah.

"I...I'm not quite sure. I can't for the life of me remember why I came here." She replied, stumbling over her words, as she rubbed her temple as if a headache were forming.

"I don't think you were coming here, dear." The Witch said mysteriously. "I found you laying out a bit from the garden wall, looked like you might have fell, or bumped your head, or maybe fainted. I woke you up, brought you in and gave you some tea to bring you back to your senses." She explained to Sarah, only the last having any truth to it because she did regain her senses when the Witch took the chalice out of the room.

Sarah continued to rub at her temple, not speaking for a few long seconds. The Witch sat quietly across from her trying to restrain the evil smirk threatening to form on her lips. Slowly, Sarah started to remember. She remembered Roy being with her... him falling against and then through the rotted wall of the shack... his hand, his punctured bloody hand. This memory caused a violent shiver to run down Sarah's spine. She remembered Jiminey and Patty McAvay heading toward the Infirmary with the injured Roy... and she was coming east because... because she was looking for... what?" Sarah sighed and then suddenly it popped into her head, The Miners!

After all the confusion, Sarah was so excited to remember something important, something that made a difference, that she jumped up out of her chair. The sudden change in motion sent a sharp wave of lightheadedness through her skull and she abruptly sat back down. The Witch only sat there and asked almost tonelessly if she remembered something.

"Yes." She replies breathlessly as the lightheadedness slowly passes. "Yes, I have. I need to look for the miners. It was supposed to be Roy and I, but he got hurt on the way to Mining Road #7. We were going to start there and work our way back toward the common area, hitting #3 and then #1. Doubt the road to #7 is even passable and they have been out there for seven days with no supplies. The chances and hope of survival are low, but still high enough to check on." A thoughtful pause as the lightheadedness completely faded, then she continued. "I must have slid off the mountain side trying to get up and fell." Something didn't feel right about that scenario, but Sarah didn't have time to sit there and ponder about it.

4

The Witch had helped her, and she thanked her gratefully for it, then she walked out of the Witch's shack and up the mountainside. The grip on the soles of her well-made hunting boots, dug into the clayey mud and she walked up the mountainside with ease. This detail did not go unnoticed by Sarah, she simply filed it away with all the other conflicting, inconsistent, and suspicious details.

Just as Sarah had expected, Mining Road #7 was impassable. She had no choice but to backtrack and hope Mining Road #3 was better. She could have taken the treacherous, possibly impassable way around to either side, but after much consideration and recalling the stories of how easily that mine flooded, the chances that they were alive were too slim for her to increase the risk. She knew none of the valley folk would blame her, especially since she was more than likely the valley's only hunter, and source of fresh meat, since Roy's accident. With a heavy heart she headed for Mining Road #3.

There, the heaviness only increased when she found a sealed cave-in only yards into the mouth of the mine shaft. Massive boulders stacked and piled, piled and stacked, clogged the shaft entrance with several yards of solid stone. She sighed and with a tear in her eye, she moved on. She couldn't even bring herself to call out their names because knowing they were still alive in that rocky tomb would only make walking away that much harder. She couldn't help them if they were alive. The entire valley could return and be up here trying to clear a tunnel through the rubble for them to get out and they would still fail. That cave-in was there to stay.

Mining Road #1 was a bit of a different story. Less than a quarter of a mile on the mining road, Sarah came across her own scrap of cloth. One of the few remnants left over from the dog packs more lively meal, but she didn't know that. She picked them up and stowed them in her coat pocket, hoping it wasn't all she would find of the miners but suspecting it was true all the same. About halfway to the salt mine, she found a couple more scraps and shreds of cloth made of the same dark blue color and the same denim-like material. She went to put it in the same pocket as the others but thought better of it, placing them in the opposite one instead. She highly suspected that the cloth scraps were part of the coveralls the miners wore, but without proof it was only speculation on her part.

She walked right by the tree where the miner had propped himself after he had broken his leg and waited for help. The man was half dead when the dogs attacked him, so the fight was minimal, unlike the kicking and swinging and squalling of the one they had mistaken as dead. The thick red blood that coated the first inches of snow had melted away with the rest of it, mixing into the mud, making it unnoticeable to the human eye. There were no signs of a struggle, no signs of the dogs dragging the body this way and that along the wide well-worn path that was Mining Road #1. The bits of leftover gore had been scavenged by smaller animals and the few insects still capable of handling the cool weather that came after the snow, and what little had remained of the salt miner had been dragged off somewhere to be gnawed upon later.

Sarah continued to the mine unaware that her efforts were fruitless. She walked about a dozen yards into the mine shaft, several steps past the end of the light that seeped in through the shaft opening. Fear gripped her and she refused to go any further into the mine; the place was eerie, and she didn't want to be in there a moment longer than necessary. So, she did the only thing that made sense to her, she yelled for the miners. Her shouts echoed throughout the tunnel, fading with distance rather than weakening sound waves. She was met with the sound of tiny pebbles dinging and pinging off the dirty rock floor of the mine. The vibrations of her echoes made the walls tremble and the fear grip her tighter. She retreated a few steps and then shouted again, braced to turn, and run at the first sounds of a cave in. The same echoing through the tunnel and the falling of the dust and tiny stones occurred but nothing more. Certainly not a return shout. Knowing it was irrational but feeling it nonetheless, Sarah headed back to the valley with the heaviness of guilt pressing down upon her. Guilt that she couldn't' bring them home. Guilt that she couldn't save them. Guilt that she couldn't save any of them.

Chapter Thirty-Four

Agenda

1

She arrived back at the infirmary shortly after the rest of the valley folks did. All were accounted for except the preacher and his trio of Sisters, the Witch, the fisherman, and Dansford Keeton. The latter two walked in minutes after she did, though. Meat from the funeral ceremony had been brought in and rationed out to the survivors. Everyone had eaten except the O'Reigan woman, who still refused to eat or drink anything and looking thinner and frailer by the hour, Roy Hoarding, who was in a painkiller induced coma from the wooden shard removal, and the two severely ill women, Beth Redley and Lena McAvay. Patty and Jiminey, unaware of Lena's condition or the death of Old Man McAvay, Jiminey's father, until their arrival at the Infirmary, had only left her side long enough to step outside for a toke of Smoke. The women were still highly feverish, their complexions almost bloodlessly pale and their lips were dry and cracked. They looked like death and smelled of rot, a sad and pitiful sight for such lovely young women.

After everyone had eaten Frank stood before the crowd and addressed them accordingly. He told them he would call on certain folks to inform the crowd of the day's accomplishments, they would discuss tomorrow's agenda and then speak of whatever else needed to be addressed. Alvin Danson was called upon first, he was none too happy with it, but he stood up and spoke to the survivors. "The entire valley has been swept and all bodies, that we could locate that is, have been accounted for and sent Heavenward. There are still some that are unaccounted for though: Earl 'Red' Redley, Ben Fariday, Joshua Jones, Sledge, the names of the six miners and a few others that were quickly announced to have left on the train for New York. He crossed those names off the list in his hand and then sat back down, his informative speech concluded.

Frank called upon Porter Sidle after Alvin. "Well, folks, we put a purty good dent in the lumber pile out dere but we built them pyre towers sturdy and true. Nothin too good for our folks, now. Need to get the lumber replaced fore long though." Short and sweet. He sat down and that was that.

Then it was Dansford's turn to tell them about the inventory in the Warehouse attached to the back of the train station. Him and the fisherman had found precious little. There were old schoolbooks and hymnals, the top layers in the wooden crates having a thick layer of dust on them. They could be used as fire fuel if nothing else, all agreed. There were a couple crates full of random material, which peaked Rebekka and Carol Jewell's interest. They had also found a few old, rusted tools and two scrapped stringless bows. There were a few coils of rope, buckets and buckets of nails, and a couple floor to ceiling stacks of tin-metal in long, four-foot-wide strips. Frank said that he and a small group would go out to the warehouse tomorrow and bring back whatever they would be able to use throughout the winter.

Sarah was next, but before she could begin, Frank, not John but Frank, asked her about the Witch. Just the mention of the sorceress clouded Sarah's thoughts and she was momentarily thrown back into that terrible confusion she had endured earlier in the day. "She wasn't feelin well." Sarah answered him too quickly and too harshly for it to be true. Frank regarded her with an odd, slightly cold look, but before he could respond she rushed into telling the group about her search of the mining roads and what she found when she made it to the mines themselves. It took several minutes to tell, and all sat patiently, if not enthralled, by it. At the end she pulled out the scraps of cloth she had found, sadly informing them that the shreds of threads in her hands was all she could find of any of them.

Rebekka Lane and Johnathan Colmes both started at the cloth scraps and then, unbeknownst to the other, they both pulled out the scraps they had found themselves. Rebekka stood and took off toward them first and Johnathan followed a few steps later. They approached Sarah, one behind the other, and showed her the cloth scraps they had found the day before. Rebekka's pieces matched the ones that Sarah had found, and everyone knew the miners wore those dark blue, denim-like coveralls. The opinion of the miner's fate was seemingly unanimous.

The pieces Johnathan held were different though. One piece was made of black, soft cotton, probably from a shirt or possibly a pair of underwear. The other was dark green and denim-like. Between Sarah, John, and Rebekka they didn't know who it had belonged to. So, they asked the crowd, holding it up for them to see in the dimly lit Infirmary. Those interested enough to do so, moved closer to the trio standing among them.

Robert Daniels was one of those that moved closer, his interest peaking at the mention of the dark green piece. He had been sneaking and hitting the Shine he had stored in one of the back rooms by the bathroom of the Infirmary, so his mind was a bit on the foggy side. He was trying to recall what Sledge was wearing when he walked out into the snowstorm. He struggled to draw the memory to its clarity through his Shine induced haze as he moved closer to the shreds of dark green cloth Johnathan held in his fingers. When he was close enough and not knowing he was going to until he did, Robert snatched the piece out of John's hand, holding it delicately in his own. The feel of the fabric seemingly cleared the haze enough for the memory of his final moments with Sledge, to rise to the surface. In that moment, he knew that the piece of cloth was part of the pants Sledge had been wearing that day, and the black piece was from his cotton tee shirt. Then the sadness overwhelmed him at the realization that Sledge probably never made it home that evening.

With the new information provided, Alvin Danson jotted the letters PD beside the names of the six miners and Sledge. He didn't cross the names off the list, but the PD stood for 'probably dead'. He decided that he should focus his attention on the other's names: Ben Fariday, Joshua Jones, and 'Red' Redley. Not that it would do him any good.

A somber silence fell upon the crowd at the realization that they, probably, had seven more dead, even if they couldn't find their bodies. That alone was odd, but no one had really wanted to explore that topic of conversation. Yet anyway. The silence drifted among them as they remembered those that they sent Heavenward that very evening, those that were still missing, and those that were wounded or ill. There was a touch of fear mingled in with the silent sadness they all felt because they all recognized that their numbers were already dwindling, and winter hadn't even begun yet.

2

Frank McGrath, after several long minutes of silence, addressed the crowd once more, assuring them that they would continue their efforts to locate the missing, scrap clothing or no scrap clothing, they would continue to search for them. Alvin Danson, deep down knowing that their efforts would be futile, only nodded in agreement. With that the discussion of the next day's agenda began. Johnathan made it clear that the meat that remained in the butcher's shop would only sustain everyone in the valley for two, maybe three, days. After that, there would be no more meat in the valley, smoked, cured, salted or otherwise. So, Frank asked for a show of hands for a large group to scavenge every standing shack and teepee across the valley for all food. About a dozen hands went up, Old Joe Brenner and Lacy's among them, and Frank sent the group off to the other side of the large room to discuss it. As the group walked off, Sarah said, "A lot of the shacks looked very unstable and should be checked before you go sending half a dozen people stomping through them. They will get crushed in collapses, like Roy almost did today.", it came out much harsher than she intended it to. Frank looked at her oddly for a moment before agreeing with her.

"You're right." He nods. "Safety of those we have left should be top priority. So, show of hands, who among us is cunning and brave enough to go ahead of the scavengers and check the shacks before they enter them?" For a moment no one spoke or moved. Finally, Johnathan stepped forward and accepted the task, but he was the only one. Frank nodded, a touch of respect intoned in the nod, and then told Dansford that he would be joining John checking the shacks the next day, rather than leading the group to clear out the Warehouse. Everyone could tell that Dansford was none too happy about it but agreed anyway.

To conclude his authoritative meeting, he ran through the list of tasks for the following day and asked if there was anything else anyone would like to discuss. No one spoke up but there were lots of whispers and hushed voices among the survivors. So, he sauntered off back into the crowd. Frank had just walked up to Sarah, looking at her in that odd way again and said, "We need to talk." Before he could continue or Sarah could respond, Dansford walked up behind Frank, placed his hand on Frank's shoulder and spun him around to face him.

"What the hell is this shit about sendin me in to check fallin-in shacks? Who the hell are you to be barkin orders at me? Just who the hell..." Dansford raved in a harsh whisper, but Frank had stopped listening to Dan's rant and looked over his shoulder at Sarah. Sarah wasn't there though. She had walked off to help Doreen change the wrappings on Roy's punctured hand. With a sigh, an intense feeling of guilt, and a sadness in his heart, he turned back to face the angry Dansford Keeton. It took almost half an hour, whispered promises, and a reassuring kiss in the dark shadows of the large room for Frank to soothe Dansford. Whenever Dan got angry and worked up, it made Frank very nervous because he was afraid that Dan would spill their dirty little secret. Dan wanted the secret out, he wanted the valley, the whole world, Hell, and the Heavens beyond, to know about him and Frank, but that's not what Frank wanted. He had convinced Dansford to keep his mouth shut for now because of Sarah. He said that Sarah was innocent in this whole bit, and she shouldn't get hurt because he was afraid of his feelings. Frank McGrath really, truly believed that but Dansford knew it was just a way for him to continue to cover up their 'relationship' and he was not happy about that, either.

About an hour later, exhaustion swept through the room and the group drifted off in slumber a few at a time until the only sound that could be heard was snoring. Snores and the slight creak of the supply room door by the bathrooms as Robert Daniels snuck in for a nip of Shine.

Chapter Thirty-Five

Beautifully Psychotic

1

As soon as Sarah Maisse, Johanthan's love affair, had disappeared into the timbers on the mountainside, the Witch headed straight for her ritual room and called upon her Master. She was unable to conceal the excitement in her voice as she did. Her excitement was justified fore she had just pulled off a feat that few others had been able to accomplish in all the live-long eras upon eras of Satan's being. She had marked a boy child for her Master, as was his will. She knew, as well as she knew the conception was fighting for its survival, and strongly too, that if the conception took it would be a boy, a very strong and healthy boy.

"It seems you are not the daft cunt I first assumed of you." The voice of Satan bellowed around her, too wrapped up in her excitement for it to be startling, coming out of the darkness. It was his way of congratulating the Witch, so she thought little of the insult. "Only time will tell if the conception has taken place. In three days from now, you will know. There will be a sign, sickness or storm, if one occurs on the third day the conception has been successful and the likelihood that the child will come to full term and be born within the tri-month increases. The most difficult part has been accomplished, and you made it seem surprisingly easy." The Witch said nothing, only nodded, a pleased smile on her face, knowing Satan could see her, feeling his eyes upon her, even if she couldn't see him. "I shall see how you accomplished this. Come Vipera." She shifted her stance, and the snake-like creature slithered its way out of her uterus, making its way toward the darkness that the voice of Satan drifted from. "In the meantime, figure out what you would like done with the demon Malum. If the conception is a success, you should be able to react your revenge soon after." An evil, knowing grin spread across the Witch's face, giving her a beautifully psychotic expression.

She wasn't given the chance to speak as the voice retreated, leaving her with her vicious thoughts of revenge. First Malum, then the valley folks, and finally Johnathan, who will be saved for last. She also had some impressive plans for Sarah once she birthed the son of Satan. The Witch knew she was going to be busy, busy, busy the next few months as winter went by. She had a lot of work to do before the reaping could start, but for the time being she could only plan and wait.

2

The next day, everyone up with the sun and ready to work, John and Dansford, equipped with long, strong, branches, went from shack to building prodding and pressing on the outer walls. If the walls held and groaned very little, they would bravely enter them, but most of them they could not. Johnathan made a mental note to mention that the unsafe buildings need to be brought down, cleaned up and salvaged of usable building materials. There were a handful of places that Johnathan stepped into, trembling from fear that the roof would fall on his head at any moment, to retrieve some much-needed food. Jars of salted blanched vegetables mostly, but food, nonetheless. The survivors were quite grateful for it.

When the scavengers searched the farm, they were quite disappointed with what they found. All the crops, missing harvest by mere days, had all died from the extreme cold, the vegetation wilted and rotted, unsalvageable. The same occurred with the livestock in the barn, but all those bodies had been removed the day before. They knew about the livestock, but they still held out hope for the crops. The crops were useless to them, but luckily, they found the O'Reigan's large cellar. It was only a third of the way full, but it was enough to sustain the group of survivors, if rationed properly, for a good fraction of the winter. It was one hell of a good find,

379

and they all knew it. The group hooted and shouted their joy as they packed it all over to the Infirmary where a couple of the group were left to begin sorting and inventorying the food found and brought in.

Frank McGrath and three others took off for the Warehouse to bring back the material, the rope, the stringless bows, and the tools. The sheet metal and nails were left in the warehouse, Frank knowing they would need them to reinforce or rebuild some of the shacks around the valley. That was for another day, though.

Alvin Danson led a much smaller group than the day before, up into the timbered mountainside. He split the group into pairs, acknowledging that very few of them had any experiencing being out in the timbers beyond still seeing the valley. He gave them very strict instructions on what to do should they get lost or one of them get hurt. Alvin was as confident as he could be in the small group and sent them off to search for any signs of anyone, alive or dead. They found no one, though, alive or dead.

That evening, the second of the three days, the variously numbered groups trickled back into the infirmary slowly and exhaustedly. Everyone, except for those sick and injured, including Frank McGrath, had worked quite hard that day. There was little talk as rationed food was handed out. It was enough to keep them going but not enough to satiate the appetite. The water was plentiful, but the food was not and there was discussion of when Sarah, being the only able hunter left in the valley, would go out hunting again. The itch was there, and she wanted to, but she also knew she was needed in the valley for other things that took priority over having fresh meat. It would have been different if they had no food, but after the cellar find on the O'Reigan farm, that was not the case. Yet. She decided to wait another day or so to see how the food situation was before going out and exhausting herself trying to feed more than a couple dozen people alone.

Even as large as the group was scavenging for food, they couldn't get through the entire valley. That would be their first task for tomorrow. They had searched the entire farm, the cellar was their biggest find by far, but a few things were found in the O'Reigan homes too. They had searched every shop around the common area and made it as far as Hussey Row in the Slums. Across the eastern river branch, they had searched through a little over half the places around the Lot, even the abandoned ones, because they all looked abandoned after the snowstorm. John and Dan had gone ahead of the group, marking the shacks and buildings that were unsafe with stones. They would take three fist sized stones and stack them like a pyramid in front of the door. The larger group would see the stones and move on to the next one. When John had to venture into an unsafe shack to get much needed food out, he would leave it piled up next to the rock pyramid-formation.

During Frank's evening meeting, Johnathan mentioned that the unsteady shacks and buildings needed to be brought down and salvaged of usable parts. Everyone agreed because everyone had the same idea in mind, to tear down the old ones so they could reinforce, and in some cases rebuild, their own. Frank agreed and put Johnathan in charge of the task, who immediately asked Ron Hellman and Porter Siddle to assist, and they agreed. The three men discussed others they could ask as well, targeting the strong.

3

The survivors fell into their own separate hushed conversations, a lot of them about wanting to return home. Frank took note of this, even if they hadn't discussed it yet, because he too wanted to go home. He looked around the large room and spotted Dansford talking with Robert Daniels and the fisherman, who was sipping on a flask of Shine. Frank took the opportunity to ask Sarah if she would step outside with him for a few moments.

Sarah watched Frank approach her and she sucked in a deep breath as he stopped in front of her. She agreed to step outside with him even though it sent pangs of dread and guilt through her. Sarah assumed they were stepping out to talk about John, while Frank was under the impression that they were stepping outside to talk to about Dansford. They were both in for a surprise.

The moon was peeking over the mountain top, casting just enough light on the valley for the darker shadows to be noticeable. It looked like it was going to be full tonight, and if not, it would be close. It was eerily quiet, no crickets singing or owls hooting or frogs croaking, but neither of them noticed. Had they stepped outside just mere minutes before they would have heard the chorused timbers buzzing and screeching with life, and then they would have heard the not-so-distant yaps and howls that had silenced it.

The valley gossip hadn't started back up again, yet, so Frank was unaware, as were most of the valley folks, that her and John had spent six days huddled up alone together in his shack. Sarah didn't know that Frank didn't know that, though, and she let it spill from her betraying lips before she could cease them. "Look Frank, I couldn't help that I got stuck at John's place during that storm. I..." Sarah rattled off in a fluster.

"Whoa. Whoa. Whoa. What are you goin on about?" Frank interrupted her, holding his hand up and furrowing his brow. A hint of anger in his tone revealed his natural twangy accent, much different than his professional tone when addressing the 'public'. "Are you talkin about the Butcher, John? Johnathan Colmes?" Sarah nodded but would not speak. "You spent the snowstorm, all six days, stuck in a shack with... with him?" Frank asked, the realization of what had happened between them dawning on him. The spark of anger in his eyes ignited into a flame of fury. She nodded again, just enough for him to see in the darkened shadow of the building they stood in.

The guilt and shame were evident on Sarah's face, but she could not bring herself to speak those few simple words that she knew he wanted, maybe even needed, to hear. If she could just bring herself to mutter those two little words 'I'm sorry', maybe she could salvage her mediocre relationship with Frank.

To what end, though? She thought to herself.

She didn't want to just settle down, and she didn't want to settle down with Frank McGrath. She wanted Johnathan Colmes. She wanted to be with him because he was more than mediocre, and he made her feel as if she was more than that too. A feeling way down deep in the pit of her stomach told her that she was forever connected to Johnathan in ways she did not and could not understand right now.

A howl from the western mountainside that went unnoticed, seemed to emphasize her thoughts.

Frank reached out and grabbed her arm, right above the elbow, gripping it tightly. "Speak! Damn you! Sp..." Frank spat in her face as he roughly shook her arm. He was stunned silent by a slap and the loud sound, like a breaking branch, that accompanied it. The pain immediately followed, the stinging and throbbing of being slapped hard across the jowls. She jerked her arm out of his grip and stepped back out of his reach.

The howl was closer the next time but still unnoticed through her rage and his shock.

"Don't you ever fuckin touch me like that again, Frank!" She told him sternly, glaring at him, her eyes telling him that if he tried her, he might win but she was going to fuck him up in the process. Frank kept his distance but the hurt and anger radiated from him in waves. (Tobias Medlin would have been able to detect the smell of dead fish in swamp water due to the emotional pain Frank was experiencing, the smell of burning wood, as if a smoky forest fire was blazing nearby because of his anger and rage, and then both scents were underlaid with a hint of burning rubber for the shame he felt over his deep, dark secret.).

Frank stood fuming, then finally asked her, "Why him? What makes him so much better than me?" He paused. "What the hell were you doin there in the first place to get stuck with him?"

"It's not what you think." Sarah lied, knowing damn well what he was thinking, and feeling guilty for knowing that not only was he right but he had every right to be pissed about it. Her fuming anger did not falter, though, because right or no right, he shouldn't have grabbed her that way. She continued but from a short distance from him. "I was on my way home after coming out of the timbers and damn near ran right into him, that's how bad the visibility was then. He refused to stop at the Bar to warm up and was almost fallin over his own damn feet when I found him. I helped him home and by the time I got him in bed and a fire goin, the snow had built up against the door so damn much that I couldn't get out. I literally got stuck in his shack with him. What was I supposed to do? Bust my way out and leave an unconscious man to die alone in a freezing cold shack? I don't know bout you Frank, but I got better morals than that." She immediately bit her cheek as soon as the words popped out of her mouth due to the sheer irony of the situation. Miss Can't-Give-It-To-Her-Beau-Frank-But-Can-Give-It-To-Someone-She-Barely-Knows talking about morals. It made her kind of disgusted with herself, but she continued anyway. "He was laid up in bed for the first two or three days, slept all but a couple hours the whole damn time."

Frank stood staring at her for a few minutes, the seconds dragging out, making Sarah more and more uncomfortable but she tried hard to maintain her composure. She did not want him to see her shaken, and she was not much on outright lying, so she had decided that if he asked her directly, she would tell him, no matter how much she didn't want to and didn't want to see him hurt. She assumed that Frank and Dansford had spent the six days snowed in together, but she thought nothing of it. She knew, but not quite as well as the rest of the valley folks, that the pair were almost always together. Her staying six-days snowed in with a man that was not her beau, but also the Witch's beau, was just absolutely scandalous in Frank's eyes, though. Finally, Frank asked her, "So, what happened after he woke up?"

Sarah swallowed with an audible click then sighed heavily. "The next couple days I fed him what little soup and tea I could manage to find in the bare kitchen, it wasn't much but it was enough for him I reckon." She paused, reluctant to continue, but had little choice under Frank's scrutinous eye. "On the fourth day we ran out of furniture to bust up for firewood, we held out as long as we could but eventually ended up huddled together under the blankets. Our combined body heat kept us alive, or I wouldn't be here to explain this to you right now." Every word was true, she had just left out a few details, that was all.

They both briefly heard the snap of a breaking branch somewhere in the timbers but that was a common sound to be heard, so they thought nothing of it.

Frank knew she was being deliberately vague and had a pretty good idea as to why. He didn't know if he was punishing himself by wanting to know for sure or hoping it would bring him some closure, but he asked anyway, much harsher than he had intended to. "Did you fuck him?!"

Sarah was abruptly taken aback by the question. She knew it was coming but everything about it stunned her. The tone of his voice, the evident pain and rage, the wording of it. She was expecting something a little less vulgar than that and it did not induce the reaction she would have expected. She got mad. No, it was more than that. She got pissed. He had disrespected her on a whole new level, even more so than the way he had grabbed her, a level she herself did not know existed until that moment. When Sarah's emotions ran high, she was apt to say the very first thing that popped into her head. Whether it was relevant, sensible, or cruel, it was always a truthful statement. Her thoughts did not discriminate, and she had almost no control over the thoughts or them slipping from her tongue. So, it was not much of a surprise to her that what came flowing past her lips, shocked even her. "Did you fuck Dan?!"

His immediate response and reaction shocked her even more, though. "He fuckin told you!" Frank shouted and the jaw-dropped expression of surprise on Sarah's face told him that HE just spilled the secret, and knowingly or unknowingly, she had tricked him into telling the one thing he had been begging Dansford to keep his mouth shut about.

They heard the final howl too, but it was only a momentary register. Wolves were known to prowl but seldom entered the valley. It sounded close but not close enough to worry about it.

It was her turn to stare at him, the bits and pieces of information she had picked up on about Frank and Dan began clicking into place like a jigsaw puzzle finally coming together. Once she considered that strange feeling she would get when he started groping her, wanting some, it all seemed to make sense. A part of her was greatly relieved at this realization while the other part pitied Frank because she could see the shame and guilt wash over him. He turned away from her and she could see that he was weeping, which made her next action that much more despicable. She started to giggle, and the giggle turned into a border-line hysterical laugh, going on for a few minutes. She could feel the anger seep out of her as she fought to control the uncontrollable laughter braying from her mouth. Tears streamed from her emerald hued eyes and a few dribbles of urine escaped her shaken bladder.

All the while, Frank stood there and endured the laughs, sobbing and speechless.

When she was finally able to stop laughing, she wiped the tears from her face and held her aching side. "I was not laughing at you, Frank, truly. I was laughing about this whole, stupid fucked up conversation." Sarah took a deep breath that came out as a half sob when she exhaled. "I understand the shame you feel, I am a bit ashamed and disgusted with myself as well, even if you can't see it. Even though nothing really became of our relationship, I really do care about you, and I never wanted to hurt you. For that I do apologize. I'd be lying if I said the same about the rest of it..." Her thoughts were obviously on Johnathan, wholly and clearly, and Frank picked up on this quickly. "...but for hurting you, Frank... for that I am sorry."

She was being sincere, Frank could tell by her tone, but he could not bring himself to speak. He stood there in the moonlight shadow of the Infirmary, in silence and waited for her to walk away. Sarah finally did, reaching out and resting her strong, petite hand on his shoulder. He flinched away from her violently, but never turned to face her, and she withdrew her hand quickly. Sarah opened her mouth to say something but abruptly closed it, the click of her teeth loud in the odd silence of the night. She turned and hurriedly walked back into the Infirmary, leaving him alone in the dark.

4

The first of the dog pack jumped off the mountainside between two of the hunting shacks along the northern end of the valley. They wandered around smelling the ground where two had stood not long before that. After about an hour of searching but finding nothing, they returned to the thick timbers in search of a much-needed meal. A pack that had once been a couple dozen only a week ago had dwindled down to about 15. Most had starved, but one had been killed by a spooked mountain lion that slashed the dog's stomach open. The rest of the pack ate well that night, once they realized the large cat had left its meal behind.

Chapter Thirty-Six

Sickness or Storm

1

The Witch had become increasingly more anxious as the last of the three days dawned. She had not slept since the marking of the unborn, had only waited and schemed. She was betting everything on the success of the ritual. If the conception took place, then the pregnancy would be successful, barring outside harm, of course. Which meant that the slut mother of Satan's unborn would have to be protected. The Witch could endure that, though. She would just tally it all up and demand payment in full at the end... and the payment would be that beau-stealing-bitch's soul.

Should the ritual be a failure and the conception be unsuccessful, then the punishment the Witch knew she would receive would make the time she spent with Malum look like playtime on the playground. She had already failed her master, the Sultan of Sin, once and such a very short time ago. It would not pay for her to fail again. The ritual had taken place around noon three days before so she would know definitively by early afternoon at the very latest. She continued to wait, constantly chewing on chamomile leaves or lavender petals, hoping to console her consistently growing anxiety.

The morning sunlight shown through the dainty window of the front room in the Witch's shack and her heart sank a little. She looked thoughtfully out at the landscape before her, the shadows growing shorter as the sun rose higher and the first thoughts of true failure flooded her mind. She took in a raspy, shaky breath and let it out in a small moan.

Halfway across the valley in the Infirmary, most had already risen from their slumber and were preparing to start their day. Another small ration of food had been passed around with hope that the evening's meal would be better. Johnathan Colmes, Ron Hellman, and Porter Siddle led the other half a dozen strong, able-bodied men and women to the first of many collapsing shacks and began the clean-up process. This task would take several weeks, but it was an important one that would gain momentum as it progressed.

On the first day of the clean-up, they had only managed to get through the western fishing pier, one of the shacks on the O'Reigan farm (the original homeplace) and part of the only other one on the farm that needed to be taken down. Alvin Danson and his small group returned to the timbers in search of any signs of... well, anything or anyone. Food was being searched for, the sick and wounded were being cared for, and other smaller but just as essential chores, such as water fetching and gathering, had been doled out accordingly.

Sarah Maisse decided to stay in the Infirmary that day and help Doreen with her four patients and the elderly that were all stricken by bone pain, what you call arthritis. She was making a point to avoid, not only Frank McGrath, but John as well. She desperately wanted to be with John, to have him hold her close and whisper softly in her ear that everything was going to be just fine. That was not possible, though, and she knew it. Even given the enlightening information about Frank and Dansford last night, she still did not want to 'flaunt' John in front of Frank. Frank was confused and angry and from past experiences and like-stories she had heard, men that were hurt and confused were dangerous. So, she told herself that she would keep her distance from them both. Frank, believing she was allowing him time and space to process and deal, and John as to not upset Frank anymore than he already was.

The widow Mrs. O'Reigan's condition had only worsened and her frail, emaciated figure only amplified the severity of her depression. The poor, heartbreakingly sad woman was slowly and painfully dying from a broken heart. She had weakened drastically due to her refusal to eat, to the point that lifting her arm and uttering a single sentence would have her panting. She was beyond the point of dehydration. She almost resembled a not-quite-dead corpse, her skin shriveled and stretched thinly across her tendons and bones, the muscles having deteriorated trying to fuel the body that had given up on itself. Doreen consistently tried to coax the depressed and dying woman to sip soup or water or anything, but she refused every time. That day, Doreen and Sarah observed the ailing woman with a sad knowledge that she would take her last breath soon, probably before the sun went down.

Lena McAvay was in a similar situation as the widow, she was very near death as well. Her fever had risen too high and had raged for too long, the hallucinations had begun late the night before and had only increased in frequency and severity since. The Apothecary aide, Doreen, had picked up a few things here and there helping people in the Apothecary for several years, and she knew that if a fever went unchecked for too long that it would roast the inside of your head. That's what was happening to Lena McAvay and Doreen was helpless to stop it. She had tried everything short of placing the fevered young woman in the just-above-freezing waters of the Collis River, and that was too dangerous to even attempt. There was a small, very small, chance that Lena's body could still break the fever on its own, but the increasing hallucinations continued to decrease that slim chance. All they could do was wait, feeling death press in around them.

Beth Redley, on the other hand, was improving. Her fever had broken hours ago and she seemed to be really resting for the first time since she'd been brought into the Infirmary. Doreen could only hope that she continued to improve and didn't regress. When she awoke a few more hours later, Beth sipped on herbal tea rather than the normal sassafras and managed to eat a small chunk of stale bread. She was able to talk but her voice was hoarse and raspy, so she kept her words to a minimum. She turned in hours before sunset and slept the night through, waking the next morning feeling almost well enough to start working again.

Roy Hoarding was a bit of a mixed case. He was in obvious excruciating pain due to the gaping hole in the palm of his hand and was given an herbal concoction that was to be chewed by him, and then spread and packed into his wounded hand. Once Doreen had it packed and coated, she would wrap it in a stained but boiled clean swatch of cloth. The packing and wrapping process was by far the worst of it and he would be delirious from the pain by the time she was finished. The chewing of the herbs was supposed to dull the senses, so the pain was more tolerable. Roy was convinced that if that were the case then having it packed without chewing the herbs first would kill him. He would literally die from the pain it would induce. The other part was the irregular waves of shock he would experience because of his hand. Sometimes it was random and seemingly untriggered, sometimes it was the sight of the hole he could peer through in his hand that caused it. Sometimes he would cry and sob, mourning his hand and all the abilities he had lost along with it, sometimes he would rage, screaming and throwing things, trying to release the churning madness within him. He felt helpless and cheated, and for the second time in a week, he thought of suicide.

3

A few hours after sunrise, the dark gray clouds began to roll in, segmented at first and bringing a ray of hope to the borderline frantic Witch. Over the course of the next hour the Witch stood at the window in her shack and watched the clouds gather, once again from the south, over the valley and densely pack themselves together. She allowed herself a small smile, more of a gratuitous grin, finally getting her emotions under control enough to stop the trembling and her heart from racing. Sorceress or not, magic or not, she was still partially human and, sometimes, those qualities shown through with a brilliance.

The working valley folks observed the gathering clouds, still leery of the weather after the last storm, but continued with their tasks. They all vowed to themselves, if not to each other, to seek adequate shelter the moment the rain and/or snow began. None ever did though. The clouds remained for some time, but eventually started to break off and float north toward their next destination.

Sensing the impending weather much better than the humans, the dogs had peaked their ears at the incoming clouds but quickly went back to sniffing around for a meal. They knew the darkening clouds were just that, clouds, but had they sensed the impending weather they would have high-tailed it back to their den to cower in the shadows of the stone outcropping.

The Witch watched with dismay as the clouds started to drift apart and away from the valley. No storm had occurred, and this frightened her badly. The eminent punishment that awaited her hung heavily in her mind. She so wanted to please her Master and she hated herself for feeling as though she had failed to do so. She allowed herself to experience these emotions for only a few moments before drawing in on herself and composing herself, almost instantly. Time is short but not up and there is still a glimmer of hope yet. She thinks to herself. How do I watch her though? It would be too obvious for me to appear in person, but my raven is dead. Then a brilliant idea occurred to her following the recollection of her Master telling her that Vipera was there to help her as well as watch her. The Witch was about to find out just how much the python could and would do. She whispered the asp's name and almost immediately she could feel it stir within her.

Once it had slithered its way out of her, the viper was coiled up, much like a cobra in striking position, bearing its rows of needle-sharp teeth at her. It did not hiss or attempt to bite, it just sat there regarding her curiously. The Witch sat staring right back at the asp, contemplating what she was about to do, hoping that it would not strike at her. The jagged teeth on the viper made her rather nervous, but she slowly extended her arm, reaching for the snake with outstretched rigid fingers that were ready to jerk back at the slightest movement from the creature. It did not move toward or away from her and once her hand was within reach, it curled its way around her arm. Vipera allowed the Witch to pick up and carry the large python.

Her movements were jerky and unsure as she slowly rose from the stone floor of the ritual room with the reptile wrapped snugly around her arm. They quickly calmed and evened out as she realized the animal was not nearly as hard to handle as she had expected it to be. The Witch was quite surprised by the weight of the snake, or lack of weight, as the case had been. The large reptile, easily a few meters or more in length, large enough to easily swallow a small doe and covering most of her arm, seemed to weight no more than a chunk of firewood.

She walked the python into the first of the two caves and stood in front of one of the wooden shelves filled with corked and lidded, bottles, boxes, vials, and jars, all correctly labeled according to their contents. "All right, Vipera..." the Witch began, and the snake hissed at the mention of its name. "... let's see if you are as intelligent and cunning as our Master implied. Show me the Juniper berries, Vipera." She instructed and then watched as the viper leaned forward and started bobbing its head up and down, left and right, seemingly reading the names of each. After several moments, Vipera paused, stuck her long-forked tongue out and gracefully lapped at the small jar with the words: JUNIPER BERRIES written upon it. The Witch's eyes grew wide with delight and awe. "Very good. What about the Hellebore?" she asked, and once again, much quicker that time, the snake delicately stroked a jar of dried leaves marked: HELLEBORE. There was a circle with an X through it at the end of the name, indicating it's deadliness. "Oh, my." She whispered under her breath in astonishment, looking at the python with a mixture of wonder and curiosity.

The Witch decided on impulse, to further test Vipera's abilities before sending it out, so she stepped over to another wooden shelving unit. That one had a couple deep wooden drawers at the bottom, so she squatted down, the snake still securely wrapped around her arm, and opened one of the drawers. It was filled with hundreds of beautifully colored rocks and amulets of every shape. "We will start with something easy, find me an amethyst." The asp spent mere moments scanning the colorful stones before releasing its tail enough to touch a small, crystalline purple amulet. Vipera flipped the amulet over, it's tinted transparency severely distorted the coloring of the stone it laid upon. "Incredible." The Witch praised.

"Chrysoprase?' Vipera flicked its tail and flipped over a rough, jagged stone the bright green of baby corn stalks. Its deep knicks and cracks were still filled with the grayish-brown bedrock it was dug out of, giving certain places on the amulet a dinghy, dirty look.

"Jasper." Another flick and a layered amulet of natural hues flipped over.

"Bloodstone." The tail flicked and a dark-turquoise-colored smooth stone, speckled with bright red dots the color of fresh blood flipped over.

"You're incredible." She told the python, staring deeply into its eyes. "Absolutely incredible. Now, listen closely my dear, go and find the woman with whom conception is occurring. You know what the Master said about sickness or storm, there was no storm, and the skies are clearing. So, it must be sickness and the sickness will fall upon her. Find Sarah Maisse. Find her and see." Immediately, the python released its grip upon her arm and slithered onto the ground, heading out of the cave and through the shack. The Witch had not noticed the incredible strength of the snake, but she had noticed the obvious purple tint her fingers, hand, and arm had taken on because of that incredible strength.

The impending doom of the departing clouds coupled with the excitement of Vipera's awe-inspiring abilities had escalated the Witch's exhaustion to a point she could no longer ignore. She finally accepted that there was nothing she could do about the situation and would only drive herself mad again, fretting over it. She decided to lay down and rest, knowing she would awaken with Vipera's arrival.

4

The only noticeable indication that any movement around the witch's shack had occurred was the slight creak of the shack door as it opened just enough for the python's thick, girthy body to slither outside. Every other snake in the area had retreated to their homes for the winter or froze to death when the blizzard pelted the valley. All the valley folks knew this so had any of them seen the large snake slithering about, it definitely would have drawn their attention. However, no one in the valley would have or could have seen it, unless they had stepped right on top of it, but no one did that either.

Aside from its unbelievable intelligence, Vipera, being one of Satan's many varmints, had a few other special qualities. One of them was its extreme chameleonic camouflage that could make it blend into any environment, matching its surroundings to the point of full transparency. That ability was the reason the snake was able to get to the Infirmary and back to the Witch's shack without detection.

Vipera made it to the Infirmary following the unique scent of the hormones Sarah Maisse was exerting and slithered up the side of the building intent on slipping through the open-shuttered window. Its long, muscular body rippled with different colors and textures. The grainy, dusty, color of the drying dirt that surrounded the building, where its tail and lower body rested before being pulled along behind the rest of the large python. Without movement, it appeared as though one could reach down and scoop up a handful of dirt right out of the viper's lower back. The bluish-gray, jagged and rough surface of the stones used to build the sturdy structure could be seen throughout the entirety of its midsection. Were one to place their hand upon the snake it would feel as though they were brushing the coarse sandpapery side of a rock. About a foot from the tip of Vipera's nose, the brown, rough-cut wood used for the glassless windowpane could be seen across its neck. The strip appeared to be real enough to cause a splinter and gave the python a bizarre resemblance to a collared pet. Its triangular-shaped head, with its forked darting tongue, returned to its deep black hue and disappeared into the shadows of the room. Vipera paused in that pose for a mere moment, scanning its surroundings before slithering all the way through the window.

Vipera wasn't aware of it, but it was in an empty exam room. All Vipera knew was that the woman was close. It could sense the hormones emitting from the impending conception. It slithered its way across the room and out the door, the only indication was the smaller than expected gap in the door the python squeezed through. The gap in the door that no one was around to notice. The asp moved down the hallway, its body the same color and texture as the rough-cut wooden slats that composed the floor. It's back and forth movement gave the floor a surreal wavy illusion that would have surely induced nausea, that unnerving sickness associated with vertigo, had anyone been around to witness it.

At the end of the hallway and at a left-or-right cross section, Vipera raised its head, its long and slender dark gray tongue flicking in and out of its closed mouth, tasting the still air around it. The asp veered to the left, toward a set of double doors built from the same sturdy rough-cut wood as the floor, only knowing that the smell of the hormones would be stronger on the other side. Vipera pushed one of the doors open with its large head, just enough to slither through it. This action went unnoticed by the sick, the elderly, and the two women caring for them, but the bang of the closing double door did not. The python stopped and when all conscious beings in the room looked in its direction, no one could see the large snake or its curvy pose.

"What the hell was that?" Doreen asked no one in particular. There was a slight panicky note to her tone that Sarah picked up on. They both, rightfully, assumed it was the stress and tension Doreen had been under caring for the ill and wounded almost single-handedly.

"I'm... I'm not sure." Sarah answered breathlessly, as she slowly stepped closer to the double doors, carefully scanning her surroundings. The smell of the hormones increased as the woman drew near and Vipera knew that was the one it was meant to find and watch. Unfortunately, the woman did not appear to be sick. In fact, she was almost vibrant with health, glowing even. Sarah Maisse, the woman who was unknowingly experiencing some life altering hormonal changes, was only a few steps away from planting her foot on the snake's midsection. Then a bone-chilling scream cut across the large room, sending the woman running back toward the others.

The few elderly folks had been getting an early start on their afternoon naps when the scream startled them all awake, jumpstarting their aged, weakened hearts. Had the small group been closer to the horrific scene that played out with Lena, they too may have suffered a similar fate as the widow. Luckily, they were too far from the sick women to see much more than Doreen trying and failing to hold down the thrashing woman, and then her falling into the floor. They could easily hear the shrieks and gasps and the scraping of the beds across the floor, but they could see very little. They knew something was terribly wrong though, when the screaming stopped and the strong, coppery smell of blood permeated the room.

Beth Redley, whose fever had broken but wasn't quite okay yet, was sleeping peacefully and restfully a couple cots away from Lena. She was in the throes of an extreme exhaustion-driven sleep, much like the Witch. So, when Lena's scream echoed through the large room, Beth simply rolled away from the sound and continued her peaceful sleep. She awakened shortly before the funeral pyres were lit with no idea as to who died and why.

Roy Hoarding was awake when Lena screamed but wished he wasn't. Oh, how he envied Beth! His only rest since the accident, three days ago, was when he had lost consciousness due to the pain. That initial excruciating, searing, nerve-blinding pain that overwhelms and destroys all senses momentarily, had passed. It had been replaced with a dull, throbbing ache that radiated up his arm and into his shoulder. Every minute movement of his hand or arm would send spears of red-hot agony shooting through his network of nerves. It wasn't enough to break the consciousness threshold though, not enough to allow him even a brief respite of mercy. The consequences of this lack of mercy were slowly killing him. His body was rejecting the food he tried so hard to keep in his stomach and would only allow him very small sips of water. The immense pain and lack of sleep combined to cause some very terrifying hallucinations, that had started the night before. To top it all off, he was still experiencing that mind-numbing disbelief and grief over the loss of his hand and everything he would never be able to do again because of it.

He needed help but Doreen couldn't do it, she had given him everything she had to give but nothing helped. To say he was desperate was an understatement. His foggy mind and fragmented thoughts were trying to devise a plan of escape when Lena screamed, and his mind automatically assumed he was having another hallucination. He watched the same situation Vipera did but from a different viewpoint, one that mercifully saved him a look at Lena's grotesque, dying face. Roy sat on his cot, his slinged arm carefully resting against his chest and pulled his knees up to him. He wrapped his uninjured arm around his legs and watched the horror unfold, keeping a careful eye on the pair of faintly glowing black eyes in the shadow across the room.

With their attentions off the double doors, Vipera raced across the room and into a dark shadow cast between a wooden shelf and a wooden desk. From there, it had a perfect view of the strange, gory, and amusing situation that followed that pain-filled shriek.

Vipera watched the hormonal woman run up beside a shorter, older woman that was trying to restrain a very pale, feverish young woman that was thrashing around violently. Blood sprayed in arches over the trio's heads, gushing from a self-inflicted bite mark on the feverish woman's left wrist. It was deep enough to have nicked the main artery; her intention fulfilled. She was trying desperately to do the same to the right wrist, but the older woman was preventing that.

The feverish woman was obviously in the throes of a very vivid, very terrifying hallucination. Her unbelievable strength came from the massive amounts of adrenaline being pumped into her dying body. The hormonal woman reached for the bleeding arm of the feverish one, but she was knocked away. The hormonal one stumbled into an empty cot but did not fall, regained her footing, and tried again. Before she could, though, the feverish one knocked the older one to the side as easily as the hormonal one, despite the obvious weight difference, and rolled off the makeshift cot onto the wooden floor. She immediately pulled her right wrist to her bloody mouth as blood spilled from the small holes in her left wrist. Sarah leapt the few steps between them and grabbed at the feverish woman with no target in mind. She ended up with a handful of hair and instinctively jerked the feverish, delirious woman's head back.

From Vipera's front row seat, the feverish woman was facing the asp, unaware of its presence, and when the hormonal woman jerked her head back, Vipera got an excellent view of the ailing woman's face. Bright red blood thickly coated her mouth, jaws, and chin; it dripped onto the grimy, sweat and blood-soaked nightgown she had been wearing since her arrival at the infirmary. The small chunk of flesh that she had ripped from her right wrist was pressed tightly between her blood-stained teeth. The look in her grayish-blue eyes were of a happy delirium, as if by fulfilling her intentions she could die happy. And maybe she did.

The hormonal woman shrieked, released the sick woman's hair, and stepped back. The blood covered lady kept her head in the same backward position and spit the flesh out of her mouth, sending it up into the air in a high arch, a trail of blood following close behind it, like the tail of a comet. It landed on the wood floor just inches from the sick woman's bent knees and relaxed arms, with a sickening splat. The feverish woman smiled wickedly, raising the hair on the other two woman's necks. The asp sensed the last rather than seen it and if a snake could smile, Vipera would have in that moment because it knew that the Master was going to find this oh, so amusing. The hormonal woman immediately bolted across the room and disappeared behind another wooden door. A few seconds later, Vipera could hear the woman retching and vomiting.

It was time to go. The python didn't wait for the ailing woman to die, it was inevitable and irrelevant, nor for the hormonal woman to return. The snake had obtained the information it was sent to retrieve, so its work was complete. Vipera slipped out the double doors, careful not to let them bang shut on the way out and went back out the same window it had entered.

Chapter Thirty-Seven

Two More Funeral Pyres

1

The Witch was wrong. She did not awaken when Vipera arrived back at the shack, less than two hours after it had been sent out to find Sarah. Nor did she awaken when the viper, also exhausted but not nearly as much as the Witch, returned to its cozy little bed-womb. The Witch would not rise for a few more hours and when she did it would have nothing to do with Vipera. It would be the first of many bargaining souls that would wake her.

There were two funeral pyre towers built that day, one for Lena McAvay and the other for Mrs. O'Reigan. During the chaotic commotion with Lena, the heartbroken widow drew and released her last breath. What they didn't know was that the same scream that kept Sarah from discovering Satan's viper, also caused the frail old woman's weak, exhausted heart to seize and fail. Doreen found her minutes after Lena McAvay bled out, sitting slumped on the floor with her legs under her and her arms stretched out and relaxed before her. She was in the same position she was in when Vipera had left. There was a broad, bloody, teeth-filled grin upon her face; a disturbing grimace that one would find in those freaky carnival sideshows. Doreen could not bring herself to touch the bloody woman after what she had just witnessed. With trembling hands and tears forming in her eyes, she tossed a moth-gnawed blanket over the slumped body and walked away.

Doreen sat down just long enough to force back the tears and get her shaky hands under some bit of control. When she was

400

able to confidently get up, Doreen walked over to check on the widow and found her sadly deceased. The emaciated woman had paled considerably, eyes half open and an unmistakable blue tint on her lips. The smell of death hung over the corpse like a shawl, but it was temporarily unnoticed by Doreen, through her shock. The floodgates broke and tears fell in rivers as Doreen broke down, sobbing. She tried desperately to get a hold on her whirlwind of emotions from the trauma she had just endured. Added to all that she knew the poor widow O'Reigan had died alone and more-than-likely scared and that broke her heart. It was all just too much for Doreen in those long, miserable moments.

Sarah returned less than a minute after Doreen's breakdown began and only had to glance at first Doreen, then the widow, to know what was wrong. She took off outside, glancing at the covered, slumped figure of Lena on her way out, only to confirm that the woman had died as she had expected her to.

She was prepared to start running around bringing the groups in herself but as she walked out of the Infirmary, she seen Dansford and the less-than-sober fisherman walking toward her carrying wooden crates full of food. "Listen boys..." Sarah panted, the shock of everything starting to catch up with her, rattling her nerves and making her body tremble. "...go round up Frank, Ron, Porter, Jiminey and Patty..." she paused, then finished, "...and John. Got two dead and need to make arrangements." She didn't know what reason she would give for John's presence, but she had a little bit of time to figure that out before they arrived. All she knew was that she needed him close to her. She craved him, in every way, like an addict craves their vice.

"Aww, shit." The men said in unison, quickening their steps to set the wooden crates beside the door of the Infirmary. "You alright there, girl?" Dansford asked the still panting and shaking woman, half-heartedly.

"Nah, but I will be. Go on and get em now." She ordered not unkindly. They obeyed, Dansford heading east toward the Slums and the fisherman heading west toward the flats where groups were gathering coal and chopping firewood.

2

Half an hour later, the group of six, along with the two messenger boys, and Sarah and Doreen, all stood in the large front room of the Infirmary where the survivors had grouped together and been staying. Sarah and Doreen told the group what happened, Jiminey McAvay only hearing a few words in all through the tremendous grief he felt at the loss of his baby sister. Patty, his wife, heard little more than he did, over his wailings, and her trying desperately to take her beloved's pain away, but knowing she never could. Patty sat with tear-filled eyes beside her husband, mere inches away from the drying blood pool Lena was resting in, holding and rocking him as the tears ran from his eyes and he sobbed like a small, heartbroken child.

Dansford and the fisherman stood by the front door of the Infirmary, listening to the women, and refusing admittance into the building until they could get the mess cleaned up. They had been recruited, only by happenstance, but would stick around to help until it was resolved. The fisherman occasionally stole a swig out of a small flask filled with Shine, just enough to keep the shakes off, that he kept in his inner coat pocket.

Dansford's eyes kept flicking from Frank to Sarah and back again. He knew they had slipped outside last night, why he did not know, but he did know that Sarah walked back in first. Alone. He also knew that when Frank returned, he looked sullen and detached. He had tried to ask Frank about it the night before when they were preparing to go to sleep, but he got no answer and had gotten very few words since then. Dan was curious as to what happened between the two of them, and he worried about the man that he cared so deeply for... even if it was the same man that had raped him only a week ago. Whenever he looked at Sarah, though, all he could feel was contempt and loathing. He despised her, despised her presence in the valley, and especially despised the effect she had on Frank. HIS Frank. His hatred for Sarah Maisse was almost as strong as his obsession with Frank McGrath.

Frank stood listening to the women tentatively enough but would not look at Sarah. He kept his eyes downcast but maintained a stern, almost angry expression. It was only a mask and Sarah knew it, she suspected that he was hiding the pain and shame from last night. She wanted to hug him and tell him she would be there for him if he wanted that, but she knew that to do so would only confuse and hurt him even more. He had his own issues he needed to work out before she could try to help give him closure with theirs. She would just have to endure that terrible look upon his face.

Ron Hellman and Porter Siddle listened to what happened, out of respect for the dead women. Porter almost married the O'Reigan widow once upon a yonder, and a small smile touched the corners of his mostly toothless mouth at the recollection of those steamy, hot summer nights they enjoyed together. The two men already knew what needed to be done but waited until the telling was done to get it going.

Johnathan Colmes was slightly confused as to why he had been called upon to hear of this before the rest of the valley folks. He had a sneaking suspicion that it was Sarah's doing and he was perfectly fine with that. Even hoped it was true because he felt as though she was avoiding him more so than just not giving him any outward attention. John missed her, wanted to hold her, and kiss her gently. Listening to but trying to block out the Apothecary aide and his beloved belle tell a sickening, terrible tale, he admired Sarah's physique and the vibrant beauty she seemed to be glowing with. He watched her, trying to take in all her radiance, with the knowledge and surety that he was looking at the love of his life.

When the telling was done, Frank shook his head and spoke to the group in a sad, pitiful tone. Nothing like his usual authoritative tone that'll snap you to attention. It was disheartening but they obeyed without question. Dansford and the fisherman were told to move the dead women into the exam rooms so Sarah and Doreen could prep them for the funeral pyre. Ron and Porter were instructed to begin construction of the towers immediately and then Frank looked at John.

The angry look on Frank's face briefly dissolved into one of confusion, as if he hadn't noticed John's presence until that moment. The confused expression led to one of irritation, and the irritation reverted to the stern look he had maintained

403

since the prior night. Frank glanced toward Sarah and then back to John, Sarah picking up on the knowing in his eyes.

"I figured since John was leading the group deconstructing shacks for usable building materials that he would be able to help Ron and Porter make quick work of the towers." Sarah told Frank more defensively than she liked, knowing the others were picking up on the tension between them. Frank's display of anger may have been warranted, to a small degree, but it did not justify throwing it all in her direction. Hadn't he done the same as she, anyway? Once again, her emotions took control before she could still her wagging tongue and loose lips. "I assumed he was a valuable asset in such manners considering YOU were the one that put him, rather than Porter or Ron, at the head of that task." Those around could hear the ice crack on the words she spoke, they came out so icily.

The glare that Sarah received from Frank melted the ice on those words and in an instant. The hatred she seen in his eyes, if only for a moment, took her aback but she held to her will and remained composed. She refused to falter, especially to a man too weak for self-analysis and realization. When Frank seen that she was not going to waver, he dropped his eyes first, but not in surrender. The final look in his eyes screamed that he would remember her insolence.

"Right you are." Frank said with a grunt, plastering a forced fake smile on his face. "John, you can aid the woodworkers. I'll go inform the others and prepare for the pyre." Then, Frank just walked away.

He made a single glance toward Dansford, their eyes locking momentarily, as he walked out the front door of the Infirmary. Frank saw the concern in Dan's eyes and Dan saw something distressing in Frank's. Something he couldn't quite pinpoint. Something that frightened him. Frank had only made it half a dozen steps past the door when Dansford looked around at the others. Almost everyone in the room was looking at him expectantly. "I think I oughta go talk to him."

"Yessum. Someone needs to and who betta than you." Porter told Dan, speaking for the lot. With that, he turned and walked toward the back door of the building, Ron and John not far behind.

Dansford followed Frank out the front, but Frank was nowhere to be seen. Dan had no idea which direction Frank would have gone in first. With a sigh, he walked back into the Infirmary to help the tipsy fisherman carry Lena McAvay and Mrs. O'Reigan into the nearest exam rooms. Dan was quiet and thoughtful as they scrubbed the blood from the wooden flooring, talking very little to the fisherman who tried on several occasions to initiate a conversation with him. They opened the shutters on every window, bundling up with coats and blankets, enduring the cold, almost constant breeze that swirled lazily around and around the valley. That was done in a desperate attempt to air out the nauseating smell of blood, that no amount of scrubbing could dampen.

While the men carried the dead off, Doreen, who lacked the confidence that she had cried out all her tears earlier, had given the elderly a lavender and chamomile tea to soothe their nerves and calm their minds. They were sleeping soundly by the time Dan and the fisherman began scrubbing the floorboards.

Roy laid on his cot in a semi-daze with his wounded hand and throbbing arm against his chest, trying to will away the ongoing hallucination. In his foggy mind, he believed that if he ignored the hallucination, it would go away on its own. It had worked a couple times before, but it didn't seem to be working that time, and Roy desperately needed it to. That was the most realistic, most vivid, and most horrifying hallucination yet, or so his mind insisted. Because of his semi-dazed state and with everything else going on, Doreen didn't bother to check on the young man.

The sun was going down behind the mountaintops by the time Sarah had finished gathering everything the women would need to prep the bodies for the funeral pyre. The men had gotten the bodies set up in the exam rooms and Doreen was waiting to get started, not out of eagerness but of force of will. She had detached herself from the situation and the women laying in the other rooms. How long it would last, she did not know but she was determined to employ it while she had it. The women began undressing and bathing the corpses, taking much care in the task. Their hair was washed, dried, and brushed free of tangles. The women, dead as they may be, looked as fresh and clean as the day they were born, with their hair fanned out behind them, giving off a halo-like appearance. They finished preparing the bodies less than half an hour before the completion of the towers, when most of the valley folks had arrived back at the Infirmary.

Dansford and the fisherman were helping the other valley folks pull together a small feast, as per custom. Ron, Porter, and John were erecting the tower in the center of the scorched earth in the common area. Doreen was wrapping Roy's punctured palm again, and the elderly were huddled around the large fireplace trying to warm up their bones. Sarah stood just outside the common area wall and watched Johnathan from a distance. She was hoping she wasn't being obvious about it but a small part of her didn't care if she was, at the same time. She also hoped that she would be able to catch a moment alone with him, she hadn't been able to yet, but the night was still young.

Frank, however, had yet to return.

Chapter Thirty-Eight

Petty Revenge

1

The Witch awoke to the sound of knocking on her door a couple hours after Vipera's return and only a few hours after she had fallen asleep. She rose feeling groggy and half-drunk with exhaustion, fighting the sleepiness back while stumbling across the room. She poked her head through the doorway between the front room and her bedroom, and hollered at whoever was beating on her door to give her a few moments. The knocking ceased, so the Witch rushed out to the cave and grabbed a small, lidded bottle about twice the size of a thimble. Attached to the lid was a tiny pipette which she used to dispense two drops of the Carnation oil held inside, onto her tongue. The Witch could feel the energizing effects of the oil by the time she had replaced the small bottle back on the shelf.

Feeling almost herself again, but knowing it wouldn't last long, she quickly made her way to the door and opened it to reveal the mystery guest that disrupted her sleep. Frank McGrath. The Witch was not all that surprised to see Frank. She knew he would eventually suspect, if nothing else, that his belle was fucking her beau, and he had come to tell her about the scandalous tragedy that had befallen them.

Frank wasn't there to tell her of their tragedy, or any other for that matter. He was there to fuck. He was there to get even with the lowly man that stole his beloved by fucking his belle right and proper. Frank had heard the small group that escorted the eldest O'Reigan daughter to the Witch's shack the first night after the thawing of the storm, talking about how astounding the Witch's transformation was. About how night and day different she looked, but still unmistakably the same sorceress they had always known, respected, and depended on. Frank found that they were right. He also knew that there was no way he or anyone else could put into words how stunning the Witch was. She was absolutely gorgeous before, which made her beauty that much more remarkable. The Witch radiated with an elegance that could not be denied or overlooked. Between her overwhelming beauty and the softness of her voice when she greeted him, he could feel himself thicken and lightly press against the front of his denim pants.

"Well, hello, Mr. McGrath." Her voice was a caress against his wounded heart, fractured mind, and raw emotions. "Please, come in." She stepped aside and Frank walked into her shack, making an obvious gesture of brushing against her as he did.

"Frank, if you will." He told her as he took a seat at the table. She joined him several minutes later with fresh coffee sitting before them. Frank was more than impressed by this, making him feel like royalty. His eyes kept running over her body, every inch of it, as if trying to memorize every minute detail about the lovely woman sitting before him. He was entranced and enchanted by her. A part of him recognized it for what it was, and he thought to himself that if it meant that he would be able to touch her silky-smooth skin, smell the sweet aroma of her hair, and caress the satiny symbol of her womanhood, she could enchant him all she liked.

The Witch caught on to his stares and the deep hunger in his eyes. How could she not, with how obvious he was making it? He resembled a boy, fresh into puberty that saw a girl for the first time that gave him that funny little tingle in the tip of his penis. She found it both cute and amusing.

"So, Frank, what brings you out here?" she asked him sweetly, with a smile that could melt snow in the Arctic.

Without hesitation Frank responded with, "You!"

"Is that so?" She could not stifle the giggle that escaped her lips, but he didn't seem bothered by it. "I assumed as much since it is my shack that you are currently occupying."

Frank smiled, but it was weak and didn't last long. "Being that your beau and my belle have been... uh... shackin up together... I thought maybe you and I could have us a little tryst of our own." He told her frankly.

That innocent giggle again that tugged at the hardness that had grown uncomfortable, pressing against his pants. "You are quite forward about your proposal, and I am quite flattered by it. As for the affair, you have told me nothing I did not already know." She told him, her tone turning icy with the last statement.

Frank didn't know what he expected her to say or how he expected her to react when he dropped that bombshell and told her of his wily intentions, all at once, but he didn't expect her to already know. He was stunned. "You...You already know?" he asked, stumbling over the words.

"Of course." She told him with a dismissive wave of her hand.

"How.... How long have you known?" he asked her.

"Since the night it began." The Witch told him matter-of-factly.

"What... How... A week? You've known for a week?" Frank's thoughts were spinning faster than his mouth could form the questions and his words came out in a flustered jumble.

Seemingly flustered by the line of questioning, the Witch's tone picked up a hint of irritation as she answered him. "Don't bother askin me how, it makes no nevermind how I know, and if it has been a week since the first night they coupled, then I have known for that long, yes. I doubt either of them know that I know, however, and I would like it to remain that way until I am able to seek the revenge I so crave."

Revenge? He liked the sound of that word, liked the way it echoed through his mind. Revenge is what brought him to the Witch's shack to begin with, he just had a different form of revenge in mind. He wasn't sure exactly what she was talking about, but he knew it didn't have anything to do with the reason he had come to see her. "Yes, revenge. That is my intention behind the proposal, as I am sure you have already deduced." He told her in a much calmer voice.

"Deduced I have. You all but put it in direct words that I would be no more than a revenge fuck for you to go rub in the face of the one that scorned you..." Frank repositioned himself in the wooden chair, suddenly feeling quite small at her blunt wording. "...so, I'd be a fool not to. However, your idea of revenge is so petty and primitive. You only want to hurt their feelings, upset them, maybe make them shed a few tears of misery. I want more, I want something bigger for them, something that will make them always remember what they did to me." She explained, the excitement apparent and growing as she went.

Frank sat listening in silent astonishment. The Witch was right. His revenge, as fun as it may have been, was petty compared to what she was speaking of. He wanted the same kind of revenge she did. He wanted to watch them, Sarah especially, burn for their adulterous deeds. "Us." He corrected. "What they did to us." The burning hatred that illuminated from deep within his eyes told her that he meant what he said.

The malicious light in Frank's eyes made her wonder if she might have a cohort before her. There was only one way to be sure. "What is it that you seek?" she asked him innocently, as if she did not understand his correction.

"Revenge, of course. The same as you, but not the... the petty kind, as you put it." Frank answered with a smile, one that was genuine and strong. "I want what you want." He finished with a strange twinkle in his eye.

2

The Witch stared at him for a long moment before responding. "We shall see." She finished off the last of her coffee and rose from the table they were sitting at. She led Frank through the shack and into the cave where she set him at a much larger, much sturdier wooden table. After retrieving her centuries old deck of brightly colored tarot cards from the first and smaller of the caves, she sat at the table across from him. "This reading will show me your true intentions and desires. It will also determine what happens next in regard to you... me... us. Understand?"

He didn't really, but he nodded his head, anyway. There was still a throbbing hardness in his pants from both the allure of the Witch and the idea of sweet revenge against that mouthy slut-bitch, Sarah. That hardness began to soften when she flipped the first card, though. It was limp after she flipped the third and in hiding by the time, she flipped the last one.

It was the first reading the Witch had done since her transformation, but not the only one she would do that day, and it was much different than the ones she had done before. Frank didn't know this because he had never been to see her for help of any kind. Their interactions had always occurred when he was checking on folks after a bad storm, disaster, or sickness, or when they crossed paths while out and about in the valley. He went along with it, though, unable to stop his curious and horrified eyes from taking in every detail of the bizarre, mind-numbing images.

First, she had Frank shuffle the cards, then cut the deck seven times in a row. The Witch laid each card delicately on the table as she revealed it, forming an upside-down cross with the bizarre cards. She flipped the first card off the top of the shuffled deck and set it at the very top of what would be the five-card cross. She was slow and deliberate about each reveal and gave Frank more than enough time to thoroughly analyze the cards before she threw down the next one. The words THE HEIROPHANT were stamped across the top of the first one. Frank's eyes were drawn to it, taking in the entirety of the picture below the title, as he would with the next six cards, as well.

It showed a weary eyed, troubled man dressed in clothes made of the finest of materials, clothing reserved for royalty and the extremely wealthy. These garbs donned by the man were no longer of royal standards, however. They had been shredded and mussed and doused with soot and mud. The man's hair was matted and tangled, his face and hands streaked with blood and dirt, and his bare feet caked with mud and grass. A top the man's head sat the universal symbol of authority, a crown. No ordinary crown, though, not by any means. The crown was a circular protrusion of needle-sharp spikes made of a deep, royal blue, the color of the ocean depths. The spiked crown sat atop the man's head, obviously penetrating deep into his skull in several places, blood trickling from the wounds. Frank felt certain that if he stared at the bright crimson of the blood long enough, he would be able to watch it seep from the wounds and drip onto the man's chest and shoulders. The same material that made up the crown, also made up a long stretch of spiked chain that crisscrossed itself around the man's body, securing him to the onyx throne he sat upon. The spikes on the chain, much like those on the crown but longer, stabbed painfully into his body in multiple places. Vividly bright crimson blood seeped from these wounds, as well. The deep blue of the crown and chain seemed almost bright compared to the black of the throne carved in a massive chunk of smooth, glass-like onyx. Hellfire burned fiercely in the background behind the throne, the colors vivid enough to give it the illusion, in certain lighting, that heat waved from the flickering flames.

Frank didn't understand the meaning of The Hierophant or the image that it displayed, nor did the Witch offer the information. He wanted to know what it meant because it didn't look like it could mean anything good. Try as he might, though, he could not make himself form the words to ask her. Even though he had never been to see the Witch before, he had heard and witnessed enough of her magical workings to know that she was no joke. His utmost confidence in her abilities, as well-placed as it was, caused the fear to seep in even before she flipped the next card.

The second card, placed directly and gently under the first one, had the words THE DEVIL stamped across the top. Frank's eyes widened at the sight of the card and the words upon it. The Witch had to repress a smile at his reaction, and wondered with a childlike imagination, if the image on the card was a true-to-life portrayal of her Master.

Hellfire burned in the background of that card, as well. Oranges, reds, and yellows, all magnificent shades of the sunset, sparkled from the ancient card. Before the fire stood a creature posed atop a mountain of corpses and dismembered body parts. From the very young to the very old, and every age in between, Frank could see the intricately detailed mountain of flesh, blood and bones the being stood upon. The horribly deformed, grotesque being that was perched at the peak of the pile of bodies in a prideful stance. It had one large claw-foot, attached to a twisted leg that bent in the opposite direction at the knee, resting upon the crumpled, heaped body of a once beautiful, light-haired young woman. The claw-foot covered most of the dead woman's back, one talon stretching across one of her shoulder blades, the tip of the talon curving over her shoulder and out of sight. A second talon wrapped around her waist, the end of it disappearing beneath her, while the third and last laid across the dead woman's buttocks, the tip of the talon disappearing under the woman's thigh. The other equally misshapen and ill-bent leg stood strong and unyielding. The creature was tall, towering high over the bodies and the flames, with a narrow, slender, emaciated figure. Its bones, clearly visible beneath its unblemished and featureless slate gray colored skin, were gnarled and malformed causing its limbs to lump and crater. The flawless gray complexion made the creature that much more heinous, giving off the illusion that it had been dipped in something like plastic. Its long arms, one at its side and hanging down to its wrongly jointed knee, ended in four-digit hands with fingers too long even for its extreme height. Its unfathomably large phallus was covered by a calf-length cloth, but the outline was there and quite prominent. In the center of the beings unclothed chest, a large gaping hole could be seen, as if a large chunk of its breastbone and ribs had been removed. In the hole was a vortex of souls spiraling into oblivion for eternity but never quite making it there. The seemingly endless vortex was filled with only Satan and God knew how many souls, all of them so small that they seemed to blur together in a sort of off-white fog. Its head, turned slightly to the right, was the most disturbing feature of the creature, with its too long snout and twinkling, beady eyes. To Frank it looked like a cross between a buffalo skull and some kind of bat... maybe? It had tall, pointed ears, resembling those of a bat but much larger, and rows and rows of small crooked, jagged teeth. A ridiculously long tongue snaked out of its mouth that was split halfway to the base, the ends of each buried deep in the nasal cavity of the severed head held within its upraised hand. It appeared to be the head of a young man with half-opened eyes and a gaping mouth, as if he had died screaming in agony.

Frank was convinced that the card meant imminent death or damnation, and he was almost panicky at the thought. Once again, Frank was desperate to ask what it meant, but again, he could not form the words. She flipped the third card before the panic could really set in and he was mesmerized all over again.

The third card was placed below The Devil card, presenting the three in a straight line. The words stamped across the top of it read THE HERMIT. The image was a black-and-white concept piece. Frank didn't care for the poorly sketched look it aimed for and succeeded at. It was of a basic human silhouette standing in front of a mirror, slightly turned to the left displaying the shadowy angles of facial features. Instead of a reflection looking back at the silhouette, the reflection was standing in front of another slightly smaller mirror that was looking at another smaller reflection in another smaller mirror. It repeated itself, every silhouette in the same position, every mirror smaller than the last. The imagery itself was dull compared to the chromatic pictures on the other two cards, but it seemed to hold more meaning.

The next card was laid gently on its side to the left of the minute gap separating The Hermit card from The Devil card. All the cards were lying close together but not quite touching, only enough space between each card for a splinter to squeeze into. The card reading THE MOON had a picture of a well sketched and colored moon but drawn from the dark side. The shadows on the moon face were evident and the line between light and dark revealed the craters and mountains scaling the surface. Behind the large-scale moon, taking up almost two-thirds of the card and leaving little room for the rest of the fantastically colored galaxy, sat the Earth. The bright sky blue of the water accented the forest green of the land, the great distance giving no obvious details to its exquisite landmarks and terrains. The image almost made Frank feel small in the way it was able to capture the vastness of space between Earth and the moon.

She flipped the fifth and final card to compose the cross titled STRENGTH and set it sideways on the right side of the upside-down cross. When the darkness consumed the Good Witch, it consumed everything connected to her, as well. The ancient tarot cards she held in her hand were no exception. The one she drew for Frank was the same as the one she had drawn for Old Joe Brenner and many others not all that long ago, but he wouldn't have noticed that it was the same had he been there to see it. The tarot cards titled in basic English, had been named in Latin before, but it was the least noticeable of all their changes. The pictures drawn and painted on them had changed, as well, becoming darker and more sinister. The Strength card, after the darkness had altered it, showed a massive tiger, much larger than it should have been portrayed, standing over the body of a fresh kill. The kill looked to be what remained of an antelope or caribou, maybe? It was hard to tell through the smears of blood and detailed gore surrounding it. The tiger stood with one bloody paw resting atop the hunched shoulder of the heaped carcass. Its claws were retracted and stuck firmly into the hide as if it feared the animal would leap up and run off. The tiger's thick coat was splattered with blood and matted with mud from the chase and the kill. Its massive head was turned skyward, a chunk of bloody meat hanging from its large carnivorous teeth. It was night in the grasslands, but the moon was full, and the light beaming from it was bright enough to illuminate the tiger and its meal.

The sixth card was flipped, and the Witch delicately placed it atop The Moon and The Devil cards, covering half of each one. That card was titled THE SUN with a picture of just that on it, painted in yellows and oranges so bright it almost hurt to look at. From the sun came brilliant sun flares that licked out of the massive fireball suspended in a beautifully depicted galaxy. The brightness of the colors and the realism of the background gave the sun a similar illusion to that of the Hellfire in other backgrounds, where it almost flickered with sparks and embers.

The seventh and last card was flipped and placed on the opposite side of The Sun card, atop the second half of The Devil card and half of the Strength card. The Devil card was, by far, the most disturbing of the bunch and it made Frank nervous for reasons he could not explain, so he was especially grateful that it was completely covered. The final card read THE LOVERS; another card drawn for Old Joe that he would not have recognized. This card had been colored to give it the jagged appearance of being ripped into triangular pieces, three of them to be exact. On the left stood a black and white drawing

415

of a woman against a silhouetted background depicting a field with a distant farmhouse or barn. A dead and rotting woman but not decayed enough to disguise the long hair and feminine figure. The obviously deceased woman stood facing away from the center and right side of the card, her back to the other sections, arms across her chest in a defiant, upset manner. On the right side of the card stood a dead and decaying man against a silhouetted city-like background, his hand outstretched toward the woman in what seemed to be a pleading manner. The center triangular rip contained a circumvoluted whirlpool of flame that almost appeared to be rotating with its intense colors. The edges of the rip seemed to be pulled in toward the eddy of fire, as well as the woman's long, flowing hair. Above the man and woman, crossing from their shaped sections into the wide top of the center rip, were two anatomically correct hearts. Both were unbelievably realistic with their combinations of reds and pinks, highlighting all the right areas to give the concaves of the muscles their proper shadows. The space between the two organs was riddled with dozens of crisscrossed threads that eerily resembled human flesh of varied tones and complexions. Each thick thread started and ended in the pierced sides of the hearts, bright red blood dripping from the punctures. Many of the fleshy ropes had been severed, hanging loosely from one heart or the other, leaving precious few to keep the two bleeding hearts tethered.

3

The Witch allowed the moments to drag on as his eyes remained locked on the disturbing images, unable to turn away from them. Finally, and mercifully, she began to explain the cards and their meanings. Frank was able to tear his gaze from the card and sighed with relief when he realized he could speak again, should he so choose. She pointed to the first card, The Hierophant, and said "What was...", she separated The Sun and The Lovers cards and then moved her finger down to the second card, The Devil. "...what is...", she continued before she moved her finger down over the third card, titled The Hermit, and said, "...and what will be." The

Witch slid The Sun and The Lovers cards together, one sliding under the other, fully revealing The Moon and Strength cards they were partially covering. She laid a perfectly manicured finger atop The Moon card and said, "Taxes...", then slid it over the Strength card and said, "...and Warnings." She separated The Sun and The Lovers cards, returning them to their proper places covering The Devil card. Pointing at The Sun, she told him, "For Love...", and then at The Lovers, "and for Loss."

Frank sat silently and thoughtfully for a few seconds before asking, "Not that I'm complaining or anything but why are these two cards covering The Devil card?" referring to The Sun and The Lovers cards.

"Because the Devil is behind your love and loss." The Witch answered quickly, with little patience, as if the question was of unimportance. "There are multiple meanings and interpretations for each card. The person, the situation, and the lay of the cards determine which meaning you are endowed with. The Hierophant is a clear indication of your authority in the valley. It is, also, the first card to be drawn, the 'What was' card, which means that this is quickly becoming a part of your past for any number or combination of reasons."

"Is there any way you can tell me what those reasons are? Please, I don't want to lose my authority, it's all I've got. It's my birthright!" Frank pleaded, almost panicked.

"There are ways, but they do poorly for me. Such dealings with the Sight have always been inconsistent, weak, and most times outright incorrect. It would be of no use to you or me. It would in fact only worsen the situation." The Witch informed him pleasantly. She enjoyed watching him squirm with panic, watch him wallow in his own fear, but she couldn't afford the time to drag it out, as much as she would have liked to. She went on to The Devil card, once again separating the two covering it, before he had a chance to respond. "The Devil shows that you are or will very soon, be in a situation that you cannot control. Entrapped in an inescapable situation. Since it is the second, the 'What is' card, it will happen very soon if not already." The Witch moves to the bottom of the cross and points at The Hermit card. "The Hermit. The 'What will be' card indicates a need for self-introspection. You, in the near but not immediate future, will have to do some self-analysis and come to terms with certain undesirable aspects of yourself."

Frank looked suddenly nervous and shameful, wringing his hands, while sweat popped out on his forehead, despite the chill in the shack. The Witch suppressed a smile but was giggling on the inside. She knew he was a homosexual; it was nothing to her what the man liked to do; she was just enjoying the misery he was in because of his shame of it. Moving along to The Moon card, forming the left arm of the cross, the Witch explained. "The Moon is a symbol for a number of things but given your situation and that it was drawn for as the 'Taxes' card, it means that you have some unadmitted truths that need to be addressed. Since it falls to the left of the cross, it falls on the 'What was' end of the lifeline, meaning that these unadmitted truths are being or will be addressed in the immediate future. More than likely, they have already begun to be revealed."

Again, Frank became flustered. He hated what was happening, hated the feeling of knowing she was pressing on him, hated the images on the bizarre cards, hated the eerily correct meanings. All of it! He hated all of it! He just wanted to leave, he wanted to get up out of his chair and walk out and go back to the common area and act like none of this craziness ever happened. He could not move though, could not bring himself to even speak again. She's done enchanted me! Lord, help me! He thought frantically through his temporary paralysis and inability to speak. What he mistook for enchantments were actually extreme anxiety attacks brought on by his own fear and guilt.

"The Strength card, the fifth 'Warnings' card, is an indication that you are apt to do harm, either to yourself or to someone you love. Its falling on the 'What will be' side is only a further indication that it is an inevitable act, but you must keep in mind that there are greater forces at work here. Forces that you couldn't possibly fathom, nevertheless understand." She placed the last two cards over The Devil card and continued her explanations. "For the sixth card, your 'Love' card, you have been granted The Sun. This card is an indication of personal gain. It could be minute or grand, time will only tell, but a gain it will be." What the Witch failed to say out loud was that personal gain would be his but only momentarily. The ultimate personal gain would belong to her Master, the Poisonous Prince.

There was some obvious relaxation on Frank's behalf upon hearing of his soon-to-be-acquired personal gain. He wondered what form it would come in, much like a child's daydream of the gifts Santa may bring, deep down hoping it would be the return of his authority. The Witch could see the corners of his lips turning upward into a small smile and quickly had to erase it before it could come to fruition. "The final card, The Lovers, placed upon 'Loss', means that you will have, in the near future this shall be, a painfully difficult decision to make. A decision that will decide your future, for better or worse, and require a sacrifice of sorts. What, I am unsure, but it is indicated that one is needed." The Witch paused, allowing Frank some time to process everything she had just told him.

After a few minutes, she concluded with an overall meaning. "You have a life-changing decision ahead of you, one that is out of your control. One that must be decided after some personal reflection and inner peace has been made. A decision that, once done cannot be undone. A decision that will decide whether you get the revenge you so crave." She watched Frank closely, trying to read his eyes for a fight or flight reaction, but could find an indication of neither.

He did not respond to her explanations and maintained a mostly expressionless face, trying to process and understand what she had just told him. She did not press him to speak or react, but after a few long minutes of his stillness and silence, she grew somewhat impatient. "Wait here," she told him with no expectations that Frank would be in any other position when she returned. She walked into the first cave and rummaged around in the amulet draw she had tested Vipera on only hours before. She pulled out a pale lavender colored crystal, much longer than it was wide but still smaller than the smallest finger on her hand. She wrapped a long piece of hemp twine around the fragile-appearing stone and carried it back into the ritual cave with her. The Witch handed the crystal to Frank, who was hesitant to take it at first. "It's an ametrine and it will help you with clarity and focus. It will allow your mind to clear of the clutter and help you to process and understand. Come to me when you have made your decision, you will know when the time comes." Frank stared at the hanging stone for another moment or two before finally accepting it. He wrapped the long pieces of twine around his hand a few times and grasped the amulet tightly.

Frank did not thank the Witch for the amulet, nor did he tell her goodbye. He sensed that their rendezvous was over, finally, so he rose and walked out. All thoughts of his original intentions with the Witch and his spontaneous arrival had long since ceased. Just like that. It was very rude, ungentlemanly, and not at all like Frank McGrath. The Witch didn't mind the rudeness however, she found it quite amusing. She had put Frank in the perfect frame of mind to destroy it. She could break him, condemning him to a life in an asylum with the rest of the crazies unfit to be in society, should she so choose. Something in his eyes told her that he had the potential to be quite a player in her little game, but only time would tell. In the meantime, she would try to devise a way to tip the scales in her favor.

Chapter Thirty-Nine

Make It Stop!

1

She felt Vipera stir within her and immediately lost all thoughts of Frank and remembered the whore-slut Sarah Maisse. Excitement, anxiety, and nervousness crashed into her in waves. She didn't want to know but at the same time she couldn't wait to find out. She was torn, but only temporarily, then awaited eagerly for the giant asp to slither out of her.

Less than fifteen minutes later, the Witch called upon her Master, all the while praising and cooing to the python-like creature. The Witch was overwhelmed with excitement several moments later when Satan's voice came booming in around her. He sounded almost annoyed at being called upon, yet again, by this so far incompetent convert. "What?!" he demanded to know. The Witch, as much as she wanted to, didn't respond, only sent the viper into the shadows and to her Master.

She sat in the ritual room of her cave, going over her plan for Malum a final time, when Satan finally spoke again. It had been almost half an hour since she sent Vipera into the darkness, and when the voice returned it sounded much less annoyed, almost with a hint of respect. "I had my doubts, sorceress, but you have succeeded. The irony of it being your unfaithful beloved and his tramp's unborn son, is the perfect insult. You upheld your end of the bargain, sorceress, you shall have your revenge."

"Against Malum?" she asked eagerly.

"If it is your wish to have it." The voice answered. "You have done me a great service, sorceress. The success of this child's future could bring down empires and destroy nations. I could bring my kingdom to Earth and mock the sky-bastard for eons to come. All at the hands of my own son!" The hopefulness and longing pleasure were undeniable in the tone and the voice of Satan laughed and laughed at the future's promising aspects.

The Witch, almost bursting with the anticipation to get her plan against Malum put in motion, had everything planned out. Her entire revenge scheme was playing out better than she had hoped. Revenge against the valley folks, Sarah, and of course, her beloved beau Johnathan Colmes, had not been forgotten. They had only been set aside until her dealings with Malum could be addressed and concluded. That business was first and foremost on her list. "This is what I need from you..." the Witch began and continued to explain, in great detail, what she needed from her Master to fulfill her much-desired revenge against the literal evil that had defiled and almost broken her.

When the Witch had finished, the strong, gravelly voice was silent for several long moments, in contemplation. "This is how you wish to get your revenge?" Her Master asked when he finally spoke again.

"Oh, yes." She responded and the maliciousness of her tone paired with the devilish twinkle in her eyes, indicated that she meant it.

"Very well. Quite impressive, your plan is. I shall do my part, sorceress. In the meantime, Vipera will remain with you until I see fit that you no longer need the extra attention." The voice informed her.

"Yes, Master." She responded agreeably and without hesitation. With that, Vipera came slithering out of the shadows but veered off to snack on one of the recently sacrificed rodents scattered about the room. The Witch could feel the voice's departure, leaving her with nothing to do but wait.

2

The funeral pyre for Lena McAvay and the widow, Mrs. O'Reigan, who had outlived her husband by less than a week, had been burning for about ten minutes when Frank joined the large group of survivors at the Common Area. Few had noticed his absence, so the same few were the only ones to notice his late arrival. All, unbeknownst to the others, questioned his whereabouts and that strange, almost sadistic look in his eyes. Only five people out of all those that were still alive in the valley noticed Frank's absence and late arrival.

Sarah noticed, of course, and was relieved when he had shown up but wondered about where he had been the past few hours. A brief here-and-then-gone-again thought swept through her mind that the Witch had been able to sink her untrustworthy claws into him. She quickly dismissed the thought though because she believed that even with everything Frank was going through, he wouldn't seek out the help of the Witch. She had been right on one account and wrong on the other but wouldn't know until it was too late.

Johnathan had noticed, too, but his wasn't as obvious as Sarah's. It was okay for Sarah to outwardly notice Frank, even with the obvious problems the 'couple' were having, but it would seem odd if Johnathan was apparent about it. John and Frank hadn't spoken outside of basic acknowledgment or task handouts in some years. John remembered the bratty little boy Frank used to be, that thought he was above everyone else and always picking on the smaller, weaker kids. Particularly the orphans, even if those orphans didn't have to live in the orphanage. John remembered those days and even though times, and the men themselves, had changed, John still couldn't bring himself to forgive Frank, let alone be friendly with the snarky bastard. So, John, as a rule and longtime habit stemming from childhood, tried to keep an eye out for Frank whenever possible. He did not like what he seen in those eyes but tried not to overthink the look. He did not know, having not been given the opportunity to speak with Sarah, what had happened between Frank and Sarah the night before. Had he known, John may have thought a little more into that look, and maybe... just maybe... things might have played out differently in the end.

Dansford Keeton had been fighting off the inner panic that was trying to overtake his senses when he spotted Frank saunter his way into the crowd. Relief replaced the panic, but part of the relief turned into dread. The look in Frank's eyes was eerily familiar, as if he has seen it before but only once or twice. That look made Dan very nervous and as much as he wanted to, he decided not to approach Frank. He would just keep his distance and let Frank come to him; he would eventually, he always did.

The feast for the most recent funeral pyre was meager, at best, but the folks partook and enjoyed as if it were fit for royalty, as was their custom. Porter Siddle had gathered his small plate and was walking out away from the heat of the fire, and the sickly smell of roasting corpses. Suddenly, the contents of his plate scattered across the ground, and he staggered to one side as someone barreled past him. "Aye!" he yelled at the passing figure in a strong angry voice, reverting to his days as a younger man that would throw hands with almost anyone. His mouth snapped shut and the anger seeped out of him when the man turned around though. It was Frank McGrath and Porter, who had watched the boy grow from knatties to knickers, genuinely feared the young man in that moment. The look in Frank's eyes was fear inducing, an obvious touch of madness that dimmed as quick as it had brightened. For a moment Porter was convinced that Frank was going to kill him, and then breathed with obvious relief when he turned and walked away.

The fifth and final person to notice Frank was the one-handed, Roy Hoarding. Roy was probably looking harder for Frank than Sarah and Dansford were, but his was out of cautious necessity. As soon as Roy had seen Frank walk away from the older, but not elderly, Porter Siddle, he snuck out the back door of the Infirmary while the elderly were watching the fire through an open window and Doreen had walked over to the Apothecary for more supplies. He took a wide berth around the common area, moving in the shadows and hoping the early dusk would help conceal his movements until he made it past the Bar. They did and he was able to make his way to the Witch's shack and back to the Infirmary unnoticed. His absence was noted by Doreen, but she cared so little, she didn't mention it to anyone.

3

The ground was still muddy and therefore slippery, so it took Roy a little longer than normal to make the trek to the Witch's front door. Twice, his foot slid out from under him and even though he did not fall, he jerked his arms reflexively. This excruciating motion sent hot, jagged bolts of pain surging through his pierced hand and fingers trailing up his arm and into the deep muscles of his shoulder. Twice, he wept from the pain, unashamed and in a misery only conjurable in dreams, but on he trekked.

Roy could sense, more than hear, movement behind the front door of the Witch's shack, almost reconsidered, but knocked anyway. The worst that could happen was that the Witch turned him away, or so he thought. The door opened a moment later and the beautifully transformed woman standing in the doorway, momentarily floored him. He had never seen such beauty and was, like most others, temporarily mesmerized by her. She seemed half surprised to see him and half expectant of his arrival. It was an odd but suitable expression that worked well on her lovely face. "Please come in, you must be chilled to the bone." The Witch offered Roy sweetly, noting the beads of sweat prickling his face and the gooseflesh running along the back of his good hand and the sides of his neck. She stepped away from the doorway in the same manner she had done only a few hours before with Frank McGrath.

In his intense upset and shock since the accident, the Witch's enchanting beauty was soon forgotten, and Roy wasted no time explaining his reasoning behind his sudden and uninvited appearance. There was no small talk or offer of tea or coffee, like with Frank. Roy was almost begging, tears hanging from his eyelashes, as he slowly and meticulously unslung and unwrapped his hand. The Witch observed the large puncture in the palm of his hand, large enough to put a coin through without touching the sides. It was festered and seeping an oily red substance, the edges jagged and puffy, as if infection were trying to set in. "Well, I can certainly find you a means of recovery if that is what you seek, but much like my new look, I do things a little differently now." The

Witch told Roy with a girlish smile. She was giddy from lack of sleep and the immense amount of suffering this man was enduring. She didn't want to end this weak and sniveling bitch of a man's misery, but she believed that if she collected enough of her own souls, she could use them to gain favor with her Master. She intended on moving up... or in this case down... the 'ladder of success' until she was seated beside Satan himself. She would be the Queen of the Underworld, the Domina of Darkness. 'His' Domina of Darkness.

The very thought made her loins ache with pleasure, but she pushed it away, reluctantly yet quickly, knowing it was not the time nor the proper company for such advantageous explorations. She returned her focus to the wounded man before her. "Please! Anything, I will do anything! Please, if you can, fix it like it was before. I don't wanna be no lame, but... but if you can't fix it, please at least make the pain stop. Please!" he cried, holding his hand out before him trying not to let it move too much through the sobs that were threatening to rack him.

"A reading must be done first, and should the reading coincide with your true intentions than a deal can be made." The Witch told him, hating the immediate relief on his face and the way he became so hopeful. It was disgusting but necessary to ensure the payment.

"Yes, anything. Let's do it." He told her eagerly, carefully rising from the chair, continuing to keep his unslung arm out before him. So, the Witch led Roy Hoarding through the shack and into the caves where she sat him down at the large wooden table. Like Frank, she explained how he would have to cut the deck even one-handed, and how all the cards had several meanings, and each interpretation is based on the person, situation, card placement, etc. With Roy, however, she explained the cards to him as she laid each one in the same carefully placed cross pattern.

The first card to be drawn was the Strength card, its title stamped across the top of the vicious tiger's nighttime feast. The Witch told Roy about the card's placement, 'What was' and that the Strength card meant recovery from injury. So, he was already beginning his recovery, even if he didn't realize it. Roy knew it was healing, it was the healing process that was part of his misery, plus the time it was taking to heal, and the added distress of not knowing if his hand would ever work right again. It was all just too much for him and he could feel himself trying to crack under the pressure.

The second card, same as Frank's, was The Devil card, with the exact same meaning. The Devil card in the 'What is' placement was almost a sure sign the Witch would have their soul and she smiled at the deep frown on Roy's face at the sight of the image.

The third card, the 'What will be' card, had the name WHEEL OF FORTUNE stamped across the top of it. The Witch told him that the card was a sign of things to come, and that they would be inevitable and uncontrollable. The images on the cards all struck Roy with the same nervous fascination that they had Frank, so the meaning went unheard by Roy, and that was just how the Witch wanted it to be. The Wheel of Fortune card showed a beautifully depicted glass ball, much like the ones seen used by the gypsies in those old travelling sideshows. It was so well drawn and painted that Roy had a brief impulse to reach into the card and pick the glass ball up, carefully of course. A pair of hands hung suspended over the ball, not aged and wrinkled, like one would expect, but soft smooth hands that radiated with vitality and youth. Had Roy been of mind to do so, he would have noticed that the hands shown on the card were eerily similar to the perfectly, unblemished hands of the Witch, herself. Inside the glass ball was another smaller image, but just as clear. The edges of the glass ball swirled with a silvery mist that almost seemed to glimmer in the light. Almost like a snow globe but with glitter instead of whatever all that white shit is. Within the metallic-like mist was a battleground, a long valley filled on both ends with thousands upon thousands of men. All of them dressed in armor and ready to fight. One side wore gold plating atop their armor, with some riding upon elephants and grizzlies. The other side wore black plating across their armor, riding polar bears and some strange creature that resembled a rhino. The skeletal and material remains of the long dead soldiers from past conflicts littered the ground around the feet of the soldiers on both ends of the war zone.

War was imminent, but was surrender still possible? Roy wondered.

She flipped the next card. "The Judgement card falls on the 'Taxes' place, on the 'What was' side of the timeline. This one has a double meaning; an interpretation for 'Taxes' and an interpretation for 'What was'. These meanings may seem quite different now, but at some point, they will intermingle. The 'What was' part shows signs of a plan already in action. One much larger than you or I. One that you will have no control over. The 'Taxes' meaning is that you have a major decision to make, and it will have to be made sooner rather than later." Before Roy could respond or even articulate words, the bizarre image on the card caught his eye and he was silenced. It showed a large set of copper-colored scales, tarnished in places but not rusted, the details incredible. There were no dials or gauge faces, there were no numbers or writing of any kind on the scales. Just two large plates of the same color as the scale, that were suspended in the air by long chains. The chains led up to a long bar balanced atop another long arm that was attached to the base of the scale. Both metal plates were occupied, one more than the other, but the one with less on it was tipped severely to the right. It must have been much heavier than the mound on the opposite plate. It took Roy a moment to realize what it was he was looking at and when he did, his stomach churned, and he feared he would retch. On the higher, less weighted plate stood a small mountain of human flesh, chunks of meat, some fresh and some rotten, and a couple bones with joints still obviously attached to the ends. The entire pile marinated and dripped with stagnant, partially coagulated blood, colored a much deeper red under the dim light of the cave. Across the bar on the opposite plate stood the stacked letters of the word DESIRE. The D stacked on top of the E, and the E on top of the S, and so on and so forth. The entire word was nowhere near as tall as the pile of flesh it stood against, yet the weight difference was awesome. The entire word, each individual letter, seemed to be made of diamond at one angle, and gold at another, and splattered with blood at every turn. The message came through clearly.

The fifth card went into the 'Warnings' section on the 'What will be' side. She flipped the card and placed it into its appropriately and perfectly aligned place in the cross. It read TEMPERANCE across the top. "In the not-too-distant future you will be torn by indecision. The Temperance card indicates the calming of the inner war, with or without peace." She explained. The colored picture on the tarot card matched the meaning quite well. It showed another battleground, it and the gold and black armies that stood upon it closely resembled those in the Wheel of Fortune card. However, the Temperance picture showed the bloody and beaten soldiers after the fighting had ceased, and both parties were shaking hands in surrender. Death lingered among the corpses of the battle, few still standing, the white flags of surrender in the background a sick joke amid the gore and carnage.

The Witch flipped the sixth card and placed it halfway over The Judgement card and half over The Devil. That one titled THE STAR. It stood for 'Love' and meant that he was bound for renewal and recovery. He could heal and be well again, she told him. The mostly black and white drawing was bleak, though, compared to the meaning she told him it held. It showed a deep black, sky-view over a desolate land, one similar to the desert but much deader. White stars shown from the night sky that took up more than two-thirds of the card and a single shooting star was streaking across the sky from the left of the picture. The only vivid color, that wasn't a variation of white or black or any grayish hue in between, was a single flower growing amidst the surrounding deadlands. It was the soft orange of a brilliant sunset that seemed to gleam in the depression it was imprisoned within.

She drew the final card of the reading off the top of the deck and placed it over the uncovered half of The Devil card and the first half of the Temperance card. THE TOWER. "A sudden conflict, one you may or may not have a hand in, will arise in the near future. The drawing of The Tower means it is inevitable and the 'Loss' placement means that it will be one that directly affects you, and probably in a negative way." The same question Frank asked just hours ago rose to Roy's lips, but he couldn't make the words pass them. In all reality, he wasn't sure if he really wanted to know if she had the gift of Sight and what that disruption would be, if she did. Roy wasn't all that convinced that she did have that particular gift because she wouldn't have looked so surprised when he unexpectedly showed up. His mind was fogged through the pain and lack of sleep. So, he decided to keep his mouth shut on the subject until he could think a little more clearly. The Tower card, much like The Star card, was done in an almost complete black and white drawing. In the center of a decimated city stood a massive circular skyscraper kind of like that one tower overseas that leans over a little. It was made of huge stones, similar to those on the pyramids, and almost a hundred meters tall. The tower still stood but there was a top to ground crack that ran through the middle of the building, splitting it in two. Both halves of the tower remained erect, and the contents of the tower were visible from certain angles. Severed limbs and bodies lay scattered amid the rubble and wreckage. Some were hanging from the edges of the split tower, debris falling from the separation. A massive bolt of lightning, coming out of the ground rather than the sky, zigzagged its way up through the widening split in the tower. It branched off in several places, into smaller jagged bolts that stretched across the darkly clouded sky suspended above the ruined city. The only color in that image was the vibrant bright golden yellow of the lightning bolt. It beamed against the darkness of the sky, enhancing its radiance. It was a chaotic, nerve-inducing image that Roy struggled to tear his gaze from.

"As a whole, the tarot reading indicates that you have a decision to make, very soon, and the implications of the decision will cause a ripple effect that may or may not impact a full recovery from your injury. This decision will cause a great inner war, your choice will determine whether it ends in peace or disruption." The Witch concluded the reading.

In his desperation, Roy Hoarding put next to no thought into what came out of his parched mouth and cracked lips. "If it will give me my hand back, and soon, the decision is a simple one." He did not regret his words in that moment, but he would.

"Very well, then..." the Witch said with an oddly sweet smile, "...follow me." He did and she led him out of the caves, but instead of taking him back into the shack, she turned right and led him into the garden.

4

She took Roy to the same place she had taken Alvin Danson and his group only days ago. Even though Roy didn't know it, the garden had changed as drastically as everything else the darkness touched. The plants maintained their healthy vibrance and lavish colors, but they all gave off a nightmarish aura. As they walked along the garden path, Roy found himself unconsciously avoiding touching any of the plants, even so much as brushing against a leaf. He became increasingly more anxious the further along the path they went, and when he thought he wouldn't be able to stand being in the dense jungle-like garden a moment longer, they entered a clearing. It was the same clearing with the same furniture as before, but with no congenial offer of tea.

The Witch had Roy kneel under the archway and place his injured hand, palm down, flat on the ground in front of him. It took a long time, a lot of tears, and a lot of strong will, but Roy managed to do as she instructed. It took a lot of willpower on the Witch's behalf as well, to keep from laughing at the crying wimp's tears of pain.

Less than a minute later, a large spider that looked like a mutated cross between a tarantula and a black widow came crawling off the foliage covered archway. It was a shade lighter than onyx with a bright red upside-down cross on its back. It had twelve legs instead of eight and far too many eyes that glowed that strange back light. Its sharp fangs protruded from its gaping mouth and dripped with a pale pink liquid that sizzled on contact. Roy was repulsed and wanted to immediately draw away from it, but his willpower held him in place, wanting the pain to end and his handy abilities back.

The odd arachnid crawled across the back of his hand, all around, and in the puncture on his palm. Roy anticipated the pain but received an opposite, more pleasurable sensation. It felt almost as if he were being tickled, which made him notice that the overall pain was more than tolerable. He just hoped that it would last. As the spider made its way around, in, and through Roy's wounded hand, the Witch's eyes took on that bright black glow as she began to chant the spell backwards.

> Labor to ability mans this restore to,
> power the arachnid this allow.
> sounds and sights, scents the amid,
> around be that powers the to.

With the last of the enchanting words spoken, the strange light in the Witch's eyes slowly faded and then diminished completely. The large, deformed spider crawled off Roy's hand and returned to its previous place on the greenery-shrouded archway. He watched with revulsion as it skittered up onto a dark green leaf, in a mild state of shock at having allowed such a grotesque creature to touch him. When the arachnid was out of sight, Roy looked up at the Witch who stood, smiling, before him. Still careful of his wounded, but not as painful, hand, Roy knee-walked forward, reaching out for the hem of the Witch's long deep purple colored, hooded cape. She took a single step back, out of his reach, looking down at him disdainfully. Not as if a healthy person would look at someone ill with something contagious, but as if she were royalty looking down upon a peasant. Roy took up the hint immediately and lowered his upraised hand, but went into a gushing, sincere fit of 'thank you' and 'I am forever in your debt' on a repetitive cycle. She allowed him to grovel in his gratitude for a few moments before quickly tiring of it all.

"Yes, yes. Be gone with you now." The Witch told him with a casual wave of her hand in the direction they had come from. "Your hand shall be restored within a week."

"Yes, madam... Thank you! Thank you! Thank you!" Roy stammered as he clumsily got to his feet and took off down the path that they had entered the clearing from. He took none of the special care rushing out of the garden as he had walking into it. He was at, through, and out of the shack in less than half the time it took going in.

5

Back at the Infirmary, most folks had gone to sleep for the night, but there were a few that were still awake and moving about. So, Roy snuck through the back door and into the bathroom when he was sure no one was paying any attention, and after a few moments walked out and to his bed as if he had been there the entire time. A couple of people looked over at him as he returned to the comfort of his bed, the exhaustion setting in quickly, but no one seemed to notice that he had been missing. Doreen was one of them, and the only one that knew he had left. A part of her was curious as to his whereabouts, a part of her was relieved to see that he was okay, and another part was slightly disappointed at his return only because it meant another person for her to care for. The strain had been a lot on Doreen, and it had only intensified with the horror she had witnessed earlier in the day. She was much closer to her breaking point than anyone, herself included, really knew.

When Roy returned to the Infirmary there were seven people awake, himself included, but only three, himself included, were in attendance in the large open room they all stayed in. He might have noticed the absence of the other four had he not been so damn exhausted. Within a minute of laying on his bed, Roy Hoarding fell asleep with his wounded hand, still hurting but very tolerable, rested on his flat stomach. It was the best and most restful sleep he would ever get in his life.

Chapter Forty

Not So Petty Revenge

1

Doreen went about sorting the following day's supplies before she headed off to bed. Danny Bailey and Betty Jones, both still very 'active' at the end of the day, had snuck off to one of the exam rooms, for a little alone time together. And Robert Daniels was seriously considering sneaking off to the storage room for another nip of his own Shine before going to sleep.

After some, but not much, contemplation over the subject Robert, partially intoxicated, decided that 'anotha nip a Shine would be jist fine 'fore he started countin them swine.' Not that his tipsy ass really needed another drink, but he slowly got out of his bed, his joints creaking from the chill the fireplace couldn't quite tame. Doreen had paid him no mind and Roy had been asleep for several minutes already as Robert made like he was heading for the bathroom. He went a little farther down the short hallway than was necessary for the bathroom and stopped at the storage room door where he hid his bottle of Shine, still ashamed that he had picked up the habit again after so many years. The only other person that knew of his Shine stash was the fisherman, but Robert knew the man was passed out drunk again, snoring loudly in the large quiet room. Doreen would be the only other person that would have any reason to enter the storage room and she had already gathered everything she needed from there earlier in the evening. Which made the sight he seen upon entering the storage room that much more surprising.

Robert opened the door, soundlessly, just enough for him to slip his thick, but not overweight, body through and silently closed the door. The room was dark except for a moonbeam of light filtering through a small, square window. It didn't take but a few moments for Robert's eyes to adjust to the darkness and they grew ever wider at the sight before him. It was Frank McGrath, completely nude, standing behind, an equally nude, Dansford Keeton, who was bent slightly at the waist. Both hands were gripping a wooden shelf in front of him and there was an expression of pain mixed with pleasure on his face. Frank, with his pelvis pressed firmly against Dans backside, moving in a circular grinding motion, had one hand on Dan's hip and the other wrapped around toward the front of Dan's waist. Mercifully, the action was out of Roberts sight, but the movement of his arm gave a pretty clear indication as to what he was doing to Dan with that hand of his.

Robert Daniels registered the action taking place, smiling broadly like an innocent young man at a gentlemen's club, long before he registered the participants of the action. By that time, they had already noticed his intrusion and had separated, frantically trying to throw some sort of clothing over themselves. In their flustered rush, Robert noticed the equipment that the participants were packing and that is when the 'who' registered with him. He looked from Frank to Dansford and back, over and over. Both men had managed to get their pants back on but were now glaring at Robert waiting to see what he would do. The fact that he hadn't made so much as a sound yet told Frank that he probably didn't want anyone to know he was coming in here. Why, was the question, and could he use it to his advantage?

It didn't surprise Robert, who was almost 20 years their senior and watched the boys grow up, that they had a homosexual relationship. Most people suspected it anyway. What did surprise him was the fact that they were being so secretive about it. Why were they hiding it? It was unspoken of but generally known that the valley folks were incredibly tolerable of all choices, races, preferences, etc. Whatever choices they made were on them, if it was not causing harm to unwilling participants, that is. They were nonjudgmental people and proud of it. Even the valley gossip wasn't done teasingly or judgingly, more of a means to keep everyone informed of each other.

In his semi-drunken state, Robert started laughing, but it was 'an under your breath' whispery laugh, as not to be heard. He laughed long and hard but very quietly. Frank and Dansford finished dressing and looked at each other uneasily. Robert wiped tears from his eyes with only a few small giggles left, and then took a step toward the two young men so they would be able to hear him whisper. "Don't fret boys, ain't nuttin to be ashamed of. Love is love and lust is lust in any form. What y'all sneakin round for?" Neither of the men answered, only looked at each other again uneasily. Like two little boys that got caught playing in the mud wearing their Sunday bests.

When he realized that they weren't going to answer him, he took another couple of steps forward, closer to Dansford than to Frank. Then, he leaned forward, and for a moment, Dan feared that Robert would try to kiss him. Instead, Robert leaned a little more toward the shelf Dan had been gripping hard enough to turn his knuckles the color of cream and snatched a half empty bottle of Shine shoved inside a stack of folded blankets. Robert took a long swig from the bottle, and Frank got a brilliant idea as he watched the Shine-maker's Adam's apple bob up and down with each gulp.

Being lifelong friends, there was a short line, almost telepathic wave of nonverbal communication between Frank and Dansford from time to time. That was one of those times and Frank gave Dan a look that said, go with it but don't do it. Dan was unsure what exactly that meant but he trusted his best friend, hopefully lover, and endearing obsession. When Robert finally released the bottle from his lips, Frank immediately asked if he could have a sip as well. Robert happily obliged, thinking maybe the Shine would loosen their tongues.

The bottle went around and around the trio until the last drops were drunk, and Robert Daniels was drunker than a skunk trapped in a wine barrel. Frank and Dan, however, were seemingly unaffected by the strong spirits they had consumed. Had Robert not been as intoxicated as he was, he may have noticed that the alcohol level in the bottle did not decrease after leaving their lips, but this was after the second go around with the bottle, just to make it convincing.

Frank's plan had worked, and Robert was drunk enough to be confused about what he had seen that night, come morning. Robert woke up with his, becoming normal, hangover and could vaguely remember an odd dream involving... what was it? Sex? Frank McGrath? It didn't matter anyway, he thought, as he slowly got out of bed, rubbing his crinkled face. Half an hour later, with his face washed and semi-unwrinkled and a little food in his gut, the fogginess of his thoughts had cleared enough that he decided that he wanted to go home.

He mentioned that desire to the fisherman as they waited for the daily tasks to be handed out, just as Carol Jewell, Rebekka Lane, and Sue Ann and David Bailey walked by them. "Wouldn't that be nice?" Sue Ann asked her husband, the only one of the four that caught the passing words.

"What's that, love?" he asked in return, genuinely unsure of what she was talking about.

"Going home, of course. Wouldn't that be nice?" she repeated her question.

"Oh, yeah it sure would be." He said, realizing he had been too caught up in everything going on to be homesick. The thoughts of home brought homesickness with it, however, and wave after wave crashed into him almost buckling his knees. "Yeah, it sure would." He repeated in a softer, longing tone.

"Then, go home." Rebekka told them kindly.

"Why not?" Carol added.

Sue Ann's eyes lit up at the idea of going home and being able to sleep in her own bed snuggled up to her adoring husband. The same man she was convinced had been another victim of the sudden and vicious blizzard that struck them not all that long ago. "Can we, honey? Oh, can we please?" she pleaded, grasping his hand with both of hers, unable to keep the excitement out of her voice.

"Well, I uh... I'm not sure, dear. We will talk about." He said suddenly confused. David Bailey had never been the leader type and was never the first one to do anything. He had been and always would be an easily manipulated follower and that wasn't going to change because his wife asked him to. If anyone else left for home, then and only then, would they leave too. Period.

Having been married to the man for years and known him much longer, Sue Ann knew by his response that he would not walk out of the Infirmary before anyone else. Based on the nonchalant tone of Robert Daniels, she had little faith that he would either. She sighed heavily and walked on.

2

While Robert Daniels was debating the pros and cons of getting up for another nip before interrupting Frank and Dan, the Witch had just finished dismembering a small groundhog out of boredom. As soon as Roy left, she went back to the first and smaller of the two caves. She grabbed some Sleep Wort, pressed it, and rubbed the oil on her temples. The sleepiness it induced was quick, and she was barely able to make it to her bed in the shack. She awoke a few hours later feeling rested and refreshed, as if she had just slept for a day and night through.

All she could do was wait and the anticipation was dancing in her nerves to the beat of her own rushing heart. She knew that Satan had released Malum of its confines under the guise that she had failed, just as she had asked of her Master. She also knew, that with its vengeful heart... or lack of... the demon would be coming for her. What she didn't know was when, but she felt that it would be sooner rather than later. She believed that the demon would not be able to control its rage for very long and since it couldn't be directed at Satan, for he was far too powerful for Malum, it would happily direct it to the witch bitch that had it confined. That's exactly what she wanted too, she just had to wait for the malicious being's arrival.

Robert Daniels was well on his way to being stoned drunk with Frank McGrath and Dansford Keeton in the storage room at the Infirmary, when Malum finally came for her. It did not appear before her as the incredibly handsome man it once had nor as its true, hideous self. In fact, it didn't appear before her at all. Instead, it brought her back to her own personal Hell, the setting the same as before. Only her consciousness, though, her body remained in an uncomfortable heap on the floor of her shack.

In Hell, she struggled to her feet after landing hard on the stone floor of the large room. She got as far as her hands and knees and then got kicked hard in the ribs by a large hoof, knocking the breath from her seized lungs in a strangled, half mad squall. The force of the kick sent her flying the few feet to the wall, slamming her into it, her back taking the blunt of the impact. The wall cracked under the pressure, sending a jagged bolt halfway toward the ceiling, chips of stone and small pebbles fell from the small indent left in the rock caused by her body. Before she was able to regain her senses, she felt long, sharp claws grab her by the throat and upper right leg, but not tight enough to puncture her skin. She went flying once more, that time longer than the last, anticipating the abrupt and brutal pain the impact would cause.

To her surprise, she landed on a mound of softness, like a giant pillow. She realized with panicky fear, even though this was very much part of her revenge scheme, that she was lying on a bed. Malum's shadow stretched across her and the fear intensified. She knew but did not know, at the same time, what Malum was about to do. She tried to raise herself up with her elbows, but the vile demon struck her hard across the face with its taloned hands, leaving three long gashes that immediately began to seep blood. Her senses wavered with the blow, but she could feel Malum pulling her closer and raising her layered dress, almost ripping the lower half off, preparing to impale her.

The hiss of the snake and the need to seek her revenge is what brought her back to her senses, as much as possible for the situation anyway. She tried to prepare her body for the imminent penetration but could not, and what little preparation she had managed got wiped away when her eyes laid upon its tool. Malum was stroking it but the more it did the more barbs and thorns pushed up through the sickly skin and protruded from the phallus it intended to rape her with. Its laughter rung in her ears, mingled with the thudding of her heartbeat and created a depressing half-melody that almost drove her mad.

She could hear the hiss of the snake from behind the demon but had yet to see the abomination. She hoped it would make its appearance before Malum stuck her with the spiked, way too long, baseball bat sized member he held in his hand. It did not though, and the Witch had to endure being literally shredded by the pounding Malum inflicted upon her. Her agony-filled screams bounced around the large room and mingled with the sadistic, rage-filled laughter of Malum.

After several minutes, Malum retreated from her bloody, barely recognizable cunt, then leaned over her to lick the salty tears of pain from her ashen face. With that done and smiling down at her, without warning, it flipped her over and slid its eager, bloody cock between her butt cheeks, scratching but not slicing her. She bit down on her lower lip hard enough to puncture it with her front, top six teeth, when Malum shoved its way into the tightness and unwillingness of her rectum. Blood poured down her chin, as well as from below, as she tried desperately to retain the scream bubbling down deep in her throat. Blood splattered the wall behind the bed when the scream escaped her bloody lips despite her efforts.

3

The unconscious body lying on the floor of the shack had a surprisingly large pool of blood collected under it. The bottom half of her black dress and knee-high leather boots were soaked with the bright red blood that flowed from her nether regions like a stream. The red on black was unnoticeable, but the shiny, sticky coating it left behind wasn't. Had anyone seen the Witch in such a state, they would have, understandably, taken her for dead.

Fortunately for the Witch, she only had to endure a couple minutes of that heinous act before she could bring it to an abrupt and painful end. She felt the mutated snake slithering up her back, its forked tongue seeking a particular destination on her body. Slowly, trying to fight back the pain of the assault, she slid the dagger she had brought hidden in the long flowy sleeves of her dress, out and into her left hand.

The edge of the knife blade had been sharpened to a razor fine peak just for this occasion. The snake head was at the base of her shoulder blade and still inching forward. For a moment, the asp-like tail paused and veered a little to the left but then corrected and continued toward the right side of her neck. Time seemed almost to pause in those few moments it took for the snakehead to reach the destination she wanted it to find.

The moment had come to enact her revenge and she couldn't have executed it any better if she'd wanted to. She reached up over her shoulder with her right hand in a swift, fast motion, seizing the snake-tail at the base of its deformed head. It immediately began to writhe and wiggle in her grasp, but only for a moment, because she brought the dagger up with her left hand and sliced the head off with a single, quick flick of the wrist.

The severed head plopped onto the bed and acidic poison spewed from the headless tail. She maintained her grip on it, careful to keep the spouting pale pink liquid from getting on her. Malum screamed in outrage as he withdrew from her and she took the opportunity to roll over onto her back, bringing her legs up to her chest as she did, the headless snake-tail held carefully to the side. She kicked both legs out simultaneously, her feet connecting with the base and balls of his preferred torture device. Malum bent to grab himself, stumbling backwards, a surprised and painful expression on his hideous face. One that quickly intensified into shock mixed with fear as the demon felt itself being penetrated by something much, much larger than itself, had to carry. Malum knew of only one, Satan himself.

The Witch had to take a moment to relish the fear in her abuser's eyes before she completed her revenge. With the poison spewing tail in hand, she stood up on the bed, to be eye to eye with the vicious spirit. Satan took a step toward the bed, forcing himself deeper into Malum, who let out another agony induced scream and stepped forward with him. The Witch grabbed Malum's disgusting, chin and forced his mouth open. It was easily done given the situation Malum was in, and she shoved its tail down its throat, letting the acidic poison drain back into the diseased body that created it.

Quickly, but painfully, the Witch stepped off the bed as the thrashing demon threw itself forward, still impaled by Satan's unbelievably large member. Satan himself, enjoyed the feel of the tightness and thrashing, and soon was matching each thrash and movement with a rough one of his own.

The demon, Malum died a horrible death deserved by none better. Smoke drifted in tiny gray swirls from its abdomen as the acid ate its way through its disease-infested skin. A light pink sudsy liquid trickled out of its mouth from around the headless tail it chocked on, and dark green blood flowed from its backside as Satan continued his molestation long after Malum took its last breath and lay motionless beneath him.

The Witch watched Malum's final agony filled moments with pleasure and accomplishment. She wanted her revenge and she had gotten it. The feelings of accomplishment and the relief that she wouldn't have to look over her shoulder for the vile demon anymore, caused a bodily reaction that she never would have expected. It turned her on despite the savage brutality that her womanhood had endured at Malum's hands... or should I say cock? "Send me back, please." She told, not asked, her Master. He did without hesitation and without missing a pump. Satan was getting rougher with the deceased demon's body, his uncontrollable lust taking over his normally contained demeanor, as the Witch's consciousness drifted back into her quickly dying body.

Chapter Forty-One

Gettin' Home

1

The movie pauses and Dr. Gerard is, finally, able to reassert a small amount of control over himself. With a shaky hand he lifts his drink and downs the whole thing, leaving only the ice to settle back to the bottom of the decanter glass with a light tinkling sound. Ice? How is there ice in my glass? I've been reading for hours, how is there ice in my glass? He wonders to himself as he goes to fill it up again, needing one more before heading off to bed. A brief glance at the clock on the wall stops him in his tracks though. Only two minutes have gone by since Warren removed the letter from its envelope for the umpteenth time.

Finish it! You are running out of time!

He doesn't argue or deny the voice this time. That feeling of impending doom is growing ever stronger within him, and he now believes that what his inner voice has been saying all along is true. He needs to finish the letter. The whole mess he has found himself in has reached the point of inevitability. Warren doesn't know how, but he is certain that he WILL die very soon if he doesn't finish the letter, and there is a very high probability that he will die even if he does, his chance of survival just slightly higher. He also knows that despite everything, he is not ready to die. He will finish the letter and do his best to handle whatever may come his way after.

Leaving his decanter glass unfilled on the small table the set is kept, he returns to the sofa and picks the letter up again. Dr. Warren Gerard, once again and for the final time, un-pauses his in-mind movie, determined to see it through until the end.

As it turned out, word got around in the Infirmary and the majority of folks were more than ready to return to their homes and beds. Try as he might, Frank couldn't change their minds. He wanted to keep the group together, they were easier to herd that way. It would be much harder to keep an eye and an ear on things if they all scattered out and went home. Frank could feel his authority slipping away from him and knew that if they left, it was just a step further in losing it. He got them to agree to go out in groups to assess the damage done to their homes, so they would know how much material they needed. It was merely an attempt to keep them there a little longer, giving him more time to try and figure out a way to keep them there, but he never could. He could not in good conscious, he told them, allow them to return to unfit homes. They were free to return home after repairs had been made and Ron or Porter deemed them safe.

Ron led the group that lived in the Slums, while Porter led the group that lived in the Lot. The Bar-owning twins, Old Joe and his two female employees checked out their own places. The three farmhands headed back to see how the homesteads held up and Doreen remained in the Infirmary with those that had nowhere else to go.

The Bar was fine, sans the leaky roof in need of a new boarding, but the shacks on Hussey Row were not, including Old Joe's. It took a couple weeks but two of the original five had been rebuilt for Lacy and Sugar, Old Joe working on the other three throughout the winter. He was able to repair, rather than rebuild, his own shack, as it wasn't as badly damaged as the other smaller shacks the girls lived in. They were all able to move back into their own places by Mid-November. Allowing for time to soothe the still open wounds of so much recent loss in the valley, Old Joe waited until the beginning of December before he had the girls go back to work.

Over on the western side of the valley, Alvin Danson, David Bailey, and Betty Jones were checking the stability of the structures that remained on the farm. The one-room farmhand shacks and the chicken coop that butted up against the western branch of the river, were gone. There was a large hole in the barn roof and two of the four shacks on the northern end of the farm needed to be torn down. The other two were in fairly rough shape, but the trio thought they could salvage enough lumber from the two that needed deconstructed to fix them. It was cold and rough going for the first couple weeks, but they started staying on the farm that night. By the time Mid-November rolled around Alvin had his own place, while Danny and Betty shared the other, only meters away. With the homestead repaired the trio began discussing trying their hand at winter crops.

Porter had to inform Sue Ann and David Bailey that their shack needed repaired before they could stay in it, so they would have to remain at the Infirmary until further notice. It was like a gut punch to Sue Ann and she almost cried over it. Carol Jewell's, Roy Hoarding's, and Abigail Fariday's places were outright destroyed but could be rebuilt over some time. Carol was upset, but not homeless because Rebekka Lane had already told her she could stay with her if necessary. Abigail, who was still grieving for her missing and assumed dead husband, Ben, was devastated to learn that she had lost everything in her little shack too. Sue Ann comforted Abigail, as best she could, and offered, without consulting her husband first, to have her stay with them at their place once it was fixed. Roy was told upon their return, but he seemed indifferent about it. They thought little of it, chalking it up to his pain. Frank McGrath and Gary Brown, the merchant, got off lucky with very minimal damage to their shacks and were told they could move in immediately. Frank wouldn't go home just yet though.

In the Slums, Ron Hellman, ironically, had the only downed home. Robert Daniels', Jiminey McAvay's, and Porter Siddle's shacks sustained little damage and could be lived in immediately. While Sarah Maisse's, Rebekka Lane's, and Johanthan Colmes' shacks had to be repaired before they could return to them.

While the others were looking at their homes, Beth Redley, the only surviving follower of the Witch, much better but still on the mend, snuck off to assess the damage to her own little tent. There were no crazy expectations that her small place survived that storm, but she still needed to see what was usable, if anything. She found little among the rest of the flattened tents but used what she could and rebuilt her small tent into a sustainable, if maintained, teepee that would be more than adequate for just her. It took her little more than a week to get it built, but she did it alone and stayed at the Infirmary in the meantime, resting well at night with the sickness still fleeing her body and the calmness of knowing she would be home soon.

Everyone returned to the Infirmary but those that could packed their precious few belongings and headed for home.

2

By the middle of November, though, everyone had returned to their homes and most returned to their work. Doreen remained at the Infirmary to care for the three elderly folk, Old Man Daniels and Mr. and Mrs. Jones, and anyone sick or injured that needed tending to. The fisherman would stay at the Infirmary on the occasion he didn't stay on Hussey Row or pass out somewhere between the two. It was a wonder the man never froze or caught his death out there. Roy Hoarding had stayed at the Infirmary for about a week after the incident with Lena McAvay and then disappeared one night, never to be seen by any of the valley folk again.

The augmentation period had started the moment the Witch uttered the last word of the enchantment over Roy. It took exactly six days, six hours, and six minutes for the augmentation to complete and when it did Roy's hand was healed and restored to all previous abilities, just as promised. The way it was restored, though, brought Roy to the brink of madness, from which he could not return. His impulsive, unthoughtfully made decision sealed his fate, playing right into the arms of the Witch.

Roy had just walked into the Infirmary bathroom, six days after the widow Mrs. O'Reigan and Lena Mcavay's funeral pyre and his fateful meeting with the Witch, his hand no worse or better. Suddenly, he felt the puncture in his palm start to tingle. At first, it was an odd but not unpleasant feeling that slowly evolved into a bone-aching vibration that surged up his arm and into his shoulder and armpit.

To his absolute revulsion, he realized that the tingling was caused by the hundreds of nail-head sized baby spiders that came scurrying out from the inside of his hand. Everyone was identical to the last and looked like a tiny version of the large one that had crawled over his hand a week before. All black as night and covered in coarse thick hair, with that bright red upside down cross displayed proudly on their backs. They crawled around the edges of the puncture, burrowed into the exposed bloody muscle inside his palm, and some scuttered in loops through the hole in his hand and around either side. In a panic he started shaking his arm trying to dislodge them but not a single spider fell away. Out of desperation he slapped the palm of his hand against the wall a few times, but stopped when he realized that though it resulted in no pain, there weren't any squished baby spiders, either. He was shrieking in terror by the time it was over, having hated spiders since he was a young boy.

It lasted for six minutes, the baby spiders running this way and that, crawling over each other, almost swallowing his hand with their numbers. At the six-minute mark, the horrid spiders stopped and parted to the outer edges of his hand, displaying their work. A slowly healing puncture wound that was there minutes ago had been transformed into a densely threaded, intricately weaved zigzag of shimmery, black silk that connected the hole in his palm in every direction. The spiders quickly rushed back over the 'sewn-up' wound and began melting into large drops of blackish slime that seeped down between the threads. It took only seconds for the hundreds, if not thousands, of baby spiders to dissolve into his hand. With the last blackish drop of slime, the vibration stopped as quickly as the tingling had started, and his palm was whole again without so much as a scar or blemish. The accident had been completely erased from his body. He balled his hand up into a fist, expecting pain but finding none and was so elated he momentarily forgot the absolute horror show he had just witnessed. Roy Hoarding did the only thing that sounded like a good idea to him in that moment of relief, excitement, and madness. He went to see the Witch. Who was the only person to ever see him alive again.

3

Abigail Fariday, who would be going to see the Witch herself soon enough, moved in with Sue Ann and David Bailey once their shack was repaired, which didn't take nearly as long as expected. Carol Jewell moved in with Rebekka Lane around the same time as the Bailey's, while Ron Hellman moved in with Porter Siddle, where he had stayed during the blizzard. Except for a few, everyone was back at home and trying to regain some sort of normalcy in their lives by Mid-November.

A few days later, though, after the explosion and Abigail's mental failings, normalcy had become a bleak idea.

Chapter Forty-Two

Secrets Must Be Kept

1

The night the Witch got her revenge on the demon Malum, who by Mid November had been dead for a little more than two weeks and was still being used as Satan's personal fuck toy, she had returned to her body much closer to death than she ever wanted to be again. The Witch with all her power and confidence, had never known fear as she had upon coming back into herself and having so little life left. "Heal me, Master. Please!" she begged in a harsh whisper, her forehead pressed against the blood covered wood floor of the shack. Over and over again she cried and begged. Finally, she got a response. "You snivelling little witch whore!" the voice shouted at her with a slight pant. "You needy fuckin bitch! Who are you to ask more of me?!" The voice didn't come from the darkness, like before, that time it was only in her head.

"Please." She whispered, and it was so weak it was almost inaudible. Clearly on the verge of death.

Satan screamed his outrage... or maybe it was from a lower outburst... and then the Witch could feel the vitality surging back into her. She immediately wept tears of mixed emotion, overwhelmed by the complete fear and panic she felt but could not express. The voice didn't speak another word, but the scream continued for several moments before tapering off into a silence that left an underlying ring in her ears. She didn't have to watch it happen to know what was going on, her body was healing itself, inside and out, thanks to her Master, the Cruel Czar. When the healing was done, she was left sore and exhausted, but otherwise very well. She slowly got up off

449

the floor and into her bed, only to sleep the rest of the night, and the following day and night through. She awoke that morning ready to take on the world! But she would settle for the valley instead... for now anyway.

Roy showed up at her shack five days later, with two very able hands. The Witch was delighted about his half-delirious mindset, and when she ushered him into her shack, she knew he would never leave again. A small, still sane part of Roy knew it too, but that small part could not be heard over the much larger, not sane part of Roy Hoarding.

2

Days before the Witch's next visitor, Roy the only one she kept, Robert Daniels' distillery exploded. He had been home since the beginning of November and had been running the distillery alone, trying to keep his supply kept up. He had a stockpile of Shine in a hole under his shack floor, but since he was drinking his supply too, he was afraid he would run out. The day of the explosion, Robert had taken a dozen bottles of Shine to the Bar, which was almost double what Nonna and Nonni usually got. They didn't question the extra or the fact that he didn't expect any extra for it. The truth was, Robert had realized the night before how tired of the drinking he was already and hoped that if he kept little of it in his shack, the temptation wouldn't be as bad.

While Robert was out delivering the Shine, keeping an extra bottle in his carrying bag to trade Jiminey some Smoke for, Frank and Dansford had snuck into the back room of Robert's shack, where the distillery was. They plugged up the hoses and tightened the pressure valves, knowing that either the pressure or the flammable fumes from the backed-up ethanol would do the trick. They were in and out in minutes, no one paying any attention to them wondering around, talking to whoever was out and about.

Frank had been edgy and nervous since the night Robert walked in on him and Dan in the storage room. His panic and paranoia only increased, rather than decreased, with each passing day. Two days before the duo snuck into Robert's place, Frank decided that Robert had to die to ensure his silence.

Frank would never let anyone know his secret and would kill or die to protect it. Sarah was the exception, but hers was coming too. The shame would just be too much for him to bare, he believed, having fought a war of conflicting emotions since he was eleven years old and started going through the man-change. It was the only way, but he had to make it look like an accident. The idea for the distillery explosion came and formed quickly, allowing Frank to rest peacefully that night for the first time in weeks.

Dansford was reluctant to follow Frank on that rendezvous, but he did. Partly due to his love for and obsession with Frank, partly because of his people-pleasing personality, and partly due to fear. He knew Frank had been acting odd since the snow-in ended, but he had gotten progressively worse and was turning to violence. Frank had never been the type to unjustly harm another, and in his own way Frank was convinced that he was still being the same way he had always been. Only Dan, looking from the outside in, knew how much and for the worse Frank had changed recently. All that aside, though, Dan really didn't want the valley to find out via the mouth of a drunkard, like Robert Daniels. When, not if, but when the valley found out about Frank and Dan, Dan wanted it to come from them. However, he did not want to see the man burst into a million pieces for it.

Less than ten minutes after the men left Robert's distillery, they passed him heading back from Jiminey McAvay's place. He nodded at them as they walked by each other, Frank giving him a courteous nod in return while Dansford tried for a weary smile that just made him look as truly nervous as he felt. If Robert noticed Dan's unusual smile, he made no outward sign of it. About ten minutes after that, the whole valley was silenced by the explosion that roared and echoed its way through the mountains they lived on. Clusters of birds took flight as the rush of wind rippled the mostly-leaf and needleless trees. Several people screamed, men and women alike, and everyone clapped their hands over their ears as the intense sound vibrations threatened to burst their eardrums. Most talked louder than normal for several hours after the explosion, but no lasting damage had occurred. Not that it really mattered in the end.

The only death to occur was that of Robert Daniels, who within seconds of the explosion came running out the flame-swallowed shack, fire engulfing him from heel to hair. First his layered clothing fell from him in burning strips and by the time all the fabric had burned from his body, so had all his hair. Then his skin began to melt, adding to the trail of burning scraps, the most recent omitting a sickly crispy meat smell. Robert tried his best to make it to the river before the flames completely took him, unable to retain the screams that erupted from his charred throat. He fell face first into the thin layer of snow, unmoving, as the flames slowly tried to turn him to ash, unable to spread but only smolder and feed on the limited fuel it had.

Some of the valley folks watched it unfold before their eyes, shocked into paralysis and unable to react or help the dying man before them. Even if they had reacted properly, done everything right down to the very last second, the end result would have been the same. Robert Daniels was a dead man the moment he opened the storage room door at the Infirmary that night two weeks ago. No one, especially not Robert, knew it then, though.

A few people's paralysis finally broke, and they sprang into action, grabbing buckets and running back and forth to the river, while others grabbed handfuls of snow to toss on the burning man, until the flames were out. The heat still coming off the body was immense, and the smell was nauseating to say the least. Most folks had already put a fair distance between themselves and the vile, odorous body. As terrible as it was, Robert's still smoking corpse was left where it lay to cool off before being retrieved, no one able to withstand the smell long enough to keep a proper watch over it.

Ron Hellman and Porter Siddle had heard the explosion and the screams that followed it. With heavy hearts, they had already started gathering the materials to start building funeral pyres when they were informed that, to their surprise, there was only one death. A few hours later, David Bailey and Gary Brown, the merchant, went out to retrieve Robert's body only to find that it had been dragged off up the mountainside. The idented wide path in the snow, streaked with black and gray, was a clear indication of that fact. There were numerous paw prints surrounding where the body was, leading up the mountainside and out of sight. At first glance the prints were undoubtedly canine but looked too big to be timber wolves. One never knew in the mountains, though. The men took all this in, in a matter of moments, and then rushed back to the common area where funeral preparations were being made for a pyre that was no longer required.

3

From her shack in the northeastern corner of the valley, the Witch didn't even so much as start at the thunderous sound of the explosion, but Roy did, though. The Witch had been laying, propped up on her bed, as Roy sat at the foot of the bed by her feet. He was using his strong hands to massage the sole of her right foot, moving his thumbs in a circular motion that he knew she enjoyed. All the while his eyes were locked on her bare breasts, and his mouth was greedily sucking on the two smallest toes of the same foot he was rubbing. When the explosion occurred, rattling the shack on its stone foundation, Roy jumped, clamping his teeth together around the base of her toes. The chomp was quick and painful but did not draw blood, it just left a very well-made impression of his teeth on her skin.

The Witch shrieked in surprise and pain, jerked her foot out of his mouth, and drew her knee up to her exposed chest. When she kicked her leg out as forcefully as she could, the heel of her foot smacked him in the nose hard enough to send him flying off the bed and on to the floor. His shattered nose poured blood down his mouth and chin, his eyes immediately swelling with large tears. The Witch jumped off the bed, "You incompetent, stupid fucking fool! How dare you..." she ranted and raved at him.

Roy, being her lovestruck pet, endured her ravings, pleading for forgiveness and agreeing to every insult she hurled at him. Until... she insulted his mother. That was unacceptable and inexcusable, and Roy reacted without thought, immediately regretting his actions. He was standing before her and as those words came blurting from her lips, he brought his arm back and slapped her hard across the face.

Silencing her and busting her lower lip as it collided with one of her perfectly straight teeth.

He knew he fucked up by the way she looked at him and smiled, a few drops of blood spreading over her just-off white teeth, making her appear that much more vicious. The fear in his eyes was evident and she enjoyed seeing it, but she enjoyed seeing pain mingled with it even more. So, with a flick of her finger, the same hand he used to strike her with, shot out to his side, Roy having no control over it. Suddenly, his shoulder popped up and out of its socket and his elbow bent inwards, in the opposite direction it should. Roy tried to scream his pain out but could not, the Witch had seized his vocal cords, as well. His elbow was followed by his wrist that bent at an unnatural angle, and then one by one his fingers began to deform. They bent at every joint in a way they shouldn't be able to, and it was, by far, the most agony Roy had ever experienced. It made him wish for the pain from his punctured hand again, because even that pain was pie compared to what she was doing to him.

That malicious smile of hers never wavered. She stepped closer to Roy until she was eye to eye with him. Hers clearly evil and his tear-and-pain-filled. When she spoke, it was in a pleasant whisper that the words did not correspond with. "If you ever raise your hand to me again... I will rip your arm off and fuck you to death with it." Their eyes remained locked for a few moments before she asked just as sweetly, "Have I made myself clear?" Roy was trying to vigorously nod his head but only succeeded in a barely perceptible one. She released her enchantment, the pain instantly dissipated, and his arm returned to its former completely usable state.

Roy was fascinated by this and when he widened his eyes in surprise, the pain from his nose shot daggers through his face in all directions causing more tears to form. "Oh, come now..." the Witch soothed him, reverting to her usually cheery mood of late. "...let's go get that nose of yours all fixed up." Roy didn't respond but allowed himself to be led into the caves.

Chapter Forty-Three

Heartaches and Heartbeats

1

Abigail and Sue Ann were heading off into the timbers to try to see if they could find anything to gather. Abigail told Sue Ann she was going to wander off a little way, because she needed some time alone. Sue Ann, worried about her friend, was reluctant but agreed if Abigail agreed not to go off too far. Abigail agreed but with no intention of standing by her word. She needed to see the Witch and she would get there if she had to knock Sue Ann on her ass to do it. It didn't come to that, though, and Abigail took off toward the east while Sue Ann continued north.

About a week after Roy showed up at the Witch's shack and two days after the explosion, Abigail Fariday made her way toward the Witch's shack rather than the timbers and came knocking on the Witch's door. Abigail didn't know or care if anyone seen her and made no effort to conceal herself. She desperately wanted her husband back and would do anything to have him. As much as she appreciated Sue Ann and David allowing her to stay with them, she hated seeing the two of them together because it made her yearn for her Ben that much more. She had even started fantasizing about killing one or both of them just to ease her own suffering, and that was when she knew she needed help.

The Witch sensed someone coming and sent Roy, his face giving no indication that it had been brutalized only two days before, out into the garden. Roy was her toy, and she didn't want to share him with anyone else, not even his company in cordiality. She answered the knock and ushered the mourning woman into her shack. As soon as the Witch noted Abigail's desperation, she knew that she would have another soul, but needed to do the tarot reading as a deciding factor. She was completely convinced, though, when The Devil card had been drawn for her second and 'What is' placement of the tarot card cross, just as with Frank and Roy.

Abigail observed each of the seven beautifully depicted, yet bizarre cards drawn for her reading, but asked very few questions and was as compliant as the Witch's new pet. When the reading was completed and explained, the Witch gathered up a small bundle of incense including Acacia, Sweet Sedge Root, Juniper, and Henna. Then, she rummaged through the amulet drawer until she found a moldavite, a crystal resembling a jagged chunk of colored glass. It was the color of swamp water and could easily get lost on a bed of moss. She tied a bit of hemp rope around the crystal, then took it and the small bundle of incense back into the altar room. The Witch flipped a few pages in the Opera Magicae, found what she was looking for and then turned her attention back to Abigail, who was sitting there waiting patiently for instructions. She placed the amulet around Abigail's neck and told her that she mustn't take it off, for if she did her husband would die. It was the price of help; Abigail was told, and she swore she'd never take it off. The Witch stood in front of the sitting Abigail and lit the incense bundle, waving the smoke above their heads as her eyes took on that eerie black glow. Abigail did not see the Witch's eyes and couldn't make out the words that tumbled from her mouth, either. Then, after only a few seconds, the Witch stepped back with a sweet smile, and set the smoking bundle in a bowl on the disgusting altar.

"Your husband awaits you outside." The Witch informed Abigail with a smile that didn't soften the maliciousness in her eyes.

"That's it?" Abigail asked with disbelief, but the Witch only looked at her without responding. So, she got up and the Witch escorted her through the shack and out the front door.

Abigail had only made it a few steps past the rock wall separating the garden from the valley, the amulet laying against her bare chest under her shirt, when she spotted her beloved husband, Ben. He stood there in the softly falling snow, looking as healthy as the last time she'd seen him. She didn't dare question the how or what happened, because she really didn't care, she had her husband back and she was mad with elation about it. She rushed to him, wrapped her arms around him and his arms wrapped around her. She could feel the warmth of his body and smell his manly musk that she had missed so much. Standing there she wept with joy against his chest.

From several yards away but with a perfect sightline, Beth Redley watched Abigail Fariday from the slightly parted entrance of her teepee. Beth watched Abigail enter and exit the Witch's shack with a smile and knew from the looks of Abigail that whatever enchantment the Witch used, it was strong and working well. Beth had watched Abigial walk past the rock wall and then stop as if startled. Then her face twisted in emotion, and she took off running only to stop again a few yards away, with her arms stretched out before her and slightly bent as if trying to wrap her arms around a tree that was not there. She kept her head in one place, crying and sobbing, remaining that way for a few minutes before finally dropping her arms and moving her head. Abigail had taken a step back, then raised one arm that was slightly bent and walked off, as if she were walking with someone that Beth could not see with her arm around their waist. 'What the fuck did you do?' was all Beth could think watching this strange woman interact with the air in such a way.

2

As Abigail and her 'husband' wandered about the valley, Sarah Maisse was stalking the timbers for more signs of whatever type of canines took Robert's body. She had no unrealistic ideation that she would find Robert, the survivors were all aware that he was resting in the guts or shit piles of whatever starved creatures took him. She was, however, on a hunting mission to exterminate them. If they were stealing the bodies of the dead, and so brazenly, they were a problem that would only get worse. So, being the only hunter left in the valley... no one had any idea where Roy went or what happened to him, so he was added to the list of missing... Sarah had been tasked with hunting down and killing whatever canine pack was terrorizing the valley.

It was her second day out and she had found plenty of tracks, too many really. There were so many that it was almost impossible to tell how many she was dealing with, what they were, and which direction they were denned in. The day before, she found blood-stained snow with paw prints around it that ran in all directions, but no corpse and no canines. She did, however, come across a couple rabbits and brought them back to add to the valley's quickly diminishing food supply. The fur went to Rebekka for material, and Old Joe Brenner and the fisherman split the rabbit bones between them, making a meal of the spongy marrow within.

She had no such luck the second day, in fact, her luck seemed to have turned sour overnight. Sarah was moving slowly, decked out in her winter camo, the mostly white and brown coloring allowing her to blend in almost seamlessly with the timbers she was roaming. She had heard nothing for several minutes and it was causing a disquieting nervousness in her that she was not used to experiencing, especially out in the woods where she felt the safest and at her most capable. She had her bow at the ready, just had to aim and shoot, already proving she was quite the shot. There was the snap of a branch to her left, immediately followed by one on her right, then one from behind. She knew instantly what was going on, just not what was doing it. She was being circled by a pack of creatures; the trees too densely packed to see anything more than quickly moving blurred shapes. She watched their movements, noting that they were growing closer with every few loops they made. They moved constantly to avoid becoming sitting targets and Sarah knew that these animals were far from stupid.

She raised the bow and centered her aim on a place in the distance between a couple of trees less than a yard away from each other. One blur went whizzing by the place at her aim, then another and that's when she released the arrow. It went flying between the trees and then pierced the chest of the third blur, popping its lungs like overfilled balloons. It was allotted a single short, high-pitched yip and then it dropped mid-stride, crashing to the ground and sliding in the few-inches thick snow. The creature came to a stop several yards from where it was shot, but Sarah made no move to go investigate her kill.

She already had another arrow strung and at the ready when the animal yipped unsure of what the rest of the pack's reaction would be. It didn't take long for her to find out though. A moment later there was a howl that caused her heartbeat to triple, not far from where Sarah stood, followed by another, and then another, until the timbers seemed to vibrate with the sound. The intense howling disguised the sound of the pack rushing at her. She was able to drop one of the five dogs that surrounded her before another one clamped onto her leg, causing her to fall on her butt in the snow, still gripping her bow. Sarah kicked the dog in the face as hard as she could with her free foot and the dog released her in its pain and surprise. She immediately drew her bow and shot an arrow through its eye socket, dropping it at her feet. Before she could get another arrow strung, another snarling dog latched onto her arm, the one holding the bow. Sarah shrieked, the noise carrying away into the timbers. The fourth dog snapped at the hand holding the arrow, while the fifth stood at a safe distance, barking and growling. She slashed the arrow through the air in the snapping dog's direction, causing it to back up a few steps allowing her the precious few moments she needed to jam the arrowhead deep into the dog's throat, the one gnawing on her arm.

Realizing that it didn't go the way it was supposed to, the two remaining dogs had enough sense to leave the human be. They were reluctant to pull away from that force nagging at them to destroy the evil before it could be, but their instincts told them they would be of no use to that cause dead. So, the dogs left, tail between their legs and ears back, in a look of shame. Those that were left would regroup, eat, and maybe try again.

Sarah watched the dogs hightail it northwest, toward the silver mine on Mining Road #2 but did not pursue. Instead, she got up off the ground slowly, trying to will the shock away so she could assess her bodily damage. She noticed the two dead dogs were from the Lot and was curious about how she had just been treated by them, since they were usually all friendly by nature and particularly comfortable with the hunters. She had taken most of the dogs out hunting with her at least once. She just couldn't understand it.

Then she seen the blood drops on the snow beside her foot and knew she needed to get back to the valley. Almost two hours later Sarah came limping off the mountainside behind the Church, weak, dehydrated, and stumbling. Sister Virtue watched the pale woman stagger toward the common area from the confines of the Church. Father Robin had been resting and preparing for the evening sermon, or she would have been nowhere near the window to see Sarah. If only she could have gone out to help that poor soul, but the Sister knew she couldn't because that would be a sin. Father Robin said so and whatever Father Robin says, goes.

Luckily for Sarah, Carol Jewell and David Bailey had been coming back from the Schoolhouse, out searching for extra stowed away material. Each were carrying a small armload of various thread spools and fabrics that hit the ground the moment they noted Sarah's appearance. She was pale, barely on her feet, and the whole bottom right leg, mid-calf down, on her camo pants were stained a bright red color and leaving a blood-drop path behind her. As they rushed to her, they noticed that her arm was also bleeding, but likely not as bad at her leg based on the amount of blood on the camo. David didn't give Carol a chance to help Sarah keep her balance, he swooped her up and into his arms as easily as if he had lifted a small child. He told Carol to go on ahead and have Doreen prepare for a bloody wound of some kind and the cold sickness. She rushed off without question.

As chaotic as it was when Sarah was being brought in, examined, and treated, the valley folk were still mindful of the obvious situation between Sarah and Frank. When Sarah was brought in, Frank was obviously distressed but instead of trying to be by her side the entire time, he walked out the back door of the Infirmary and stayed gone. Dansford didn't follow him, but after everyone knew Sarah was going to be okay, he left when a lot of the other folks did. It also became obvious, since Johnathan Colmes had the reaction that everyone expected Frank to, Johnathan was the one that had come between them. Of course, they never suspected that it would or could have been Dansford that got in the way.

At that time, Frank was still a very well-respected man of authority in the valley. He could feel it slipping from between his fingers, but the valley folks couldn't yet. Because of this there were some folks that soured to Sarah Maisse and Johnathan Colmes. Not enough to wish her dead, of course, but enough to feel as if she deserved what she got up in the timbers.

As it turned out the bite on Sarah's arm was a shallow one, just breaking the surface of the skin in a couple places enough for it to bleed, soaking into her sleeve. The one on her leg, however, needed more than a little cleaning and bandaging. The dog had caught its teeth around her leg under her thick camo trousers, but still biting into two other much thinner layers of clothing and then her skin. It was a hard bite that required stitches in multiple places around the back of her calf. Only inches lower and the dog would have bitten through her Achilles tendon, rendering her foot useless. Doreen cleaned the wound as best she could both before and after stitching each tooth mark closed. It took almost an hour to get them all and Sarah had passed out, regained consciousness, and then passed out again due to the pain, during that time. She was still unconscious when Doreen finally finished cleaning the wound for the last time, so they left her alone to rest.

3

The following day, Sarah woke with a sore leg and arm, which was to be expected, and queasy, which wasn't. Doreen checked all her vitals, noting that her heart rate was still up, which she would have assumed was due to the pain, but her blood pressure didn't indicate the same. Sarah's temperature, although not high enough to register a fever nor did she look or feel feverish, was still higher than normal. Doreen had her suspicions but wasn't about to announce them in front of a group of people in the Infirmary, so she helped Sarah hobble her way into one of the exam rooms. In there she took out 'the cone' and, instead of putting it to her chest or back, she had Sarah lay back and placed 'the cone' on her lower abdomen. She listened intently for several long seconds, broken thoughts swirling through Sarah's mind like a cyclone while she waited for Doreen to say something... anything.

Finally, Doreen exclaimed, "There it is! I thought so." and raised up from 'the cone', looking at Sarah with a sense of reserved pride.

"There's what?!" Sarah asked in a panicky tone. "What are you talking about?!" she asked with tears in her eyes, having no idea what the Apothecary aide was about to tell her. "Please, tell me!"

"Calm down, child." Doreen soothed and tittered a little, taking one of Sarah's thinner hands into her plumper ones. "That's all it is, really, it's just a child." Sarah stared at her dumbly as if not comprehending the words that came from Doreen's mouth. "You gonna be a momma, honey." She told Sarah with a genuine smile.

Sarah was speechless. Frozen. Unthinking. Doreen either failed to notice or did not care and persisted with information. "By the sound and strength of the heartbeat I would say you're about eight to ten weeks in."

Those words brought Sarah back to reality with a hard slap. "That's impossible. I can't be eight weeks in. I mean I've had relations recently, but it has only been within the last three weeks not three months. Before that, well let's just say that I would have a walking tot by now. So, how could I be eight weeks in if I could have only conceived at the earliest, three weeks ago??" Sarah was almost hysterical explaining this to Doreen, but she could not help, given the circumstances, how she reacted to her uncontrollable emotions. She tried but would often fail.

Doreen looked at Sarah for a long time not responding, as if she were trying to read Sarah's mind. Finally, with a minute shake of her head, she told Sarah that she was upset and therefore was probably mistaken about the timing. It happened quite often with new mothers finding out so unexpectedly. Sarah tried to argue that she was not mistaken but Doreen only shushed her and soothed her. She was so convincing that Sarah, actually, started to believe that she was wrong about the timing and that much more time had gone by than she realized. The logical part of her knew that

Doreen was wrong, the timing was wrong, and the pregnancy was wrong, but the emotional, irrational part of her believed that she had to be mistaken and that Doreen was right.

Sarah, after enduring several minutes of Doreen's soothing, cooing tone, fell into a mild state of shock at the news she had just received. She allowed herself to be led back out into the main lobby of the Infirmary, where Doreen briefly considered having her smoke a bit to calm her nerves. Ultimately, she decided against that and just gave Sarah some herbal tea to help her rest for a bit. She took it willingly enough and then laid in her bed, crying silently until she dozed off for a late morning nap.

4

Speaking of Smoke, Jiminey and Patty McAvay were able to return home in the beginning of November and Jiminey, immediately, started pouring his grief into tending his crops. And smoking it, of course. His wife helped him tend to the plants, ensuring that trade was done strictly for food and always keeping enough for themselves. Not that they would run low anytime soon between the beginning-to-bud crops and their stash, they had enough Smoke to last them months or longer. Trading strictly for food worked well for them in the beginning before the rationed food supply ran dry at the end of November. They were able to keep themselves fed through the winter with what they had been able to accumulate, though.

The merchant, Gary Brown, and his wife were able to return home at the same time as Jiminey and Patty. Gary immediately returned to work the next day with his wife tagging along at his heels. She was an unusually paranoid woman that mostly kept to herself. She was known to be uppity, odd, and a little crazy around the valley, but Gary loved her dearly. She was hysterical when the storm began and her husband wasn't home with her, and because of that she refused to let him leave her sight for longer than a few minutes at a time. Gary didn't particularly like that she was the way she was, but he accepted her, held his patience in check, and appeased her. It turned out that she was quite the help to him in the mercantile, cleaning and sorting items that hadn't been touched in ages.

The end of November was also the end of the valley's food supply, and as the cherry on top so to speak, the first noticeable, yet unnoticed, drop in the water level of the river. The beginning of December brought a fend-for-yourself attitude, that came with fights and unfair trading. Due to Sarah's condition, who was showing with a small baby bump come the beginning of December, she was not able to hunt anymore and since Roy was still missing, there were no hunters out in the timbers trying to feed the valley folk. Sue Ann Bailey was the only gatherer left in the valley come December, but she could barely find enough to feed her and her husband. There was no way she alone could gather enough of anything in the timbers to feed the 30+ surviving valley folk, so she, understandably, didn't even try.

Chapter Forty-Four

Seeking Lost Men

1

Abigail Fariday walked with her 'husband' back to Sue Ann and David's shack, where they would be staying until Ron and Porter could get theirs rebuilt. Since her 'husband' was back, she wanted to be in her own home with him. Sue Ann was still out gathering and not due back until almost dark and David was working, due home around the same time. Abigail and her 'husband' had some time to themselves and were alone, so she decided that they were going to make the best of it. On Sue Ann and David's bed, without a care in the world, Abigail and her 'husband' made love as if they were young again. She could feel him throbbing within her; the veins pulsating as he spilled his seed within her at the same moment that she let out a wail that expressed her climaxing ecstasy.

Had anyone been around to see such doings, they would have found it both unnerving and quite comical. They would have witnessed a naked, sweaty woman thrashing around the bed, switching positions every so often for about half an hour. Abigail was panting and moaning, grabbing and clawing at the air as if embracing someone. Her mouth would pucker and contort, open and close, her tongue darted in and out of her mouth as if she were in the deep throes of love making. Her arms bent and touching, were raised above her head, as if wrapped around something. Abigail's intense solo act ended with a screech that matched the pleasure that coursed through her. It was a strange scene and luckily, no one had to endure seeing it. Except me, of course, and all because of that goddamn Witch.

Anyway, David arrived home before Sue Ann later that evening and was quite confused when Abigail became so upset with him for not acknowledging her 'husband'. He had come back to her, she told David, the least he could do was welcome him. David didn't know what she was talking about, there was no one in the shack except for the two of them. He did not want to think that she was losing her mind, she was a friend of his and a good friend to his wife, so he hated thinking such unkind thoughts about a grieving wife with a missing husband. Her actions, though, made it difficult to keep those thoughts at bay. He made a point to be outside and waiting when Sue Ann arrived home so he could let her know about Abigail's mental state before she got blindsided by it, like he did.

Sue Ann and David talked about it and decided to play along with her 'husband' charade until they could go talk to Doreen the next day. They weren't sure if Doreen could help them, but she was their only option, other than the Witch and rumor was that she was ill and not seeing anyone. This, of course, was not true but it kept the traffic down to a minimum allowing her dirty little secrets to remain that way.

Doreen had no idea how to handle such a situation, but she told them that as long as Abigail wasn't hurting herself or others then she didn't see the harm in it. David and Sue Ann were not completely convinced that that was the right way to handle the situation, but Doreen did have a point. They decided to keep going along with it the best they could, and it drug out that way for a couple weeks. At the beginning of December, however, Sue Ann heard Abigail and her 'husband' arguing outside one brisk morning, by which it was just Abigail crying and yelling at someone only she could see. Then, Sue Ann heard Abigail shout, "Wait! Where are you goin? You can't just walk away from me like that!" She took off trudging through the several inch thick snow, toward the eastern bridge connecting the Slums to the Lot where the Bailey's shack was. Abigail shouted with every step but kept walking, following someone only she could see.

466

That was the last time Sue Ann would ever see her friend again, and though she would mourn her, she believed that death was a mercy for Abigail compared to the mind-bent life she was destined to live in her grief.

Abigail Fariday followed her 'husband' through the Lot, across the bridge, and through the eastern end of the Slums to the Witch's shack. Abigail was so winded from the energy exerting snow walk that she barely noticed where they were when her 'husband' finally stopped. She sat upon a knee-high flat-rock wall beside her 'husband' and tried to catch her breath. She put her head down, took a few deep breaths, and when she raised her head back up her 'husband' was gone. The foliage of the dense trees and plants on the other side of the wall were waving as if someone had just passed through them. She cursed her 'husband' under her breath, still panting but not as badly, swung her legs around to the other side of the wall and took off in the same direction the leaves swayed.

She didn't know it, but she was walking through the Witch's garden.

2

For three days, she stumbled about the jungle-like terrain avoiding the strange creatures that lurked and watched the timid human from a distance. She didn't know it, but when she entered the snowless foliage of the garden, a branch snagged the hemp twine on the back of her neck, breaking it. The amulet fell from inside her shirt the first time she stumbled, just steps past the rock wall. She quickly lost her 'husband' and called for him relentlessly but to no avail and would hide and watch at any sight, sound, or smell she did not like. She would sip from the streams of fresh, naturally enriched water, but dared not eat anything for fear of poisoning. On the third day, the hunger pains bordering excruciating, she was reconsidering it, contemplating what would be worse: death by starvation or death by poisoning? Had she known what beheld her immediate future, though, she may have happily opted for either one.

Abigail wandered into a small clearing that was scattered with peculiar circles made of stones, mushrooms, or flowers, all with varying colors. Tiny creatures floated and darted about them, not many, though and too far away to tell. She didn't know that they were fairy rings, but she found them beautiful and fascinating. As much as her deprived body and mind would allow, anyway and she took off walking again, through the clearing. She drew very close to, trying to identify the small insect that was buzzing around the tops of some neon-colored mushrooms aligned in an almost-perfect circle, when she stumbled from weakness. She did not fall, but she took a step forward to keep her balance, and her foot landed on two of the toadstools comprising the fairy ring, and the insect was nowhere to be seen. Abigail quickly moved her foot and immediately seen the small dark splatter behind the tiny, crushed body that laid upon the squashed neon orange mushroom.

She felt a pang of grief, through her exhausted delirium, for the tiny thing but couldn't tell what it was in its mangled condition. She decided not to get too close to the others as to not do it again, but she was never given that chance. As she took a step back, she felt something slam into her ear causing her to violently shake her head and claw at her hair and the side of her face for a moment. She stopped when she felt it crawling through her ear canal, but before she could react to that bizarre sensation, another one slammed into her face and scurried up her nose before she could knock it away. It was followed by a third that flew into her gaped mouth. Another landed high up on her cheek and she knocked it aside, but only as far as the other side of her face. It darted for her eye, shoved her eyeball to the side and slithered in behind it via the corner. This went on dozens of times, each one scurrying its way into one orifice or another. Luckily for her she was wearing trousers rather than a dress that day she left Sue Ann's, or they would have had a few other entrances as well.

Abigail could feel the violating effects of the fairies' intrusion on her body, and she died an agonizing death because of it. She would have screamed, but her vocal cords were the first to go. Every organ in her body, large and small, was stabbed and sliced, had chunks ripped from them and large gashes left to gush blood. Her ligaments and tendons were severed causing her limbs to become drawn in places and useless in other's. The fairies chiseled and chipped away at her bones, leaving them brittle and frail. She had been paralyzed soon after her voice was taken, and she crumpled to the ground in the clearing in an unnatural heap, most of her bones snapping upon impact. Finally, her brainstem was sliced and cut up, but not completely disconnected, and all her veins had been gashed open for maximum bloodletting. Abigail Fariday died a miserable death as blood gushed from her eyeless sockets, disabled ears, ruined nose, as well as other places that wearing trousers had done nothing to prevent.

The whole ordeal lasted less than 15 seconds but to Abigail, the agony made it feel like 15 lifetimes. With their revenge taken, the fairies no longer wished to look at the disgusting being that killed one of their own. So, they sent out a small group to bring back a few of the satyrs. They were a vicious breed of equal parts humanoid and goat, but there was a mutual respect among them and the fairies. This meal offering would only strength that. The satyrs arrived soon after and dragged the body away, grateful for the meal. Later that night, the moonless-midnight-colored unicorn came strutting into the small fairy ring clearing and lapped at the congealing blood that painted the soft grass. It was gracefully mindful of the fairy rings and glided by each one without disturbing a thing as the unicorn strolled through the clearing and into the trees beyond.

The fairies watched the massive unicorn stride out of the clearing from the safety of the trees around it. They both marveled and loathed the unicorn for its elegance, grace, and power. For there was only one other being, aside from their life source, the Witch, that even the majestic unicorn feared... but that creature could be only legend among the fairy folk, too.

3

Abigail Fariday's disappearance was only the beginning of the loses December claimed that winter decades ago. It was not the bloodiest month the valley endured during the Witch's winter, but it was probably the most mentally exhausting.

December was the work that put the calluses on the hands of the valley to toughen them up for the rest of the winter job.

It was only days later that Beth Redley disappeared, but before that she had become more and more distraught over the whereabouts of her brother, knowing that the longer time went on the less likely they would be to find him at all. She prayed that he was still alive, but her hopes were slashed more with every passing hour. One evening in the beginning of December, she decided on impulse to walk over and see if the Witch would help her find her brother. If anyone could, at the very least, point her in the right direction, it would be the Witch.

As Beth stepped out of her teepee, the Witch was preparing to sexually abuse her boy-toy, Roy and it irritated her that someone was interrupting her just as she had finally slid into her skin-tight leather bodice. "You stay where you are." She told Roy sternly as she spun her long, flowing hooded cape around her. She let it rest on her shoulders and then cinched it at the waist, where it accentuated her breasts and hips the most, causing Roy to shiver with excitement. She had already walked out of the altar room when the irony of what she had just said sank in. Roy, who was chained to the altar by his wrists and ankles, couldn't have left if he'd wanted to. He could move his hands and feet and the chains weren't tight enough to cut into him, but he was still held in place. He had never 'played' like that before and highly anticipated it, almost finishing before she even returned from dealing with Beth Redley several minutes later.

Beth had been a long-time follower of the Witch, running away from home and to the Witch's doorstep at just 15 years old. Because of this, there was no need for a tarot reading because the Witch already knew that she would own Beth's soul. So, the two women sat and spoke for a few minutes and then the Witch told Beth that she would return momentarily, and she did. She was carrying a Blue Kyanite amulet hanging from some hemp twine. Beth's eyes sparkled with curiosity and hopefulness at the sight of the layered stone. It had several shades of deep blue, that intermingled with layers of gold, bronze, and a light coppery color. It had all the colors of a cloudless sky just as the sun begins to set over the ocean.

The Witch placed the amulet around Beth's neck, but before she tied the ends of the twine together, the Witch's eyes widened and then started emitting that eerie black glow. Beth could hear the Witch mumbling something and what few words she was able to pick up made no sense to her.

Repentance for her admonish or,

content hearts her until give.

True is that way the her show,

blue of stone ancient this with.

Beth Redley had this overwhelming yet very brief bout of dread wash over her. It only lasted a few moments and then was over, but she had felt her fate being sealed in that moment, she was just unaware that that's what it was. The Witch ceased her mumbling and even though Beth didn't see them, the Witch's eyes returned to normal. The knot was tied, and the beautifully hued amulet hung from Beth's neck like a charm. "This stone will lead you to your brother. It will illuminate your path but be weary that it doesn't enrapt you along the way." The Witch cautioned Beth, who was paying little attention to the Witch's words as she observed the guiding light laying upon her chest.

Beth left soon after following the light radiating from the amulet. The Witch, making sure that Beth was gone, returned to Roy in the altar room of the cave where she began their abusive romp session. By the time it was over, Roy did not wish to participate in such violent activities again. It went on for hours and at one point the Witch sent Vipera, the girthy python, exploring Roy's bowels while she rode his enchanted cock. He had grown sorer and sorer with every thrust and had been throbbingly hard for hours. It was all just too much for him, but he would only have to do it again, once more.

Beth followed the lit amulet that took her across the eastern bridge and into the Lot. She walked along the rows of shacks, some still standing and some in pieces on the ground yet to be sorted, paying little attention to anything except the light before her, it already threading its way into her thoughts. She passed the train station and then the railroad tracks, continuing through the dense, tall trees that created an eerier canopy of darkness at night. Beth paid no attention to the dark or anything that may be lurking in it. She just

471

kept following the light, adjusting her direction by a few steps whenever she though the light was dimming out.

The grieving woman looking for her lost brother, the first victim of the snowstorm that set upon the valley, was so entranced by the illuminated amulet that she didn't realize she had exited the small forest separating the valley from the waterfall. She didn't realize how deafening the sound of the waterfall was that close to it, and she didn't realize she was living her final moments.

Four steps from the edge of the plummeting mountainside. The light grew brighter.

Three steps from the edge. The light brightened even more. Beth squinted her eyes.

Two steps. The light was blinding. She raised her hand to shield against it.

One more step. Beth tried frantically to see around the light but still did not stop.

Beth Redley fell from the cliff, realizing in midair that her beloved Witch had betrayed her. The words "But why?" slipped from her lips in a hushed whisper just before her body disintegrated with a SPLAT! on the rocky surface of the pool edge below. Blood, bones, brain, and flesh splattered the surrounding landscape and water. Steam rose from the point of impact where a large portion of her flattened torso remained. Small carnivores would find bits of her to munch on for weeks to come. She landed several yards from her brother, who had met his demise at the hands of an icy bridge and rushing river. She was unaware of it in death, but the Witch had fulfilled her promise and Beth had been reunited with her lost brother.

Chapter Forty-Five

David, My Love

1

During the first ten or so days of December, a lot of minor occurrences happened that set the rest of the season on its destined path. The path of revenge the Witch swore to take on the valley and her 'beau'. The same beau that impregnated another woman but hasn't been to see his 'belle' since the blizzard. Of course, she knew what was going on, but Johnathan's blatant disregard for her and her feelings enraged her all the more. She held on to that rage the same way Frank held onto his rage toward Sarah. The Witch had promised him that Sarah would be his and he fantasized daily of numerous ways to torture, abuse, and kill her.

While Frank became more obsessed with his revenge on Sarah, knowing that her death would destroy Johnathan Colmes, Dansford was trying to come to terms with his overwhelming guilt over the death of Robert Daniels. He didn't think it would bother him as much as it did and he desperately needed to talk to someone, anyone about it. The only person he could talk to was Frank, but every time Dan tried to mention it, Frank would become angry and shush him. The anxiety was tearing at Dansford's sanity, and he didn't know for how much longer he would be able to keep their secrets.

A few days after Abigail's disappearance Carol Jewell, with her own much milder obsession, made her move on David Bailey. She used her grief over her mother and the other recent losses as leverage to draw the man in and it worked as he attempted to comfort a mourning friend. Rebekka was nowhere in sight and David was genuinely surprised when Carol grabbed the crotch of his pants and planted a sensual kiss on his lips. This was unusual behavior for Carol because she had never really been attracted to anyone, male or female, sexually or otherwise, and the thought of having a partner never really appealed to her. Until seeing how David looked at Sue Ann the day all the survivors met up at the Infirmary and she wanted someone to look at her that way. No, that's wrong. She wanted David to look at her that way, and therefore made it her mission to have him. She did not consider that he might reject her, she did not take Sue Ann's feelings into account, nor did she debate any consequences her actions might bring on. She wanted him and she would have him.

David was unsure of how to react, having been with Sue Ann for years he hadn't had to fumble his way around such a situation in almost a decade. His memory came back quick though, and he soon realized that he not only enjoyed but missed the feelings that Carol's touch was inducing. Feelings that Sue Ann's touch hadn't been able to induce in ages. His biggest mistake in that moment was confusing his wife's loving, caressing touch of comfortability with lack of passion and love. And so, the affair began.

David and Sue Ann just got a feel for each other's bodies, over the clothes, of course, during their first make-out session, under the clothes during the second, and all out naked and at it by the third. A tear fell from the corner of Carol's eye as her virgin blood spotted the wooden planked floor she lied upon, and then shrieked in ecstasy during her first ever mind-numbing orgasm beneath David Bailey. Then, just like that, she was addicted to him.

During all their secret meetings, and there were a lot of them in the short time it went on, sometimes as many as four or five times a day, Sue Ann was out trudging around in the thickening snow and much colder temperatures trying to forage anything that her and her husband could consume. She had spoken briefly with Sarah on a few occasions, who explained to her how to set snare traps to catch small game like chipmunks and rabbits. She was trying as hard as she could, doing everything she knew how and still went home most nights with barely enough for one. It was discouraging but she kept going for her husband, David. Had she not been so busy and exhausted much of the time, maybe she would have caught on to the affair, but in the end, it was probably better that she never did.

2

Alvin Danson, Danny Bailey, and Betty Jones were trying their hand at growing their food. They planted cabbage, mustard greens, turnips, parsnips, radishes, and a few others. None of them had ever done the planting but they had plowed and knew to start there. The plowing was hard to do with the ground half-frozen in the middle of November, but they managed, and then they just popped a few seeds into finger dug holes, like they had seen Old Mr. O'Reigan do. Maybe if they had planted the seeds deeper, they would have taken but more likely it was just too cold even for the winter crops. The trio waited until the end of December before letting the despair take over, knowing the seeds would not sprout.

The lack of food in the valley was a serious issue. Ron Hellman started hoarding and hiding food, knowing that the elderly Porter Siddle was starving. It would take Porter a couple weeks to figure out what Ron was doing, but he would. Doreen was only eating the smallest amount in an effort to give more to the elderly, and the lack of food quickly showed through her rapid weight loss. Though her martyrdom was commendable it would also prove to be fruitless and foolish.

Old Joe Brenner put Sugar and Lacy back to work, trading in food only. They had very few customers but two regulars that came most nights and therefore, they stayed fed. Old Joe, usually taking his cut of the trade before giving the girls theirs, let them keep whatever they could get. Old Joe started going over to the Bar each night, talking with the twins and the fisherman who also came in most nights. The fisherman would usually saunter off toward Hussey Row to get him a taste of Sugar once he was well-intoxicated, though, leaving Old Joe and the bartending twins to themselves. Rebekka Lane started seeing Lacy and quickly became fond of her, preferring her company over that of Carol Jewell most nights.

Rebekka suspected Carol and David's affair but never asked about it. Not that it mattered much because it was a brief one, ending after only 16 days, on the day that Sue Ann began her slow journey toward death.

For the two weeks between the beginning of December and the middle of it, whatever trades came in for the clothing were divided among the three of them, food included. In his lust-sick fantasy come true, David was sharing that food with Carol rather than taking it home and sharing it with his wife that spent all day trying to find food for the two of them. He would always eat what she managed to find that day, never offering her any extra of his. David was well fed, averaging being able to eat twice a day and looking more-or-less the same, while his wife, having only eaten on average once every other day, was malnourished and far too thin.

The day her husband's affair ended in the middle of December, Sue Ann awoke especially weak and pale. David noted this but said nothing and cared little about anything other than trying to meet up with Carol before work. David wished his wife luck on her gathering as he did every morning, gave her a quick kiss, and then rushed out the door hoping she wouldn't notice that he was leaving about ten minutes earlier than the day before, which was 15 minutes earlier than his normal, before Carol, time. Sue Ann was too exhausted to notice, though, feeling only the slightest bit better after two cups of sassafras tea.

She didn't want to be out at all, but Sue Ann went foraging on the western side of the mountain, beyond the farmland and behind the barn and silo, hoping that she would have better luck over there. A little less than an hour later, she still hadn't found anything to eat, but she did find a slick patch of snow that whipped her feet out from under her. She straightened her arm to catch herself, grasped at anything but missed everything, before she landed. Her hand took the blunt of the fall and she felt her wrist snap under her meager weight. Only a moment later and before the pain in her wrist could register through the shock of the fall, her head smacked the ground. There was an agonizing jolt of pain as her brain hit the inside of her skull from the sudden impact. Her sight glazed over and doubled as she looked at the smear of blood on the jagged rock, she had hit her head on. She had just enough time to register the intense pain of her immovable wrist and the warmth and stickiness of the blood dripping down the side of her face when she mercifully lost consciousness.

Sue Ann awoke sometime later, how long she did not know, but long enough to be covered by a thin dusting of snow. Her face, especially her nose, was numb and she feared frostbite as the temperatures had dropped into the high teens and had stayed there for days. Her joints felt as if they had frozen. They were stiff and creaky when she tried to get up off the ground, and it took a few attempts to first sit up and then stand up. She still wasn't sure if her legs were strong enough to carry her off the mountainside, but she was insistent that she would die trying and took off walking. She had carefully tucked her arm into her thick jacket and moved slowly off the mountain, praying she wouldn't fall again.

Luckily, she didn't but there were a few times that she felt it safer to sit down and slide down a steeper part of the mountain, and the action of sitting would always jar her wrist. No matter how careful she was or how well she thought she had her arm secured against her chest, it would always shoot a bolt of pain through her hand and up her arm. The bleeding from her head had stopped and the blood was not dry but frozen to the side of her face. She tried to scratch it off but could feel her skin coming off with it, so she left it be. Sue Ann fought off waves of lightheadedness and dizziness that would cause her to have to make brief stops to keep from falling. She would lean against a tree, wait for it to pass, and then move on. It took her almost three times longer to get off the mountain than it should have.

3

Alvin and Danny were out in the barn when they heard shuffling on the mountain behind them. They thought little of it, having animals roam about all the time, and continued with their work. When it continued and only got louder, they stepped outside to see what it was. The two young men watched a woman, unsure of who it was from the distance, slowly and carefully inch her way down a steep boulder, on her rear. They took off at a sprint along the side of the large barn, stopping at the base of the mountainside, Alvin hesitated due to his fear of heights, but Danny did not and scrambled up the massive rock.

Sue Ann was deep in concentration, knowing that one false move could send her tumbling, leaving her even worse for wear at the bottom. So, when her husband's brother, Danny, appeared before her seemingly out of nowhere, it startled her badly. Her heart pounded in her chest hard enough to physically hurt, she sucked in an icy cold breath that stung her throat and froze her vocal cords, and she tried to turn and scurry backward one-handed. One of her feet slipped at the same moment her hand did and she landed on her stomach with her broken wrist wedged between her and the snow-slick boulder. Her thick coat and layered clothing did little to cushion the blow, while the bone-deep cold only intensified her misery. Sue Ann tried to scream out the immense pain, but it only came out in a raspy, croak that was disheartening to hear. She began to drift off into the darkness that was trying and succeeding in swallowing her, thinking that the sensation of sliding that she was experiencing was only part of the drifting.

But she was wrong.

Alvin used one hand to stop her limp body from sliding down the rock by grabbing the back of her leg firmly, using his other hand to brace himself from falling with her. He planted one foot and slowly slid Sue Ann's body down until her crotch was resting on his planted foot so he would have the use of both hands to steady himself before trying to get her off the mountain. He told Alvin to move closer to the rock, so he could slowly lower Sue Ann down to him, her thinness made it slightly easier for them.

It took them several minutes to get her off the boulder, and Alvin had her laying on the ground, her head in his lap, trying to get her to wake up, when Danny was able to join them. She had been out for too long and Alvin did not like the way the cut on her head looked. Danny looked at her closely and agreed that she didn't look good at all. He told Alvin to have Beth get the cart out and then run ahead of them to have Doreen prepare for her. Alvin carefully moved Sue Ann's head from his lap and then took off without delay. David immediately swept her up off the ground and took off slowly, his legs weak and rubbery from the climb and excitement but willing them to keep him standing.

Alvin made it to the Infirmary about 15 minutes before Danny and Betty arrived with the still unconscious Sue Ann. Doreen sent Alvin to go find David, he needed to know of his wife's condition and hopefully be there when she arrived. If Alvin had shown up five minutes earlier, he would have caught his best friend's brother with Carol Jewell. They had already finished their final romp, not knowing it was their last but one of their best, and even though they were obviously still flushed from their activities, Alvin assumed it was from the brisk wind.

David's entire demeanor and attitude changed in that moment Alvin informed him of Sue Ann. Carol picked up on its origins but of course Alvin did not. It was guilt that changed him, and she watched the stormy clouds begin to gather in his eyes. Did he blame her? Carol wondered to herself as she regarded the cold way his gaze crossed hers as he rushed off to the Infirmary. "I'll go get Rebekka and meet you over there." She called to the men, but namely to David. Neither gave her a response and she did not like the uneasiness she felt growing inside her. An uneasiness that she would have to live with, among other distressing emotions, for the rest of her short life.

She arrived at the Infirmary with Rebekka Lane at her side, shortly after David did. She immediately found him sitting by Sue Ann's bed, his tear-filled eyes on her and her alone. Carol knew she was the furthest thing from his mind and that broke her heart. She, being completely new to this whole romance bit, was naïve and therefore couldn't understand why he didn't love her that way, or even at all. She had mistaken his lust for love, a mistake most learn from much earlier in life than her 30+ years. It went unspoken but Carol knew at that moment that she and David were done. She tried to repress the tears, but they fell anyway and were regarded as a slightly dramatic response to Sue Ann's accident and nothing more.

4

David Bailey had managed to shove his way through the small group standing in the Infirmary doorway just as his brother, Danny was laying Sue Ann on one of the cots. She was coming to but still incoherent, not responding to their voices or touch. David sat at the head of her bed as Doreen and Sarah Maisse, who was by coincidence already there getting a check-up of her own, began assessing her injuries. Doreen quickly examined the head wound, noting the frozen blood and skin irritation beneath and moved on to the wrist. Cold or not it could be reset and splinted.

Sue Ann rolled her head from side to side, mumbling under her breath, as Doreen and Sarah prepared to tend to her broken wrist. David who almost had his ear pressed against her lips couldn't even make out the words she was mumbling. His heart surely would have broken if he had, though, for she was saying, 'David, my love' over and over. The mumbling was brought to an abrupt halt by the scream that tore through her throat when Doreen twisted and jerked on her hand, moving her bones back to their proper places.

Sue Ann had regained consciousness for a few moments as she was being taken into the Infirmary, the warm air hitting her like a brick in the face. She was bleary eyed, faces and voices going in and out of focus, but nothing impressive enough to register. Suddenly, there was a brilliant, blinding pain in her wrist and a distant scream that may or may not have been coming from her own throat. She was swept away into the peaceful, pain-free abyss of unconsciousness, once more.

More than an hour later, Sue Ann with a blood-free bandaged head and splinted forearm seemed to be resting comfortably enough in the same cot she had been treated on. Her husband had yet to move from his place at the head of the bed and he sat stroking her hair, silently crying, his tears falling and wetting strands of her auburn hair the color of autumn leaves.

Doreen was cleaning up from the treatment while Sarah sat in a nearby chair resting. She tried to help Doreen with the clean-up, but she would have none of that, telling Sarah that she had already done enough, probably too much, in her oddly fragile state. Doreen was one of the only two people that knew of her being with-child, Sarah being the other, and since Sarah was showing with a little, rounded baby bump already, she would have to tell Johnathan soon. She wouldn't be able to hide it under her layered clothing and coats much longer, especially at the rate she was growing. Sarah had never been pregnant before, but she knew something was wrong with the whole thing.

Doreen had been absolutely sure that Sarah was wrong about her timing the day Doreen confirmed the child's heartbeat, but when Sarah returned to her this morning, being 14 weeks in according to Doreen's count, but really only six at the very most, Sarah was showing signs of being in her 21st or 22nd week. Doreen could barely comprehend it and would never have believed it if she hadn't seen the evidence with her own two eyes, and she certainly couldn't explain it. Her concrete surety that Sarah's timing was wrong had turned to mud, but she had to push all that aside when Sue Ann was brought in.

Being so few of the valley folk left, most folks caught word of incidents quickly and they gathered around to watch the situation unfold. This was partly done out of curiosity, that blessed curse of an emotion that usually gets the best of humanity eventually, and partly out of concern. Everyone knew everyone much better since the storm, and well enough for it to be almost intimate, too. There were some that kept to themselves, though, such as Jiminey and Patty, the merchant and his wife, and the Witch, of course, who had only been seen by a handful of people since the snowstorm.

Chapter Forty-Six

Sacrifices

1

The Witch was becoming bored with her new toy after weeks of playing with him, tiring of their increasingly kinkier 'games'. The satisfaction she had felt from enacting her revenge against the demon, Malum, set a lust-driven fire deep within her. That fire was finally, after weeks of daily 'games' with Roy, starting to extinguish and his usefulness was dissipating. So, the day after Sue Ann's fall and two days before his death, while Roy had his face buried between her long, flawless legs and his left thumb placed firmly in her rectum, she decided to kill Roy Hoarding.

On that cold, snowy day in the middle of December three situations occurred that would seriously impact the better part of the valley. Roy's death was the only one of them that directly affected most everyone, while the other two had both direct and indirect consequences.

The first of the two minor ones was that Sue Ann Bailey had struck with fever. The fever was the first sign of the cold sickness, and still being extraordinarily weak from hunger her immune system was barely capable of fighting off that. It would soon lead to an infection in her broken wrist that would spread into her blood. During her last dying days, her body pumped poisoned blood through her body as her lungs filled with fluid. Sue Ann Bailey died a slow and painful, miserable drowning death, that started on that snowy day three days after her fall. Her husband, David, never left her side. Her sickness led to her death, and her death directly affected her husband, David Bailey, and his mistress Carol

482

Jewell. It would indirectly affect Rebekka Lane, Sarah Maisse and Johnathan Colmes.

The second of the minor two directly affected Betty Jones and Danny Bailey and indirectly affected Alvin Danson and Gary Brown and his wife. Betty went to see the Witch, hoping she could make a deal with her, but before I tell you about that, you need to know about the Witch's sacrifice.

2

Earlier that day, under the guise that they were going to 'play', Roy reluctantly allowed the Witch to chain him to the altar again. He was nowhere near as excited about it that time around, and with good reason, but he agreed anyway knowing she could easily control his every movement should she take a notion too. While his naked body laid chained to the cool slab of the altar, the Witch wrapped a black cloth around the upper half of his face, leaving the bottom of his nose and mouth uncovered. It wrapped all the way around his head and was pulled tight. It greatly muffled his hearing and completely blinded him, his lack of senses causing his heart rate to increase drastically.

For a long time, Roy just laid there, the anticipation haunting him, trying to hear what was going on around him, but failing all the while. The Witch was preparing for the sacrifice. The one she would make to her Master, the Lord of Ludicrousness, for the power of Sight over the ones she wished to seek her revenge on. Those in the valley that have used her and worse yet, those that have scorned her.

Candles were placed in specific places around the defiled altar and set in small groups scattered about the room. Some were black, some the green of army fatigues, and some the sickly yellow of infection. Four ceramic bowls, of unknown age and origin, were placed at the four points on a compass. In each one she placed a smoldering bundle of herbs containing: Myrrh, Vervain, Cinnamon, and Frankincense wrapped in Black Rose Petals. The Witch's delicate copy of the Opera Magicae was carefully placed on a small pedestal beside the altar where it was displayed and easy to read. She had already located the necessary spell, the large book opened to the proper page. The final tool she needed was her athame. An ancient dagger, as old or more as the deck of tarot cards, made of pure Tibetan Tektite and much stronger than the fragile, dark volcanic glass it was comprised of. She gently laid the beautifully crafted, Damascus-esque, bladed dagger in the center of Roy's chest. It's smooth handle, inlaid with magic symbols, laid in the hollow of his breastbone, his skin rippling with gooseflesh from the sudden coolness of the glass.

The Witch stripped off her clothing and ignored the gooseflesh that rippled across her own body from the icy drafts of the cave. Her body was still but, on the inside, she trembled with anticipation and her heart raced with excitement. She slowly climbed onto the altar, crawled atop Roy, and carefully lowered herself until she sat on his pelvis. He felt her sit down on him, tensed at the unexpected touch, and then braced himself for the coming cruelty. She positioned herself on top of him to where his soft penis laid between the trim swatch of hair between her legs. She grabbed his maleness with one hand and snapped her fingers with the other. That action extinguished the lighting candles around the cave, lit the ritual candles aflame, and set the incenses smoldering in an instant. The rest of the large cave was dark, the candles illuminated the altar and a small area around it, casting eerie shadows that melted into the darkness. She stroked him until he was hard enough to penetrate her, which didn't take long once Roy realized she was being gentle compared to her usual roughness. She guided him into her and slowly rotated her hips. This gave her little pleasure, her mind solely on the sacrifice and this being a small part in it. She moved in ways that brought him to climax much, much quicker than his usual, surprising even himself considering less than five minutes ago his dick was as limp as a willow branch.

When she could feel him twitching inside her, she raised the knife from his bare chest. In his near eruption, the lifting of the dagger went unnoticed as did the initial slashing of his throat. As if caused by it, her eyes took on that black glow the moment her fingers touched the weapon and she began chanting the spell backwards, as it was written in her precious spell book. Roy hunched his hips upwards, driving himself deeper within her, ejecting his spill as the words tumbled from her lips.

> May thee if sight the grant to,
> pay thy as blood spilled the take.
> Within power great thee's upon call,
> kin species thy of blood spilled the let.
> Sight of ability the thee upon bestow,
> night blackest the of forces those all calling.

She drove the dagger blade into the side of his throat and jerked it to the side in a single swift movement, the sharp blade slicing through his throat like fresh butter. The cut was so quick and clean that it was almost painless. Roy felt the blood spilling its warmth onto his chest before he felt the burning in his nerves as they registered their abrupt disconnection. She dropped the dagger ignoring its nerve-crunching CLANG! as it landed on the stone floor of the cave. Then she bent over him, his softening member slipping free from her womanly depths, placed her hand on his forehead and forced his head back causing the slash in his throat to gape open. Blood gushed from the open wound and the Witch buried her face in it, sucking greedily at the spilling blood as the life ebbed out of Roy Hoarding.

A minute later she rose from her bent position, panting, blood dripping from her mouth and chin. Her near perfect teeth were stained the bright red of life, making her smile appear that much more malicious. Then came her Master's voice booming out of the darkness. The same Master that seemed rather impressed by her sacrifice and granted her the ability of Sight that she had inquired about. With that ability she was able to view the doings of anyone in the valley, from a secular view, upon proper meditation.

3

The Witch had tossed Roy's body into the far corner of the cave, where he would stay until the following day when she cut him up into bit sized pieces for Vipera. She was considering cleaning up the bloody mess on the altar when she sensed the coming of a visitor and found it to be the distraught Betty Jones.

Given the gory mess in the altar room, the Witch left Betty sitting in the shack while she went to retrieve the deck of Tarot cards, after Betty had informed her of the reason behind her visit. She desperately missed her brother and worried about his health and well-being. It had been weeks and still no one had seen hide or hair of him. Betty did not mention the type of work she did, her beau or the rest of her family that was stuck in New York; she only spoke of her missing brother Joshua. She knew the Witch could help her but hoped that she would be willing to do so. Of course, the Witch knew that Joshua had took off into her garden where he met his fate at the hands of the tree elves, but she didn't tell Betty that. She would use Betty, if the cards deemed her fit to be taken, to kill Danny Bailey. Betty had never been to see the Witch before now, so she was only guilty by association. Danny, however, had been to see her on two separate occasions: once for a wearable incense that attracted females and some time later for an herb to take care of the 'crotch rot' he had acquired from one of the said females. He had used her the same way he had used that incense to lure those women, and the Witch hated him for it! Hated every man for the sins of one and she would have her revenge!

Betty Jones' tarot reading, however, did not give the Witch the same surety that Roy's and Frank's had given her, even though The Devil card had been drawn for the 'What is' place in the seven-card tarot upside-down cross. The third card, the 'What will be' card, was the reason for her uncertainty as to whether the Witch would have Betty's soul, or not. She had drawn the Temperance card which indicated that with strong will and determination the right outcome would prevail. Tarot had been and always will be a game of interpretation, a game that the Witch had mastered as well as her enchanting abilities, but this read could go in either direction. There was no doubt in the Witch's mind of how strong Betty's will was, and if she so chose then the Witch's plan for revenge would go along without a hitch. On the contrary, should Betty decide to go against the Witch it could upheaval any number of things in the Witch's plans. The Witch made a quick, yet calculated, decision to trust her instincts, that rarely led her astray, and decided to extend her offer to Joshua Jones' sister, Betty.

"I could help you find your brother..." the Witch began. The emphasis she had put on the word 'could' did not go unnoticed by Betty, who initially was hopeful and then only distressed at the note of inflection. "...but I doubt you have the... oh, what's the word I'm looking for, oh yes... I doubt you have the ability to provide the payment for such a service, though."

Betty was genuinely shocked by this remark and the look of surprise on her face made the Witch want to crack a smile, but she repressed it. "That's awfully presumptuous of you to say so." Betty told her with an air of sophistication that the Witch hadn't seen in almost a century. How does she know what I'm capable of? Betty wondered to herself in a prideful, willful way. The Witch almost wished that she had known that Betty before Johanthan Colmes had broke her heart, she would have made one hell of a follower. Maybe she still could be. Only time would tell, though.

"Is it?" was the Witch's only response to Betty's uppity remark, but she continued with her proposal anyway. "The price is the heart that holds your own, that of your beloved beau, Danny Bailey."

Betty gasped, not knowing what to expect of the Witch's payment, but knowing that was definitely not it. And how did she know about Danny? How could I choose? Betty thought to herself as she stood speechless while her grief-stricken mind slowly and carefully processed each word and brought them to full clarity and comprehension. It took several long moments, but she was finally able to speak. "What..." Betty tried but it came out inaudible, so she cleared her throat and tried again. "What, exactly, does that mean? It's a riddle or something, right?" Betty asked with hopelessness that she tried to mask behind false hopefulness.

"I meant the very words I spoke." The Witch told her. "Bring me the heart of Danny Bailey and I will help you find your dear brother, Joshua." She clarified, inwardly enjoying the conflicting emotions that stirred beneath Betty's outwardly surprised but calm demeanor. "You need not make your decision now; the offer will stand. Let it be known, though, that you cannot deceive thee. I will know if it's the heart of your beloved. Any trickery will lead to..." The Witch finished with action rather than words. She lifted her arm and pointed a long, elegant finger at the stone fireplace that was burning strongly, providing ample heat for the shack. A large stone, roughly the size of a small watermelon, first wiggled and then popped loose from the other stones that surrounded it. It drifted, eye-level with the sitting women, in the air toward them, stopping just out of their reach. The stone suddenly separated into a dozen oddly shaped chunks of stone that hovered in the same place, the space between each piece painstakingly apparent. The point had been drawn and Betty understood it, understood it loud and clear.

With a twitch of her finger, the Witch solidified the large stone and then replaced it back into the fireplace, dried mud holding it in place and all. The results were as if nothing out of the ordinary had occurred. Betty wasn't sure how to respond to such a threat, so she didn't.

There was nothing left to be said between the two of them after the Witch's display of talent and heart-wrenching deal, so Betty left with a heavy heart and a muddled mind.

Chapter Forty-Seven

Selfish Sumbitch

1

Less than an hour after Betty Jones left the Witch's shack and headed back to the farm, Sarah Maisse sat down at the small, familiar wooden table in Johnathan Colmes' shack. She had asked him if she could come over to his place, earlier in the day, and he had agreed but tried not to appear too eager about it. Sarah made the question public, not caring who heard her or what they might think of it. As discreet as the two of them had been, most of the valley folks knew about John and Sarah due to Frank's attitude of late and Johnathan's reaction to Sarah's injuries. Most felt sorry for Frank McGrath, seemingly love-sick and broken hearted, which caused a resentment toward Sarah, a resent that came along in part due to her still being a new resident of the valley. She hadn't even lived in the valley for six months yet and would only make it weeks past that mark upon her death.

Johathan offered tea and she accepted cordially enough. She was polite but awkward, he had noticed. There were no affections or endearments like which he fantasized, nothing of which he would have expected from her in the safety and privacy of his own repaired shack. Neither said much of anything as he prepared and served the sassafras tea, but she got straight to the point moments after he sat down across from her.

Sarah left her tea unattended, giving it no notice, but Johnathan carefully lifted his to his lips, not to take a sip but merely to lightly blow across the top. He had always found this to be soothing, watching the surface of the tea ripple and wave. The concentrated breathing so as not to blow too hard or too softly and the thought-dissipating way it entranced him. He allowed himself only a moment of adoration before redirecting his attention toward the love of his life. John hoped that she was about to tell him that she was done with Frank, but he couldn't shake the feeling that she was going to break up with him, instead, which was making him nervous. The light blowing on the tea continued, but absent-mindedly.

"I'm having a baby... your baby." She told him bluntly, never moving her eyes from his. He gasped at the words and sucked recently boiling tea into the back of his throat. The mug full of tea fell from his hand, spilling its hot contents across the wooden table but Sarah was fixated on John's twisted, contorted face. In an instant his eyes had tripled in size and bulged from his head, his mouth was stretched open as far as possible and bent at an uncomfortable but not unnatural angle, his tongue hanging out the side of his mouth. It was a comical facial expression of surprise, pain and embarrassment all rolled into one, but what made Sarah laugh so hard was the single abrupt noise he made. It was a cross between a squawk and a cough. It was loud, sudden, and completely unexpected.

Sarah could not retain the giggle that turned into a full on laugh the more she thought about his face and replayed that noise in her mind. John had rushed over to the water bucket and drank greedily, trying to soothe the searing holes burned into the back of his throat. She was still laughing almost a full minute later when he returned to his place at the table with a rag to sop up the spilled tea.

"Find that funny, didya?" John asked in a raspy voice, with no attempt to hide the irritation.

"Quite, actually." She told him, frankly, trying to sober up from that comic relief she needed more than she realized. "I'm sorry, but it was rather amusing. Not the part where you were hurt, of course... it was just the combination of your face and that..." she let out a small giggle. "...that noise you made." She finished and then immediately burst into another much shorter gale of laughter.

"Finished?" John asked her after a few long moments, still irritated.

"Possibly." She answered sarcastically, which only added to his irritation.

John had had enough, he stood up from his chair and leaned over the table, causing her to sit back in hers. "What the hell, Sarah?" he shouted. "You ask to come to my house, tell me you're havin my baby, and then throw around a hysterical bitchy attitude to me. Fuck no! Come back when you're ready to be a damn adult about this, because I don't find anything about it to be a goddamn joke!" He pointed at the door of his shack, the same door she couldn't get out of all those weeks ago, then sat back down in his wooden chair at the table, one of the many places they had made love during those snowed-in days in his drafty little shack.

Sarah glared at him with eyes that screamed fury. "Alright." That was the only answer she would give, and with it, John knew that he had made a mistake. He wasn't exactly sure what that mistake was, but he knew he had made one. Sarah rose from her seat and walked toward the door without another word, swinging her oversized coat on as she went. John tried to stop her, but she ignored his words and jerked away from his touch without looking back. She walked out the door, closing it gently behind her. Johnathan considered chasing after her, but his anger won out and he decided against it.

For three days, Sarah avoided Johnathan. She would be civil with him in public but nothing more. The pair would finally sit down and discuss the too-quickly growing child the evening after Ron Hellman and Porter Siddle had their fight, if that's what you could call the beatdown Porter received at Ron's hands.

2

Porter, who like many others was only eating on average once every other day, was slowly starving to death. So, when he found Ron's stash of food hidden under the floorboards in the attached outhouse, Porter took it as a sign that his luck was changing. Porter sat on the outhouse floor, too weak and excited to take the loot into the main/kitchen area and ate until he was sure his stomach would explode. Porter was in slight misery from being so full, but he had been so hungry for so many days by then that he missed it, pain and all. He didn't eat everything he had found, but he certainly put a large, noticeable dent in the pile. He swept everything back into its hidey hole, trash and all, and replaced the floorboards. He knew but did not care that Ron would be back soon and find his stash so heavily depleted. He slowly got up off the floor, strode into the bedroom like a king in a castle, and plopped down on the bed. He was asleep moments later, happier than he had been in ages.

A couple hours later, Ron returned to the shack with his latest looted bundle of food. He noted Porter asleep on the bed and relaxed a little about trying to get his loot into the hidey hole in the outhouse floor without being noticed. He walked in and popped the floorboards up, ready to drop his loot and replace the boards, so he could check on Porter once more before indulging in his latest find. What he found angered him to his core. There was little left of the food he had managed to scavenge and keep to himself and there was only one person that could have eaten it. Only one person that would have left it so obviously amiss. Porter Siddle.

Ron considered waking the sleeping Porter Siddle, but ultimately decided to let him wake on his own. He, also, briefly considered beating the older man to death while he slept, but he decided against that too. Ron wanted Porter to know and fully comprehend the beating he was going to get and why he was getting it. So, Ron pulled up one of the wooden chairs from the small wooden table that occupied the main/kitchen area and settled into it in the doorway of the bedroom. He waited for almost an hour for Porter to wake up and even allowed the man to go take a piss before confronting him.

Ron met Porter as he stepped out of the outhouse still buttoning the front of his trousers. "You found MY food." Ron said, not bothering to ask. It was a direct statement and his eyes dared Porter to deny it.

He didn't. Porter stood up a little straighter, his unbuttoned pants momentarily forgotten, and he stared daggers through

Ron. "I did and you ought to be ashamed for hidin it thataway." Porter told him in a fatherly sort of way.

Already in a foul mood from finding his stash depleted as much as it was, especially since the loot finds were decreasing by the day, that admonishing comment enraged Ron. He drew back his fist and punched the older man in the bridge of his nose, drawing back slightly at the very last moment to prevent obliterating his sinuses. Porter was not expecting the punch, honestly never thought that a younger man would have the balls enough to strike him, out of respect if for no other reason. He was Ron's mentor, to boot, and Porter couldn't believe that Ron had just struck him even as he fell on his ass and his face exploded in a spiderweb of pain. Porter could feel his eyes begin to puff up by the time he made it to his feet again, Ron standing before him huffing and puffing in anger.

"You had no right to take what wasn't yours!" Ron shouted at Porter, who swayed on his feet from the blow to his face.

"And you had no right hiding it from a starving man kind enough to give you shelter." Porter quipped, knowing it would cut at Ron and possibly earn him another blow, but he had never backed down before and he'd be damned if he was going to back down from that no-good sumbitch.

His words enraged Ron all over again because they were true, and Ron didn't know how to deal with the shame of it other than by inflicting pain on the person that pointed it out to him. So, Ron caught Porter in the ribs with a blow from his right fist, knocking the air from his lungs and doubling him over. Ron grabbed the back of his head and brought his knee up into Porter's face, connecting with his left eyebrow and forehead. The blow knocked him back on his ass, once again, and blood dribbled down his face in thin lines from a gash in his eyebrow that would require four stitches. Ron began stomping and kicking the man laying in the floor, trying to move into the fetal position but being too slow about it. Ron stomped and kicked, kicked and stomped at the defeated man until he was breathing heavily, and his legs felt like rubber.

Porter Siddle lay on the bedroom floor, very nearly unconscious, bleeding, broken, and whimpering. Ron stormed out of the shack and wasn't seen until the following night.

When Porter was sure Ron was gone, he slowly crawled to the bed and used it to help him get up on his feet. The first attempt to stand failed due to weakness, the second attempt failed due to his sagging, unbuttoned pants, but he was finally successful on the third. He buttoned his trousers with shaky blood-stained hands and very slowly made his way to the Infirmary.

3

Sarah wasn't in the Infirmary that time, so Doreen examined and treated Porter from head to toe, by herself. He was in bad shape, having very few places on him that wasn't cut, scraped, or bruised. She had to put stitches in his eyebrow and two in his lip, but luckily his nose was not broken just badly busted. The entire left side of Porter's abdomen had already started turning a deep purplish black, and his ribs, though not broken either, were severely bruised, making it hard for him to breathe. There were numerous bruises across his back and legs, some in the exact pattern on the bottom of Ron's boots. Doreen, looking paler than usual, much thinner, and with dark circles under her eyes that were more prominent than before, had Porter stay at the Infirmary that night to keep an eye on his breathing, ensuring there were no broken ribs. She cleared him to go home the following day with instructions for recovery.

Ron Hellman showed up later that night, the blood-dried scuffs on his knuckles evident, and just walked right into the shack as if nothing had happened. It didn't much surprise the battered but still headstrong Porter Siddle, that the arrogant sumbitch would be so ballsy, and it didn't much surprise him when Ron asked, "Ya learn your lesson, old man?"

"Reckon so. Learnt yer an ungrateful, selfish sumbtich and I don't want you in my place no mo'." Porter told him truthfully and sternly as he slowly stood from the chair, he had sitting in by the lit stone fireplace.

To Porter's surprise Ron began to laugh, an odd laugh, an untrustworthy laugh, as he slowly walked toward Porter. "Oh, Porter..." Ron said as he approached his mentor, who refused to cower before him. That did not go unnoticed by Ron, and he did not care for the lack of fear or respect Porter displayed. Suddenly, Ron lunged at Porter wrapping his arms around the beaten man and pinning his arms to his bruised sides, as if in a friendly bear hug. Ron squeezed just enough to get a wince and small gasp out of Porter and held the pressure as he whispered in his ear. "I ain't goin nowhere old man, this be MY place now, and maybe... just maybe, I might be kind nuff not to kick your scrawny useless ass out in the cold."

Even in his beaten and weakened state, Porter was deeply angered by Ron's words and struggled in the younger man's strong grasp. It was a fruitless attempt but an attempt, nonetheless. Ron increased the pressure on Porter, and he not only stopped struggling but stopped breathing, his lungs and chest compressed and unable to expand to take a breath. Ron held this position for a long moment. "Understand, old man?" he asked in the same harsh whisper. Porter could only nod, but with it was released from Ron's crushing hold on him. He fell to the wooden floor, gasping and sucking at the sweet warm air of the shack while Ron looked down at him with disgust and then walked away.

In that moment, Porter decided that he would just have to go along as Ron expected until he was strong enough to do something about it. So, for the next two weeks Ron would only take enough out of Ron's food stash to go unnoticed and only when he had to. The two men resided in the same shack but rarely spoke or acknowledged each other, Ron going out and doing whatever it was he did while Porter sat in his shack, healed, and got stronger.

Ron had made a habit of going out after the work was done for the day and scavenging the empty shacks and buildings for food. He knew the ones that had been marked to be knocked down had been checked for food but not thoroughly. He was rechecking them all and had found quite the hoard doing it. When he was feeling especially generous, he would take a small portion of a great find and go share it with Sugar or Lacy over on Hussey Row, whichever one wasn't already occupied. That did not happen often because most of the time his hand did the trick and would save him a usually unfair trade. On those certain particularly bad days, though, or as a reward for an excellent find, Ron would saunter into the Bar and trade Nonna and Nonni a bit of food for some Shine.

The twins and Old Joe Brenner would watch him catch a good strong buzz off the Shine but never get drunk, grab his usually bulging leather bag and head out the door. The trio would always discuss his quiet arrival and departure, refusing to make conversation or exchange words with anyone. He asked for his drinks, drank them, and left. It perplexed them, as did the odd but intriguing feelings sparking between the three of them. Old Joe Brenner and Nonna and Nonni Brookes. They all sensed them, they all feared them, and they all refused to acknowledge them.

Chapter Forty-Eight

Too Big, Too Fast

A few hours after Porter had been sent home from the Infirmary and a few hours before Ron Hellman returned to Porter's shack, John showed up at Sarah's place. He knocked on her door timidly, almost changing his mind and returning to his place multiple times. The butcher's shop had been forgotten with no meat in the place and none coming in, it didn't make much sense to keep the place open. If anyone did happen to catch or kill an animal, it was theirs and theirs alone. The valley rules had changed with the severe lack of food and the obvious depletion in the river. Everyone was managing to keep the panic at bay, but just barely.

John almost walked away before Sarah answered her door, wrapped in a moth-eaten robe, a few moments later. She had been lying down and had barely heard his knocking. She didn't seem particularly pleased to see him, but she didn't turn him away either. Instead, she allowed him in but skipped the offers of cordiality. She left him sitting in the main/kitchen area, without a word, and stepped into the bedroom, leaving the door open but moving out of his line of sight. When she returned after a few minutes, she had redressed in thick insulated pants and an oversized sweater that hid her physique quite well. Sarah went about preparing tea in the kitchen, silently, as John sat and watched her. He withstood as much of it as he could, watching her go about her day as if he didn't exist, as if the child they had created wasn't growing inside her at that very moment.

"Sarah..." John spoke but she either did not hear him or chose to ignore him. So, he repeated her name a little louder the second time, hoping he kept the building irritation out of it, but the result was the same. "Goddamn it, Sarah! Talk to me!" He shouted at her from his place at the table.

"What, John?!" she screamed at him and then slammed one of the ceramic mugs down on the cast iron stove top, shattering it in her hand. Somehow, she had avoided being cut by any of the sharp jagged pieces that scattered the floor, stove top, and the piece she still held in her hand. "What the fuck do you want me to say? You want me to tell you how fuckin wonderful this whole fucked up situation is? You want me to tell you just how goddamn excited I am and how we're going to live oh so happily ever after? What, John? What the fuck do you want from me?!" She dropped the piece of ceramic mug, the boiling water forgotten, covered her face with her hands and wept.

John did not expect that sudden outburst and rant, nor did he feel that he had provoked it. Learning from their last discussion, he smartly did not respond with anger. Instead, he walked over to Sarah, wrapped his arms around her, much like Ron would do to Porter later in the evening, and just held her until the weeping subsided. "Sarah, honey..." he soothed her, using a tone opposite the one that had started the whole bit. "...we need to sit down and talk about the baby." he finished.

Sarah, who had calmed down and was a little more rational minded, agreed. "You're right. We do, because there's something wrong with it." She told him matter-of-factly, but with tears in her eyes. A knot of dread began to form in the pit of Johnathan's stomach, but he tried to ignore it.

"That seems a little extreme, don't ya think? I mean you are a new ma as I am a new da. I know I'm about scared to death so I'm sure you are. You sure it's not just you bein scared?" Then, almost as if it were a spoken thought, he added, "Lords, I hope I'm not sayin all this wrong."

She eyed him for a moment, before she replied. "You're doin alright, so far." She moved away from him to sit down, and he helped her along, the relief on his face apparent. Once she was seated, John went about making their tea and she continued. "I am scared. I really can't express how scared I am, both for and of the child. There's something wrong with it and I'm not the only one who thinks so."

That small bit of information did not go over well with Johnathan, and he stopped mid pour and turned to face Sarah. "Who the fuck knew before me? Why was I not the first person you told?" He could not repress the anger at finding out that he was not the first person to find out about his child.

Sarah's one word answer, "Doreen." was given calmly and without anger, diminishing John's and making him feel small and insignificant by consequence. Of course, Doreen knew because Sarah needed medical attention in her state. He felt like a jackass for his reaction but allowed his actions rather than his words to be penance. John returned to preparing the tea, without another word.

"How much do you know about a woman being with child?" Sarah asked him after a few moments.

John was thoughtfully quiet as he served their tea and answered her between tiny blows across the surface of his steaming hot mug. "I know it takes about nine months, their bellies and... other body parts... grow and sometimes stay. I know how they enter the world, if that's what you're askin." he told her, blushing at the end.

"Honey, you're a grown ass man, I would hope you do." She paused to collect her thoughts before continuing. "Okay, this baby could only have been conceived during those snowed-in days at your shack. You are the only man I have been with since I've been in the valley. So, therefore I could only be at most six- or seven-weeks in. Right?" She asked him, hoping he was following along.

John sat thoughtfully for a few moments, deciding that she was being truthful. He believed that he was the only man she had been with, at least since her arrival in the valley, and after some quick addition, said. "Yeah, that's my calculations, too. Seven on the outside. Hell, I know women that don't find out til 12 or so weeks in." He told her, remembering seeing multiple women throughout the years grow and birth children.

"Exactly. Does this look like I'm seven weeks in?" she asked, as she stood up and raised her sweater. Her lower stomach protruded from her small frame, as if a cantaloupe was growing beneath her skin. She looked like she was well into her second trimester. "My stomach was flat four weeks ago when Doreen heard its heartbeat through 'the cone' for the first time." She told him.

That took him aback. She had grown that much in a month. She was right. There was something wrong with it. But what?

Chapter Forty-Nine

Never Shoulda Been

1

The days faded into nights, and they too passed. Food grew scarcer for humans and animals alike. There were less than half a dozen left in the dog pack by the year's end, and they were fiercely struggling to survive. Some had frozen or starved to death and then been consumed by the remaining living pack. Food had almost become a luxury in the valley during those last two weeks of the year and the lack of was a major factor in the aggressive, depressed mood that seemed to overtake the valley and its residents.

By the end of December Alvin Danson, Danny Bailey, and Betty Jones had lost all hope that their winter crops would take. Whether they had done something wrong, missed a step, or it was just the harshness of the mountain winter, made no difference or provided any comfort to the trio. They were disheartened to say the least and each tried to deal with that loss on top of the numerous others, in their own ways.

Alvin was struggling to find something to live for. He had no family in the valley. He had, like Sarah, just shown up in the valley one day hoping the place would stick, and it did. He did not regret his decision to stay in the valley and try his hand at their strict, yet provocative way of life, but Lords, it was a hard one. One he wasn't so sure he could survive, especially after the loss of his belle, Anna Weston. Though she had been one of the victims of the blizzard, the grief and hurt was still very raw and fresh for Alvin. He tried to keep his grief in check, only mourning her in his alone time, and tried even harder not to resent his best friends Danny and

Betty for their love. A part of him wanted to hate them for having each other and their lack of loss and heartache, while the other part of him knew that was unfair of him. Of course, they had endured their own heartaches and losses but there was no way, he believed in his grief-stricken mind, that they were hurting like or as much as he was.

His pain was so great that he tried everything he could to ease it. Out of desperation, he visited Hussey Row one night. Lacy was good, maybe even the best he'd ever had, but the guilt he felt both during and after was astounding so he didn't try that again. Alvin thought that the arms of another may help him temporarily forget his pain, but it only amplified it, instead. He had tried Smoke but it, too, amplified his emotions and he would more-often-than-not cry himself sober. He had tried taking to the Shine but once he got drunk enough to forget he was sad, he got pissed and ready to fight. The last time he had gotten drunk he took a swing at Betty after a heated comment and Danny knocked him on his ass with a single quick blow. Apologies were doled out and all was forgiven the following morning, but that was the last of the Shine for Alvin Danson. He was drowning in his sorrow, and he was quickly running out of options.

Danny Bailey didn't realize the intense pain his best friend Alvin was in because he was too focused on his belle, Betty Jones. He was disappointed about the crops because they were relying on that as a food source, even if it wouldn't yield anything for weeks or more, but he was deeply concerned for Betty. She had changed recently, he couldn't pinpoint when it had happened, it was more of a gradual change, but it wasn't one for the better. Of course, he had no knowledge of her visit with the Witch and the proposition placed at her feet. All he knew was that she had become distant and defensive. They didn't talk about things like they did before, and they were fighting a lot more. She was less affectionate and endearing with him, but their sex life had maintained its vigorous consistency, only having gotten rougher and slightly kinkier.

Danny, right and wrong simultaneously, assumed it had to do with her missing brother and her grief for him, seeming to have hit her full force after the shock of everything wore off, so he tried to give her what he thought she needed. Space when necessary and a loving hand to hold when she wanted it. He loved Betty Jones with everything in him and his heart broke over her sadness. He wished he could take her pain away, for he would gladly bear it as his own if it meant he could see her lovely smile once more.

Sadly, up until moments before his death, dealt at her hands, he was convinced that Betty was going to end things with him, and he found that the thought was almost unbearable. Ultimately, Danny wasn't wrong. He literally spent the rest of his life trying to please the love of his life, his beloved, his murderer, his belle, Betty Jones, who in a different life may have married Danny Bailey and bore his children.

Betty had changed in all the ways Danny had noticed and more. She had finally gotten past the shame of even considering the death of her beloved for the whereabouts of her missing brother and was seriously contemplating it. This consideration had created a war within her that was at a brutal standoff. One side desperately wanted to find her brother, the only family she had left but unsure if she was able to kill to find him. The other part of her loved Danny Bailey and wanted to spend the rest of her life with him. He could be her family, but she wasn't sure if she was willing to trade her brother for him. Ironically, she believed that her brother would never leave her and there would always be the possibility that Danny could.

This inner tearing, paired with her grief induced depression was having some major effects on Betty's mood, especially toward Danny. She knew there was no way she could talk to anyone about the proposition she had been given by the Witch and having to keep everything in and having no one to help her through it was not only frightening but heart-wrenching. Danny was supposed to help her through everything, that's how it was supposed to work, but he couldn't, and even though it was completely her fault, a small part of her hated him for it.

Betty was being particularly moody toward Danny the day Sue Ann died. They had a bad fight before leaving for the Infirmary to check on Danny's brother David, and his deathly ill wife. The squabbling continued but to a lesser degree all the way there, only to discover that she had passed not too long before. In fact, had Betty not started a fight with Danny that morning, they would have left earlier, and Danny would have been at the Infirmary to console his devastated brother. That did not go unnoticed by either Danny, who quickly forgave his beloved for it, or by Betty, who didn't much care at that moment if he hated her for it. Or for any other reason, for that matter.

2

David Bailey was devastated. Doreen had told him for three days that Sue Ann's fever had been too high for too long and that her lungs had filled up too much, too quickly and there was nothing she could do to help her. She had done everything she knew to do and even tried a few things she wasn't sure of out of desperation, but nothing helped enough to make a difference in the end. On the first and second of the three days, Doreen had tried to talk the couple into going to see the Witch, but they steadfastly refused and dropped the subject. Doreen didn't bother to try on the third day because she knew by then that it was too late for Sue Ann Bailey, and she died only hours later.

Doreen had spent the past two weeks, tending to the needs of the three bedridden elderly folks, and the worsening Sue Ann, all while having precious little to eat. Sometimes she would go three or four days without any food, only water and tea, and then eat a small chunk of stale bread. She lost her formerly plump appearance, dropping an excessive amount of weight in only a few weeks, which caused her skin and clothes to hang from her like drapery. She grew paler by the day and the hollowness of her facial features gave her a ghostly appearance that was almost creepy. She wasn't the only thin person in the valley that winter, but she was certainly the most, sickly appearing.

Danny and Betty walked into the Infirmary to find David sobbing and weeping uncontrollably. Tears streamed from his eyes, snot from his nose, and drool from his lips as he openly cried and mourned his deceased wife. Danny's heart broke at the sight of his big brother, and he went to him immediately, tears stinging his eyes, as he hugged David against his chest. Betty couldn't handle the sight of the grieving brothers in her temperamental state, so she helped tend to Sue Ann's body, instead.

After awhile the tears ceased and David calmed down, way down, to the point of being in shock. He sat in the Infirmary for a long time after Danny and Betty left, who had insisted that he join them but gave up after a while without receiving any kind of an answer. After some time, he just stood up and walked out. He had spent the last two weeks in the Infirmary beside his wife, tending to every need and want he was able. He hated himself for betraying his wife, even though he believed that she died never knowing of his sins, and he hated Carol Jewell for tempting him the way she had. He knew that he could not live without his beautiful wife, and he certainly couldn't live with the guilt of what he had been doing, which was the eventual cause of him losing her in the most final of forms.

The solution: his death, but he wasn't going out alone.

Usually, Sue Ann's body would have gone out to the common area for the funeral pyre as soon as she had been prepared for it, but the weather had its own agenda. The snow was coming down in sheets, by the time she was prepped, allowing for very little visibility, with even less than during the blizzard that had snowed them into their shacks, tents, and teepees, not so long ago. The falling snow was accumulating quickly and adding to the inches of snow already laid down. The daily temperatures had been hovering in the high-teens and low-twenties since around the beginning of December, but this small and fierce snowstorm dropped them into the low-teens, high-singles and brought an icy wind that would catch between the mountainsides, like most did, and swirl through the valley. Pleasant in the summer and autumn when a cooling breeze was needed and cold enough to freeze the bones in the winter and spring. The combination of the wind and quickly falling snow prevented the valley folks from sending Sue Ann Bailey heavenward the day of her death.

The snow had only begun to fall, but the wind was continuing with its ferocity, when David Bailey had left the Infirmary. He had gone into shock when the tears stopped but it was only a mild state that he snapped out of soon after. He continued with his shock-like expression though, as his suicide plan began to take form. David left the Infirmary when he had everything planned out and had gone over everything more than twice. He grabbed a random coat made of leather and lined with rabbit fur on his way out, sliding it on over his own. With the hood of the coat over his head he could be anyone heading anywhere and easily mistaken for someone else.

He made it to his place, the newly rebuilt shack that he had spent so little time with his beloved wife in, having only been there twice in the last two weeks, unnoticed. He built a fire, made tea, and ate whatever he could find in the kitchen that hadn't frozen or rotten in his absence. He changed into his warmest clothes, stuck a large-bladed knife handle up, into this leather belt and left for his next and final destination.

It was a slow trek to Rebekka Lane's shack since the snowfall had increased so much and was still pouring down steadily when he arrived. He stood in the darker shadows of cloudy dusk and watched for some time to see if Carol was there, which she was, and if Rebekka was too, which she wasn't. There were no thoughts of regret, no guilty conscience, no remorse for his intended actions. He wanted to do it. Every time he thought of his wife, which was almost constant, the thoughts would lead to her final choking gasping breaths. The gurgling sound that came from her throat and the bubble-popping, crackly sound in her chest would haunt him for the rest of his very, very short life. He had relived her drowning in her own sickness over and over since her death, and believed... no, he knew... that his guilt would always keep that hurt fresh and alive for him to endure anew.

He waited and watched through the small murky window until Carol walked into the bedroom and then stepped into the shack, knife in hand but held behind his back, closing the door behind him, without a sound.

3

Carol Jewell had spent the last two weeks in a heartbroken daze, of sorts. The first heartache from a lost love that seems completely unbearable, as if your entire world crashed down around you in an instant. A few days after Sue Ann's fever sank its greedy fingers into her, Carol went to the Infirmary to check on her, and David, of course. David had paid little attention to her arrival as he did with everyone else. He sat watching Sue Ann sleep and stroking her shoulder-length hair, shivering occasionally from the fever, even under the layers of blankets laid upon her. Sweat lightly beaded the bridge of her nose and, not only reflected off the dim light seeping in through the shuttered windows but reflected the false hope that the fever was breaking, as well.

Carol spoke briefly with Doreen and Sarah Maisse, who was there helping Doreen that day with the elderly, before approaching David. She knew Sue Ann was asleep when she walked in and breathed an internal sigh of relief, because even if she didn't know about her and David, Carol didn't want to speak with the woman her love chose over her. As it turned out, she didn't get to speak with David either.

David seemed not to notice Carol walk up to where he was sitting at the head of Sue Ann's cot and squat down beside him. He did notice her, though, the moment her hand rested on his forearm, and he jerked away from her so violently that had anyone seen, they would have thought he had been touched by fire. Carol hadn't even been able to utter a word yet and knew not to with the look he gave her. That look induced fear, panic, and ever-increasing heartache in Carol Jewell, and she knew that she was the last person he wanted to see. She left quickly but returned two days later, and then on average every other day after that.

It was risky and Carol feared how David might respond should she approach him or divert his attention from his ailing wife in any way. So, while there she kept her distance and inquired of Sue Ann's steadily worsening condition from afar. She cried on more than one occasion during those visits to the Infirmary. The reality was the tears were caused by the immense pain she endured knowing her love was so close and yet so far away. However, she told anyone who inquired or attempted comfort that it was because she couldn't handle seeing Sue Ann, or anyone else, suffer so much since the death of her beloved mama.

Carol's visits to the Infirmary were for herself and as Sue Ann's health decreased with each passing day, a spark of hope flared within Carol. It began in the form of a single unfinished thought, 'When she dies...' and that hope grew into a perfect, small bud that exploded out into a beautiful blossom upon hearing the news of Sue Ann's death. It took actual willpower for Carol not to smile but she managed. Her thoughts went wild, and she began to fantasize about David showing up at the door one night and carrying her away with him. Not now, it was too soon, of course, but next week, maybe...

Well, David did show up but that was the only part of her fantasy that came true, and it was much, much sooner than she ever expected, even in her most outrageously wild dreams.

Rebekka had gone to see Lacy again and because of the heavy snowfall, would not be back until the following morning, when she would find their dead bodies. Not that David knew where she was or that she would be gone all night. He went into the shack expecting Rebekka to show up at any moment or for Carol to scream, drawing the attention of the nearest neighbor. Neither of which happened but the deaths were quick, nonetheless.

Carol stepped out of the bedroom, noticed the figure standing in front of the door and stopped. She recognized David the moment he pulled his hood back and turned toward him, beginning her plea before he had a chance to leave. "Oh, David, I'm so sorry about Sue Ann..." she was only steps away, with her arms extended and ready to embrace him. "...but maybe..." she was only a step away from him and ready to wrap her arms around his neck but caught the strange light in his eyes and stopped. She was able to stop her body but could not stop her mouth. "...maybe we can finally..." and that's all she was able to say before her blood gushed down the front of her sweater, running out of her slit throat.

David endured the sound of her voice as long as he could, but it quickly reached its end when she said 'we'. That did it for David. He brought the knife out from behind his back and swiped it quickly and strongly across her bobbing throat as she spoke. Her words were cut off as his began. "There is no 'we'! No 'us'! There never damn will be and there never should have been! I hate you for guiling me with your sympathy, you wicked bitch! I hate that I betrayed her so! And I hate myself most of all! All because of you and your damn temptations! To hell with you, I beg of the Gods! That is my dying wish!" David Bailey concluded his raving speech by slitting his own throat.

The blade slipped from his hand, landing on the floor of the shack with a dull thud that went unnoticed by the present company. David slowly slumped to the floor, blood gushing from his gaping throat and joined Carol, who was moments from death herself. She died looking at the man she loved, a man that wasn't hers, with a combination of undying love and horror at the realization that he truly did not love her as she had so hoped he had. And then there was nothing for Carol Jewell.

Less than a minute later, gasping and choking for breath, clawing at this bloody throat, and suddenly wondering for the first time why he had gone to such an extreme, David Bailey followed her into that darkness of nothing.

4

The following morning dawned bright and brilliant but cold. Rebekka Lane returned to her shack the following morning to walk with Carol to the shop so they could begin the days work. Which at that point was repairing old clothes for what very little anyone had to trade and there were so few people that they would go days without a customer. The merchant, Gary Brown, could relate and attest to that because he too would go days without a customer only to get one with so little to offer. It didn't induce anger, only pity and disappointment, which was worse.

The last thing Rebekka expected to find that morning was two dead bodies lying side by side so close to the door that it would only open halfway. "What the hell?" she muttered as she shoved on the shack door to no avail. She stuck her head through to see what was stalling the door and first seen the face-up body of David Bailey. His eyes were closed, and the dark reddish-brown blood had soaked the front of his coat and pooled under the back of his head and upper back. Her initial thought was that Carol had murdered him in self-defense, but then her eyes shifted to the other body, over to the knife lying at David's feet and then back to Carol, and she knew that she was wrong in her assumption. She noted the front of Carol's sweater, also blood soaked, and the pool of blood beneath her that was less than an inch away from connecting with the puddle under David's body. Her eyes were open in a forever stare and Rebekka knew that when Carol had died, her murderer was the last person she had seen.

David had killed them both, but why? That was the question.

Rebekka took in the entire scene in a matter of moments, gasped loudly and jerked her head away from the door so quickly she stumbled causing her to fall backward into the snow. By happenstance, Ron Hellman, who only lived three shacks away in Porter Siddle's place, came walking out of the shack when Rebekka stumbled and fell. Without thought or hesitation he rushed over to help her up, but stopped just short when he caught a glimpse of the bodies through the partially opened door. The sight stopped him in his tracks, momentarily forgetting about the middle-aged woman, 20+ years his senior, sitting in the snow. "What the hell happened?" he asked, not expecting an answer and somewhat startled when he received one.

"I'd like to know the same thing, young man. I came home to it, and it knocked me on my ass. Now, if you'd be so kind..." she said the last with a stern motherly tone and finished the statement by lifting her arm toward him.

"Oh, yes, of course." He complied, blushing through the shame of his lack of manners. He helped her to her feet and then looked at her almost accusingly. "So, you didn't do this? I mean if this is your place than why are you coming home shortly after the sun is up?" He was afraid that she would scold him for questioning her, but he would endure it given the circumstances. He was right to ask, and she must have recognized that because she answered him honestly, sans the scolding.

"I spent the night with Lacy." She told him matter-of-factly. "The snowstorm kept me there, not that I much wanted to leave anyhow." Rebekka mistook his look of shock at her answer for one of doubt and added, "Ask her if you doubt me."

Ron blushed a deep red, having spent a few nights of his own with Lacy, but he never would have suspected such doings from Rebekka Lane. As far as Lacy and the rest of Old Joe's 'employees' on Hussey Row, they were paid to fuck anything that was horny and had something to give in return, with or without a dick. "Oh, no. That won't be needed I don't reckon." He replied obviously embarrassed, and he left it that.

Word got around quickly and within two hours of their discovery the whole valley knew, what few were left to hear, that is. Aside from the initial shock of seeing two dead bodies in her shack, Rebekka seemed to be handling it rather well. Eerily well, actually. The bodies were taken out of the shack, but Rebekka couldn't bear to stay there any longer, so she gathered her things and moved into Sue Ann and David Bailey's newly rebuilt place instead. Rebekka had known David well, loved and cared for him like a son and Carol like a daughter, so it was a comfort to be living in David's place. It was a little farther away from Lacy on Hussey Row since she was now staying by the Lot rather than in the Slums, but she didn't mind it.

David Bailey was sent heavenward in the valley's ritualistic funeral pyre with his wife on his right side and his mistress-for-a-short-time on his left, but only one of the three actually made it there. They were, also, the last of the valley folks to ever be sent heavenward in such a traditional fashion.

Chapter Fifty

Ice, Slice, and a Price

1

Three days went by after the deaths of the Bailey's and Carol Jewell, and all the valley folks could do was speculate on what they thought happened as to why David killed Carol and then himself. It was obvious once they all thought about the days before Sue Ann fell on the mountain, but it didn't lessen the hurt of losing more friends and loved ones. They would have to endure yet a few more before that year ended and the next one began, only two days from then. The survivors just wouldn't know of these last few deaths until after the start of the new year, and even then, they would only find three of the four bodies.

The ice storm that brought in the new year for the folks of the valley was a harsh one, but all survived except for the elderly and their caretaker. They did not and it wasn't so much a direct effect of the ice storm as it was a direct effect of Doreen's death. It began the afternoon of Doreen's passing, an hour or so before sundown, and ice pellets the size of small pebbles fell from the sky in a torrent. It fell well into the night, and when it finally dissipated and the dark storm clouds parted ways, everything was coated in an inch or more thick layer of ice. Windows, the few that still had glass panes, cracked but remained sealed through the thick ice that would take days to melt away. Valley folks were trapped wherever they had sheltered, and it was a long four days stuck where they were, but they endured.

Doreen rushed around the Infirmary, it was just her and the three bed-stuck elderly folks, trying to shutter and lock

512

all the windows, close off all unnecessary entryways and bring in as much wood as she could before the storm worsened. While she scrambled to accomplish everything else, the fire had burned down low and that was when she started bringing in firewood. She hoped that the fisherman would pop in at any time so that she could set him to doing such chores. She assumed that he was on Hussey Row with Sugar, though, and she was right, he was. No matter, she would endure, or so she thought.

One of the front double doors of the Infirmary flew open with a BANG! that startled the three elderly folks confined to their beds. Doreen came stumbling in and fighting the ice-imbedded wind managed to kick the door closed without losing a single chunk of the first bundle of firewood piled up in her arms. She took off across the large waiting room of the Infirmary toward the stone fireplace, she walked slowly but seemed to take smaller and smaller strides with every step. Doreen was more than halfway to the fireplace when she side-stepped, catching the attention of Old Man Daniels. He directed his attention in Doreen's direction and Old Mr. and Mrs. Jones followed his line of sight out of curiosity. They watched from their beds as Doreen's eyes rolled, her head lolled and then she slowly released her large armload of firewood. It spilled from her arms a few pieces at a time, almost as if in slow motion, and more than one of them landed on the tops of her booted feet. Whether it hurt or not, Doreen gave no indication as she swayed on her feet and then fainted dead away. She crumpled to the ground, partially atop the loose pile of firewood, in an incredibly uncomfortable position, where she would remain until her body was discovered days later.

Doreen did not die immediately; instead, she slipped into a malnutrition-induced coma and then fell away into the depths of forever a few hours later. The elderly thought she had died long before then and had ceased calling to her to wake up and watching her for movement. None of the three of them were close enough to see if she was breathing and her head was turned away from them so they could not see her eyes. They had full visibility of one hand and one of her feet, and for a while watched her. She twitched a time or two, but it only instilled a sense of false hope in them.

The last of the flames in the fireplace died out less than two hours after Doreen had fainted, not that they were putting off much heat anyway. The hot coals and orange embers lasted a few hours longer, but it did nothing to fight off the bitter cold that seeped into their old, frail bones. Mr. and Mrs. Jones were wearing their flannel pajamas opting not to have dressed that day, and they each had a few blankets a piece. They had scooted their beds together long ago and even sharing their body heat, Mrs. Jones a little plumper than Mr. Jones, they were not able to withstand the cold. They froze to death in each other's arms in the darkest, coldest hours before dawn, mere hours after Doreen had drifted away into her own oblivion.

Old Man Daniels' awoke the following morning, waited for some time for them to wake on their own before trying the wake them himself. When he realized that they weren't going to wake up, he lay in his bed and wept. His bones ached more than the others, more than likely a side effect of his very thin, very frail body type. So, Old Man Daniels dressed in layers all winter long, no matter if he was bed ridden or not. As the first of his three days alone drew on and the sun began to set, he knew that if he was going to survive the cold of night, he would need more than the blankets he had. The only ones within reach of him and his bed, though, were the ones covering the deceased bodies of his friends, Mr. and Mrs. Jones. He asked the Gods for forgiveness and then reached over and took all but a single blanket that he draped across them both. That added five more to the four he already had.

He survived the second night and even the third by spreading the blankets in layers over him from head to toe, occasionally lifting a small edge of the blanket to allow some fresh air into the staleness of his own warm breath. He rested little but dozed more and more often as he slowly dehydrated, his skin tightening and shriveling against his bones. By the morning of the third day, the second day of the new year, he awoke from a restless short fit of sleep too weak to sit up or even move the blankets off him.

Old Man Daniels, lying in the fetal position beneath his multi-layered blankets, died a couple hours later, resembling a mummy straight out of the crypts of Egypt.

2

About three hours later, Johnathan Colmes was the first person to break the ice away from his door and end his iced-in entrapment. He had been with Sarah at his place when the ice storm started, so they endured the four days together and were elated to have the time and privacy to think and talk everything out. They had almost accomplished that too, but then Sarah became very weak. They had had very little to eat and Johnathan would always give at least half of his own to the woman carrying his child. The woman that looked as if she were in the throes of her second trimester but was really only about eight or nine weeks along. It was astonishing, frightening, and eerie, but no matter how much he tried, John could not deny the intense love he felt for his child. His son... according to Sarah, who claimed she knew it was a boy, but didn't know how she could know.

Due to Sarah's extreme weakness from lack of sustenance, John forced his way out of the shack and took off toward the Infirmary, fighting off his own bouts of weakness, to get Doreen. She would come for Sarah; he knew she would because she was just as intrigued by Sarah's extraordinary child as its parents were. The last thing he expected to find after busting his way through the back door of the Infirmary, though, was four dead bodies. There was no smell, the deep cold dampened it almost to the point of nonexistence. Doreen was still in the same position she had been in when she fell, sprawled across the loose chunks of firewood. He found Old Man Daniels under a heap of blankets and his body was still slightly warm to the touch having just died a few hours before. He was the most disheartening to look at because the smallness and frailness of his body gave him an almost child-like appearance. Finally, he uncovered the bodies of Mr. and Mrs. Jones. The couple was facing each other, both lying in the fetal position, so close their noses almost touched, and their fingers were entwined and resting between them. Because they had froze instead of starved or dehydrated their bodies were perfectly preserved from the moment of death.

John was initially in a flustered panic, not knowing what to do since the only person that could help Sarah was dead and frozen to the floor. The panic turned to fear as he realized that Sarah could very well die if she didn't get help, but he didn't know how to help her. If only I could find her something to eat. He thought to himself and that thought led to the next and the next and so a plan began to form. Within minutes he was on his feet and in action, relieved and hopeful for a future with Sarah. A future that a deep part of him knew he would never have.

Less than an hour later, Johnathan stood in the back room of his Butcher's shop, tying his stained apron around his back, with a nostalgia-like feeling. He was perfectly calm and unregretful of his actions. The way Johnathan Colmes looked at it, he had a family now and that meant taking care of them at any and all costs. He was hell-bent on being the father he never had. That was one of the few things they had yet to discuss before Sarah took ill. Well, not ill, she was just extremely malnourished, but Johnathan was about to fix that though.

He removed his meat clever from the peg on the wall, remembering and adoring the feel of its worn and scarred wooden handle on his fingers. Then he slowly sauntered over to the long wooden table where the body of Old Mrs. Jones laid in wait. He had stripped her down and cleaned her the best he could in the cold conditions, numbing his fingers in the process. With everything prepared and ready for his use, he began by hacking off her hands and feet at the ankle and wrist joints. Then he would set the cleaver aside to replace it with an incredibly sharp knife with a deer antler handle. He used it to slice what little meat he could off the palms of her hands and the soles of her feet. He then tossed the parts he could not use into a bucket off to the side and moved on to her head, repeating the same process with every other body part of hers.

Even though she was noticeably better fed than her husband, Old Man Daniels and Doreen, there was still precious little that Johnathan could carve off Old Mrs. Jones. He took all he could off her legs, arms, torso, sides, and back but it was only enough to maybe feed Sarah for a couple weeks, at most. Even less once he told Sarah where they were going after she felt better and was strong enough to walk a little way.

He tossed the 'scraps', the remains of Mrs. Jones' corpse, dismembered and sliced and carved in so many places she was unrecognizable as a human, never mind who she was, into the whirlpool-like convergence of the east and west branches of the river. John watched them swirl in the water and then quickly float downstream. He walked back into his shop and finished preparing the meat by dicing the sliced off strips of flesh into bite sized pieces. Most of it was still frozen, some almost completely solid, but some were beginning to thaw from being handled and a few drops of blood were visible. He gathered the meat and wrapped it in half-frozen, half wilted massive cabbage leaves, as was his normal before everything went to Hell, and tied the hemp twine as tight as he could get it around the leaves with his numbing fingers. While also carrying what little bit of food he was able to find in the Infirmary, the package of meat held up well enough on his way back to his place, where Sarah awaited him. Only two tiny drops of blood had escaped it, painting the pure white snow with its crimson color. Only two tiny drops that would go unnoticed by humans and animals alike and be covered with fresh snow by morning.

3

John did not see a single other living person that day while he was away from Sarah, so he decided he would go around helping others get out the next day. He needed one more night alone with the love of his life to get everything settled.

Sarah awoke at the sound of Johnathan walking into the shack, but she did not try to sit up. She opened her eyes enough to register that it was, in fact, Johnathan and not someone else, like Frank McGrath for example, that had just walked in. She was relieved but knew that had it not been Johnathan there was nothing she could have done about it while she was in her current state. Sarah closed her eyes again and dozed off without being aware of it. When she opened them again, she was met with confusion believing that she had only had her eyes closed for a moment, for just a touch longer than a blink. What she discovered when she opened her eyes, wasn't a sight but a smell. A delicious, mouth-watering, seductive smell of cooking meat that was delirium-inducing. I'm dreaming. She thought to herself with a self-pitying tone and then closed her eyes once more.

She was awoken sometime after that and to her it had only been a moment or so since she had closed her eyes again. She was slightly irritated about being awaken so suddenly. She couldn't understand why Johnathan was waking her up anyway. It was obvious that she was with child, hell she felt like she swallowed a cannon ball and looked the part too, and she was weak from hunger on top of that. So, why was he trying so hard to wake her up? She opened her eyes and meant to ask him so just as harshly as she had thought it, but then she smelled the food again and her eyes immediately found the steaming bowl sitting on the floor beside the bed. All harsh thoughts drifted away as her hunger overtook her. She was ravenous and regardless of how big she felt she looked she knew she was far too thin to be nourishing a child. A normal one or otherwise.

Sarah, with Johnathan's help, sat up in bed but her arms were too weak to hold her bowl and spoon. She tried but almost spilled the hot meat and gravy all over herself, so John took over. He sat there and patiently fed and listened to her as she wept about feeling so weak and useless. She protested his help but took every bite of her food, and he endured her crying and ranting all the while. He even encouraged it at times when he thought she was faltering. He knew that the louder and more worked up she got the better she felt. At that point, he hadn't been able to get her past a shout, but she was starting on her second helping, so time would tell.

It did and by the end of her second bowl, one that she was able to eat the last half of by herself, she was sitting upright. Her strength and color had come back completely, and she was just about screaming at him about something he had lost track of minutes ago. If Sarah wasn't completely back to her normal self, she was very close.

Once he got her settled down, he told her that they only had that night to finish clearing everything up between them. She agreed and told him to make them the last of the coffee she had found weeks ago. He did and brought their mugs into the bedroom where she remained but was still sitting.

And, so, the conversation continued.

They had already discussed Sarah and Frank's relationship, as well as John and the Witch's. They talked about Sarah being with child and if anything had happened to have caused its strangeness. The longest and most heated part of their conversation was the baby and how they were going to handle the situation if it really wasn't a child at all.

John initiated the conversation by asking Sarah about her and Frank. She told him about their last conversation and how she had told Frank about her and John being snowed-in together. "He kinda connected the pieces, ya know? I didn't confirm nor deny it, but he knew." She had told him. Then, she revealed the deep dark secret that Frank McGrath didn't want anyone in the valley to know, his homosexual love affair with Dansford Keeton. John was dumbfounded, not because of Frank and Dan's affair, but because of how easily it had slipped from Frank's lips. It would have been amusing if it wasn't so pitiful.

That led Sarah to ask John about him and the Witch, giving John no other choice but to confess that he hadn't seen or spoken to her since the night Joshua Jones' wife and baby girl died. It was then Sarah's turn to be dumbfounded by the blatant disregard and disrespect he had shown the woman that he was not only in a relationship with for some months, but he had also betrayed in the most love-murdering of forms. To completely ignore her existence, on top of everything else, was like pouring salt into a bleeding gaping wound. He should have been ashamed of himself and then without thinking, she asked him, "Is that the kind of man you want your son to be?"

John sat thoughtfully silent through his reprimand, but tears pricked his eyes as she asked the last. If she was trying to get her point across, that certainly did it. "You're right. I should have handled the situation better, but I did the best I could at the time, and I didn't think I could face her

519

until I had everything figured out. Now, I think I do." He continued by telling her how he believed that the Witch had enchanted him into loving her, if you could even call it love if it was enchantment-induced. He went on to explain how coming out of the enchantment was like emerging from a thick mist that swallowed everything around you, how it was so confusing and almost suffocating in its intensity. It took him much longer to come out of that mist than he cared to admit, but when he did, everything resumed its natural color and beauty. Everything became clear again. He was as sure that Sarah helped him emerge from that mist, as he was that the baby Sarah was carrying was his.

Sarah understood why Johnathan didn't want to face the Witch in such a state. She also believed that, even if he wouldn't admit it, that he was afraid the Witch would just suck him back into her clutches. It was by no means an excuse for treating the Witch with such disregard, but it did help to soften Sarah's anger and strengthen her empathy.

When John and Sarah began talking about her being with child, it was touch-and-go at first because Sarah was so reluctant to talk about it. He eventually got through to her that it was necessary and okay to be vulnerable with him. That she could step out of her extra tough exterior that carried her through all her hardships in life, only strengthening as it went. He reassured her that he would never hurt her, and he could tell her why he never could, but first they needed to talk about her being with child.

Eventually, John convinced Sarah and she agreed to be open with him. She was too; she opened up to him like a flower blooming in the late spring. Sarah told John how she feared the child she carried, and even though she didn't know how, she knew that there was something wrong with it. She disliked the situation for more womanly, vain, and humanly reasons as well. Her growing and changing body, the surprise and awe of growing an entire other human being, her raging hormones and uncontrollable emotions, all the sacrifices she would have to make for a child she never even asked for, didn't know, maybe didn't even want. At the same time, though, seeming to exist in isolation and loneliness, was that unique love only a mother can feel for her child.

A part of her wanted to, as bad as it sounded, to kill the child at birth, if not before, and take the first train out of the valley without John and never look back. That same part of her wanted to blame Johnathan for what ailed her unborn son. An opposite part of her wanted the child to be born in the best of health, she and Johnathan could be married, and they could live happily forever as a family of three, and maybe more later. But that was a fairytale fantasy, the makings of a love-sick child dreaming of later, better years. Those opposing parts of her were at war, and she was deeply torn because both choices felt right but wrong at the same time. It was confusing and just added more stress to an already hard decision.

John was not appalled by her thoughts and feelings, did not judge her in any fashion. He listened to her, patiently, taking in everything she said. He could empathize with both sides of her divided psyche because he too was torn quite the same way. Not nearly as intensely or nearly as long as Sarah's inner conflict, though, and he had resolved his quickly. He was not ashamed of it, but he wasn't the one literally connected to the baby either, so he completely understood why it was so much harder on Sarah. He knew that he may not agree with her decision, but if that were to be the case then so be it. It wasn't, though, and in the end, they decided that if the child was born a normal healthy baby, then they would treat it as such. If it came out as anything but that, they would 'dispose' of it. Simple as that and they would figure out the details when the time came.

As John pondered on what could have caused such an incredible anomaly as her rapid growth, he asked Sarah what she did the days after the snow-in. If she had known the term for it, she would have said that John was interrogating her, having her go over each day, time and time again. When she mentioned that she had to stop and inform a few others to meet at the Infirmary one day shortly after the snow-in, the Witch one of them, he focused on that. She could almost see the pieces connecting in his mind, forming the larger picture, and exposing other missing pieces. Sarah insisted though, that she never set foot in the Witch's shack. She knocked on the door, the Witch answered, Sarah told her they could use her help over at the Infirmary, but the Witch said she wasn't feeling well so Sarah left her be. It was short and to the point.

John didn't buy it. Something didn't feel right about it, but he couldn't say how or what or whatever. The more he thought about it, the more he convinced himself that the Witch had somehow enchanted Sarah too, and that more than what she believed happened, actually happened. Aside from confronting the Witch directly about it, which could fare very badly for him, Sarah, and their unborn baby, John didn't know how to find out what was going on with his child. It was something that needed further contemplation.

4

When Sarah's weakness began, they both thought it was from her getting over-excited about their emotional, heated discussion about the baby and John's stressful interrogation-style questioning. It worsened quickly and they soon realized it was more than that, much more. That was late the night before, and she had been in bed ever since. They sat sipping the last of the coffee from chipped mugs almost 20 hours later, a night and day difference in Sarah's strength, and John changed the subject to a much more disheartening and grimmer one. He told her about Doreen and the elderly, omitting what he did after that.

Sarah wept, of course, for her friend Doreen and initially asked what had happened to her. Before John could answer, she changed her mind and told him not to tell her, that she really didn't want to know. John kept his theories on what happened at the Infirmary to himself. He done the best he could to comfort her through her grief and when she quieted, he reminded her of when he had told her that he would never hurt her. "I told you that I would tell you why I could and would never hurt you, and you can believe that that goes for our little one..."

"Our son" she spoke with finality, interrupting him.

"Forgive me." John told her with a small smile. "...that goes for our little boy... tenfold.' He corrected, paused, and then sighed. "I became an orphan shortly after my seventh birthday..." he continued thoughtfully, being thrown back to that fateful day that he suddenly realized had changed his life forever. John told Sarah about his worthless, abusive father, about his mother's murder, and finally what he had done about it. He finished the recollection with how he came to be raised by Ms. Rebekka Lane. He thought he seen a look of dismay or, maybe it was disgust, on her face and quickly added, "Honey, I swear on my mama, my soul, our baby, or whatever you want me to, that I have never intentionally hurt any living creature since that day." That was the truth, too. No matter how big or how small. It seemed ironic given his career choice, but it was the truth, nonetheless. "Even at that young of an age I knew how dangerous I can be when pushed to that point, so I have dedicated my life to never reaching that point again. Please, my love, believe me when I say that I would NEVER hurt you or our son. I want to be the husband and `father to you and our baby that me and mama needed but never had." He finished by taking her hand in both of his, her facial expression softening.

Sarah went without responding for so long that John started to think she was never going to. Finally, she asked, "What did she look like?... Was she beautiful?... Do you look like your mother or your... father?" Her questions startled him. Of everything that John had anticipated her saying, none of those questions were among them.

He stammered over his reply before he was finally able to give her an answer. He described his mother to her, the best he could, that was. It had been more than 15 years since he had laid eyes on her, and they didn't have photos in the valley. A few had drawings but that was all, and if there had been one of his mother and father, or the three of them as a family, John had never seen it. He also told her that he very much resembled his father, but he was not as big as his old man, and certainly not as mean. His father had been a beastly-sized man, a lumberjack, but John was a couple inches shorter and not quite as muscular.

Sarah never mentioned the deaths of John's parents after that but would occasionally inquire about his mother. Very rarely his father, though. Sarah actually done this because she could feel the love he felt for his mother and wanted to keep her memory alive for him. He always seemed to perk up a bit whenever she would ask some random question about her and it usually followed with a story, most of which she genuinely enjoyed hearing and Jonh genuinely seemed to enjoy telling.

After their first discussion about his mother, he returned to the subject of Rebekka Lane. John told Sarah of his plan for the two of them to go stay with Rebekka. She would be better fit to help him take care of Sarah and she was also one of the few that didn't harbor resentment toward either of them because of Frank McGrath. Sarah had done business with Rebekka on several occasions, but didn't know her beyond that, and she certainly never would have thought that Rebekka had raised the man she fell in love with. John didn't know who else to turn to, and since he had to leave Sarah to take care of her, he couldn't do it alone. She would be too vulnerable, he thought to himself, having no idea just how protected she was. Just as long as she had Satan's unborn, marked son within her, that was.

Sarah was reluctant to agree to going to stay with Rebekka, but John swayed her, getting her to understand how easily overcome she would be if someone or something attacked while he was out scavenging for things to take care of her. He didn't want to play on her vulnerability but felt it necessary for her to see reason. She finally agreed to it, willingly enough and then asked for another bowl of meat and gravy.

He felt uneasy about it but allowed her that third serving of the night. She took it gratefully, feeding herself, and ate it greedily. When she was finished, she wiped her mouth with the sleeve of her flannel nightgown and initiated the conversation about the 'food' he had acquired. It was as if she had just realized that she had been eating meat that she had not hunted and killed herself.

"You suddenly learn how to hunt?" she asked him in a light-hearted teasing manner.

He eyed her strangely for a moment before answering, "Somethin like that."

That remark earned him a strange look, and another question. "Seriously, what is it? Deer, rabbit, bear?" That time she wasn't teasing, though, and was becoming genuinely curious about the meat that tasted so good to her and even better to the child inside her. She could almost feel her unborn child's strength increase with each bite of the savory, slightly tough, uniquely flavored meat.

Johnathan skirted the question by asking a couple of his own. "Do ya like it? It's not upsettin yer stomach or anythin?"

"No, not upsettin me at all. It's delicious! At first, I thought it was just because of how hungry I was, I think anything would have tasted amazin when you first woke me this evening. That last bowl I ate was better than the first two, though. The baby likes it, too. I can feel him gettin stronger and I know that whatever kind of meat that is, it's good for our baby. So, make it a permanent item on your shoppin list, honey." She told him with another sweet, teasing little smile.

John did not verbally reply, he didn't trust his voice to, but he returned her smile with a small one of his own. The uneasiness that he felt earlier had spread like cancer into dread, but he would not allow himself to be regretful. Sarah was stronger for what he had done and given her, and according to Sarah, so was the child. Why would he regret that? How could he?

They sat thoughtfully in silence for a few long moments and then Sarah blurted out, "What will become of us John?"

He looked at her, obviously confused about her meaning, but replied with the safest answer he could think of. "I'm not sure, to be honest with ya. I really don't know what's goin on to be able to answer that right now. I reckon I could go give the Witch a visit..."

Sarah immediately objected with a harsh "NNNNOOOOO!!!!" She provided no further explanation and immediately silenced, so that he could continue.

John stared at her for a moment and restarted. "I reckon I could have Rebekka ask around for me and see what she can find out. Maybe I can answer you when I have some more information."

The answer would have to be suffice, like it or not, Sarah decided, believing it was the best she was going to get. John could see the disappointment on her face and knew that even though she would accept that answer, it wasn't filled with the reassurance she was looking for from him. So, he added, "Regardless of what trials and tribulations befall us, love, we will face them together. We will stand against them, with our child in our arms and our hearts, and best whatever comes our way as one." John told her, relapsing into the wordage of the stories he grew up hearing and then reading of the olden days of elegance and regality. Those olden days that allowed him the fantasies that filled his mind, and carried him through his childhood years, of grand adventures, cunning enemies, and beautifully attainable noblewomen.

The reassurance that John so hoped had emanated from his last bit, worked and Sarah was much more pleased with that answer. So much so that she rewarded him with a lovely, sensual smile and then wrapped her arms around his neck, pulling him to her. She kissed him long and slowly. It was the first one since they left his shack after the blizzard and neither of them had realized how much they had missed the touch of the other. They were nearly panting with passion when they pulled away from each other, staring deeply into each other's eyes as the silent communication that only those within the bounds of true love can possess passed between them. A moment later John leaned in for another more playful kiss, laying her down as his tongue fondled hers and his hands roamed about her beautifully changing body.

They made love for the first time in weeks. It was slow, gentle, and sensational. The two of them collapsed into each other's arms right after they climaxed together, and Sarah was asleep in minutes, resting the way only those inflicted with pleasurable exhaustion can. John, however, lay awake long after she fell asleep nestled against his side. He lay there listening to the rumbling of his hungry stomach and wondering what exactly the meat was doing to Sarah and the baby, why it was making them stronger. He hadn't and wouldn't eat any of the meat, he had decided that while butchering Old Mrs. Jones. He was torn about telling Rebekka, though. He couldn't tell her not to eat it without telling her what it was, and he didn't feel right about not telling her and letting her eat it anyway. He could tell her that it was a special diet for Sarah but that would come with a lot of other questions.

He was still pondering that and everything else when he drifted off into a fitful sleep.

Chapter Fifty-One

Bloodless Hearts

1

The beginning of January was the bloodiest part of the winter in the valley, the valley folks losing a total of ten survivors in the first ten days of the year. On the third day of January the death of Old Man Daniels was the only one of the new year, at that time. Johanthan Colmes, after taking his beloved to Rebekka Lane's new place over by the Lot, went around helping those few that remained in the valley out of their shacks. The only person that had lived in a teepee was Beth Redley, but she joined her brother at the bottom of the waterfall a while before the ice storm demolished her newly rebuilt place. No one knew that, of course, they just knew they hadn't seen her for some time.

Lacy, one of the only two left of Old Joe's employees, had rather enjoyed her little break during the ice storm. Sugar did too, just not in the same relaxing way as Lacy. The fisherman was with Sugar when the ice storm started, and they ended up stuck together for the next few days. They had very, very few customers, but their regulars, Rebekka and the fisherman, were as needy and exhausting as a few of the others combined. Neither one minded it, though, it kept them fed-ish, and was a pleasant distraction from the constant death and loss that loomed over the valley that terrible winter.

Even though Old Joe Brenner frequented the Bar every day, enjoying the pleasant company of the twin bartenders and owners, Nonna and Nonni Brookes, he spent the ice storm in his own little shack on Hussey Row. He went three days without seeing them and it did the opposite of easing that sexual tension he felt equally toward both women. The little spark felt among the three of them had only strengthened over time, each very aware of their own personal feelings and desires. No amount of self-pleasure was enough; in fact, it seemed to make the yearnings even worse. It still had not been recognized by the others or acknowledged by any of them. The feelings just continued to fester and intensify. Nonna and Nonni, who were so closely linked they could almost read each other's thoughts, hadn't even mentioned the sexual tension toward Old Joe to each other. It was the longest secret the twins had ever kept from each other in their entire lives.

Speaking of secrets, Johnathan tried much harder than he should have had to, not to give Frank or Dansford, the indication that he knew of their secret affair when he helped them get out of Frank's place. It was apparent that neither of them was fairing too well under the pressure. Frank was half out of his mind with intense rage toward Sarah and paranoia over their deep dark secret being exposed. Most of the time he took the anger that boiled over when he thought of it too long and directed it at Dansford. It happened so often that it had almost become a routine. Beginning with Frank becoming outraged over something insignificant causing them to argue. The arguing led to throwing and the throwing led to hitting. Frank would never use a closed fist on Dan's face because that would leave an evident mark; he saved those for the body. He would try to fight back, but Frank had always been the bigger and stronger of the pair. At best, he could get in a hit good enough to bloody his lip or nose. The hitting always, somehow, led to a very rough and painful session of intimacy. Ones that left Dan in tears and Frank in a fitful, restless sleep.

Dansford Keeton was still distraught over the death of Robert Daniels, the guilt ate at his psyche and his soul. Frank knew how guilty and ashamed Dan felt about it and he used that to his advantage. Used it to distill fear in him, making him easier to manipulate and keep quiet. In a moment of weakness, however, Dansford attempted to at least try and make it right with his God. All those years he had been forced by his parents to attend the valley Church, had made him believe in a higher power capable of forgiving and erasing all past sins. He could only hope murder was among them.

He knocked on the Church door for a long time, circled the place trying to peer into shuttered windows, but he seen and heard no one. With a heavy heart and slumped shoulders, he returned to the place he shared with Frank, praying to his God that there would be no fighting or fucking that night. He was still bruised and bleeding from this morning, but his prayers went unanswered.

John let someone else discover the bodies in the Infirmary and let someone else point out the fact that Old Mrs. Jones' body was missing. John also stepped back and watched a disheveled Frank McGrath as he attempted to get some sort of control over the situation but failed to. Ultimately, Doreen's body was lifted, frozen in its awkward position and laid on a bed by the elderly dead men. There the three of them remained. Speculations were that the same dog pack that took the other bodies, like Sledge and Robert Daniels, took Old Mrs. Jones too, even if there wasn't any sign to prove such a thing. It was easier for them, to a person, to believe that it was the wild dog pack running around than it was to believe that one of their own had done something to her.

Aside from the few in the Infirmary, the rest of the valley folks had survived the ice storm with minimal damage to anyone's shack. When repairs and rebuilds were being done, winterization of the shacks was too, which was the biggest reason they all survived the freezing cold temperatures.

Jiminey and Patty McAvay, and Gary Brown and his wife, were the only couples that didn't gather with the rest of the survivors at the Infirmary over the deaths of Doreen and the elderly. They just continued being the antisocial couples that they were. The two pairs were civil enough, but not quite welcoming, with those who came with something to trade for their products. Other than that, they kept to themselves and were left alone to do it.

The Witch was the only other person in the valley that didn't converse with the rest, but it wasn't due to any antisocial reasons. She had simply been too busy for such things, not that mingling with the valley folks and their drab lives really appealed to her anyway. More about her and her doings later, though.

2

It was, in fact, the decisions of two people that started separate domino effects that led to the other nine deaths by the tenth of January. Betty Jones and Porter Siddle. Of course, the Witch had both a direct and indirect influence over how those dominoes fell, and she made sure that they fell perfectly aligned with her plans.

Betty Jones had made her decision regarding the Witch's offer after learning of the deaths of her grandparents, Mr. and Mrs. Jones. She believed that she had made the decision on impulse due to her overwhelming grief over losing more of her family. She still believed that her brother Joshua was alive and desperately wanted to find him. What she didn't realize was that over those past few weeks, she had been pushing Danny away, guarding and preparing herself, long before she consciously made up her mind to kill him. The day after Johnathan Colmes helped everyone bust out of their shacks, the fourth day of the new year, Betty did just that.

She waited until Alvin had left the farm, watched him cross the bridge headed for the common area before feeling sure enough that she had enough time to complete her tasks. Betty found her beau, Danny Bailey beside the barn busting firewood. She approached him casually, knowing that as long as she didn't give him any reason to be suspicious that she would be able to get the best of him. She would just have to make that first hit count, because that one was the only one that really counted.

Danny watched her stroll around from the front of the barn and his first thought was that she had come to start another fight with him, or worse, tell him that she was finally done with him and leave. He knew, could feel, that she was pushing herself away from him, no matter how desperately he clung to her, but he never could figure out why. He loved her so much and it tore at his soul that she was going to end things. There was never a single malicious thought toward her though, just heartache and a touch of pity. The deaths of her brother, niece and now her grandparents, on top of her family being stuck in New York, had been much harder on her than he originally thought. That was his assumption,

530

anyway. There was no other explanation, that he was aware of, for her unloving behavior.

Instead, she told him that she was making tea and wanted to know if he was going to come in and warm up for a bit. Not at all what he was expecting but he didn't put too much thought into it, either. After a very quick self-deliberation he decided that she was in one of her increasingly rare, good moods and he planned on taking as much advantage of that as he could. All thoughts of her leaving him faded away and were replaced with images of him making love to her in front of the blazing fireplace. When he agreed, she kissed him on the cheek and took off around the front of the barn again as if headed back to the homestead.

Betty knew that he would finish the dwindling pile by the barn before coming in, the continual whacking of the ax confirmed that, so Betty snuck through the barn. She grabbed a hatchet off the barn wall, one well weighted that she had used on multiple occasions, but never for anything so violent as what she intended to do. There was a narrow path, just a touch wider than the handcart, that ran the length of the barn and silo, nestled between them and the steep rocky mountainside. She moved silently up behind him, only moving when he did to cover the sound of the snow crunching beneath her feet. The sun was out but casting her shadow behind her so she knew that that would not give her away. She flipped the hatchet so that the flat end would be her weapon of choice for the first critical blow. She could pull it off, she knew she could, but she would have to have her timing just right, and she only had one chance to do it.

She was only a step behind him, hatchet in hand and ready to strike, but she paused until he raised the axe above his head, straightening his body and bringing his head slightly back. As soon as he was in the position that she wanted him to be in, she brought the flat end of the hatchet down on the center of his head as hard as she could swing it. Betty was a farmhand, just as strong as Danny and Alvin, proving it anytime she could, so the swing was considerable. Danny Bailey's head split like a hatching egg, gray matter slowly seeped out from between the cracks, a cloudy white liquid oozed from around it and mixed with the rush of blood from his lacerated scalp. He pitched forward slightly, dropped the axe to his side, and stood there for a long moment before falling face first to the ground.

Luckily enough for Betty, she had been behind Danny, so she was spared the sight of his face as he died. The sudden and powerful impact caused one of his eyes to bulge from the socket and the other one to completely pop out. It laid against his cheek, hanging by the optical nerves they were still attached to, and a small trickle of blood had escaped the corner of the eyeless socket. As he fell his right hand twitched twice and his left foot once, as his body registered the sudden death of his brain.

He fell to the ground, on his face, busting his lip and bloodying his nose on the hardpacked snow. His whole body seized and then began thrashing and jerking violently, creating a bizarre smear of images as his bloody face beat against the ground. It only went on for a few moments before he finally laid still and unbreathing. Betty watched all of it in horror, the full reality of what she had just done hit her like a brick in the face. She dropped the hatchet on the ground beside her and then fell to her knees weeping.

After some time, she was able to get herself under control again, and regaining her confidence decided that she would not let Danny's death be for nothing. She had killed him for a reason and since the worst of it was over, she would finish it and try to hold her head high doing it. With a renewed spirit, she grabbed the hatchet and crawled over to her dead beau's body. As soon as she rolled him over, she leaned over and vomited up a mouthful of bile leaving behind a terrible aftertaste. The jerking and thrashing had shredded his lips and cheeks, the lower half of his face a mask of frozen blood and small bits of torn flesh. The dangling eyeball had detached and was lying in the snow right above Danny's shoulder. Betty tossed a couple handfuls of snow over it so she wouldn't have it staring at her. It wasn't as bad as the other bulging eyeball, though, the one she couldn't cover so easily with snow. It had a snow speckled wood chip lodged into the side of it, almost touching the dark brown coloring of his eye.

For obvious reasons, Betty didn't want to look at it, so she tried to turn his head so the grotesque eye would be out of her sight. His head seemed to be frozen in place, though, so she applied a little more pressure. Suddenly, there was a loud noise that sounded very similar to a snapping tree branch causing Betty to cringe harder than she ever had in her life. Every muscle in her body tensed at the same time, and she released Danny's head, which immediately flopped unnaturally over onto his shoulder. Tears streamed from her eyes, hating that he died so terribly and knowing that she would never be able to forgive herself for what she had done. It never once occurred to her that her brother was dead or that she had been deceived by the Witch, but then again, neither did the rest of them either.

With the spiked eye out of her sight, she cut through the layers of clothes Danny wore to his chiseled chest and abs that were toned but pale and tinted a soft blue. She used the hatchet and with three good, well aimed swings she cut a triangle out of the center of his chest just large enough for her fist to fit through. Ignoring the blood splattered across her face, arms, and chest, she snaked her hand through the newly made hole. She was forearm deep in his chest cavity before her fingers wrapped around his still warm heart and she ripped it out of the hole in his chest, ignoring the slice on her finger from a jagged rib bone.

She carried it carefully as if it were the most precious element on Earth and took it into the barn. With bloody hands she carefully wrapped the heart in a rag and then tied the rag to it with hemp rope. She then tied another piece of the rope to the wrapped heart, tucking it securely into her coat pocket. The other end of the rope was tied to her wrist so she wouldn't lose it as easily if it were to fall from her pocket.

She left Danny lying beside the barn, bare chested and heartless in the snow for Alvin to find whenever he returned. She was most of the way through the Slums, on her way to the Witch's shack, before that happened, though.

3

The Witch had three visitors in less than 36 hours, and Betty Jones was the first. The Witch sensed her coming but was unsure as to the nature of her visit. It was probably going to be a refusal or a futile attempt at another deal, but maybe... just maybe... She could have used the Sight, but it would have required drawing it away from her present viewings and they seemed more important than the reason Betty was approaching her shack. Besides, the Witch didn't mind a surprise, disappointing or otherwise, every now and again. It kept things lively.

She was not at all disappointed by Betty's surprise visit, was in fact almost giddy about it. She laughed maliciously, quite pleased with how everything was unfolding before her. The Witch lifted the heart to her mouth, holding it as carefully as Betty had. Her eyes took on that black glow and she mumbled incomprehensibly. Then her eyes returned to normal, the mumbling stopped, and for a moment she only stared at Betty, making her even more uncomfortable than she already was.

Betty was just trying to understand what her eyes were telling her she had just seen. Then the Witch sank her teeth into the bloody muscle, ripping away a small chunk and Betty just stopped trying to process what she was experiencing. She was in too deep to back out by then, anyway, and she knew it. The Witch held the heart out toward her. "Drink and it will show you the way to your brother." Betty hesitated but only for a moment and then leaned forward, pressing her lips against the concavity from the missing piece. The Witch kneaded the heart as Betty sucked on it, reluctantly at first and then more greedily. Blood spilled from the corners of her mouth as she drank for several long moments.

When she was satiated, the Witch led her through the shack and pointed her in the direction of the garden. Betty took off without so much as a thank you or good-bye, and it did not go unnoticed by the Witch. "Ungrateful cunt!" she muttered as Betty disappeared into the jungle-like foliage of the Witch's magnificent garden, but she said it with a smile because Betty was going to get hers.

Just like the rest of them would.

Betty Jones trekked through the garden for a few hours, following a sense only she could feel, that she believed was going to take her to her brother Joshua. Of course, she didn't know that Joshua was dead or that she was in the same place he died. Nor did she know that the sense leading her to her brother wasn't even leading her to the tree elves that consumed him, as some sort of sick joke. It was leading her to something undiscovered, something amazing, and something that would be her doom. That something was the only creature that inhabited the garden that the mighty unicorn feared and avoided.

The desperate farmhand looking for her brother was about to be the first person, aside from the Witch of course, to ever lay eyes on that creature. She wasn't allotted enough time to appreciate or regret following the sound that led her to it, though. She was, however, allotted just enough time to register the fact that she had never seen anything like it, but everlasting darkness overtook her before she could ponder on it.

4

She wasn't sure what she was hearing at first. The sound of rain? A new kind of bird chirping from afar? It was strange but it was the first out of place sound she had heard since she began her walk through the garden. She followed the noises, coming upon a swiftly running stream, and realized that she had at least gotten the water part right. She could hear another noise over the running water and decided that it needed further investigation as well.

First, she drank from the cool refreshing stream, satiating her more human thirst. She walked through the shallow, slightly-higher-than-the-ankle deep, water in the direction of the noise she kept hearing. Betty walked several yards still unable to pinpoint what kind of animal was making that noise or if it was an animal at all.

Then she was stopped dead in her tracks by a sight like nothing she had ever even imagined.

Several yards ahead of her, sunbathing atop a massive flattish boulder that made up a large section of the bank laid a creature unlike anything she had ever seen. It spotted her at the same time she spotted it and it immediately coiled into an obvious attack stance. It was longer than any anaconda ever known but as broad as a buffalo from hips to neck. It had a long, spiked tail and two stubby but powerful hind legs. It had no arms but two large wings that appeared to be feathered all along the edges. They were positioned about a quarter of the way down from its head, protruding from its muscular back, and each wing seemed to be as wide as she was tall. Razor sharp spikes ran up from the spiked tail and tapered off just past its hind legs, and then resumed just before the wings, dividing them, and continued up its neck and merged at the top of its massive head with the clump that occupied it. It was a small patch of the same feathers that lined its wings. The head was an odd elongated triangular shape, like a deformed viper would have. Its eyes, set just a little too far apart, were large and a brilliant orange color, vibrant enough to be seen from yards away. Its nostrils sat at the end of its long snout, much like a crocodile, and its huge jaw-unhinging mouth was lined with three rows, top and bottom, of needle-sharp fangs that oozed a bright orange venom. Except for the feathers and the spikes, the creature was covered from snout to tail with scales a shiny, almost metallic, black that shimmered in the sunlight. The spikes beginning at the base were black but quickly melted on the way up the spikes, into the same bright orange as the venom that leaked from its slobbering jaws. Its feathers matched its eyes, spikes, and poison.

Betty had time to hear its half-bird, half-banshee screech and see the feathers on its head and outstretched wings vibrate, creating their own strange clicking noise. Something large and dark came rushing into her view so fast that she had zero chance of reacting. The blow was so sudden and forceful that her death was mercifully instantaneous.

A second creature, one a little larger than the one Betty had her staring contest with, removed its spiked tail from her face. It swished its massive tail with enough force to sling the gore from its spikes as Betty's body collapsed into the stream. Betty Jones was no longer recognizable. The creature had obliterated her face, concaving it, leaving behind a large bloody, featureless crater where her pleasant face had been only moments ago.

It was called a Basiliragon, the Witch's own creation with the mythical dragon and basilisk in mind. It sauntered off to rejoin its mate up the stream. When the one on the boulder had settled down, the three much smaller, python-sized offspring went about slither-crawling through the stream, resuming their play.

Awhile later, hungry and tired from their hard play, the young feasted on Betty's corpse, and it served to be quite a fine meal for the three little ones.

Chapter Fifty-Two

What to Do with the Dead?

1

Alvin Danson returned to the farm shortly before Betty made it to the Witch's shack, but he didn't find his friend, Danny Bailey, for a few more hours. In fact, Alvin barely thought of Danny or Betty until later that evening, lost in his own grief-filled thoughts of his lost love, Anna. Betty or Danny, either one, would walk over to get Alvin every evening around the same time to eat with them. The meals were becoming more and more meager but at least they still had something, which was more than others in the valley could say. The evening that Betty had killed Danny, neither of them showed, and that's when Alvin became curious.

Of course, the first place he checked was their shack. No one there, and no sign that anyone had been there in some time. So, with a lit lantern in hand, he went outside, into the darkening evening in search of his friends. His breath puffed from his mouth and nostrils in small puffy clouds, the icy cold wind rippled his layered clothing, and the snow crunched loudly under his feet in the eerily quiet dusk.

After some time and some fruitless beckoning, Alvin never found Betty, but he did find Danny. His entire body, what Alvin could see of it, was cast with a blue, icy tint, and the ragged, gory edges of the hole in his chest sparkled with ice crystals. Alvin was hit with a wave of nausea at the sight of his friend but had nothing in his stomach to expel. He sat by his friend's side and silently mourned until his fingers and toes had grown numb in the bitter cold.

He drug Alvin's body into the barn and covered him with several old grain bags. It saddened him to see his friend in such a manner but there was nothing else he could do for him that night. So, Danny was left to lie frozen in the barn while Alvin went back to the warmth of his shack, only to cry himself to sleep with an empty stomach.

The following morning Alvin woke with a newfound purpose. A dream, or maybe it was an epiphany, came to him the night before. He walked out to the barn where Danny still lay; somehow, his scent evaded the small, viciously hungry dog pack roaming the timbers around the valley. Alvin knelt beside his deceased friend and with tears in his eyes, he said his final good-byes. Then he stood up, struck a wooden match off a barn post, and flicked the lit match into the bales of hay stacked on one side of the barn. Within seconds the tiny flame had grown to that of the size of a blazing fireplace, and seconds after that half the bales were smoking and smoldering.

Alvin stood in the barn beside his friend until he could stand the heat no longer and then slowly backed out. When he finally turned his back to the flames and headed for the western bridge, he never looked back.

He had one destination in mind, and he refused to be diverted. He had his entire heart and soul, or so he thought, set on finally getting the help he needed... the help he deserved. Unfortunately for Alvin, though, it didn't go the way he envisioned. Of all the scenarios he had played out in his head of how the Witch would help him, being outright denied was not one of them.

2

Alvin Danson was her third and final visit within the confines of that 36-hour limit, but it did not go as planned for either of them. The Witch had invited him in, heard him out and even began his tarot reading, feeling as though she would be adding yet another soul to her devilish resume. She drew and laid the first card, as expected. She drew the second fully expecting it to be The Devil card, which was her sign that his soul was ripe for the taking. Alvin's second card, however, was The Sun, which was the opposite, much more optimistic version of The Devil card. It signified all that the Witch had renounced and despised. All that her Master resented.

She quickly gathered her tarot cards, refused to help, or even see Alvin Danson again, and then sent the pleading man away. Alvin beat and banged on her shack door, alternating between screaming profanities and begging her for her help, for some time before finally giving up and walking away. To where, the Witch did not know nor care.

Alvin felt an unbearable weight of hopelessness crush him as he walked away from the Witch's shack. He didn't know what to do or where to go as he slowly, mindlessly, walked through the Slums during that early afternoon. He passed Hussey Row and then felt his knees buckle under the crushing weight of his own heartbreak and emotions. So, he made his way into the Bar and took a seat. He made no attempt to ask for anything, and after several minutes, Nonni walked up to him.

She noted his dark, baggy eyes, tear-stained cheeks, and the deep look of depression or desperation upon his face. "Ya look like ya could use a drink, hun... or maybe two." She said to him, partly as an offer and partly for conversation.

"Ain't got nothin." He said, shortly.

"I's see." Nonni responded softly and then turned to leave him be, once more. A few minutes later she returned with a bottle of Shine and a glass. She sat both at the table before him. "On me today, hun." She told him, gave him a wink, and then headed back to the bar again.

He stared at the bottle for a long time, unmoving. Finally, he leaned forward and uncorked the bottle. He poured a mouthful into the bottom of the glass, picked it up and swirled it around thoughtfully. He done this for so long that Nonna and Nonni Brookes, standing at the bar and watching him without being obvious about it, weren't sure he was ever going to drink it. Finally, he brought the cup to his mouth, swallowed the contents, and slammed it down on the table, startling the identical women. He paid no attention to them, just poured another mouthful into the glass, and repeated the process of swirling, drinking and then slamming. Each time the swirling ended sooner than the last.

After about a third of the bottle of Shine had been drunk, Alvin decided it had grown too warm in the Bar for him, so he grabbed his bottle, left the glass, nodded his head in thanks in the direction of the bar, and walked out into the much colder, failing light of late afternoon/early evening in the mountains. He stepped around to the side of the Bar, relieved himself, and then headed for the western bridge.

He had forgotten about setting the barn on fire until he seen the orange glow against the mountainside as he stopped and stared just as he had passed the Mercantile. Of course, everything else on the farm went up in flames with it but it would go no further than there. In his hazy Shine-soaked mind, Alvin knew he couldn't go there but didn't know where else to go. So, he turned around and stumbled up onto the small porch of Brown's Mercantile, where he sat and consumed another third of the bottle of Shine.

By then, Alvin was out of his mind with grief over his lost friends, the ghastly images of Danny replaying in his head, and the Witch's constant denial on repeat. The Shine was in full effect, amplifying his emotions and exasperating his mentality until he could stand it no longer. He refused to live in such a way. He took another swig from the bottle and then walked into the lockless Mercantile. Alvin only grabbed one thing, a coil of thick, strong hemp rope, and left what was left of the Shine as payment for the use of it. He took one last, final long swig from the bottle and then stepped back out onto the porch. Alvin swung the looped end of the rope over one of the porch rafters and tied it securely to a post.

Alvin Danson's final thoughts were of relief at finally being able to end his pain.

3

The following morning, the sun was high but not nearly high enough to peak over the mountaintops and be seen by the few surviving valley folks when Gary Brown and his wife sauntered up to their shop. His wife was in one of her incredibly rare, delightful moods and Gary was watching her walk up onto the screened-in porch of the Mercantile, thinking that he couldn't love his wife any more than he did in that moment.

His loving husbandly thoughts were jerked from his mind by the unnerving screech that ripped from his wife's throat, and he rushed to her side. He seen what made her scream a mere moment before the words, "What the hell?" popped out of his mouth, unable to stop them. He stepped between her and the hanging, deceased body of Alvin Danson, shielding her from his frozen dead stare. Gary held his wife tightly against his chest, her still screaming all the while but not fighting his touch. He was able to lead her into the Mercantile and set her down behind the counter. Luckily, that position did not have a direct line of sight to the end of the porch Alvin had hung himself on. It took quite some time before Gary could calm his wife enough to be able to step away from her for a few minutes. He patiently held her while she screamed and cried out her most recent of nightmares, he soothed her, reassured her, and told her how safe she was until she believed it herself.

When he was finally able, he went back out on the porch and untied Alvin's body. It dropped to the weatherworn wood floor with a sickening crunch that caused Gary's stomach to churn. He belched back the nausea behind sealed lips, certain that if he opened them that the vomit would immediately follow.

He had no idea what to do with the body, so he hesitated for a long moment before grabbing the corpse by its ankles. Gary didn't know who he should tell, with Doreen dead and Frank McGrath a step away from completely losing his mind, or if he should bother telling anyone at all. It was obvious the man wanted to die, or he wouldn't have hung himself. Why on his shop porch? Gary had no idea, but it made no difference anyway, he still had a dead body to dispose of. As soon as he grabbed the stiff, frozen legs of Alvin Danson, he released them. He was not expecting them to feel that way. He didn't know what to expect, but it wasn't that. He decided with very little deliberation to take the body to the closest place that it could be found without his wife coming across it again.

He steeled himself and grabbed the ankles again, dragging the body off the porch. Once on the ground, he looked around quickly, hoping no one would choose that time to come strolling through. No one did. He spotted the Butcher's shop to the right of the mercantile, briefly considered it, almost rejected it, but ultimately decided it was as good a place as any. Gary drug the dead body to the back of the Butchers shop and propped Alvin against the wall beside the back entrance.

He pushed all thoughts of guilt and shame away and replaced them with thoughts of his wife. Of course, he knew Alvin, but not well enough to know why he would kill himself. It was easy for Gary to detach himself from anything that did not directly affect him. Alvin's death and body removal was an inconvenience but nothing more. Gary's only goal in life was to care for his beloved wife to the best of his ability.

The Mercantile didn't open the day Alvin died, he took his wife home to rest, instead. He seen the note and the two-thirds empty bottle of Shine upon his return from disposing of the corpse. He took both with him when he took his hysterical wife home. Three days later, she still refused to leave the house and couldn't stand him leaving her sight for more than a matter of moments. It made very simple tasks very difficult, but Gary prevailed patiently. Any hope he had of returning to the customer-less Mercantile dwindled with each day that his wife settled into her hysteria.

The Mercantile never did open back up in the valley and he would live that drab, stressful life for almost two months.

4

A few hours after the merchant safely got his wife back to their shack, Johnathn was heading over to the burned flat O'Reigan farm. If anyone was on the farm during that fire, they had plenty of time to get across the bridge, otherwise they did not make it. They couldn't have because the only things still standing was the stone fireplaces, and those were crumbled in places. Just about everything else was ash.

Before he started for the bridge, he walked around to the back of the Butcher's shop to make sure there weren't any blood spots on the ground, or a piece of Old Mrs. Jones caught on a rock or branch. It was the first time he had had a chance to double check the area with better lighting. What he found instead of any evidence that he had been back there, made his heart jump into his throat. Alvin Danson's dead body propped up by the back door of the Butcher's shop. Coincidence or the blessing of a higher power? It really made no difference to John; he had a family to feed, and this was his only current option.

He dragged Alvin's body into the Butcher's shop through the back door, tied his apron around his back, and went to work. It was executed in a very similar way to that of Old Mrs. Jones but coming away with less meat because he was a lean young man before the lack of food issue.

Sarah and Rebekka had both grown incredibly worried for Johnathan, who had been gone since dawn, just having dropped Sarah off at and with Rebekka. He finally arrived back at Rebekka's well after dark. He had brought another cabbage leaf wrapped package of meat and a small bag of the precious few other things he could scavenge.

Sarah enjoyed the fresh meat much more than the first batch, claiming it was slightly sweeter, more tender, and much more flavorful. She then proceeded to tease him good naturedly about spoiling her with such fine food while others in the valley starved. "The others aren't my concern." He retorted softly, without bitterness. It was a terrible way to be but Sarah and, more importantly, his child, came first, and it was something John was unequivocally unregretful for.

Chapter Fifty-Three

Sinner!

1

Porter Siddle's decision resulted in the deaths of five more, his own included. He knew he was strong enough, maybe not completely healed, but still strong enough, to enact his own revenge against that sumbitch Ron Hellman. Porter needed help, though. He knew he couldn't best the much younger man in a fight, but fighting was never done fair. So, Porter went to see the Witch.

He was her second visitor and showed up less than three hours after Betty Jones disappeared into the garden. The Witch invited him in and listened to the reasoning for his visit. Porter skipped all the cordialities, not caring if he came off as rude in front of a lady, and got straight to the point, his thick mountain drawl becoming more prominent the more worked up he got talking about Ron Hellman. She could feel the waves of hatred flow from him, and it gave her a giddy schoolgirl-like excitement listening to him rave about how badly he wanted to kill that sumbitch.

When he finally calmed down, she was so overwhelmed with the giddiness, it was almost a turn-on, but she pushed those thoughts away. She left him fuming in the altar room of the caves to step into the first and smaller of the two. That was one of those rare occasions when the Witch could skip the tarot, partly because she knew the hatred oozing from his very pores was genuine, and partly because there was no actual sorcery involved this time. She was only gone a few moments and returned with a small vial half-filled with white powder.

545

"This is White Hellebore. Just sprinkle it in or on his food." Simple enough instructions to follow.

"I's preciate it, but I ain't go nothin to give in return." He informed her, sliding the small vial across the table to her. She made no move to pick it up, only gave him a sweet smile that seemed to be hiding something much more venomous.

"Oh, but you do." she said ominously, and continued before he could comment. "We can deal with such matters another time, however. I have matters I must attend to, and you have one of your own." She placed the small vial in his hand and then escorted him through the shack and out the front door. With Porter on his way back to his place, the Witch returned to her state of meditation.

Porter returned to the shack in the Slums a few hours before Ron did giving him ample time to distribute the Hellebore. Ron had never bothered to find another hiding place for his food stash, so Porter found everything tucked neatly under the floorboards in the attached outhouse. He added a generous amount to a quarter-full jar of handmade applesauce, he sprinkled a little on a stale chunk of bread and what few pieces of jerked meat he had found wrapped up in an old swatch of leather. He added some to the few nips of Shine left in the bottom of a small ceramic jug, and what little remained he dumped into the partially full jar of blackberry jam. Porter replaced the floorboards, nice and neat, making sure everything was exactly as he found it, feeling quite pleased with himself. He stoked the fire and waited for Ron.

What the Witch failed to tell Porter Siddle was that even though she had given him twice the amount needed to kill Ron he would have to consume the entire amount of Hellebore within an allotted time to get the desired effects of the poison. Porter didn't know it, but he would have been better off putting half the vial in one item and half the vial in the other. He had distributed it too much and the only way it was going to work properly is if Ron ate half of his stash or more in one sitting, which wasn't going to happen.

Later that evening, Ron returned around his usual time and spent his usual amount of time in the outhouse. Porter felt certain that Ron had eaten something with the Hellebore in or on it, and it was confirmed the following morning when Porter woke to find a very ill Ron Hellman had been up most of the night vomiting and shitting. He was quickly deteriorating into weakness and bouts of unconsciousness, the violent regurgitation and diarrhea were starting to contain blood, and it wouldn't be very long before he had his first seizure.

Ron pleaded with Porter to help him, but Porter refused, at first claiming that he didn't want to catch whatever sickness he had. Then, Porter decided that it didn't matter if he told Ron the truth because he was a dead man anyway and that realization brought a vicious part of him to the surface. A part that the Witch had only glimpsed but would have found quite impressive. So, Porter told Ron the ugly truth, but didn't get the satisfaction he expected from it. Ron was too weak to have much of a reaction and that was disappointing, but the satisfaction came from watching Ron beg for simple things like a drink of water and having the bloody vomit wiped from his chin and chest. Porter would do none of those things for him and by the following morning, Ron had stopped asking and come to the realization that he might actually deserve the treatment Porter was giving him... maybe.

Nothing changed the rest of the day and most of the next. Ron remained pale and sickly, the vomiting and diarrhea had tapered off in intensity and rate only because he had next to nothing in his body to expel, but when it did, it was still bloody. The seizures were random but mild and he had a total of four of them, Porter refusing to help in anyway. He would just stand across the room and watch with a look of disgust upon his face.

Several hours after Ron Hellman's last seizure, he sat up in bed for the first time in days. He really didn't have much choice, it was 'get up or lay there and die'. He needed water, badly, and hadn't had any in over 24 hours so he slowly stumbled his way out of the bedroom, his legs shaky and barely able to support his weight. They finally collapsed under him just as he made it to the nearly empty water bucket. He drank what was left, slowly and deliberately, taking his time. He hadn't seen Porter in a little while and wasn't sure where he had gotten off to. What he was sure about, though, was that Porter was going to die. If Ron was able to get a bit of his strength back before Porter returned, he was going to beat that old man to death.

So, he laid on the wooden floor in the kitchen area of the shack, resting and waiting.

2

Porter had been out scavenging for food, he didn't dare eat anything out of Ron's food stash, not even the items he didn't put Hellebore on. He had found a nice little stockpile of food in Rebekka Lane's old shack, Carol Jewell had been hoarding food much the same way Ron did, and Porter had been the one lucky enough to find it. He wasn't about to share his findings with Ron, who he so hoped had died while he was out, so he left it all sitting on the side of the shack in a small crate.

He opened the shack door, stepped in, closing the door behind him and had a quick look around. Nothing was out of place and Porter couldn't see the bed from his place at the front door, but he assumed since nothing was moved or missing that he would find Ron still laying in bed. The biggest mistake he made that night was not checking to confirm his assumption. That mistake may have very well been the reason he died that night.

Porter turned to step back outside and retrieve his stash, but as he did, he caught a quick glimpse of Ron standing in the corner behind the door. Porter didn't see him coming in because the door was open and obscured the sickly man gripping a chunk of firewood in his thin, dry hands. There was no time to react between seeing Ron propped in the corner and the firewood cracking him in the center of his forehead. He fell straight back, stiff as a board, rattling the shack when he landed. A beautifully shaped, rounded knot began to form above his brow, colored the bluish purple of early dawn.

Ron felt that old familiar rush when he swung that chunk of firewood at Porter's head, could feel the adrenaline pumping through his exhausted body. He would deal with the consequences later, but at that moment he meant to utilize the energy he had while he still had it. Ron swung that chunk of wood over and over, hitting Porter anywhere he could hit him, until blisters formed on his hands, burst, and then bled. Porter's blood splattered Ron's filthy underclothing, arms, and face, but the blood on his hands was his alone. He went on for several minutes until his arms were weak from the exertion and felt rubbery.

When he finally stopped, Ron slumped to the floor, letting the chunk of wood slip from his bloody fingers to lay beside Porter's mangled face and broken body. He was recognizable but just barely. As the adrenaline dissipated so did the undeserved hatred and anger he felt toward Porter, the full realization of his actions consumed him in that moment.

Ron Hellman wept for some time before finally collecting himself enough to get up off the floor. He needed to rest; he knew he did, but he also needed to try to make amends for his actions. So, he bundled up and took off toward the woodshop to retrieve the handcart. It would make for a makeshift funeral pyre but at least he tried. He never did make it to the woodshop, though, the Sisters took care of that. Not that it would have made much of a difference, anyway, the starving dog pack found Porter Siddle's bloody and bashed body before Ron had enough time to return with the cart. They dragged it back to their den in the northwestern side of the timbers and the four remaining dogs feasted well for a few days.

As Ron trudged through the snow by moonlight toward the woodshop, having already passed Hussey Row and the Bar, he was stopped by a sweet, low voice. He was unnerved by the voice that got louder as he approached the Church and by the moonlight, he seen three figures standing on the steps. He could not make out who they were, only that there were three shadowy people, much like silhouettes beckoning him. He remained silent but moved a little closer to the calling shadows, not enough to allow features but he assumed they were women based off their figures. Then it clicked with him. "Sisters?" he asked relieved at the revelation, answering the voice for the first time.

"Yes, Ron." One of them whispered to him, almost seductively. If he had known what a Siren was, the mythological beings that would lure men to their deaths, he would have associated the Sisters with them in that moment.

"Is..." he croaked, uncomfortable, exhausted and in pain. "...is there something I can help you ladies with?" he asked.

"Oh, yes, Ron! Hurry, come quick! It's Father Robin!" One of the Sisters answered in a rushed whisper. Ron didn't know nor much care which, but he felt ashamed for misconstruing their concern and discretion for... well something else. Ron took off at a fast walk, the best he could manage in his weak and exhaustive state, toward the women standing on the Church steps. It was several yards to the doors, but Ron was making the distance quickly, the adrenaline pumping again. When he got within a few steps of the bottom stair something hard and heavy smacked him in the face, splitting his cheek. It startled him and he stumbled backward before the pain exploded in his face. Another object hit him in the chest, and then another in the neck. He put his head down to protect his face and at his feet he seen that they were small fist sized stones being pelted at him. "What the hell are you doing?" is what Ron Hellman tried to ask the Sisters, but a stone caught him in the mouth, shattering two of his front teeth. Jagged pieces of bone shredded his throat as they were swept down with the sudden gasp as the pain set in. He fell to the snowy ground choking on blood, teeth, and torn flesh. The Sisters continued to throw stones at him, from a seemingly never-ending pile of them, long after he was still and lifeless. They chanted a single word the entire time they stoned a man to death from the steps of the Church, and that word was 'sinner'.

3

Father Robin had been off to himself, resting and preparing for the next 'sermon', as he liked to call them. They were just sessions where he would humiliate and torture the three Sisters. He would name each and every one of their supposed sins and used them as a reason to treat them so heinously, which Father Robin disguised as 'punishments'. Some 'punishments' were milder than others depending on the transgression. A mild example was when he had them kneel for 12 straight hours without moving. If they so much as shrugged their shoulders or arched their backs, he would whack them with a studded staff. Their sin: they weren't praying hard enough. An example of a severe punishment was when he cut off all their hair, even though it was always hidden under the headdresses they wore, and sewed their vaginas closed. Their sin: Their womanhood and beauty had caused Father Robin to have impure and distracting thoughts about them. Sister Virtue had her lips sewn shut for three days when she dared ask him why they were being punished for how God created them and the thoughts that went on in his head.

Luckily, for the Sisters, they didn't have to deal with such tortures from the psychotic man they feared too much to run from, for much longer.

Father Robin heard the chanting and the thumps and stepped out of his quarters to see what was going on. He was instantly enraged the moment he realized the Sisters weren't in the Church. He stomped down the aisle between the wooden pews and threw open the double doors. There stood the three of them and he relaxed, but only a little. They did not move or even turn in his direction, and he was sure they heard him open the doors. They had to have, as hard as the doors banged off the outside walls, but they hadn't given any indication that they had. They were staring out at something beyond the Church steps, so he pushed himself between them to see what it was. "Oh, my." He muttered and took off across the snow to check on the man laying dead in front of his Church.

Father Robin, after confirming that Ron Hellman did not have a pulse, demanded to know why they would do such a thing. Not one of them could answer him, though, and it infuriated him even more. They were weeping their sorrows out by the time he ushered them back into the Church. Ron Hellman was the first and last person in the valley to ever see the Sisters alive again, but he was in no position to tell anyone that. As far as the few remaining valley folks were concerned, the fire was an accident and the four of them burnt up in the place they loved the most.

That's not what really happened, though.

He made the three frightened, confused, and weeping women stand together in the middle of the aisle and left them there for a few moments. When he returned, the Sisters were huddled together even closer, partly for warmth and partly for comfort. Father Robin carried a wooden unlidded box but did not offer to set it down or show them the contents. Instead, he told them to remove their clothing until they stood in nothing but their thin undergarments. They immediately obeyed, violently shivering all the while. Their former lovely locks had been reduced to lousy thin patches of hair in random places and at various lengths across their scalps, gooseflesh was evident across the entirety of their exposed and unexposed skin, and the transparency of their undergarments left next to nothing for the imagination. He stared at the trio for a long moment before finally placing the box at their feet and the trio peered inside with a look of confusion. It was full of wooden pegs, mallets, and chisels.

4

Several hours later the third and final wooden cross was being erected and stabilized. Inside of the Church looked as though a cyclone had run through the place, wood in every direction. Only a few untouched pews remained, the rest had been deconstructed and recycled when possible. The three Sisters had worked nonstop the entire time, their muscles overworked and aching, their hands bloody and raw, their thin attire damp from sweat that chilled them with every draft. They were thirsty, filthy, and exhausted and all they wanted was to rest.

Father Robin brought in a tray with four steaming ceramic mugs balanced precariously, just as the women were hammering in the last of the wooden pegs. "Well done, Sisters! Very well done. Please, come sit and rest." Not at all his usual tone or demeanor but the Sisters were so thirsty and tired and fed up with him that they didn't much care what he was up to. He had told them that building the crosses would be their atonement for the murder of Ron Hellman, even though none of the Sisters could remember throwing a single stone or why they would have done such a terrible thing to start with. As far as they were concerned, to a person, looking down at their bloody torn fingers, they had atoned for their sin.

Unfortunately for Sister Harmony, Sister Grace, and Sister Virtue, Father Robin did not agree.

He had spiked their herbal tea with some very strong hemp, ensuring that the exhausted women would sleep through just about anything. It worked too because they were all strapped to the laid over crosses before they woke up. He started with Sister Grace, driving railroad spikes into each of her wrists and through her crossed ankles. Her agonizing screams drowned out the ranting of Father Robin as he named her sins with each hammer blow. Small trickles of blood oozed from around the spikes that were flushed with her bruised and reddened skin. Next was Sister Virtue, the process repeated, and finally Sister Harmony, who was half-delirious from fear having endured the screams of both her spiritual sisters. They both lay weeping quietly through the pain as Sister Harmony screamed through her own. When all the Sisters were nailed to the crosses accordingly, he securely placed a 'crown of thorns' upon each of their nearly bald heads. A crown of thorns created by twisted rusted barbed wire that ripped at their skin sending rivulets of blood down their tear saturated faces.

Father Robin hoisted and maneuvered the crosses back into place until they stood like Jesus had on the day of his death. Due to their lofty position, Father Robin had to use a jaggedly broken broom handle but succeeded in stabbing each one in the side, leaving behind a gaping bloody puncture wound. Several minutes later, he used the same broom handle to shove vinegar-soaked rags into their side wounds causing fresh screams to erupt in the echoey Church. Another rag was shoved into their mouths causing the women to retch and gag at the bitter taste but unable to spit the rags out.

Sister Harmony succumbed to her pain, first, slowly sagging on the cross until she hung limply enough that the three spikes holding her in place groaned, threatening not to hold. They did, though, but barely.

Father Robin 'preached' to the dying Sisters about God's word and the Commandments, about atonement and forgiveness, about morals and faith, about... on and on he went. Sister Virtue went before Sister Grace, and she took her last ragged breath a little more than two hours after the nailing of the railroad spikes. Two agonizingly painful hours.

5

Father Robin paid no attention to the Sisters when or after they passed. He was too enthralled in his manic ravings to notice, nor did he notice the deep rumble of thunder that went on for a minute or longer, increasing in intensity as it drew out, almost shaking shacks on their stone foundations by its climax. It ended with a massive bolt of white lightning that sprang from the cloudless, star-studded sky above and struck the steeple of the Church. The steeple exploded into hundreds of splintered shards of wood that sailed in every direction, while the jagged edges of the Church caught fire.

The deafening crackle of the lightning finally got Father Robin's attention, but he didn't have enough time to wonder about it when he heard the explosion of the steeple. He dropped to the cold, wooden floor of the Church, covering his head with his hands as flaming debris rained down into the wrecked Church from the large hole in the ceiling. When the sound of falling objects had subsided, Father Robin took his chance and bolted for the double doors at the front of the Church. He slid to a stop in front of a large fallen ceiling beam that was ablaze with fire blocking the main way out. He turned on his heels and darted down the aisle, jumping over and dodging the larger chunks of debris, some on fire and some not.

He stumbled on an unused broken piece of pew and fell to the littered floor with a sound that was silenced by the crackling flames that were quickly overtaking the Church. His Church.

That stumble saved his life... well, prolonged it by a few moments, anyway. As he raised his head off the floor, slightly confused by the fall and the sudden turn of events, he watched a ceiling beam larger than the one blocking the front entrance, land only feet away from his face. He gasped at the abruptness of it, immediately breathed a sigh of relief, and then began praising the Lord above for sparing him. Had the fire not been so loud inside the Church, Father Robin would have heard another deep rumble of thunder. One that sounded even less approving than the first if it were possible.

The bases of the large wooden crosses caught fire and quickly engulfed the three dead ladies in flames. Their thin undergarments and meager patches and stubble of hair caught first, followed by their skin. Had they been alive they would have been able to smell the sickly, sweet aroma of charring flesh, hear the spinal fluid surrounding their brain boil behind their ears, and feel their organs roasting inside their torso. Luckily for them, they didn't have to endure such tortures.

Father Robin laid on the Church floor whispering his praises, as much smaller, but still aflame pieces of debris fell around him. One landed only inches away from his left shoulder, another by his feet, one by his right hip and one landed squarely on his back. He didn't feel the debris land on him and by the time he felt the heat of the fire through his layered clothing, half his back was ablaze. Naturally, the 'Godly' man panicked and started rolling back and forth on the debris covered floor. He bumped into jagged pieces of wood that gouged his skin, some of them, also, on fire. The bottom of his right pant leg went up in flames and quickly crept up his leg. It was almost to his knee when he realized that what he was doing was useless. He jumped up, only made it a couple steps, and stumbled over another piece of pew, sprawling to the floor once again. That time he busted his lip and gashed his cheek, but those minor injuries went unnoticed, hidden behind the unbearable agony of his skin and clothing melting into one.

He got to his feet, again, that time much slower trying to make his way outside and into the snow through the back door. The flames spread, his pain intensified, and his breathing became more labored with every step he took. He was only steps away from the back door when he collapsed under the weight of the pain. He died from the extensiveness of the burns a minute or so later, in complete misery and relentless pain, only to be thrown into the depths of Hell, where the hottest fires burned, to spend eternity enduring the pain, humiliation, and torture he bestowed upon his three ever-so faithful followers.

Sister Grace, Sister Virtue, and Sister Harmony were taken in the arms of angels to Heaven's Gate. There they were blessed by their God and granted entrance into Heaven, for he knew the truth. He knew that free will was moot in the stoning of Ron Hellman and therefore the Sisters were as innocent as any human can be.

Chapter Fifty-Four

Another Found

1

Johnathan Colmes was walking across the eastern bridge into the Slums when the thunder began. He checked the sky in every direction but couldn't find a single cloud against the star spotted clear night sky. At first, he assumed it was a distant storm approaching but quickly dismissed that idea when the prolonged rumbling of the thunder grew louder. It grew so loud that it made John's teeth ache in his mouth, and he let out a small, startled screech that he was glad no one was around to hear when the bolt of lightning struck the Church. He watched the steeple explode in a rain of sparks and debris that he could hear hitting the ground, even from his lengthy distance.

The next morning, when the rest of the valley's survivors noticed the burnt down Church, it would strike John as odd that no one else seemed to have heard the thunder, the lightning, or the explosion. To him, that was one of the most mysterious parts of the entire situation.

John took off toward the Church at a dead run, moving as fast as he could through the thick snow. The Church was burning brightly enough that John could clearly see the Bar by the time he made it to Hussey Row, and he could feel the heat on his face by the time he passed the Bar. He knew by the time he made it to the Church, that if anyone was alive in there, they were on their own and had very little time, if any, to get out. He wouldn't even be able to make it to the building before the heat baked him in his clothing. He circled the building from a distance that still made him sweat beneath his layered clothing, hoping to hear or see anyone that might be trapped in there.

The only person he did see was the body of Ron Hellman laying only yards from the Church steps, bloody and broken, his face swollen and his lips retaining a bluish-purple hue. Dozens upon dozens of fist sized stones riddled the body and the bloody ground around it, some scattered and rolling a few feet away. Half the body was lying in an indented mound of red-dyed snow while the other half was lying in a puddle of fire-melted snow, the crimson of his blood staining and distorting the colors of both sides.

Johnathan saw another opportunity and took it, but this was one he would come to regret. It was unnerving carrying the body of Ron Hellman all the way to the Butcher's shop, but he managed it undetected. He repeated the process with Ron Hellman the same way he had with Old Mrs. Jones and Alvin Danson, starting with the hands and feet.

A couple hours later, Johanthan had tossed out the last of the 'scraps' and had packaged the meat. He decided to swing over to Ron's place and see if Porter was home. If not, he would check the place for food and get back to Rebekka's where he was sure Sarah was worried sick.

As it turned out, John didn't even have to step foot into the shack. He seen the many sets of paw prints in the snow, by the moon and star light, before he made it to the shack where Porter and Ron lived. In the partially opened doorway, the burning fireplace cast shadowy light across the floor and out into the blood-stained snow, revealing the bright red streak that began in the shack and disappeared into the timbers several yards behind the shack.

John's eyes traced the bloody trail around the side of the shack and quickly noticed the dark silhouette of a box-like object against the shack in the shadows. He moved it carefully out of the shadow and into the light of the moon, nervousness and curiosity mingled in his gut. He was elated to find a boxful of food; food that he himself desperately needed. Rebekka refused to take any food from them, stating that Sarah needed it to nourish the child, strange as it may be, and John needed it to have the strength to take care of Sarah and their child. She would find her own food, she told them, and she always did.

He placed the wrapped meat on top of the wooden box and packed it back through the Slums, across the eastern bridge, and through the Lot. Sarah was indeed worried. She could not understand why it took him so long to acquire the meat she had been consuming, the meat that was strengthening her and the unborn child within her. She knew she couldn't have the meat and his time too, but she didn't have to like it.

Sarah was hungry, too, of course, so John fixed her a small portion of the fresh meat. She enjoyed every single bite of the meat that wasn't quite as good as the last batch but still very tasty. She praised him and then laid down to sleep as he added the meat to the remaining first two batches. Only about half of each was left due to her voracious appetite and John was starting to wonder how long he would be able to continue providing her with such a special diet. Finding them dead was one thing, but he wasn't sure if he could kill for it, though. The thought was repulsive, and he shoved it away.

After cleaning up, he laid down on the floor beside the single bed that Sarah occupied and tried to rest. Rebekka was staying with Lacy for the night, having left minutes after John returned with the box full of food. He offered her a decent-sized chunk of bread that was slightly soggy from the snow and half a jar of wild strawberry jam. Rebekka, normally, wouldn't have taken it but she knew that Lacy had a soft spot for wild strawberries. So, she took the jar of jam and the chunk of bread gratefully, fully intending on it sharing it with her girl-toy.

The two ladies enjoyed their sweet meal and for dessert... each other.

John laid there restlessly for a long time before he was finally able to drift off, his thoughts running wild about everything from the strange unborn child he shared with the love of his life, Sarah Maisse, to the burnt down Church and those within it, to the Witch herself. He couldn't help but wonder if the Witch had anything to do with the plague of events that had struck the valley since winter began. He drifted off to sleep with those ponderous thoughts swirling around in his head.

2

He awoke some time later, how long he wasn't sure, to the sound of water being dumped out. Was it water, though? And why would anyone be wasting it with the river running as low as it was? He sat up and blinked the sleep from his eyes as he heard the gush and spray again. He looked around the room and seen Sarah partially raised up in bed and leaning toward the opposite side. She was vomiting. It was projectile and violent. He rushed to her side, almost slipped, falling in her upchucked bile, but managed to regain his footing. He grabbed a rag and began wiping her mouth of vomit and the sweat off her forehead. This wasn't the first time she had thrown up, it seemed to be a normal regular part of being with child. Morning sickness, he had heard it called before, even though it would happen at any time day or night.

"He don't seem to care for that kind so much, does he?" John asked rhetorically, light-heartedly teasing her. He hoped he could draw a smile out of that pale, miserable face of hers, even a faint one. She usually took to the teasing well, throwing a snippy, light-hearted remark right back at him. There was no such exchange this time and that worried John more than what she told him next.

"Some... thin's... wrong... with... the baby." Sarah whispered breathlessly. She took several shallow breaths before continuing. "Sick... John... he's... sick... save... him." She passed out, a light blue tint to her lips. She was breathing in quick raspy breaths that made John incredibly nervous. He tried desperately to fight off the fear that threatened to overtake him, and he won for a while.

In a panicked rush, John threw on as many layers of clothes as he could, slipped his boots and thick coat on, quickly kissed his dying love with tears of sorrow and desperation in his eyes, and raced out the door. It seemed to John to take eons to get from Rebekka's place by the Lot to Hussey Row, but there was no noticeable movement of the moon in the night sky to confirm that. He beat on Lacy's small shack door, nonstop, until a sleepy, bleary-eyed Lacy cracked the door open. She was wrapped in a deer skin blanket and was wearing next to nothing beneath it, but John didn't notice given the current situation. "Where's Rebekka?" John asked before she could say anything.

Lacy, still half asleep, couldn't come up with the right answer through her foggy mind, so she only stared at him blankly. "God damn it!" John yelled, startling Lacy and then jerked his arm out in front of him, hitting the door with the palm of his hand, opening it the rest of the way. Lacy stumbled back with a low squeak of surprise and fear. "Rebekka!" John called stomping through the small one-room shack with attached outhouse. The bed was hidden behind a makeshift wall of drapes and that's where John found Rebekka just coming awake from all the noise. "Rebekka! Oh, thank God! Hurry! Sarah is sick, and she says the baby is too. I think she's dying, and if she does then the baby surely will. I need to go see the Witch. I know Sarah would never approve but I must save her, Rebekka. I must!"

Rebekka sat up on the bed, taking in everything John was saying through a foggy, sleepy mind, but she managed to take in enough to understand the stress and anxiety he was experiencing. "I know ya do, boy, but you must remain calm. I understand your pain, but you ain't gonna be no good to her or that baby by gettin all worked up and not thinkin straight. The Witch may be able to help, I would almost bet she could, but the question is: will she?" Rebekka paused and looked at John sternly, much like his mother would when he was much, much younger. "You wronged her, boy, and you's know it. If you do this right, you just may come outta it alright, but if you don't, you be sorry." She told him straight-forwardly, like she's done since the night he showed up on her doorstep in the pouring rain a decade and a half ago.

John was thoughtfully silent for several moments. The thought of the Witch refusing to help Sarah and a defenseless unborn child because of the pain that he had caused her, hadn't occurred to him. In hindsight, it wasn't much of a surprise because his decision to go see the Witch was a carelessly planned, impulsive one made from desperation and lack of options. He realized there was a lot he hadn't thought of, once he took a moment to really do so and knew that he would have to be extremely cautious when visiting the Witch for several reasons. He needed time to think about how to approach her for help, so he abandoned his plan of sending Rebekka back to Sarah alone, while he went on over to see the Witch.

He waited by the fireplace, warming himself by the freshly stoked fire, while Rebekka dressed and said her goodbyes to Lacy. They made it back to Rebekka's place a while later, speaking very little on the walk there, John mostly lost in thought and sick with worry. Sarah had vomited at least once more, maybe twice, since he'd left but she was sleeping, and her breathing was a little better. They kept quiet as not to wake her while John gathered the few things that he needed to make the trek back across the bridge and the Slums to the Witch's shack.

Chapter Fifty-Five

The Gift of The Sight

1

Three weeks ago, just after Betty Jones had left the Witch's shack with a heavy heart and burdened mind due to the deal the Witch had placed in her lap, the Witch was unwinding from sacrificing Roy Hoarding, her former boy-toy. When all was said and done, she was quite exhausted. She slept the sleep of the peacefully dead and awoke hours later feeling fresher and more revived than she had since her Master had healed her after her final confrontation with the demon, Malum.

She began preparing for the meditation ritual that needed to be performed to set the power of Sight in motion for her, so to speak. It would be a long and tedious ritual, having to be done exactly right with every element aligned properly, but it would be worth it in the end.

Starting with clearing the magic circle engraved into the stone floor of the cave, she set variously colored candles in certain places around the circle and in small groups outside of those. Each colored candle she used strengthened a particular element of the magic. Orange amplified adaptability, power, and energy, while yellow amplified divination, intellect, and knowledge. Green was to represent Mother Earth and nature, the strongest of the natural elements for the meditation ritual. Violet for divination, the third eye chakra, and spirituality. Silver for psychic ability, psychic development, and divination. Brown represented Earth and the animals, and amplified concentration, while Indigo was for meditation and insight. The grouped, unlit brightly colored candles looked bizarre in the dimly lit ritual room of the cave.

With the candles carefully arranged and in place, the Witch moved on to gathering her incense bundle. That was a quick and simple task, only needed to strengthen the natural elemental magic during the ritual. Each incense represented one or more of the four natural elements. Cinnamon and Rosemary represented Fire, the deadliest of the natural elements. Cinnamon, Lavendar, and Sage represented Air, the swiftest of the four. Mugwort represented Earth, the most adaptable of the natural elements, and finally, Thyme represented Water, the most powerful. With the small bundle tied securely with hemp twine, she set it in a small ceramic bowl and placed it in the center of the magic circle.

She took the mortar and pestle, her ancient athame, the mind-bogglingly old Opera Magicae, and a handful of amulets, carefully chosen from the hundreds she possessed, to the center of the magic circle. The Witch had grabbed every magical stone she had that would intensify the power of the Sight. She set a different stone between the carefully coordinated candles, creating a magical pattern. Sodalite, Moonstone, Blue Kyanite, Barite, and Apophyllite were the strongest among the amulets, while Chrysocolla, Desert Rose, Fluorite, Lapis Lazuli, Magnesite, and Moldavite were weaker but still incredibly powerful.

Once the stones were arranged, she returned to the smaller of the two caves to retrieve all the ingredients she would need to create the anointing oil for the meditation ritual. Sandalwood would promote the Sight, Acacia to develop psychic powers, and Nutmeg for meditation. Anise for divination and clairvoyance, Magnolia for meditation and psychic development, and Camphor to strengthen psychic powers. She also grabbed Lilac to induce clairvoyance and Lotus for meditation. She took all the small bottles and vials into the ritual room and placed them beside the tools of her craft.

2

The moon was bright and full that night, exactly as she needed it to be, and it was high in the sky by the time she was prepared to begin the ritual. She stood naked in the cold, damp cave facing North with the ancient athame held securely in her hand. She ignored the gooseflesh that rippled across her skin with every chilly draft that blew across the stone floor of the cave. When the moon was positioned just right, moonlight trickled down from the hole in the cave ceiling to cascade over the magic circle. The incense bundle smoldered in the ceramic bowl, a thin line of smoke trickling up into the moonlight, and the Witch began the meditation ritual to induce the power of Sight.

She stuck the tip of the sharp athame into the tip of her index finger hard enough to draw blood. She let a single drop fall from her finger and then spoke the words, "I bid this blood sacrifice as payment to the Earth element, aid me in my endeavor." She took three steps to the right and faced East, allowed another drop of blood to fall from her finger, and repeated the sentence almost to the word. "I bid this blood sacrifice as payment to the Water element, aid me in my endeavor." Three more steps to the right and she faced South, repeating the phrase but replacing the natural element with Air. She said Fire facing West. The moment she stepped back into the same place she stood when she recited the words facing North, the colorful candles surrounding the magical circle lit up instantaneously, their flames burning bright and strong.

The Witch breathed a sigh of relief because she knew that the natural elements accepted the sacrifice, and all was going well. She took her place in the center of the magical circle, everything set up and ready to be utilized. She began combining ingredients using the mortar and pestle as it was instructed in the Opera Magicae. Dried leaves from the Acacia, a few drops of Camphor and Sandalwood Oil, dried Lotus, Magnolia, and Lilac petals, Anise seeds, and powdered Nutmeg all created the meditation anointment oil. The final ingredient was a small splash of water. She held the unmixed ingredients over a candle flame for seven seconds, and then waved the incense bundle atop the herbal concoction for another seven. She mixed all the Earth found ingredients together very carefully with the mortar and pestle. With the oil ready, she dabbed some on her index and middle fingers of each hand and rubbed a little on her temples. With another dab on her bloody finger, she marked an upside down cross on her forehead and her chest. The blood from her finger mixed with the anointing oil gave it an eerie orangish color that Satan would have found tasteful. It was the same color orange that her eyes began to omit, much more unnerving than the glowing black eyes she had always possessed before. Had the Witch been able to see her reflection, she may have scared herself with those terrifying eyes.

The flames of the colorful candles began dancing on their wicks as the Witch assembled the oil. The small flames cast giant, creepy shadows the Witch paid no attention to. The more she progressed with the herbal concoction the faster the flames moved, swayed, jumped, and jittered in place. The flames resumed their former strong, bright flame once she had anointed herself with the herbal oil. The Witch knew the dancing fire was only a sign of a progressing ritual, one that was succeeding, but she still didn't want to get her hopes up for success just yet. The hardest part of the ritual had yet to come when she had to recite the lengthy meditation chant seven times without fault or fail. The meditation chant was almost as old as the book it was written in, the Opera Magicae only predating the chant by a few centuries, and all the much older spells were written, and therefore had to be recited, in Latin.

The eerily colored anointing oil was visible on her chest and forehead in the dimly cast light of the candles. She was vaguely aware of the slight burning sensation behind her eyes much like what she experienced when they glowed with that strange black light and assumed it was the same or too alike to matter, and she was right. The burning sensation or the glow of her eyes did nothing to distort her vision and she was able to read from the Opera Magicae easily enough. The pronunciation was the hard part, and even as careful as she was about it, she still had to restart the chanting more than once.

"*Elementa Terram, aquam, Aerem et Ignem appello,*"
I call upon the Elements Earth, Water, Air and Fire,
"*I. magicae Visus ut est desiderium meum.*"
I ask for the magic of Sight as it is my own desire.
"*Alii mean attentionem, quam videre et observare cupio,*"
The others of my attention that I wish to view and observe,
"*contempsisti me modis plusquam merui.*"
Have scorned me in ways that is more than I deserve.
"*Mihi visum tribuas, elementis loquor,*"
Bestow upon me the Sight, to the Elements I do speak,
"*quae mihi dulcem sinit ultionem obscuram quam peto.*"
Which will allow me the sweet dark revenge that I do seek.

The Witch made it halfway through the first chant when the candle flames started sputtering and popping on their wicks, indicating that she had made a mistake and the chant had failed. The word 'observare' had been her downfall on that first try, but she took a deep calming breath, restarted the chant and the flames regained their complacency. She made it through the first and second chant without fail but again messed up on the third one. That second time, it was the mispronunciation of the Latin word 'ultionem' that caused the flames to pop and sputter.

The Witch had been kneeling in the same position for over almost an hour by then and was starting to feel the crampy effects of it. So, she stood up and walked a few rounds around the shadow-filled dank cave that was her ritual room, the candle flames still popping and sputtering. Initially the failure brought tears to her eyes, but her pride forced them away while her determination demanded her pessimism to remain silent, and it did. She walked to clear her mind and stretch her muscles, and when both had been accomplished, she knelt back down in the center of the magic circle with a newly discovered sense of self-worth and optimism.

The mental outlook done well for her concentration, allowing her third try to be successful. The Witch had recited the Latin chant seven times in a row, while her eyes glowed a bizarre orangey color, and the flames burned bright and strong. The words glided off her tongue and past her lips as if controlled by a force much stronger than herself. If that was the case, she welcomed it gratefully. The flames of the brightly colored candles scattered around the circle blinked out, all at once, when the last of the seven chants were complete, indicating the ritual was a success.

3

Vipera had been out roaming around the valley when the Witch performed the meditation ritual. The asp's absence worked out in her favor because she needed to test her new ability. The Witch concentrated on Vipera, concentrated on mentally connecting with the beast sent to her by her Master. It took her several tries, but she finally succeeded. She was able to see everything that Vipera could see and speak to the snake telepathically. After repeating the process over and over, the Witch was able to connect with Vipera almost instantly, anytime she pleased.

Since she had mastered that part, and in less than a week, the Witch had branched out her concentration, attempting to connect with other wildlife. After many, many attempts she had connected with a rabbit, a few squirrels and chipmunks, and a variety of small bugs. She could see everything they could and even control them as if they were puppets and she were the puppet master.

This new-found power of hers was how she was able to influence some of the valley folks and their actions, or lack of in some cases, to ensure the dominoes fell just the way she wanted them to. And they did.

Most of the incidents in the valley from the night after Roy Hoarding's death were at the hands of the Witch, whether directly or indirectly, but most indirectly. What could have happened to the valley folks, had the Witch not interfered as intrusively as she did, is anyone's guess. All I know is what did happen and how the Witch had only to twitch her fingers or to mutter the correct series of words to make it happen.

Sue Ann Bailey's fall in the mountains was one of pure coincidence as was her falling ill with fever a day or so later. A single drop of Vipera's venom in Sue Ann's herbal tea, was how the Witch ensured that her sickness worsened too quickly to mend and that she would die a miserable drowning death. Not that Sue Ann had ever done anything to particularly deserve such a terrible death, the Witch just enjoyed the agony of others, almost feeding on it.

David Bailey, usually the most reasonable of men even in the worst of situations, had been persuaded by the distant enchanting whispers of the Witch to kill Carol Jewell and then himself. The man loved his wife, Sue Ann, dearly, and could only surmise that his brief physical affair with Carol was a character flaw, a mistake never to be repeated. The Witch emphasized on his guilt over the affair, intensified it until it was a crushing, unbearable weight, and when he was half-mad from it, she began whispering sweet nothings in his ear. Only at first, though, lolling him, drawing him in, until she convinced him that Carol didn't deserve to live when his wife couldn't, and he damn sure didn't. The Witch gave David more credit than he deserved, turning out to be much weaker than she anticipated, leaving the Witch unfulfilled and yearning for a challenge.

It didn't take long for the Witch, with her new power to watch anyone at any time, to realize that the general mood of the valley was one of desperation and depression, among many other negative emotions. She could accomplish a lot more if she could amp up those emotions until it brought most, if not all, to the brink of madness, driving them to do things they usually wouldn't do. A touch of additional coaxing would seal the deal for most once the enchantment took hold of them. With that realization, the Witch had found her challenge.

No one knew if it was pressure, an electrical current, or what, but they could all sense when any type of storm was coming in, but they had no way of telling what that storm would bring, or how bad it would be, until it arrived. The Witch couldn't conjure storms or any type of weather, for that matter, that was beyond her or any sorceress' powers. She could strengthen them, though, and that's just what she did with the ice storm. The ice storm that welcomed in the new year for those in the valley had been amplified more than double its original strength, which kept them holed up for days. She needed to strengthen the storm to hide the intense energy of the simple, yet incredibly powerful enchantment she used to amplify the emotions of those left in the valley. The amount of energy she had to expel to cast such an enchantment had been felt by all living creatures, young and old, natural and mythical, across the valley. All said creatures, two-legged, multi-legged, or no-legged alike, stirred restlessly for the duration of the enchantment's casting, even becoming overwhelming to some at its climax before tapering away to nothing. The Witch had bet that the valley folks would assume that unnaturalness in the air was only a product of the intense storm that pummeled the valley. She was right, they did. She also needed the few days that they were confined to whatever shelter they had taken to get out of the storm, so that she could rest after exerting the power and energy needed to enchant the entire valley. Everyone except Johnathan Colmes and Sarah Maisse, that was.

The Witch had been watching Doreen care for the elderly, ill and wounded for the couple weeks between the Witch gaining the Sight and Doreen's death. She had watched the Apothecary aide grow thinner and weaker with each day, believing she was sacrificing so the elderly could thrive longer. The Witch knew that it wouldn't be long before Doreen passed, all she had to do was wait.

The Witch couldn't have planned it any better herself when Doreen fainted dead away at the very beginning of the ice storm. The only glimpse of anyone she had gotten before falling into a coma-like sleep that lasted almost three days. Doreen's faint left the three elderly folks on their own, each to die their own awful deaths. The enchantment intensified Old Man Daniels desperation for water and help, driving him to a maddening delirium in the agonizing hours before his death.

The enchantment did not cause any emotions to develop that weren't previously there. It would only amplify that emotion, no matter how small or insignificant, and it always targeted the emotion that would cause the most damage and misery in the end. For Jiminey and Patty McAvay, it worsened their grief, slight paranoia, and self-seclusion.

It intensified the feelings Sugar was developing for the fisherman, believing that he genuinely enjoyed her company when the reality was that he just genuinely enjoyed the way Sugar worked her cunt. The fisherman's alcoholism worsened, eventually leading to him stealing Shine from the Bar.

That spark of sexual tension between Old Joe Brenner and Nonna and Nonni Brookes ignited into a strong, bright flame. Lacy was becoming irritated with Rebekka, only because Lacy preferred dick to pussy and Rebekka took up a lot of her time. The enchantment amplified that irritation into anger and Lacy took that anger out on Rebekka in bed, aiding in Rebekka's menopausal horniness that, too, was amplified by the enchantment.

It worsened Dansford Keeton's guilt over Robert Daniels and the anxiety of keeping a secret that should never have been shameful to begin with. For Frank McGrath, it intensified his rage and hatred toward Sarah Maisse and Johnathan Colmes, but mainly toward Sarah. He hated that she was John's, he hated that she was having John's child, he hated that he was the way he was, and he hated Dansford for making him that way. The enchantment played on all that hatred, fueling his fury and he, too, began taking his anger out on Dan in bed.

4

The day after the survivors emerged from their shelters following the ice storm, Betty Jones had accepted the Witch's offer, the only one she would extend, which led Betty to kill her beau, Danny Bailey. That decision, pressed to be made by the enchantment, not only caused her own death but set off the first of two domino effects that resulted in a total of ten deaths within the first ten days of the new year. Alvin Danson's visit to the Witch, his rejection, and subsequent suicidal hanging, the last suggested by the whisperings of the Witch. The merchant's wife finding his body and the hysterics that followed, Gary Brown's hidden depression and relentless devotion. The hysterics and the intensified depression driven by enchantment.

Porter Siddle's decision to go see the Witch, driven by his amplified hatred for Ron, was the start of the second of the domino effects, leaving with a small vial of the deadly herb, Hellebore. Ron Hellman came very near death but survived

571

the poisoning. Porter's death at Ron's hands, the initial rage and then Ron's subsequent guilt and eagerness to send Porter's body heavenward, all intensified by the enchantment. Coaxed to the Church steps on his way to do just that, the three Sisters had been enchanted by the Witch to stone Ron Hellman for killing Porter Siddle. It was not yet his time to die, and since Ron's poisoning failed there was no deal, and therefore no soul for the Witch. Which was unacceptable.

The Witch had no influence, aside from the valley enchantment that intensified his deranged thoughts and actions, over Father Robin's crucifying Sisters Harmony, Grace, and Virtue. In fact, she found the act of mockery overdone and distasteful, finding someone else to look in on whenever Father Robin finished nailing the first of the three Sisters to their crosses, perfectly content with losing that soul.

The Witch snapped out of her meditation soon after, when she heard the deep rumble of thunder, immediately and instinctually knowing what that sound meant. She was scared. Genuinely afraid and unsure of how to handle it, having never have truly angered a higher (or lower) power before. She did the only thing she could think of to do in that moment, she called upon her own power... her Master, Father of the Faithless.

Though her Master tried to assure her that if that God wanted her dead, she would be, but since she was still alive to hear the rumbling, chances were that that God wasn't after her, it did little to put her mind at ease. The Witch was jumpy and on edge long after the lightning struck and the thunder faded away.

Father Robin was the opposite of the 'Godly' man he proclaimed to be and though he believed that his God was watching over him, he was a disgrace to those that really were of the 'Godly' type. He believed that his God loves all, but his God's patience was certainly tried by the likes of Father Robin and the way he twisted everything to fit his unhealthy view of 'Godliness'. His crucifying of the three Sisters was the final straw, so to speak, for his God and his God had had enough of Father Robin's self-righteousness. Father Robin had angered his God for the last time and his God gave him a mere taste of what his eternity would be filled with.

If the Witch had had any doubt that the thunder and lightning strike that burnt the Church flat, leaving behind only the stone fireplace and chimney that crumpled to the ground in the early hours before dawn, was the wrath of a pissed off God, she had only look at the buildings around the Church. The Infirmary to the south and the Schoolhouse to the west of the Church was unscorched and untouched. The immense heat that was omitted from the burning Church didn't even touch the surrounding buildings. Long, thick icicles were still hanging from the short eaves of the Infirmary and Schoolhouse, and there was still frost on the few remaining windows with glass panes, the following morning when the fire had burnt itself out. The fire didn't even catch the grass around the Church on fire, the only things that burned were the Church itself, the three corpses within it, and Father Robin. Everything except the stones of the fireplace burnt to ash.

One of the main reasons the Witch wanted the power of the Sight was so that she could keep an eye on John and Sarah. She quickly grew tired of that, though, days before the ice storm, finding them rather boring. The two of them just sat around the shack all day, John only left when necessary, and both acted as if everything were perfectly fine and not completely fucked up. Due to Sarah's hormones, one moment they were awkwardly cooing to each other, looking more in love than possible, and the next they were on the brink of arguing, snapping at each other like yipping dogs. It disgusted the Witch, so she decided to only glimpse in on them every other day or so, just to make sure that Sarah was in good health. A part of her believed, though, that if anything should happen to the child, she would sense it before being told, and if not, then her Master certainly would and bring the wrath of Hell with him when he came to inform her.

The Witch chose not to have any influence over John or Sarah. It was a personal choice on her behalf, not wanting to harm Sarah because of the baby and so that John would remain as confused as possible for as long as possible. If anyone was to catch on to her doings, it would be John. Despite her choice not to enchant John, or even try, she believed that because of the pure, true love that John and Sarah shared, any enchantment she did try would only fail. Enchanting Sarah was out of the question until she was no longer needed by the child, she carried, that was marked by Satan.

Because of her lack of attention toward the couple, the Witch did not know that John had changed Sarah's diet. She was resting from the ice storm enchantment when he butchered Old Mrs. Jones body, was sending Porter on his way with a vial of Hellebore when he found Alvin Danson's body, and was speaking with her Master, her attention his and undivided, while he carried Ron Hellman's body to the Butcher's shop. So, when Johnathan Colmes came knocking on her shack door needing her help, she was quite surprised to find out why.

Chapter Fifty-Six

Whatever the Cost

The snow had been falling for quite some time, adding several inches to the several inches that already blanketed the valley. It crunched under John's weight as he trudged through the mid-calf high fluffy white snow. The warmth of his breath mingled with the frosty coldness of the air sending puffs of steam from between his bright red lips. He had made it through the Slums and could see the Witch's shack up ahead. He went over what he intended to say one more time, as he approached her place, the cabbage leaf wrapped package of meat tucked securely in his coat pocket.

To say he was nervous was a massive understatement. Johnathan Colmes had never been so scared in his life as he was standing at the Witch's door knowing her answer would decide not only his fate, but that of his unborn child and Sarah's, forever. He never would have considered to what extent the Witch would or could go to get what she wanted in return, though. He took a long deep breath, steadied himself, and rapped three times on the shack door that was opened almost immediately.

He was greeted by a glare of pure hatred so strong he could not resist dropping his eyes and then his head, unable to gaze upon her furiousness. He could not bring himself to speak so he only stood there waiting to see if she would slam the door in his face or allow him in. Luckily for him, she chose the latter, stepped aside, her glare a little softer, so he could walk in and then she rudely slammed the door behind him. Johnathan winced at the loud, abrupt sound, certain that she wished his head had been against the jamb when she slammed the door. "What the fuck do you want, John?" she asked, the edge in her tone sharp enough to cut glass, as she

575

returned to her seat at the small wooden table in the kitchen area.

"Look... I need to apologi..." John began, quietly, reciting the speech he had intended to orate. He was interrupted by the loud smacking sound of the Witch slamming her hand hard against the tabletop, silencing him.

"Goddamn you, Johnathan Colmes! You are not going to come in here after all this time telling me how fucking sorry you are! You don't get to do that after everything else! You're obviously here for a reason and I know that this bullshit your trying to hand me isn't it! So, tell me what you want and then get the fuck out of my place!" The Witch screamed at him from across the table, startling him in her ferocity.

He swallowed hard, considered trying the speech again but one look at the hatred in her eyes told him not to. Fuck it! He thought to himself as he made the impulsive decision to tell the Witch about Sarah being sick. She hadn't kicked him out yet, so he went for it.

The Witch cringed at Sarah's name but stirred restlessly when he told her that she was sick. When he told the Witch what Sarah told him about the baby being sick, she was visibly concerned. John was quite surprised to find the Witch so eager to help him help Sarah, but he feared what her reaction would be if he questioned it. So, with more effort than it should have taken, he shoved those willful questions aside and focused on what the Witch needed to come up with the cure for Sarah.

John took the package of meat from his pocket and carefully unwrapped it so that the pieces wouldn't spill all over the table. He explained how he didn't know which was which because it all looked so similar in color, not specifying what kind of meat it was, only that there were three separate kinds. The Witch looked at the pile of meat for several long moments, her eyes glowing an unappealing brilliant orange color, that awed Johnathan.

When she finally spoke, she told him that Vipera would be arriving soon and then they would know which was which. Johnathan didn't know what she meant by that until a large snake-like creature came slithering into the shack. It curled up, much like a striking rattlesnake a few feet away from the

Witch. He had never been particularly fond of snakes, nor did he really fear them, but he did not like the way that one caused the hair on the back of his neck to stand up or the gooseflesh to ripple across his skin.

The Witch tossed a chunk of the meat to the snake that wasn't really a snake and the beast caught it in mid-air, chomping on it with its multi-rowed teeth, before swallowing it down. She waited about half a minute and tossed Vipera another piece of flesh, the asp repeating its previous process. This went on for more than five minutes before the creature rejected one of the chunks. It swallowed it down but within a few seconds it started chocking and gagging, finally regurgitating the chunk of meat it had just swallowed.

Vipera looked down at the piece of meat it had just expelled and then up at the Witch. The snake opened its wide mouth and hissed viscously at her, obviously angry. "Oh, don't be so upset." She cooed to the snake. "The marked one is ailed, and I can cure him now that you've helped." The Witch whispered to the snake as she bent down to retrieve the slimy chunk of flesh off the wooden floor at her feet. Vipera calmed at that statement and slithered off into the bedroom.

Johnathan had to repress a gag as he watched the Witch pick up the chunk of flesh covered in clear miry saliva, speckled with bright orange bleeding dots of venom, with her bare fingers and then drop the piece of flesh onto her outstretched tongue. He watched her tongue retract and her lips close. He watched the movement of her jaw as she rolled the meat around in her mouth and then her throat contracted as she swallowed. Then she opened her mouth and plucked the saliva-and-venom-free piece of flesh off her tongue.

"Good as new." She said with a smile, knowing how disgusted he was by her. "Come. Time is not on her side." The Witch told him as she walked through the bedroom and out the backdoor of the shack, heading for the caves. They never made it into the ritual room. The Witch was in such a hurry to complete the healing potion that she concocted it right there upon one of the desks that held many of her vials, bottles, and small containers filled with a variety of herbs and oils.

Using the mortar and pestle, the first thing she did was grind the freshly clean piece of flesh into a gory pulp. The smell, whether from being a slowly rotting piece of flesh or due to the poison in contained, was awesome to the point of being almost overwhelming. The Witch didn't seem to mind but John had to take a step back from both the sight and the smell of it. He watched from a couple steps behind her as she added several other ingredients to the bloody mess. A couple brittlely dry Carnation Petals, a pinch of dried and ground Lavender, and a few drops of Sandalwood Oil. Dried Narcissus Leaves, Rue Oil, and Lotus petals came next. Finally, a touch of ground Rosemary, Violet petals, and a couple drops of Myrrh Oil. The Witch combined the lot of it with the mortar pestle until it had a syrupy consistency.

She carefully poured the pale purple-colored contents into a small bottle and handed it to John. "She only gets a thimble full at a time, anymore will make her sicker, so pay close attention to the time and amount. Time and amount, John, it's very important!" she told him seriously. "She must take that sip every two hours until it's gone. This will cure her and the unborn child if you don't fuck it up." She finished, adding an accusatory touch to the last remark.

John took major offense to that statement and his anger got the best of him before he could repress it. "Fuck it up? You really think so? Then why don't you just cast one of your damn spells to make sure I don't? You make sure to get whatever you want, by any means, but you gotta use your precious magic to do so because you know, deep down, that you're not only uncapable of attaining what you want on your own, you're unworthy of it." John concluded his shouted rant standing before her, bottle in hand, huffing and puffing as his chest heaved from the pumping adrenaline. He stared daggers through her and that time she was the one that dropped her gaze first, knowing that he had figured out that she had enchanted him.

His first thought was: Goddamn that felt good! But it was followed by the thought: Fuck! I should have kept my damn mouth shut! With that though, his anger melted into fear, and he was genuinely afraid for his life when she looked up at him again.

He did not get the response he expected, even though he didn't know what to expect. She smiled sweetly, startling him, and when she spoke, the softness of her voice and the pleasantness of her tone matched the innocent look upon her face. It made her words that much more ominous. "Oh, but you are wrong, my dear, John. I do know my worth and my capabilities, which is why I am able to get what I want, and usually when I want it. If my magic is required to make that happen then so be it and I will not apologize for that. I work hard for what I want, just not in the same way that others, like yourself, do. So, when something I worked hard for is lost or... taken, I will go to almost any length to see it returned in one form or another. Some would consider it a flaw in my character, but I choose to embrace it, use it to my advantage. You can fool yourself into believing that I am giving you the cure for your beloved Sarah's ailment out of the kindness of my heart, but I will get what is now owed to me, John... and one day, you will get yours."

John stood silently, perplexed and scared by the words she had spoken. He looked down at the bottle in his hand, thought about how sick Sarah was when he left and how sure she was that she would be dead soon. He felt sure that his life would be the payment to save Sarah and the baby, and he was content with that. He looked back at the Witch. "It's worth it... whatever the cost." he whispered.

The Witch only laughed, and it struck Johnathan as strange. They were wasting time with that back-and-forth nonsense that was doing nothing to help Sarah, so he didn't question her amusement. He thanked her in a quiet shaky voice and then quickly left the shack, the Witch still cackling.

Chapter Fifty-Seven

Vanity Potion

1

The death of Father Robin marked the tenth and final death in the valley during that first month of the year. A lot of death had occurred in the valley in the recent days and the Witch realized that at the rate she was killing them off, there wouldn't be anyone left in the end except for those in the Witch's love-lost revenge triangle. That wouldn't do, though. She wanted those that were left in the valley to stew in their misery and depressive thoughts and feelings. She wanted to feel their agony and pain at its fullest before taking their souls. So, she let the next few weeks pass into the first week of February with very little interaction with the valley folks. She simply sat in her shack, content with using the Sight to watch over them from afar.

She watched Johnathan Colmes nurse the with child, Sarah Maisse, back to health with the healing potion she had given him, and then watched as Sarah grew stronger with each day. Johnathan hadn't fed her anymore human meat, leaving what was left for the Witch to do whatever with. In the middle of January, though, while walking the timbers and gathering fresh roots and nuts, he came across four very scrawny, frozen dog carcasses. The furs were useless with the hide-makers dead, Rebekka had stopped making any clothing having no one to make for, there were no dogs for the guts and bones, so most of it went into the puny excuse for a river. He was able to scavenge precious little meat off all four dogs and the three of them ate well for two days.

She also watched as Sarah's stomach grew much quicker than usual, her navel starting to protrude from its previously concaved position, indicating the time to birth the child was drawing near. The quickness of her growing belly did not go unnoticed by John, Sarah, or Rebekka and when John noticed her belly button, he and Rebekka done some quick math. They determined that Sarah's time with child was going by almost three times faster than a normal woman's. Which meant that, if they were right, she would be having the baby within the next couple of weeks.

The Witch watched as Old Joe Brenner and the twin Bar owners, Nonna and Nonni, squirmed through their awkward sexual tension. Old Joe started being the first and last, and more often than not the only one, to walk into the Bar each day. It had become so strong among the three of them that they could all sense it but didn't begin to speak of it until it became overwhelming during the last few days of the month.

She noted that Gary Brown stayed in his shack with his wife, tending to her and trying to keep her fits of hysteria to a minimum. He done that with great patience, love, and adoration for his wife that could rival the likes of any gentleman. Which disgusted the Witch. However, deep down in the depths of the darkest part of his soul festered the depression and hatred he felt for his life and his beloved wife's sickness, but it was apart of her, one that she had no control of, and therefore he could never tell her how much he despised that part of her. The Witch could sense that small part of him and only had to wait for it to erupt.

Jiminey and Patty McAvay stayed holed up in their shack only trading with those few that came around with some food item to trade or maybe a bit of Shine. They had done well for themselves, rationed their food, smoked as much as they wanted, went after firewood together, retrieved water together, maintained the shack together, etc. The Witch looked in on them, like Gary Brown and his wife, on occasion, but mostly she found them boring.

Frank McGrath and Dansford Keeton had made themselves scarce after Doreen's and the elderly folks' deaths. Frank had accepted but was not proud that he had lost his authority in the valley, and probably most of his respect too. Both men were overwhelmed by their own terribly depressive emotions. Dansford was dealing with the guilt of everything while Frank was dealing with his personal rage toward Sarah. The misplaced tension between the men, who lived together in Frank McGrath's place, was almost palpable. They glared and passed snarky, mean remarks to one another in passing, always meaning to hurt the other. They were like a bitter couple amid a devastating divorce being forced to live together. Despite the growing tension between them, though, there was no loss of love. Dansford still loved Frank and though not as obsessed as before, still wanted to be with him and have the life that he believed they had always deserved. Frank was still internally conflicted over who he really was and couldn't get past being rejected by Sarah for the Butcher, Johnathan Colmes, of all people. A part of Frank wanted to be with Dan, like the two had always fantasized about, but the guilt and shame he felt about not being 'normal', overwhelmed the late-night pillow talk fantasies they shared.

The Witch found the pair rather amusing, observing their arguments with delight at the venomous slights they hurled at each other, knowing it would result in a physical altercation eventually. However, her entertainment came from watching the fisherman toy with the emotions of a temperamental and probably unstable woman by the name of Sugar. Sugar had proven to be quite the customer back when the valley was normal, coming to the Witch several times for various reasons. Some of those reasons were malicious, like the time she wanted to blind that one young man who told her she wasn't attractive. The Witch, good for the sake of goodness back then, couldn't and wouldn't help her blind him, but she did tell her about a commonly found flower that would give him major intestinal upset for days. Other times was for pure goodness, like when Sugar needed help finding her Ma. The Witch had helped, and she recalled how good it had made her feel that day when they did find Sugar's Ma, only mildly injured but unable to get back on her own. The Witch shoved all those goody-goody recollected feelings away with disgust and repulsion and focused on how Sugar was part of those that took advantage of her magnificent powers with little appreciation or gratitude. Thus, her revenge upon the valley ensued.

2

Sugar had grown quite fond of the fisherman believing the feelings were reciprocated because he chose to spend so many of his evenings with her. She didn't know that he just preferred her pussy to Lacy's, but he wouldn't tell her any such thing, either. He wouldn't tell her that he didn't have the same feelings for her that she thought he did. He wouldn't tell her that he was just using her. He allowed Sugar to continue thinking that he felt the same way she did. His love and attention were on his Shine, and his Shine only. There was no room for anyone or anything else. Had he told her about these things at any point between the ice storm over new years and the beginning of February, maybe things would have turned out a bit differently.

After the ice storm, Sugar became more and more clingy with the fisherman, and he would have had to have been all but completely blind not to see that she was acting more like a girlfriend than the hussy she was. So, naturally, he started spending less time with Sugar and more time with Lacy. Lacy welcomed the mix-up from her usual with Rebekka Lane. It initially irritated Rebekka but once she realized that Lacy was more into with her, after being with him, she didn't mind it so much. Rebekka enjoyed Lacy's company, but it was solely for pleasure, and she kept the emotions out of it. The fisherman was adamant about his and Lacy's secrecy, though, not wanting Sugar to find out. He didn't want to hurt her, but he was trying to distance himself from her while maintaining his high libido. It took Sugar less than two weeks to figure it out and she was furious.

Sugar had let the deception fester for a few days before she had decided what to do about the fisherman and that slut-bitch Lacy. It was much harder than she expected it to be, going on those few days as if she knew nothing of the fisherman and Lacy's trysts of late. Typically, such problems never would have arisen between the two women, work was work, and that was that. However, only a day or so after they were able to get out after the ice storm, Sugar had told Lacy about her feelings for the fisherman and how sure she was that he felt the same about her. Lacy had seemed genuinely excited for Sugar and her new-found love interest, and it went unsaid that the fisherman was 'off limits', but in hindsight Sugar wondered if that excitement had only been a cover for her jealousy.

She had contemplated on and dismissed a multitude of ideas about how to deal with her current situation, none of them seemingly harsh enough to match the pain and humiliation they had put her through. So, she decided to go to the Witch for help. She always had before, but the Witch had never helped her seriously harm anyone. This time was different though, she thought to herself, it wasn't just some snide comment from a boy too young to know if he liked cunt or cock yet. This was serious and it required a serious consequence. She just had to convince the Witch of its seriousness.

On the third day of February, Sugar trudged through the blindingly white snow to the Witch's shack. The Witch had opened the front door and invited her in before she even had a chance to knock. Sugar thanked the Witch and stepped into the warmth of the shack out of the single-digit temperature of the outside. The smell of steeping tea molested her nostrils and entangled them in their herbal aroma. She sat at the small wooden table, not for the first time but unaware that it was her last, without being invited to do so. She felt comfortable around the Witch, always had, but this time was different. Sugar felt even more comfortable with her, almost as if she belonged with the Witch. So inviting and warm. So seductive. Sugar felt as if she could tell the Witch anything and everything.

"I was expecting you, so I made us some tea that will help soothe your nerves." The Witch told Sugar. Sugar wasn't surprised much by the Witch's expectation of her arrival, but she wondered how she knew that she needed the calming tea. She had visited the Witch enough to know that she usually sensed those approaching a bit before they knocked at her door, but never had she been able to read minds and all that. "I know why you are here, child..." The Witch had always called her that, and many others, and most found it odd because of the Witch's immense beauty and seemingly eternal youth. She had not aged a single day that any of those that lived in the valley could attest to. So, it was strange having someone who looked your age or younger, calling you 'child' as if she were your 80-year-old Grammy. But Sugar overlooked it as she always had. "...I know of many doings in this valley, but you may tell me about it, if that is your wish." The Witch finished.

Sugar was silent for a long moment, thinking about how odd that sounded, even for the Witch. Even she had her limits and couldn't know of everyone's business at once, especially since she never left her damn shack anymore. Still, she wondered. As if on cue, thoughts of the fisherman and Lacy sprawled across Lacy's bed in a tangle of arms and legs and sweat and erotic musk, swept through her mind. Tears pricked her eyes and her heartache doubled. Yes, she wanted to talk about it and as the words spilled from her lips, the tears spilled from her red-rimmed eyes. She went on about it for over half an hour, taking small sips of her lovely aromatic tea as she spoke, concluding by pleading with the Witch for a way to get her revenge on them both.

3

The Witch ate up Sugar's misery. Her heartache. Her humiliation. Her wounded pride. Her hatred. She devoured and enjoyed every bittersweet morsel of it. She knew that Sugar was one client she didn't have to get a tarot pass for. Sugar, even without her elevated emotions, had a mean-streak in her wide enough to attract the attention of Satan himself, so she would be easy to attain once the deal began. The hard part was finding the proper combination of herbs and oils to create the 'vanity potion' Sugar would need.

It took her a few hours and several failed attempts to get it right, but the Witch had finally concocted the right herbal concoction. It required a few drops of Camphor, Cypress, Hyacinth, Melilot, and Narcissus Oil that was then added to an herbal mixture. The herbal mixture consisted of just the right amounts of ground Willow, Cactus, Walnut, Holly, Rue, Ivy, Rosemary, and Peony. Together, the herbs and oils created a pale-yellow watery substance that very much resembled urine. Sugar was instructed to throw the herbal oil into Lacy's face, the sooner the better, and then just watch from a distance. The effects would be rapid.

The second part of Sugar's revenge was the perfume she needed. The perfume was a delicate but complicated mixture of more than 15 oils. Some were of the more common variety, such as Cinnamon, Ginger, Jasmine, and Rose. While others were much less common, like Ylang-Ylang, Cyclamen, Orris Root, and Neroli. This 'love potion', as it was called by the less educated, was a very commonly used herbal concoction that could grant the wishes of most love-stricken souls. In fact, the Witch gave out this 'love potion' so often that she made it up in large batches so she would have multiple vials on hand.

She grabbed one from the shelf she kept them on, and the bottle with the vanity potion in it, then walked back into the shack where Sugar still sat, obviously bored. Sugar straightened up from her slumped position at the table and wiped away her finger-tip drawing done on the wooden tabletop, with the cold leftover tea in her cup. Her eyes lit up with anticipation when the Witch walked in with the vials in hand.

"Listen carefully, child, the instructions I give you must be done as I say, or you will not get the revenge you seek." The Witch continued to tell her what to do with the pale-yellow mixture in the small bottle. "Now, with this one..." The Witch said, holding up the small vial with the bright red, almost blood colored, perfume. "...Dab this behind your ears, between your breasts, and right below your navel. You will not be disappointed with the effects of either." The Witch finished with a sly smile that hid the viciousness behind it.

"What's gonna happen?" Sugar asked, suddenly feeling uneasy about the whole situation. The touch of conscience that she did possess was trying to make itself heard over the rest of her that desperately wanted to get back at the fisherman and Lacy for hurting her so. The desperate part won out, of course. The Witch wouldn't have had it any other way.

The Witch's smile broadened becoming even more wicked. "Just sit back and watch, child... they will get what they deserve... and so will you." was all that she would say.

Sugar, though still slightly uneasy, nodded and gathered her things. The Witch saw her out, reminding her that she must follow the directions as she told her. Sugar swore she would and disappeared into the darkness of the Slums as she headed back to her small shack on Hussey Row.

Chapter Fifty-Eight

Revenge on Hussey Row

1

She didn't see the fisherman or Lacy that night, not expecting to as late as she had gotten back, but she made a point to see them the following day. She waited until she knew that the fisherman and Lacy were together in her shack, only two doors down and decided to just walk right in on them. Luckily for Sugar they hadn't commenced to their fucking just yet, but from the look of their heavy breathing and puffy, slobbery lips, it wouldn't have been long.

Lacy and the fisherman were startled out of their tongue-wrestling session when Sugar walked in, slamming the door behind her, never breaking her stride. She had put the perfume on, just as instructed, before she walked out of her shack and the aroma was still very pungent. Sugar stopped just a few steps from the bed. Lacy let out a small squeal and the fisherman jumped to his feet. The moment the smell of the perfume wafted in his direction he walked straight up to Sugar, wrapped his arms around her waist and buried his face in her hair. He began weeping, profusely apologizing, begging for her forgiveness. She knew his reaction was the result of the perfume and she enjoyed seeing the flow of his tears, enjoyed the begging and pleading. She wanted him to suffer more, wanted to prolong it. So, she shoved him off and told him to get out of her face, that she would deal with him later. He obediently stepped aside.

Lacy sat on the bed astounded by the fisherman's immediate and unexpected reaction. His actions contradicted everything that he had convinced her of with words and she couldn't fathom it, he had no reason to lie to her either way. She was still sitting on the bed, contemplating, when he stepped out of the way allowing Sugar the chance to douse Lacy with the pale-yellow herbal concoction. It splashed a long, thick shattered line diagonally across her face, stuck to the hair around her left temple, soaked the eyelashes of her left eye, and dripped from her jawline. She squealed again, but that time from fury rather than fright. She wiped the odd smelling substance from her face, as she demanded to know what Sugar had just thrown all over her. She would only smile in response, though, wondering about the strange liquid herself, and then turned and walked out of Lacy's shack. Lacy screeched curses at her but never attempted to follow her out, but the fisherman did, right on her heels.

2

Over the course of the next two days Sugar took full advantage of the effect that the perfume had on the fisherman, making sure to keep herself well-perfumed. For the first two hours after they had returned to Sugar's shack after catching the fisherman and Lacy together, the fisherman had said everything he could to try and convince her that he was worthy of her forgiveness, and how he would do anything, literally anything, to prove it to her. Eventually, she decided to test that 'anything' claim and had him performing more and more degrading acts. Everything from licking her boots clean to crawling around on the floor like an animal for her entertainment. He obediently performed every request without question.

In between the acts of humiliation, Sugar had the fisherman satisfying her in every sexual form she could imagine. Yes, he had hurt her. Yes, he had humiliated her. Yes, he had deceived her. Yet, he was still a hell of a lay with a thick cock so she figured she would make the most of it while she had him around to play with. After all, her high libido, even from the young age of ten, had been the main reason she had pursued such a career. She wasn't about to let such an ample opportunity go to waste.

Several times over those two days, Sugar made a point to walk over to Lacy's shack and sneak a peek at what that urine-colored liquid was doing to her. She wanted to make sure that Lacy was getting what she deserved. Sugar certainly thought so as she watched the grotesque transformation occur and all she could think about was how fitting the consequence was. Lacy always had believed herself much more attractive than Sugar, and a better fuck too, better than all Old Joe's 'employees'. She wasn't so pretty and fuckable upon her death, though.

Lacy, on the other hand, had a much worse time over those same two days. She had used what precious little water she had left to wash the strange liquid off her face and out of her hair once Sugar and the fisherman had left. She felt odd, out of sorts, but thinking it was just the shock of being intruded on, didn't put much thought into it. But by the time she had come back in with the buckets of snow, she knew it wasn't just shock.

The river was too low to draw water from, for the first time since anyone had lived in the valley, but those still there tried not to think about what that would mean for them in the future. If there was snow on the ground, they had water to drink. Most folks were just trying to survive the day-to-day of finding food, which left little time for anything else and worrying about the future was one of them.

Her throat was too dry, and she desperately needed a drink of water, but the snow wasn't melting fast enough. She had taken off her layers of coats and shirts but still she felt too warm, almost feverish. She couldn't see it, but a bright red welt appeared diagonally across her face and covered every tiny place on her skin that the 'vanity potion' had touched. The rest of her face looked pale in contrast to the redness of the welt, in the dim light of the small shack. It seemed like an eternity had passed but Lacy finally got that drink of water she so desperately craved, then curled up in bed and waited to see if Rebekka would show up.

She did a few hours later, horrified by what she saw. By that time, the red welt across Lacy's face had broken out in large blister-like pustules. The variously shaded yellow and green pus that oozed from them was gut grasping. Rebekka had to clamp a hand over her mouth to stifle a disgusted cry of horror. The skin around the edges of each pustule had turned black and flaky, giving off a sweet, rotting smell that was overwhelming once she got too close.

"I don't feel right, Bek... I think I might be gettin sick or something." Lacy said in a drowsy tone, seemingly unaware of the seeping infection rolling down her face, sometimes over her lips and dripping down into her mouth.

Rebekka swallowed back the knot in her throat before speaking. 'No, Lace, ya sure don't look too good... let me... uhh... yeah, let me go see if I can find something that might make ya feel a bit better." Then, she turned and walked back out into the bitter cold before Lacy could reply.

Lacy knew that Rebekka wasn't coming back so she got up and locked the shack door with a wooden peg that slid over the edge of the door, keeping it closed from the outside. The shacks on Hussey Row were the only ones in the valley that had them and they were only used as an indication that business was in progress. If the door was open, so were the legs, if the door was closed, they tried again at another time. It wasn't very often that Old Joe had to run off some drunk belligerent bastard because he didn't want to walk away when the door was closed. Despite his name, Old Joe wasn't one to be trifled with and neither were his 'employees'.

Lacy had been wrong, Rebekka did return the following morning but since the door was closed, she assumed that Lacy was with the fisherman. She knew that horny bastard would fuck anything with a willing hole and Lacy was always willing, so she left with no intention of returning.

When Lacy heard the rattle of the door trying to be opened, she assumed that it was the fisherman trying to hit her up for another lay, so she didn't bother to get up and unlock it. Had either woman taken the few extra moments to confirm their assumptions, maybe everything would have turned out differently for Lacy. She wasn't sure if she would be able to make it to the door without falling over something anyway. She had woken up that morning, after a fitful night of sleep, with her eyelashes fused together by a kind of crusty, yellowish-green, goo. Her eye was swollen and irritated causing her vision to be blurry, by the time she managed to get it all cleaned out enough so that she could open it.

The pustules had erupted and spread across most of her face and down her neck giving it a hellish-landscape appearance of bright reds and pinks, sickish yellows and greens, and the blacks and grays of her decaying flesh. The pustules that had erupted had grown over with the rotting black flesh that surrounded it, with new pustules already beginning to form atop the blackened skin. Lacy's skin, as grotesque as it was, did not cause her any physical pain. She could feel the pustules oozing, feel them erupt, and could feel every lump and crater on her once beautiful face with her fingertips. However, fear of what she would see had prevented her from looking at her reflection in the bucket of water. Her vanity and pride wouldn't allow her to look upon the fate that she knew way deep down, she really did deserve.

Later that afternoon, Lacy was attempting to comb her badly tangled hair, being careful not to brush against the sides of her face. The section of hair around her left temple that had caught some of the urine-like liquid the day before, was tangled worse than the rest as she had expected it to be. It wasn't long before the comb got caught up in a particularly stubborn knot of hair that wouldn't let the comb free. She did the same thing she always did when that happened and gave the comb and tangle a bit of a jerk. She heard a wet ripping sound, close enough to almost echo in her ears, and assumed that she had ripped a small bit of her thick hair out, which happened most of the time anyway. The comb was loose in the tangle, so she gave it another solid jerk. That was followed by another, louder and more violent ripping sound that made her cringe. Her arm shot away from her head still gripping the comb handle and she stared at what she held in her hand in disbelief. Her eyes followed the swatch of hair from its finite tips, up into the stubborn knot that still entangled the comb and back down the other side to the roots of her hair. What was so bizarre about it was that the roots were still firmly implanted into the small patch of scalp that had ripped away from her skull with her hair. She could feel the blood running down the side of her face, filling her ear, but she could not feel any pain. It was as if her entire body was numb, and she was grateful for that if nothing else.

3

By the end of the second day and mere hours from her death, Lacy had even less hair than the three Sisters after Father Robin's vanity sermon, and much less skin too. Most of her scalp was missing, exposing her bloody skull, with only a few small patches of hair scattered across her head. The pustules, still growing but over black, flaky rotten flesh, had covered her entire face, going no further than her hairline but creeping down her neck. Any sign of the red welt had been completely eradicated. They lined the oval shape of her right eye, allowing her sight to remain undisturbed by the unnatural pustules. One pustule had formed at the corner of her left eye and another on the same eyelid while she slept the night before, erupting back-to-back less than an hour before she woke. The infection spilled across her eye and pooled in the deepened socket. When she woke and opened her eyes, the pooled infection spilled into the left one and for the first time in days she had felt pain. The pus burnt like acid and no amount of snow or water would soothe that burning pain. Lacy's vision had blurred over, thick mucus crusted her eyelashes, and everything had a distorted milky cast. Her eye remained that way, pain and all, until her death.

The 'vanity potion' didn't just affect her hair and face, it affected her entire body, inside and out. Lacy gained more than 50 pounds during those two days even though the only substance to pass her lips was water during that time. Her slim hips broadened, her firm ass became droopy and unshapely, her lovely thighs and flat stomach ballooned, complete with stretch marks and cellulite, and her perky breasts dropped and sagged. She had become the very image of herself that she only seen in her nightmares and most depressing thoughts. She had become the hideous person that she had always feared to be.

Lacy's heart fluttered and skipped beats more and more with every passing hour, and her breathing became raspier, as if her lungs were filling up. She no longer sounded like the sweet and sexy young woman she was three days before. Her stomach was plagued with painful cramps that doubled her over and brought her to her knees. Every time she went to the outhouse and sat down maggots fell from inside her. Her bones ached as if they were brittle, her hands trembled, and her feet felt too heavy most of the time, tripping her up. She could feel everything wrong on the inside of her body, but her skin was numb, and she remained grateful for that, even when the internal pain became unbearable.

She believed that she would find sweet relief in death.

Sugar had kept travelling back and forth between her little shack and Lacy's, watching Lacy slowly transform into the hideous, miserable being that she had become. Late on the second night, Sugar, allowing the fisherman to accompany her that time, returned to Lacy's. Instead of peeking through the small window, Sugar had the fisherman break the door down. With so few folks left in the valley and all of them scattered, they didn't worry about anyone hearing the pounding, cracking, and splintering of wood. If anyone had heard it, they would have just assumed that a tree was falling somewhere nearby, which wasn't uncommon.

The initial commotion of the fisherman ramming his body into her shack door startled her, but she was fully immersed in her overwhelming pain again by the time Sugar and the fisherman stepped inside. Lacy was lying on the bed, sprawled naked and weak. It was the first time that the fisherman had seen Lacy since Sugar had walked in on them two days before and was absolutely astonished by her appearance. His first thought was 'She looks like an overweight burn victim!' that was followed by a bewildered spoken thought. "What the hell happened to you?"

Lacy followed the pair with her right eye, her good eye, while the left one sat idle, cloudy, and oozing a thick light pink liquid. When the fisherman spoke, Lacy raised herself to a sitting position, slowly, then raised a trembling finger to point at Sugar. "That... crazy... bitch... did... this!" Lacy rasped, accusatorily.

The fisherman looked over at Sugar who was looking down at Lacy with an evil, vile smirk upon her face. She wouldn't respond to the accusation because the look she gave Lacy said enough. Sugar was proud of her work... well, the Witch's work... but the fisherman and Lacy didn't need to know that. After a long moment of silence, Sugar broke her gaze away from Lacy and looked over at the fisherman. "Come. I need to speak with you outside." Then she abruptly turned and walked out, stepping out of eyesight of the broken door.

During the few moments she had outside alone, Sugar reapplied the last few drops of the 'love potion' perfume behind her ears, between her breasts and finally, below her navel. As the fisherman stepped through the broken door, Sugar watched the deeply concerned look upon his face melt into one of love-sick obedience, as he drew nearer to her. She leaned against the outside of the shack and allowed him to wrap his arms around her, bury his face into her hair and let his hands roam about her body. The feeling of power and satisfaction Sugar got from looking at Lacy's destruction created a pleasant burning sensation deep in her lower belly, one that the Witch would understand well. But it was not the time for such doings, there were other matters to attend to.

As the fisherman rubbed one hand up her inner thigh and the other over a perky breast, Sugar began to whisper in his ear. She told him how miserable Lacy was in her new form and how it would be a mercy to end it for her. She told him how all their troubles were Lacy's fault and that it had been her plan all along to split them up. Sugar had half-convinced herself of that much. The more she whispered, the quicker her breathing became and the rougher his hands and grip became in anger. While one hand was rubbing vigorously, almost painfully, between her legs, the other was squeezing one of her breasts hard enough to leave bruises. She told him what she wanted him to do to Lacy as she climaxed, moaning softly in his ear.

When her breathing had calmed, he removed his clammy hand from between her clothed legs and turned to walk back into the shack without a word. Sugar adjusted her clothes and then followed him inside, realizing that it was going much better than she could have hoped.

4

The fisherman had already pulled the knife out of his back pocket by the time Sugar could see Lacy again, and the fear in her one good eye was delightful to see. Lacy, in her raspy voice, began crying and begging the fisherman not to hurt her, that she didn't want to go out so painfully. The fisherman disregarded her pleadings and advanced on her viciously, stabbing her over and over. Blood slung from the knife with every jab of his arm, splattering the wall, the ceiling, the bed. The high arc of his first few stabs sent speckles of blood across the floor behind him. Over and over, he stabbed her, releasing every disgusted thought and all the pain and humiliation he could muster. He hated what he was doing but was unable to stop himself. He screamed to keep from crying.

Finally, after what seemed like an eternity, he was able to drop his arm and subsequently, the knife fell from his cramped fingers. The fisherman huffed and puffed, catching his breath as Sugar stood behind him, giggling at how well he had performed. She was almost giddy over it. When he turned to look at her, her laughter broke for a moment. The fisherman was almost unrecognizable beneath the mask of blood and gore that coated his face and upper body, but what caught her attention was his eyes. He had an odd, unfamiliar look that gave Sugar a moment of unease. He looked away quickly and she resumed laughing but it tapered off soon after.

Sugar approached Lacy's lifeless, mangled body, wanting to get a better look at the damage he had caused. The fisherman had stabbed her more than 50 times in the face, neck, chest, and stomach. There wasn't much more than a bloody holey mess to look at, but Sugar wanted to see her up close anyway. She even bent down to get a better look at a chunk of bloody black flesh hanging off the side of what was once Lacy's face. The fisherman took that moment to take Sugar by surprise.

As Sugar approached Lacy's body, the fisherman was trying to work most of the cramps out of his fingers while she was still distracted, with his adrenaline pumping due to the anticipation of his intended actions, it didn't take long. He found a lengthy piece of hemp rope, used for Lacy's kinkier clients, and secured each end tightly in his hands. The fisherman, trying to control his breathing, just hoped that he still had enough strength to see it through, otherwise he was a dead man. He approached her slowly and silently, and as she was bent over the body, with one swift motion, he had the rope around her neck and tightened to the max. Her face began to puff up, turning bright red and then deepening into purple very quickly. Her boot heels, the only part of her feet touching the floor, tittered in place and she clawed at the air behind her head, sensing he was there. She made contact once causing him to momentarily loosen his grip on her neck allowing her a tiny acid-laced gasp of air that felt like a firecracker explosion to her oxygen starved lungs. It only prolonged her death.

The fisherman's arms felt heavy and useless by the time he was sure Sugar was dead and not just unconscious. That would be a bad mistake on his part. He had snapped out of his trance the moment Lacy died, even though he couldn't make his body stop stabbing her. It felt as if he was being controlled by someone else, like a puppet, until they had had their fill of it. He hated killing Lacy and hated Sugar for entrancing him and making him do it. Sugar deserved what she got. The fisherman left the two dead women where they lay and walked out, thinking about how good a nip of Shine would taste.

Chapter Fifty-Nine

Bits and Pieces

1

The following morning, Rebekka left the shack she was sharing with Sarah Maisse and Johanthan Colmes, to go get a couple buckets of coal. Usually, John took care of such chores, but he and Sarah were in the midst of a heated argument that morning, so she decided to do it herself. She had tried hard not to think about Lacy but found it more and more difficult to do. Rebekka hadn't seen her since she had left in a panicked rush two evenings before and couldn't seem to shake that odd impending doom feeling. So, Rebekka decided to stop by Lacy's shack on her way to the Coal Flats and try the door again.

Rebekka Lane had roughly the same startled reaction to finding Sugar as she did when she found David Bailey and Carol Jewell, sans the falling part. She had entertained the idea of Lacy's death only because of the condition she was in the last time Rebekka had seen her. She had tried to prepare herself for that possibility, couldn't quite get there, and then gave up. She tried to convince herself that Lacy was probably fine but definitely alive, but she would check to make sure, anyway.

Moments after Rebekka seen Sugar, swollen and blue-faced, laying on the floor, she spotted Lacy's body lying face up on the bed with her legs and feet dangling over the side. Rebekka's mind fogged, her eyes filled up with tears, a knot formed in her throat, and her heart broke. Her hands trembled, her knees weakened, her chest tightened, and the rage boiled over down deep in her soul. The fisherman's

598

bloody pocketknife, one she and many, many others had seen time and time again repairing and rebuilding after the blizzard, laid at Lacy's unmoving feet. There was no doubt as to who had killed Lacy. The fisherman did it. The fisherman did it! THE FISHERMAN DID IT! Rebekka's mind screamed until it felt like the top of her head was going to pop off. She had to let out a scream of her own to release the pressure that she was sure would have killed her.

Her tears began to fall as she kissed Lacy's lovely, blood splattered hand and realized in that moment how much Lacy had truly meant to her. She had never denied that she had feelings for the harlot, she had just never tried to figure out the extent of those feelings. She knew then that she loved Lacy, and she would avenge her death by killing that fucking fisherman!

As much as it pained Rebekka to do so, she left Lacy on the bed where she took her final, pain-filled breath, and continued toward the Coal Flats already devising her plan.

The Witch, through Vipera's eyes, had watched Sugar's confrontation with the fisherman and Lacy, and seen how effective both of her herbal potions had been. She watched with eagerness and delight as Lacy spiraled in her pain and anguish as she transformed into her worst nightmare. The Witch didn't mind that Lacy and Sugar were dead because she just added two more souls to her collection, and she knew that she would have the fisherman's, too, whenever he got his. However, the Witch believed that if she played it right, she might be able to snatch an extra one. So, she refocused her attention and began whispering to Rebekka, not that she needed much encouragement to keep her rage boiling over Lacy's death.

It took Rebekka almost a week to find the fisherman, but when she did, she was ready for him.

2

Rebekka was the only person, besides the murderer and the Witch, of course, that knew of Lacy and Sugar's deaths. Old Joe was too involved with Nonna and Nonni Brookes, having taken up spending most of his nights in the Bar, too, to have noticed. Nothing had happened between the three of them, yet, but they could all feel the heat rising. Old Joe was too caught up in his own hormones to notice that his only two 'employees' had been killed and would die without ever bothering to find out.

As the beginning days of February passed and faded, each one just another day the valley folks had survived, they could all feel that something was coming. It was similar to the feeling of impending doom, that many of them knew too well, and not one of them was comfortable with that feeling. That feeling would come to its peak in a matter of days and then blow off their hearts like a leaf caught in the wind. Even after that feeling had come and gone, though, they couldn't say, to a person, which event, exactly, it was that had caused them such uneasiness to begin with. Was it the fisherman's disappearance? News that Frank McGrath was missing? The death of Old Joe Brenner? The birth of Sarah and John's baby? The missing bartending twins? The death of Dansford Keeton? Or was it a culmination of it all? Too many things had happened in the valley between the start of that feeling and its departure. Of course, we know what that something was, but they sure as hell didn't. Some didn't much care what it was, they were just glad that the depressing feeling wasn't weighing on them anymore, well the ones that survived through mid-February, anyway.

Even though the fisherman was a known drunkard, he was also known for his hard work, so it didn't go unnoticed that the fisherman wasn't out working shortly after the sun came up the morning after Rebekka found him. He was believed to be missing by the end of the second day, around the time Rebekka was beginning her third and final session with him. By the fourth day, he was assumed dead, but no one had recovered his body nor had anyone bothered to go out searching for him. Those few that could still go out searching were too weak to do so. Rebekka Lane was the only person, aside from the Witch, that KNEW he was dead and not just missing and assumed so.

She had found the fisherman passed out drunk, empty bottle by his hand, curled up in front of a cold, fireless fireplace in an empty shack. He was dressed in several layers but there was a blue tinge to his lips that made it obvious that he wouldn't last much longer out in the cold. She bound his hands and feet, just in case he woke up along the way, and dragged him through the snow to the Mercantile. She didn't bother to hide the obvious track his body left in the snow, nor did she care if anyone found it or him. Truthfully, she didn't see anyone coming to this end of the valley, and if they did, they probably wouldn't pay much attention to it, paw prints or not, after those canines took off with Robert Daniels' body.

Once in the Mercantile, she built a warm fire, leaving the fisherman laying in front of it, still tied up, and then went outside to fill a couple buckets with snow for water. After about an hour of performing minor but necessary chores and regaining feeling in her fingers and toes again, she was able to begin her work. She untied his bindings and used scissors to cut every layer of the fisherman's clothes off. Left sprawled and naked on the cold wooden floor of the Mercantile, he still hadn't awakened from his drunken semi-coma.

She dragged him into the back storage area where she had placed a large straight-back wooden chair in the middle of the large room, a coil of rope sitting nearby. She struggled but finally managed to get the limp fisherman seated in the chair well enough to tie him into it. The fisherman slept through the whole thing and longer, allowing Rebekka plenty of time to rest and ensure she had everything she needed.

Of course, the fisherman panicked when he came too, quickly realizing that he couldn't move or even speak. She had placed a large piece of cloth over his mouth to muffle the cries and screams, and it had worked. It took a few long moments for his eyes to adjust to the dim light of the room, and even then, he had no idea where he was. He didn't see anyone, but he could sense that someone was nearby, and he was none too eager to find out who it was.

He was surprised to see Rebekka appear from behind him on his left and wondered why she, of everyone in the valley, was doing this to him. Then he remembered how often Rebekka would frequent Lacy's shack and how Lacy had told him that even though she didn't mind being with women, she didn't enjoy it nearly as much as Rebekka did. But... a paying customer was a paying customer. Then he questioned how she, or anyone for that matter, could fall for a whore. He, himself, answered his own question only a moment later when he, also, remembered that odd, entranced feeling he had whenever he was around Sugar. He didn't have any romantic feelings for Sugar, never had and never would, but no one could have been able to tell by the way he acted with her. It had to be the work of magic because nothing else made any sense, so maybe the same thing had happened to Rebekka and that was why she was so upset over Lacy's death. Still yet, he thought, if that were the case than she would have to kill him to break the enchantment, the same way he had to kill Lacy to break Sugar's enchantment over him. That wasn't quite right, but the fisherman didn't know that. All he did know was that he probably wasn't going to escape that situation alive, and on that account he was correct.

That run of thoughts went on for only a moment or more. but the realization that accompanied them brought tears to his eyes. Even if she could have understood him through the thick cloth covering his mouth, his attempts to weep and plead would have fallen on deaf ears. Rebekka went about her preparations, knowing he had awoken, with a set determined look on her face and a malicious hatred in her eyes.

She had planned his demise to be executed during three sessions. Between each session she tied him up by forcing his knees to his chest and wrapping his arms behind the bend in his legs. She placed his hands over his elbows, tied his forearms together tightly, then finished by tying his feet together. The thick cloth covering his mouth stayed in place from the time she put it on him in the front room of the Mercantile, until the beginning of their second session. Once tied up, she dragged him over to an unlidded, overturned crate and shoved him most of the way into it. His movement was restricted, only able to wiggle around a bit, and not very well, so he didn't have enough time to get out of the crate before she tipped it up right from the other side. It landed with a loud SMACK! that echoed in the large room, and the fisherman's already cramped and contorted body toppled on itself. His extremely painful head and face were at the bottom of that bodily heap and try as he might he wasn't able to wiggle enough in the crate, that was just barely big enough, to relieve the pressure from it.

The fisherman was kind of relieved when Rebekka put him in the crate after the first session, believing that she had left him in there to die. After hours of being in the crate, however, he was almost in tears at the relief of being let out of it. He was ready to go back into it by the end of the second session, though, and that time hoping and praying that she really was leaving him there to die. He had no such luck though and was much more scared than appreciative when she dragged him out of the crate for the third and final time.

He couldn't speak but followed her with his pleading, tear filled eyes, as he sat tied to the straight-back chair she had placed him in. Rebekka refused to acknowledge him until she had everything she needed, just the way she needed it to be. When she finally did look at the fisherman, she stood before him in an old moth-eaten sweater and thick, fur lined men's trousers, both much too large for her. In her hands she held the same pocketknife that he had used to murder her beloved Lacy with... dried blood and all.

She knew by the look in his eyes that she didn't have to explain anything. He knew why she was there and why she had him there. She was out for revenge, and he knew it. What he didn't know was how sweet it would be for Rebekka Lane, who had always had a sick fascination with how much pain the body could endure before death became it. It was the first time she had been provided with the motive and opportunity for experimentation, so she was going to find out if he could survive longer than Lacy did with everything that she had endured during the two days before her heinous death. Rebekka didn't know that he hadn't had anything to do with Lacy's transformation, not directly anyway, but she wouldn't have believed him had he been given the chance to tell her that. If she hadn't had run from Lacy when she seen her during the beginning of her deformity, Lacy would have had the chance to explain to her what Sugar had done. Even though Lacy had no proof that the two events were connected, she had a strong suspicion that they were. It may not have made any difference in the end, anyway, because the fisherman was still responsible for wielding the weapon that took Lacy from her, and that was really all Rebekka needed to know.

3

She started on the right side of his head, grabbed a tuft of his shaggy dark brown hair, pulled it taut, and using his own bloody pocketknife she sliced a plum-sized piece of scalp from his skull. Blood swelled around the tip of the knife blade as it punctured the skin, and then dripped into his hair and down onto the back of his neck, sending a pain-induced shiver down his spine. The fisherman tried to kick his feet but only rattled the chair slightly. He tried to scream but only a muffled sound escaped that no one would be able to hear. He tried shaking his head but that only drove the knife blade deeper into his scalp, so he quickly abandoned that idea. There was nothing he could do but endure, and try as he might, it wasn't something that could be endured gracefully.

She made her way around his head, a sweet but sadistic smile upon her face all the while, and sliced off variously sized pieces of his scalp, some only the size of a coin while others as large as an apple. He cried, sobbed, wept, and screamed throughout the entire session, not caring how shameful it was. When she sliced off the third piece, the fisherman urinated on himself. The flow started out as an arch that went up and out onto the floor and ended as a small trickle that spilled between his bare legs on the wooden chair. By the seventh, he had defecated on himself, all the squirming and wiggling had smeared it across his backside and the constant stench assaulted his senses.

He was still conscious, somehow, by the time she was satisfied with the results. Rebekka had sliced off more than a dozen pieces of his scalp, leaving very few scattered about, much like Lacy's had been upon her death. Blood ran in torrents from his scalp-less skull, and she expected him to pass out at any time from blood loss. She couldn't allow that, though, because that was a step closer to death that she didn't need him to take yet. He couldn't die until she was ready for him to do so. So, she grabbed a couple handfuls of salt out of a large feed bag that was filled with it and coated his bleeding scalp. Fresh waves of searing pain brought on another round of screams that went unheard. She coated his skull with the salt until blood stopped dripping down his neck, accomplishing stopping the bleeding as she had intended. Finally, and mercifully, the fisherman lost consciousness, but only for a few moments.

The first session wasn't quite complete yet, and he was brought out of his peaceful darkness by blinding pain. She was leaning over him, her face only a couple inches from his. She had one hand across his forehead, pressing down, keeping it in place, while the other hand's fingers were hooked behind his left eye trying to pop it out of the socket. Only a moment after he realized what was happening to him, she had succeeded and he felt the wet plop of his eyeball as it settled on his cheek, still attached to the optical nerves. Through his screaming and limited thrashing, Rebekka somehow made quick, light work of the detachment by retrieving the pocketknife she had laid within reach and severed the tethers with a flick of her wrist.

She made sure that he watched her with his only eye as she dropped the extracted one to the floor at her feet and then stomped it. It popped like a balloon filled with water, and not-quite-clear liquid splattered across the floor in a jagged arch around the toe of her boot. The fisherman's remaining eye fluttered as he wavered in an out of consciousness for a moment, equal parts pain, fear, and shock all playing their parts, but he remained conscious, as much as he wished that he wasn't.

Rebekka tossed him in the crate, lidded it, changed clothes, and then returned to her shack to check on Sarah Maisse. It was late morning when she left the Mercantile but wouldn't be able to return until after midnight, leaving the fisherman in the crate for almost 15 hours.

She returned to the Mercantile, that second night, to begin their second session, after John had finally returned from scavenging and completing chores for the day. It was hard living during that winter, but most of the valley folks managed well enough, until their deaths, anyway. More death was coming to the valley, though, and the fisherman was only the beginning.

Rebekka unlidded the wooden crate and then knocked it over onto its side, landing with another loud echoey SMACK! The fisherman didn't tumble out as she had expected, he had barely moved, only having slid a little way out of the overturned crate. She dragged him out onto the floor, the sudden movement to his cramped body caused him to let out a weak scream that was muffled behind the cloth. She quickly untied his forearms but rebound his hands, expecting him to extend his legs, but again he barely moved. She grabbed the rope binding his feet together and dragged him over to the straight-back chair. The jerk she gave him extended his stiff bent knees, quickly and painfully, causing them to loudly POP! like a burning pine knot. Again, he screamed in pain and misery, adrenaline fueling his emotions, but the weakness was still evident. Rebekka never even hesitated at the sound, just kept dragging, and after several long minutes she had the fisherman secured in the chair and ready for their second session to begin.

She did allow him a cup of water to drink, only because she didn't want him to die before she was done with him.

He was relieved when she unlidded and flipped the crate, but the pain of moving, even the slightest bit, was excruciating, making it almost not worth it. Rebekka had helped with that, though. Then he relished every single drop of the cool refreshing water that she had given him. The thought of poison had briefly crossed his mind, but his need for water won over the suspicion and he drank greedily and gratefully. The moment the water cup was empty she shoved the same cloth but wadded into a small ball, deep into his mouth. He choked and gagged a couple of times, trying to spit it out but couldn't. Finally, he gave up, trying to preserve his energy. He never had the chance to beg for his life.

Using his only eye, the fisherman looked around him trying to get an idea of what may be next. He seen a bulging feed sack and a large metal serving spoon sitting on the floor. Moments later, Rebekka appeared with a plate full of burning beeswax candles, about half a dozen in a tight cluster, that she set carefully beside the full feed sack. She reached into the feed sack, using her body to shield its contents, then rose with whatever she had retrieved hidden in her hand behind her back.

"You did quite the number on Lacy." Rebekka said, an undeniable viciousness to her tone.

The fisherman couldn't speak but he violently shook his head and tears welled in his eyes, sincere tears of guilt. Rebekka mistook those tears for those of fear and smiled for it. She nodded her head slowly, maintaining her pleased sadistic smile. "Yes, you should be afraid. You will die much like she did but much more painfully!" Then she brought her hand out from behind her back and in it she held a fist sized stone.

His first thought was that she was going to throw it at him, and he tried to brace himself for that impact, but she approached him instead, stone in hand. She stepped to his right side and using her free hand, held his head at an awkward angle. She placed the stone on his forehead, just above the temple and began rubbing furiously. Within seconds his skin became raw, and blood speckled. She stopped only a minute or so later, tossed the stone behind her, grabbed another out of the feed sack and repeated the process only right below the first mark.

It wasn't pleasant by any means but compared to the literal scalping he had endured that morning a little raw skin was easily tolerable. Rebekka repeated the process with multiple stones, making her way over his entire face, outlining his ears and chin, and stopping at his scalp-less skull. The raw skin was burning fiercely but it was still tolerable.

The fisherman hoped that that was the end of it, but knew it wasn't when she reached into the feed sack again and pulled out another larger, coarser rock. He knew that it was going to be more painful the second time, but he had no idea how much. Rebekka went over his face, ear to ear, missing scalp to jawline, with several larger rougher stones that gouged into his already partially skinned flesh. Once the stone became soaked in blood it lost its rough effectiveness, so she had to discard it for a new one. Rebekka went through the stones until the feed sack was empty, scrubbing the flesh right off his face.

When she tossed the last stone behind her, the fisherman's face was an unrecognizable mask of blood and shredded flesh. Some places were deep enough to expose bone, while others were just shallow enough to bleed. His head wobbled on his neck, obviously losing consciousness and again Rebekka worried that he might bleed out, so she quickly began the next step. She had anticipated the need to stop the blood the second time but had wanted to prolong the whole thing. She wanted to wait as long as she could but knew that time was quickly running out.

4

She grabbed the long metal spoon and held the serving end over the flames of the beeswax candles until it was hot enough to instantly evaporate a drop of water. With the heated metal spoon ready for use, she took the couple steps toward the fisherman, who was still wavering on the brink of consciousness. Rebekka jerked him away from that knife-tipped edge back to reality when she stuck the spoon to his bleeding forehead in the same place she began. There was an immediate sizzling sound that very much resembled that of frying bacon and the sickly, sweet aroma of burning flesh and boiling blood. The unbearable pain combined with the horrid smell of his own skin being broiled turned his stomach over in large, folding waves. It caused him to regurgitate the refreshing water he had been given not long ago, that was mixed with the acrid taste of his own stomach bile. The cloth in his mouth prevented the regurgitation from exiting and he was forced to swallow what didn't soak into the cloth. It was swallow or choke, and his body chose for him.

To the fisherman, it felt like lifetimes went by before Rebekka finally removed the spoon from his face, but it had only lasted a few seconds. She took the couple steps over to the candles and held the serving end of the spoon back over the open flames. Back and forth she went, between the slowly melting candles and his bloody and burnt skin until she cauterized the fisherman's entire face. She even flipped the spoon around, heating the metal handle to have a narrower tool for the harder places, such as around his nose and ears.

The whole process of stopping the blood loss took hours, only because Rebekka was so meticulous about it, enjoying her revenge and the results she reaped from the work. Luckily for the fisherman, he had passed out during the fourth round with the spoon. His exhausted, pain-wracked body remained dormant and unfeeling until well after she had put him back in the crate and left.

He didn't know it, but it was midmorning when Rebekka left the Mercantile. He was left in the crate for a few hours less than the day before but was in so much more pain, when his weak and miserable self, had awoke in the crate. As much as his cramped and dehydrated body needed to move, he was more scared than relieved when Rebekka returned almost 12 hours later.

He remained in the wooden crate for some time while he listened to her rummage about the shop, her footsteps increasing in volume when she was in the back room and decreasing when she walked to the front. Finally, overwhelmed with fearful anxiety, he heard her approach the crate and tried, but failed, to brace himself for the jarring impact of the tumbling crate.

Once settled and secured in the chair, Rebekka went about gathering the handful of things she needed for their third and final session. The fisherman watched, with his right eye, his only eye, as she walked into the front room and returned only moments later with a full feed sack held upon her shoulder with one hand, and a two-tined metal fork and the bloody pocketknife he knew so well, in the other. She set everything down in the same place she had everything the night before and returned to the front room.

The fisherman was examining the full feed sack, sure it didn't contain stones that time because it didn't bulge oddly in places as the other one had. With no indicating mark on the sack, though, he wouldn't know what was in it until Rebekka wanted him to. When she walked back in, she was carrying another tray clustered with tall, thick beeswax candles that burned brightly. He tried to swallow but his parched tongue and throat would not allow it. His heart rate increased, his breathing deepened, and his fear triplicated.

609

The only clear thought in his mind was that he hoped his death would come quickly.

With everything prepared, Rebekka stood before him with the bloody pocketknife in hand. She had opened the feed sack, but he still wasn't sure what it contained, the angle of the sack and the poor lighting in the room made it impossible for him to tell. He would have cried had he not been so dehydrated, and he would have fought had he not been so weak. However, given his condition, the fisherman could do little more than sit there and endure, even when he had convinced himself that he couldn't.

Due to the Witch and her advanced powers, the fisherman was not given the luxury of losing consciousness. He felt every moment of that final session right up until his death, Rebekka ensuring that it was long, drawn out, and only completed when she was satisfied.

She didn't speak a word to the fisherman, knowing there was nothing to be said. He knew why he was there and why she was doing what she was, and that's all that mattered. So, she began by kneeling in front of him and slowly ran the tip of the pocketknife from the top of his bare foot, up his calf, over his knee, and to his inner thigh. There she applied more and more pressure until the tip slipped into the flesh of his leg where much less blood than expected trickled out. She dug deeper with the blade, slicing into his leg, leaving a four-or-five-inch gash.

The fisherman squeezed his eye shut and jerked his head from side to side as she sliced into him. A low moaning sound, barely audible, could be heard over the wind swirling about the eaves of the Mercantile, but he lacked the strength for any more of a reaction. He sensed rather than watched Rebekka reposition herself to reach into the feed sack. Fearful curiosity got the best of him for only a moment, and he opened his only eye to see what she had in her fisted hand. He watched her sit the knife aside and use her free hand to stretch open the gash in his leg. His head jerked back as a response to the intense pain, but he recovered quickly enough to watch Rebekka use her fisted hand as a funnel to pour salt into his fresh wound. The burning, searing pain of the salt on the exposed nerves sent lightning rods of pain through his leg, lower back, groin, and lower stomach. His body almost tingled from the horrendous pain, his nerves vibrating on high alert.

With the gash on his leg packed with salt, Rebekka moved on to his ribs repeating the slicing and separating process. She had to massage the salt into the rib wound instead of pouring it into it, but the results were essentially the same. She went over the entire front of his body, sparing his genitals, gashing and slicing and then pouring or massaging salt into them. She had cut him more than 50 times and had tediously salted every one of them.

The fisherman, still conscious, trembled through the pain, looking more alienish than human. Most of the front of his body was a crystalized pink giving him a bizarre appearance, with his scalped head and skinless, charred face. All he wanted was the sweet relief of death.

Rebekka stood back to observe her work, and after several long moments she walked back into the front room. She had three buckets of snow melting by the fireplace and after a little stirring she had three half-full buckets of water. She poured one bucket into another, creating a full bucket of water and then used the third half of a bucket to take a long slow drink from. After satiating her thirst, she picked up the full bucket of water and packed it into the back room with her.

Again, she stood and observed her work with an appreciative eye for several long moments before continuing with their session. She doused him with the icy cold water, rinsing away most of the salt that coated his body. The shock of the cold water reanimated the fisherman for a few minutes, causing him to stiffen and straighten up in the chair. His right eye widened, his heart rate and breathing increased, and he began thrashing around. The adrenaline didn't last long, though, and he quickly resumed his slumped, dying position, shivering violently.

"It's almost over." Rebekka told him snidely. "Not that you deserve death, only cause you're past savin. There's just one more, small matter to deal with fore then." She finished with a malicious tone and a smile to match.

The fisherman looked at her the moment she spoke, shaking the whole time, his head jerking against the back of the tall chair. He was relieved to know that death was near and hoped it would be quick. He just wanted the excruciating pain to end, but he knew there was more to endure by her tone.

5

Rebekka walked over to her small bundle of supplies and picked up the two-tined metal fork. The fisherman thought that she had replaced that with the bloody pocketknife but once she was in full view of him again, instead of at an awkward angle, he realized that she had one in each hand. The knife in her dominant right hand and the fork in her left as she slowly stepped toward him. The sound of air rapidly being pushed into and out of his nostrils was loud in the large back room of Gary Brown's Mercantile.

He watched as she stepped to the left of him, the weapons held tightly in her hands. "I never did care for the likes of ya too much, usin and treatin wimmin the ways you did. Just so you's..." she raised the double tined fork, "...could satisfy..." with her arm extended she brought the fork down swiftly, "...your pathetic excuse for a prick!" An audible high-pitched noise could be heard from behind the balled-up cloth shoved in the fisherman's mouth as the two fork tines stabbed into his genitals. Both tines slid straight through the middle of his shaft, exiting the opposite side. One metal tine missed a testicle as it punctured his sac, ripping a jagged slash across his scrotum before it hit the chair seat. The second fork tine struck the other testicle, piercing it, the metal sliding effortless through and out the bottom, until it met the resistance of the wooden chair the fisherman sat upon.

Rebekka pulled the fork out and away from his body, with no intention of ripping his member off because that would have been too quick, she pulled it just enough so that the skin became taut. Then, in short, slow sawing motions, she sliced off the fisherman's manhood with the pocketknife. He screamed but couldn't be heard, he thrashed but couldn't move, he wept but couldn't cry, and he prayed but couldn't be saved. When the last of the flesh had been sliced through, she pulled his speared genitals away from his body, presenting it in front of his face so he could get a good look at it. It dangled limply, the jagged severed base dripping blood, the bright crimson color off setting the pale, wrinkly organ it clung too.

She quickly dropped the knife and grabbed a handful of salt from the feed sack and rubbed it vigorously into his bloody, wounded pelvis. The shock, cold, and pain caused him to tremble so violently that one would have been convinced that he was having a seizure. The thrashing and shaking had caused the hemp ropes he was tied to the chair with, to dig deeply into his wrists and ankles, glimpses of bone visible in places. Despite everything he had been through, though, he was still alive... and conscious.

With the meaty member hanging from the fork, Rebekka slowly heated the dismembered body part over the flames of the beeswax candles. The blood sizzled and blackened while the flesh broiled and charred. She removed it from the candle flames and immediately stepped in front of the fisherman, the fork in hand. Using her free hand, she ripped the balled-up cloth from his arid mouth, allowing him to suck in a raspy burst of chilly air. Before he could exhale, Rebekka shoved his smoking, blackened genitals into his mouth. The edges of the metal fork tines were so hot they melted the corners of his mouth before she pulled the fork free.

The fisherman immediately began to gag as the large, burnt fleshy phallus was roughly shoved toward the back of his throat. The retched taste that settled on his tongue from the charred skin, amplified his thirst almost to the point of insanity. His right eye bulged, his throat contracted, his chest hitched, and his stomach tried to expel contents it did not have. One of his last complete and sane thoughts was that he was going to die chocking on his own dick and balls.

Rebekka stepped back, letting the fork fall from her hands and clatter on the wooden floor. The satisfied expression that settled on her face as she looked upon the fisherman was undeniable. She favored her artful revenge for a long moment, letting her pride indulge, and then stepped over and picked up the pocketknife again. She returned to her place directly in front of him and stared into his wide, almost bulging right eye. The fear, pain, and agony were evident in his gaze, and she knew that he was begging her to kill him. Rebekka's hands hung at her sides, unmoving, her right one grasping the bloody pocketknife. She stood and watched as his fear grew and his throat contracted as he choked. She watched him struggle for breath through his anxiety and shake uncontrollably.

Rebekka watched as the fisherman struggled at the brink of death, wavered between this life and the afterlife, all with a pleasant, content smile, as if all were right in the world once again. Suddenly, with a single rapid movement, she raised her right arm and swung the knife in a wide sideways arc that ended when the blade impaled the fisherman in the side of the throat. The blade disappeared, buried to the hilt, severing his jugular on the way through. The tip of the blade pierced and stopped in his esophagus causing a snuggle fit, and she had to wiggle the blade to get it to pull free.

When it did, a single small spurt of blood shot out directly behind it but quickly tapered off into a slow stream down the side of his neck and onto his shoulder. The choking and gagging noises coming from the fisherman turned into bubbling, gurgling sounds, and Rebekka wondered if he would die from blood loss, chocking on his own dick, or drowning in his own blood. She didn't know it, but it was the drowning that got him. Most of the blood that would have seeped out of his punctured neck poured into his lungs instead.

The fisherman could feel death looming about him through his misery and pain, begged it to take him into its peaceful solace, but still it only lingered. Even after Rebekka stabbed him in the throat, it lingered but still would not take him. He sat in his agony, feeling the warmth of his own blood trickling into and filling his lungs. His breaths became shallower and shallower until his only good eye began to fog and blacken. The pain was still unbearable and though his body seemed to be lifeless, no beating of the heart, no breaths taken, his mind was still very much awake. Trapped within his own dead body, feeling every cut, slice, burn, and puncture he had endured. Every grain of salt still coating the exposed nerves across his body, the severe thirst and dehydration, and extreme loss of blood. It was excruciating and he all he had wanted was the peacefulness of death. However, he would not... could not die, until Rebekka Lane did.

Exhausted and finally completed with her work, Rebekka left everything, including the fisherman were it was. She had no reason or intention to return to the Mercantile since he was dead, so she dampened the fire, dressed, and left, returning to the shack so that she could rest and prepare for the birth of Sarah and John's baby. The fisherman left strapped to the straight-back chair, trapped inside his own mind, remained exactly where she had left him until her own death, weeks from then. The constant pain and misery drove him mad after days and the way he cursed his God bought him his own personal Hell when he was finally taken by the ever-lingering death.

Chapter Sixty

Raging Hormones

1

Death made its way around the valley, touching many but taking only a few, during those days that passed through the middle of February. The temperature had risen out of the fierce single digits during the day, staying steady at about 20 or so degrees. They had been lucky enough to not have more than an inch or so added to the knee-high snow amount they already had to trek through.

The snow nor the cold could stop Old Joe Brenner from trudging over to the kitchen in search of a little cinnamon bark, though. The sexual tension between him and Nonna and Nonni was to the point of being almost unbearable. They had to have each other, like hormone-enraged young adults, the very thought sent shivers through them. The only issue was that Old Joe had trouble getting his prick to work. The twins had tried on several occasions, and it wasn't from their lack of trying or his lack of desire, it just wouldn't stiffen like it was supposed to.

The three of them discussed options to help or cure his affliction, trying the ones they were able, but they were all fruitless attempts. Nothing worked and it was disheartening for all involved. The night of Rebekka's third session with the fisherman, as Nonna and Nonni took turns trying to stroke some life into his limp dick, Nonni remembered something that their grandmother had told her once when she was a young lady. Her grandmother had said that she had to give her husband some cinnamon tea every once and again to keep the manhood working strong.

About an hour after that recollection, the twins had put their heads together to remember the ingredients their grandmother had used in the tea. She had never told them anything other than the name but remembering back to those days with their little old Granny, they had seen her make it many nights before sending them off to bed. They had most of the ingredients, the ginger, the sassafras, a touch of mint, Shine, and water of course. They only lacked the cinnamon, a generous piece of bark steeped with a touch of mint, sassafras, and ginger, then splashed with a nip of Shine was supposed to act like that little blue pill they've got out, these days.

The following morning Old Joe dressed in thick layers, laced up his boots and headed out of the Bar in the direction of the Common Area. He knew that the Kitchen had been blasted and coated with back soot, but the Twins were sure that the cinnamon bark would have been kept in a glass, lidded jar and therefore unharmed by the coal dust and ash. The trio was quite anxious to see if the tea would work, so Old Joe decided to go check and see. If he couldn't find any there, he would check the butcher's shop knowing Johnathan had used cinnamon in some of his dry rub seasonings, and if not there then the Mercantile. It was the only other place he thought that would have cinnamon bark and he really didn't want to go shack to shack looking for a stray jar with just a bit of cinnamon in it.

He lucked out, though. The Twins were right. After about ten minutes of searching the many cabinets and shelves filled with jars of all kinds of different food stuffs that no one else had bothered to check on, he found several small chips of cinnamon bark in a small glass jar behind a few others. He took it back to the Bar, quick as he could, excited to show Nonna and Nonni what he had found.

The Twins, their sexual desires overriding reason, decided to let the tea steep for a few hours rather than the permitted minutes. They began preparing it whenever Old Joe had shown them the cinnamon and had let it simmer until well into the night, occasionally adding more water to the strengthening brew. The smell of cinnamon enveloped the shack and could be smelled from the outside before the door was even in sight. When it was finally time to serve the tea, they added a vigorous nip of Shine to the mug. Old Joe sat and sipped on the steaming hot cup of cinnamon tea, the potent aroma caused tears to well in his eyes and the taste overwhelmed his palate, but he drank it... every, last drop.

Half an hour later, when he was still as limp as an overcooked noodle, Nonna and Nonni gave him another cup of tea. He wanted to tell them that they should probably just wait a little while longer, but he was as anxious to be with them as they were to be with him, so, he agreed and choked down another mug of the strongly brewed tea.

About ten minutes later, the first signs of life came into his manhood via twitches that quickly grew stronger and more pronounced. When it was partially 'awake', Old Joe informed the Twins and with eager snickers and smiles the three of them retired to the back room where Nonna and Nonni, and more recently Old Joe, slept.

Old Joe fondled the women, one hand on each body, wanting them both at the exact same time in the exact same way, regardless of the impossibility. He would kiss one, then immediately kiss the other, wishing there were two of himself to be able to handle it all. Nonna's hand gripped his enlarging organ, stroking him slowly and intently, while Nonni massaged his testicles with the same intention. They wanted him as hard as they could get him, and he was just going with whatever they wanted, enjoying every moment of it.

The first two or three sharp pains in his chest went unnoticed given the circumstances and the next two or three were noticed but ignored. The final ones, however, were too strong and too painful. He clutched at his chest, loudly gasped several times, then fell forward, face down between his slightly spread, outstretched legs. Nonna and Nonni watched in horror as Old Joe's demise unfolded before their eyes, motionless from shock. Unsure if he was dead or just unconscious, Nonni reached over and pushed his body back up into the slight sitting position he had been in to start with, propped up on a pile of feather pillows. The bluish cast to his puffy tongue and lips, his unmoving chest and dull eyes all told the Twins that he was, in fact, dead.

2

Neither of them could stand to look at his face but as they turned away in unison, their eyes caught sight of something else. His very hard, very erect, penis. The women looked at each other, knowing what the other was thinking. Together and unspeaking, they decided to push away the shameful thoughts and satiate their sexual appetites that still burned fiercely within them despite their current situation, while the opportunity presented itself. They spread a blanket across his face, so they didn't have to see what they were really doing and proceeded to take turns pleasuring themselves with Old Joe Brenner's stiff member. While one sat atop Old Joe the other played with themselves or fondled the other.

They went well into the night, the Twins experiencing one mind-blowing orgasm after another until they finally fell into an exhausted sleep, one on each side of the dead man they had spent the late hours of the night fucking. They awoke the following morning to the brilliant sunlight filtering in through the small, shuttered window and piercing the dimness of the shack.

The women rose within minutes of each other, having been almost perfectly in sync with the other since birth, theirs was more than the typical twin connection. They were groggy and initially confused, looking around the room and then settling their eyes on the dead man between them. They didn't have to remove the blanket over the corpse's face for all the memories of the night before to slam into their minds like an oncoming wave, and the overwhelming shame of what they had done followed directly behind those memories.

Nonna and Nonni Brookes sat on their bed with the stiff, deceased body of Old Joe Brenner laying between them, clung to each other, and wept. The sobbing and weeping were followed by panic and anxiety. They didn't know what to do or who to tell, or if they should do or say anything. The Twins were sure that they didn't want to try to explain the situation to anyone for any reason. With their sexual appetites quenched, it amazed and disgusted them both that they had found anything appealing about Old Joe Brenner. It was completely out of character for the women to do any such thing as... well, Old Joe, and the extent that the three of them had gone to make it happen. The consequences had been fatal, and they wouldn't... couldn't explain why everything had happened the way it did. Only the Witch could do that.

The women could only see one way out of their mess, they had to leave the valley or die trying. They knew that Old Joe was well-respected in the valley, not loved just highly regarded, and they believed that the valley folks would want their heads for killing him. They had a slight chance of survival if they went across the mountains, but a lesser chance if they stayed in the valley. So, in a hurried rush they dressed in as many layers as they could handle wearing, grabbed a couple blankets each and tied them into sacks. They filled the blanket sacks with whatever food they could, several bottles of Shine, and extra clothes. With everything packed as quickly as they could, they snuck out the back door of the Bar and took off toward the timbered mountainside with the sacks in hand.

They had barely made it past the tree line when they realized that they had packed too much and couldn't carry the extra weight. So, they abandoned the extra clothes and some of the less sustainable food they had packed, but kept every bottle of Shine they had brought, passing one between them when they headed deeper into the timbers.

Old Joe Brenner was the last person to ever see Nonna and Nonni Brookes alive. They had made it quite a way over the mountains, but never made their destination. Their bones remain where the women died, only hours apart, a couple weeks after leaving the valley. Their food and Shine had run out days before and they became too weak to go on, their immobility finally causing their frozen deaths.

It has been decades since that winter in the valley with the Witch, but the now buried bones of Nonna and Nonni Brookes have yet to be recovered and possibly never will be.

Chapter Sixty-One

Too Much Tension

1

A few days went by and the dozen or so remaining folks in the valley were too preoccupied to notice that the Twins were gone, and Old Joe had died. Gary Brown was fighting to keep his increasingly more violent and depressive thoughts at bay while caring for his mentally unstable, hysterical wife.

Jiminey and Patty McAvay stayed inebriated from dusk until dawn, spending their days hiding from the world and the death and misery that had taken hold of it. They spent their nights in their own personal escape, wrapped up in each other's arms, thinking of nothing but themselves.

The tension between Frank McGrath and Dansford Keeton was coming to its inevitable climax. Frank's rage over Sarah had been solely directed at Dan, and Dan's guilt and shame over Robert Daniels was directed at Frank in the form of anger, in retaliation. For weeks their emotions had been mingling and steeping into a fetid grotesque cancer between them, one that needed to be lanced.

Rebekka Lane and Johnathan Colmes were preparing for the birth of Sarah and John's baby, knowing that at any time Sarah could tell them that the birthing pains had started. She hadn't said any such thing yet, but they knew it wouldn't be long until she did.

Johnathan took care of the chores while Rebekka watched over Sarah and made up some clothes and blankets for the coming child. He trudged through the snow, back and forth across the valley with a handcart gathering firewood. It took him a full day, but when he was finished stacking it neatly

621

on one side of the shack, there was enough to last a week or longer. The next day, he shoveled a wide area of snow that spiraled out away from the shack. Every shovelful was tossed against the shack creating an insulating wall of snow that would be easy to fill buckets from. The wall of snow stretched all the way around the house, stopping at the stacked wood pile beside the door, and the shoveled area went as far as a few shacks over from theirs. Only a small portion of the top of the outside walls and the roof were visible when John finished with the snow.

Scavenging was the worrying part. He didn't want to be out, even though it was necessary, when the child came. Rebekka whistled a quick but high-pitched tune from an old nursery rhyme she had been told as a child. It was unlike any song or chirp of any bird so it would be distinguishable among the sounds of nature. The whistle would echo around the valley and if he listened carefully, he should be able to hear it anywhere. That tuneful whistle would let him know that he needed to return to the shack as quickly as he could.

So, off he went to see what he could find but a threatening storm was blowing in, and John didn't want to chance getting stuck elsewhere, so his trip was cut short. He returned empty-handed after being out for only a couple hours, both Rebekka and Sarah surprised to see him back so soon.

Due to his earlier than expected return, John and Sarah expected Rebekka to take off toward Hussey Row so she could spend the night with Lacy, as was her usual, unaware of the demise that Old Joe's 'employees' had succumbed to. They both noticed Rebekka's lack of eagerness to leave, but John was the one that noted the touch of sadness in her eyes when they mentioned if she was going to go see Lacy. A simple 'no' was all she would give them in response. Rebekka didn't elaborate and John and Sarah didn't question it. They had heard her mention that the fisherman had been frequenting Lacy's shack more and more lately, and though she wouldn't admit it, John knew that it bothered Rebekka. He assumed that the fisherman was the issue, so he dropped and changed the subject. It was never brought up again.

The storm had come and gone throughout the night but the three of them had slept through it, undisturbed. John took off early the following morning, hoping to find everything he needed and quickly, so he could get back to his beloved Sarah. Rebekka whistled the old nursery rhyme tune as a reminder, as he stepped out the shack door and into the blindingly bright morning.

Sarah made it through another night without the start of the birthing pains, but she grew more and more nervous as time grew shorter and shorter. She had all the typical new mother fears and worries, the typical womanly vanity, and the even more basic 'What the fuck am I going to do?' questions. All those thoughts and questions swirled through her mind, threatening to overwhelm her, and that threat increased when the other more atypical questions began to form in her mind. 'What is my child?', 'Is it even a child at all?', and 'What do I... we do if it's not?' were a few among many. She didn't know, nor know anyone that did, the answer to any of those questions. Only time could give her that.

Sarah got a few of those answers a lot sooner than she realized. On that day, four days after Rebekka's third and final revenge session with the fisherman, the birthing pains began. At first, she thought that the baby was moving about, kicking her a bit harder than normal, but when she felt the warmth of liquid slowly pool beneath her in the bed, she realized what was happening. Rebekka looked up from sewing a small baby's quilt when she heard the snap of the blankets as Sarah threw them back to reveal that her water had broken. Rebekka took one look at her wet night gown and mattress, set her quilt to the side, stood up and walked to the shack door. She stepped out into the late afternoon sunlight, waited for the breeze to die down and then whistled the tune for John to return. It was much, much louder than when she whistled in the shack, and she could already hear the first of the echoes as she stepped back inside.

John had been scavenging for hours, having found most of the items he had gone searching for. He still needed to find some metal pins to keep the baby's nappy on. He searched all over the Seamstress shop, Rebekka adamant that she had some, but he hadn't found them yet. He had found everything else, but not those. He was searching through a littered shelf full of small boxes, lidded containers, jars, and bottles of assorted small things that sat propped against the wall beside a glassless window. One of the shutters had broken off and was hanging from a single hinge, allowing the icy breeze and sunlight to flow in. He may not have heard Rebekka's whistle if he had been away from the window, but he did hear it. Faintly, but surely.

2

Frank McGrath and Dansford Keeton had been bickering all day, the tension between them more intense than it ever had been. The two men had been together since birth, literally, and were so used to having the other around that separating was never even a thought on either part. However, it had gotten to the point that both men had briefly entertained the idea, but not at a realistic level, of killing the other.

Frank's homicidal thoughts were an extension of his desperate need to relieve the relentless rage he felt, all the time, broiling inside him. Like a beast trying to claw its way out of its cage, a wave crashing against the dam that contains it, or an unborn child's pain-filled journey to enter the world, it needed to be released. All the fighting and fucking they had been doing were meager, temporary fixes to his emotional upset, much like putting a band-aid on a skull fracture. He thought, maybe, murder would release that rage. Though these murderous fantasies were emotionally based, rather than logically, Frank wondered if he really could do something like that to Dan.

Dansford's homicidal thoughts were born out of sheer revenge, but his not as profound as Frank's given his immense guilt over killing Robert Daniels. He did fantasize a bit though, only because of how cruel and hateful Frank had been to him in recent weeks. He didn't know why Frank had taken to being so heartless and sadistic, only that it had something to do with Sarah Maisse. It was as if Frank was enjoying his heartache and anger from the mean, hurtful things Frank would say and do. These fantasies didn't last long, though, because he couldn't imagine his life without Frank. Regardless of how barbarous his behavior had become, Dan still loved him more than anything in the world and would continue to endure for as long as it took for him to get through whatever it was that he was dealing with.

The same afternoon that Sarah's birthing pains began, Frank and Dan were in the middle of a particularly violent argument. Frank had awoken that morning in a much fouler mood than usual and Dansford knew, minutes after he walked out of the bedroom, that Frank was itching for a fight, and a good one at that. It just so happened that Dan was in an unusually temperamental mood that same morning, and impulsively decided that if Frank wanted a fight, that he would give him one. Hell, Dan thought to himself, it might even do him a bit of good to get a taste of his own medicine for a change.

Both men's odd temperaments were a result of the Witch 'fueling the fire' so to speak. As they slept the night before, the Witch, using the eyes and tongue of her devilish pet, Vipera, whispered of things both true and untrue, turning their peaceful dreams into nightmares. Their subconscious minds absorbed every word like an arid sponge, which fed Frank's inferno of fury and strengthened Dan's flare of anger toward Frank, into a blazing bonfire. The Witch had all her dominoes in place and if everything fell the way she wanted them to, and they almost always did, then she was in for quite a show that night.

The argument had begun shortly after they had awoken, while outside stacking firewood. Of all things, how the wood should be stacked triggered the disagreement that escalated gradually throughout the day and into the night.

At the same moment that Sarah realized that her water had broken, Frank was kicking Dan in the stomach with a socked foot. When Frank brought his leg back to give him another, Dansford rotated on his socked heels and drove his shoulder into Frank's lower abdomen, sending them both flying back into the wall. A stunned Frank didn't have time to react before Dan was using his forearm to pin Frank to the wall.

There was a window only inches to their left, shuttered but glassless, and when they slammed into the wall, the jarring had knocked one of the shutters partially open. Dansford was using his free hand to deliver multiple short punches to Frank's ribs when they both heard the distant but evident high-pitched whistly tune. They both hesitated for a moment, stunned by its suddenness and mystery, which allowed Frank that moment he needed to react.

3

John forgot all about the jar of little metal pins when he heard Rebekka's 'come back' tune. He grabbed up everything he had acquired and raced back to the shack as fast as he could. When he walked in, Sarah was lying on the bed, propped up in a sitting position with some pillows, her head laid back and to the side. She appeared to be sleeping, but then her face suddenly twisted and contorted as another pain rippled through her midsection. He rushed to her side, not taking the time to remove any of his layers, just dropped the stuff he carried in and went straight to the bedside.

Sarah grabbed his hand frantically, fighting through the pain and trying to stifle the screams and moans threatening to erupt from her throat. When it finally subsided, she whispered, "John, I'm scared."

"So am I, love... so am I." he whispered back, before gently kissing her hand. She seemed to be alright for the time being, so he released her hand, kissed her softly on the mouth, and then returned to the door to shed some layers and remove his boots. 'Ready or not, here comes baby.' Johnathan kept thinking, hoping that they were ready enough for it. Whatever it is.

He was helping Rebekka put away the items he had found when another pain hit Sarah. Rebekka got to the bedside before John and after helping her through the pain she checked the baby's placement since her pains were getting closer and closer together. Rebekka had aided in more than a few births, a lot of the women in the valley old enough for grandbabies had and knew the many signs and steps of the birthing process. In the valley, the doctor wasn't called to a birth unless something was wrong with either mother or child. Sarah and John didn't have that option though, so they were relying on Rebekka to handle everything. John knew the Witch wouldn't help him again, he had nothing else to offer her. He just hoped that Sarah wouldn't suggest it in desperation, if something were wrong.

Given the baby's placement, Rebekka suspected that the baby would be born before the rise of the sun. She had never witnessed such a sight as Sarah Maisse, from conception to birth, it had only been a little more than three months. Aside from the rapidity of the unborn child's growth, all the symptoms and steps were the same, just done at a much quicker rate, and she expected the birth to be much the same way.

She wasn't wrong. Sarah continued to fight through each birthing pain, resting between them when she could. Rebekka checked the baby's placement every quarter hour, knowing the unborn child could speed up or slow down the process at any given time. Either scenario would present its own set of issues and Rebekka wanted to avoid any complications if she could.

About an hour and a half after John had returned to the shack, all was going as expected with Sarah and the baby. The frequency of her birthing pains had increased to only a few minutes apart. John grew more and more nervous as Sarah grew more and more exhausted with each tick of the clock, while Rebekka remained focused, trying to be ready for anything.

4

Frank was used to Dansford fighting back during their quarrels, he almost always did once he realized that de-escalation wouldn't work, but he had never fought back so hard as he did the night that Sarah and John's son was born. Dan surprised Frank on several occasions that day and night, repeating many of the same brutal things that Frank had done to Dan at some point over those past weeks.

When they heard Rebekka's whistle, Frank used that moment of hesitation to shove Dan away from him. His foot caught on an overturned broken chair as he stumbled back, falling hard to the floor, landing in front of the fireplace. Frank stood leaning against the wall, panting, waiting to see what Dan was going to do but he only sat there.

The men remained in their places for several minutes, catching their breaths and taking a brief respite, both knowing that it wasn't over yet. Frank was the first to speak, tossing out the starting comment for the next round. "Just think that none of this woulda happened if ya had just kept your goddamned mouth shut!"

"I nevva said a damn thing til you came over tossin my stack all over!" Dansford retorted hatefully.

"Cause you were doin it wrong, you dumb sumbitch!" Frank shouted, just as hatefully as Dan.

"Don't you talk bout my mama dat way!" Dansford yelled, the anger in his voice evident. Without thinking, he reached toward the side of the fireplace and snatched up a busted piece of firewood. It was about a foot long piece of solid oak, and he chucked it at Frank as hard as he could from his sitting position. As soon as the firewood left his hand, he was on his feet and ready to fight, but watched it hit Frank in the cheekbone instead. Dan heard the smacking sound as it contacted Frank's face, loud in the suddenly silent room, that was followed by a muffled cracking noise. The dazed and crazed young man slowly slid down the wall to a sitting position as he drifted off into unconsciousness.

It was not the result Dan had expected but it was one he could work with. It was time for Frank to get a taste of his own doings. So, Dan dragged Frank's unmoving body toward the fireplace and roughly jerked his layered bottoms down to his calves. Frank's consciousness was suddenly slammed back into wakefulness when Dan shoved his barely lubricated manhood into Frank until his testicles touched skin. They had been 'intimate', if one could use such a term, on dozens and dozens of occasions but only twice had Dan been in that position.

Frank tried to struggle but Dan was ready for it and held him in place. It was very nearly a repeat, just in swapped positions, of their very first romp during that October blizzard. And much like that first night, just reversed, Frank hated every moment of it while Dansford loved every moment of it. It was more the satisfaction of knowing that Frank's pride was hurting much more than his asshole, than it was the action itself, though Dan did find it quite pleasant.

When Dan finally exploded in Frank, releasing a lot of the built up anger he felt toward him with it, Dan immediately punched Frank in the side of the head, returning him to his state of unconsciousness. Dan knew that Frank was just waiting for him to finish so he could react, but Dan didn't give him the chance. He pulled free of their entanglement, stood up, pulling his pants up as he did, and left Frank where he laid.

Frank wasn't out for long, only a few minutes, but was confused upon awakening. It took him a long moment to realize where he was and a longer one to remember what had just happened to him. It all felt kind of hazy, though, like a dream. He only had to look down at his bare legs and genitals to know that it wasn't though, and then as if on cue he became aware of the stickiness oozing out beneath him. He slowly rose, having to hold the mantel on the fireplace for support until the wooziness in his legs dissipated. He had gotten his layers of pants back up around his waist when he realized that Dansford wasn't there.

Chapter Sixty-Two

Deep Cuts

1

Dusk turned into night, and it darkened with the passing time as Sarah's pain increased in both intensity and frequency. John was almost sick with worry over Sarah and their baby that may not even be a baby at all. He watched as Sarah grew more exhausted and weaker with each contracting pain, he wiped the sweat from her brow, watched her complexion pale, and whispered words of encouragement when he thought she needed them most. He longed to take her pain away, to release her from her agony, but he knew that he could not and he loathed the impossibility of it all.

When the time came that Sarah had only a minute or less to rest between pains, Rebekka had her stand up beside the bed, then squat down as low as she could with her knees spread as far as possible. With John at her side the entire time, Sarah began to push and rest when Rebekka said so. Tears streamed from her eyes, sweat rolled from her forehead and dripped from her nose, and try as she might she could not stifle the screams that burst from her mouth. The sharp rippling pains that vibrated through her lower abdomen combined with the excruciating burning sensation that radiated from the womanhood between her legs, was overwhelming and agonizing. She had never known such pain in her entire life, and she feared what the outcome of it would be.

"Stop!" Rebekka shouted. "No mattas how bad ya want to... do NOT push!" Rebekka told her.

"What's wrong? Rebekka! Answer me, Rebekka! What's wrong?" John asked, the panic threatening to overwhelm him.

Though Rebekka was concentrating hard on whatever was going on with Sarah and the baby, she stopped and looked at him sternly. "I don't know if there is anythin wrong. John, I know you're scared, but my attention needs to be on her..." Rebekka said as she pointed at Sarah, "...and not soothin you outta your fears. The time it would take me to do that could mean the death of em both. So, less ya want your worse fears to come true, you needs to let me do this." Rebekka told him in a stern but loving, motherly way.

"You're right. Forgive me." he whispered. He bowed his head in shame, took a deep breath, let it out shakily and then returned to his place beside Sarah. Rebekka immediately diverted her attention back to the coming baby.

After a few moments of intense inspection Rebekka took off into the kitchen only to return moments later with a small-bladed knife and a thick handled wooden spoon. "John, I needs ya to stand hind Sarah and when I say so, ya keep a good firm grip on her shoulders... and don't ya let go, boy, I mean it!" she told him pointing a long, bony finger at him. John was taken aback by her adamancy and knew he better do as she instructed. He feared what she was about to do, even though she had not divulged that information yet, and what would happen should he fail to keep Sarah still.

"Sarah..." Rebekka began, handing the exhausted and panting Sarah Maisse the wooden spoon. She accepted it with a trembling hand. "...You needs to place that in your mouth to bite down on. What I gotta do, it gonna hurt fiercer than the rest, girl, trust me. You gonna want that so ya don't go bittin a hole through your tongue." Sarah barely had enough energy to nod in response and slowly lift the slightly shaking spoon to her lips. As soon as Rebekka seen her chomp down on the wooden spoon handle, she dropped to the floor, lying on her stomach but looking up between Sarah's legs, where she could see the very top of the child's head.

All had been going smoothly until the baby got stuck. Rebekka could almost watch the baby's head slowly deform from the pressure and she had to do something to get it out. "Now, boy!" she yelled as she used the small bladed but rather sharp knife to slice a small gash into Sarah, just below the child's head. Sarah let out a high-pitched scream from behind

631

the wooden spoon held tightly in her teeth. She tried to jerk away from Rebekka, but John's strong and quick reflexes held her in place.

The gash she made in Sarah wasn't deep enough, so Rebekka had to run the blade over it a second time. Blood gushed in a pool beneath both women and Rebekka knew it was time. She quickly scrambled to her feet and though Sarah was screaming she had stopped trying to thrash around and jerk away. Rebekka dropped the knife and placed her hands between Sarah's legs, all while ordering her to push as hard as she could.

2

For hours, Frank McGrath and Dansford Keeton played a kind of cat-and-mouse game. It took a little time, but Frank had found Dan in the kitchen, kneeling before a bucket of water trying to clean up some of his injuries. Frank saw his opportunity and took it. Catching Dan off guard, Frank leaped onto his back, shoved his head down into the bucket of icy cold water, and tried to drown him. Dan managed to knock the bucket on its side but by the time the disorientation wore off, Frank was gone. He found him a bit later, though, hiding in one of the two bedrooms.

The bedrooms were both simple, square rooms that sat side-by-side along one side of the house. Each had two doors: one led to the opposite bedroom and the other out into the living area. Frank was hiding in the corner of the room, between the bed and the wall, mostly hidden from sight of either door. So, Dan tossed a kitchen knife at Frank, with no intention of hitting him with it, but when it stuck into the wall just inches from Frank's face, Frank took off at a dead run toward the door to the other bedroom. He knew the knife had been thrown from the living area doorway and therefore believed that it was his safest bet. He didn't know that Dan had tossed the knife and then sprinted to the opposite doorway knowing that's where he would go.

As soon as Frank stepped through the doorway, Dan swung a piece of wood from a broken table and caught him in the mouth and nose with it. Blood splattered across the walls in both bedrooms as the force of the blow knocked him back through the doorway. Frank remained conscious, just dazed for several moments, laying flat on his back. His mind tried to register what had just happened, and when it did, he realized what Dan had done. A part of him was impressed with Dan and his simple cleverness, but a larger part of him was furious with him. He finally sat up, gingerly touched his face, winced from the pain, and pulled away a handful of blood. He spit two of his teeth out on the floor beside him, along with a few mouthfuls of blood, and then slowly got to his feet, groaning and panting all the while.

Frank stumbled around the house for quite some time before he came across Dansford again. That time, Frank attempted to stab Dan in the chest with the same kitchen knife he had thrown at him earlier, but Dan moved too quickly, and he only managed to cut his arm. Frank swung the knife again while Dan was examining his bleeding arm, but again Dan was quicker than him. Instead of gutting him as he had intended, the knife was buried to the hilt into the top of his thigh. Dan squalled in pain and fell to the floor as Frank darted from the room, leaving Dan like a stuck pig.

Dansford had enough sense to know that pulling the knife free would be like popping the cork on a bottle. The blood couldn't really spill out until the knife was removed, so he left it there. He sat in that same room, resting and planning, until he felt strong enough to deal with Frank McGrath.

A few hours had gone by, and Dan hoped that it had played into his favor, that Frank had dropped his guard a bit since so much time had passed. It seemed that he had because Dan found Frank in the living area, seated by the fireplace. He appeared to be sleeping, so, as Dan smiled at his luck, he quietly approached Frank.

3

Sarah pushed with everything she had. Her sweat-damp hair stuck to the sides of her face, veins popped out on her neck and forehead, her temples throbbed with the beat of her own heart and sweat glistened across her flushed complexion giving her an angelic appearance. Her eyes were tightly closed, her nose scrunched, her jaw set, and her teeth clamped down hard enough to leave very deep impressions in the wooden spoon. She screamed, loudly and painfully, to the point that she feared her throat would rupture, as the baby widened the fresh gash trying to make its way into the world.

She pushed so hard that she started to see dark spots invade her vision, her body slowly numbed, and she wavered on the brink of consciousness. She could hear John and Rebekka talking to her, from a distance, but couldn't understand their words. She assumed that Rebekka was telling her to 'Push!' but she couldn't feel her body at that moment to do so. She could see and feel nothing and hear only distant, muffled sounds, but the coppery smell in the air and taste of blood in her mouth was overwhelming. She wouldn't realize it until a few hours later, but she had bitten the wooden spoon so hard that she had jabbed a splinter into her upper gum, causing it to bleed.

Sarah Maisee forced her way back from that brink when she heard the faint and distant sound of a whimpering baby. The wooden spoon fell from her mouth and left a bloody trail down her nightgown as it rolled down the front of her body, seated then instead of squatted, and it clattered to the floor. Her sight slowly came back into focus, Rebekka kneeling before her, her downcast head between her legs, the first thing she had seen. Slowly, Sarah turned her head and found John at her side but turned away from her. She tried to call his name, but her parched throat wouldn't allow her to speak, and she was too weak to reach out for him.

When he finally turned toward her, she immediately noticed the wrapped bundle he held in his arms, causing her heart rate to triple. She wanted desperately to ask what it was and not in terms of gender. She wanted to know if her baby was... well, a baby, and not some demon creature or something. A part of her yearned to know what was concealed within the newly made baby blanket, but another part of her feared it.

After several long moments, John finally realized that Sarah's eyelashes had stopped fluttering and her eyes had focused once again. They weren't looking at him, though, only at the bundle-o-baby he held. The fear and wonder were evident in her eyes and that's when he realized that she couldn't even see the baby. The way John was holding the newborn and the blanket covering all but the small round face, she was just staring at the blanket. He moved toward her and her stare broke, moving her eyes to meet his. Though she couldn't speak just yet, he knew what she was asking about from the frantic look in her eyes. That same look that immediately melted away when Johnathan Colmes gave her the most genuine smile of relief and happiness. He kissed her forehead, oblivious to the sweat beginning to dry there, and whispered in her ear as he carefully laid their newborn son upon her chest. "He's a prefect baby boy. He's wonderful and so are..."

"Here boy! I need your hand a moment." Rebekka interrupted. John didn't mind and immediately moved down closer to Rebekka. Without realizing it until the pair were thoroughly soaked, the three of them were almost wading in Sarah's blood. Panic threatened and he knew Rebekka could sense it when she removed one hand from the blood-dripping rag she held to Sarah's genitals and grabbed his arm. "You hold this here, tight, boy! Tight! Focus on that ONLY until I get back. Hold it tight!" She released John's arm, leaving a noticeable blood smear of her fingers around his wrist, and he could only nod as he shoved both hands over the bloody rag and pressed hard enough to jar Sarah, who seemed not to notice.

A very nervous, very wary, very doubtful Rebekka Lane was tossing old moth-eaten blankets out of the bottom of a wooden trunk. Self-doubt was eating at her, and she was fighting back the panic and hopelessness that was threatening to overwhelm her as she gathered up the blankets and headed back into the bedroom. As she walked by the table in the kitchen area, where a mostly sewn quilt had been left and forgotten, she seen her needle and thread. The sight was followed by a brilliant idea, so she snatched it up and headed quickly into the bedroom.

An hour later, Sarah laid resting uneasily, very pale, very weak, and very near death. Rebekka had done all the necessary afterbirth removal as quick as she could and then sewed her up, but she was still bleeding. Not as heavily but that could have very well been due to her having so little of it left. John and Rebekka were cleaning up the massive amount of blood off the floor, while the newborn baby boy slept in a wooden bassinet beside the bed. All they could do was wait and see if Sarah would recover or not.

4

Given the worrisome circumstances that Sarah and the baby were in, neither of the three of them noticed, nor would have cared if they had, that quite the weather anomaly was forming in the sky above them. From the North came a lightning storm to rival all others. The clouds were an infectious black and flashes and streaks of bright blue bolts descended in crooks and forks toward the Earth. Thunder not only rolled, but trembled across the clouds, causing the very ground beneath it to vibrate. It formed and remained over the northern end of the valley, creeping its way south to cover the southern end.

However, a different storm formed across the southern end of the valley that was made of light gray clouds. If thunder rumbled from the southern storm, then it was drowned out by the roars of the darker northern storm. The darker clouds formed when Rebekka moved Sarah into the squatting position on the floor. The Witch had nothing to do with the storms, but she felt as if she should not use them for any such matter, like with the New Year's ice storm. Everything was going too well for her, and she didn't see why she needed to exert the effort. She, also, didn't fear the dark storm because she knew it was only her Master's way of ensuring the marked child's survival.

The Witch became very nervous when the lighter gray storm formed across the southern end. She knew it wasn't the same God that the fucked-up preacher and the three Sisters worshipped, but it was certainly a higher power, or one very close to them.

The much lighter colored storm didn't move or drift, it just held its place and lingered. Seeming to stand against the darker, seemingly more powerful storm. The southern storm's forming seemed to have only antagonized the darker, northern storm causing the rumbling thunder to intensify and the lightning strikes to increase in frequency and ferocity. It went on consistently for several minutes, the southern storm appearing pathetic and meager against it.

The few remaining folks in the valley would have noticed the electrified air, the constant clash and bang of thunder, the vibrations in the ground, and the flashes of light bright enough to blind, had the higher powers behind the storms willed it so. The Witch was the only one in the valley that could see and feel the powers of the storms. The two very conflicting, yet very powerful storms. She feared and respected one while she loathed the other.

The northern storm went on and on with its trembling roars of thunder and constant flow of bolts of lightning. Its power never wavered or diminished but seemed to hold strong, if not increase. Yet, the southern storm remained unaffected, unmoved, and refusing to dissipate.

When John and Sarah's son... the marked child of Satan, himself... drew his first breath, the southern storm struck a single bolt of lightning toward the dark, northern storm. That single bolt of lightning contained more power than the entire several minute display the northern storm had just performed. That single bolt of lightning stopped the northern storm's rumbling and flashes, caused the clouds to waver, then slowly dissipate.

The southern storm finally began to dissipate when there were only a few puffs of sickly black clouds left over the northern end of the valley. The powers behind the southern storm knew that the child had survived, but that was only due to the agreement both sides struck. They had won a small battle against their wicked foe but had failed to solve the problem, before it could become one. If anything, they had given structure to the issue. Both sides had won and lost that night, but time would tell which side would win it all.

Chapter Sixty-Three

Hateful Hysterics

1

Dansford Keeton quietly hobbled his way toward the seemingly asleep Frank McGrath as he sat slumped over in a chair pulled up close to the fireplace. There was a chunk of firewood resting on Frank's thigh, his hand resting upon it but not tightly, which aided Dan's belief that Frank was asleep. He still hadn't figured out exactly what he was going to do with Frank, but he figured he would start by getting him out of the chair and tied up.

Dan let the coil of hemp rope slide softly to the floor, knowing he would need both hands to get Frank out of the chair. He balanced himself the best he could on his unwounded leg and set his body to shove Frank as hard as he could, soundless all the while. Just as Dan was ready, Frank tightened his grip on the firewood, swung it as fast and as hard as he could, nailing Dan in the bridge of the nose.

He fell back, stumbling on his hurt leg, landing hard on his back on the floor, covering part of the coil of rope. It knocked the breath from his lungs as stabbing pain spiderwebbed across his face. He wished for unconsciousness as his vison wavered and dimmed, but it would not come. Confusing and frightful for a moment, he watched a featureless being appear before him but quickly realized it was Frank. Without thinking, Dan kicked out at Frank, solidly catching his right knee. It buckled but did not bow, and excruciating pain exploded across his kneecap, sending shards of pain up into his thigh and groin, and down into his calf and ankle. He stumbled backward, caught himself on the mantle of the fireplace and immediately straightened up. The flames had caught the back of his pants, though, catching them alight while the heat on his bare back was undeniable and intense.

Dan had just gotten to his feet when Frank dropped to the floor and started rolling back and forth frantically, trying to put the flames out before they could engulf him. In his flopping struggle with the fire, Frank knocked into Dan's good leg sending it out from under him and Dan fell atop Frank in an awkward fashion. He quickly rolled off Frank and scrambled to his feet just as the last of the flames were smothered.

He had had enough. It had gone too far. He had a knife sticking out of his leg and Frank had almost gotten cooked. It was all just too much, and Dan was done with it. He looked down at Frank, who was still laying on the floor, panting, and asked, "Ya alright?" Hoping that like so many other times that they could just let it all rest for the night.

Frank didn't respond with words, instead he grabbed Dan's good leg and jerked it out from under him, rolling away as Dan fell to an awkward heap on the floor. Dan was beginning to feel all the bruised and tender places across his body where he had fallen so much in those last few minutes. He tried to ignore the pain in his leg that intensified with every jarring motion but found that he could not. As he struggled to his hands and knees, trying to get back up on his feet, Frank was already up and ready for another round.

He grabbed the chair he had been in when Dan found him, looking crazed with it held high above his bloody and busted face, smoke still rising from the back of his scorched pants. He broke the chair across Dan's back driving the wounded man back down to the floor, pieces of the chair breaking and flying in all directions. The combined pain of the already hilt-deep knife driven ever deeper into his thigh, the explosion across his bruised back, and his broken nose's contact with the wooden floor, Dan was momentarily numbed, his body in shock.

Dan was oblivious to everything around him as Frank jerked his layers of pants down and then grabbed one of the broken chair legs. It was about two feet long, slender, and rounded. Much like Frank earlier in the evening, Dan was slammed back into reality when Frank rammed that chair leg inside him, half of it disappearing immediately.

Frank was madder than he ever had been in his life. The rage boiled uncontrollably within him and the beast clawing at its cage door had escaped. The same thoughts played over and over in his mind, fueling that raging fire within him. Sarah chose him over me! It's Dan's fault I am this way! She chose John! That should be my baby! Among many, many others. His intense rage was a direct result of the birth of Sarah and John's baby even though he wouldn't find out until later about the birth. His sanity had fled with his self-control and his only purpose was to ease his own suffering, in any way he could.

While Sarah was wavering on the brink of unconsciousness due to exhaustion and blood loss, Frank grabbed the coil of rope and looped it around Dan's neck. He pulled it tight enough behind him to jerk his head upright and back, way beyond the limits of comfort. Frank wrapped the rope around one hand, keeping it pulled just as tight, freeing up his other. He reached down and gave the chair leg a good, hard jiggle which sent Dan into a frenzy of shaking and jerking, then he shoved his hand down the front of his pants.

The faster Frank moved one hand, the tighter he pulled with the other. It didn't take him long to finish, but by the time he did, Dan was already dead, strangled to death by the love of his life. Frank had no intention of killing Dan and Dan, even as frightened as he was, really didn't believe that Frank was going to kill him. They both kept telling themselves that Frank would let go before it went too far, since he always had before. Dansford Keeton still didn't believe that Frank was killing him even as he blacked out into the darkness of eternity.

Frank released the rope and his shriveling self, stepping away from Dan as his body slumped face down on the floor. He stood there panting by the fireplace, waiting for Dan to get up. Frank was expecting Dan to get up ready to fight again or try to call it quits, and if he did that Frank considered taking that offer. He was exhausted, hurt, and humiliated but seemed to be calmer. The fury within him had dampened, temporarily anyway, and Frank wondered with cautious relief how long it would last.

Several minutes went by and Dan still hadn't moved from his face down position on the floor. Frank became panicky and nervous when he realized how long he had been standing there, knowing he needed to approach Dan's unmoving body but finding himself very reluctant to do so. A few more minutes went by before Frank finally walked over and knelt beside Dan's body. Frank was tense, every aching muscle in his body was taut, and his nerves were quaking causing him to tremble as if cold.

He slowly reached over and shoved Dan's body to the side. The body tilted up but caught, the handle of the knife catching on a floorboard, so Frank shoved a little harder. Frank got Dan rolled over onto his back, ready to place his ear to his best friend's chest. The moment he saw Dan's face, though, he knew that there was no need. There would be nothing for him to hear.

Dan's entire face, from hairline to rope line, was a dull reddish, purple color. His facial features were somewhat distorted beneath the swollen, puffy skin. His wide almost bulging eyes were an intricately detailed maze of red and white outlined by the deep purple of bruising. His lips had a blue cast, and his tongue was equally as swollen as his face. Frank couldn't bear to look at what he had done to Dan, but he knew that it wasn't his fault.

No.

It was Sarah Maisse's fault.

2

That eerie feeling that those left in the valley could feel but not identify, had dissipated with the morning light the day after Sarah gave birth to a beautiful baby boy. Perfectly healthy. Perfectly normal. Perfectly human. Even those directly involved didn't know exactly what happened that night to cause that feeling to finally evaporate. It had lingered for days, setting heavily across the valley like a thick wet, moldy blanket. It had affected the moods of everyone, sans the Witch, but everyone, except for Sarah Maisse and Dansford Keeton, felt a little brighter, a little better, that morning.

Sarah Maisse survived the birth of her son, the marked child of the Witch's Master, but just barely. She was very near death for days and kept in bed by Rebekka and John for weeks after. Even upon her death almost six weeks later, her once beautiful naturally tanned complexion remained an unappealing ashy gray. Rebekka and John were grateful, for the child if no other reason, that Sarah had survived the birthing process but wondered if maybe it would have been easier for her, if she had passed that night.

Most of her time was spent sleeping and when Sarah was awake, she was nursing the baby. John and Rebekka were constantly giving her water, tea, and soup broth regardless of how much she insisted she didn't want it, even gently pouring it between her lips as she slept to ensure she stayed hydrated enough to feed her son. John and Rebekka did everything else with and for the child, who thrived and grew spectacularly.

Though Sarah wasn't clear-headed enough to approve of it, John felt that she would, so he started calling the baby boy, Owen. She had stated more than once that she wanted their son to be named after his father, but John didn't want his son to be called Lil John or something to that affect his whole life, so he used his middle name instead.

Well, baby Owen was seemingly no different than any other infant. He would grow like that of every other child his age, meeting the same milestones, only slightly advanced in certain areas up until young adulthood. About the time he turned 21, though, Owen ceased to age like everyone else, slowing down almost tenfold.

I have yet to see the man since he was an infant, but I would assume that even at his 30+ years he would look like a recent high school graduate. I also know that his name is not and hasn't been Owen in over two decades.

There are higher powers at work that will do their best to ensure you fail your part of this, but there are also powers to ensure that you don't. You are way beyond the point of no return, Doctor, even attempting to do so would result in your death, so please continue reading. Gather the information. Learn. Teach. Prevail.

3

The Witch, through Vipera's eyes, watched as Sarah lingered on the brink of death for days. She was uncertain of Sarah's future, uneasy all the while. She needed her Master's marked son to be healthy and thrive, and only the mother's milk could ensure that. Once the child was a bit older, the Witch would take him, keep him, and raise him in her Master's image, but she needed Sarah to survive in the meantime. It was close but she did.

After a couple weeks of merely watching the valley folks survive day to day, the Witch had grown bored and irritable. So, during those last few days of February, she decided to entertain herself by inducing a particularly intense fit of hysteria upon Gary Brown's wife.

Gary had just stepped outside to grab an armload of firewood when he heard the shattering of glass from inside their shack. He dropped the firewood, chunks falling around him and rolling in several directions as he sprinted back inside. His wife was standing in front of the fireplace, both hands white-knuckle gripping the mantle, her hair hanging loosely around her face, concealing it. He glanced at the opposite wall and beside the doorway leading into the bedroom, was a loose pile of ceramic mug pieces scattered on the floor.

"Honey..." Gary breathed soothingly unsure of his wife's state and what her response could be. She didn't respond or even move as he slid out of his coats and hung them beside the entrance. He stepped closer to her, reaching his hand out to gingerly touch her shoulder. Before his fingers could even brush her nightgown though, she spun toward him and the bizarre expression on her face took him aback. He stepped away from her as her eyes locked on his, a hatred in them that he had never seen before. Her breaking things were normal, the scowls and distorted facial expressions were normal, but the look in her eyes was not. For the first time since his wife's hysteria began, Gary Brown feared for himself rather than her.

She started side stepping, hands raised and hooked into claws, circling him like a predator does its prey, and Gary knew he needed to do something and quickly. So, he waited until she took two more steps to her left and when she was lined up with the bedroom doorway, only a few steps from it, he rushed toward her. Her scowl transformed into a look of surprise, and she stumbled backward unsure of his intentions. She stumbled right into the bedroom, as he intended and before she could realize what was going on, he slammed the door closed with it between them. He held the handle tightly as she slammed into it with the entirety of her body weight, which wasn't considerable by any means, but seemed to be, by the way the door shuttered.

His hands were trembling from the exertion and beads of sweat were popping out on his brow as she beat and battered at the door with a strength that neither of them knew she possessed. Each hit, kick, and slam caused the door to creak and shake in its frame. He spotted a broom sitting off to his left and risked releasing a hand to grab it, knowing that he only had one chance to succeed or fail. He succeeded in grabbing the broom handle and slid it through the door handle and out along the wall, securing the door. The broom handle immediately creaked and cracked against the strain, so Gray quickly grabbed a chunk of firewood to replace the broom handle. The piece of firewood did much better at handling the poundings on the door.

Slightly relieved, he sat at the wooden table, catching his breath, and debating his next move. The beatings on the door went on for several minutes as his wife spewed curses and vile names at him the whole time. As the filth ran off her tongue, Gary Brown could only weep for the woman he had loved so dearly, as well as the marriage they had had, and the end of it all that he knew was drawing near. She had grown considerably worse in the weeks since finding Alvin Danson's body on the front porch of the Mercantile and Gray no longer had any kind of hold over it. She loathed him. He didn't understand why, though, because he had hardly ever even raised his voice to her over their decades' long marriage, but he knew by the look in her eyes that she hated him.

The grief of losing his wife, even though she was still alive and breathing, was more than Gary could handle. He made his decision in that moment based on pure emotion and began seeing it through. After checking that the bedroom door was still secure, he grabbed his coats, and headed for the Mercantile.

It had been days since Rebekka had been there and the fisherman's body still sat in the tall straight-back wooden chair, frozen in death but still very much alive. Gary Brown would have found him had he needed anything from the back room, but the only two things he needed were stashed under the front counter. He was in such a hurry, though, that he never even glanced through the doorway leading into the large back room.

One of the two things Gary had gone to retrieve was a small wooden box containing his own personal reserve of Smoke. It was kept in the far back corner on the top shelf beneath the front counter of his shop. It was hidden in the shadows, and nestled behind an array of jars and glass containers filled with a variety of herbs, flowers, roots, etc. Gary Brown kept a small shelf full of these Apothecary/sorcery items for medicinal purposes, for those that were ailed but could not afford to get well. He didn't indulge in the Smoke often, but he liked having a bit around for when he felt that he needed it.

The other was a small jar of an herb called Datura. It was used for medicinal purposes, and he kept it in the shop for those who couldn't afford to see the valley doctor or the Witch. His grandmother had been a healer of sorts and used a lot of herbs and flowers for their healing properties. So, when he took over the Mercantile, he put that knowledge to use and tried to make deals with the gatherers whenever they would come across any. The only problem with Datura was that it was fatal if used incorrectly or the dosage was wrong. Gary had never given any more than exactly, or less, than what they needed at the time. He never let the herb leave his Mercantile unused. It would have been too dangerous to allow.

He returned to his shack, as quick as he could with the small wooden box of Smoke and the small jar of Datura tucked safely among his many layers, making good timing since little snow had fallen and the snow had been tracked down quite a bit. The bedroom door was still closed when he walked in and there was silence from the other side of it. He resisted the urge to go to the door and check on her, and instead prepared the Smoke and grabbed the two-thirds empty bottle of Shine

Alvin Danson had left, from a shelf in the kitchen area. There was more than enough Datura to treat twenty or more people in that small jar, but he dumped all of it into the bottle of Shine, giving it a few good swirls.

Gary grabbed the bottle and the freshly rolled hemp joint and walked over to the door. He removed the chunk of firewood, quietly setting it on the floor among the broken ceramic pieces and slowly opened the door. His wife was squatted down by the bed on the opposite side, all but the top of her head and eyes were concealed. It was an eerie sight that caused a ball of nervousness to form in the pit of his stomach. He tried to swallow the knot forming in his throat as he gently closed the door behind him.

Without breaking eye contact he side stepped toward the end of the bed, his wife staring at him, unblinking and intently all the while. "Ya feelin any better honey?" he asked in a hoarse whisper, trying and failing to keep the fear out of his voice. She did not move or answer, just continued staring as he slowly stepped around the end of the bed in a wide arc. He couldn't tell for sure, but he felt like the hateful expression in her eyes may have been a little softer, and he hoped that it wasn't just wishful thinking on his part.

When he made it to the other side of the bed, still several steps from her, and she came into full view of him, he immediately noticed her bloody hands and the drying streaks on her soiled nightgown. Her hair was a mess of knots and tangles, and her face was crazed and smudged with blood. He forgot about how dangerous she could be and rushed to her. His sudden and unexpected movements sent her into a panic, and she screeched like a banshee. She jumped up, meaning to get across the bed and out the door, but he was faster than her and grabbed her before she could. They both landed on the bed, his arms wrapped around her waist. She immediately began squirming and wiggling, fighting fiercely to get away from the monster that she believed he was. Before he was able to restrain her, she clawed him across the face, her lengthy fingernails tearing the skin from his cheek in three long gashes. He straddled her abdomen and used his hands to pin her wrists to the bed. It would have been sexy if she didn't look like she had just murdered someone escaping an asylum.

She screamed terrible things at him, called him every horrid name she could summon to mind, went into great detail about how much she hated him, and condemned him to Hell for eternity.

Gary held on for as long as he had to, he tried to ignore the terrible things she kept saying to him, but the tears came anyway. He watched as drops of blood from his deeply scratched cheek and the tears that fell from his eyes splatter down onto the front of his wife's filthy nightgown. After what felt like an eternity, she fell into an exhausted sleep, and he was finally able to straighten his long aching back and legs.

As soon as his muscles would allow it, he went and found some hemp rope and used it to tie her hands to the bedposts. With that done, he pulled one of the wooden chairs from the kitchen area into the bedroom, rested, and waited for her to wake up.

It wasn't long before she did, and he was relieved to find that she was mostly her normal complacent self. As always, she awoke with the initial confusion but once the memories of her actions came to her, she began tearing up and profusely apologizing. He didn't know if it was just an aftereffect of what he had just gone through with her, but he got the sense that her apology wasn't as genuine as it had been in the past. As if the hatred he had seen in her eyes had spilled over into her soul. He knew in that moment that he had made the right decision to get the Datura.

He untied her hands, helped her clean and redress, then they settled into bed. Her hands were covered in scuffs, small cuts, and splinters. It took him almost half an hour to de-splinter and clean her hands. Once settled, he retrieved the bottle of Shine and hemp joint from the bedside table. He had unmindfully set it down sometime between entering the room and rushing toward his wife. He didn't remember doing it, but he had found them sitting there when he finished tying up her hands.

At first, she adamantly refused the hemp joint but after some time he talked her into it by convincing her that it could help with her fits. He didn't know if it would or not, but it didn't matter, he needed to smoke it to calm his nerves. Since she fed off his emotions, she needed to be calm too, which is why he didn't tell her about the Datura, just encouraged her to drink the Shine. More out of desperation than anything else, she agreed and quickly relaxed about it after the first two cough-inducing hits.

About halfway through the joint, with dry mouth setting in quickly they started passing the partially full bottle of Shine between them. Gary loved watching his wife smile and giggle, something he hadn't seen in months or maybe even years. He was content with going out that way, with that version of his wife so fresh in his mind. They finished the Smoke and continued passing the diminishing Shine until it too was gone.

They laid there in each other's arms enjoying the tingling, buzzed feeling of the Shine and Smoke when Gary's wife started jerking and shaking uncontrollably in his arms. Her eyes rolled up under her eyelids leaving only the veiny whites exposed, a grayish colored foam oozed from between her bruise-colored lips, and he could hear the gurgling in her throat and chest as she choked to death on the poison that he had given her.

Before he could react, he himself began jerking and shaking uncontrollably, his movements intensifying as his wife's tapered off beside him, the life leaving her body. He could feel the grayish foam fill his stomach, his lungs, surround his rapidly beating heart, ascend his throat, and invade his mouth. It tasted like salty black licorice as it spilled across his tongue and escaped past his parted and paralyzed lips. He hated himself for putting his beloved wife through that agony and he prayed that she would forgive him. His last thoughts were of his wife's radiant smile, the sound of her voice when she whispered his name, and the feel of her lips upon his. When he finally blacked out, he was able to join his loving and forgiving wife in the afterlife.

Chapter Sixty-Four

Deviating from the Plan

1

The deaths of Gary Brown and his wife went unnoticed by the few remaining valley folks, the Witch being the only person that knew anything of it. It had been quite a show, but the ending was terrible. Much, much too sappy for her taste and it had left her quite disappointed. Though, she had to give Gary Brown credit for the Datura. That was a nice, unexpected touch that she respected. Yet still, he had to ruin a good thing with all that emotion. She was growing wary and anxious anyway. It had only been two weeks since his birth, but she grew impatient, wanting her time with the child.

She called upon Frank McGrath as February faded into March, whispering to him during his restless nights of sleep. He finally appeared at her shack on the second day of March looking haggard and beaten. His bloodshot eyes were encased in dark sunken pits, his cheek and jaw bones prominent on his gaunt face, his nose a busted and crooked mess, and his soiled clothes hung from his scrawny body.

The Witch took one look at Frank standing in the snow, the sunlight reflecting off the brilliant white bright enough to blind, and she knew that her plan would have to wait a bit longer. She ushered him inside and stripped him down to nothing, socks, undergarments, and all. She wrapped him in a large, doubled over, bear hide blanket and placed him in a chair in front of the fireplace.

Over the next three days, the Witch fed him multiple times a day, forced herbal tea and water into him when he wasn't eating and as soon as he was strong enough, she had him working in her enchanted garden to rebuild his lost muscle. Of course, the herbal tea she was giving him was really a healing potion and it worked wonders, because by the fourth day, Frank McGrath was almost the same muscular size he was that day in August when Sarah Maisse showed up on the train.

Food wasn't the only thing the Witch was feeding Frank, either. She was constantly feeding his ego, encouraging him, preparing him mentally for the task she was about to bestow on him. When she wasn't feeding his ego, she was feeding his rage toward Sarah by remarking on how happy her and John seemed with their new baby boy, how wonderful John was with her and the baby, and how radiant Sarah was being in love. Just little comments in passing, nothing direct, but enough to keep that fury burning bright and fiercely hot.

On that fourth day, the Witch sat Frank down and told him what she wanted him to do. She was very precise with her instructions and very adamant that he didn't deviate from them. She assured him that he would have his revenge on Sarah, and John too if he wished once the task was completed. The Witch knew that what she was asking of Frank was going to be quite the challenge for him, but she was confident enough in him to believe that he could control his anger long enough for her to get her hands on her Master's marked child.

Given Frank and Sarah's history they both knew that it was going to be hard to gain entrance into Rebekka's shack, and therefore access to Sarah and the baby. So, they decided on, hoping against hope that it would work, to use their history as a means of entrance. The Witch anxiously sent Frank off toward Rebekka's place while an exhausted Vipera rested within the Witch. She had no way of knowing how it had gone until Frank returned because the cold kept all the insects away, even the termites in the wood of the shacks were buried too deep to be able to see or hear anything. The Witch was impatiently patient as time ticked by, the minutes turning into hours.

Frank knocked on Rebekka Lane's shack door, looked curiously at all the snow piled up around the small place and wondered why they had done that. Then the door opened, and the warmth of the inside splashed his exposed face and he understood why. It was Rebekka who answered the door and Frank was able to sigh with relief since it wasn't John.

"Ms. Lane..." he began in his formal, addressing the public tone, "...I have heard that Ms. Maisse and Mr. Colmes welcomed a child recently and I have come to offer my congratulations to the father." Frank paused and cleared his throat before continuing, able to feel Rebekka's odd gaze on him. "I have also heard that Ms. Maisse had taken ill and died after giving birth and I feel a great need to ascertain or discern this information... for my own personal reasons." He finished, allowing the vagueness of his final statement to run loose in Rebekka's mind. They hoped that Rebekka would sympathize with him and want to believe that Frank meant no harm to anyone, therefore letting him into the shack.

It worked just as the Witch had intended and Rebekka allowed him inside. Before she let him step inside though, she made sure he knew that he could only stay a few moments and that the only reason she was allowing him inside was to prove to him that both Sarah and the baby were alive. He nodded in acknowledgement and tried to resist the urge to smile at his success. The Witch was adamant that once he was inside, he was not to leave until the task was complete.

Frank knew that it was going to be hard seeing Sarah, but he did not realize just how emotional he would get. He stepped through the entrance to the shack, immediately scanned the place from left to right, from the kitchen area to the bedroom door. It was ajar and he had a direct line of sight to the bed that Sarah sat in feeding her almost three-week-old baby. John stood dutifully at her side, his back to the door and Sarah's head downcast, adoring her beautiful baby boy while she could, before John took him away from her again.

Every muscle in Frank's body tensed at once and his heart rate went into overdrive. His stomach knotted, his throat swelled, and tears pricked his eyes. He quickly blinked them away, though, and forced the rage back down as he removed his coats but left his boots on. He sat at the table, as per Rebekka's offer and sipped on sassafras tea as he waited for John and Sarah.

After about ten minutes of small talk with Rebekka, who wouldn't divulge any more information than, "It was hard on her.", about Sarah's childbirth, John exited the bedroom, alone, closing the door behind him.

"They're both resting." John said, more to Rebekka than to Frank, then joined them at the table. Rebekka poured John some tea and topped off Frank's cup as the small talk proceeded. Another fifteen minutes went by when they heard the small cries of an infant drifting from behind the closed door of the bedroom. John immediately moved to get up, but Rebekka stopped him with a hand on his forearm.

"Ya sit and rest, boy, I'll ten to him." She got up and left before he could respond, so he settled back into his chair. Both men were quiet until Rebekka closed the bedroom door again.

"So, what brings ya here, Frank? Really?" John asked, seriously but without hate or resentment.

"I have been sent to collect your payment." Frank replied matter-of-factly.

John's brow furrowed with genuine confusion. He did not associate Frank McGrath with the Witch and therefore was sincere when he asked, "Payment for what?"

Frank made a show of rolling his eyes dramatically. "The Witch sent me to retrieve the payment that YOU owe HER!" He said forcefully in a loud whisper.

It suddenly dawned on him what Frank was talking about. Of course, she wanted to be paid. "Three weeks..." he whispered after a long, drawn out, silence. "At least she gave me that, I reckon." He was fully prepared to die for Sarah and his son Owen, but that didn't make the pain of knowing that he was going to miss out on all those amazing years with them hurt any less. He sighed deeply. "So, are you here to escort me back to her place? Make sure I don't try to skip on my end of the deal?" he asked with an icy tone. The anger was setting in and the only one to direct it at was Frank, even though John knew he didn't really deserve it.

Frank took his tone in stride though and even cracked a small smile. He leaned over his folded arms to get a bit closer to John and asked in a low voice, "Did she tell you what the payment would be for saving the life of your beloved Sarah?" Obviously, adding a touch of sarcasm to the word 'beloved'. A touch that did not go unnoticed by John.

John almost gave an immediate, 'yes' response but stopped and thought back to their conversation that day in her shack. The answer was no. No, she didn't tell him what the payment would be. He just assumed that she would take his life for it, eventually. Of all emotions, hope began to fill his heart and mind. "No, she didn't." he told Frank, bewildered at the revelation.

Frank looked at John for a long moment trying to decide if he was lying or not, finally decided that he wasn't, and then sighed loudly. "Well, that's unfortunate. I was under the assumption that you already knew the terms that you agreed to."

"Sarah's life was at stake..." John stammered. "I just assumed..." He was clearly flustered. "I don't know what else she could..." His eyes darted back and forth in his head as his thoughts became more and more jumbled. "If not me, then..." The panic was rising quickly, as was his heart rate, breathing, and blood pressure.

John watched through hazy eyes as Frank's expression grew into one of concern.

Frank watched as John's face quickly went from bright red to almost purple as his eyes fluttered to remain open. Then, John gasped loudly and fainted, falling face first from his chair, landing stomach down on the wooden floor. The realization that the Witch wanted Sarah or Owen as payment, instead, was much more than his psyche could handle at that moment.

2

It only took a few seconds for Frank's shock at John's fainting to wear off and recognize the opportunity he had been presented with. With John down for however short a time, it was just two women, one of them sickly, standing between him and the baby that the Witch wanted. The Witch would be pleased when he presented her with the baby boy, and Frank was all but lost in fantasy as he opened the bedroom door.

Frank caught movement in the peripherals of his left eye and turned his head in that direction. He didn't know it, but

Rebekka had been eavesdropping on their conversation and had come to the same conclusion John had but much sooner. She anticipated that Frank would try to rush in and take Sarah, the baby, or both, so she was waiting and ready, when he did. She stood to the left of the door and waited until he stepped in to swing the broom handle that she held. Since he was turning his head at the same moment, the blow that was supposed to smack him in the bridge of the nose, connected with his right temple instead, opening a small gash at this hairline. He dropped like a feed sack to the wooden floor, unconscious but breathing.

Rebekka dropped the broom, quickly jumped over Frank's unmoving body, and knelt beside John, who was moaning softly while slowly swimming back to consciousness. She shook him roughly, yelling at him to wake up. "...up, boy! Get up! Gotta get em out! Get up!" He listened as her voice slowly rose to the proper loud volume that she was yelling at him in, as he slowly raised himself up on his hands and knees. From there he managed to get up on his feet, Rebekka yelling stern encouragement all the while. She grabbed his arm and took off, John forced to stumble his way behind her. "Don't trip over him." She said as she dragged him by his wrist over Frank's body. John could see the bright red trickle of blood seeping from the gash on Frank's head as he awkwardly stepped over him but was still too hazy minded to wonder what happened.

Once over Frank and into the bedroom, the sound of baby Owen's whimpering cry brought most of John's senses back to him in a flood. He seen Sarah was out of bed and trying to dress in as many layers as she could get on, Rebekka helping her as best she could. The baby lay in his bassinet, swaddled in a blanket while several more had been laid to the side for him when they walked out.

He knew they had to leave before Frank woke up but as an added caution, he tied Franks hands and feet together. Afterwards, without questioning anything, John began adding more clothes to his already layered wardrobe. Then he went into the kitchen and helped Rebekka pack up as much food and stuff as they could handle carrying. Rebekka sat on the bed and rested from the exertion of dressing. She did not hold but tried to soothe her crying son as he lay in the bassinet, sensing the tension around him.

Luckily for them, John hadn't returned the handcart he used for firewood yet, so they had a way of transporting Sarah and the baby, easily. They had little daylight left so he knew they couldn't go far. He loaded first Sarah, cradling the sleeping baby Owen, into the handcart, then placed a small crate of food at her feet. They were gone within minutes of Frank being knocked unconscious.

When Frank came to, sometime after they had left the shack, but long enough for the blood on his face to dry, he headed back to the Witch's place. He held his head low in shame and disappointment as he explained how Rebekka Lane had bested him with a broom, catching him off guard. The Witch was furious and made sure that Frank knew how upset and angry she was over his insolence. He endured the tongue lashing he received with humility and as much pride as he could muster.

It was his fault the trio had gotten away with the child the Witch wanted and he knew that before the Witch insisted on telling him repeatedly during her rantings and ravings. He had not been informed of the baby's importance, that he had been marked by Satan himself as his own, or why the Witch was so adamant about having the child. Frank assumed that she was so upset because she was so used to getting what she wanted, when she wanted it, that she wasn't used to not getting her way. He, also, assumed that she just wanted the child as a sick and twisted way of getting revenge on John for his disloyalty and unfaithfulness. He didn't necessarily agree with her way of revenge, but he understood it because he felt the same way about Sarah. He wanted her to hurt, he wanted to see the pain in her eyes as he inflicted it upon her. He just wanted his revenge to be in a more physical, face-to-face setting, compared the Witch's more indirect emotional pain.

He had made a promise to himself weeks ago that he would have his revenge on Sarah and so far, that evening had been the closest he had been able to get to her, and it was all because of the Witch. When she first approached him with the task of retrieving the baby boy, Frank was reluctant, but eventually, as a means to an end, he had agreed to help the Witch in return for that face-to-face time he needed with Sarah. As harsh as the Witch's words were, as they rolled off her tongue, he knew she meant no real harm because she needed him as much as he needed her at that moment. He didn't understand why but he knew that she herself couldn't just walk in and take the child. If she could, she wouldn't be going through all the trouble of having him do it for her. Not that he really cared much either way, as long as he got his time with Sarah Maisse before the end.

3

The days and nights blurred together over the next several days in the Witch's frantic search for John, Sarah, or Rebekka. She knew that if she could find any of them that they would lead her right to the child. She had Frank out searching by day and she sent Vipera searching through the nights but had recovered none of them. She knew they were staying on the move, always seeming to be one step ahead of her, but she didn't know how. She didn't dare risk any harm to the baby by using her sorcery, so she couldn't find them with enchantments, and she didn't dare grovel to her Master for help. The point of the whole matter, beyond her own personal need for revenge against John and the rest of the valley, was to assure her Master of her worth. She believed that when she presented her Master with her own collection of souls, as well as the marked boy, her Master would be pleased enough with her to grant her Malum's status or maybe even higher.

The anticipation of it all and the underlying panic that she would fail just added to the Witch's overwhelming whirlpool of emotions. As each new day dawned without the child in her presence the Witch grew warier and warier of her predicament and wondered if a higher power had joined the game. This revelation made sense of a lot of things for the Witch, like the way John had been able to evade her for over a week, and how she wasn't able to sense their whereabouts the way she could others.

If she had more to present than a hunch and a few explainable circumstances, then she would bring it to her Master's attention, but she knew at that point that her Master would only scoff at her inability and desperation. She was on her own until she had more to go on about the higher power theory or she found one of the three that would take her to the child. She pushed all those thoughts out of her mind for the time, then almost immediately fell into her meditation state as she viewed the valley from above, through the eyes of a dove looking for a meal. Frank was on foot searching the Slums for the umpteenth time, while Vipera rested within the Witch's womb.

The Witch's patience had grown so thin it was almost nonexistent by the time Frank had finally spotted John out trying to scavenge for food, eleven days after the men's conversation in Rebekka's shack. Frank was just strolling between shacks, scanning for movement, and listening to the sounds of nature coming to life in the melting snow.

The birds chirped and squirrels and chipmunks chittered from the timbers. It had been unseasonably warm over the last few days and much of the snow had melted, revealing sprouts of grass. Frank knew that it wouldn't be long before the spring lilies would be popping out up out of the ground, too. The river had been reduced to little more than a small stream rolling its way over the large rocks that lined the deep bed of the river. The valley seemed almost unnatural without the roar of the waterfall that had gradually decreased in volume over the last few months, and it hurt Frank's heart a little to know his once beautiful, thriving valley had crumbled because of an early winter blizzard.

Frank was all but lost in thought when he suddenly heard the creak of a door or window shutter. Had there been a breeze he would have thought nothing of it, but the air was as still as could be, so it caught his attention. He was just passing by one of the shacks across from where Robert Daniel's place stood, when he seen a boot disappear behind the shack he was about to walk by. Frank quickly considered his options. He could chase John down but even if he did catch him, Frank knew that John would let Frank kill him before he told him where Sarah and the baby were. He could follow him and see if John led him to where they were staying, but he would risk not only getting caught by John, but he wasn't sure what he should do once he got there. It wasn't a situation that he could or should improvise in, he needed to inform the Witch... immediately. So, he proceeded on his stroll taking very careful note as to where he seen John and slowly sauntered his way back to the Witch's place. Frank didn't want to seem any different than he did just a few moments before he heard that creak just in case John was watching him. He didn't want John to have any indication that he had been spotted, so Frank showed no emotion until he was inside the Witch's shack with the door closed securely behind him.

Frank returned a couple hours before dark and was all but bubbling over with anxious excitement. Initially, the Witch was upset that Frank came to her instead of pursuing John, but once Frank explained his thought process behind it, she understood and even agreed. They needed a plan and about an hour after night fell, they had one. A good one.

The Witch sent Vipera out with instructions to begin searching the area in the Slums that Frank had spotted John in, and the asp-like creature slithered away as commanded. Then her and Frank sat down to go over the plan one more time, allowing Vipera the time she needed to locate them. Vipera had been gone for about half an hour when the Witch checked in the first time. There was nothing but the constant searching movement to see so the Witch disconnected and waited impatiently.

She checked again fifteen minutes later only to find the same thing, and then again fifteen minutes after that. This went on for a few hours and the Witch became more and more overwrought with the same outcome. Frank was becoming more and more nervous around the Witch every time she came back out of her meditative state, unsure of her reaction. He was betting on their plan and his major part in it to keep him safe from her lashings, but the more time passed, the less he thought he could place his hope on a plan that may never be carried out.

A few minutes after midnight, though, the Witch finally got the result she was looking for and Frank knew it because she had stayed in her meditative state longer than all the other times. When she finally disconnected, she looked at him and smiled maliciously. It induced a fearful, odd smile from Frank in return, but he understood her evil grin when she informed him of John, Sarah, and Rebekka's whereabouts. They were at Frank's place, and the irony of it made it almost comical.

With a weapon in hand, Frank took off for his place as soon as the Witch was sure that he knew the plan and his part in it. He made it there rather quickly, not having inches upon inches of snow to trudge through anymore, but he did slip on a couple of slick patches in his rush, though. He recovered without incident, knowing he was lucky on both accounts but couldn't fathom the consequences he would have to endure at the hands of the Witch, if he had wounded himself bad enough to not be able to do his job.

Once he crossed the bridge by the Lot, Frank kept to the shadows just in case any of them were on watch. He was right to do so because he seen Rebekka walk to the windows and peer out several times in the ten or so minutes it took him to get from the eastern bridge of the almost waterless river to the house. A pang of grief struck his heart at the sight of the house because that was where him and Dansford had lived, fucked, loved, and tried to kill each other, only Frank succeeding. He pushed all thoughts of Dansford Keeton to the back of his mind, unaware that they were only fueling the rage that was threatening to boil over as his thoughts switched to Sarah Maisse.

Frank circled the house, carefully scanned everything through every window, multiple times before he finally accepted that John wasn't there. That wasn't part of the plan and Frank wasn't sure what the Witch wanted him to do. They had no reason to believe that John would be anywhere other than with them since he appeared to be out scavenging earlier when Frank spotted him. He knew Vipera was around there somewhere, but even as many times as he had walked around the house and looked in it through every available angle, he had not seen the Witch's pet.

He decided to go through with the plan they had devised, and the part that included John would just have to wait until he showed up, if even did. That thought instilled a sense of hope within Frank that it might end up being easier than he was expecting it to be. It turned out that it kind of was.

4

Frank McGrath gripped the large carving knife in his right, dominant hand as he watched Rebekka make another round checking the windows. As soon as she started across the kitchen, Frank silently opened the door enough to slip inside, knowing that Sarah was in the bedroom he had slept in. He hunkered down beside the table, obscured by the shadows, and watched as she walked into the main room where the fireplace was alight with a small, almost pitiful, fire.

Earlier that day, John had seen Frank before Frank had seen him, but John wasn't aware of the fact that he had. So, he fell for Frank's nonchalant, emotionless stroll through the Slums back to the Witch's shack. Nonetheless, it made John quite nervous that Frank had come so close to discovering him, so he figured that the last place they would suspect them of being, was at Frank's place.

It wasn't the first time they had stayed there since they had been running from the Witch and Frank McGrath. He had discovered the body of Dansford Keeton the first time but was able to remove it before Sarah or Rebekka had seen it. He did warn them of the highly unpleasant smell in one of the bedrooms and suggested it remain unused. It did and still was.

Frank watched Rebekka, from the shadows of the kitchen, walk from window to window throughout the house, scanning the outside perimeter of everyone. When that was done, she opened the bedroom door that Sarah was occupying, noted that she was sleeping, as was baby Owen, and then silently closed it.

While her back was turned to him, he retrieved a second, smaller bladed kitchen knife from the tabletop and switched it over to his right hand, while sliding the much larger one into his belt. When Rebekka walked back into the kitchen and turned away from the table toward the stove, Frank emerged from the dark shadows with the smaller bladed knife ready to use. He silently walked up behind her and in a quick motion he placed his left hand over her mouth as he wrapped his right arm around her, driving the blade into the hollow of her throat.

He released her and the knife handle at the same time, as Rebekka spun around to face whoever grabbed her, momentarily unaware that she had been stabbed. She recognized Frank and immediately began screaming but the knife blade wouldn't allow anything more than a soft whistle to escape her lips. Rebekka collapsed to the floor, unwilling to even touch the knife protruding from her throat to remove it. As she fell, her eye caught the glint of metal as Frank raised a second, much larger knife. She knew death was imminent and her mind wanted, even insisted, that she fight back, to not just lay there and die willingly. Her body would not cooperate, however. Try as she might, her shocked-into-paralysis body, would not allow it and she was forced to suffer through every agonizing wound as Frank stabbed her over and over, totaling a few dozen times.

Frank finally stopped when he realized that Rebekka had died. How long before he had stopped, he wasn't sure, but it didn't really matter anyway. He felt much better about the success of their plan and his ability to enact his revenge upon Sarah Maisse for wounding his pride, choosing Johnathan Colmes over him, then tricking him into telling her that he was really a homosexual and laughing about it. She needed to be punished for toying with his emotions and then be so openly amused at him for falling for her trickery.

Frank stood up from his kneeling position over Rebekka's body, leaving the knife buried hilt deep in the middle of her face, cutting her nose in half horizontally. Blood seeped from every stab wound across her upper body and head, as she lay breathless and unmoving in death. He stretched the muscles in his back and legs well before approaching the bedroom door that Sarah slept behind.

When he opened it, he did not find Sarah and the baby asleep in their beds as he had expected them to be. Instead, Sarah had taken the baby from his bassinet and hidden him. Frank could not see him anywhere in the room and it reignited any rage that had been dampened from killing Rebekka. Owen wasn't on or under the bed. He wasn't on or under the chest of drawers, or the desk, or the chair that sat before it, or the small table that sat beside the bed. Sarah sat upon the bed with a defiant, stubborn look upon her face, daring him to approach her.

Sarah's attempt at fierceness was recognizable but underwhelming. Her thin, frail body combined with her ashen complexion screamed weakness and she couldn't display that motherly instinct to protect her child that she could feel coursing through her body. She watched Frank try to conceal an amused grin at her failure and realized that she was going about it the wrong way. She let her emotions take over for a few moments and tears flooded her eyes. Through them she watched that hateful, amused smile flicker and then fade as sympathy or maybe even a change of heart passed over him.

It was gone as quickly as it came, though, along with any hope Sarah had of playing on his feelings for her. She knew that the only feelings he harbored for her were of hatred, resentment, and an undying need for revenge. The thought was barely complete in her mind before he was standing in front of her with his hand raised. He had backhanded her hard enough to split her lower lip and rock her head to the side, splattering blood drops across the animal hide blankets strewn across the bed.

The tears stopped immediately, and Sarah was flooded with anger. She vowed in that moment that she would see that sumbitch dead before she was, and she meant it with every fiber of her being. "Tears will not help you, you snivelin lil bitch!" Frank told her and the harshness in his tone was undeniable. "Tell me where the child is!" he demanded.

Her and John's worst fears came true with those six little words, knowing that the Witch wanted their baby instead of her life. Frank would have that as payment for getting her the baby. It all came together like the last few pieces in a puzzle, connecting the whole picture. John had come clean to Sarah about going to the Witch, why she was sick, and the payment for her help the night Frank showed up at Rebekka's shack. It was a lot for Sarah to process and she went through a hurricane of emotions before accepting what she could not change or control. They hadn't gotten to her baby yet and she would die making sure they didn't. That was all that really mattered in the end, protecting her son.

She wouldn't answer Frank, only looked up at him with an unnerving snarl like grin that made him uncomfortable, so he slapped her again. The blow delivered to the same side of her face widened the split in her lower lip and a bluish knot started to form on her cheekbone where a bright pink welt had been only moments before. She expected that hit so her head didn't rock nearly as much as the first time and the lack of response from Sarah not only wounded Frank's pride but enraged him even more. Maybe she would have lived longer had she resisted the urge to be so crass.

Frank could no longer contain the ever-raging inferno of fury within him, the beast that could not be caged, the wave that could not be contained, that inner demonic child that could no longer go unlabored. He balled his strong hands into fists and swung with all his power, connecting with her already bloody mouth, shattering her front teeth. Sharp shards of bone sailed into her mouth and down her throat, shredding her tongue and esophagus.

Sarah wasn't expecting that blow, and it knocked her backward on the bed, dazed but conscious. She could taste the blood on her tongue before she could feel the pain of her obliterated mouth. She tried to rise into a sitting position before the blood rushing into her throat could choke her, but Frank knocked her back as he leapt on top of her. For a few unimaginably frightening seconds Sarah was convinced that Frank was going to force himself on her and she was actually relieved when he punched her again, instead.

Frank screamed until his throat felt raw as he punched Sarah in the face over and over, switching from one hand to the other. After several blows, he stopped, panting while still straddled across her unmoving body. Believing her dead, he got up off the bed and angrily paced back and forth across the room, huffing and puffing, partly from exertion and partly in rage. He thought that killing Sarah would make him feel better, but she did not beg and plead, or scream and cry through her suffering, and that was what he had wanted to see. It had been unfulfilling, and he was pissed at the disappointment of it all.

Owen's soft cries could barely be heard from the chest of drawers, the very bottom one, that was ever so slightly open.

Frank's screaming was what had awoken the child, and his cries is what brought Sarah back from the brink of death. She was fading quickly into the eternal darkness only to force her way back toward the light and the pain at the sound of his cries. Her face exploded with pain at every slight movement, but she forced herself to try to roll over on to her side, anyway.

Frank noticed that Sarah was awake and even though he wouldn't admit it, even to himself, he was relieved, but the fact that she was still alive after such a beating enraged him. He was about to scream at her, asking how, why, whatever, but then he heard the soft whimpers of a baby. His heart raced and he focused only on the sound of the cries, softly creeping around the room until he came to the chest of drawers. He found baby Owen, swaddled in a blanket, nestled snugly in the bottom drawer, and gently lifted him out of it.

5

Sarah had managed to get on her feet but couldn't stand without holding on to the footboard of the bed. Her eyes were swollen, bruised, bloodshot and blurry, but she could see well enough to know that Frank was holding her baby. She was too weak to do anything as blood poured from her unrecognizable face. She stumbled and fell awkwardly to her knees as she released the bed and tried to walk toward Frank and her baby. "Please!" she tried to say. "Please don't take my son! Please! He's only an infant, he needs me! Please, Frank!" All that would come out, though, was garbled noises, blood drops, and teeth fragments as she spoke, but Frank knew that she was begging.

He enjoyed it. He enjoyed seeing her trying to crawl to her child, pleading for him, trying to protect him. He enjoyed seeing her fail at it too. He wanted her to hurt, he wanted to take from her the way she took Dansford from him. There were no thoughts of the Witch, no thoughts of their plan, no thoughts of remorse. He wanted to hurt Sarah Maisse's heart and that's exactly what he did.

Frank made a show of removing his small-bladed pocketknife from the front of his jeans and pointed it menacingly at Sarah as she struggled to crawl toward them, very slowly shortening the distance between them. "You broke my heart Sarah, and then spit on it with your laughter. You took from me, so now I must take from you." He said almost sadly, and then immediately stuck the knife blade into the side of the baby's throat. The sharp blade sliced easily through his delicately thin skin and into the vibrant blue veins beneath that almost pulsed with activity. Owen's eyes widened, then his face contorted as if to cry but didn't, then immediately widened his eyes again as Frank removed the knife. A small arching spurt of blood followed the knife and then tapered off as it spilled down his small body and soaked into his unraveled blanket. He closed his eyes as if falling asleep and gasped his last little breath.

Sarah let out a scream of pure tortured agony that literally ruptured her already wounded throat. Frank looked down at the tiny bloody corpse he held in his arms and then tossed it across the room in disgust. Baby Owen's lifeless body landed with a sickening thump on the wooden floor several feet away.

John, who had walked in just as Frank was finishing his little speech, could only stand in shocked paralysis, unable to move or comprehend what he had just witnessed.

Frank was already dead, and Sarah was only minutes from it by the time his paralysis broke.

Chapter Sixty-Five

Basking in Agony

1

The moment Frank killed John and Sarah's baby boy, Owen, the marked son of the Witch's Master, all of Hell knew it because Satan was furious. Moments later, the cloudless night sky over the valley cracked with a rumble of thunder so powerful it rattled shack doors and shutters. Those very few left in the valley felt it even if they were unaware of what it was. Jiminey and Patty McAvay, sleeping soundly in their bed, both stirred and rolled away from each other uncomfortably. The Witch flinched, lost focus, and disconnected with Vipera at a very crucial moment, but immediately fell back into her meditative state. John swayed on his feet but remained still and unblinking, still processing.

Sarah crawled as quick as she could, which was sadly very slow, across the floor trying to reach her son. Tears spilled from her swollen and blackened eyes. Whimpers, moans, and attempted words escaped her lips. Every ounce of strength she possessed was poured into getting to her son, but she never could. The vibrations from the thunder made her arms tingle and give out under her weight. She spilled forward on to her still healing abdomen, almost smashing her already busted face on the floor. When she failed to raise herself back up on her knees, she tried to crawl on her stomach, reaching toward her bleeding son only a foot or two out of reach. She knew that she was getting almost no ground at all, but she kept trying to until her last dying breath, oblivious to what was going on around her.

After tossing Owen's corpse aside, Frank stood over Sarah and watched as she cried and mourned for her baby. He could almost feel her pain and heartache radiate from her in waves and Frank loved every second of it. It was exactly what he wanted to see from her, that agony, and it was doing wonders for his anger. He felt tears prick his eyelashes as relief flooded him, knowing that the nightmare he had been living the last few months was finally over. The idea occurred to him that he should do something special for the Witch, since she was the one that allowed him that blessed relief, whenever he delivered the baby...

Frank's eyes widened until they almost bulged from their sockets when he realized how bad he had fucked up by killing that little boy. Panic rose within him, and his mind jumbled with fear. Only a few seconds after this realization and less than 90 seconds after he had killed the child, Frank McGrath was punished for just that.

When Vipera had finally come across the trio and the child entering Frank's place, the snake slithered under the house through a break in the foundation and entered it through the opening in the attached outhouse. There were no windows in there so, the Witch, through Vipera, wasn't worried about Rebekka coming in there constantly. The snake-like creature hid in the darkness of the night shadows in the outhouse doorway. There were only two small candles and the pitiful fire to light the place, so not to attract attention, especially while John was away, so it would be easy for the snake to move around if necessary.

The Witch, using Vipera's eyes, had a direct line of sight to the confrontation with Frank and Rebekka and she was quite pleased with how he handled it. She was worried that he wouldn't go through with the plan since John wasn't there and taking him out was such a crucial part of it. She figured that it was simpler and easier that he wasn't, and if Frank kept an eye out, it should all work out accordingly. She was glad to see that they followed the same line of thinking, and he was carrying through with it as planned.

Vipera had slithered out of that doorway and into the bedroom only a second or so behind Frank, unnoticed. With Vipera settled in the dark shadows of the corner, the Witch watched Frank's brutish pounding on Sarah and enraged huffing fit afterwards. She heard Owen's cries about the same time that Sarah did, and she too became overeager, her heart racing much like Frank's was. Relief and joy washed over her as Frank pulled the baby from the drawer, seemingly healthy as could be.

The Witch thought nothing of it when Frank pulled the pocketknife out and waved it at Sarah. In fact, she was quite fond of his confidence in being able to kill Sarah while holding her baby. His words were muffled because Vipera couldn't perceive sounds like people do, so the Witch was absolutely dumbfounded when she watched Frank use the knife on the infant instead of Sarah.

Shocked to the point of disbelief, the Witch could only gasp and stare. Vipera hissed viciously and loud enough to be heard, but was drowned out by Sarah's tortured, heartbroken scream. Just as the Witch's shock wore off, the thunder erupted and the Witch's intense startle disconnected her from Vipera, who she had just sent out of the shadows toward Frank.

Vipera stopped dead, confused by the sudden and unexpected disconnection, and unsure what to do. The asp was far enough out of the shadows to be seen in the dim room but went unnoticed by Frank, Sarah, and John. Moments later, the Witch was back and was absolutely irate. Vipera was feeding off her Master's rage, as well, wanting to literally bite Frank's throat out. So, the Witch allowed the snake-like creature from Hell to do just that.

Vipera slithered up the bedpost closest to Frank, silently and unnoticed as he watched and basked in Sarah's misery. Frank's revelation that he had made a massive, probably life-ending mistake, came just as Vipera was positioned and ready to strike. The timing couldn't have been anymore on cue if it had been mercilessly rehearsed. Frank turned toward the bed just as Vipera lunged off the bedpost, mouth wide open, unhinged, displaying rows of small needle-sharp fangs while venom dripped from its mouth.

Frank felt the creature smash into his chest and seemingly millions of teeth sink deeply into the sides of his neck. Blood had just begun to seep from the puncture wounds, almost tickling his sensitive nerves as it trickled down onto his collarbones, when the ripping began. He could feel his flesh tearing, his nerves and tendons being stretched until they separated, and the blood gushed down his chest and back, as the creature slowly closed its massive jaws, taking a large bite out of his throat. The pain was enormous and unending, and he wished for death, begged for it, but it would not come until Vipera had succeeded in pulling away from him, with over half his throat lodged between its teeth. Frank's eyelids fluttered as death finally took him. The weight of his head quickly became too much for his mostly missing neck and it wobbled first forward and then backward, falling against the nape of his neck. A large spurt of blood shot out onto the floor as Satan's asp finished chewing and then swallowing Frank McGrath's throat.

2

The sound of Frank's body hitting the floor is what brought John out of his shock-induced paralysis. He looked around, quickly scanning the room and then sprang into action. An indescribable feeling came over John and his only purpose in the world at that moment was killing the bizarre snake-like creature that just slithered away from Frank's body and was heading in the direction of baby Owen. With a strength that John knew he couldn't possibly possess even with his large, muscular physique, he sprinted toward Vipera and wrapped both hands securely around the tail. The creature was much longer than John was tall and the room too small to allow what happened to have happened, but he still swung the asp high over his head, bashing it against the floor repeatedly on both sides of him. The weakening snake was roughly slung across the ceiling, tearing scales from its body before each connection with the floor. Blood and bits of bone splattered against the walls, floor, and furniture as the battered creature hissed in pain, anguish, and a touch of surprise.

After the fifth or sixth hit, John dropped the lethargic slithering body and stepped toward its head. He wrapped his fingers over the top jaw of the large snake, and then grabbed its bottom jaw with his other hand, oblivious to all the tiny teeth shards stabbing into his fingers. John slowly pried Vipera's jaws open until he felt each one snap under the pressure. Initially, the snake-like thing wriggled violently, lashed out with its tail, and tried to snap its jaws shut. All attempts were fruitless, so Vipera stopped moments after starting. When the creature died, John dropped its head and its jaws fell in opposite directions. Satan's viper was no more, and John could feel that indescribable strength as it evaporated.

Blood pooled under the upper part of Frank McGrath's twitching body, as John stepped over him to get to Sarah. She was still trying to slowly crawl her way toward her dead son lying in an unnatural heap just out of reach, moaning and crying through her grief. Even in the dim light of the room, Sarah's brutal facial wounds were evident, and John was taken aback by the viciousness of the beating she had received. Sarah didn't acknowledge John, even during her last dying breath, her eyes, thoughts, and focus on her son Owen, and Owen only.

John held her hand through her death anyway, knowing what she was looking at and reaching for and why, but he could not bring himself to look. He could only stare at Sarah's beaten and bloody face, remembering the beauty beneath it and all the memories they shared during their short time together. He let the tears fall and splatter to the floor as she took her final raspy breath.

He wept quietly in the silence of the night, still holding the hand of his beloved Sarah Maisse, lost in his own grief and tormenting guilt. Suicide was the thought first and foremost running through his mind. He was desperate for a way out, for a way to get away from the pain. He wasn't yet 25 years of age and he had already suffered so much loss and pain, how could he survive another 50 years or more? It was his fault. All of it. He didn't protect his mother from his father! He made himself an orphan! He fell for the Witch! He fell for Sarah! He deceived them both with his lies and cowardice! He wasn't there to save Rebekka or Sarah! He wasn't there to protect his only son! Everything he had ever loved was gone and it was all his fault! All of it! No family or friends left, no love, no child, no home, no business. It was gone. All of it. Gone. So, why? He asked himself, why should he stay?

Lost in his whirlwind of negative thoughts and emotions, John didn't notice that the much smaller blood pool under baby Owen was decreasing in size. His ashen, bloodless complexion began to brighten as the wound in his neck began to draw in and reabsorb the blood. Within two minutes, baby Owen was breathing, healthy, uninjured, and full of life, but was highly uncomfortable.

3

When Frank tossed his lifeless body to the side, Owen landed on his stomach with his head tucked to his chest and his left arm and right leg bent oddly under him. Nothing was broken, but if it had been, that would have healed too. Being less than six weeks old and unable to move, all he could do was cry. It started out as a soft, whispery whimper that grew in volume until he was almost wailing in frustration. John heard the cries before he accepted them, believing them to be a figment of his overworked, overstressed, grief-stricken mind. When he willed them to stop and they wouldn't, he entertained the idea that the cries were real and finally forced his eyes to drift in Owen's direction.

John was shocked to find his son almost screaming and wiggling around in an odd heap on the floor, not a single drop of blood to be seen anywhere. Not on the floor, not on the blanket still partially wrapped around his legs, and not on Owen himself. He immediately dropped Sarah's cold and lifeless hand, crawled over to his son, quickly but gently picked him up, and wrapped the bloodless blanket around him once again. Owen stretched in his arms but continued with his wailing fit as John hugged him to his chest, crying, and cooing over him.

How? John wondered, through it all. I know what I seen. I watched Frank kill him. I watched the blood exit his body and spill down his tiny chest and soak into his blanket. I watched Frank toss his lifeless body away. So, how could this be? How am I holding and soothing him right now? How is he alive? And unharmed at that? These were questions that he wouldn't know the answers to for decades to come. Johnathan Colmes learned those answers through a series of dreams while institutionalized at the N.D.A.M.A. and would go on to write down everything he had learned from those dreams. He would then leave this writing in the form of a letter to a certain Dr. Warren Gerard in the hopes that he would fulfill his part in the Greater Plan. So, if you haven't figured it out by now, Dr. Gerard, and I am confident that you have, I am Johnathan Owen Colmes and my blood runs through the man that is destined to bring Hell to Earth.

A war has been raging between the Higher Powers and the Lower Powers for centuries with Earth being the battlegrounds. Both sides know that if the war continues, eventually there will be no more souls left on Earth to take and therefore a deal had to be struck. Each side would have a five-decade long period, beginning sometime before the tragic events that befell the valley, to find and prepare a warrior for their side. On a currently unknown date and time, a battle between the Powers will ensue. The battle is inevitable, but the outcome cannot be foretold.

John and Sarah's son Owen was the Lower Powers choice as their warrior. When Frank killed him, the Lower Powers lost their warrior and were not powerful enough to bring him back. The thunder over the valley was the Lower Powers' outrage over the loss being released. That indescribable feeling that possessed John was a gift from the Higher Powers only for the purpose of killing the creature. John was the messenger sent to deliver the Lower Powers a simple statement; Vipera's death being a payment of sorts. Had baby Owen's death been at the hands of the Lower Powers or a natural one, the Higher Powers would not have intervened. However, given the circumstances of the child-warrior's death, the Higher Powers brought Owen back to life, healing and strengthening him.

Knowing what I do now, I wish they would have let him stay dead… but if they had, someone else would have just taken his place. As unfortunate as the outcome could be, we must have hope in the Higher Powers warrior. The warrior that you will father with the lovely, young Vivian Lancing. I know that that statement alone is a lot to take in, so take a moment to process. I know what I'm saying, crazy as it sounds. I am literally asking you to have a child with a woman you

672

barely know, and then teach and train your child to kill my own son one day. It's a lot, I know.

I was quite distraught when I found out why you were the one that I was writing all this for. The Higher Power wants me to try to convince and prepare you for this coming omni-important task that has been placed upon you. You should know that this task is also an inevitable one. The child will come, a part of you and a part of her; an unholy reunion blessed by the Higher Powers. It is up to you to decide whether you prepare your child for what faces them in the future or let them die at the hands of my son, allowing Hell to rise and reign.

4

We got a bit off track there, so let's redirect. The Witch stayed with Vipera through the beating and was finally disconnected upon the violent death. The Witch was stunned speechless, completely dumbfounded about what had just happened to her Master's pet. She could not understand how I had been able to do that because, as far as she knew, no mere mortal could defeat a creature associated with the Higher and Lower Powers.

The Witch was still new to being evil and therefore knew nothing of the stories of all the other beasts, creatures, and demons that had been bested by mere mortals temporarily endowed with the abilities of the Higher Powers. She had learned of the stories where the beings of the Higher Powers had been defeated, on rare occasions, by those strengthened by the Lower Powers, during her schooling. She was a very young sorceress then and she had long forgotten most of those stories over the decades upon decades that had passed since that time.

She called upon her Master, meaning to inquire about the strength that I possessed to do that to the creature, and immediately wished that she hadn't. Satan's voice boomed from the shadows of the alter room, undeniable fury in the tone, that struck fear deep within her. The Lower Power blamed the Witch for the circumstances that had quickly spiraled out of control, all because she sent an enraged and unstable Frank McGrath. She would have been sent to the deepest level of Hell had she not shown so much promise, even after her massive fuck up, and her being the closest one to the marked child.

"This task was of too much importance for you to delegate to such an insolent being! You should receive the harshest of punishments for your inadequacy! Idiotic cunt!" This was followed by a long slur of insults as the fear encompassed her.

When the anger had tapered off some, Satan continued in a lower voice. "And yet I still see a potential in you that cannot be ignored. Though I have lost my precious Vipera, it has been brought to my attention that the Higher Powers seen it fit to revive and heal our warrior." The Witch gasped with shock and then sighed deeply with relief, for she knew that the child was her only saving grace at that moment.

"As punishment you have been stripped of your ability of Sight and will receive no further assistance from the Lower Power. You are on your own. Bring me the child, immediately! And do not disappoint me, sorceress!" Satan bellowed and then the voice dissipated with the echoes bouncing around the cave.

The Witch was left alone to wallow in her own guilt and shame but decided to save it for another day and crawled into the comfort of her bed. She fell asleep quickly hoping that her dreams would bring about an answer. She slept like the dead and woke only an hour before sunset the following day.

Chapter Sixty-Six

Find Him

1

I had managed to evade the Witch for more than a week and with each day the hope that my son and I would survive that winter in the valley, grew. Most of the snow had melted away by the time the train was due to arrive, leaving behind the destruction that the weather and the valley folks, or lack of, had caused. It was a sad, sickening, almost post-apocalyptic sight that hurt my heart to look at and even think about now.

We survived on melted snow and a couple jars of jam I had found, but I was deeply worried about Owen in the beginning, because he wasn't receiving the nourishment he needed from nursing. It was a fruitless concern because he remained as healthy as could be on what little we had, while I continued to wither down to a slimness that bordered sickly. It was as if he didn't require the same sustenance that everyone else needed. At the time, though I did not and still do not believe in God, the Gods, or any other higher (or lower) power, I was eternally grateful to whoever gave me my son back for that added benefit.

The train was due on the second day of April, and each day that I was able to keep my son out of the hands of the Witch, was another day toward getting my son on that train and out of the valley. I only had a day left to wait, if the train arrived on time, when the Witch finally found us. She seen me skirting behind a shack with Owen tucked into a blanket sling at my chest but was too far away to catch me. She was quick, but I was just a bit quicker and stayed just out of reach. The Witch finally exhausted herself to the point of giving up, so she could devise another plan since that one was clearly not working.

Well, she did, and it worked. The Witch used the only other two people left in the valley, Jiminey and Patty McAvay. It was simple yet brilliant. She just waited until the next time they cuddled up in their bed and lit one of their hemp joints, which was only about two hours later, and then she put them to sleep. The joint fell from Jiminey's fingers and landed on the animal hide blanket they were covered up with. As deep sleep took them both, their bodies naturally settling into the bed, the blanket shifted and the joint rolled onto the quilt that separated them from the pokey, straw mattress beneath. It left behind a smoking, slowly spreading patch of smoldering fur that glowed brilliant orange in the dimness of the room. The quilt beneath the lit joint began to smoke and then smolder as it burned through the layers of fabric the quilt consisted of.

Luckily for Jiminey and Patty, they were lost in a coma-like sleep and felt no pain as their bodies were engulfed in flames. Once the fire hit the dry straw beneath the quilt, it went up like a matchstick. Their transition from sleep to death was a smooth, easy one that led them into the light. The Witch knew that she would not be able to obtain those two souls, but that sacrifice was worth it to flush me out of hiding. It worked too. Not immediately, but all she had to do was wait.

By the following day, most of the Common Area and all the shops around it and the Slums were mostly burned flat, the fire spreading across the valley and down toward the Lot. Since the O'Reigan farm had already burned to the ground before the new year's ice storm, the fire had no fuel to the west, so it maintained its steady, fiery course through what little remained of the Slums, spreading into the Lot.

Remarkably, the fire stopped just shy of the Witch's shack and her magnificent garden. It would be the only place still standing when the fire finally went out completely, days later. Aside from a handful of blackened, crumbling stone chimneys and the railroad tracks bisecting the valley, the Witch's place was all that would be left in the end.

2

Owen and I had made it to the train station, the farthest and one of the few remaining havens untouched yet by the flames, just minutes shy of the time the train was supposed to arrive. It didn't though, and I could sense more than see that the Witch was closing in on us. I had developed almost a sixth sense when it came to her during those final days in the valley. I was in pure survival mode, knowing that I and I alone were the only hope that my son had. So, with Owen held tightly to my chest, I darted back toward the immense heat of the fire and the thick smoke trailing to the west on the light breeze.

I swerved through the maze of shacks, some burnt and smoldering on the ground, some fully alight and engulfed in flames, while others were somewhere in between. The air was thick, gray, and acrid, stinging the eyes, lungs, and sinuses, reducing visibility to mere inches. I had wrapped a thick blanket around my own first, and then Owen's head before leaving the train station, knowing the risks, and believing them still better than him choking to death in the smoke. I hoped that my risky attempt to lure her away would work and the Witch would follow me as I led her deeper into the fire and the thickest of the smoke. She did and we were almost to the bridge leading into the Slums when I sensed that she was very close. Almost close enough to touch, but that's when I heard the rumble of the train as it entered the western tunnel.

The Witch heard it too, momentarily startling and distracting her, allowing me a few precious moments to make my escape. I darted through the thick smoke, coughing and choking for breath, trying to keep Owen pressed tightly to my chest and the unraveling blanket over my mouth and nose. I heard the brakes of the train as they engaged, it coming to a full stop as I ran for my son's life toward the sound.

I finally exited the flames and the worst of the smoke but could still feel the tremendous heat of the fire on my backside. It turned out that the unraveling blanket had caught fire as I skirted past the flaming buildings and was threatening to catch my tattered clothes on fire. I ripped the blanket from my head, letting it fly back behind me to land on the ground where it burned to ash. I never looked back but slightly loosened my grip on Owen since the smoke was a lot thinner by then.

I knew the Witch was still chasing us, but I had gotten a several second head start on her. The adrenaline coursing through me allowed me to run faster than I ever had in my life, putting a bit of distance between her and us. I didn't bother going back to the train station, I just headed straight for the train, itself, hoping that the Conductor was still on it.

I leaped across the tracks and skidded to a stop at the train entrance where a young man with apparent physical and mental deformities stood. I sensed that he was kind and sweet and after inquiring if he still lived with his mother, I left my son with this young man to take home to her. That young man was my son's saving grace and the only option I had in the moment. I quickly unwrapped Owen's head, needing the blanket, kissed his forehead gingerly leaving a gray smear of soot behind, and handed him to the young man on the train. I snatched a piece of wood stacked up by the train door and took off into the timbers that separated the tracks from the waterfall knowing that the Witch had gained some ground on me. I wrapped the wood in the blanket as I ran through the timbers, toward the waterless waterfall.

I stopped at the cliff's edge having nowhere else to go, holding the blanket tightly to my chest as I had before, when the Witch came sprinting out of the tree line. She demanded that I give her Owen, but of course I refused, which immensely angered her. I was unaware of it but the Conductor, not the young man on the train, but an older late-middle aged man by the name of Jimmy Moran, had spotted us running in the direction of the waterfall and followed us. Upon my refusal, the Witch screamed at me in anger, its power enough to blow the hair off my forehead and cause a momentary lapse in my balance. Conductor Jim watched me stumble so close to the edge of the cliff it caused him to gasp loudly, drawing our attention.

The moment I seen Jim I had every intention of telling him what had happened since the last time he had rolled through, not knowing nearly the amount that I know now, and who was behind it all. The Witch had other plans, though, and enchanted me instead. It was spoken in a sort of riddle, so I hadn't the slightest idea what she said, but then she blew some powder into my face, momentarily blinding me. There was no pain or burning and I recovered quickly, but I instinctively put my hands to my eyes, dropping the wrapped piece of wood. The Witch caught it before it landed on the rocky surface of the cliff edge, believing she had finally gotten her hands on baby Owen.

She soon realized that she hadn't though, when the blanket unraveled in her hands exposing it for what it really was. I grabbed her upper arms while she was still in shock and though I said the words in anger, I cannot deny the truth in them. I whispered, "I never really loved you.", and then using the slight element of surprise that I still had, I hurled her over the edge of the cliff.

I watched the Witch's eyes widen, almost bulging, as she realized what I had just done. The force of the scream that escaped her lips was fierce and full of fury and hatred. She released the chunk of wood wrapped in the blanket, the two objects separated and free-fell with the Witch. The wood hit the ground only a moment or two after the Witch, while the soiled blanket still fluttered through the air.

The Conductor came running up to the edge just in time to watch the Witch land at the bottom of the monstrous cliff and dart for the miniscule trees beyond the base of the waterfall. Her defiant scream reverberated off the stone faces of the mountain until it had faded out of existence.

3

Of course, Conductor Jim struggled to understand what he had just witnessed, having no knowledge of the events that had transpired since October when he had last been through the valley. I could tell that he struggled to recognize me, someone he had known since I was still in school, but it was understandable since I didn't much resemble the same man I was, months prior. I was considerably thinner and less muscular. I was filthy and covered in ash and soot from the still blazing fire. My clothes were shredded and in tatters, hanging from my almost emaciated body, and though

I wouldn't know it for a few days, a lot of my hair and facial hair had burned off. With the adrenaline losing its power, weakness and exhaustion began to set in and I was just too tired to offer my name or any other information at that moment. I knew the questions were coming, so I just waited until they began.

My assumption was that his first question would have been 'Who are you?'', but it wasn't. Instead, it was "Who was that?" referring to the Witch. Maybe things would have gone a bit differently if it had been his first question, but we will never know. I obliged him with an answer as we walked back through the timbers toward the train. Well, I tried to oblige him, anyway.

The moment I spoke the Witch's name, the proper sounds coming out of my mouth became jumbled and unclear and then there was an intense, burning sensation in the back of my throat. That sensation amplified, crawling into my mouth, overtaking my tongue, gums, and teeth, until the inside of my mouth felt hot enough to melt my tongue. I was wrong in that assumption, though... it wasn't melting my tongue... it was disintegrating it. The pain became too much for me to bear, added to an unimaginable level of exhaustion, fatigue, and hunger, I passed out in the middle of the timbers.

I would not have blamed Jim Moran if he had just left me among the trees to die, hell I may have even welcomed the option had I known what I do now. He didn't, though. He dragged me through those winding trees until he got me on the train. I never had the chance to thank that gracious man for not leaving me in that valley that day, and my only true regret in life is never having had the chance to do so.

My son was safe. I had succeeded in that and keeping him away from the Witch, and that was all that had really mattered at the time. I assumed, up until I woke up in the N.D.A.M.A six days later, that I would either die in the valley protecting my son or I would be reunited with him once I had deterred the Witch. I never thought that I would have lived for this long never to lay eyes on him again.

I could have twisted some story and gotten myself out of here, and seriously considered it in the beginning, but ultimately and heartbreakingly came to the realization that

Owen was safer without me. If the Witch was going to try to find him, and I was sure then and know now that she was, she would use me to do it.

This is the only way you were ever going to know the whole story of what happened that winter in the valley. If I had given you any of my information, even my name, you may have been able to deduce some of the bizarre events that I had lived through and could have tracked Owen down once he had become of age. I didn't want you to know who I was, so you wouldn't be able to find him and bring him back into my life. Not that I wouldn't have loved anything more, before I learned of everything I know now, but I didn't want that added danger and confusion brought on him.

4

You need to find him. I don't know what name he goes by; it had been changed and hidden from the Higher Powers since he was six years old. Tobias Medlin, the mentally challenged young man that I left my son with, did indeed take the boy to his mother and she raised him as her own. When Owen was six years old, Mrs. Medlin was taking Owen and four of his friends to the park one Saturday summer afternoon. Owen had light brown hair, greenish-blue eyes, and was the size of a typical, healthy six-year-old boy. Coincidentally, all four of the friends riding with him that day, had very similar-colored hair and eyes, and were approximately the same size as him.

The official report on the 'accident' was brake failure that resulted in loss of control of the vehicle. It had flipped several times before being stopped by a massive oak tree. We know that the Witch had discovered that the Medlin's had the marked child and that she orchestrated the entire 'accident', killing everyone in the vehicle except for one of the six-year-old boys that claimed his name was not Owen. Everything around and about my son has been obscured to the Higher Power, courtesy of the Lower Power since that 'accident'. We don't know what name he gave the authorities, where he was taken, or what has become of him since. Nor are they, or I since my death is imminent, able to find out... but you can. You

681

should. The more you know about my son, the more you can teach your offspring about him. Knowledge is power, use it. Learn. Teach. Prevail.

I know nothing more about Owen, and very little more about the Witch. Beware of her, should she find you, and believe that she will. Hell hath no fury like that woman scorned. Her powers have strengthened over the decades, and you would do best not to underestimate her cunning, her mind can be as powerful as her sorcery.

As disheartening as it is, there isn't much more to say. I have proved credible with my ability to know things I shouldn't with the three new arrivals, but I understand that you are reading a letter written by a man locked up in an insane asylum for the past three decades. I can see and understand why you wouldn't, even believing you shouldn't, believe me, but you should because not believing will result in an end to everything you have ever known and loved.

The only other bit of information of any real importance I must give you is the Witch's name. I don't know exactly what will become of me once I write those letters on this paper or even if you will be able to read them, only that a form of death for this life will occur. However, it is imperative that you know her name. It has power over her now, like so many other demons before her, but it is unlikely that she will possess her true name or features. Like my son, you should learn as much as you can about the Witch before your offspring meets mine.

Finally, and maybe most importantly, I want to extend my deepest apologies for throwing such a massive endeavor in your lap even though I am truly only the messenger. I can't apologize on behalf of the Higher Power because they are beyond such emotions and wouldn't be sorrowful even if they weren't. You and Vivian were chosen to raise the Higher Powers warrior, to prepare them for the ultimate battle between the Powers. The choice is yours and hers to accept or refuse but know that your choice will greatly impact the child's future and outcome, either positively or negatively.

You and Vivian can do this, even in those moments when you are convinced otherwise. You must. And remember: Learn. Teach. Prevail.

Sincerely,
J.O.C.

P.S. Her name, the Witch, is Araylia Travee.

Chapter Sixty-Seven

No Proof

Dr. Warren Gerard reads the last two words over and over, memorizing every letter of the unique name. Less than five minutes have passed since he began reading, but to him it feels like a lifetime. His mind has not only accepted everything he had just seen in his 'movie' as true, but as normal as going to work. The hard part is going to be interpreting between the two. That, and convincing Viv that he hasn't lost his mind.

He sets the last sheet of lined paper upside down on the top of the stack, intending to go to the phone and call Vivian. He knows she won't believe him if he tells her, so he will show her the proof instead. She won't be able to 'watch it', like he did but she can read it… with a magnifying glass… especially the part about them having a child together and that the child is inevitable. And since they have already been together on several occasions, it's safe to assume that she already could be.

Suddenly, the stack of papers bursts into a brilliant black light that evaporates the pages in the blink of an eye. The only thing that remains is the worn manilla envelope that they had been stored in, but he knows she won't be able to read what is addressed on the front of it. Only he can because of his eyes. She, nor anyone else, knows what had happened to his eyes. He is adamant about making sure his colored contacts are in anytime he is or will be face-to-face with anyone.

Warren sits and stares at the spot on the coffee table where the stacked letter sat only moments before in utter shock. *How am I going to convince her now?* He wonders to himself as the shock slowly breaks. He walks over and picks up the phone to call Vivian anyway, when he hears a knock at the back door.

"Dang! She's got some good timing." He mutters to himself, as he places the phone back down in the receiver and goes to answer the door. Thoughts of how to go about explaining what he had just read without any proof are swirling through his head when he grabs the doorknob. His distraction causes him to just assume, rather than check that it is Viv at the door, and he opens it carelessly.

His breath lodges in his throat, his eyes widen, his chest tightens and his heart flutters. His knees weaken, his legs tremble, his hands shake, and his mind scrambles. He tightens his grip on the doorknob to keep himself steady as his mind processes who is standing at his back door.

And it isn't Vivian Lancing.

To Be Continued...

www.ingramcontent.com/pod-product-compliance
Lightning Source LLC
Chambersburg PA
CBHW032249020726
47495CB00001B/24